RETROSPECT:
THE SALVATION OF MAC SCOTT

A NOVEL BY
BY A.J FORTON

ISBN-978-1-8384559-1-0

Cover design: May Dawney
Editor: Charlie Knight

Find out more at: ajforton-author.com

Those that I love, know I love them.
This time I want to thank my readers, who have stuck with me through Mac's journey, through cliff-hangers, angst and feels.
You are my favourite people.

AN AFFECTIONATE THANK YOU FROM THE AUTHOR TO…

Sue Forton, Evie Hawkley & Althea Valentine – My beta readers, your patience with my typos is not to be underestimated.
May Dawney – My book cover designer who is not only an incredible artist, but also an awesome friend.
Melissa Tereze – Whose encouragement and friendship in moments when I really needed it have made all the difference in the world.

***

I would like to acknowledge my indebtedness to the various movie quotes that have enriched Mac Scott's character, along with my firm favourite song, 'Sweet Home Alabama' which made its way into my prose, this novel wouldn't be the same without your inspiration.

CONTENTS

PROLOGUE

10 months and 15 days. 319 days. 7656 hours. Since I burst back into the world. Rebirth, resurrect, revive. I returned - my existence restored. I re-entered the world, my world, or at least…it used to be. My life was shelved, regarded superfluous. An old user manual hidden at the back of a cupboard. There, but unnecessary unless there came a need for it. The need for it has come.

I began my crusade to conquer those who sought to end me. I, the monster you contrived from fire and blood, broke the ties that bound me. I vanquished the demons that hunted me only to find that the real enemy was hidden behind the curtain, watching me flail through the impossible with frivolous eyes and a cold heart. That enemy is far more formidable. An unyielding force, impregnable and immense.

How does one slay leviathan? By capturing his trust, infiltrating his heart, and then betraying it mercilessly. I will forge a bond with you; I will do unforgivable things, things that will tear at my already tattered, expendable soul to secure that bond. I will expose the poisonous hive that facilitates you, dismantle the pillars that support you, and then, Father - you will fall.

Your blood runs through my veins, an itchy, salted crimson flow. This will afford you no favour. Just as it didn't me when you stood by – allowing me to be stolen from the world, to pay the high price of your crimes. You instigated our common enemy. You guided the blades that cut my skin. You fuelled the fire in which they punished me relentlessly with. You inspired the evil they bought to my heart, and it is that evil that I will use to destroy you.

You, the founder, the instigator, the catalyst of hatred that has extinguished the lives of countless innocents. Ruling with cruelty, thriving on coercion, in your wretched acts of terror. You hold the world hostage. Life is balancing on a knife's edge, and whatever your plan, however you seek to divide the world in the coming calamity…I will stop you. I will reign incendiary upon The Culling.

Your path of destruction ends here.

My name is Mckenna Scott. Most know me as Mac, few know me as Agent Scott. I am 32 years old, and I *exist* in London. I was a photographer, but I am many things, thanks to you. I was lost but now… In the quest to seek retribution, I have found myself. It is my vow; it is my purpose, and no matter the cost, I will pay it. It takes a monster to catch a monster, so live or die - *I am coming for you.*

CHAPTER 1

Awakening

"You have got to be fucking with me! How does that even work?" I gape doubtfully.

"Nope, no joke kid. Basically, it's an earpiece communication device, but it's implanted into your inner ear just under the skin. The head of it is barely visible. You program it with a phrase, and when you say it, it activates the implant. I can hear you, and so can Lexi if she's activated and vice versa. To shut it down, you just repeat your programmed phrase, and it deactivates. Lexi already implanted mine last night. Stings a bit but no big deal," Alfred explains with a shrug.

"Big sister is listening," Anna chimes in.

"Amen to that," I reply, not looking at her.

After last night's encounter, I made the decision I would never again allow myself to get hurt that way by Anna. I will be civil, friendly even - it isn't like I want to lose her completely - but I will definitely find it easier to keep my distance from now on. It hurts to be around her, but I am focused on the job at hand, and I'm doing my best to let the darkness take the wheel. I clearly cannot be trusted to make sensible decisions when it comes to protecting my own heart.

"What's your phrase?" I ask Alfred, and he beams.

"'Elementary, my dear Watson.' It has to be something you're not likely to say in general conversation, or you might accidentally activate it. All I have to do is flick the switch on the side of the injection gun, wait for the light to go from red to green, and then you say your phrase clearly. When the light goes back to red and flashes, it's ready to be implanted."

I look at the gun-shaped piece of steel in Alfred's hand with unease. It reminds me of those guns used to pierce ears, only Star Trek seems to have stolen it and given it an upgrade. I don't like this. I am not bothered about the pain; it just feels like an invasion of my right to privacy.

What rights? You're a mass murderer working off a prison sentence. Suck it up.

"Okay, let's do it," I confirm, cringing.

It does sting, there is no denying that, but it's over quickly, and now my ear just feels hot. Alfred laughed as I uttered my phase: 'Houston, we have a problem.' My mind went blank, and it was the first line that came to mind. And that was directly after the lyric 'I like big butts, and I cannot lie,' was stuck in my head. We test the sound; I walk down by the fire pit, and I can hear Alfred in crystal clear quality sound. Then Anna and Alfred join me by the fire to run through everything Lexi told me last night.

"To be honest, she didn't say that much. Most of it was warnings. Don't get arrested, don't get dead - that kind of thing. She said that my advert for Barrett will be in this morning's newspaper and that I'll be meeting two instructors today."

"Yeah, I know about the instructors. I'm supposed to be setting you up a parkour run for some new agility training, but I think I may need a hand shifting all the gear. Hope you're feeling fit, kid." Alfred winks.

"I can help, but what the hell is parkour?"

"It's basically free running. A little like the doom dash but harder and faster. It's a physical discipline of training that helps you move with agility and speed either through or over any terrain. There's a lot of running, jumping and climbing. It focuses on strength, fitness, balance, spatial awareness, coordination, precision, and control. It's ideal for combat in urban areas, and you have to think fast, or you'll go splat. Let's just say I'm glad that it wasn't a part of my training back in the day."

My stomach clenches a little; my first day doesn't sound like it is going to be an easy one. I think I have seen videos of people doing this on YouTube. People jumping around like spiderman without the safety of his web. Leaping across building gaps and running up and jumping across walls and faces using opposing forces.

Yeah, this is going to suck.

"Well, when you put it that way – I can't wait." I utter feigning enthusiasm.

Alfred heads inside to make some bacon butties for breakfast before we start the heavy lifting. Now, I am sat opposite Anna, feeling a thick atmosphere that I really don't want to be around. I catch her eye; she looks tired and troubled and yet still so annoyingly gorgeous. She is wearing a warm-looking baggy navy jumper that hangs off of one shoulder, her rusty red hair dancing off the soft skin of her collar bone in the light wind. She has the most gorgeously prominent collar bones. The longing in my chest begins to burn, and I force myself to look away.

"I'm just going to give him a hand." I huff, lunging myself out of the camp chair.

"Mac…"

I pause and groan internally, turning back round to face her, and I beat her to the punch.

"Whatever you're about to say, I probably don't need to hear it. What has happened has happened. No point going over it."

"There is a point. Will you please just let me explain? I know you are hurt, but you don't understand. Mac, last night - "

"I understand perfectly, Anna. There's no need to explain. So, let's just leave it at that, okay?" I dead pan, my voice measured, but Anna's eyes still tighten before she looks away from me.

I am hurting her feelings, and even though she hurt mine, I don't want that. It's so hard for me to turn and walk away. The gravitational pull she has on me is relentlessly strong, but somehow, I manage to do it. My heart yells at me to go back to her with every step I take away from her. At this point, I don't want to hear anything that I know will only cause more pain.

After my fill of bacon sandwiches, I set to work with Alfred building the parkour run. Alfred has made some platforms from scaffolding with wooden beams across the top of them. All the platforms vary in height and depth and are spaced out irregularly. I can already see that if I misjudge my speed or spatial awareness, I am going to come flying off the platform, and the highest is a 15-foot drop. The first platform has a long make-shift ramp to run up to give me speed to launch myself off. Some balance beams have been assembled out of scaffolding bars, and there are also some high up too, I assume to grab and swing off of. There are haystacks piled up. Some big wooden crates, boxes, and the big, blue plastic keg drums that Alfred usually uses to fill with water and loads onto his tractor to go round feeding the animals are stacked up too.

"How are things?" Alfred asks, and I snigger.

"You really don't do subtle, do you? *Things* are fine; I don't want to talk about it. What's done is done."

"Yes, well, be sure you know what you're doing before you shut the door on her completely. She was in pieces last night. Sent that Danni girl home not long after you left."

"I really don't want to talk about it. She made her choice, and I just want her to be happy. Can we just leave it at that?"

"Sure, kid, whatever you say."

The course is beginning to take shape, and the more I look at it, the more nervous I become, but I am also excited. It's like a grown-up playground with no soft landings. Alfred seems to have been constructing the parts of this course for a while. We drag more and more parts out of the big red barn till it becomes practically empty. When we finish, the course spans the size of a football pitch.

"That should do the trick. I'll give you the heads up just once, kid. I will be moving parts of this course around regularly so that the terrain always changes. So, I wouldn't get too comfortable or cocky, or you are likely to jump to something that you expect to be there but has moved. The idea is that your mind learns to think fast in *any* terrain," Alfred warns.

"Noted. Thanks for doing this. I seem to have taken over your farm and your life with my bullshit and baggage. I hope you know I appreciate you having my back and that I've got yours too - always."

"Don't mention it, kid. Like I said to you last night, we'll get through this together. You and me, we are partners, and we are going to bring The Culling down together." Alfred grunts, clapping me on the back. "Meet me by the fire; I have some more things to give you from Lexi."

I trudge over to the fire pit and re-join Anna there. She looks up when I arrive with the same troubled eyes, and I give her a smile which she returns weakly. I'm determined to make things as smooth with her as I can. I need to be able to be here, and I don't want either of us hurting more than we need to.

"Looks like you are in for one hell of a day," Anna says evenly, and I chuckle.

"Nah, it will be a piece of cake." I wink at her, and she smiles, looking more like herself. "What are you up to today?"

"Well… Danni is coming over in a bit. I was going to just stay here for a while, but with you training – I don't want it to prompt questions that I can't answer."

Anna speaks warily and watches for my reaction, so I do all I can not to give her one. Although an emerald-eyed monster is attempting to claw its way through my chest like a scene from an Alien movie, I think I succeed.

"Don't feel you have to leave on my account. This is your home; I don't want to disrupt your life. Just say that I'm training for the army or something. Don't make it a big deal, and it won't become one." I shrug with a smile, but she doesn't return it. Instead, she looks back at me intensely with glassy eyes. Her expression is as honest as always, and pain is written all over it. Pain I don't really understand.

"It's your home too, Mac."

I look away to hide my grimace, quickly replacing it with a half-hearted chuckle.

"Well, I do seem to have taken over the yard with that monstrosity of a course. Maybe I should just pitch a tent there and call it quits."

"That would mean leaving your glass mansion behind." Anna jibes, sounding much more like the girl I know.

"True, it's worth it just for the open fireplace and coffee machine."

"You still owe me a movie by that fire," Anna simpers.

"Ah well, you win some – you lose some."

There is no way that's happening.

Alfred re-joins us carrying a duffle bag. He sits down with a huff and unzips it. From inside, he pulls out a pair of combat boots, a small black box and a knife. I frown with confusion; I'm not sure what I was expecting. It's not like I was expecting an umbrella that also doubles as a machine gun, but the sight of these objects is rather underwhelming. Alfred hands me the small black box, and I open it.

"They are autonomous contact lenses, amazing little things. Through the lenses, you will be able to receive augmented vision assistance from Lexi and I, and also, when you wear them, we'll be able to see everything you can. They can continuously stream video wirelessly, and the video link frequency is tied into both Anna's and Lexi's computers. When Barrett makes contact, we will be able to support you. When you get close to him, you could sneak a peek at documents, and we will be able to screengrab them and copy the information without detection as quick as a camera flash." Alfred rambles excitedly, and I smirk.

"You're a little excited about this, aren't you? Okay, I have to admit that's pretty cool, but what if I need to pee or something? Can I turn them off?"

"Just close your eyes and think of England, kid, because with the ear implant active, we will also be able to hear you tinkle in stereo sound clarity," Alfred snorts, and I scowl at him.

"Alright, Alright, moving on."

Alfred hands me a knife. The blade is roughly six inches long, the handle wooden and smooth. It has an old look about it, weathered and worn, but the blade is as sharp as you could want and quite thick. About an inch away from the point of the knife is a curved hole. It feels heavy for its size but balanced in my hand. I look up to Alfred, sceptical.

"Don't let appearances fool you. That may look like any old tactical knife, but it's actually a gas-filled tactical knife. The handle contains a canister of pressurised carbon dioxide. There is a trigger that vents it through the channel of the blade. When you stab someone or something with that blade, it causes an internal explosion. There is a tiny trigger mechanism hidden in the hilt. If you don't hit it, then nothing will happen. If you do hit it while it's inside someone… Well, let's just say it's going to get messy."

I look for the hidden trigger; it's hard to find because it is perfectly camouflaged as a part of the steel hilt. I press it and jump as a loud and forceful puff of air releases in a high-pitched hiss. Alfred hands me a small box, and inside it is crammed full of tiny C02 canisters.

“Twist the hilt, and it will click, and the handle will fall away from the blade. Then you just drop out the used canister and replace it - clicking it back into place. Then you’re good to go again. Each canister is good for about three triggers depending on how long you hold the trigger.” Alfred instructs.

I follow his instruction. It’s quick and easy, but I wouldn’t want to be carrying a box of tiny canisters around with me. I shudder at the thought of what this would do when inside the body of a person, and I am in no hurry to find out. Alfred hands me a pair of combat boots that look remarkably like the ones I practically live in, only newer. Mine are a fashion statement, not real combat boots, and these give the same vibe.

“Lexi had these custom made for you. They’re designed to look like your boots, but you will find them much more comfortable, supportive, and equipped to deal with the demands of combat. They also come with some upgrades. Inside the left heel is a small stick of C4, and the laces of the left boot are copper wired, so you can pull out the copper wire and set a small remote charge. To release the heel, you just pull back on it and twist it to the left. Inside that heel, there is also a tracking device.”

Again, I follow Alfred’s instructions, but I struggle to open the heel. I twist and tug, and then I notice Anna giggling.

“Mac, you are turning it to the right, not the left.”

“Oh… right, yeah. Thanks.” I blush, twisting open the heel.

Just remember to unscrew the left heel, turn it left. To activate the right heel, turn it right. You don’t want to be getting them mixed up. Inside the right heel is a dose of cyanide. If you twist the right heel, after a 30-second delay, a small needle will penetrate inside of the sole of your boot, entering the heel of your foot,” Alfred said grimly.

“Why would she need that?!” Anna snaps.

“In case my cover is blown, and I’m captured. Lexi already told me that there would be no rescue. This is just insurance because they don’t want me to spill information under torture. It’s actually a smart move,” I determine.

“How is that smart? Why doesn’t that bother you, Mac?!”

“Because I know what it’s like to be captured and tortured. It’s not something I’m willing to repeat again, and I know too much. I would be a threat to national security. Everyone breaks eventually, and I wouldn’t want to be a source of information that Barrett can tap into." I hold her gaze, and there is no mistaking the disgust on her face, so I look away and begin taking off my old boots to try on the new ones.

If anything, I feel more secure knowing there is an easy out if the worst should happen. On the boat, it was a luxury I didn't have, and that was the worst torture I experienced. The pain - day in, day out and having no way to stop it and feeling like it would never end. I would have given a lot back then for a quick and easy death.

"I think you'll appreciate the last upgrade being the movie nerd that you are. In the toe of your left boot is a magnetic activation chip. If you kick the back of your right heel to your left toe, it will retract a small blade in the right toe." Alfred grins with excitement again.

Lacing up the boots, I notice they do feel much more comfortable than what I am used to, but they are also heavier, something I will have to adjust to. Following Alfred's instruction, I stand up then kick my right heel with my left toe. The action feels a little odd, but the effect is smooth and immediate. A small, pointed blade flicks out silently from the right toe; it resembles the head of an arrow, only wider like a squashed triangle. The blade is only an inch deep, but it is obvious the kind of damage that it could inflict. It looks razor-thin; I wouldn't have known it was even there.

"Now that's awesome. I feel totally James Bond now." I chuckle, "How do I make it go back inside?"

"Just point your toe to the floor and push the blade back in. It's thin, but it is made from Japanese steel, so it's far from flimsy," Alfred informs.

It seems I prejudged the gadgetry; I feel pretty pumped up about it all now. Both Alfred and I bounce with excitement while Anna remains quite reserved. She is present and joins in the chat every now and then, but she has a constant troubled look like she is trying to work out a maths problem. All in all, things are a lot less awkward than I could have hoped for, but I can't escape the dread that fills my stomach, knowing that at some point today, I will inevitably have to meet the new woman in her life.

That thought is thankfully interrupted by the arrival of an unfamiliar silver van pulling up onto the farm. Both front doors open, and two people get out and make their way towards me at the fire pit. When they arrive, nerves begin tingling in my stomach. Just in front is a woman with very light natural blond hair tied back loosely. She is attractive, but there is nothing distinctive or eye-catching about her face. Her features are soft, and her eyes warm and honey-brown. She has an easy, welcoming smile that is slightly crooked as she extends her hand to me, and I take it, shaking it politely.

"You must be Agent Scott. I'm Kate Dixon, but you can call me Dixy. This is Agent Callum Lambert, my partner. We are here to kick you into shape." She winks, and my nerves dispel a little.

Standing just behind Dixy is a heavy-set man with deep eyes and heavy eyebrows, making his dark eyes look even darker. He has a strong jawline, a stubbly face, and he is quite good looking in a rugged kind of way. He nods at me in greeting with a slight brooding smile. He is hugely muscled; the khaki t-shirt sleeves are stretched tight around his biceps. Both instructors are wearing army greens and look raring to go.

"Thanks for coming; this is Anna and Alfred. Hopefully, I'll be able to keep up. Where would you like to start?"

"First, we need to see what your capabilities are. I know you've had some training in hand-to-hand combat; that's Lambert's field more than mine, as is weapons training. I'll be working on your fitness, movement, and field tactics. So, let's get you running on the course, see how you move, and then get you sparing with Lambert. Once we get an idea of what level you are at, then we know where we can push you further. After that, I have some field tactics to run through with you that will help you blend in when trying to maintain your cover. It's important that we get you comfortable with the unknown. Being able to react appropriately given anything that is thrown at you is vital when working undercover. There's a lot to cover, so I would buckle up." She quirks an eyebrow and grins.

As I stand at the foot of the ramp to the 15-foot platform, I feel watched, and it is making my muscles tighten. I can feel the eyes of Alfred, Anna, Dixy, and Lambert burning into my back, and it's intimidating. I need to focus. If I don't, that loss of concentration will probably lead to a mistake that will not only hurt but be mortifying. I take a deep breath, trying to shut down all the overactive thoughts shouting in my head. I focus my eyes straight ahead, trying to channel my inner doom dash. I can vividly remember the feel of my feet lightly springing, how being loose and fluid made the dash almost feel like dancing. I begin to feel steady and alert, so when the whistle is blown, I blast into a run.

My boots make contact with the ramp, and it springs under my feet as they pound into it. When I get halfway up, I see two platforms. One to the left that only has a foot of floor space and one to the right, which is bigger but too far away for me to jump to. There is a steel high bar halfway between that I could make, and before I know it, I am jumping off the edge and soaring through the air towards it - hands outstretched.

My hands connect with the bar, and I panic as my own weight almost pulls it out of my grasp. I grip on and feel the friction burning my hands. Swinging back, I gain some momentum, and with the upswing, I let go, launching myself towards the next platform. I didn't quite make enough air or speed, and I know I'm not going to land smoothly on top of the platform. I bring up my knees and extend my hands out. I hit the side of the platform, my knees absorbing the impact, my hands gripping the edge, and I grunt at the pain.

Clinging to the side of the platform, I climb around the side using the grip with the toes of my boots and knees to gain traction to stop me from sliding down. My mind is in overdrive, trying to move fluidly and not stutter with over-thinking, but I know it is taking me too long to plan my next move. I launch myself off the platform using my legs and land clumsily to the next lowest platform.

I tiptoe down the balance beam propped against the platform, then hit the floor at a run. I vault over a course of haystacks; some I am able to jump over cleanly. Some I use my hands to push off from; some have been made into small bridges that I can slide under smoothly with enough speed. This part is fun, and adrenaline is starting to fuel me making me run faster and approach obstacles more aggressively. My feet are starting to move light and confidently.

Then, I run hard and fast towards a rope that is hanging from another platform. Just in front of it is a wooden crate. Running at high speed with gritted teeth, I use the crate to launch from gaining the extra height I needed to reach the rope. My hands connect and grip the rope, and I pull myself up onto the top. My feet connect with the top of the platform, and I straighten up, letting go of the rope. I feel a smile tugging at my lips - confidence is beginning to return, but it is fleeting.

Out of nowhere, I feel an impact hit me square in the middle of my chest. I lose my balance and then my footing and topple backwards off the edge of the platform. A horrible swoop of shock and fear hits my gut. My hands flail out, trying to find the rope I just used to climb up, and I manage to grab it. My hands grip the dry fibrous rope and slow my fall, but the speed I am falling drags the rope through my palms, burning my hands all the way down. I land on my back with a mercifully light thud. I drag myself up to my feet, annoyed at myself, and see that the impact was from one of Alfred's sandbags. I hear fast footsteps approach, and Dixy bursts around the corner.

"Agent Scott, are you okay?" She grabs my hands and assesses the damage, but my pride stings more than my hands.

"Yeah, I'm good but for the record, it's Mac," I pant, catching my breath and she smiles.

"Well, Mac, I learnt a lot from that. Let's go patch your hands up."

I follow Dixy to the firepit, where I find Anna and Alfred waiting. As I sit down, Lambert throws a first aid kit to Dixy smoothly. Like they were waiting for me to get injured because - they probably were. Dixy pours antiseptic over my hands, and I suppress a wince as she begins wrapping a light bandage to both of my hands.

"You move quite fearlessly and with aggression, and you're light on your feet, but you don't plan your moves very far ahead. I need to work on that with you. Plus, you get tunnel vision. You were so focused on speed of movement that you didn't notice the sandbag being thrown at you, so I'll work on your awareness too. You caught that rope mid-fall; you may have burned your hands on the rope, but you saved yourself worse injuries on impact so, your instincts are good." She looks up at me with an excitable grin. "Yes, I think I'll be able to kick that butt of yours into shape in no time."

"Bring it on, girl." I taunt, my smile darling.

Don't flirt with the instructor – ugh.

Dixy begins bandaging my other hand, and my eyes fall on Anna, who is staring dazed into the fire. I feel a pang of guilt, and I am not even sure why; I am itching to go over to her and check she is okay because if I have learnt anything about that blank expression, it is that it means that she's not okay. But I don't trust myself to keep my distance, and distance is the goal.

None of your business

"Can I get you guys a coffee or anything?" Alfred asks, snapping me out of my inner monologue.

"Yes please, if it isn't too much trouble." Dixy accepts but Lambert declines, shaking his water bottle in response.

He doesn't seem to talk much, and *seriously* - could they have picked a bigger guy for me to fight with? As I watch Alfred leave, I see another car I don't recognise, and my insides clench as I realise the loan figure walking down towards us must be Danni. My heart seems to lag, a slow dragging pound. Danni has long, mousy brown hair and olive skin. She wears simple jeans and a vest that is much more feminine than I was expecting to see. Her features are harsh, her face slightly round. She takes a seat by Anna, and I look away, turning to Dixy.

"Mind if I take 5 minutes?"

"Of course. Are you alright, Mac?"

"Yeah, I'm good. Just going to grab some water," I lie before turning to Lambert.

"Lambert, I'm heading inside for some water. Would you like me to top that up for you?" I offer.

"Yes please, Mac. Thank you."

His voice is gravelly and monotone but his tone more polite than I was expecting, and that makes me feel more at ease. He is a scary-looking guy and breaking the ice makes me feel a little less intimidated. I head towards the house, avoiding the firepit and trying to keep my head up, unphased. Inside though, it hurts. As I make my way to the kitchen, I find Alfred loading cups of coffee onto the tray.

"How you holding up, kid?"

"I'm good, a little bit nervous over fighting a man-beast, but I'm good."

"Use your strengths. He has strength, but you have speed. Just go for the soft spots, weaken and tire him. I reckon you can take him." He winks, and I scoff. Clearly, he vastly over-estimates my ability.

I follow Alfred back down to the fire, walking slowly in the attempt to put my game face on, but the game face isn't for Lambert. I walk directly over to Anna and Danni. As I approach, I make considerable effort to not meet Anna's eyes and give Danni my best charming smile as I extend my bandaged hand to her.

"Hi, Danni, is it?"

Danni looks up at me. Her eyes scrutinise me swiftly and then fall into my gaze. My blood runs cold, and I feel myself freeze, the smile dying off my face and my chest tightening. Her eyes are so cold upon mine, not even her smile warms them.

"Yes, and you must be Mac." She takes my hand and shakes it politely, gripping it unnecessarily hard. "I've heard a lot about you."

"Well, I feel for you there – I'm not that exciting," I quip, gripping her hand back and ignoring the burn in my palm. "Listen, it was nice to meet you, but I have to get back to work." I let go of her hand to walk away, but she keeps a hold of mine.

"Ah, yes, Anna told me you are training for the army. Mind if I stay and watch?" Danni requests, and my eyes flick to Anna quickly, who is doing all she can not to look at me.

"Um, sure. Why not." I shrug before pulling my hand free and walking away towards Lambert, the hairs still raised on the back of my neck.

Well, she and I are going to be best buds.

"So, what are we going to be doing?" I ask Lambert.

"Well, that depends. I'd like to warm you up a little first, then I want to work on improvised weaponry with you. What kind of fighting have you done the most of?"

I explain to Lambert about the stick fighting and boxing I went through with Billy, along with some disarming techniques, and he listens intently. Now that I am talking to him, I see that as scary of a fella he may look, he also has a calm presence about him. His voice is oddly soft-spoken and hypnotic.

"Right. If that is the case, like Dixy. I need to assess your ability. When you are undercover, it's never as simple as pulling a gun. A lot of the time, you don't even have one because it can risk blowing your cover. That's the reason we learn to fight effectively with improvised weapons - everyday things you have around you. Whether that be a frying pan or a piece of wood or even a length of rope – you need to be able to use your surroundings to your advantage, and that's what I intend to teach you. Stick fighting is an ideal way to start, so I'll grab some batons from the van if you want to get ready."

The nerves tingle; I am at least starting with something I have a little confidence in but this guy is huge, and I have an audience that is impossible to ignore. I keep my back to everyone at the fire pit, and Dixy comes over to join me.

"Are you stick fighting?" she asks, and I nod.

"Don't hesitate and don't pull back. He won't go easy on you," she warns, and I turn to her grinning.

"I wouldn't have it any other way."

"Oh, I see a little badass in your eyes there, Mac. I've been waiting for that. Just a tip, he favours his right side massively – I'd really enjoy it if you got a good hit in. He's such a sore loser."

"I'll do my best. Thanks for the tip."

I step forward and take the sticks from Lambert with a nod. They feel familiar in my hands, almost comforting, but it has been a long time since I have done any stick fighting. The last time would have been in training with Alfred just before the battle with Jakub. That feels so long ago now, but I guess it really wasn't. I pace, spinning the stick around my wrist. The bandages are making the grip feel loose and obstructed.

"You ready, Scott?" Lambert calls.

I take a sideways glance at him and exchange a goading grin with him. The excitement suddenly fizzes in my veins, and I turn to face him. He lunges forward without warning bringing his right swing down hard, and I block. The baton slides straight out of my grip, and I step back angrily and storm off towards Dixy.

"Take them off," I growl, holding my hands out - my pride stinging.

"Mac…that is going - "

"I can't grip the sticks with them on. You can bandage me up afterwards if you like. Just do it; it will be worth it." My eyes implore intensely, and after a few seconds, she relents, begrudgingly unwrapping the bandages from my hands.

I pick the batons back up, and it stings for sure, but I feel much more in control. Out the corner of my eye I see that everyone at the campfire is staring this way, and I shake the image away. I grip the batons and focus on Lambert's eyes, willing the rest of the world to disappear. This time I lunge for him, catching him off guard.

Clank, clank-clank-clank, clank, clank.

The familiar satisficing noise of batons clashing fills the air. He hits so much harder than Alfred or Billy ever did. Each collision sends vibrations stinging through my palms and down my arms. I feel a calm coming over me; I love that feeling. The muscles in my torso, hips, and back loosen up, and I begin to move more fluidly, using my speed and flexibility to my advantage. He is fast, and he hits harder, but I am able to bend and sweep away faster than he can.

Clank-clank-clank-clank. Clank-clank-clank-clank.

The hits are picking up speed, and I fight to try to find an opening in his defences. Dixy is right, he is weaker on his left, but the problem is - so am I. My teeth grit as sweat pours off of me, pain searing in my palms, and I focus. My heart is pounding, but it's a good pound, a thrum of excitement. I feel the calm inside me slow everything down. I can see the frustration building on his face, and I take the opportunity.

I see his right swing hammer down, and I block it. I feign a right step forcing him to pivot right, then step left - just wide of the left swing that's pummelling towards my face. I drop to one knee, ducking below the right swing, then I hit my baton hard against his. My hit forces his own baton upwards until it smashes into his face. I feel the contact and hear him yelp as he stumbles backwards, and I roll back onto my feet.

"Ahhhhhhh!!! Nice one, Mac!" Dixy cheers, running over to me, and gives me a high five.

She isn't the only one cheering, but I keep my eyes well away from the cheers by the fire pit. Dixy hands me a water bottle, and I chug it thirstily;

my t-shirt is sticking to my skin, so I whip it off and pour the water over the back of my neck. The cool relief feels immense.

"He's going to come back twice as hard now; stay focused," Dixy warns.

I wipe the sweat off my face with my t-shirt, throw it on the floor, and I turn back to Lambert. He spits a mouthful of blood and grins at me.

"You just made this so much more fun," he taunts.

He lunges at me before I am ready, but I manage to recover just in time. I can tell from the look in his eyes, he is determined. His hits are coming harder and faster, and then he takes a step back, crossing his batons together like a shield, and barges towards me with force. I mimic his movement, crossing my batons, and he pushes on them; I sidestep backwards fast and stumble a little as I spin out of his grasp. He turns on me before I have a chance to catch my breath, and I block his right swing as his left swing clips my eyebrow. I wince at the sting and then feel the warm flow of blood trickle down my face.

"Time out!" Dixy yells, running up behind me. She presses my sweaty t-shirt hard against the cut on my eye, stanching the blood.

"You need to stop?"

"Nope." I smile. My pride is stung, but I am actually enjoying it. All the anger inside that has built up is finally finding a place to release, and it feels good.

"Go kick his arse then." She winks, and I walk back over to Lambert slowly, giving my chest a chance to slow its gasping heave.

"Gwarn kid!" Alfred booms, and I can't help but smile a little, a heated blush reddening my cheeks.

"Nice little coffee break?" Lambert goads but I ignore him, my eyes focused on his, and I stand still, forcing him to make the first move.

I see his eyes harden, and I brace myself just before he bursts into a run. This time, I am ready. I am attacking with dominance. Instead of just blocking him, I am stepping into him and forcing him to block and step backwards. The pain in my hands is gnawing at me but I keep pushing, harder and faster than I ever have.

Then I take a step backwards, bringing both my arms out wide. I swing them both inwards with all the force I have, trapping his batons between mine. I shift my weight onto my back foot, bringing my front knee up, and I kick out so hard, a loud growling grunt escapes my mouth. My foot makes contact with Lambert's gut, and he buckles, falling on his butt. Cheers erupt, and goosebumps race excitedly across my skin. I look down at my hands, wincing. The pain in my hands is ridiculous. There is blood trickling down my wrists, and I wipe them on my trousers.

"Next point wins, guys." Dixy announces, and my heart sinks.

I don't know how much I've got left in the tank, but there is no way I am backing out of the fight now. I walk back over to Lambert, and there is no mistaking the pissed look on his face. My arms are so heavy, but I raise them, indicating that I'm ready. Lambert doesn't hesitate; he launches towards me furiously, and his first powerful hit sends a shockwave of pain through my palm. I grit my teeth and grip the batons, pained grunts coming out my mouth with every hit.

Clank-clank-clank-clank. Clank-clank-clank-clank.

Adrenalin kicks in, and a second wave of energy hits me. We dance together in circles, the hits coming faster and harder. Lambert changes direction, his baton swings up for an uppercut too fast for me to block. I dive out the way and roll back onto my feet before he can lunge at me. We circle each other - staring each other down. The tension is discernible, not a sound coming from the fire pit. We both lunge at the same time, and Lambert bursts at me with furious power. I push with everything I have left in the tank.

Clank-clank-clank-clank. Clank-clank-clank-clank.

The power in his hits is painful, and the batons in my hands begin to slip in my bloody palms. I miss the block, and he slams his baton down hard on top of my left baton with his. It slides out of my hand, and his right swing hits me hard in the gut. I bend over, crying out, but no noise escapes my winded lungs. Then I am blindsided with a fast uppercut to the chin. My head shoots back in the force of the hit, straightening me up in reaction. Lambert moves impossibly fast; his left swing comes back around and hits my ribs, and I buckle to my knees.

"What the hell are you doing, Lambert? She was disarmed!" Dixy barks furiously, a sound she doesn't look capable of barking.

On my hands and knees, I choke on the blood pooling in my mouth as I try to get air and crawl over to my t-shirt. I just manage to grab it when I feel a hand on the bare skin of my back. I recoil and jerk away in a panic, getting to my feet too fast and yanking my t-shirt back on. As my head pops through the head hole of the t-shirt, my eyes fall on Dixy. Her eyes are scrunched in confusion.

"I'm fine," I choke, sputtering blood down my front. I hold my hand out in front of me. "Just give me a minute."

I turn away, spitting blood and feeling mortified because I really needed today to go well. I needed to feel like I warrant the faith Lexi has put in me. Instead, I feel like the same jumpy mess I always do. I catch my breath and try to straighten up to find Lambert approaching me, taking wary measured steps, his shoulders slumped.

"I am *so* sorry, Mac. I got a little carried away."

"Don't worry, bro. No big thing," I reassure him because he looks absolutely disgraced with himself.

"Take a walk, Callum. Now!" Dixy growls, her face a mask of fury.

"Dixy, it's really fine," I reassure, but Lambert walks off towards the van, and Dixy turns her attention on me.

"No, it isn't. He lost control. I need to check your ribs." She takes a step forward, and I step back, my hand raised, warning her.

"They're fine, I'm not so good at…" I trail off. "I'm fine. Honest."

Dixy frowns at me, and I feel the familiar embarrassment crawling over me. She takes another step forward, and I flinch back yet again.

"Tell me what to check for," Anna demands, appearing out of nowhere, and Dixy looks taken aback as Anna steps between us.

"Oh, for the love of God! My ribs are not broken, damn it!" I growl, and Anna steps up to me, close, her eyes adamant but soft.

"It is her, or it's me," she whispers, laying her hands on my hips.

She doesn't take her eyes off of mine, and the look she is giving me is completely disarming. Warm, full of knowing and a hint of bossiness. Pain sears in my chest, God I have missed that look. That look has a way of making me feel so damn precious, like I am the only person she sees. And even though I know that's not true, I can't help but succumb to her. I am livid at my own weakness; all I can do is nod.

Anna keeps her eyes on mine as she slides her hand up my shirt. She holds the hem of my shirt with her other hand keeping my torso hidden. Her eyes are so intent on mine as the warmth of her hand slides further up my shirt, dragging against my skin in a slow caress. It is impossible for me to hide the breath that catches in my throat at her touch. Pleasure and pain – in perfect tandem, as always. It is also impossible for me to miss the way the bright green of her eyes darkens at my reaction or feel the way her hand trembles for just a moment.

"Find her top rib and run your fingertips along it, pressing it gently. If you feel movement or the bone feels out of place in any way, like sticking further out or sunken in – then there's a break," Dixy instructs, and I snap out of my reverie.

The anger resurfaces. This is ridiculous; I've had enough broken ribs to know when one is broken. Anna's fingertips lightly press down my ribs, and I can feel her gaze firmly set on me as I fixate on the grassy ground. I just want to walk away. This didn't need to be a big deal, and I didn't need Anna to jump in. Now I can feel eyes on the back of my head and the longer I stand here, the more pissed off I get.

"I feel swelling, but there isn't any movement, I don't think." Anna confirms, pulling her hand out of my shirt, and I turn away from her the second I get the chance. My body missing her touch. My heart aching for more, and my head barking angrily at her screwing with my head. It feels like a game, and I know she would never play it, she is too… good for that, but it doesn't change that it hurts.

"Can I take five, Dixy?"

"Of course, Mac. Can you meet me by the start of the assault course? I think you've had enough for one day, but I need to talk to you before I go."

I pick up my water bottle on route and swill the blood in my mouth, spitting rosy-red water and then I walk towards my usual spot on the back fence. I don't know why I am so pissed; they were both only trying to help. It is like the colder I feel, the easier it all is to cope with the loneliness and pain – right up until someone tries to touch me, and then it is worse than ever.

My limbs are trembling, I feel the heat burn across my skin, and I growl at myself as tears overcome me. I don't even know where they are coming from. I grip the fence and focus on the physical pain of the wood digging into the open wounds in my hands, and it helps, the lump in my throat sliding back down. I feel the cold icy darkness freeze in my veins, and I begin to steady myself.

Overreaction. Get over yourself.

I walk slowly. My feet dragging in the brush of the overgrown grass. My eyes fall on the fire pit where Anna is sat next to Danni, so I look away and watch my feet walk instead. When I get to the assault course, I find Dixy is sat waiting with her hands busy inside the first aid kit. I take a seat in front of her, mirroring her cross-legged position on the grass.

"Can I fix your hands, please?" she asks with wary eyes, and I feel a pang of guilt as I hold my hands out to her, palms up. She starts cleaning the blood off of my wrists and forearms.

"Sorry, if I was a jerk."

"You weren't, but I do need you to be upfront with me. I'm going to be pushing you hard, both physically and mentally. There will be more injuries, and you're probably going to hate Callum and I by the end of this. But if I don't know how to respond when something goes wrong then, I can't push you as hard as I need to - to help you. If you won't trust us, then you'll be fighting this training uphill when it will already be hard enough, trust me."

I gulp, anxiety fluttering in my chest. I need this to work, it's the only chance I have of destroying The Culling, but that doesn't make what she is asking for any easier. Dixy finishes cleaning my hands and begins wrapping them with clean bandages.

"I… am not very good at being touched. I'm… better t-than I was but…" My hands shake a little, and Dixy holds them steady.

"I thought that might be it. Hands seem to be okay, though?" She smiles warmly as she looks down at her hands holding mine.

"Yeah, most of the time. There was a time I couldn't do that. Now, I can cope with more but not…"

"But not your bare skin where you're scarred?" she states. I frown at her, and she laughs softly. "You were choking up blood after getting ten bells knocked out of you… yet you still managed to drag your scrawny arse up and put your t-shirt on like your life depended on it."

"That's creepily observant."

"Well, durr – I'm a spy," she mocks playfully, and I am happy to be laughing, breaking through the tension. Dixy lets go of my hands and shuffles closer. "Do you mind if I clean your face? You look like an extra from a vampire movie."

"Sure."

The antiseptic is so pungent I can taste it. For someone so dainty-looking, Dixy is not shy about manhandling me. She grabs at my chin as she wipes the massacre from my neck as if I hadn't just told her that physical touch is difficult for me. It's hard allowing her that close, but I know I have to try.

"He didn't knock ten bells out of me, more like… three bells. Don't give him too much of a hard time; he did apologise."

"That isn't the point, Mac. He's a sore loser; he shouldn't have lost control that way, but I don't think you did his ego any good. No guy wants to be beaten by a girl, and you were even till the end - probably rattled him." Dixy snorts.

"It was fun. Well, it was till I lost."

"You said you're better at being touched now than you were. That wouldn't have anything to do with the fiery redhead sending daggers my way, would it? – Don't look." She adds quickly, making me freeze and just nod.

"Thought so. She doesn't keep her eyes off you, and she certainly moved fast when I tried to check your ribs. I'm just going to continue washing your face; it is driving her *crazy*."

"Stop, you are terrible! She's just… protective."

"Yes, that is exactly the vibe I am getting. Step off bitch, I'm being protective."

And just like that, I relax, laughing so freely my ribs wince in protest. I like her sarcasm, it's a welcome breath of fresh air, but soon, the smile falls from her face. She looks back at me with contemplative honey-brown eyes.

"Mac, thank you for being upfront with me. It helps to understand, and I'll try to be more aware with touching, but Anna isn't always going to be around. If you get hurt and she's not here, then I don't want to have to fight you. If I'm worried about you getting injured because you won't let us near you, it means I have to be more careful and not push so hard."

I somehow knew the words were coming, yet it doesn't make them easier to take. Anna let me go, and not only is what she did today painful, it doesn't help me move on or trust my instructors. This has to be about beating Barrett. Maybe for me, the hardest battle isn't the pain or the fight, it is the letting go of the scars that weigh me down and trying to trust people again. And hardest of all, letting go of the one person whose touch doesn't scare me.

"To be honest, I don't want her to come running anytime something goes wrong; I have my own reasons for that. So… in the future, if I need help, don't take no for an answer. If I have any chance of beating what's coming my way, I need to be pushed out of my comfort zone, and that's what you are here to do. I can't afford to let anything get in the way of doing whatever it takes to stop Barrett. So, don't hold back, don't take any of my shit. Be as hard on me as you need to be."

Dixy smiles at me proudly, heating the flush in my cheeks.

"Well done, Mac. I see what Lexi is going on about… you are brave. I can appreciate what a big step that is for you. Don't worry, I'll have you ready for Barrett in no time."

Dixy orders a night of rest, promises that tomorrow will be a less physical day, and she walks off back to her van with Lambert. I lay back on the grass, somehow feeling lighter than I have in a while - acceptance is a powerful thing. Goosebumps start to irrupt as the chill of the night freezes the sweat on my skin. The frame of Alfred comes towering above me with a crooked grin.

Nice fighting, kid."

"You know I lost, right?" I hold my hand up, gesturing for him to help me up. He takes it and lifts me with ease to my feet.

"Maybe, but you fought well against a guy twice your size, with far more fights under his belt. I'd say you did awesome."

"Thanks, Pa," I blurt without thinking, and he raises an eyebrow. The instant cringe shuddering through me is gross.

"Sorry! Oh God, how weird was that? I think I'm just so used to hearing Anna call you that, my brain farted."

"You can call me Pa. I like it. I'm an excellent Pa." He puffs his chest out and chuckles.

"You are; I heard you cheering me on. Thanks for that, by the way. I think I'm going to scoot. I'm beat. I'll be back in the morning."

"I will have coffee waiting. Well done today."

"Thanks, Pa," I call over my shoulder as I walk off.

***

I drive, but somehow, it isn't my house I end up parked outside of. I make my way out of the car walking like an old man up the pathway of the well-kept garden. I rap my knuckles lightly on the mahogany-coloured wooden door. Alisha's face lights up, then her eyes fall upon my appearance, and her smile fades.

"What the hell happened?" She gasps, reaching out to cup my face.

"It's nothing, just been training. Now, are you going to let me in, or do I have to watch a movie and drink whisky alone?"

Her laugh is musical as she grabs me by the collar. Alisha pulls me inside, shuts the door behind me, and pushes me against the wall. Her lips move against mine softly. Somehow, she is sexy even when she is being gentle with me.

"This is a nice surprise," she mutters into my lips.

"Mission accomplished." I wrap my arms around her, and she melts into me. Her floral scent engulfs me, and she holds me a little too tightly.

I cringe and grunt at the pain in my ribs, and Alisha flinches and pulls back. She pulls me by the hand and leads me to the living room, and I collapse on the sofa. Alisha disappears out of sight, and I frown after her till she comes back into view. She sits down on the coffee table just in front of me and hands me a bag of frozen peas and a glass of whisky, her rich hazel-brown eyes tight with concern. I wince at the cold when I lay the frozen peas against my ribs and then I drain the whisky in one. I look back up at her, her expression expectant, and I cringe because I can't actually tell her the truth. I didn't really think about that before I impulsively drove here.

"You are going to tell me what is going on, Mac. You can't just turn up with cuts and bruises and not explain that."

"I can't tell you what is going on. I'm not being a jerk; I actually can't."

"Has this got to do with the reason you were so quickly released from prison?" Alisha hints, amplifying the cringe. I guess I can't blame her for putting two and two together.

"Yes, it has. I just can't give you the details. I would if I could, honestly."

Alisha looks down at the floor, nodding, then she goes back into the kitchen and fetches herself a glass and pours us both another generous measure of whisky and sits back down.

"Is it… dangerous? Whatever you're doing?"

"A little, yeah."

"That means a lot. You're a crap liar, Mac the knife."

Alisha stares into her glass with concern written boldly on her face. I am not used to this side of her; she always has such a good poker face. This kind of honesty hasn't really been a part of our relationship.

"If it means I stay free, there isn't anything I wouldn't do. I'll be okay; I'm not that delicate, you know."

Alisha puts her drink down and gets to her feet. She stands over me with her hands braced against the sofa, either side of my head. A smirk is playing sexily on her lips as she grazes her nose against mine.

"You better be okay, or I'm going to be really pissed at you." She smoulders, her whisky-soaked lips growing hungry against mine.

I shuffle forwards and sit her on my knees, and her hands fall on my chest, gripping the collar of my shirt. As her lips stroke deep and slow, I coax them with my tongue and delight in the heavy huffed breath as she welcomes me into her mouth.

"You shouldn't kiss me like that."

"Why?" I mumble into her lips.

I feel her silent answer when her fists tighten around my collar, and her hips buck. While my body tingles with arousal, my chest tightens with fear. Alisha pulls away as if she can feel it; she climbs off my lap and leads me up the stairs. I follow her, a little head spun by the sudden change and still clutching the bag of peas to my ribs as I trail after her. Alisha sits me on the end of her bed and starts unlacing my boots, pulling them off. She stands me back up, her hands unbuttoning my jeans, and I can't stop it. My hands grab for hers.

"It's okay, hey… I'm just changing your clothes; they are covered in blood, and you are not getting in my bed like that," she explains, and I let my hands fall.

Alisha takes a t-shirt out of her chest of drawers and shows it to me, reassuring me that she is going to cover me right up again. She lifts off my shirt, and my arms instinctually cross over my chest. I don't have time to panic; she wastes no time on easing the soft cotton t-shirt over my head, and then she leads me into the bed. As I lay back, she places the ice pack on my ribs, pulls the duvet over me, and tucks inside the covers with me. I am immersed in her scent, my head falling against her shoulder as she turns the TV on.

"Thank you." I mumble sleepily.

"Thank you for letting me - you stubborn pain in the arse."

I chuckle and watch the wall-mounted TV as she flips through the channels, her fingertips stroking my forehead. A warm heaviness spreads over me; I feel like I am sinking into the bed, but a sadness pangs deep in my chest. Sadness and conflict.

"You keep doing that, I will fall asleep before you find a film."

"Would that be so bad?" She turns, her lips on my forehead.

"It would be rude; I only just got here."

"You are here. That's enough for me, Mac."

CHAPTER 2

Overload

Eyes.

Perverse and cruel eyes.

Dark dilated pupils zeroing in like a camera lens.

Unapologetic, probing, excited eyes.

Watching my pain, feeding his pleasure.

Brutal, unyielding force.

His poison infiltrates my system with his unauthorised entry.

Desecrating my body, devastating my soul.

"Mac…"

"No… stop… please."

"Mac… Wake up…"

Fast, painful, rhythmic blows.

"Argghh!"

"Mac!"

Sweat stings my eyes as they fly open, pain sears in my ribs as I bolt upright. Terror is vibrating in my limbs, his eyes still etched so clearly in my sight.

"It's okay. You were dreaming; I couldn't wake you up." Alisha soothes, grabbing my face, and I flinch away harshly.

"Baby, it's me," she utters softly. She holds her hands up, eying me warily.

I look at her, trying to clear the horror from my mind, and my breathing starts to slow as I realise it was just a dream. A memory of a monster I have long since slain, yet his hauntings are still plaguing me.

"Sorry… I…"

Alisha moves slowly towards me, her hands lightly laid on my chest. She looks frightened, and the sadness I closed my eyes to awakens at the sight. I never want to be the reason that fear is widening anyone's eyes, but how could I not be?

"It's okay. Just tell me what happened?"

"It's nothing, was just a dream. I'm okay."

"That was not just a dream. You were screaming, and I couldn't wake you. It was a memory, wasn't it?" Alisha probes, wiping the sweat off my face.

"Alisha, I'm fine. I'm sorry for scaring you, but it's nothing. What time is it?"

"A little after 5am," she advises, and I get out of the bed and pull my jeans on.

"Where the hell do you think you are going?!"

"I have training. I need to get home and shower and get ready," I ramble as I pull her t-shirt off and quickly replace it with my bloody one. She gets out of bed, walks over to me, and grabs my wrists lightly.

"Stop. You are running from me. If you don't want to tell me what happened yet that's fine, but don't just bolt. I don't deserve that," she snaps, breaking my momentum.

"You're right; you don't. I'm sorry." I lean into her, my thumbs stroking her cheeks as I kiss her lightly. I pull back, and she smiles a little.

"Okay, you're almost forgiven."

"Almost?"

I kiss her deeper, my lips moving firmer against hers. My hands moving off of her face and sliding down her waist. I pull her closer, and she smirks into my mouth.

"Okay, fine. You're forgiven."

***

I drive back to my apartment in the darkness, the sun not yet making its warm appearance. Icy frost is creeping around the edges of the windscreen, my breath steaming in a visible, misty judder as I shiver. My chest is tight, the memory still jerking at the edges of my psyche. I blast the music on the car stereo to quieten the loud booming thoughts invading my mind.

Inside the apartment, I shed my dirty clothes as I walk and step eagerly into the hot, pounding water of the shower. I scrub my skin too harshly, making it red and angry – as if scrubbing hard enough will wash away the violations that he poisoned me with. No amount of scrubbing can wash the ugliness away. I sit on the slippery shower floor, the water as hot as I can stand it. With my arms wrapped around my knees tightly, I rock to the rhythm of my pounding heart. Even the darkness inside me has abandoned me, the pain rains down, and I absorb it with wide, unblinking eyes as the shower water stings them.

Please, let me forget again.

***

My feet crunch on the frost-bitten grass as I walk with heavy legs towards the fire pit. I load more wood onto it, stoking up the embers with my shaky breath as I blow on them. The flames re-ignite, and I take my usual seat, my arms tightly wrapped around myself as I wait for the warmth of the fire to thaw me out. The hissing and the cracking of the fire and my shivering breath are the only sounds on the pitch-black farmland. All the lights in the house are off. The darkness is so impenetrable, it's a wonder I made it to the fire pit at all with only a few small embers to guide me, and yet no amount of darkness is vacating the evil behind my eyes.

I have to pull myself together; this is not the time to fall apart. It's in the past - he's dead, I killed him. So, why now? Why is he now haunting my dreams and terrorising my present? His eyes are so clear in my mind. No matter how hard I blink, they are there. My skin crawls as though ants are scurrying all over me, an all-over itch I can't quite reach. A deep ache in my tummy making me feel hollower than two years of hunger ever did.

"You alright, kid?"

"Jesus!" I snap, jumping out of my skin.

"Sorry, I didn't exactly creep behind you. You were away with the fairies." Alfred flinches, almost spilling the contents of both coffee mugs he's carrying.

"Yeah, sorry. I must have zoned out. I didn't mean to bite your head off."

"No worries. Looks like you have a lot on your mind."

I survey him from across the flames; his eyes are wary and concerned. Very much the same look Alisha gave me and Dixy when I got injured and flinched away from her.

I'm just freaking people out left, right, and centre. Brilliant.

"I'm fine, brother. Don't worry."

"Well, this might be the perfect time to show you something I fixed up for you. Come with me," he grumbles, getting to his feet.

I follow him curiously; we walk the 20 odd feet behind the fire pit to the big red barn where Alfred keeps his scrap. I hesitate; the last time I spent any real time in here, it was with Anna, watching movies on the big screen he rigged up for us. The memories materialise before I can stop them. Her warm, gentle touch exploring my scars. Her lips adoringly gracing my scars.

"I've never wanted you more."

The memory burns deep in my chest like wildfire, clenching my fists and catching my breath. I stand behind Alfred as he unlocks a brand-new padlock, and I couldn't want to enter the barn less. He hands the padlock and key to me, and I take them, confusion quirking my eyebrow up questioningly.

"Come on in," he encourages, his crooked smile young and excited on his lined face. There is no way to say no to that face, and that is what carries me forwards.

And then I see it.

The barn has been transformed; the upper-level guard rail is laced with thousands of fairy lights giving the whole place a warm glow. On the upper level, I see my old punch bag rigged up along with my weights and climbing ropes. The lower level is completely opened up; along the far back wall are big bull's eye targets taped to haystack towers and next to that, a selection of throwing knives.

My jaw drops as I take everything in. To the right is a bed made from pallets; on the bedside table is my camera and tacked on the wall, the photos that I took on the farm during my time hiding here from Jakub. Anna's selfie somehow making me smile through the pang in my chest. There are mismatched rugs laid on the floor, giving the space a rustic warmth. The big screen is still hanging where it was; now, though, there's an old beaten couch lined up in front of it with a coffee table that has my old laptop sat on top and a bottle of whisky.

To the left is a hanging rail with pairs of combat trousers, khaki t-shirts, and jumpers all lined up in military precision. To the side of them, my Carbine rifle, Glock, and the knife Alfred gave me are all mounted on the wall proudly. In the centre of the barn are some crates all bunched together with sheets of plywood bolted to them, making a large desk. Lamps and candles are placed in the centre with old wooden chairs surrounding it. The lump rises in my throat, my eyes blur with tears.

"Alfred…" I breathe.

"Hey, what happened to Pa?" he grumbles in mock offense, and I turn to look at him, gobsmacked and touched.

"How… why… I can't believe you did this," I struggle, and he blushes, redness glowing through the white whiskers on his cheeks.

"Well… um… I thought it would be good for you to have your own space to retreat to. I've seen you need it; I saw it yesterday when you went up to the back fence. You're like me; you need a door to shut when things get bad. Now you have that. You can train in here now. It's getting colder and you need to have somewhere to pass out that is better than the grass or camping chair. I managed to get Lexi to have the police release the rest of your property, and it was dropped here last night."

I stride towards him and wrap my arms around him, and he chuckles, giving me a bear hug. He smells like hay and engine oil; it's familiar and homely and thickening the emotion building in my chest. Because here he is, yet again – protecting me.

"Thank you so much, Pa," I mumble into his chest.

"Anytime, kid. You know that. Come and take a seat."

I let him go and take a seat on the old couch, and as I do, I see a puff of dust float up around me. I don't know where he got it from, but it is very worn leather. The sort of sofa you would see in an old rich man's smoking room. I like it, it's soft, smooth and tatty. Alfred sits opposite me, eying me.

"Are you going to tell me what's going on? Don't bullshit me with the 'I'm fine crap.' I'm not blind; you look rougher than a badger's arsehole, and you're rattled. So, spit it out," he grumbles firmly, and I sigh, defeated.

"Memories keep coming back. They are all similar and all a-about… one person. I don't know why but I can't seem to stop them. Awake, asleep, doesn't really matter. I can't stop them, and I need to. I don't need this right now."

"They're being triggered by something; you're just not sure what yet. They will probably slow down once you figure out what that is."

I nod absentmindedly. "Probably. Look, I'm okay – I promise. You don't need to worry about this. I'm just tired; it will pass. And now at least, like you said – I have a place to run to when things get bad." I smile, but he doesn't look altogether convinced.

"Well, you know where I am, kid. We are partners. We pull each other out of the suck."

"Don't worry, I'll rub some dirt in it."

I sit back out by the fire while Alfred goes back into the house to make breakfast. One of these days, I really should make him breakfast. I have tried, but my reputation as a horrific cook precedes me, and he always politely declines my offers to help. I watch the flames dance; the sun is finally up, and the frost is melting on the grass.

If Alfred is right and these memories are being triggered, then what could possibly be triggering them? He has to be right; I've never gained memories back without something triggering them, like a video or something someone says or does. There is nothing to trigger these, though. I killed him right before I killed Jakub. I watched the life leave his sadistic eyes as I stabbed him in the heart. So, why now?

I hear movement behind me, but I keep my eyes on the fire. It makes me wonder how I know she is coming. Her footfall is so feather-light compared to Alfred's, and yet I always know when she is approaching. I see her move to the chair opposite me in my peripheral vision. I feel on edge; I am not in a good place for a deep chat right now. I twiddle the padlock key to the barn between my fingers.

"I'm sorry about yesterday. Danni insisted on staying. I wasn't happy about it." Anna croaks in her groggy 'just woke up' tone.

"It's fine. None of my business. I wouldn't worry about it."

"I heard about the barn."

The cringe is instant. I didn't even think about the fact that it might make her uncomfortable for Alfred to do that. Now I feel like a jerk.

"I'm sorry. I didn't know he was going to do that."

"I don't know why you're sorry; it was my idea a long time ago. I just never got round to..." She trails off, and I chance a look at her which is a mistake. Her eyes are pained and burning into mine, and it's enough to make me ache. Even when I try so hard not to, all I seem to do is cause her pain.

"If it helps, I'll be trying to stay away from it as much as I can. I have an apartment to sleep at; I don't need to be here anymore than necessary." I reassure.

"You think that's what bothers me? That you will be here too much?"

"I, uh..." I shrug. All my words abandon me.

"Can I see it?"

I get to my feet, and Anna follows me over to the barn. With a tug and a groan, the barn door swings open, and I stand aside to let Anna inside. I stay in the doorway, watching her take the place in. She moves around the barn slowly. Her fingertips fan through the clothes hung up, her eyes pausing at the guns mounted on the wall.

"He told me you called him Pa last night."

"I did. It was an accident."

"It's sweet. It made him happy." She smiles softly.

Anna runs her fingers over the grip of the carbine rifle. She hesitates, her eyes spending what feels like far too long examining the weapons.

"I can still picture you with this practicing when Pa was training you. It always looked so big in your arms, too big. Till the battle on Eastfields Street, then it was like it was a piece of you. You moved so comfortably with it that suddenly it seemed smaller."

"Well, you were watching through binoculars. I'm sure it wasn't easy to see much, which is probably a good thing – harder to see how much I was bricking it," I joke, and Anna turns away from the gun to face me.

"I saw everything, Mac. You were scared; who wouldn't be? But you were also...*glorious*. And that might sound horrible considering what you were fighting. But you were, you were glorious, just – this unstoppable force and somehow still... beautiful..." Anna pauses, her eyes bright and disarming, and I look away. "Sorry... I..." Anna struggles, clearly worried she has upset me, but I look back up and smile through the painful urge to kiss the hell out of her.

"Don't be. It's not every day someone calls you glorious." I wink, and she beams, the relief on her face obvious. She turns and walks along the back wall and then stops dead in front of the bed.

"It is just like the warehouse, only..." She chokes.

"Warmer," I finish her sentence, and then I turn and walk away.

That is enough wandering down memory lane for me. When Anna comes out, I lock the door behind her and walk off to towards the house. I can feel her dawdling behind me. I feel like I can't walk fast enough. So much for distance. Why do I keep doing this to myself? And then she calls me, and I freeze to the spot. She catches me up, crossing past to stand in front of me.

"For the record, you can be here as much as you want to be. Don't stop yourself because you think that is what I want. It's really not. This place is your home; it always will be."

"Thank you, Anna. That's nice to hear."

"Anytime, Mac-attack."

I am relieved to see that easy smile on her face, and I hope it lasts. We get inside and sit at the table, and Alfred places breakfast in front of me. He is such a feeder – there is no way I could ever finish a portion he plates up for me.

"Looking forward to training today?" Alfred asks.

"Well, I won't be getting beaten up by a man-beast today, so it is bound to be an improvement on yesterday," I joke, and Anna laughs, the sound making me smile harder.

"I wouldn't hold your breath, kid."

"What do you know that I don't?"

"Not much but enough to know that if they aren't kicking your butt, they'll be poking your brain. They need to cover as much as possible, as quick as possible, because Barrett could approach you at any time. They need to make sure you can convincingly lie, maintain your cover, and not get rattled by him. Which means…"

"They're going to rattle me. Ugh," I groan, my mouth running dry.

"Afraid so. You'll be alright; Dixy knows what she is doing."

Suddenly I have lost my appetite. My mind isn't exactly being my friend right now; surely that is going to make it worse. The dread in the pit of my stomach is nauseating and is making my head spin. I hold my icy cold hands over my face, and it feels good, grounding somehow. This is not going to be a good day; I can feel it. I close my eyes, pressing my palms into them to calm the spin in my head, and then flinch as the ghost of those vicious eyes flash in my mind.

"Mac, are you…"

"I'm good, just going to get some air. Back in a minute." I flash Anna a brittle smile.

Making the conscious effort to move as casually as I can, I make my way back outside, and as soon as I am out of sight, my walk speeds to a clumsy jog. An unnatural feverish heat is burning across my skin; I can't tear my jumper off quick enough. The icy morning air freezing the sweat off of my skin feels soothing, but it is not enough, not nearly enough. My breath is getting caught in my chest, and I know this feeling well. This is panic. I need to stop it, and I need to stop it now. I choke on absolutely nothing as I see his eyes burn into me, his grip around my throat squeezing the fight out of me. My hands find soft wood as I stumble towards the back fence and grab it, the world moving beneath my feet.

My head sloshes up at the sound of a growling engine and tyres crunching gravel, and I look in horror as the silver van pulls to a stop metres away. The panic accelerates as I spot Lambert and Dixy exiting the van and trudging towards me. I need it to stop; I need it to stop right now. They can't see me like this, they can't. My head swims, the horribly familiar heavy sensation weighing on me as the memory begins to swirl.

"Stop... STOP... Get off of me!"

"Oh, mala suka – I have only just begun to have fun with you.

I am out of air; my vision is blurring in a wash of colour, and then...

Darkness.

***

"Can everyone just back the hell up! She doesn't need to wake up to an audience," Dixy commands.

"You don't even know her! Where do you get off telling us to back off?!" Anna snaps.

"Savannah, stop – she knows what she is doing, come on."

I feel fingers press against the inside of my wrist, then hands delicately lifting my head and mapping my scalp.

"No bumps; her pulse is slowing. Would you go down to the farmhouse and see if Alfred has anything sugary?"

"Mac..."

Stinging taps to my cheek rouse me awake, my eyes squint against the brightness of the sky. Dixy leans above me, her expression soft, the corner of her mouth teasing a smile.

"Oh, for fuck sakes," I groan.

"Well, hello to you too."

I push myself up, dragging my butt until my back is against the fence. I am mortified. This day could not have started any worse, the chagrin level at an all-time high.

"What happened?"

"Low blood sugar. It's nothing." I shrug, rubbing the disorientation from my eyes.

"There was me thinking you were smart. Lying to your instructor isn't smart. I can't help you if you lie to me."

"You can't help me with this. It's irrelevant. I'm fine."

Callum walks up behind Dixy and hands me a bottle of Dr Pepper and a Kit Kat. I thank him, and he nods and walks off again. He really doesn't talk a lot; it's quite nice. There is too much talk lately. I drink the Dr Pepper, but the idea of eating anything right now turns my stomach. The last thing I need to top the embarrassment is to puke on Dixy.

"Do you know why Lexi assigned me to you?"

"No, just assumed it was random," I admit, finally looking at her again. The change of conversation easing the embarrassment a bit.

"Nothing Lexi does is random. I was like you; I didn't see myself as an agent because it wasn't something I chose to be. My background isn't exactly clean."

"I'm sure, though, that you weren't a mass murderer working off a prison sentence."

"Oh, you have that sexy, smouldering, self-loathing thing down to a T, don't you," Dixy jibes playfully.

"Funny…"

"I thought it was. No, I wasn't working off a prison sentence. I was rescued by Lexi, completely by accident. She was tasked with the mission to take out the drug kingpin that kept me as a pet for over a year. By the time she found me, I was angry, damaged, and messed up. It wasn't pretty; I was basically feral." She laughs darkly, and now my attention is peaked. "I knew a lot of the faces of his… associates, and Lexi persuaded me to work with her to identify them so she could bring them all in. Over time, she trained me. Before I knew it, I was an agent of MI5, and I felt like an absolute fraud. I had done some bad things to survive. I was stuck in a spiral of self-hatred, thinking that I didn't deserve good things, and I was icy cold."

"I find that hard to imagine."

Dixy turns around and lifts the back of her shirt, revealing her back, and I stiffen at the sight of the slash scars that slit angrily across her back. She pulls her top back down and turns back to face me with a calm yet knowing expression. Suddenly, Lexi's choice makes sense.

"I'm so sorry."

"Don't be. If it wasn't for that, I wouldn't be who I am now. It took a long time for me to break the cycle. I have no idea what you went through on that boat. There's only so much a file will tell me. I know you had it worse, but once, a long time ago, I was sat where you are now, and my instructor was sat where I am now. I was faced with the choice of trusting them or running away which I was very good at back then. Now, you have to make the choice, Mac. There is a way out of this, I'm proof of that, and I *can* help you. You just have to be brave enough to take the chance."

I feel completely exposed. The lump in my throat rises, and my eyes well. I want so much to believe there is another way to live, to feel. To believe I can live instead of just existing. The more time goes on, the further I am pushing everyone away, scaring them. How long before there is no one left? How long before there is nothing of me left? I close my eyes taking a deep breath, and the tears roll, stinging my face hotly. Then, I look at her and hold my hand out, and she takes it, squeezing it.

"Good choice, Mac. Now, tell me what happened."

"Memories keep coming back, when I am asleep, when I am awake. I don't know what's triggering them. They only ever used to come when triggered, but these ones of this man – They keep coming out of nowhere, and I can't stop them. I saw you guys coming, and I was already panicking. I guess I freaked that I wasn't going to be able to stop it before you got here, and then, I passed out."

Dixy squeezes my hand a little tighter, her smile small and full of empathy.

"That's okay, we can deal with that; I can show you how, Mac."

"Did this happen to you?"

"Not memories, no, but I did get flashbacks. I still do sometimes but now I know how to control the effect they have on me. I don't think these are just memories; they're flashbacks too. If ever there was a classic case for PTSD – it would be you. A flash back, is basically a vivid experience of reliving a traumatic event as if it is happening now, but there are ways of breaking through them and showing yourself, they are not real, ways I can teach you. Your memories are slightly different. To you, the memory isn't past tense in the moment that you regain it, as you have forgotten that it ever happened to you but also, somewhere, your mind hasn't forgotten. That makes the experience more real and harder to snap out of. I think because no matter how traumatic the memories are, your mind and you – *want* to remember."

Dixy flashes me a knowing, sympathetic smile but it doesn't stop the fear of God rippling through me.

"Don't tell Lexi please, I don't want her pulling the plug on me. If they throw me back in prison, I won't survive it again, Dixy," I ramble fearfully, and the thought starts to spur the panic on again, making my arms shake.

"Mac… I absolutely will be telling her because this is exactly what she hoped would happen! That you would let me help you so you can face Barrett from a place of strength. You are not going back to prison, Mac! You're not a fraud; this isn't just blind luck. Lexi is doing this because she sees in you what she saw in me. You are an agent; it's inside of you. My job is just to help you see it, to help you believe it and get you there, and whatever the fuck it takes – I'll make that happen! *Now get up!*" Dixy orders, and I gape, shocked.

"Did I stutter? Get up, Agent Scott!" Dixy demands, even firmer, and I find myself obeying, dragging myself off the floor. My jaw is clenched as I face her, panic still trembling in my limbs.

"Now, I want you to close your eyes and picture the happiest memory you have. It has to be easy to picture. The sounds, smells, everything about that picture must be clear. Do it." Dixy urges, her tone just as firm as the hold she has on my wrist. It doesn't feel bad, usually I would pull away from anyone holding my wrists, but it doesn't feel like she is restraining me. It's more like she's letting me know in some way that she is still there while she barks orders at me.

As I close my eyes, I see myself camping as a kid. I am rifle shooting, a sherbet lemon lollypop in my mouth, the gun kicking in my shoulder. The sound of my friends laughing when I miss the target. The smell of the nearby campfire burning away, the scouting neckerchief knotted around my neck proudly. My very favourite campsite, I must have spent half of my adolescence there. The memories sweep across my mind vividly.

"Do you have it?"

"Yes…" I breathe.

"Good, now pinch your thumb and index together as hard as you can. Keep the memory, the sound, taste, images, and pinch as hard as you can. Do it."

I follow her instructions feeling like a complete prat, but I do it.

"Hold it, hold it, and pinch. Let the memory fill every corner of your mind and pinch harder. Hear the sounds, smell the scents and pinch harder."

I let the memories play over in my head. There was no place I felt more myself than when I was camping with my scout troop. The discipline, the unity, and sense of family it brought me. The opportunity to think innovatively and problem solve. The first sense of being responsible for myself and my friends. The fun of getting muddied up and learning survival techniques, it was a simpler time, and it is easy for me to go back there.

"Open your eyes and look at me," she growls, and I obey. Her jaw is set, and her eyes are tight. She takes a deep breath, her eyes hard and intense, and her grip on my wrist tightens.

"You are going to see the man, the man in the memory, and when you do, instead of trying to stop the vision, you are going accept it and let it run its course! When you see what you don't want to see, pinch your thumb and index finger together and picture the good memory. Interrupt the connection, it will slow it down, and that is the first step to controlling it."

"Don't make me do this!" I spit, pulling away, but Dixy steps forward, grabbing the collar of my shirt and ramming me hard against the fence, her expression livid, and it rocks me. Who knew someone so soft-looking would be capable of such hardness?

"I gave you an order. I suggest you follow it!"

I grit my teeth, glaring, and she doesn't blink. She's not messing around; I have to trust her, I know I do, but the fear I feel of provoking this is staggering. A whimpering "Fuck…" escapes my mouth as I close my eyes; my legs weaken as my head begins to swim heavily. I feel Dixy tighten her grip on my shirt and plant her feet, bracing me with her forearms against my chest. I wish it wasn't so easy to see him, to feel him, but I knew it wouldn't take much to summon him. It's as if he is there waiting. His eyes burn in my mind, and the memory swirls.

Facedown, my cheek sliding on my own urine. Nails digging into the back of my neck, and I can't breathe.

"No…" I choke. I screw my eyes up tight and pinch my fingers hard together, wheezily sucking in air.

My mouth fills with the taste of lemons, and I hear laughter and the images flicker. I kick, and I flail, and he lifts my head and slams it down on the pissy wooden boat deck floor. My head spins as he uses his knees to part my legs. My thighs shaking and clenching as I fight to squirm away.

"ARGH." I cry out pinching my finger and thumb harder, so hard it stings.

The rifle kicks in my shoulder, and I see the target. I watch the pellet swoop wide of the bullseye, and I huff in frustration as I hear the jeers behind me.

"Ha-ha! What a miss, Mac!"

"Best out of three?" I suggest.

The smell of firewood is burning in my nose, the twigs snapping under my boots. The campfire songs being sung booming in my ears, loud, festive, and out of tune.

I gasp… my eyes fling open, and Dixy is there, her eyes glittery and haunted. Her fists still gripping my collar tight. I wait for the memory to come back, eyes wide… but nothing happens.

"You made it stop, didn't you?" Dixy whispers.

"I… think… I - "

The realisation hits. I *did* make it stop. Maybe it doesn't have to be this way. Maybe one day, I won't have to relive this anymore. Maybe one day, I can live in the now.

"T-thank you…" My head bows, and I break, and as if she was expecting it, she pulls me by the collar and holds me through the sobs. It is an awkward hug, rigid, and it isn't just me making it so.

"Well done. The first time is the hardest. It will get easier now, I promise. I need you to keep practicing tying the memory to pinching your finger and thumb. One day, it will become so ingrained that you could have a flashback, and no one will ever know it is happening to you. You will gain control, and it won't hurt so much anymore," she mumbles in my ear, rubbing my back.

"You were right." I half smirk. "I'm starting to hate you a little bit."

"If you are going to be a spy, you are going to have to learn to lie better than that." Dixy giggles. "I'm sorry I had to push you so hard; that wasn't an easy thing for me to do. I remember how bad it feels, so forcing you to have a flashback didn't feel good."

"Where would I be if you hadn't?" I point out, and she smiles gratefully.

"Right. I would love to say that is it for the day, but unfortunately, the day has only just begun. However, I think we both deserve a strong drink and a decent length break. Are you game, Agent Scott?"

"Thought you'd never ask, Agent Dixon."

We walk back down towards the farm, my legs dragging in the ice-licked grass, and I feel shell-shocked and edgy but, surprisingly, lighter. Dare I say it – I feel hopeful. When we reach the fire pit, Lambert and Alfred are chatting together. A disagreement unfolding about which semi-automatic rifle is the best. I listen to the three of them swap war stories and laugh as the whisky trickles down my throat, warming me.

"… And then she shouted, 'I'm the king of the world!' at him!" Alfred booms, and my cheeks pinken as everyone booms into laughter.

"I'm never going to live that one down, am I?"

"That is priceless! Tell me you at least got a swing at the guy," Dixy gasps excitedly.

"Did she ever? A swift head butt broke his nose!" Alfred cheers.

"Not so pretty anymore," Anna sings.

My chest warms as I hear her behind me, the memory making me smile. I crane my neck and see her, the smile dying off my face before I can stop it as my eyes roam to see her fingers interlocked with Danni's. I look away, the monster crawling in my chest as green as her gorgeous eyes. They stand there awkwardly as all the camp chairs are taken, and I just want the ground to swallow me up.

"Here, Anna, take my chair – I need to stretch my legs anyways," Dixy offers, springing out of her chair.

"Thanks, Dixy. It's okay, though; we were just going to head inside."

"Nah, let's stay. Looks like everyone is having a drink. Let's join," Danni quips.

What the hell? Is this girl immune to awkwardness or what?

Danni pulls Anna toward the empty seat by the hand, and Anna sits down, her smile sheepish and not touching her eyes as Danni sits on the floor between her legs. I pour myself another whisky, busying my hands while trying to put out of an air of 'I don't give a fuck.' Inside, I am fuming. At this point, I feel like Anna is just trying to punish me. I have tried to be as friendly and easy as I can be with her. She knows I passed out earlier, and now she brings Danni here. I don't know, maybe I am overreacting, but my blood is boiling, hurt burning in my belly like acid. I have no right to feel this way, I know that. Why should she care if I am okay or not? If my day has already been hard enough? But she is Anna. Thoughtful, pure-hearted Anna. This doesn't feel like the Anna I know. This feels… cold.

Maybe she didn't care as much as you thought she did.

A game of truths begins, and if I didn't want to leave before, I most definitely do now because a good-natured game is the last thing I'm in the mood for. But I keep my eyes away from Anna and Danni, and I soon get absorbed in the stories being told around me.

"Alfred, what was your biggest rookie screw-up?" Lambert asks, his grin boyish.

"Oh, hells bells, there were so many! Okay, up in the mountains of Pakistan, high altitude in sub-zero temperatures. There is zero visibility, and we are all packed like sardines in this tent, and the tent is pitched on this tiny ledge. You can't get out of the tent till daylight, or you risk falling 20,000 feet. So, me and my buddies – we prepared, we all bought two water bottles each, you know… one for drinking water and one to pee in. The water bottle with the pee in would get warm, so we would put it inside our jackets to keep us warm and well… At some point in the night, I wanted a drink, reached inside me jacket, and chugged a good few gulps of my own cold piss before I realised I got the wrong bottle."

Laughter irrupts. I love Alfred's stories, and he has no shortage of them. I laugh easily, and right now, that is exactly what I need. I sip my whisky and feel its caramel warmth trickle through me.

"Okay, okay… Who is next?" Alfred asks.

"It's my turn, isn't it?" Danni asks. "Yeah, right. Mac," I turn to look in her direction, surprised she is throwing a question my way. "What is your biggest regret?" she asks, grinning, but her eyes are staring me down icily. I hold her gaze, and inside, my chest freezes.

"Come on. I bet you have *loads* to choose from; it can't be that hard to pick just one," Danni goads.

My eyes flick to Anna, who is staring into the fire, her expression blank, and it cuts. Dixy sweeps in front of me. She sits down at my feet and rests her back against my legs.

"That's a bit of a loaded question. I thought we were having fun? I think it's time to get back to work anyway, Mac."

"Just playing the game," Danni replies, unphased.

The awkward tension is thick, and adrenalin fizzes in my limbs as Danni stares me down, her glare as cold as ice. Dixy gets up and stands by the side of my chair; she places her hand on my shoulder as if to warn me not to bite. As I get to my feet, Danni gets to hers too, and she takes two measured steps towards me.

"Sorry, Mac. Didn't mean to cause any offence," she utters lightly, but she eyes me hatefully and the hairs rise on the back of my neck. Then she turns away and stalks off towards the house, leaving my heart thumping in my ears with a heavy pound.

"Mac…" Anna chokes, her eyes imploring, and my anger flares. I hold my hand up, glaring at her, and I turn away from her before the hurt etched on her face breaks my step.

"Dixy, Lambert. Let's get back to work."

I walk away with tingly legs, adrenalin fizzing around my system, filling it with an agitated energy I don't know what to do with. I make my way towards the barn, unlock the door, and hold it open for them both. Once we are inside, Lambert makes a beeline straight over to the guns, his eyes hungry.

"Mind if I take a look a closer, Mac?"

"Go for your life, brother."

Dixy is curiously circling the place, and I take the moment to calm myself down. The anger is subsiding, making way for a painful pang of betrayal, only I am not sure where it is coming from. It's not like I expect Anna to have my back, but what the hell has she said to Danni to make her despise me so much? The look in her eyes was unmistakable; that was real hate. Maybe Anna hasn't said anything at all. It's hard to believe she would do that to me, and it isn't like the war I inflicted on Eastfields Street is a secret. It's been splashed all over the papers. Danni's contempt could come from that.

Who could blame her?

"I didn't know you lived here," Dixy pipes up, snapping out of my inner monologue.

"I don't. Alfred wanted me to have my own space. I'm also quite good at running away, which he doesn't like. So, he wanted to give me a place to run to. He only showed me this place this morning. Lexi managed to get my stuff released from my old hideout, and Alfred put this together for me," I explain, my voice monotone.

"Are you okay?"

"Yeah, I'm fine. A little pissed off but fine."

"Not surprised. That girl was clearly baiting you."

"You noticed that, huh? Glad it wasn't just me; I was worried I was overreacting."

"No, not at all. Everyone noticed that, even Anna. What did you do? Piss on her cornflakes?" she jokes, lightening her probing.

"Your guess is as good as mine. Thank you, though, for having my back."

Lambert, Dixy, and I sit at the makeshift desks in the centre of the barn and get to work. My mind is quickly blown by an information overload, but I am relishing in it. I hang on their every word, determined that I will soak up every detail.

"The first thing we need to teach you is how to effectively maintain your cover. This means you must be in control of your reactions no matter what stress or danger you may be in. Everything from your body language to your voice must be in your control. You must be able to lie convincingly and be able to think fast under pressure to maintain the lie. Barrett will try to pick you apart; to operate for this long without being caught means he's skilled at reading people and very careful who he allows into his inner circle."

My lungs clinch tightly. I am a terrible liar, and now my life depends on being able to become a master at it. As I listen to Dixy explain how vital it is, self-doubt begins to creep in, but I know I have to have some faith. Lying is a skill; skills are learnt; no one is good at everything. I just have to learn.

"So, the first thing I am going to do is subject you to a lie detector test. I expect you to fail miserably, so try not to worry. It is that failure that will help me teach you how to pass it later on. If you can pass a lie detector test, you will understand how to manipulate your own reactions to your advantage." Dixy gives me a half-crooked smile, and I gulp.

"I can't wait," I manage, and Dixy laughs.

Lambert sets a laptop up on the table and begins connecting wires in the various ports down the side. My mouth is dry as I try to get a handle on the nerves swirling in my stomach. Dixy wraps two wires around my upper and lower chest, then straps a blood pressure monitor to my arm. It inflates but not fully, just holding a firm grip on my bicep. Cuffs with wires attached are wrapped around my fingers, and then Lambert turns the laptop around to face me.

"The two corrugated wires wrapped around your chest are there to measure your breathing and respiratory rate; that is the top blue wiggly line. The blood pressure monitor will detect any changes in your heart rate and pulse; that is the second red wiggly line. The cuff on your index finger measures skin conductivity which relates to how much you sweat during questioning, that is the third green wiggly line. First, I'll establish a baseline by asking you easy questions. Are you ready?" Dixy asks.

"Yes."

The monitors spike up and down erratically, and the beeps of my heart rate pick up speed.

"That would be a lie," she informs me with a smirk, and I laugh, relaxing a little.

"Is your name Mckenna Margo Scott?" Dixy asks, and I scowl at the use of my much-despised middle name.

"Yes," I growl.

"Don't worry, I won't tell anyone. Are you 32 years old?"

"Yes."

"Have you ever committed a crime?"

"Yes."

"Was that crime indecent exposure?"

"Maybe next time," I retort, and Lambert chokes on his whisky.

"Right, that should be enough," Dixy surmises.

The door barn door groans open, and I hear Alfred shuffle in. He walks around to my view with a tray loaded with bacon sandwiches, and my stomach growls. Close behind him is Anna, carrying a tray of coffees. I keep my eyes on Alfred but that doesn't stop the heart rate monitor beeping faster and faster, and I catch Dixy's eye. She steps forwards and hits a button on the laptop, and the beeps stop immediately. I have never been so grateful.

"OH, Alfred, you absolute gem!" Dixy squeaks, her eyes hungry. Alfred turns his gaze to me, chuckling, and I glare at him playfully.

"Lie detector test, is it? Oh dear, kid, what a compromising position to find yourself in. You are going to have fun with her, Dixy. She's a useless liar."

"Oi! Shush you and give me a bacon sandwich." I pout.

Anna leaves the barn and takes the awkward energy with her. It is a relief; I know at some point she is going to want to talk about what happened. Right now, I feel ready to blow, and I don't think a candid conversation with her about her weirdo girlfriend is going to cool my head. Alfred soon follows her, and Dixy gets on with the questions. They are a little bit more stress-provoking but nothing too bad. I guess they need to push a stress response to read my reactions. As everyone suspected, I failed miserably. It is a relief when Dixy removes all the wires, and I can move around freely.

"Right, Mac. The baseline questions to any lie detector are the most important of the test. They seem easy, but that is where the patterns begin. If you answer calmly to five questions and one of those is a lie, it creates a faint blip in your results no matter how small the lie is. That blip is the point of reference to the whole test. When the real questions begin, if your readings reach anything near those readings of the faint blip, then it's clear you are lying. If the readings are less than the blip, they will read as truthful. Follow me so far?" she asks, and I nod.

"So, what if you were able to accelerate your readings in all of the initial base questions? What do you think would happen?"

"I would have lots of blips, stronger ones?" I guess.

"Exactly. Say you were able to raise your heart rate, maybe make yourself sweat a little, and then you were to answer the base questions. Your readings would be elevated even in the truthful answers. Then when the harder questions come along, your heightened readings will not look so different to the baseline questions."

"So, if I was able to think about bad stuff, make myself anxious in the beginning, it would make the end result inaccurate?"

"Yes! But you don't have to stop at bad thoughts. Physical pain speeds your heart rate, breathing and causes you to sweat. You could discreetly bite your tongue; the pain would elevate the results too."

"So how does this help me lie? Barrett may not subject me to a lie detector test." I point out.

"Because I'm trying to teach you how to manipulate your own body reactions and control your emotions. This is just step one of that. When you infiltrate The Culling, you're going to have to persuade him and the rest of his cell that you are loyal, believe in the cause, and will do anything to serve them. You will also have to hide any disgust you feel towards their ideology or their plans to kill more people. Controlling your emotions, your lying tells, body language – it's all vital in persuading them that you are one of them."

My brain feels like it is going to explode, but I feel an ember growing inside. A warm determination that is glowing more and more as information fuels it like oxygen. I want to be ready; I will do all it takes to be ready. Dixy tells me that I will have another lie detector test in a few days. Hopefully, I can give a better result next time.

***

The truck rumbles along quietly as I drive, feeling a little awkward under the watchful eyes of Lambert. This is the first time I have spent any alone time with him. While I enjoy that he doesn't talk much, it is a little uncomfortable driving with him so quietly. Dixy has taken the van and is meeting Lexi at MI5 headquarters to give her a progress report, and I am going for a coffee with Lambert. I wish it was going to be that laid back, but it is actually another part of my training.

Walking the streets of London, it feels great to have a change of scenery. It is good to see actual people walking around living their actual lives. I hope one day, after all of this, I might get the chance to do that. To live in the now, experience life again. Dixy has made me feel more hopeful that maybe that is possible for me, but hope is a scary thing to have. You can't be as easily disappointed if you are always expectant of the worst.

Dodging passers-by, we walk side by side, weaving in and out of streets. It seems so loud and fast; I am now so used to the quiet peace of the farm or my apartment that I feel overwhelmed by the movement and speed of the outside world. We come to a stop outside a coffee shop called Umber.

"This should do. After you, Mac," Lambert announces, nodding to the door.

I enter the coffee shop, and the smell of bitter coffee and sweet pastry hits me hard. I salivate; I love the smell of coffee. The walls are all exposed brick, and the domed steel ceiling lights are dangling low from chains. Everything is brick and steel, giving an industrial vibe. The seating is rough wooden benches built into brick surrounds, and towards the back, there are some comfier-looking tub chairs. It is quite busy inside, the murmurs of groups chatting filling the air with a light buzz.

"Pick somewhere to sit, and I'll bring us over some coffees," Lambert offers.

I look around. Although it is busy, there are plenty of places to sit. In the end, I settle for a seat by the window. I wait for Lambert to return, but he doesn't.

"Mac, over here," Lambert calls.

My head shoots up in the direction of his voice, and I see him walking away towards the back of the coffee shop. I follow, a little confused as to why he bothered to ask me to pick somewhere to sit but eager to have my caramel latte. I find him at the back of the restaurant, and he slides my drink over as I sit down.

"Why did you choose a window seat?" Lambert asks.

"It isn't something I've had the chance to do much after being in hiding."

Lambert nods and keeps eye contact with me; his eyes are actually quite kind, soft even. It seems so alien on his rugged face. His brow is furrowed and dark, his jawline strong, and his face rough with a five o'clock shadow – all of which make his eyes look softer somehow.

"That makes sense. I moved us to the back here because I have a view of the entire restaurant. My back is against the wall, which means no one can approach me from behind. To my right is a fire escape which is an easy out if needed. I assess every building and outdoor space I come across. I am always alert to every weakness that can be exploited to make me vulnerable. This keeps me safe. At first, it's a matter of pushing yourself to remember to do this, but it quickly becomes habit."

It is quite easy to zone out when Lambert talks because everything that he says sounds the same. There are no highs and lows in his tone. No exaggeration, quirks, or identifiable markers that make him sound uniquely him.

"Don't run scared, run smart," I state – Alfred's words repeating in my mind.

"Basically yes. You always have a back-up plan, and you never enter somewhere blind. If there isn't a clear exit strategy – change location. This will be important when you make contact with Barratt. You need control over wherever he approaches you, but you don't know where that will happen. If you've already properly risk assessed every area you visit, then you already have control of the location no matter where he approaches you."

"Makes sense. This is at least something I have some experience in." I huff with a half-smile.

"You are doing better than you realise, Mac. Have some faith in yourself," he encourages. "The other thing vital to maintaining your cover is to be able to blend in. Right now, you are in a coffee shop. It may sound simple, but if you are in a coffee shop, then drink the coffee. Partake in the activities around you, pick up a magazine, read a little but multitask. You need to read enough that if someone asks about what you are reading, you can give a convincing answer but also not so much that you are not mindful of your surroundings. It requires balance and a cool head."

"What if I make a mistake?"

"That's where the ability to control your emotions and lie effectively comes back into play. You will make mistakes; the trick is to keep calm under that pressure and improvise. A good musician can play a bum note but manage to keep playing and cover their mistake so that no one listening would ever notice that a mistake was made. Panic is what will blow your cover, not mistakes."

I take a deep breath, and Lambert's words actually calm me down. I don't have to be perfect; mistakes will happen. My head is beginning to pound. This has been such a long day of brain prodding and filling already; it feels like it is never going to end.

"There are some things I want you to practice from now on. Once you infiltrate The Culling, the game will change. You'll have to blend in, yes, but a massive part of your job will be to get information and not be caught. So, when you go to a restaurant, I want you to choose a civilian and practice tracking them. Study their behaviour discreetly, watch them without being caught, and eavesdrop on their conversations without drawing attention. You would not believe how helpful eavesdropping can be. Also, I want you to start watching movies on mute. You are going learn to read lips and understand the facial expressions that people give away without hearing what is being said."

I nod at him, a little awestruck. This man's mind is like Alfred's, only somehow, even more analytical. I feel very lucky; both of my instructors are very good at what they do. The longer I sit with Lambert, the more I see that everything he does is by design. He is very still; his movements don't attract attention, but he moves just enough that he doesn't look rigid or out of place.

"The last thing I want you to practice before I make your brain go pop," he smirks boyishly, "is improving your night vision and hearing. Work in the dark: assemble your weapons, read, anything that requires your concentrated sight - do it in the dark. With your hearing, it's easy to get distracted and overwhelmed by so much noise and distraction but hearing the right thing at the right time can save your life. If you'd heard the swoosh of the sandbag being launched at you yesterday, you would have reacted. That's about awareness as well as hearing. So, blindfold yourself, take away your sense of sight, and try to pick out sounds one by one."

"Does that actually work?" I ask, unconvinced, and Lambert smirks at me deviously.

"Table across at 9 o'clock. The blondes name is Sara, and she is sitting with a brunette named Kerry who just got off work from her secretary job. She's having problems with her husband. Sara hasn't spoken much; she can't get a word in edgeways while Kerry rambles about her lazy husband Steve.

Instead, she is picking at a cinnamon whirl, smiling and nodding when she feels it's appropriate." Lambert didn't take his eyes away from mine, and he laughs as my jaw drops.

"Wow, okay, that's just showing off, dude."

"Maybe a little, but I had the same training as you are having. Granted, we are having to ram it into a lot shorter time, but if you apply yourself and trust us – you'll get there."

I do actually feel like my brain is about to pop, so I am relieved when he stops rambling at me. My head hurts from trying to take in every piece of information, but I am so grateful for it. The more I learn, the more confident I feel.

"We should get back, but before we do, I wanted to apologise for yesterday. I had fun fighting you because you fight on instinct not just trying to recite moves. It's rare to get that in a sparring partner. I got over excited and lost control; I'm sorry for that."

"Callum, I was carried away too; you were just better than me. I need you to push me. Like I said to Dixy, don't hold back – push me hard because it is the only chance I have of beating Barrett. Don't be too hard on yourself, alright?" I reassure, and his face relaxes in relief.

"Thanks, Mac. Let's get going."

It was nice to get to know Lambert better. Both he and Dixy have managed to make me feel more hopeful and determined in one day than I could have ever imagined. My brain feels like a heavy, waterlogged sponge, though. Even driving is requiring much more focus, my mind slow and fatigued. When we pull up back at the farm, night is starting to fall, and the silver van is already back along with a car I don't recognise.

"That is Lexi's car," Lambert informs me as if he can read my mind, and suddenly, I feel uneasy.

We walk down to the fire pit where everyone seems to be congregated, my legs feeling heavier with every step. As I get closer, I see Anna and Alfred sat on camping chairs, and stood just away from the fire are Dixy and Lexi, deep in conversation. I walk straight over to them, and they stop talking and turn my way. Both of them look stressed, Dixy especially.

"Agent Scott. There has been a development I need to brief you on. Is there somewhere we could talk more privately?"

CHAPTER 3

Thank You

That feeling you get as a kid when you have been sent to the headmaster's office. Yeah, this is that, multiplied by 100. Dread is knotting in the pit of my stomach as I watch Lexi perch on the end of my dusty sofa. Her black fitted suit and stark white starchy shirt look so out of place inside the rustic homeliness of the barn. I wipe my sweaty palms down my thighs as I try to figure out if I have done something wrong, but her expression is unreadable.

"Mac, I hear from your instructors that you are doing very well," Lexi begins, and I exhale a little.

"If that's the case, why do I feel like I'm about to get bad news?" I deadpan, and her eyebrows raise.

"It's always straight to the point with you, isn't it?" She smiles a little. "Okay, the police managed to apprehend a man in Bosnia. He was badly beaten and rambling madly about The Culling. We have some sleeper agents in place there, so we were informed quickly but not quickly enough to get a lot of information. What we did get wasn't good news. The man was sleep-deprived and delirious from heatstroke."

Heatstroke? In October?

"He mentioned the words 'reconditioning' and 'ritual.' Unfortunately, before I could get him transported here for further questioning, he succumbed to his injuries. Medical examination points to heart failure, and there was evidence of asphyxiation. Water in the lungs - not enough to kill him, but the prolonged use of waterboarding weakened his heart."

I choke but do not drown; I drown but do not die.

"He was tortured to death," I breathe, my throat instantly parched.

"Yes. I think that this reconditioning is hazing or something that you have to pass to be a member of The Culling. A ritual that Barrett has created, and whatever it is, this man failed," Lexi explains grimly, and I can feel her watching me as I nod absentmindedly.

"A reconditioning that I'll have to go through in order to infiltrate The Culling."

Lexi doesn't answer, she just looks at me, and that is answer enough. I get to my feet and turn my back on her, panic threatening to overtake me. My heart palpates unevenly, and I feel the darkness creeping over the edge of me, and I let it. I welcome it. My fear turns to anger; it boils up so fast, I could scream. I kick out at one of the chairs at the desk hard, and it flies across the room, crashing against the barn wall.

"FUCK!"

"Mac…" Lexi approaches me silently, making me jump.

"Sorry. I…"

"Don't be. As you were, Agent. If ever there was a time to lose it a bit, it's now."

When I turn back round to face Lexi again, I see a hint of worry. It's small, but it is there, tugging at her jaw.

"This doesn't change anything, Lexi."

"You still want to go forward?" Lexi frowns, but I see her jaw loosen. She is relieved when I nod. "You are going to make an extraordinary Agent, Mac."

I look away. I am not trying to be a good agent, and hearing that just pisses me off; I am trying to keep myself from a fate that I know I won't survive; I cannot go back to prison. Plus – who else is going to stop Barrett?

"Do they know?" I ask, my eyes fixed at the barn door.

"I asked Dixon to inform them while I spoke to you, so they do now. Though, they don't know you want to go forward."

"They know. Is there anything else I need to know?"

"Not at the moment. Is there anything I can do, Mac? Anything that will help?"

"I'll let you know if there is. For now, I could use a few minutes to process this."

"Of course. Please, if you need anything. It may not feel like I'm around but trust me, I am fighting in your corner – every step of the way."

"Thank you, Agent Holt."

"No, thank you, Mac. I can't imagine… the sacrifice you are making. I am grateful for you. The world would be too if they knew."

Oh, please…

I follow Lexi to the barn door, and without another word, I turn in the other direction, walking away from the fire and into the darkness. Every step further I get away from everyone is a step closer to losing control of the hurt I feel threatening to suffocate me. It seems like every time I find a little hope, something comes along and dashes it.

Inevitably, I end up at the back fence again. There isn't really anywhere else I want to go. Sitting down in the grass, my back against the fence, I watch Lexi's headlights beam eerily across the farm, and then the darkness fully saturates my view. The night is frigidly cold, but I find the feeling soothing. It is helping to keep the panic at bay.

I knew it wouldn't be long till someone found me. I wasn't exactly hiding; I just want some peace.

"I really don't have a pep talk in me right now," I utter.

Alfred sits on the grass next to me, groaning on the way down. He puts a glass in front of me, fills it with whisky, and hands it to me before filling himself up a glass.

"I didn't come to talk; I came to drink."

We sit in silence. Every time I empty my glass, Alfred just tops it up again. Soon the warmth starts to penetrate, my head becomes heavy, and I lean it against his shoulder. Alfred sits with me, quiet and strong. The safety I feel breaks my resolve. The tears come, and I grip the sleeve of his over-worn denim jacket as if holding on will keep me safe.

"I'm so sorry, kid. I wish I could go in your place. I'd give anything for that."

"I know you would, and you know, I'd never let you."

***

I open my eyes, confused about how I ended up in the barn and my head pounding in a whisky fog. It is cold outside the bed, so I layer up, and when I go outside, the cold hits me in the face, clearing the cobwebs in my mind. It is still dark but that bluish darkness that happens between night and sunrise. I stoke the fire, breathing life into the embers, and then I walk over to the parkour run. I walk the course, the physical action making me feel less fizzy with nervous energy.

After three circuits, I begin to speed up, the anger and the fear less suffocating the harder I run. The hangover is making me feel sluggish, but I power through it. I am not really training, not thinking about improving my ability. In fact, I am not thinking at all. The more I run, the harder my feet pound across the platforms, the harder I tug my weight with my hands, the less hemmed in I feel. Pain is grounding. After all this time, it has become a friend.

Soon, exhaustion hits me, my stomach uneasy and sloshy with alcohol. I sit by the fire and hope the queasy feeling will pass. There is a part of me that would like to hope that Barrett wouldn't subject his own daughter to any kind of reconditioning, but it is so obvious that he is not capable of any kind of empathy. The man is a narcissistic psychopath, and he will afford me no special treatment. That hope is foolish.

I miss the days when I thought Jakub was my biggest problem. At the time, it felt like an impossible mountain to climb. Now, it feels like child's play in comparison to this. The more I learn about The Culling, the more I want to take them down. They are monsters revelling in their nihilism and driven by creed and lunacy. There is no line they won't cross, no moral they won't tarnish. They are a force hell-bent on devastation. Really, when you think of it that way, the cost of what is left of my tattered soul in return for destroying them – doesn't seem like such a high price. I feel a calm sweep over me… Yes, that helps. I will make them burn. Every last demented one of them.

It takes a monster to catch a monster. I am coming for you.

Burn, burn, burn.

I close my eyes and let the anger calm me like a heavy blanket. I feel heavy; the sun is glowing sunset orange through my eyelids. That happened quickly; it was dark, and now it's not. I feel a warm hand on my face, stroking my cheek gently. That feels nice. I feel safe; there is safety in that light touch. I must have fallen asleep; I don't want to wake up. The blanket is soft and cosy, and the touch against my skin is warm and comforting.

"Shhhh," Anna coos. Her hand lightly moves my head to the side, and then she moves it back, and my face rests against something warm and soft. The scent of candy perfume fills my nose, and I smile.

"So cute," she whispers.

That can't be right.

"Why don't you just wake her? Doesn't she have a bed to go home to?" Danni hisses sharply, but Anna's fingertips move undeterred, softly stroking my cheek.

"She's probably been training; she's had a rough night, and she likes it by the fire. I have no reason to wake her," Anna replies, her hand stalling on my cheek, her thumb brushing my bottom lip.

My insides fizz, a mixture of warmth from her touch and ice from the cold eyes I feel boring into me. Confusion has me paralysed. When Lambert told me to practice eavesdropping, this wasn't exactly what I had in mind.

"You are always watching over her; she doesn't appreciate it. The sooner you see that and let her go, the better off you will be, Anna."

"I have told you; I have no intention of letting her go. I've been clear about that from the start and if you *ever* push her like that again…" Anna growls an angry hiss, and my stomach drops.

What the hell?

"Don't threaten me, Anna. We have been over this," Danni spits.

My mind is reeling, too sleepy to understand. I am missing something here, but the guilt still hits me hard. I have no idea what I have missed, but she clearly had my back more than I gave her credit for. Her words echo in my head over and over, and I still can't make sense of them. I feel her warm lips on my forehead, and I can't suppress my flinch or the warmth that spreads through me. Anna pulls back a little, her hand still stroking my face, and my eyes fall on hers. She looks more tired than I do and a little fearful.

"Sorry, I didn't mean to wake you. Go back to sleep," she whispers, pulling her hand away, and I stop her. I lay it back on my face and hold it there. She smiles at me, a little taken aback, and my eyes droop.

"Thank you..." I mumble.

"For what?" she whispers with a shaky breath.

I don't answer; I fall back to sleep feeling peaceful. She did have my back after all, and I may not understand any of what I just heard, but all that matters is I feel peace in knowing she didn't betray me. She still has my back – she is still Anna.

The next time I wake up, it is to the voice of Alfred and the smell of bacon.

"I see how it is, I make you a bed, and you still sleep by the fire."

I rub my eyes and wait for the hangover to hit again; it is a relief when it doesn't. I look around, trying to shake the disorientation. I sit forward, and something soft falls into my lap, and I pick it up. The material is heavy and dark red and flecked with orange. I run my fingers over the cable knit pattern of Anna's favourite jumper, and the constant dull ache I feel intensifies. So that wasn't a dream then. The conversation replays in my head, and it still doesn't make any sense to me. The anger in Anna's voice, the hate in Danni's. I have never been more confused.

Alfred hands me a coffee and a plate of bacon and egg sandwiches. My stomach churns, but once I force myself to start eating, it settles, and I feel much more human.

"Pa... How much do you know about Danni?"

"Not a lot. You know me; I stay out of Savannah's...stuff. Why?"

"Something feels...off."

"Are you sure that's not just jealously talking?"

"No, it's not. Something in my gut... I don't know, Pa; something doesn't feel right. I can't say anything because that is exactly what Anna will think. Can you just keep an eye on her? That's all I'm asking."

Alfred sighs, scratching the hair behind his ear and fidgeting in his chair.

"I can do that."

"Thank you. Do you mind if I grab a shower? I feel gross."

"Since when do you ask?" He frowns, and I grimace. The understanding soon hits him.

"She isn't here; she's at work covering your shifts. Lexi has delayed your return to work for a while. Given the new... information, she wants to focus on your training. It's looking more and more like Barrett is in Bosnia, but that still doesn't give you much time. Lexi has all of the airports primed to notify us if he makes a move."

"Maybe he won't come at all, and they will just throw me back in prison, and everyone can go just go home," I joke darkly.

"If he doesn't come, we will be going to Bosnia. Lexi told me last night; she's preparing for every eventuality."

How messed up is it that hearing that is actually a relief?

When I get outside, showered and feeling much more human, Alfred is busying himself on the parkour run. Moving things, adding things, and the silver van pulls up as I watch him. The figures of Dixy and Lambert make their way towards me, and my stomach clenches in anticipation as I wonder what hell is going to rain on me today. Lambert has a large duffle bag, and he breaks away in the direction of Alfred and drops it on the floor in front of him, greeting him with a high five. I smile as I watch the 'bromance' blossom.

"Agent Scott," Dixy greets me, taking a seat.

"Do you have to call me that?"

"Yes, I do, actually. Eventually, you'll get used to it."

"Don't bank on it."

"How are you doing?" she enquires stiffly, and I look at her. She looks haggard; her smile is brittle and doesn't reach her eyes.

"I could ask you the same thing. You look more stressed than me."

"Oh, that isn't possible," she jokes, and I don't laugh. I just hold her gaze, and she lets out a strained sigh. "I suppose I might be a tiny bit stressed out. We are going to have to change the direction of your training. I admit I don't like the direction or the reasons for the change."

"You think I should have backed out?"

"No, I completely get why you didn't, Mac. I never thought for a second you would; I don't think any of us did."

"Then what's the problem?"

"We came here to help you, and it's huge that you're letting us. Now, the only way to help you is to cause you more pain. I don't know how to do that; I don't know if I can."

"Are you abandoning me, Agent Dixon?" I say lightly, but I don't think I'm quite able to hide the worry in my voice.

"Nope. No one can kick your arse like I can."

"You got that right. So, what's first?"

"Well, I'm hoping that maybe we can go a long way by teaching you to cope with things that may happen to you. Everyone has weaknesses. So, I guess I need to know what yours are so that I can try to find coping mechanisms."

"Whisky, Haribo eggs, and bossy women." I joke, and she laughs, which is good. She looks more like her normal self now.

"Nice deflection. Only you can tell me what you're going to struggle with the most. If we can break down those fears, we have a better chance of getting you through whatever this… reconditioning might be."

I cross my arms and then uncross them. Learning about body language is making me uncomfortable. Crossing my arms is a sign of me trying to put distance between Dixy and I, protecting myself. Now that I know this, it is making me fidgety and self-conscious.

"Touch might be a problem, but you already know that. I'm not so good at constant darkness and silence; a segregation cell taught me that. Being restrained is also not great. Mostly I…"

The memory flashes, and I feel my throat tighten. I screw my eyes shut, trying to shake the sickening images flashing through my mind.

"Mac… are you still with me?" Dixy asks, and I snap back.

"Yeah, sorry."

"Will you tell me what you just saw? Because that is what you are afraid of."

Dixy looks at me, waiting patiently, and I cross my arms again. His eyes flash in my mind, and I flinch, jumping to my feet. My thumb and index finger pinch together hard, and the images distort.

"Mac…"

I feel her hand on my wrist; she lifts it up and then puts it down again but doesn't let go. Instead, she holds it, and somehow, it helps. The happy vision is easier to see, and my vice type press on my index finger and thumb loosens as I gain control.

"Check you out," Dixy whispers, and I manage a laugh. She lets go of my wrist, and I sit back down, eyes wide and heart pounding. The image of his eyes is still faintly etched in my mind's eye.

"I can't tell you about him; those things tied to him aren't relevant. They're not something Barrett is likely to do, but I can tell you about the rest."

"It's all relevant, Mac, but for now – let's start with what you *can* tell me. What else came straight to your mind other than the man?"

It's not that I can't talk about this, it is easier than it used to be, but it just seems like memories are being triggered so easily that talking about it feels like I am just inviting more memories. I take a deep breath and speak mechanically.

"Dry drowning, electrocution, forced suicide and self-harm, hallucinations, the box," I list indifferently.

Dixy almost doesn't react. She has a good poker face but not perfect. I see her jaw clench, and then I look away.

"They were the worst things, apart from the man?" she asks softly, and I nod with my eyes on the floor.

"Can you tell me what the box is?"

"A plastic box. I was kept in there sometimes. Smelled like piss, my own piss. When you gotta go, you gotta go," I joke darkly, but my tone is too dead to pull it off.

"And the hallucinations?"

"Sleep deprivation and whatever drugs they gave me. Benzos and something else, they call it truth serum."

"Why did the hallucinations make the worst list?"

"Because they were of people I missed, and I'd think I was going home or already home, but I wasn't. I wasn't sure what was real anymore, and when reality would straighten out again - it hurt. Plus, some hallucinations were not so nice."

"Thank you, Mac. That…helps. I will work on that," Dixy says, and when I don't respond, she comes and kneels in front of me. "What would help, right now?"

"Anything physical. Running, fighting, anything."

"I have just the man. Just give me a sec."

I sit on the edge of my seat, knees jumping as I bounce on the balls of my feet. Fear is kicking my arse. If this is how much of a mess I am just talking about the torture, how am I going to get through it happening again? Pain is fine, I can deal with pain, but…

"Mac, come with me?" Lambert calls, snapping me out of my trance, and I follow him to the barn. The nervous fizz is pumping through my limbs, just itching to be expelled somehow. He walks over to the throwing knives and picks one up, then he flicks it up in the air and catches it. He nods to himself and then turns to me.

"Have you ever used throwing knives?"

"No, they aren't mine. I guess Alfred intended to teach me, and that's why they are there. I never asked."

"Well, I'm going to teach you. It just so happens; I'm pretty good, and it will help the first leg of your hand-to-hand combat training anyway. Remember what I said about using improvised weapons?"

"That you rarely carry a gun because it can blow your cover, so you learn to use what is around you as weapons."

"Good. So, learning to throw knives is really helpful. If you can learn to throw a knife accurately, then you could throw practically anything, which is useful because it's a distance hit. Hand-to-hand combat can all be very close quarters, but in reality – do you really want to be overwhelmed by hostiles all trying to fight you at once? Even the best fighter would eventually lose. So, if you can take down oncoming hostiles from a distance, then you thin down the immediate threat."

I nod, my jaw set – I am feeling calmer already. As my brain soaks up the information, it takes up some of the room the anxiety is dominating. As always, Lambert's voice is monotone, taking on a hypnotic quality that I very much appreciate right now.

"There are three types of throwing knives. Handle heavy, blade heavy, or balanced knives, and they all need to be thrown differently. A balanced knife like this is easiest to learn with because the centre of gravity is balanced. It makes nice circles when you throw it, and it is easier to guess the trajectory."

"There are two types of grip: the hammer, which is self-explanatory, and then there is the pinch grip. You can try both and see which feels more comfortable, but when you start throwing with heavy handle knives, you have to throw by the blade, so you have to use the pinch grip, or you'll slice your hand."

Lambert picks up a good handful of knives and puts them on the table just behind us. He demonstrates the different grips and explains the movements you can use to throw them.

"The blade must do at least one full turn if you throw handle first or one and a half turns for throwing by the blade for the tip to land in the target."

Lambert picked up four knives, demonstrates handle and blade throws in both his right and left hand. Both throws so smooth and accurate it is as if he doesn't have a more dominant hand.

"Your turn. Come and stand here, placing your non-dominant leg forward with no weight on it. Raise your dominant hand in front of you, bending your elbow so that the knife is alongside your ear, and then hold the position."

I follow Lambert's instruction, and I freeze in the position, knife poised.

"When you are ready to throw, shift your weight from your dominant back leg to your non-dominant front one. At the same time, swing your forearm forward from the elbow so that your arm ends up straight in front of you. When it's at that straight point, that's when you let go of the knife. So, when you are ready, give it a go."

Suddenly, I feel very self-conscious. I try to focus, then I swing my arm forward and let go. The knife barely spins once and hits the target with the flat of the blade with a slap, then slides down the target and thuds as it hits the floor.

"Right, can I show you what went wrong?" Lambert holds his hands up, his eyes wary.

"Go for it." I smile reassuringly. Poor man is terrified of touching me.

Lambert readjusts me back into the throwing position and then holds my elbow and wrist lightly in his hands.

"The power of the throw comes from your elbow and hips, but the spin comes from your wrist. The further the target is, the more spins you need and the more of an angle and flick you need from your wrist. It is judgement at first, but it will become muscle memory."

Lambert explains while he manipulates my arm in slow motion, going through the actions and exaggerating the movements.

"Right, now try again and try to relax. If you grip the knife too hard, it will drag when you release it. This is about finesse – not power."

No one ever relaxed because someone told them to, but I already missed. The nerves of embarrassing myself have melted away. I take a deep breath and try to relax the muscles in my shoulders and arms. I swing my arm forward, making sure I sweep it in a straight, swooping, arch movement and flicking my wrist a split second before release. The knife launches into the air in a spin. My breath held; my stomach muscles tight. The tip makes contact, and the knife hits the target with a light thud. It stays there, statue-still and poker-straight, and my chest tingles with elation.

"YES!!! Well done, Mac! That was bang on!" Lambert booms, giving me a palm stinging high five, and I feel giddy with excitement and adrenalin.

"Now keep going, keep practicing. When you feel you have nailed the motion, move positions, distances, and even swap hands, and soon you will be as good as me." He beams, showing off a little.

"Just how good are you?" I ask because I get the feeling he is bursting to show me.

Lambert picks up all of the knives, at least five in each hand. He stands still, his arms hanging at each side loosely. Then, he explodes into movement. His arms flick left and right fast in fluid motions but not just overarm throws. He flicks them underarm and spins the last two like frisbees simultaneously, his arms crossing over each other. I turn to him with a gulp.

"Dude…are you Batman?"

I spend time practicing with him, laughing and joking, failing and succeeding. By the time I stop, I manage to have a roughly fifty percent hit rate. For a few hours of work, I am happy with that. I feel lighter and giddy; it is just the fun and focus I needed to clear my head. I don't actually want to stop throwing because the satisfaction of hitting the target feels that good, but soon, we make our way to the fire pit, and Alfred and Dixy are waiting for us there.

"You look much more like you." Dixy smiles.

"Yes, apparently some light violence brings out the best in me."

"Well, I hope you are feeling fit because you and I are running the parkour run. I'll lead; you can try to keep up."

***

Dixy runs, and I follow her, not to chase as much to observe, and it's a good job since she is twice as fast as me. Her movements are like liquid, smooth and naturally flowing. It is mesmerising to watch. I feel very alert as I traverse the obstacles, wary a sandbag could be thrown any moment. As I mimic Dixy's movements, I find that I am moving faster and with a lot less effort and exertion. I am able to move more deftly and expend less energy in the process. Still, I am nowhere near as flexible and fast as Dixy.

"I have big plans for the run tomorrow and your awareness. So, we are going to work on that. First, I'm going to blindfold you, and you are going to use your hearing and instinct to listen for movement. If you hear one of us, you'll point. Then when you get into the swing of that, we will kick the game up a notch. Are you game?" Dixy asks.

"I'm game."

Before I know it, I am standing in the middle of the field, blindfolded, and my body tensed in focus. It doesn't take me long to master that; the grass is so long that when either Dixy, Alfred, or Lambert move, it is relatively easy to pinpoint the location. The game steps up a notch, and this time, they are all going to take it in turns to either tackle me to the ground or they will throw a sand bag. All I have to do is move out the way.

I manage this with varying degrees of success. Alfred and Lambert have a heavy footfall, so I dodge them easily. Dixy, however, is able to knock me down more times than not. The sandbags, I am not so great at dodging; it is difficult to hear them being thrown, but I'm improving slowly. Apparently, it will get easier when they are thrown at me on the parkour run; when I have my sight back, it will feel like a superpower. I can only hope.

We sit down to eat, and every time I stop moving, it's like this cloud of doom comes over me, and my thoughts get too loud. As soon as that happens, I feel the panic begin to rise, and I start to lose control. I am scared, and I am doing my best not to show it, not to admit it. Not because I, as always, hate showing weakness. It is because if I admit how scared I am to anyone, it is like admitting to myself that I can't do this.

Torture - a short word that means a long length of time of pain, fear, and suffering of both my body and mind. I am so mad at myself for being scared. Whatever I could go through with Barrett couldn't possibly be as bad as what I have already lived through on that boat. Yet I can't shake the fear that this time, I won't survive.

It was a fear I had at Sennybridge camp when I knew that I was going to be held by Billy and his brothers. Fear was definitely there, but I knew it was a game, and I held on to that. There were points, though, where I was losing grip of that, where I started to forget it was a game, and I started to lose myself. Just like I did in the segregation cell in prison. Whatever I may go through trying to infiltrate The Culling, it won't be a game. I won't know when it will end. There won't be lines that shouldn't be crossed. Time… an infinite amount, under torture, not knowing when it will end. Not knowing if I will be able to keep a hold of who I am. My sanity, my fight, my soul… Me.

"Not hungry, kid?" Alfred mumbles, cheese sandwich rolling around his mouth.

"Not really, no. I think I might just stretch my legs."

I get up from the table, flashing a smile, and walk away. I walk and walk and walk, circling the farm and trying to calm my thoughts. I run over the things I have been learning. I try to remember every tiny detail, muttering to myself furiously, and I keep walking. Every time I feel the unnatural fever start to burn across my skin, I walk faster and think harder.

"Mac, are you good to go?" Dixy yells, and I turn on my heels and stride back towards her, feeling anything but good.

"Right, this next part is going to be just you and me. It's going to require you trust me. Can you do that?" Dixy asks.

"Um, yeah. What are we doing?"

"Well, in order to work on your fears, we need to provoke them. There are a lot of ways we can do that in a controlled way, to build up your resistance to the effects it can have on you."

"You mean like exposure therapy?" I ask, my mind flicking back to therapy with Alisha.

"Yes… how did you know that?"

"Not important. So, what are we doing first?"

"The box. It's the easiest one to start with. We can put you in, and I will check on you every 15 minutes. I think if we can aim for an hour, that would be a good first step, but if you need to come out before, you will know that I will be back every 15 minutes, and I can get you out. If it really becomes too much you can buzz me," Dixy reassures, tapping her ear.

An hour, no moving, with too much time to think, to panic. The fear hits me square in the chest. I want to run. The irrational instinct to run is so powerful, but this is the first step. If I back out of it, then what chance do I have really? How could any of them have faith in me then?

I walk with weak legs to the middle of the field, and then, right there in the centre, I spot a wooden trunk. It is bigger than the box I was put in on the boat. One of those trunks that look like a treasure chest, with an oval top and a black metal catch on the front. My chest tightens as I realise there will be no getting out unless Dixy lets me out. Even with no padlock, the metal catch makes escape impossible.

"Are you ready?"

"Yeah…"

Dixy lifts the lid, and my mouth loses all its moisture as I step inside. I lay on my side with my knees crammed in against the side of the box and pressing up against my chest. Immediately, I can feel the restriction my knees are having on my breathing.

"Right, Mac, I'll be back in 15 minutes. See?" Dixy holds up a kitchen timer, and I nod rigidly. "Okay, focus, Mac. You can do this. See you in 15."

Darkness.

The reaction is almost instantaneous. The unnatural fever burns at my skin, and I forgot to take my jumper off. My breathing turns ragged, and I feel like I am suffocating. My body begins to convulse in violent shakes that burst from my chest and radiate into my limbs. Shakes so powerful they hurt my muscles. The effect takes hold in 30 seconds, and it feels like 30 minutes.

Stop… You have to stop. Come on. You can do this. It is 15 minutes. No, it's an hour. An hour of panic, of suffocating, being trapped… I am trapped…

The sweat pours off of me, and I start to whimper and rasp, tears mixed with sweat burning my eyes.

STOP! Suck it up, buttercup! You are not trapped; she will be back in 15 minutes. You can do this. Just keep thinking and breathe.

I can't breathe... I can't...

My head swims, the darkness and fear saturating my mind, and the memory swirls.

"Let me out! Let me out! Please!"

"I need the toilet!"

"Let me out, you piece of fucking shit!"

I feel a swoop and a crash as the box is picked up and thrown across the room. My head is jerked backwards and smacks hard against the back of the box in the impact. My head spins in a nauseating spin, and I gag, my stomach too empty to bring anything up.

Fear rocks me, my breathing tight and my body aching from repeated impacts. I feel the box swoop, and the impact sends a jolt of pain through my spine. Warmth spreads through me as I lose hold of my bladder and piss all over myself.

I choke and splutter as I snap out the memory, and I find myself just as trapped. I kick and flail, I try to scream, but nothing comes out but raspy whimpers. I pound my fists against the lid of the trunk uselessly.

"Mac? MAC! What the hell!?"

The lid flies open, and I scramble out, tipping over the trunk in desperation and landing on my chest. I choke trying to get air on all fours, and I feel hands on me, trying to turn me over.

"Jesus, you are soaked. Mac, it's me! Stop fighting me; it's okay. MAC!" Anna yells.

She manages to roll me over and pull me upright, and the oxygen hits my lungs with a long raspy wheeze. Anna grabs my face with soft cool hands that feel like heaven against the burn of my heated skin.

"Hey… Mac, it's just me – I've got you, just breathe, it's okay," Anna coos softly, her hands firm on my face.

My eyes meet hers, lingering for just a moment too long. Glassy and vivid green, pained and tired. Instantly, I feel a longing so deep it hurts. I pull away sharply, crawling away from her and stumbling towards my truck. I hear Anna yelling my name as I slam the accelerator pedal down. My vision swims as I drive, my eyes wide as I try to focus. I open all the windows letting the cold blast of air keep my eyes open and my mind lucid. I drive too fast, my phone vibrating in my pocket. I screech to a stop as I answer the phone.

"Alfred, I am safe... just give me… a few hours. Please."

"Oh, thank God. Okay, kid – roger that. Thanks for answering."

My head spins, making the garden pathway wobble. I thump into the wooden mahogany door, and I knock on it. The wood feels so cool against my forehead. I hear movement, but I don't register the sound quick enough. When the door opens with me leant against it, I stumble to my knees and through the door.

"Mac!" Alisha shrieks pulling me to my feet. She hooks my arm over her shoulder and starts leading me through the hallway, my vision darkening.

"What the hell happened?"

"I'm going to p-pass out."

"No, no, no… Baby, I need to get you to…"

Darkness

***

Tap, tap, tap.

"Mac…"

"Ugh, stop slapping me… Stings," I whine, and she laughs in a relieved sigh.

I open my eyes, and the light is jarring. Black spots fly across my vision. I can just about make out Alisha's face, although it is fuzzy. I am lying on Alisha's living room floor with my head in her lap, her fingers running through my hair.

"Hey…"

"How long was I out?"

"Not long. Ten minutes maybe."

"I think I can get up now."

Alisha helps me sit upright, and I pull myself to my feet using the door frame. I walk a little wobbly to the sofa and sit down. I am getting deja-vu as she sits on the coffee table opposite me with concerned eyes. She's waiting for an explanation I can't give.

"You're not going to tell me what happened, are you?"

"I can't do that."

"How convenient," Alisha snipes.

"What's that supposed to mean?"

"There is always a reason you can't tell me something. First, you come here bruised and bloody. Now you are covered in sweat with bashed-up knuckles and passing out. You won't tell me about the bad dreams, you won't let me touch you, you won't talk about what happened to you. I don't even know how you feel about me. What exactly am I here for, Mac?"

That hit me where it hurts, a painfully truthful dress down. I look down at my knuckles, and my brain registers the sting as I see the chunks of bloody skin grazed along them from pounding the lid of the box.

"I'm sorry, I know – I get it, but I don't know how to change that right now."

"There are things you are not allowed to tell me; I get that, but the other stuff, that's your choice. You are choosing to shut me out. Do you ever plan on opening up to me?"

"I haven't got room in my head to think about that. Truthfully, what I'm doing right now takes up all the space in my head I have. I'm barely holding on right now, Alisha. I'm sorry, I never meant…"

Alisha moves towards me, kneeling down between my legs. Her hands find my face, and she pulls me closer, kissing me deeply. Her lips move on mine, firm and slow, the emotion bursts from her kiss, and her intensity rocks me. A whimper escapes her lips, and she pulls back, leaning her forehead against mine.

"Not so long ago, I told you that there were some things I wanted to say to you. I haven't because I don't want to push you away. Sometimes it's easier to accept that you won't give me more because at least you're here. That's something I've wanted for a long time, but it is not easier. It hurts."

I pull back from her, my hands holding hers, guilt gnawing at me. I can barely look at her; I am hurting her. She is so strong, so good at hiding her feelings it was too easy for me to persuade myself that everything was okay. I didn't want to see that it wasn't. Alisha lifts my face by my chin. Her deep hazel-brown eyes are powerful and determined and glittering with tears.

"Mac… I love you. If you can't let me in, then… Let me go. You don't have to give me everything, just something to show you are in this with me."

My insides freeze, all of my words – disappear. I pull her in, kissing her, and she kisses me back at first. And then she pulls away harshly. She gets to her feet and turns her back on me.

"Alisha…"

"Mac, I need you to leave, and unless you can start to let me in, unless you can decide what it is that you feel for me…don't come back." Alisha's voice breaks, and I step forward, my hands gently on her hips, turning her, but she steps out of my grasp.

"Go, Mac!"

I walk out the front door, pain searing in my chest as I realise how much I have hurt her. Is there anyone I won't hurt? She deserves so much better than this, than me. I find myself driving, aimlessly at first. Not knowing where to go or what to do. Then I realise there really is only one place I want to go right now, only one face I want to see. When I arrive, I spot her through the window, washing up. She sees me, and her face lights up like Christmas morning. I let myself in through the front door; the familiar smells hit me nostalgically. Mum comes bursting around the corner with a big smile that fades a little as soon as she looks at me.

"Come on, love. You need a cup of monkey tea," Mum comforts.

Monkey tea is actually PG tips tea; we call it monkey tea because of the adverts on TV. No one makes a cup of tea like my mum, and it is her go-to remedy for anything from a cold to a broken heart. Soon, I am sipping a steaming mug of homely warmth, sat at the dining room table.

"You look exhausted, McKenna. It's so good to see you, but I can't pretend it is easy to see you looking so beaten up." Mum lays her hand over mine, and I feel the lump in my throat rise.

"I know it looks bad, Mum, but I'm really doing okay. Everything is moving well; training is going okay. I'm working hard, that's all."

"Then why do you look so sad, darling? I'm your mum; you think I don't know when you are hurting? It comes in the mother's training manual, right next to how to give the best hugs."

I chuckle weakly; the tears fall, and she wraps her arms around me, holding me tight. She does give the best mum hugs; she is warm and smells like lavender.

"I'm just… h-hurting everyone, Mum. I feel like such a horrible person." I sob, the ache in my chest intensifying.

Mum gives me another squeeze, and then she pulls back. She smiles at me sweetly, eyeing me a look of understanding, a mothers' look.

"I see. This is about a girl… or maybe, *two* of them."

"How…"

"I was at the hospital; I met them both. When I got there - before you woke up, they were both in the waiting room, arguing with Alfred. Both wanted to see you, and Alfred was having a hard job keeping them away. So, what happened?"

I take a deep breath. I explain, first what happened with Anna, then Alisha. I leave a lot of details out, telling her just enough for her to understand.

"… Alisha told me she loves me, and I froze. I hurt her badly. I don't know why because I do love her, I … I just…" I falter, my head in my hands.

"Do you want me to be honest with you, love? Or do you want me to sugar coat it?"

"Honest, always Mum. You're not Willy Wonka."

"When you finally came home after I lost you for so long – you were so guarded and distant, it broke my heart. You wouldn't let me touch you; your eyes were cold, you were rigid and coiled up like a spring. I felt like I lost you all over again; you were here, but not here. You wouldn't say a word unless it was in answer to a direct question. You never laughed; you were a ghost.

"Then I came to the hospital, and of course, I was devastated to hear what you had gone through and that I was going to lose you all over again. I was so scared of the moment you would wake up because I was expecting that you would be even colder than ever. Then you opened your eyes, you held my hand, talked openly with me, and you hugged me. I can't tell you, how shocked I was. I was so happy. I was losing my daughter again, but I also had her back.

"Now, ask yourself. How did that happen? How is it that right now, you are openly crying with me, telling me how you feel, letting me hold you? If you answer yourself honestly, I think you'll find that the conflict in your heart is not as complicated as you think it is."

I break as I hear her read me openly like a book. The pain overcomes me, and she holds me through it. I ugly cry like a child, and the hurt crashes over me, wave after wave, but eventually, I calm down, and she lets me go.

"Darling, you're not a horrible person. The problem is, you believe you are, and it's that belief that keeps you thinking that you are not worthy of love. But you are so *wrong*, and if you don't find a way to realise that, you will lose the love of your life forever."

***

When I find myself back at the farm, it is getting dark. The silver van is still there, and I see Dixy walking up the hill towards me. I wait, bracing myself. The passenger door opens, and she gets inside and shuts it. She doesn't say anything. I feel like she is waiting for me to talk, and my brain is so battered that I can't think what to say.

"I pushed you too hard," Dixy states eventually, breaking the silence. I gaze out the windscreen with my hands still on the steering wheel.

"No, you didn't. I wasn't honest with you; I was panicking before I got in the box," I confess. I see her head snap around at me harshly, and I brace myself.

"Why the hell wouldn't you have told me that?! Don't you think I needed to know that?!" Dixy spits angrily.

"Because I don't know how to do this. I have no choice, and I will do it, but I'm scared of going through this again. I'm scared I won't be able to come back from this a second time. Admitting that means you could all lose faith in me, and right now, that faith is all I have to hold on to."

The words flow out of me easily, so easily that it even shocks me. There is no point in hiding it anymore. It isn't going to make me stronger; it is just obstructing any chance I have of succeeding.

I feel her hand grab for mine, pulling it off the steering wheel and into her lap.

"You found out you are likely to be tortured again, and you haven't blinked; you have barely spoken about it. You don't think that maybe, I was waiting for you to break? You needed to; anyone would need to. It isn't going to stop us from believing in you if you show a sign of weakness. You're not invincible, and no one expects you to be."

"I'll try to bear that in mind." I turn my head to look at her, relieved to find no anger there.

"Good. And next time, don't drive off in a panic because one, you will probably crash, and two, I really don't want to have to deal with a fiery redhead losing her shit at me again."

I wince. "What happened?"

"It's nothing I can't handle, don't worry. She went nuclear at me for putting you in the box. That girl has some bite, I can tell you."

"Oh, I know, believe me. Sorry about that. I'd say I would talk to her, but I will probably just make it worse. I always do." I chuckle.

"I think Alfred already beat you to it."

"That man is always saving my bacon."

"He is pretty awesome. Listen, I know you think you can't get through this, but I know you can. You just have to be honest with me. Tell me when it's too much, tell me why it is too much, and we can adapt. Flooding you with fear is not exposing you, it is drowning you, and that won't work. You don't have to wait for me to suggest things; if you have any ideas then tell me because I can't read your mind, and you are not the most forthcoming person in the world."

"If that is the case, I think you should try again, but this time, I want you to tie me up and blindfold me."

"That's very forward, Agent Scott. Who knew you were so kinky?" She grins daringly, and I choke on a laugh.

"You have no idea." I scoff. "No, in the box, it was too much because it wasn't just triggering the claustrophobia. It was dark, and I was cramped, so I felt restrained, which are two more separate fears. Maybe you could just restrain me and blindfold me, use a timer like you were before. Then do the box when I can handle that."

"That is a fabulous idea!" Dixy squeaks.

"Okay, you are far too excited about this."

***

I find myself sat in the middle of the field on a wooden desk chair, my hands and feet bound and a rope holding me securely to the chair. Dixy went a little overboard, I would say. The blindfold covering my eyes has left me in complete darkness, the panic did start to bubble at first, but I was able to slow it to a simmer. I can breathe, and the cold night's air that's kissing my face is soothing. That automatically makes it easier than the box.

When the anxious thoughts start to overwhelm me, I start playing games with myself, just like when I was bound and blindfolded by Billy and his brothers. I am starting to understand the driving force of the fear. When I was on the boat or waiting for Billy and Jakub to come back and interrogate me, the fear was the pain I knew was coming but couldn't see coming. I couldn't even hold my hands in front of my face to protect it because I was restrained.

Right now, no one is going to hit me, and I know that. The fear is driven by the darkness and silence because, in those, I have nothing but my dark thoughts to keep me company. It is those thoughts that broke me in segregation. Without those thoughts, the darkness would just be dark, the silence would just be silent. Knowing this means I know I have to stop those thoughts, however possible. Understanding that takes a little bit of the power away from the fear, like when a magician reveals the truth behind their illusions.

"Mac, you copy?" Alfred's voice sings in my ear, and I jump. I had forgotten all about the earpiece implant.

"I copy. How did you do that? I didn't activate my earpiece."

"Our earpieces are connected. If you activate yours, it automatically activates mine and vice versa," he explains.

"Oh, that is pretty cool. You mean, I could ask for a cuppa practically any time I want?"

"You could ask… Don't mean you are gonna get it, you cheeky git." He chuckles gruffly. "I just thought I'd check on you. You've done 30 minutes. Do you need Dixy to pull you out?"

"No, I'm good. It's helping. Thanks though. Check back in 15, but I want to make the hour."

"Roger that, Mac-attack."

I take a deep breath and focus. Half way there. My fists are clenched, and it's making my grazed knuckles sting. I make a point of releasing my grip and rolling my shoulders, stretching the aches and trying to hang my arms loosely. It helps, like I am trying to fool my body into believing there's no reason for the tension.

The chill of air the is getting bitter. I try picking out the sounds around me one by one. I hear the light swoosh of the long grass every time there is a puff of wind. If I strain, I can just about hear the faint crackle of the fire, but the smell of the smoke is much clearer. I hear clattering in the kitchen, pots and pans being moved around with voices and laughs in between. I hear the crunch of feet walking over gravel...

"Who's there?"

"It's Danni. I'm waiting for Anna to come back from work."

It's automatic; my body stiffens. This is not what I need right now. I hear a faint foot fall in the grass as she takes a step closer.

"I think that's close enough," I warn, and Danni sniggers. She takes another step closer, my fists clench tighter, and I hear the ropes creak as my arms strain against them.

"You know, she doesn't want you here. I should know, she told me. She just feels sorry for you," Danni taunts with a light, sickly voice. She takes another step forward, and I smirk.

"You really think that's going to work? I know her a lot better than that. I don't know what your problem is with me, but I'd let it go before you lose her. Just some friendly advice."

I feel her take another step forward. She is too close.

"There she is, holier-than-thou… You," she taunts, jabbing my chest with the point of her finger, "are one messed up cookie. You know that right?"

I can feel how close she is, her breath hot on my face. Her finger still jabbed against my chest. I lunge against the ropes binding me.

"Back the fuck off!" I shout.

"Mac? What's … Danni? What are you doing?" Anna asks nervously.

"Hey, we were just catching up while I waited for you to come home. No big thing," Danni lies so smoothly it shocks me. Fury inside me burns like acid.

"I wasn't aware we had plans," Anna replies with an edge to her tone.

"We didn't. I thought I'd surprise you."

"Okay, well, meet me at the fire pit. I need to talk to Mac about work, and then I'll be right over."

I hear footsteps walk away. My heart is hammering, adrenalin rushing around my system making me jittery. I feel her hands untying the knot of the blindfold, and she kneels down in front of me holding the arms of the chair.

"Are you okay? What did she say to you?!" Anna frets, anxiety thick in her throat.

"Nothing I can't handle. Don't worry."

"I didn't ask if you could handle it, Mac. I asked you what she said?" Anna presses, and I look up from the floor. Her expression is fearful, and then I understand.

"Nothing that I believe."

The relief that washes over her is astounding. She exhales loudly and bends forward, resting her forehead against my knee so lightly, I can barely feel that she is there. Her breath comes out fast and heavy.

"It's okay, don't worry. You better go, Anna."

Anna gets to her feet and ties the blindfold back into place, and I am back in darkness. I feel Anna's hand lightly on my shoulder and her lip brushes my ear. She lingers there, just a few seconds too long, her breath shaky in my ear, and tingles irrupt inside me.

"Thank you…" she whispers.

CHAPTER 4

The Butcher

It sucks; it *really* goddamn sucks! I lay in bed in my apartment, my heart heavy, my eyes puffy, and I have no desire to move again, ever. My mind plays the events of last night over in my head. A useless, painful movie stuck on repeat. It is thoroughly deserved pain, though. I own it; it's mine.

The memory swirls.

I stand in her living room, and she watches me with hurt eyes. My heart is in my mouth, the lump in my throat is screaming for me to let go, but I can't, or I will never find the words that I need to say.

"At the hotel, I knew instantly I was going to fall for you. You had me so quickly it was terrifying. When I left, I walked into my home, and I was ambushed. The next time I opened my eyes, I was on the boat. I spent a lot of time hoping I would get to see you again. The problem is, when I finally did, I had no idea who you were. I've been trying really hard to connect who I was then with who I am now. Make all the pieces of myself go back together again. But the truth is, I am on a path that may mean I could end up more dismantled than ever. I may never be completely whole again."

"I do love you. There is no doubt about that. I ..." I struggle, pain strangling my throat.

"But you love someone else...more," Alisha states flatly.

"It's not that simple, Alisha. I promise you it's not. This isn't just about Anna."

"I know it's not. Why do you think I stayed? But in the end, it is the only part that matters, Mac," Alisha concludes, her voice finally starting to break.

I turn my back, pain overcoming me. I sob into my hands, and she grabs me, pulling me in. I don't think I have ever held someone so tight. It is tearing me up. I am going to lose her, and there is nothing I can do.

"Oh, God. I am so... sorry. You don't know how much," I sob.

"I do know. I'm always going to love you. So, I do know, and now - you are going to kiss me, and then you are going to walk straight out without looking back," Alisha cries.

I blink hard as my mind slides back to the present. No…I don't want to move, but if I don't move, someone will make me move, I know it. Yet, I can't seem to move. I just sit in bed watching a muted TV, trying to lip read, and getting distracted by my thoughts of Alisha.

The truth is, regardless of how I feel about Alisha or Anna, it wasn't about that. In those very few seconds when Anna held my face after she got me out of the box, the longing I felt was all-encompassing, both in desire of her and need of her. I know if it wasn't for Danni or Alisha that in that moment, I would have let her be that light for me she's always been because I let her get that close. And I can't seem to do the same with Alisha. She deserves someone that can, and I just have to hope there is a way to not only stop wanting Anna but to stop needing her too.

Just like clockwork, my phone starts to ring. I see the name Dixy flash across my screen and groan.

"Hello?"

"You are late, Agent Scott."

"I'm aware of that, Agent Obvious," I snipe.

"Oh, someone is pissy today."

"Yep. I'll be there in 15."

***

My mood hasn't improved by the time I get to the farm. My chest aches with grief, and I am angry at myself more than anything. I hope I get to hit someone today; that would be really good. I enter the farmhouse and find Anna in the kitchen, and I tense. She has her back turned, and she doesn't turn as I speak.

"Hey, um...have you seen Dixy and Lambert?"

"In your barn, I think," she replies in a tight voice.

"Are you okay?"

"Yeah. Fine," she replies, clipped. Her voice is too high to sound normal for her.

"Then why am I talking to your back?"

Anna turns around. Her eyes fall on mine, and they're red and puffy and full of tears. They are also ringed with darkness; she looks exhausted. The sight has my heart feeling clogged with cement.

"What's wrong?" I ask, taking a step forward and then stopping myself.

"I can't...please don't ask. I'm fine. J-just need a minute. You can go; it's okay."

I walk over to her, trying not to think too much, and I sweep her into my arms. She breaks down immediately. It hurts but nothing compared to whatever is hurting her right now. I have only ever seen her break like this once, and that was when I spent weeks not looking at her and left her thinking our time together was a lie. This is so much worse. She sobs violently into my neck, inconsolable, her fists grabbing the back of my shirt. I hold her, the pain searing in my chest, but I hold on anyway.

"It's okay, I've got you. Whatever has happened, no matter how hard it might be for me sometimes, I'm always here for you, Anna. That will never change. I promise."

Her sobs begin to slow instantly. Her tense body loosens and melts into me, almost like she is falling asleep. I pull back from her and look at her to find - she is falling asleep! Jesus, what the hell is going on with her? I pick her up, and I know there is no way I can carry her up the stairs. Then I see Dixy and Lambert leave the barn, and my legs start moving. I walk towards the barn, and Dixy catches me en route.

"Shh – can you open the barn for me?" I whisper.

Dixy runs ahead and by the time I reach the barn door, Anna is a dead weight, completely asleep. I get inside the barn and make every effort not to drop her too hard onto the pallet bed, but it's so low to the ground, I don't altogether manage it. Her eyes open, and she grabs my hand.

"Stay till I sleep," she slurs.

I hold her hand and stroke her cheek, and it doesn't take long, but I stay a bit longer anyway. Something is going on with her, and I stare at her as if it will help me figure out what. My first instinct tells me it is Danni, but that doesn't make sense; she is a strong girl, and she doesn't take any crap. She wouldn't stay with someone who makes her miserable. Letting go of her hand carefully, I cover her with a blanket, creep out of the barn, and find Dixy waiting at the door.

"What happened? Is she okay?"

"No, she's not. She won't tell me, but something is really off. Do you know where Alfred is?"

"In a meeting with Lexi. Left just before you got here, *late*." She quirks a disapproving eyebrow.

"Alright, lady, I get it. I had a rough night."

"Well, I hope you are feeling fit because you are getting your butt kicked today."

"I'm good to go, and to be honest, I could do with a physical day."

"Good. Lambert will call us over when he is finished setting up."

I am keen to get moving. I just want my brain to stop shouting and my heart to stop hurting. I am busted up over Alisha, and now, seeing Anna like that – I ache to be there for her, but I know that I can only take so much, and it isn't really my place anymore. I feel uneasy; not knowing what is happening to her to make her so broken is driving me crazy. All I can do is watch over her from afar and hope that whatever is wrong becomes right for her again.

I walk over to Lambert impatiently to see what he is up to and see that the parkour run is completely different. There are a lot more platforms and ropes. Standing back from it, it looks like a mini skyline picture of skyscrapers. There are now some even higher platforms that make my legs wobble just looking at them. Some ladders have been fixed horizontally like monkey bars.

As I walk closer, I notice lots of smaller items that seem out of place dotted randomly around the course. There is a broomstick leaned against one of the smaller platforms; on top of the largest platform, there is a cargo net screwed up in a messy ball. As I let my eyes analyse, I see lots of household items: a frying pan, a plant pot, washing line cable, a paint roller, garden sheers, inflatable beach ball, an umbrella, a mop and bucket, a garden hose. Some of it is easy to spot; some I see are cleverly hidden. My stomach starts to clench as I realise what we might be doing. The nerves are there, but I'm excited too. This is exactly what I need right now.

I hear a car engine, and I see Alfred's truck pull up.

"Houston, we have a problem," I utter. "Pa, you copy?"

"Loud and clear, kid," Alfred sounds inside my ear.

"Meet me by the fire pit."

"Roger that."

"Houston, we have a problem," I say, deactivating the earpiece, and I smirk a little.

That really is handy.

I tell Lambert that I will be back in five and jog over to the fire pit. I know I will feel better if I tell Alfred. I want to be there for her, but I also don't want to complicate things with Danni for her or hurt myself in the process.

"Alright, kid?" Alfred asked with a furrowed brow.

"Yeah, I am, but I'm worried about Anna."

I explain what happened, and his frown grows deeper and deeper. He scratches his ear, something he does a lot when he is worried.

"You think it's Danni, don't you?" he grumbles.

"It doesn't make any sense that it would be. If she wasn't happy, you know she would just end it."

"Yes… but you still think it is Danni, don't you?" he presses.

"Yes, I do."

Alfred nods, scratching the whiskers on his cheek. He has that thinking face where his eyes flit rapidly, and you can almost see the cogs turn.

"So, what are you going to do about it?"

"What do you mean? I can't do anything. She knows I'm there for her, but I can't step on toes. That isn't fair on her."

"Screw toes, Mac! She needs you! She hasn't been right for ages. Ever since her birthday, anyone can see that," Alfred growls.

"What do you expect me to do!? She is with someone else; it isn't my place!"

“Yeah, and so are you. Hasn’t stopped you watching over her, has it? Or her you, for that matter!”

“I’M NOT WITH…” I yell, and then I stop. I don’t want to yell at Alfred. I take a deep breath and cool my head. “I’m sorry. I will watch over her, you know that I will, and I’ll try to find out what’s wrong. There isn’t anything I wouldn’t do to protect her; you must know that,” I implore, and his eyes soften.

“You would do *almost* anything to protect her. Anything, except tell her the truth. You really think she has been better off not knowing how you really feel about her?” he says softly, his eyes sad and making me feel like the worst human ever.

“I’ll watch over her. You do the same, and let me know if you find anything out.”

I walk away, fuming. Now I need to hit something more than ever. When I get back to the parkour run, Lambert explains what we will be doing. His eyes are bright beneath his bushy eyebrows with excitement.

“This is improvised fighting and evasion. It’s about tuning your senses into everything around you. Awareness and concentration are key. This course is bigger, higher, and more complex than it was before, but that actually makes moving easier. There are more places to run to, and you’re going to need them...” He smiles gleefully.

“I’m going to be chasing you. Your objective is to try not to let me catch you, and if I do, to fight me off and escape again using the random objects around to help you. Improvise, adapt, and be aware of your surroundings at all times, because I’m sure there are more sandbags around. Are you game?”

“Yep. Let’s do it.”

I stand at the foot of the ramp, my arms and legs twitching with nervous energy, but inside, I’m excited. Dixy is on the side-line watching, and I notice that there are some sandbags piled up near her and a bunch of little bean bags too. The sight doesn’t fill me with joy but fixates my focus because I really don’t want to come a cropper with one of those again.

“Mac, on the whistle, you will run; Lambert will go on my second whistle 10 seconds later,” Dixy yells, and I give her the nod and then chuckle.

Who does she think she is? John Anderson?

I can see from the bottom of the ramp that there being more platforms does make it look easier to move. There are more places to run and jump to, but that also makes it easier for Lambert. 10 seconds is not much of a head start; he has long legs, and he's good at practically everything. He will be on me quickly, so maybe the smart play is to obstruct the path to slow him down.

My eyes roam urgently and then spot a small wooden crate by the side of the ramp, and instantly, I know what I am going to do. The whistle blows, shrill and ear-splitting, and I bolt up the ramp, picking up the crate as I go. At full speed, I run and jump to the first platform. From mid-air, I can already see my next move. I land lightly on the top of the platform and quickly lay the crate in the middle of the platform to block Lambert's path.

I try to stay aware, focused, and loose. Not moving as fast but moving smarter and more fluidly, I move with ease to the next platform, which is five feet lower. I chance a look over my right shoulder and see that my block worked and has forced Lambert to change direction; he has chosen right, so I move left. The next platform is higher but has a ladder leading up to it laid down like a bridge between them.

Balance isn't my best ability, the nerves hit me, but I have no time to second guess. I step gingerly on it, swaying as it inclines, then changing tack. I move on all fours instead. I am relieved when I make it across to the other side, legs slightly wobbly. My senses are in overdrive, making me edgy, but it has to be a good thing because out of the corner of my eye, I see a sandbag hurtling towards me. I drop to the platform, landing hard on my chest and only just narrowly missing being hit.

When I get back up, I feel awesome, the surge of adrenalin from successfully dodging the sandbag is pumping through me, and I am smiling. I jump up three platforms in quick succession, and I have looped back around, and now Lambert and I are facing each other. Moving like chess pieces, every time I jump, he makes a move towards me, and I make a move to avoid him. I need to think because eventually, we are going to collide.

I try to stick to the higher platforms as I know that Dixy won't sandbag me from those heights because the fall would be too dangerous, but there are not so many of them. I reach the highest one; Lambert has pushed me in this direction, and now I feel the fear, my legs weakening at the height. I see the cargo net and pick it up. There is only one way down that doesn't mean getting caught by Lambert. I sit down, sliding my butt to the edge of the platform, and let my legs dangle. My head spins dizzily when I look down.

Ugh, crap.

My stomach swoops with nerves as I loop the cargo net over the rope attached to the corner of the platform, wrapping the ends of the cargo net securely around each hand. My heart is in my mouth; it's a long way down. Taking a deep breath, I slide off my butt off the edge of the platform, and my bodyweight tugs the cargo net tightly around my hands. I slide fast, ziplining down the rope, and I hear Dixy whoop. The excitement is intoxicating, and I grin from ear to ear as I glide through the air. The speed is more than I expected, and if I don't get the timing right, I am going to hit the lower platform hard. I lift my knees and brace myself as the impact sends a jolt up my spine, but it is bearable. I scramble to my feet. Lambert is gaining on me fast, and my stomach drops when I see a frying pan in his hand.

My legs are tiring, and my chest is heaving, trying to catch a breath. I can't keep running. My eyes scan for the nearest weapon, and then I spot it. The broomstick leant up against the second-highest platform. I run and jump; it feels like I am moving in slow motion as I soar through the air with no time to worry about the height. My feet make contact with the platform hard, my knees taking the impact. I dive on my chest and reach over the edge of the platform, my hands groping for the broom handle, my jaw clenched, trying desperately to ignore the head swimming height. My muscles are tight like coiled springs just knowing he is seconds behind me.

Rolling onto my back, I see him; I get to my feet just as his jump lands him right in front of me. He swings the frying pan, and I manage to block just in time. The broom was a mistake, it is too long with him stood this close, so I can't get a full swing; I can just barely block his hits. There is no way to manoeuvre, nowhere to run. He is just too close. My mind registers talking but just barely a second before...

"NOOO!" Dixy screams.

It is too late, I know it is going to hit me, and so does Lambert. He drops the frying pan just as the sandbag hits me. I fall sideways, a wave of sickening shock whooshing through my stomach. I see Lambert dive, grabbing for me as I fall, and I grab for him. My fingers make contact with his, and for a split second, I stop falling. My fingers slip uselessly through his. It slowed my fall, but the landing is hard, and the pain is blinding. Everything goes white as I scream out. I can't move for the pain.

Lambert skids to a stop right next to me, panting. "Mac, don't move, okay, soldier? Just in case anything is broken," Lambert orders, holding my head still.

"Alfred, get her the fuck off of this land before I kill her myself!" Dixy roars.

"Oh, God!" I cry.

"Mac, stay still. Tell me what hurts so I can move you," Lambert commands.

"My hip, j-just my hip!"

The pain is unbearable, and I am terrified. I can't afford anything to be broken right now; I don't have the time to waste to recover. I feel someone grip my hand, and I grip back as Dixy leans over me.

"How bad?" Dixy asks, her face flush and her jaw clenched, a vein throbbing down the centre of her forehead.

"Without an X-ray, it's hard to be sure. We need to take her in *now*. If it's a pelvis break, the blood flow could stop. I need you to hold the weight of that leg; keep it off her hip while I carry her."

"Wait!" Dixy Snaps, "You need to stabilise her first, take off your belt. We need to immobilise her and secure her hips in place," Dixy orders.

With a nod, Lambert slides off his belt and with the help of Dixy, ties it securely around my hips. Then Lambert slides his hands beneath me, lifting me smoothly and with complete ease – the pain is harrowing, and I can't suppress my scream.

"I know, I know – I'm sorry, Mac. We just need to get you in the van." Dixy cringes.

Dixy braces my leg by my ankle and knee and straightens it, and I scream so much my head swims, my vision beginning to blacken, but once my leg is straight and supported, it eases the pain some. They begin a slow walk, trying not to jolt me, my head sloshing and bobbing against Lambert's shoulder.

"Mac! Oh, God! What happened!?" Anna shrieks.

"Your girlfriend threw a fucking sandbag at her, knocking her off a high platform – that's what happened!" Dixy snaps.

My chest flares in anger; that makes sense. I knew Dixy wouldn't sandbag me from that height. I knew Danni hated me, but this is a whole new level of hate.

"Dixy, it's not… her fault – chill!" I groan.

"You're right. Sorry, Anna. I'm just so pissed. Why the fuck would she do that!?" Dixy snarls.

It feels like it takes forever to get to the van, but I don't mind. The pain feels less with the lack of movement. It gives me a chance to breathe and try to calm the fear threatening to make me bawl like a child.

"Callum, we need to stop. Anna, grab my keys from my back pocket, unlock the van, and open the back doors," Dixy orders. She is a lot calmer now, and I am glad. The way Anna was earlier, the last thing I want is her blaming herself for this.

We reach the back of the van, and Lambert steps inside, carrying me as if I am weightless. He lays me on the floor of the van carefully, and Dixy keeps hold of my leg. I wince but the pain is definitely decreasing. Lambert jumps out of the van, and Anna jumps in. Her face is a mask of fear, her eyes dazed and unfocused.

"How are you doing, Mac?" Dixy asks.

"It hurts less than it did. I-is that bad?" I ask her, my voice shaky and obviously scared. I don't care; screw my dignity, I am scared.

"Hey, it's okay. That could be a good thing. We are just being careful, just in case. You're going to be okay. We've got you," Dixy reassures, and then Anna slides across the van floor towards me. She takes my hand, holding it tight, and I feel her hand shaking in mine.

"I'm so sorry," she whispers, the pain on her face evident.

"Not your fault, girl."

"Yes, it is."

The van's engine comes to life, and I feel movement. The floor of the van vibrates up my back as the wheels start to revolve over the gravel of the driveway. I brace myself, my jaw clenched, and it hurts for sure, but the blinding pain is gone. Now it's a constant sharp ache that is making my head swim.

My head flops around as my eyes droop, the motion of the van jerking me awake. Anna lifts my head and slides her leg under it. She holds her hand lightly on my face, stopping my head from jerking around. I want with all my heart to push her away, to not be comforted by her. I know it will only hurt me more later, but as her fingertips sketch softly down my cheek and through my hair, I lose all the will I have to fight her, and I fall asleep.

***

My hip feels unnaturally stiff like someone filled my joint with cement. The pain is definitely decreasing, but until I know what the damage is, I know the pit of dread in my stomach will continue to grow. The nurse removes the belt and wheels me down for an X-ray and MRI. The X-ray is easy enough, but the MRI makes me feel like I was in a coffin. Asking someone like me to keep my fidgety, anxious butt still while they scan me is asking the impossible.

I am wheeled to a private room to await the results. The atmosphere is thick with tension as no one really speaks to each other; I can tell Dixy is livid at Anna, who sits by my bedside with her eyes glazed over. The blank look on her face, the statue still position she sits in, makes her look like she is about the shatter like glass. Lambert has left to get everyone coffee and food, and Dixy is stood at the foot end of my bed, rambling at me to try to keep me calm.

"I didn't think you'd zipline. You looked about ready to crap your pants on that platform," she teases.

"Yeah, apparently, I'm not such a fan of heights. My butt cheeks were definitely twitching,"

The door to the room swings open, and a man in a long white coat appears. His appearance is neat; a blue shirt and perfectly knotted blue striped tie are peeking out beneath the white collar of his coat. He has a serious face, with short and grey curly hair that looks too old for his face. He is carrying a large brown file and greets me with sober eyes that make me nervous.

"Miss Scott, my name is Doctor Corbin, and I am head of Orthopaedics. I have some good news; there are no new breaks showing up on your X-rays," he informs me with a smooth voice.

I exhale, leaning back into the bed. The relief is enough to make me want to cry, but I don't. My eyes catch Dixy's, and she looks as relieved as me.

"However, there is significant swelling. I believe the fall aggravated your previous internal fixation repair. Can I ask where you had this surgery performed?"

"Sorry, Doc, I don't know what you're talking about." I frown.

He may as well have just spoken to me in German for all the sense that made. Doctor Corbin opens the file and pulls out two sheets of glossy black plastic. He walks over to the wall at the end of my bed, and Dixy moves to the side of the bed, sitting opposite Anna. Doctor Corbin slides the X-rays under the catch on the wall and flicks a switch. The X-rays glow, and he turns back to me. I see my hips and pelvis. To my untrained eye, they look normal to me. Then I see something out of place, and my stomach swoops.

"Right here is a pin that has been placed in your hip. It is a repair that is made on broken hips only; this method is prehistoric. Although it seems to be working and holding properly, by today's standards of medicine, there are much cleaner methods."

My mouth is dry. I have no memory of this operation, no memory of an injury. Which means…

"I don't know… I… How…" I struggle, and Anna stands up. She takes my hand and presses her lips against my head. I turn to look and find devastation in her eyes like I've never seen before. The sound of the doctor's voice snaps my head back.

"Miss Scott, the X-ray shows other fractures. Here, can you see the fuzziness? The lines are faint, but they are there."

I squint, though I don't know why I am bothering. I don't understand a thing I am seeing. Does this mean that I had surgery on the boat? The blade-like smooth and arching scar that runs from my groin, over my hip to my tail bone, flashes in my mind, and my stomach churns.

"T-that isn't my hip."

"No, these are pubic rami fractures, maybe two years old. They are more common in children that have suffered - "

"Okay, Doc! I think we just need to know how to help Mac now," Dixy interrupts, getting to her feet.

My stomach bottoms out as understanding hits. I let go of Anna's hand and cross my arms across my chest. His perverse eyes flash savagely in my mind. My thumb and forefinger press together, and my head starts to swim. I look at Dixy wide-eyed as the images start to flash.

"Doc, maybe we could take this conversation outside, give Mac a moment to… process, and you can talk me through the treatment plan." Dixy puts her hand on Dr Corbin's arm and lightly glides him towards the door. As soon as it shuts, I start to gasp, and Anna grabs for my hand, but I pull it away.

"I n-need you to go," I snap as my head starts to spin.

"Mac…don't…please," Anna chokes, her hands on my face, but I pull away.

"*Now…*"

She lets me go. I hear a sob as she leaves the room, and as soon as the door closes, my vision blurs, and the memory swirls.

Fight... Kick... Struggle... Flail.

Not again, no more.

You must battle, Mac. You must attack... Fight!

I snarl a furious, rabid, feral snarl.

I scratch out at those savage eyes that are intent upon me.

Blows, sharp and stunning.

Oxygen forced from my lungs; All power leached from my limbs.

Not again, no more.

Fight, Mac. Fight!

My knees thrash, my fists pound.

The chain jangles, cold around my wrists.

I wrap it around his throat.

Pull Mac, pull!

His savage eyes bulge, his face ruby red.

Rage... Vein throbbing rage alters his face.

My thigh pushed against my stomach; I pull and pull and...

His hand rams hard against my knee, forcing it sideways.
A pop… A loud and blinding pop bursts from inside.
Agony. I scream with every thrust till...
Darkness.

***

"Tomasz, you greedy fuck. She is no good to me dead," Jakub spits.

"Sorry, got carried away. Mala suka tried to strangle me," Tomasz chokes, rubbing his throat.

"Call the butcher; he will fix her."

My eyes open, my chest heaves, and the hospital room morphs back into my focus.

"Tomasz…" I growl.

The door opens, the tiny click enough to startle me. Dixy comes into the room alone; she approaches me cautiously. I feel frozen in place, unable to move, not even able to look up.

"The man?" she whispers with a slight growl. All I can do is nod.

"The doctor is going to inject your hip with steroids and anti-inflammatory. He said you will feel better in a day or two. You need to rest and move it regularly to stop it from stiffening up. As soon as it's done, we can take you home, okay?"

***

The injections sucked. The needles were huge, and my language was colourful, making Dr Corbin flinch. He gives me some crutches, and I am taken home to my apartment. Protests are made as both Dixy and Anna insist I go back to the farm, but I refuse them. Now I am on my sofa, feeling numb and battered. My mind is a heavy fog of whisky, and I pass out quickly in a drunken haze.

The need to pee wakes me, and with how long it takes me to precariously and painfully drag myself up the spiral staircase, it's a wonder I made it to the bathroom in time. I take advantage of being upstairs, taking the chance to shower, and then lay on my bed.

"Mac, you copy?" Alfred's voice grumbles from inside my ear, and I flinch. These ear implants have annoyingly good range.

"Yeah."

"Can I come see you in the morning?

"Since when do you ask?"

"Since I was a bit of a dick to you this morning."

"It's already forgotten, Pa," I reply, and he sighs.

"I'll see you in the morning, kid. Rest up. If you need anything before that, holler."

"Houston, we have a problem."

***

The next morning, I notice the cement stiffness in my hip is less. I can't bear much weight because the pain is ridiculous when I do. The crutches are necessary, but I am relieved when I don't feel as bad as I was expecting, and I can move and bend the joint. I plonk down on the sofa, watching the TV on mute. It is boring, and I have no idea if what I am lip reading is actually correct. The door knocks, and I shout for Alfred to walk in. He trudges toward me with his head hung. He has a childlike unease on his face like he has just been given a good hiding for stealing a cookie.

"Hey…"

"Okay, what's eating at you? Spit it out," I tease, and he chuckles.

"I'm sorry for yesterday. I pushed, and it really isn't my business. I wanted to apologise, but then everything kicked off before I had the chance."

"It is your business; you are worried about her. I get that; I am too. Especially after yesterday. I know you meant well; you just can't help but be a meddler!" I wink, relieved to see him smile. "What exactly did happen? No one told me much."

"Well, according to Dixy, Danni came over and started talking to her; she was asking her questions about the parkour run, casual like – you know? Dixy didn't think anything of it. She asked about the sandbags, and Dixy explained what they were for. Then out of nowhere, she picked one up and said, 'Like this?' She threw it before Dixy could stop her. I heard her shout, and she launched herself at Danni, knocked her flying trying to stop her, but it was too late."

I can see it happening crystal clear in my mind. I remember the feeling of falling and the pain of landing. I shake my head, trying to clear the images.

"That seems really random and out the blue, don't you think?"

"Not really. She came to the house looking for Anna. I had to tell her that she was asleep in your bed and that I didn't want her waking. Her face said it all."

Ugh, that makes a little more sense, but still, that was a ballsy move, and it seems like a serious overreaction. One thing is for sure: that girl is dangerous.

"How is Anna?"

"I don't know. She locked herself in your barn. I haven't seen her, and she won't talk to me. She is obviously going to blame herself for this. Lambert camped over by the firepit; I asked him to stay just in case Danni comes back. After what she did to you, I don't want her anywhere near Savannah."

"It's not her fault. I'll help her see that. I don't want her carrying this. Danni doesn't want to show her face, though. A bum hip won't stop me from snapping her in half."

Alfred chuckles. "I think you might have to get in line kid. Dixy was terrifying, and Lambert is fuming; he's mad he couldn't stop you falling. And that's not to mention me," he scathes with fire in his eyes. "Anyway, how are you feeling? Dixy told me it was rough, although she didn't elaborate."

"I'm fine. It sucks, but the Doc said it should be better in a few days. Just got to rest and move it regularly."

"Is there anything you need?"

"Actually, yes. I could do with getting out, and I have some stuff I want to practice that Lambert showed me. If I can't move around, I can at least practice the stuff that doesn't require me moving. I just need a ride to a coffee shop."

"No problem. How about you buzz me on the earpiece when you're done? I'll come get you, bring you back to the farm, and maybe…you could try to have a talk with Anna for me," he mumbles awkwardly. "I wouldn't ask, but I think you're the only person she's going to listen to right now."

"I can do that."

***

I sit in Umber, my back against the wall, the fire exit on my right. I watch, and I listen, pretending to read the latest copy of Empire magazine, sipping my coffee with my ears pricked. I am learning a lot about the people around me. My eyes flit around, and I try to be conscious of my body language and the way I move so that I don't draw attention to myself.

After about three hours of this, my heart feels a little fluttery from too much caffeine, and I have observed and eavesdropped on an American tourist couple, a group of giggly girls on their lunch break, two businessmen complaining about the state of the economy, and a family of four squabbling over cake. Then, I realise – I am delaying the inevitable.

I want to be there for Anna, but there is no way that she didn't pick up on what the doctor was trying to say yesterday. In fact, it felt like she understood before I did. I don't want to talk about it. I don't want to be pushed, and she has a way of breaking through my barriers regardless of how hard I fortify them. Plus, I know she is going to be hurting – it hurts to be close to her, it just… hurts. The fact is, she is hurting too and I need to stop that if I can. I roll up the magazine and put it in my bag, then drain the coffee mug empty, my eyes curiously people watching and then, it happens…

There is only one way to accurately describe that feeling that rocks me. My stomach falls out through my arsehole, and I freeze when I see a familiar face. His eyes sweep the restaurant, his big, round, and piercing grey-blue eyes.

"Houston, w-we have a problem." I choke.

Then his eyes fall upon me. He smiles slightly and walks towards me slowly, his hair perfectly styled and peppering with grey specks around his ears, his face clean shaven and handsome. He pauses at the chair to undo his double-breasted blazer and then sits down smoothly in front of me.

"Mac, did you mean to activate?" Alfred booms from inside my ear.

I take a deep breath and exhale with a small smile, smoothing myself out calmly. Inside my guts twist, and my mind races. Like a duck on water.

"And there was me thinking there was no way you would respond to my message, after all this time," I mutter lightly.

"McKenna, I have waited a long time to meet you. Of course, I came."

"Well, thank you, *Barrett*. I'm glad you did," I utter, purposefully dropping his name.

"Oh shit! Alright, kid. Stay cool, Dixy is patching in. I'm on my way."

"That is nice to hear. After missing so much of your life, I feared you would be too angry to reach out to me. I am… pleasantly surprised," Barrett muses. He is watching me, analysing me.

This is a test; he doubts me already.

"I was angry for a very long time. You abandoned me; I hated you for that. Maybe I still do, but the anger I had for you started to subside when I realised you were trying to save me. I started to want to believe you cared. Maybe that was foolish of me." I look down at the table and try to portray a little vulnerability.

"No, no, McKenna, that isn't foolish. I do care; I always have. I only left you because I had important work to do, and I couldn't protect you if I stayed." Barrett speaks with a softness that churns my stomach, but I feel relieved.

"Well done, Mac," Dixy sounds in my ear.

"I hope you mean that, because in the end, it didn't matter that you left me to try and protect me. I was still taken."

Barrett reaches out and lays his hand on top of mine. It takes all my will not to flinch away, not to react in any way. I just hold his gaze keeping my face slack.

"Will you give me the chance to show you that I do mean it?"

I take my time answering, trying to show some signs of being unsure. I look at his hand and then back up to his eyes.

"Yes. Call me crazy but – I want to give you that chance. So…don't screw it up." I quirk an eyebrow, and he laughs easily, squeezing my hand, and I let myself smile a little.

I'm going to need to shower after this.

"Thank you. We have much to talk about, but I don't have much time right now. I will be in touch. It is so good to see you, McKenna.

"You too, Barrett."

I watch Barrett walk away smoothly, his movements exuding confidence. He pulls the door open, and I watch it swing shut as he leaves and then I exhale.

"I'm clear," I puff out, my chest heaving in relief.

"Mac…you little bad ass! That was extraordinary! I'm so impressed," Dixy beams in my ear.

"Ugh, God, I feel dirty." I groan, and she laughs. Then, I see Alfred stride towards me, his face bright with pride.

"Nicely done, kid. Are you alright?"

"Nothing a shower and a whisky won't fix."

***

The drive back to the farm is quick, but I've been sitting prone for too long; the weight pressing on my hip is causing my pain to escalate. I am desperate to lay down and take the pressure off or even just stand up. When we finally pull in, the pain is starting to make me sweat. Alfred helps me out the Landover, and I wobble on my feet wincing.

"You're not looking so hot; can you make it?"

"Umm…yeah, I can get there. It's sitting that hurts. I either have to stand or lay down."

"Okay, I have an idea. Let's just get you to the fire pit, and I'll sort it," Alfred assures me.

I hobble over, the crutches getting caught in the long grass with every stride I make, and it is definitely slowing me down. Alfred walks with me anyway, keeping pace. When I come into view, Dixy and Lambert boom with cheers, and I feel heat redden my cheeks. Finally, I make it. Alfred heads into the house and Dixy jumps up, ruffling my hair and grinning from ear to ear.

"You fucking legend, Agent Scott!" She beams.

"Alright, chill out. I had no idea what I was doing."

"You did, you just don't realise it. You had complete control of that meet even though you were caught off guard. You had him eating out of your hand!" she shrieks.

"Urgh, gross stop. I already feel like I need a shower."

When Alfred returns, he is dragging the cushions from the sofa in the living room along and hooked on his wrist is a plastic bag clinking away which he hands to Dixy.

"Oh yes, definitely!" She whoops, pulling out a bottle of Jack Daniels and some glasses.

Alfred starts dragging a big, old, and rusty digger bucket towards the fire pit. It still has flecks of yellow paint, and the teeth on it look menacing. Lambert is on his feet helping him when he sees Alfred struggle to drag it along.

"What are we doing with this, Sarg?" Lambert gasps through gritted teeth.

"Stop here. We need to flip it," Alfred grunts.

They flip the digger bucket over, so the inner scoop is underneath, and the teeth dig into the grass. The underside swoops in an arch, and Alfred lays a sofa cushion against it, then he lays two more in front of it. I can see that he has made me the worlds quickest assembled lounge chair. He looks at me, grinning, quite proud of himself.

"Genius!" I giggle.

Lambert takes my crutches, and he lowers me to the floor with ease. The relief on my hip is incredible, and I moan in delight, and everyone laughs brightly. A glass of Jack in my hand, the pain dulling, it starts to become more of a reality what has just happened. I just held hands with the devil. The game is on.

"You alright, Mac?" Lambert asks.

"Yeah, just…things are moving, and I can barely walk. Feel a little exposed." I admit, and he nods, his smiling fading.

"I'm sorry I wasn't able to keep hold of you. Wasn't a good feeling, you slipping through my fingers like that."

"Don't be a doughnut, Callum. You slowed me down; if you hadn't, it would have been a lot worse. You could have gone down with me, the way you dived for the edge like that. So, thank you for having my back."

"Thank you for saying that. As for feeling exposed, I don't think Barrett will move that fast. He's going to want to be careful. I'd be more worried about the psycho who knocked you off the platform. That…was a cold move and bold. Which tells me she's probably capable of doing worse." He huffs bleakly.

"Yeah, that's what I thought. Thanks for staying to watch over Anna. Maybe I should start carrying some throwing knives in my jacket," I scoff.

"You can laugh, but I slept with my knife last night. Not that I thought anything would happen, but I've learnt when your instincts are firing never to ignore them. She clearly has it in for you. As your instructor, I'd advise you carry till you're sure the threat is neutralised. Actually, I have something for you. Give me a minute." Lambert gets to his feet and stalks off.

"O…kay…"

I listen to Dixy and Albert talk and laugh, not really paying attention to their conversation; I feel exhausted. My mind is overloaded with a barrage of constant murmurs and shouts. Barrett, Tomasz, Danni, Anna…round and round and round. The whisky is certainly doing its job, making me sleepy. I find myself staring at the barn door, knowing Anna is in there. At this point, it's obvious she's hiding in there with no intention of coming out.

Lambert returns and hands me something black, a strap of some sort made of neoprene that has been wrapped into a tight roll. I unwrap it and see that it is actually a sheath. The strap was hiding a small knife. The handle is skeletal, a thin outline made of steel and covered in a black over-mould grip with a hollow centre. I pull the knife out; it is feather light and balanced in weight. The blade is also black and about three inches long.

"Woah…"

"It's a ghost strike knife, completely concealable under your trouser leg and lightweight. You will forget it's there," Lambert explains kneeling down.

"Can I?" he asks, pausing with his hands over my trouser leg, and I chuckle, nodding.

Lambert lifts the trouser leg of my uninjured leg and straps the sheath to my shin just above the top of my combat boots. Then he pulls my trouser leg down, and he is right, you would never know it is there.

"Keep it; I have another. Wear it every day, keep yourself safe – That's an order." He smirks boyishly, holding his hand out, fingers pointed up, and I smile, giving him a high five. My chest swells a little at his big brotherly gesture.

"Thank you, Callum."

I feel silly admitting it to myself, but I actually do feel better, knowing it's there, and I am touched. Who knew big beastly Callum Lambert was such a softy? However, this fearful buzz is still gnawing in my gut.

Alfred heads inside to make us all some lunch and Callum offers to help him; he must be a decent cook because Alfred actually lets him. Dixy comes over and sits on the floor next to me, and inside I groan because my head is heavy, and my eyes want to close, and the last thing I want is a serious talk.

"How are you doing?"

"Ugh… stop it. I'm fine," I grumble, and she laughs.

"You can't blame me for checking."

"I guess not. Thanks, for…"

"That's okay."

"I don't want to talk about it," I mumble.

"I know. I'm just going to sit with you while you fall asleep."

"You creep," I joke, and she giggles.

It isn't till she is sat with me that I realise how unsafe I feel. My stomach is full of nervous tingles, and my chest is heavy with a tight ache. Tears well in my eyes, and I rub them roughly, sending my vision screwy.

"You're not sleeping."

"Nah, I'm good," I lie, clearing my throat.

"What did I tell you about breaking?"

"Not happening."

Dixy shuffles closer so she is sat on the cushions with me.

"It will happen, sooner or later Mac – trust me. Don't let yourself be alone when it does."

"Bossy," I grunt.

"Is that why you find me irresistible?" she jokes.

"Shut up; I'm trying to sleep."

I lean my head against her shoulder, and I feel her giggle silently. I realise that for all the things I've lost, I have also gained so much. Callum and Dixy are here to teach me how to protect myself, to survive, just like Alfred did. Somehow, I know that there isn't anything they wouldn't do to protect me. They would go to the bat for me, and I would do the same for them in a heartbeat. I am not alone in this fight.

Barrett…WE are coming for you.

CHAPTER 5

Keep the Faith

When my eyes open, it is just starting to get dark, and the first thing I see is Anna sat across from me. As soon as I open my eyes, she looks away. Now she is staring into the fire and doing all she can not to look at me, her eyes puffy and exhausted.

"Come here, please."

She hesitates, then she gets up, closing the gap between us, and sits on the ground in front of me. She sits cross-legged with her hands in her lap, her eyes downcast.

"This wasn't your fault, Anna."

"Yes, it was. If I were you, I would stay away from me. It shouldn't be too hard; you do it most of the time anyway. Please, just stay away from me," Anna sniffles, her tone completely defeated.

That stung.

"Anna…what's going on with you?"

"Who says there is anything going on with me?" she snaps evasively.

"I do. This isn't you."

"What would you know?!"

She is trying to push me away. I am trying so hard not to bite; I feel like she wants me to be mad at her. Why would she want that? I feel the worst pang of guilt I have ever had deep in my gut.

"If nothing is wrong, why won't you look at me?"

Anna huffs; her jaw is set when she looks at me. She still looks so tired, and she is looking at me so blankly. I've never seen such coldness in her expressive eyes, eyes that make me feel everything they say. Right now, they say she can't stand to look at me. They say I've lost her, and really, it's no one's fault but my own. I feel like my chest is being stretched open. I look down, and I take her hand, and it's cold; I have never known her hands to be cold. I take both her hands and rub them in mine, warming them up.

"Did I do this to you?" I choke, and pain washes away the coldness in her eyes.

"Why would do think that?"

"I thought maybe something was wrong with Danni, but you are worse since she is gone, not better. After everything I put you through, I couldn't blame you. Now you are telling me to stay away from you. Makes sense that it would be me. I was always so scared of breaking you, of tarnishing the magic of you. It's not hard for me to believe I finally have. I just need to know. I … I can stay away, as much as I can, if it w-would help."

Her eyes begin to well, and her hands shake inside of mine.

"No… Please, don't think that. Don't ever. You have always … Please, Mac, don't." She sobs; she is starting to break again. Anna bows her head down, her forehead resting on my hands. I keep hold of her hands and stroke her cheek with my thumb.

"Hey, it's okay. I'm sorry. Please, Anna – tell me what's going on. You look scared, and I'm worried; I have been for a while. Something is tearing you up – please, talk to me."

"Please stop," she whines.

"Is it Danni? If you don't tell me, maybe I should ask her myself," I ask with an edge to my tone, and her head shoots up, her eyes furious.

"You don't talk to her! You don't go near her, ever! Just stay out of it, and stay the hell away from me, Mac. I am not your problem anymore. You made sure of that!" she snaps with venom.

Anna pulls her hands harshly from mine. She gets to her feet and storms away towards the house, leaving me feeling bitch slapped. My head spins, trying to understand. Part of me believes she just wants me gone because it is just so easy to believe that. I have hurt her so much. The other part is fighting to believe I know her better, the part that aches at the thought that she is lost to me forever.

"Houston, we have a problem. Pa, you copy?"

"What's up, kid?"

"Can you come to the fire pit?"

"On my way."

I look up at the house, and I see Anna's bedroom light turn on. God, what I would give to be inside her head for just a moment, to understand what the hell she is thinking. I see Alfred skulking down towards me, and he is carrying a plate of food. Even in my anger and hurt, I can't help but laugh. The man is such a feeder. He hands me a plate of sandwiches covered in cling film and takes a seat.

"I take it you spoke to Savannah."

"Yes, I did. Why?"

"She came in crying, went straight past me up to her room."

"She was crying, not angry?" I press.

"She didn't look angry. What are you getting at?"

"Something is tearing her up. She wouldn't tell me, but it was going okay till I mentioned Danni. I told her if she won't tell me, then maybe I should talk to Danni. Then she flipped; she completely lost it at me. So why when you saw her, literally a minute later, was she crying and not mad?"

"Can you stop talking in riddles? You've lost me, kid."

"I think she *wants* me to think she is mad; she is pushing me away as hard as she can, but that wasn't anger… she is terrified. She lost it when I threatened to go near Danni. I think she's afraid of her, but if it's over – then why is she so scared?"

I see the understanding flicker in his face, then it turns to anger.

"Because it isn't over," he growls. "She must have some hold over Savannah. After what Danni did to you, she wouldn't go near her again if she had a choice. I know she wouldn't."

"She absolutely cannot be left alone. I could be overreacting, but I will not take that chance on her, and I can't shake how scared she was, Pa. I don't know, the things she said were either designed to make me *think* she is done with me and doesn't want me anywhere near her or…she actually feels that way, and I've lost her. My head keeps flitting back and forth. I just...I can't…"

My head is in my hands, pain burning me. I don't know what to believe anymore. Have I lost her? I mean, like – all of her? I know I lost her a long time ago, but I never felt like she was gone…till now. I feel a giant warm hand on my shoulder, and I look up.

"Don't lose faith now, kid. Not when she needs you to have it the most. I don't know what she is doing or why, but the one thing I know with absolute certainty is - she would never just let you go. She needs you, Mac," Alfred says, squeezing my shoulder.

My memory flashes.

"I have told you; I have no intention of letting her go. I have been clear about that from the start, and if you ever push her like that again…"

I nod my head, Anna's words repeating in my head, over and over with every nod. I don't know what is happening, but I can't give up on her now.

"Then we protect her until I can find a way to make her safe again, and God help Danni if she so much as touches a hair on her head," I spit.

"That sounds more like it. Are you alright?"

"Yeah… I think I just need to go sort my head out for the night. I don't want you leaving Anna; one of us always needs to be here. Will you see if Dixy or Lambert will give me a ride back?"

***

It is a relief to be at the apartment. I go through the motions, eat, shower, bed. I put a movie on, listen to music, but nothing I do will quiet the noise in my head. I met my father for the first time, and I feel nothing but revulsion and hatred. I feel a constant gnaw inside, a dread for whatever is about to come. The lack of control, not knowing what will happen next is exhausting.

The pain I feel over Anna, is exhausting. It always has been, but now it is worse because I feel like I have lost her. It is so hard to hold onto the hope that she doesn't want me gone. I lost my shot with her a long time ago, but I think I always hoped that one day, there might be a - one day. More than anything, she doesn't seem like the person I knew; I barely recognise her. And I feel that loss the most. Did I destroy her?

The grief I feel over losing Alisha is exhausting. The loss of her, after all this time, after everything she came to mean to me, hurts. I have said goodbye to Alisha many times since our first encounter at the hotel but the finality of this goodbye is… sharp, because the scales finally tipped; I just wish I hadn't hurt her so much before they had. I hurt her, I hurt Anna…maybe Anna is right to tell me to say away from her. Maybe when this is all over, that is exactly what I have to do for her.

***

Not much sleep was had; my brain just doesn't want to shut down no matter what I do. I am loading up on coffee when I hear the doorbell chime. I hobble over and open the door to find no one is there. Then I see a cardboard box on the doorstep with a white envelope on top. The envelope is thick and white with an embossed pattern of damask that is glossy. It feels expensive, and the box is so light it feels empty. My mouth dries up. I don't get mail here really, only the odd fast-food menu is dropped through the letterbox. I turn the envelope over, there is no address written on it, not even my name.

I slide my finger along the seal and pull out the thing thick card inside. My heart flies as my eyes freeze on the raised triangle screaming out on the card.

Miss Mckenna Scott – Plus one

The pleasure of your company has been formally requested at our charity Masquerade Ball.

The Royal Café – 68 Regent Street

Saturday 5th October – 8pm

Δ

The 5th is only two days away. I didn't think Barrett would make contact so soon, and even when he did, a masquerade ball is the last thing I expected. I tear open the cardboard box carefully. Inside are two masquerade masks. One is black and silver, quite simple, elegant, and edgy. The other is green and gold and is more feminine and extravagant. My mind flashes to Anna; she always looks stunning in green.

"Houston, we have a problem. Alfred, you copy?"

"Morning, kid. You alright?"

"Yeah, Barrett made contact. Looks like the game is on," I announce grimly.

"I'm on my way."

"What about Anna?"

"Don't worry, Dixy and Lambert are already here. I've filled them in, and they will watch over Anna. Dixy already wants to kill Danni, so it won't be a problem if she turns up."

"She can get in line. See you in a bit."

I am able to walk using one crutch now. The pain is still there, but it must be getting better because I keep forgetting I have the injury, use the leg as if it is perfectly fine and then curse as I hurt myself. Now more than ever, I need my hip to get better. Alfred walks straight in, and I hand him the box which he carries for me, putting it in the back seat, and soon we are on the move. You can definitely tell that winter is close; I am shivering in the front seat of Alfred's Land Rover since his air conditioning no longer works.

"Just a heads up, Lexi is on her way too," Alfred informs me.

"I didn't think it would be long before she came, not after Barrett found me."

We pull up on the farm, and I see that everyone is by the fire in their usual spots. Dixy and Lambert are in deep conversation, and Anna is sat separate, her eyes glazed over. She doesn't look up when I arrive. Maybe I am way off; maybe she is mad at me after all. I hobble over to a camp chair and wince as I sit. I don't want to be laid out on the floor when Lexi arrives. For some reason, I don't like the idea of how weak it makes me look.

I don't have to wait long. Soon, I hear the crunch of car tyres on gravel as she arrives. Lexi moves behind me silently; I never hear her coming. Alfred offers his camp chair like a perfect gentleman, and now she is sat opposite me, staring expectantly. Actually, everyone is except Anna, who is clearly pretending I don't exist.

"So, this was dropped on my doorstep this morning. No name or address. It's an invitation from Barrett, but I suspect that it won't just be him in attendance," I explain, reading out the invitation and showing everyone the masks.

"What makes you think it won't just be Barrett?" Lexi asks.

I hold up the invitation so that it can be seen, my index finger pointing to the raised triangle, and then look back at Lexi, her eyebrows raised.

"The triangle of truth, I see. So, it is probable that other members of The Culling could be in attendance. This meet is vital; it will be the first time that we have had a glimpse of other members. Makes sense that he would choose an event where people have to wear masks. How you handle this will be pivotal to how easily they except you within their group." Lexi speaks calmly, but there is a fire in her eyes. An excitement that rubs me up the wrong way.

"I agree." I'm trying to seem unphased when really, I need a nervous pee.

"So, who will be attending with you?" Lexi asks.

"I wasn't intending on taking anyone. I don't see why that's necessary."

"The invitation is plus one, and he has sent you two masks. To not attend with someone makes you too conspicuous, and he is clearly expecting you to, so you *will* be taking someone."

"I don't have anyone to take," I admit, keeping my voice level and my eyes firmly away from Anna.

"What about Dixy?" Alfred suggests, trying to bail me out.

"That isn't an option. If they look too closely at Agent Dixon, it could blow your cover. It has to be a civilian. How about Anna? She is a part of this and fully briefed on the situation. She is a part of your life; you will be able to act naturally together - she is the ideal choice."

I tense up, anger starting to boil up, but I have to keep in control. Lexi is basically my boss and also the only person keeping me out of prison, but still…I am pissed.

"You want me to take a civilian, exposing them to an unknown number of Culling members? No, that's not happening. She didn't sign up for this, I did. Besides, that isn't something she is going to want to do. There has to be someone else," I assert firmly, but Lexi merely sighs.

"Anna, would you be willing to allow Agent Scott to escort you to the charity ball?" Lexi asks with exaggerated exasperation.

My head shoots in her direction, and she looks fearful at first, but her expression quickly turns blank and cold. She looks back into the fire.

"Yes," she says in a dead voice, and I turn back to Lexi.

"No, I'm not doing that," I growl, getting to my feet. Lexi gets up too, taking a step towards me, her eyes livid.

"Agent Scott. That is a direct order!"

My eyes flick over her shoulder to Dixy, who is giving me wide "shut the fuck up" eyes and shaking her head discreetly. I take a hobbled step back, my eyes burning with anger, and I take a calming breath. It barely helps.

"Understood," I growl through gritted teeth, and I sit down, trembling with rage but also, my chest burning with pain. I don't want to take Anna because I don't want to put her at risk, but also, she looked like the idea of going with me repulsed her.

"Very well then. If you listen to your instructors, there is no reason why you won't be able to keep Anna safe. Hopefully, we can learn a lot from this event. If you would, keep me up to date, Alfred."

"Of course," he agrees respectfully.

Keep Anna safe? She doesn't care if Anna is safe; she cares about the mission only. I get that. It is all I am working for. I understand and accept that I am expendable, but Anna is not. I am seething, and I am relieved when Lexi leaves, so I don't have to worry about losing my temper. The tension she left behind is still here. It takes too long for anyone to speak. Eventually, Anna gets to her feet and walks towards the house without a word.

"Well, that was fun." Dixy snorts, defusing the tension.

"She is going to have to play nicer than that if she's going to be your escort. She will draw too much attention, and that's the last thing you need," Lambert chimes in.

"Ugh, that is because she doesn't want to go with me! She shouldn't have to go," I groan.

"Doesn't matter, Mac. She will just have to channel her inner actress; both your lives depend on it, and so does our chances of dismantling The Culling. It is not the time for petty disputes."

"I'll let you tell her that, brother."

"Better Lambert than me. Pretty sure she hates me." Dixy giggles. "Besides, you and I have plans."

"We do?" I ask, confused.

"Yes. You are going to the ball, Cinderella; it is time to go shopping!" Dixy shrieks, her face glowing with excitement, and I cringe.

"Oh, Jesus. Can this day get any worse?"

"Bitch all you want, Mac; you're not going to ruin my fun." Dixy beams. I look at Lambert, who is smirking. "Shoot me. Shoot me now."

***

In the passenger side of the van, I pout. I hate clothes shopping at the best of times, but Dixy's excitement over shopping fills me with dread. Girls always want to take me clothes shopping like I am some fun, real-life mannequin for them to play with. The more I protest, the more fun it seems to be for them.

"Cheer up, Mac. This is going to be fun!"

"I already have a perfectly good tux; I don't see why I need to buy another." I sulk.

"Has Anna seen that tux?"

"Why does that matter?"

"Oh, come on! When are you going to admit you got it bad for the girl? You two are like some tortured Romeo and Juliette story. Both watching each other from afar like it is some forbidden love. No wonder you are so brooding and glooming," she teases.

"Yes, that's right – she is absolutely swooning over me. The excitement about going with me was just gushing. I'm sure she is at the farm right now trying on every dress she owns while watching The Princess Diaries and scrawling my name in love hearts all over her books."

"Oo, I hit a nerve. Okay, so yes, she looked pretty pissed about going, but she isn't exactly herself right now. I barely know the girl, and even I can see that. Trust me, that girl wants you. I'm a girl; we know these things."

"I'm a girl," I point out, stating the obvious.

"Yes, but you're oblivious."

"Ugh, change the subject or take me home, woman."

I stand under a union jack flag that is proudly flying above the doorway. The building I am faced with screams expense and luxury. Gieves and Hawks Bespoke Suit Tailoring is emblazoned in gold across the white pillars of the entrance. My stomach twists.

"Seriously, can't I just wear the suit I already have? I don't want to go in there," I whine.

"Why not?"

"Because I have been to these places before. They don't like a girl coming in trying to be fitted for a man's suit – Trust me, I've been there. Much easier just to send measurements and order online."

"We have 48 hours; online ordering isn't going to work. Now suck it up, princess, and get inside." Dixy huffs, pushing me inside.

The inside is worse. I limp inside the tailor's, feeling twitchy and out of place, and my eyes widen at the sheer size of the place. It opens up to a wide and brightly lit space; there are shirts neatly pressed that are impeccably folded and displayed inside lit up glass cases - like the ones you see in jewellery stores where they keep the diamonds. Built into the walls are lit up pigeon holes that house shoes, and the suits that are displayed range from military to bespoke modern, tuxedos, silk smoking jackets, tweed hunter style, and sports blazers. My eyes light up, and I forget just how nervous I am for a moment as I see the display of ties and bow ties, pocket watches and rotary watches. I am in heaven.

"Wow…" I gape, wide-eyed and in awe.

"Oh, you're almost drooling," she teases, giggling.

We walk over to the front desk, where a suited and booted man greets us. His top lip is sporting a curly moustache, he is wearing round-rimmed glasses, and his hair is parted down the side in a comb-over that does nothing to hide his bald spot. He eyes me exactly how I expect, with malcontent curiosity.

"Hello, welcome to Gieves and Hawks. Do you have an appointment?" he asks, his voice quiet and pompous. He is definitely looking down his pretentious nose at me. This is exactly why I didn't want to come in. I refuse to fidget.

"I don't need an appointment; I would like to place a new order with Holt security access. I need a bespoke dinner suit fitted for my friend here. Something in silver and black, not shiny – more a subtle sparkle, slim fitting and sexy as hell. I need all the extras, plus the usual upgrades, and I need it ready and *perfect* within 24 hours," Dixy asserts sassily. She takes a card out of her pocket, lays it on the desk, and slides it towards him. The moustached man gulps and tightens his tie.

"Oh…I see. Right you are, miss, right you are. Of course. I am sure we can accommodate your needs. Let's get you both comfortable, and we will begin with the measurements. RICHARD! Can I offer you both a beverage? RICHARD!"

"Oh, I would love a cappuccino with chocolate sprinkles. Mac?" Dixy turns to me smirking, and I suppress a snort.

"Same, please."

A young man comes dashing over, skinny and lanky and dressed in a plain blue suit.

"Yes, Mr Sinclair?" he huffs breathlessly.

"Richard, please see that these ladies have everything they need to make them comfortable, starting with two cappuccinos with chocolate sprinkles on the double." Mr Sinclair orders.

"But sir, w-we don't have any chocolate," Richard stutters.

"Then *find* some!"

I lean over to Dixy and whisper in her ear, "You are evil. You know that, right?"

"Shut up. You love it."

I actually do; I can't help but get a little pleasure out of seeing Mr Sinclair squirm. To me, he is just another person standing in the long line of people that look at me in a way that makes me feel unacceptable. I don't look or act like the socially acceptable norm, and I can't help but enjoy the moment that one of the people in that line gets a dress down that I have always myself wanted to give - this is fun!

We are taken to a private dressing room which is fancier than most hotel rooms I have stayed in. The room is decorated in thick black and silver striped wallpaper. Along the wall are photographs of various famous people in suits;

the background of the photographs showing the same striped wallpaper. Grinning faces of members of the royal family, famous sportsmen, and actors looking dapper.

I am measured and try on various demo suits to try to establish the perfect fit. Mr Sinclair dashes around me with chalk and pins while humming a jolly tune, and Dixy orders him around. She is clearly enjoying every moment.

"No, tighter in the legs and butt. She's not a man – show that pert little butt off," she orders, and I raise an eyebrow. "Don't look at me like that; I know what I'm doing."

Once the measurements are completed, we look at fabrics. Dixy does practically all the talking. Although she asks me if I like the things she chooses, I get the feeling she is having far too much fun to care if I said no. Luckily, she does have good taste…so far. The fabric of the suit is very dark silver mixed with black. It isn't shiny, which I am glad for. It glitters slightly in the light and is more of a gunmetal grey than silver. The lapels are slim black velvet, with a waistcoat to match.

There is a flutter of excitement in my chest because never have I worn a suit that fits me correctly. While I love the masculine style, I have a feminine body which means that it never looks as flattering against my frame as I hope for. The prospect of finally wearing a suit exactly the style I love that actually fits, has an excitement building inside me that resembles a child trying to sleep the night before their birthday. And I can't help it, try as I might to ignore the voice inside my head, it is annoyingly loud and perversely satisfying…

Can't wait for Anna to see me in this suit.

We move onto the accessories, and my eyes light up; I could spend a lot of money in this place. I want to touch the shiny silks and the soft velvets, but everything is so neat and perfectly lit up. My instinct tells me I should probably keep my hands to myself. In the end, I am fitted a black dress shirt. It is silk lined and again, not shiny but has a soft feel. The shirt has to be taken in a ridiculous amount with so many pins, I fear if I move a muscle, I will be pricked like a pin cushion.

"Does it really have to be this tight? Feel like if I bend over, it's going to split," I whine.

"Yes, it does. We want sexy, not comfortable."

I huff; I don't see why it has to be sexy at all. Not sure that will help me infiltrate The Culling. It feels like I've been in this shop forever. We finish by choosing a matching black skinny silk tie, and Mr Sinclair hands Dixy a velvet box as we leave. He smiles politely, but his eyes clearly hope that Dixy never darkens his doorstep again.

***

We stop at a restaurant to get some lunch, sitting in the very back and facing the entrance. The restaurant is large and busy with the lunch time rush – perfect for blending in. After ordering food, Dixy slides the velvet box towards me, and I open it. Inside is a pair of cufflinks, a watch, and a tie pin, all in silver that shines in the light. I look up at her with a raised eyebrow, and she chuckles.

"These are the 'upgrades' I requested. All the suits used by MI5 Agents are made and distributed by a shadow company hidden within Gieves and Hawks. The waistcoat you will be receiving is lined with Kevlar and is bullet proof. Make no mistake, though – you get shot when you wear it, you won't die, but it will be agony.

"The watch has been resized to fit you, it reads your vital signs and sends them back to us so we can monitor you. If your heart is to stop, we can remotely activate the lifesaver feature, which will inject you with a shot of adrenalin on the inside of your wrist and send an electric charge to restart your heart. It also has a distress beacon, compass, and if you turn the face of the outer face of the watch until it is upside down, you can click it, and it can send morse code signals to us."

"I don't know morse code."

"Yet." She winks.

Dixy takes out the watch and hands it to me. It is a skeleton Rotary watch; I have always wanted one. It is stunning, masculine but not too big or out of place on my wrist. I smile as I get lost watching the little cogs turn inside.

"I saw you eyeing them like a kid in a candy store. Figured it's the least you deserve." Dixy smiles softly, her eyes downcast.

I turn the watch over and see words engraved in the back. 'Make every second count – D.' I look up at her, a little gobsmacked, a lot touched, and her cheeks redden.

"Hopefully, it will remind you that you're not alone in this. You are a part of this family now, and we will be in this with you, every second till the very end."

"Dixy… I… Wow…" I choke, and then I chuckle, embarrassed. "Agent Dixon, who knew you were such a softie," I tease.

"Shut up! Don't think I don't see you getting all misty eyed. Just put it on and let's move on before you fall madly in love with me."

Dixy picks up the tie pin. She twists it and flips it inside out. A little like when you use a pair of nail clippers. In the hinged end, a small needle pops out. It must be roughly a centimetre long.

"This is a poison dart; push the needle in hard, and the impact shoots a concentrated dose of snake venom into the bloodstream; the victim dies within 20 seconds. The needle is strong enough to pick locks too."

I hope I don't look as dumbstruck as I feel right now. I don't know whether to be excited or creeped out.

Both, definitely both.

"The cufflinks double as garrottes. Push and twist the back fastening, and when you feel a click, pull the fastening," Dixy explains, and I do as she instructs; I feel the click and pull, and the front of the cufflink separates from the fastening clips, revealing a long, thin wire.

"It looks flimsy, but it isn't. You could zipwire from that thing, it's more than capable of strangling someone."

"Damn… that is…" I struggle, shuddering.

"Yeah, wouldn't be my weapon of choice either, but you never know when you might need it."

I let go of the fastening clip of the cufflink, and the wire retracts back inside like a measuring tape, just as fast but silent. I really hope I never have reason to use those. The food arrives, and the conversation inevitably steers towards the charity ball.

"How are you feeling about it?"

"Fine. I'm more concerned about Anna than anything. I really wish I could just go on my own. Feels like a train wreck waiting to happen."

"Okay, seriously. What happened with you two?"

I explain, though I don't know why. Maybe because I am about to go undercover with her and the tension between us is worrying me. Maybe I just felt like I needed to talk about it, maybe both. It actually feels like a release being able to talk about it.

"You are quite the masochist, aren't you?" She smirks, and I glare at her playfully. "I get why you felt the need to protect her from Jakub. The fact that psychopath took Alisha is proof of the danger she was in, but it sounds more like you feel you need to protect her from yourself. Why?"

"Despite what it may look like now, she is so bright, positive, and warm. I always told her, there's a magic about her, a light. One I was always worried I would snuff out with my darkness. Now, it looks like even though I tried to stay away, I may have still succeeded in doing that to her anyway. I don't know what is going on with her. I know there is more to it than just me, but…" I trail off, unsure what else to say.

"You never told her how you really feel about her?" Dixy asks, sucking strawberry milkshake through a straw.

"I nearly did the night of her birthday. I was about to…that's when I found out about Danni," I say, flinching a little at the memory of that perfect kiss. The blow of having my hope dashed still hurts.

"Ouch. That had to suck. Doesn't make much sense to me, though. The Danni thing, I mean. I watch people; I did it long before I became an Agent. I find people fascinating – their expressions, their behaviours, trying to work out what they are thinking. I've seen Anna around Danni; there's no warmth there, nothing in her eyes, nothing…connects. I have never even seen Anna touch her."

"She was probably just trying to spare me from seeing it. I just want to make sure Danni isn't hurting her in some way and that she is safe. I'll get the charity ball over with, and then I will leave her alone like she asked."

"Don't worry about the ball. Me and Lambert will sort her out," she assures me, and I snort.

"Are you taking her shopping too?"

"God no; she would hate every second. I'll be sorting her outfit, though; would you like me to buy her something really ugly?"

"Wouldn't make a difference. The girl would look good in a bin bag, especially if it is green." I sigh.

"I hope things work out for you, Mac. Shall we head home?"

We get to our feet, and Dixy turns to lead the way out, and I grab her wrist. She looks at me confused as I hesitate before I pull her in and give her a hug.

"Thank you for being a very irritating but relentlessly awesome human being," I whisper.

"Damn it, you were almost cute then. You had to ruin it, didn't you?"

***

It has been good to get away. As much as I protested, I really enjoyed the experience of having my own suit made, not that I will ever admit that to Dixy. I needed the time away and the laughs, and it is never dull with Dixy around. As I return to the farm, I find myself wishing I could just go back to the apartment. The heaviness in my heart gets weightier the moment we return, but I told Alfred I would be around more to watch over Anna, so it looks like I will be staying here tonight.

I get to my barn and decide to practice some knife throwing. My hip is beginning to feel a lot better, but I don't see me running the parkour run any time soon. I limp over to the table to pick up the throwing knives, and as I turn round, I notice something is missing. My eyes scan the wall where my weapons are, and the knife that Alfred gave me is gone. That's weird. Maybe Alfred is using it for something.

The practice is starting to pay off. I am no Batman, but my accuracy is improving. I am learning to judge the trajectory, how much force and flick of my wrist I need to apply at different distances. I enjoy the physical movement, the satisfaction I get from hitting the target and seeing myself improve. After nearly two hours standing, though, my hip is starting to object, so I go and lay on the pallet bed.

The smell of candy perfume puffs from my pillow as my head hits it, and I groan. I try to stop myself, but I fail. I breathe in the smell, and the memories hit me hard and fast, pounding me in the chest with incredible force. The tears begin to fall, and I resent them. I throw the pillow across the room in a rage, but that just makes the tears flow faster. I feel tormented by the hot and cold, the there - but not there. The riddle that Anna has become. I feel like she is playing with me, but I know that she would never do that.

I curl myself up in a tight ball, feeling lonely and pathetic. I swore I wasn't going to allow that girl to break my heart anymore. How weak am I that I have let that happen again? The barn door swings open, and I freeze. My back is turned; hopefully, whoever it is will think I am asleep.

"Mac, can you come to the fire pit? Lambert wants to talk to you and Savannah about some strategies for the ball," Alfred asks.

"Be right there."

I wipe my eyes; they are puffy and red, and there is no hiding that. Hopefully, the fact that it is getting dark will be enough to hide it if I keep my head down. Anna is the last person I want to see right now; I take a deep breath and hobble outside. Dixy, Lambert, and Anna are all sitting by the fire. I take a seat and keep my eyes down.

"Right, this is more for you, Anna, than it is for Mac, but it would be good for you to hear too," Lambert informs us. I nod and listen, hoping this will be over quickly.

"The moment you walk into the Royal Café, you are going to be watched. You especially, Mac, are going to have to show a little…discomfort. Try to think from Barrett's point of view; you won't know anyone there but him and each other. So, he'll expect you to stick together. He will expect that you keep to yourselves and feel a little out of place. So, you don't want to show too much confidence. Remember, to him, you are the daughter whose affection and approval he is trying to win. Don't give it to him to easily or he will be suspicious. Although, the way you handled the first meeting, I'm not too worried about you handling him.

"Anna, you have to play the escort, show you want to be there with Mac. To you, this is just a fancy date. Relax and show enjoyment because you are not supposed to be aware of a group named The Culling or feel in any danger. Don't go off on your own where Mac can't ensure your safety. Try not to watch other people too much; be natural and act like this is like any normal date because they will be watching you. They have no reason to be suspicious of you, so don't give them reason to be, and you'll be okay. You need to be convincing and if you can't do that, say now – it's not worth jeopardising the whole mission. We will find someone else if we have to."

"I understand what I have to do." Anna says firmly. She almost sounds like herself again; I suspect that is her trying to prove she can behave.

Great, just great. A pretend date with Anna, where she smiles at me, talks with me, acts like she wants me, and when it is all over, goes back to pretending I don't exist. Just fucking wonderful.

"The objective is just to get closer to Barrett, get him to want to get closer to you, Mac. Don't worry about trying to watch other people or getting information. This is going to be a long con. The only way we take them down is if you persuade him that he wants you to be a part of The Culling. He must trust you; that is all you have to worry about."

"Piece of cake." I sigh.

"We will be renting a car to take you and pick you up because we can't risk being seen, but we will stay in contact with you via earpiece. You'll need to wear your contact lenses so we can see what you see. If you feel he's on to you in any way, don't panic. Hold your nerve and lie; we will be in your ear if you struggle. Everything about this meet for him will be about him testing you and probably every meeting after for a while. Bear in mind this man may not know you, but he has been watching you your entire life. Be yourself because if you put on some act, it will send alarm bells."

I listen carefully, focusing on the calm of Lambert's monotone voice, taking in every word, soaking it all up. I nod, show that I am listening, but I keep my eyes on the fire. I value the information and instruction he is giving me, but I want more than anything to disappear.

"I see you're still limping. How is the hip feeling?" he asks finally.

"It is getting there, although I would prefer it get there faster given the meet is so close."

"Well, Lexi has passed over some medication. It is not MHRA approved, not anything you will receive in any hospital, but it will help. I have had it myself with numerous injuries. It means a nasty injection in your hip, but if you can take it, believe me – you'll feel better in the morning. What do you think?"

My stomach tightens at the idea. The last injection in my hip was horrific, but if it means that I recover quicker…

"Let's do it."

"I'm not doing it, Dixy is," Lambert says.

I look at her apprehensively. I should have guessed. Dixy seems to be the one with all the medical training.

"Come on, bed and trousers off." She smirks, and I cringe.

Could she make it any more awkward?

Laying down on the pallet bed with my trousers off, I am covered in a blanket and I still have underwear on, but I still feel very exposed. I feel the anxiety building in my chest, quickening and shallowing my breath. Dixy looks down at me apologetically.

"Sorry, I know it is going to suck, but this stuff is amazing," she encourages.

"Not worried a-about the pain."

"Oh, yeah. Didn't think about that. All I need do is place my hand on your hip and hold it to keep my aim steady. The needle will go in and out so I can inject the serum at all angles. Do you think you can handle that?"

"Just do it."

I feel her hand on my hip, and I screw my eyes up. My body tenses to try to stop the physical reaction of the panic. Then, I feel the pain and forget all about her hands contact with my skin. Pain shoots inside my hip and down my groin. It feels like there is incredible pressure building up inside and its burning.

"Urgh, mother of…!"

"Keep still, Mac."

"Easy for you to… Arghh!"

My eyes water, my fists clench, and I feel myself start to sweat. The pain isn't enough to make me pass out, though I can't help but wish it was.

"Half way there!"

"Oh, fuck my life, that sucks!" I snarl through gritted teeth.

"Okay, I'm done. Take these; they will probably make you feel like you are on another planet, but they will knock you out," Dixy says, handing me some pills.

"I'm okay with that."

"I will get you some ice, and you get you some rest."

It isn't long before everything starts to feel a bit bent out of shape, like someone is taking my vision and making stretch and warp. The pain blissfully begins to melt away, and everything becomes warm and heavy. I am sinking into the mattress; it is not a bad feeling. I hear the barn door open.

"Let me take it," Anna requests.

"I've just given her a strong painkiller and sedative. She needs rest – not stress," Dixy warns, but her tone is soft.

"I know. I'm just going to sit with her."

Anna walks over to the bed and sits on the floor next to me. She places the ice pack on my hip, and I cringe at the iciness. My eyes struggle to stay open as I watch her watching me, her expression completely blank like she doesn't want to be anywhere near me. Then why is she?

"I don't understand…you…anymore," I slur.

"I know."

Darkness…

CHAPTER 6

Fool Me Twice

"Woah…what the…"

I push myself upright in bed with my hands, bracing myself for the pain in my hip, and…nothing happens. Then I scoot to the end of my bed and stand-up feeling…nothing! My stomach does an excited backflip. I take a tentative step, then another, and…nothing. No pain, no stiffness, just beautiful…nothingness.

"Ahhhha!" I squeal.

I pull some trousers on excitedly and walk slowly outside; the farm is covered in a layer of white frost that is crunching under my careful footsteps. I watch my own legs anxiously as if something might snap at any moment. God, it feels good to walk without a limp. My weight is spread evenly between both legs, and my uninjured leg feels relief from not carrying all the extra weight. The pain is gone; it feels strong, and I am so happy about it, I laugh to myself, walking around watching my legs like a child watching their feet walk in new shoes.

"Well, would you look at that?" Alfred gasps in awe, and I look up at him, grinning.

"I know, right?! I'm fucking walking, dude!"

"I would love to know what was in that cocktail Dixy shot you up with," Alfred gawps comically.

"I don't care; I feel awesome."

"I noticed that; I shouldn't have said anything because I'm sure you were about to break into a dance." Alfred chuckles.

"Oh, you don't want to see that. It's terrifying."

I head inside the house with him to make a coffee and see that Anna's car is gone, and immediately the hazy memory of her watching me at my bedside comes into my mind. What was that all about? One minute she tells me to stay away from her, and the next, she is sat watching me, her face completely unreadable.

Whiplash.

I shower, washing off the sweaty night, and get ready for whatever this day will hold. As I walk across the landing about to head downstairs, I find myself hesitating outside Anna's bedroom door. The conflict abounds… Do I? Don't I? Do I? Don't I? I don't even know why I want to. Nothing good can come of it. Like a car crash you can't look away from, morbid curiosity takes hold of me. My hand hovers on the door handle, and my heart is in my mouth. Curiosity wins.

The room looks exactly the same as it always has. The sharp memories hit me with power. Vivid memories of waking up in here after I was shot, the understanding I felt when I saw Alfred's medals on the wall and the photos of his younger self with his military brothers. The most enduring is the memory of falling asleep in Anna's arms after I killed the mala suka man. Her lips kissing my tears away and the feeling of electricity that ran through me when she called me baby.

I walk over to the bed and sit on it and let it all wash over me, my heart aching as my eyes search over the room. Then my eyes pause on the bedside table as I see taped to it the note I left on her laptop all that time ago. The word "Goof" scrawled in my handwriting, the edges of the paper all worn and crinkled. Above her bed are new photos. Ones of me and Alfred, her and Alfred, and then one of me I've never seen before. I am sat caked in mud by the fire with my feet up on a crate, smiling easily with a cup of coffee in my hand. I'm not looking at the camera. I look relaxed…happy.

My heart melts, and it hurts; I don't remember her taking this. Why is it there? Why is the note still there? Why is she so God damn confusing? I leave the room, feeling more conflicted than ever. I don't know what I was expecting or hoping for, but I wish I hadn't gone in there. Or do I? I don't know anymore.

The day moves quite fast. This always seems to happen when something I am dreading is looming close; someone hits the fast forward button in spite of me. I spend most of the day in the barn alone, studying books on morse code and wondering how my mind is ever going to soak it all up. I practice throwing knives, work out with the punch bag, and keeping myself to myself, trying to mentally prepare.

For most of the day, no one bothers me as if they know I am trying to prepare. I am glad for that. It isn't till the evening that Dixy knocks on the barn door. She appears with a grin and holding a suit in a navy garment cover, the words Gieves and Hawks emblazoned in gold. She struts over and hands it to me.

"Put it on! I need to make sure it's perfect!" She shrieks and then leaves the barn. I chuckle.

I unzip the garment bag and gasp. The suit is stunning. All my androgynous dreams have come true. The materiel is beautiful, and I am afraid to touch it, dark gun metal silver that has the faintest glitter. I undress and pull the suit on carefully, being far too tentative and nervous about it.

"Hurry UP!" Dixy bites from behind the door.

The shirt is very snug, but it moves with the shape of my body perfectly and feels so soft to the touch that it tingles lightly against my skin. The waist coat is heavy from the Kevlar lining, but you would never know it is there to look at it. The trousers and blazer hug my body, following every curve. I look in the mirror, and I can't deny; it couldn't fit me better. I feel awesome in it.

"Alright, I am decent."

"About time! You are never decent.... Damn!" She ogles, and I blush, "Now that is sexy. Oh, I am so good at this. Admit it!" She beams with glee.

"Okay...I will admit, I'm in love with the suit. You did perfect. Thank you for being a bossy know it all."

"Turn around; I need to see the butt," she demands.

"You're not serious."

"Just do it."

I huff and turn around; I feel like a complete prat, but I don't have the energy to argue with her.

"Oh yes, definitely! Okay, take it off before I jump your bones myself. I'm going to sort Anna's dress out - wish me luck." She mock cringes, and I snort.

"Good luck."

I hang the suit up from the balcony of the second floor and stare it nervously. As the night darkens, I feel the icy darkness begin to flood my veins, and I welcome it. Somehow, my fear of what I am about to face with Barrett is measured equally against the fear of the pain that being close to Anna will inflict. I have to find a way to stay disconnected and protect myself but somehow still pull off a believable façade.

My eyes close and picture her with Danni, her angry eyes as she tells me to stay away from her. The pain in her expression at the hospital as she tells me she is letting me go. The finger-like tendrils crawl up inside me, and my blood runs cold. The numb calmness it brings is soothing. I open my hardened eyes and feel at peace as I get ready for bed knowing that this is just a game. She was lost to me long ago.

***

I fill my morning with exercise, lightly jogging around the farm and testing the strength of my hip. It feels good, but I am still feeling cautious about it. I spend time stick fighting with Lambert, burning the nervous energy out of myself.

"You ruin her face before the ball tonight, Callum, and you're a dead man," Dixy snipes, and he scoffs, giving her a mock salute.

"How are you feeling?" Lambert asks breathlessly as we battle our sticks furiously.

"Fine. It's the wait I don't like."

"Yeah, I get you. Keep yourself busy; it will help. I have to head out in a bit to pick up some extra surveillance equipment for tonight. You can come with me if you want, get away for a bit. I might even buy you one of them caramel lattes you love so much."

"When do we leave?"

***

I stay hidden in the van. I don't mind – it's good to just be away, and Lambert is a calm presence to be around. He doesn't feel the need to talk to fill the silence, and I like that. He is the polar opposite to Dixy. He is subdued, careful, and light. Dixy is brash, pushy, and intense. Both of them make up the perfect balance of things I respond well to when I need different things. Right now, that is quiet and calm.

I am sat, my eyes transfixed upon MI5 headquarters. It is a weird looking building; it is almost castle-like, made from sandy coloured brick with green glass. The building is huge and layered as if it were put together with Lego and someone added more and more when they decided it wasn't quite large enough. It is so complex, I can't even tell when the entrance is. I wonder if I will ever get to go in there. Looking at it, I am not sure that I want to, it is intimidating to look at. Lambert returns with two boxes full of wires, laptops, speakers, and a lot of tech I just don't understand. We elect to go through a drive-through coffee shop, staying in the van to lessen the risk of being seen with Lambert.

"How is Anna doing?" I ask, wiping the latte moustache off my top lip.

"Why don't you ask her?"

"Complicated."

"Well. It needs to be less complicated by tonight. She's doing okay, I think. She seems ready to play her part. I was concerned about it the same as you were, but after speaking to her, she managed to persuade me that she could do this."

"How did she do that?"

"Well, I told her that I am inclined to agree with you, that we should find someone else. She didn't like that and told me that she wanted to do it and she could handle it. She was quite forceful about it, actually."

"What?! That's bull, she doesn't want to do it at all! She just doesn't want to let anyone down. Don't worry; I'm able to separate any feelings I may have from the job. It won't be a problem for me," I assure him fiercely although I am not quite sure who I am trying to persuade - him or myself. I am pissed off. She had the option to bail; Lambert gave her an out, and she didn't take it.

"I know. You make avoiding your feelings for the girl an Olympic sport, so I don't doubt that for a second."

"Oh, dude, don't you start! You channelling Dixy or something?" I whine.

"God, no; you will get no meddling from me. I'm just saying. I know you've got this; you have pushed yourself hard with all aspects of your training. I know there is still a lot we have to go through with you, but I'm amazed at the progress you have made. Especially considering the pressures and the injury you've had to face. Anna or no Anna – I'm not worried about you, so you shouldn't be either."

"Thank you, Lambert. You had me worried there for a second."

"Anytime. Make sure you don't forget your ghost knife. You won't see it under the suit, and if anyone ever saw it, you were kidnapped, so you can easily pass it off as protecting yourself. A Glock though, not so much."

"I put it on every morning. You were right – I forget it's there – but I'm sure I'll remember if I ever need it."

***

The barn floods with the rowdy roar of rock and heavy metal music – maybe a bit too loudly. Something I always do when I am getting ready, and I bet Alfred is hating every second. For some reason, my hair, my make-up, everything goes better to the thrash of loud music. Plus, it keeps my mind quiet, and right now the combination of nerves I feel between Barrett and Anna is making my stomach churn.

Music off, and I stand in front of the mirror and scrutinise myself as I knot my tie snuggly around my neck. I don't think I ever felt so good in a suit. My right wrist is glinting with the rotary watch beneath my sleeve, my left the bangle that Anna bought me. Despite everything, I never take it off. I am struggling with the cuff links when Alfred walks in.

"Damn, kid, you look…" He hesitates, gawping.

"What?" I squint back at myself in the mirror, wondering what's wrong. Alfred walks over to me and fixes my cufflinks, and then he undoes my tie and starts retying it with expert hands.

"Is it weird if I say…that you look beautiful?"

"It's not weird. A little shocking maybe but really sweet. Thank you, Pa."

"You're welcome. You look even better with your tie knotted proper."

"How much time do I have?" I ask, my mouth dry.

"Enough time for a whisky with your Pa."

"You read my mind."

He actually did. The nerves are eating at me, the darkness has abandoned me, and my emotions are all over the place. I can only hope the Dutch courage helps me get it together. We drink in silence, and he stands shoulder to shoulder with me, lending me his strength. I can see, though, there is worry crinkling the lines on his face. It is pulling at the corners of his mouth and dazing his wise eyes.

"I won't let anything happen to her. I promise."

"I know you won't, but I don't want to lose either of you. It's not like I think anything is going to happen tonight, we're only at the beginning of this, but…it's begun. I don't want to lose you, kid," he mumbles as he stares into his glass.

My eyes get a little misty, and I swallow the pang down. I hate doing makeup; I don't want to have to do it twice. I take his hand, and I hold it. I don't think I have ever seen him this worried; it's jarring.

"You have made sure, just like Dixy and Lambert are making sure, I'm not that easy to kill. I will work my arse off to make sure that doesn't happen."

"I know that, but it isn't just your body that can die, kid. I'm going to say this once, and then I won't mention it again. You need her as much as she needs you. What is the use in having a pulse, of your heart beating if it's broken and empty? What's it beating for? You could lose yourself during this…reconditioning. We could lose you; you don't have to be dead for that to happen. You can't just fight to save the world from The Culling; anger and duty will only get you so far. You have to fight to come home to the people you love. If you close yourself from that love, it's going to be much easier to lose yourself." His words come out softly with sadness, but they hit me like a brick, and it takes me a moment to recover.

"I hear what you're saying, Pa, I do, but I'm not so sure that is what she wants anymore."

"Even if it isn't, I can see that coldness inside of you coming back. The look in your eyes, the same look I saw when you were in prison, the same look you had when you first came here bleeding from a bullet wound. It's faint, but it is there. You're shutting down, and it's the fastest way to lose yourself. This isn't just about Anna. Don't shut me out, Dixy, Lambert, your mum. Don't close yourself off. We're your people, your family."

"Did you have this speech planned or what?" I chuckle, trying to hide the welling of my eyes.

"Well, yeah – a little."

"I get what you're saying. I'm trying my hardest not to go down that road again, but sometimes it's the easiest way to cope with…" I hesitate and look away from him.

"Losing her?"

"Amongst other things. I know that in the long run, it won't help me, but in the moment, it feels like the only thing I have to hold on to. I'm aware I can't make you any promises except – I'm trying not to lose myself."

"That's good enough, for now. Your car is going to be here in 15. Savannah is probably ready now. Are you good?"

"As good as I can be. I need to put these contact lenses in, and then I'll be right out."

He claps me on the shoulder and walks out of the barn. Thankfully, this isn't my first time wearing contact lenses. Once they are in, after a couple of blinks, my eyes adjust, and they feel comfortable. They don't seem to impede my sight at all. I take one last look in the mirror and jump out of my skin.

"Holy crap!" I gasp a choked laugh.

In the top right corner of my vision, I see words flash up. Clear words in bold red text float as if by magic.

`Luck be with you, Agent Scott. P.S - Nice suit! Lexi out.`

I wink in the mirror, knowing Lexi can see me in the reflection through my own eyes. That is going to take some getting used to.

I turn away, pick up the masquerade masks, and take a deep steadying breath. It is time to fake it till I make it; I just have to pretend my gut is not twisting in uncomfortable knots and channel my inner bad ass. I will walk out of this barn, cool, calm, and as sexy as the suit makes me feel, and I will not freak out till I am home free. Barrett, The Culling, and Anna be damned. I have worked too hard for this…

I am Agent Scott.

I stride sure-footed and with swagger out of the barn door and towards the house. I hold myself with a confidence that I thought I had long since forgotten, and I am loving every single second of the rediscovery… I feel sexy. Head held high, I feel a smile playing on my lips and a determination smouldering through my eyes. My body is buzzed with adrenalin and excitement. I see Alfred, Dixy, and Lambert all standing in a line by the fire. I look over, and they whoop at me, making my smile grow larger. Then, I turn toward the house and…

I see her.

Suddenly, it is no longer my legs that keep me walking but the majestic gravity that she holds drawing me in. I am moved by her, just as I always have been but never has such magnetism pulled on my heart so forcefully. It belongs with her, and it wants to go home.

Her dress is emerald green, and it glows off her glittery pearl skin. The top half is designed in such a way to only just cover her suggestively. The lace gives the illusion that the dress is made of leaves that cascade down her chest. There is more skin on show than leaves, and as they fall down her body, they cling to her every curve. The lace smooths to a silk skirt with a tantalising spit running up the length of it. Surely, there has never before been a sight more enticing.

I step towards her and finally look at her face. Her fiery red hair is elegantly curled and pinned out of her face. Her lips are raspberry pink and juicy, her makeup sparkling with gold. My stare finds her intensely green eyes, and I feel paralysed by her. She looks at me, unsure and a little fearful.

"Every kind of beautiful," I breathe.

She gasps, the fear immediately leaving her eyes, and they flood with relief. I hold my arm out for her, and she smiles and slides her hand through the gap and onto my bicep. I feel her eyes on me as I lead her to the car. The extent of which I was blown away by her is only magnified when I see the car that until now – completely escaped my notice.

Gleaming in burgundy and white, the chrome shining proudly off its prominent headlights and distinguishable Rolls Royce grille. I step towards a scene from the 1950s. The deep rumble of the engine purrs in my chest as I step closer to the beautifully restored Rolls Royce Silver Dawn. Inside I spot a chauffeur dressed in an immaculate plain black suit and drivers cap, tapping his fingers along the steering wheel impatiently. Stepping forward, I open the door for her, and she lets go of my arm to get in the car. The interior and seats boast smooth ivory leather, and the thick pile burgundy carpet is soft under my feet, the walnut woodwork polished and smooth. My eyes fall on Anna, and she is stifling a laugh, and I look at her questionably.

"You are looking at the car like Christmas came early." She grins at me in a way I haven't seen in a long time, and I laugh an unnatural laugh, pain suffocating the joy within its sound.

We pull on our masks as the car moves off with a smooth grumble, the engine loud and the movement slow. I try to enjoy the moment; it is impossible not to feel a little special in a car like this. Heads turn to look at us as we delve deeper into the centre of London. It is also painful. This could be the most magical date – if only the girl next to me, felt an inch of what I feel for her. I keep my eyes forward, trying to remain focused. It takes a lot of will, feeling her sat next to me, looking like a goddess sent specifically to tempt me. I am going to kill Dixy; that dress could not be more perfect for her or more torturous for me.

We pull up outside the Café Royal, and I get out of the car and dash round to the other side. I open the door and hold out my hand to her, my eyes flitting around the area. She takes my hand, and I feel the pull as she steps out and stands in front of me where I can't escape her gaze, her hand still in mine. She looks at me; even in the mask those eyes capture me forcefully. I will myself to look away.

"Houston, we…"

Anna places her finger on my lips and stops me from activating the earpiece.

"Not yet…" she whispers, keeping her eyes on my lips. "I didn't get the chance to tell you… God…you look incredible, Mac Scott," she whispers; it almost came out in a moan.

She looks back at me, taking her finger away from my lips. The tingles erupting through me are intoxicating, making me wonder how I will ever get through this night without claiming her lips with mine.

"You've got this; I know you do." She squeezes my hand and turns away from me. We both stand hand in hand and face the Café Royal. I watch, my eyes scanning as limousines and sports cars stop, and elegantly dressed people vacate their cars and reveal their masks and coordinating evening dresses and suits. They walk towards the entrance of a grand white building that stands elegantly, lit up and exuding luxury.

"Houston, we have a problem," I mouth. "Eyes in the skies – are you reading me?"

"Loud and clear, kid," Alfred confirms.

"Visual and sound connection, confirmed," Lambert informs smoothly.

"Stay sexy, Agent Scott," Dixy encourages.

"Clear to proceed, Agent Scott. Luck be with you," Lexi reports with authority.

I walk forwards, feeling a calm wash over me as the building gets closer. I feel the air of excitement as I lead us both through the clumps of people buzzing with anticipation. We come to the entrance and are met with a large man dressed in a suit, a long black coat, and a bowler hat.

"Good evening. May I please take your name, ma'am?"

"McKenna Scott."

"Ah, look at that – top of the list, excellent. Please proceed to the lobby where complimentary refreshments await."

"Thank you, sir."

We cross the threshold and enter the most spectacular reception area, and I feel warmth the moment I step inside. The walls are white and terracotta marble. At either side of the entrance are two magnificent, pure white fireplaces. Heat is radiating from them as the flames glow and flicker. The ceiling is high like a cathedral and lit up with grand, glittering chandeliers.

I push Anna forward, my hand light on the small of her back. We weave in and out of masked couples and groups of people, my eyes scanning busily.

Waiters in top hats and tails glide around with trays, passing out glittering champagne flutes. I stop in the middle of the lobby where there is some space and take the place in. Ahead of us are two sets of stairs that glide in a perfect arch towards each other. A scene from the Titanic movie immediately comes to mind. They meet in the middle and lead to a doorway that is decorated lavishly in white roses. At the bottom of each staircase is a thick red rope barricade.

I feel a sharp bump barge into the back of my shoulder. The impact jolts enough to make me grunt, and my instincts fire. I sidestep in front of Anna, my hand sliding behind my back and onto her wrist while my eyes search rapidly. My gaze falls on a woman; she is dressed in a royal blue dress and mask. Her back turned to me, but her head turns towards me, eyes fixed. The hairs raise on the back of my neck as she stares at me. Anna's hands slide onto my hips, her lips at my ear.

"Who is that?" she whispers, her voice shaken.

"I don't..."

The woman in blue smirks, and it feels so familiar and yet so cold, a shudder runs through me. As quickly as I saw her, she dissolves into the crowd, leaving a heavy sense of deja-vu clouding up my mind. I sidestep back, pulling my hips out of Anna's grasp and look side on at her to see her eyes are distant beneath the mask but wide and fearful.

"I don't know who that was, but I feel like I should. Are you okay?" I ask, and Anna hesitates before giving me a stiff, unconvincing nod.

A waiter with slick, over lacquered hair pauses in front of me and tilts his head forward, holding the tray of champagne glasses before me. I take two and nod at him politely, and he glides away. Turning to face Anna, I hand her a glass, and she takes it with a sheepish smile that is adorable on her face, but I see the tension in her eyes as she looks away.

"It will be okay. Just stay in my sights at all times, and I will get you in and out – safe and sound."

"I know," she mumbles, her eyes on the floor like she can't stand to look me.

I can feel the tension coming off her as she stands next to me. I wrap my arm around her protectively, my hand firm on her waist, and I pull her a little closer while I look away, sipping my champagne. I feel her relax, and her hand slides under my blazer, across my back, and onto to my hip. Heat trickles down my spine at her touch, and it takes every ounce of my will to suppress my shudder.

"Thank you…" she utters softly, and I look at her. The look in her eyes is a mystery to me, her mask obscuring her expression and my ability to read her. Not that I have been any good at doing that lately. I give her a formal smile, and this time, it is me that looks away.

The lobby begins to fill, the space becoming tighter as the air fills with the aroma of perfume and aftershave, the atmosphere thick with anticipation. I spot movement on the stairs, and I see a man dressed in a royal blue suit with a matching mask. He is staring down on the crowd with a satisfied smile. My veins fill with ice as I momentarily stiffen, then force myself to relax my muscles. He is flanked by a beast of a man on his right dressed completely in black; his mask is harsh and haunting. On his left a statuesque woman in red, wearing a crimson dress so short and tight it is a wonder she can move.

"I have eyes on Barrett. Blue mask on the balcony," I report, and then I look away, sipping my champagne casually.

"Copy that, Agent Scott," Lexi replies, her voice firm in my ear.

"Ladies and gentlemen! What a pleasure it is to see all your colourful masked faces smiling up at me tonight. If you will please, make your way to the Pompadour Ballroom and make yourselves comfortable for what is sure to be a spectacular evening," Barrett booms with charm.

He gives a nod, and two men in suits and bowler hats step forward. They stride towards the bottom of the staircases and unhook the red ropes. They step back in unison and bow their heads. The whole movement seems rehearsed and unnatural. As the double doors at the top of the stairs open, the sounds of warm classical music flows out of them. The crowd surrounding us starts to move past us, and I wait for it to thin a little. My heart is pounding hard against my rib cage. I let go of Anna, and she takes my arm as I lead her up the stairs.

If ever there was a scene that inspired a fairy tale, it is this. We move through the doors and enter a different world, a world where it is hard not to believe that magic exists. My eyes fall on the decorative ceiling that is elaborately painted with beautiful, coloured frescos depicting scenes of love. The ornate detailing that is carved into the walls and ceiling, the series of Corinthian pilasters, and mirrored panels on the walls with lavish gilded frames laced with gold, all give the room a Louis XVI style. The room glitters warmly, the light from the chandelier's reflecting off the mirrored walls.

Along the right-hand side of the wall are large round tables decorated with white and gold sophistication. In the centre of each table is a gold tree-shaped structure; each branch is laced with white roses with crystal-like beads and tiny lights dangling from them. It is like a warm winter wonderland. To my left is a stage where musicians in red blazers with gold chains across their shoulder pads play their instruments softly, welcoming the guests on their arrival.

The centre of the room is left wide open, the floor rich brown and woody. Waiters are gliding around the room, handing out more champagne and canapes. The guests are talking excitedly, the room begins to fill, and I lead Anna to a table in the corner where I have a good line of sight around me and pick a spot where I can sit with my back against a wall.

"Well, this is subtle. I thought it would be flashier. I'm disappointed," I joke, and she giggles but doesn't look my way.

"Yes, I was thinking the same thing. There aren't even any ice sculptures. Pathetic effort," she muses lightly, and I am relieved when she plays along, but I can see how uncomfortable she is. I need things to look natural between us, not awkward.

"At least there is free champagne," I quip, taking a sip and playfully cringing. "Tastes like fizzy vinegar, but it's free."

"I've drunk worse."

"Me too. I'm still not over the trauma of Pa's moonshine."

"There is nothing wrong with my moonshine, cheeky git," Alfred booms in my ear, and I laugh.

"What's funny?" Anna asks.

"He disagrees with my distaste for his moonshine." I smile, tugging my ear, and she laughs and looks away again.

While it hurts that she can't even seem to stomach looking at me, I'm more concerned that isn't helping this seem natural. She looks tense, and I need to find a way to break the awkwardness before it becomes a problem. But I also don't want to outright say anything when everything I say is being listened to. My eyes scan the room for Barrett, and he's nowhere to be seen, but what I can see is making my muscles tighten.

"Are you seeing what I'm seeing?"

"If you mean all the people whose eyes seem to be on us...yes," Anna says, her voice shaking. I reach out and hold her hand on the table, giving it a squeeze.

"It's okay, don't worry – with you in that dress, who could blame them for staring?"

Her answering blush spreads warmth through my chest. I've missed that blush.

"Oh, you're just so damn smooth. If she doesn't kiss you by the end of the night – I will," Dixy sounds in my ear, and I clench my jaw, stifling a laugh.

"Come on. Let's go explore," I suggest.

I get to my feet and hold my hand out to her; she takes it, and we start to move slowly through the room. There is no mistaking the eyes that follow us. I do my best to ignore it and keep calm, but it isn't easy because there are just so many of them. I can feel the fear in Anna's grip on my hand. Somehow, I need to calm her down. The trouble is, everything I would normally do to do that would mean stepping over lines that I can't cross.

The room curves round to the right, revealing a series of tables with white boxes on top, and my eyes fall on a white mounted frame fixed to an easel. The sign reads 'Silent Auction' in gold fancy script. Opposite is a bar, the barmen are all dressed in white shirts, black waistcoats, and bowties. Surrounding the bar are small high tables and bar stalls, and the area is a lot less busy of people.

"Fancy a real drink?" I ask her.

"Definitely."

I pull Anna towards the brightly lit bar, and my hands touch the white marbled, smooth, stone-cold surface. It glides in a continuous oval, curving round the corner of the room. The bottles mounted against the mirrored wall are glinting, and I hear the sounds of glasses clinking as the barman loads them into the racks. I order us both a whisky and Coke, and we sit in the very back corner of the curve, out of sight from most onlookers, and I see her begin to relax immediately. She sips her drink, and I lift my mask a little, so it rests just above my forehead, and she does the same. Her eyes fall on me speculatively, and this time she isn't looking away. Her expression is unreadable, unemotional, and vague.

"Are you okay?" I ask.

"Better now. I'm sorry; they all got me a bit nervous. I'll be alright in a minute."

"You don't need to be sorry for that. Just try to tune them out. It's me they're watching – not you. I get the feeling they know I'm the evil villain's daughter." I wink, and she laughs.

"What was it like? Meeting him, I mean."

"Creepy. I needed six showers afterwards. You'll see what I mean when you meet him."

"Yeah, I can't pretend I'm looking forward to that."

"It's just a game, Anna; it's all role play. Just… pretend I'm someone else, pretend he is. Fall into the atmosphere of it all. Play along, and it will be easier."

"Is that what you are doing? Pretending I'm someone else?"

For a split second, I think I see a flicker of pain in her eyes, but it's gone so fast, I must have imagined it. Maybe I want to see it there. Her blank expression, her distant eyes are all painful when directed at me. I wish I knew that it wasn't just me finding this fantasy date hard.

"I don't have that good of an imagination. Besides – I don't have the need to." I keep my voice even and my expression as blank as hers, and she nods. "Anyway, how are you doing with…everything?"

"I'm fine, everything is fine, work is going…"

"Fine? Say fine more, that will convince me." I smirk playfully, and she laughs. This time, I see warmth in her eyes. She is beginning to relax.

"You are still a goof." She giggles, and I keep my smile regardless of the pain because it is calming her down. Her shoulders are starting to relax, and her smile is more natural.

"Hey! Shhh…less of that, lady. No one here knows I'm goofy; you're going to blow my cover. At least let me pretend that I'm a super sexy spy for a little while longer before you ruin it," I joke, and she smirks at me, a smirk so sexy it's unfair.

"I don't think you need to pretend anything."

Her eyes smoulder at me, and I can't seem to drag my eyes away. She holds my gaze, and I feel desire burn inside me. She takes a deep, shaky breath, and I make the mistake of looking at her lips, and the compulsion to lean in is painful to resist. After spending the whole time looking at me coldly or not looking at me at all, it is jarring. Jarring and completely alluring.

"Oh, the sexual tension is ridiculous," Dixy sounds in my ear, making me blink.

"Shall we go look at the silent auction?" I blurt, getting to my feet.

We walk over to the row of tables opposite the bar and on each one is a small white card very similar to the invitation I received. Each card has details written about items that are up for auction. There is a holiday for two in the Canary Islands, a sailboat, VIP tickets to various sporting events and concerts, a family holiday to Disney Land, a few sports cars, and some smaller, less exotic getaways. In front of the card is a white box with a slit to place your hidden bid for the item on the card.

"What would you bid on if you could?" Anna asks.

"That's easy, the couple's cabin in the woods. Hot tub, open fireplace, quiet and woodsy. The sort of place where you feel like you've disappeared - right up my street," I explain, and she smiles.

"Can I come disappear with you?"

She is role playing, it is what I needed her to do, but God, it hurts. It is playing with my already screwed up head, but I need to play along. It is about the mission. I step a little closer and let the smile bloom on my lips.

"Sure. You bring the champagne, and I'll pack the bags. What is it that you want to disappear from?"

This time, I know I see pain in her eyes.

"Mac, I…" she begins, but then her eyes flick over my shoulder, and I feel a hand light on my forearm.

I turn around to find the woman in the red dress standing a little too close to feel natural. Her hand is still on my forearm, and her mask is unable to hide the intensity her eyes are firing at me. My arm instinctually slides around Anna's waist.

"Hello, you must be Mckenna. I thought I'd introduce myself. My name is Farah. I work closely with your father."

Farah lets go of my forearm, and I feel myself relax. She has long, slinky, jet-black hair that blends perfectly with her black and red mask. Her lips are thin, and her teeth brilliantly white. She has a small scar that slits across her lip, interrupting her shocking red lipstick. Her perfume is strong and metallic, the kind that gives you a headache if you are exposed to it too long.

"Farah, it's nice to meet you. Thank you for introducing yourself. I'm at a bit of a loss, not really knowing anyone here," I utter smoothly.

"Well, I'm sure Barrett will catch up with you soon. He is the popular man of the hour; everyone wants a piece. Can I do anything for you? Is there anything you need?" Farah offers. There is a slight accent to her voice I can't place.

"Not that I can think of. I think we are more than comfortable but thank you."

Farah leans in a little, her hand on my forearm again.

"Well, if you change your mind. Don't hesitate to come find me."

"Thank you. I'll certainly bear that in mind." I flash a charming smile, and she blushes and walks away.

"Good work, Mac. We are running the name Farah," Lexi reports.

"Copy that," I mumble.

I keep my arm around Anna and walk towards the natural light coming from some double doors at the end of the room. They lead onto a courtyard that gives an impressive view out onto Regent Street. The courtyard is all made from creamy coloured brick and is in line with the roof of the building next door. There are wicker sofas and tables and warm lighting coming from large lanterns and fairy lights, giving the place a romantic yellowy glow.

To my left is a towering sparkly white cake. Tier upon tier of decorative white roses and extravagant icing with gold leaf trickling down one side. I see the waiters cutting up the cake and serving the slices into small white cardboard boxes, and I go over to grab us some. We walk over to the edge of the balcony, and my head spins.

"Ugh… Nope, no looking down," I groan, and she giggles.

"At least it is not as high as The Shard."

"There's the silver lining I was looking for," I grumble, and I hand Anna one of the cake boxes. "Pudding?" I grin daringly, and she howls with laughter.

The memory, although a little close to the bone, is still just as funny. It is good to see her laugh like that. It feels so long since I have seen it, that laugh that lights up her whole face to the degree that she bewitches me into laughing too. We tuck in. The cake is delicious, obviously, lemon cake with vanilla swiss meringue filling. Alfred would love this; it is decadent, it tastes of luxury, and I could totally eat a second helping.

"This is good pudding," Anna groans.

"Bah…I've had better."

As much as the light and flirty "inside jokes" are making things run smoother, it's becoming increasingly harder for me to keep an unphased façade. For me, this all still feels so raw. As she laughs at my jokes and smiles at me with her sexy grin, it is becoming increasingly harder to keep in mind that this is all a game, a role play; she is too good at it. I find myself forgetting that it is an act and getting lost in her.

"It can't be that bad. You're wearing a lot of it. Come here, you have cream…"

Anna reaches out and wipes her thumb along my bottom lip, and then she freezes with her hand on my face. The grin on her face starts to fall, her eyes immovable on my lips. The feel of her touch sends searing pain across my chest, and I cringe away harshly.

"Uh, thanks. S-shall we…head back inside?"

I hold my arm out to her and she takes it, but she doesn't say a word. Anna walks with me rigidly, and I can feel the tension coming off her again. We find our way to some seats, and she stares out into the crowd in a daze. Damn it, this isn't helpful, and it's my own fault for pushing her away so harshly. I can't have her shut down now; people are looking our way again, and she is making me nervous. I look for any sign of Barrett, but he is nowhere to be seen. The volume of the music picks up, and people start to fill the dancefloor.

I get to my feet, and I hold my hand out to her. She looks up at me hesitantly, and then she takes it. I walk her to the dancefloor, and then I pull her to me with dominance. One hand holding hers, the other against the small of her back, holding her firmly against me as we sway in time with the music. My God does she feel good in my arms. I lead her, my eyes locked onto her blank eyes, smoothly around the dancefloor. A longing ache is burning in my chest as the familiar scent of her candy-like perfume bewilders me. The torturous thirst I have to kiss her and the strength it takes not to quench it is painful. But not as painful as the feeling that I am alone in that desire.

"Don't worry. It will be over before you know it," I reassure her, unable to hide the coldness in my voice that the pain is inspiring.

Her eyes close like she is in pain, and she lets out a shaky breath. She moves towards me, her lips at my ear.

"Who says I want it to be over?" she whispers.

I feel her nose graze slowly down my neck, her breath warm against my throat as her mouth hovers there. The thrilling sensation that surges through me as I feel her lips so close is immeasurable. Then I feel the softness of them press firmly against my skin as she kisses the scar on my throat, just once, and my legs weaken. Anna lays her cheek against my chest, lets go of my hand, and lays it on the side on my neck, her thumb caressing my jawline. Her touch against my skin injects tingles of pleasure into my veins that invade my whole system with extraordinary power. She melts into me, and the world around me disappears as I wrap my arms around her, holding her close yet needing her closer still. Pain and pleasure dance inside me as I dance with her.

But the pain I feel dissolves. The need I have to keep hold of her, to keep hold of this brief moment I get to breathe her in and be with her as if nothing ever tore us apart, overrides everything. All instincts to protect my heart are obliterated as my hand slowly slides up her back onto the back of her neck and in her hair. I feel her shiver against me as my lips find her forehead just briefly. Anna lifts her face so her cheek is against mine. Her hand slides up my neck and onto my other cheek, holding me there softly.

The sheer need is exploding in my chest, and the pain of resisting is getting too much. I feel her lips brush against my cheek as she starts to slowly turn her lips towards mine. She kisses my jaw line lightly; her breath shakes heavily as her lips brush the corner of my mouth, and the pain becomes too much. My body tenses in reaction to the grief that seethes inside my heart, and I start to pull away. She looks up at me and sees the pain I know must be blazing in my eyes. Her hands on my face, I look away from her gaze.

"I'm sorry… Please, Mac…" she whispers.

"It's fine. T-that was some good acting. I'm sure you had everyone convinced; you almost had me..." I nod my head, flash her an unconvincing smile, and take her hands away from my face gently. She frowns at me, her eyes narrowed with confusion. I pull her by the hand back towards our seats, and I swallow the pain down. It feels like I might choke on it. A flash of royal blue out of the corner of my eye snaps me out of my turmoil. My arm instinctually wraps around Anna's waist, and I feel her look up at me, confused at the sudden change in direction.

"McKenna, I'm so pleased you came. You look…you sure are a head-turner," Barrett gushes.

"Barrett, thank you for inviting me. This is some party you've put together, a truly beautiful reception," I utter smoothly, and he smiles, flattery puffing out his ego. Stood just behind and at either side of him are the same two people that were flanking him on the balcony. The beast-like man in black is eying me with contempt, and the woman in red is smirking at me with curious eyes.

"Thank you. It would seem everyone is enjoying themselves, and it's all for a worthy cause, but I think the true vision of beauty is gracing your arm. Wouldn't you say?" Barrett oozes as he eyes Anna, and I feel her hand grip my hip.

"I certainly would say. My luck isn't lost on me." I grin and glance at Anna with an easy smile and then back to Barrett. "This…is Anna."

"Anna, what a pleasure." Barrett leers as he holds his hand out to her. Anna takes it, and Barrett kisses it like he just stepped out of a movie set in the 1950s. I watch her as she smiles sweetly at him. She is proving quite the actress; you would never know that inside she is no doubt cringing and probably terrified.

"It's lovely to meet you, Barrett. Thank you for having me."

"Nonsense, you are welcome. Would you mind if I take a moment with my daughter? If you would like, they are setting up for some fireworks outside. You could go to the courtyard and grab a good spot, and I will have McKenna back to you before the festivities even begin."

"Of course," she replies. I feel Anna tense a little in my arms.

I look at her and move in, my hand on her face, my eyes warm as I try to reassure her. I hold my lips against her neck, kissing her just once. "It's okay…" I breathe and then I pull back and feel the panic rise as she walks away. I watch her leave through the double doors at the far end of the ballroom. Barrett puts his hand on my shoulder and leads me to the edge of the room.

"Focus, Mac; Anna will be okay. He wants to get close to you, and hurting Anna doesn't serve his purpose." Lambert's calm voice sooths the icy fear threatening to overtake me. He is right. Hurting Anna isn't logical. I take a deep breath and smile at him.

"I wasn't sure you would come." Barrett eyes me like he is x-raying me, taking note of every move I make.

"Neither was I, to be honest."

"I am glad you did. I meant what I said before. I would like the chance to get to know you. Now that you are here, I wanted to ask you if you have had any thoughts regarding…the triangle of truth."

Barrett watches my reactions. I keep my face slack; I have been waiting for this question – luckily. How could he not ask after he revealed his psychotic agenda to me by way of video message that he had surgically implanted in my chest? My eyes flick to the courtyard doors as I see the big beefy man in black open them and step outside. Anxiety flutters inside my chest. I hate that she is out there exposed.

"Eyes on the prize, *Agent*," Lexi orders.

"I've had many thoughts, but without knowing more, it's hard for me to make any clear assumptions."

"Would you like to know more?"

"This…mission that you have, it's the reason you left me behind? I ask him, laying it on thick with pained eyes.

"Yes, Mckenna, the only reason," he soothes, putting his hand on my shoulder.

"I think…it would help me to understand if I knew more about it. Maybe then, I could let it go, and we could move forward – together."

"Then you shall know more. I want more than anything for you to be a part of this, for us to move forward together." Barrett' eyes seem so sincere, I almost believe him, "I have some business to attend to, but I would like to talk to you about this more…freely, in a secure location. Mckenna - if you are serious about knowing more, then meet me where you killed that son of a bitch Jakub, three days from now at 8pm." His eyes flare so coldly, I almost cringe back, but I manage to control myself. I look at him with a slight smile, only slight, hoping he will see it as a feeling of pride.

"I'll be there, but if you are serious about getting to know me, I need one thing from you, and I'm afraid – it's a deal-breaker," I assert seriously. He looks at me, slightly taken aback, and I smile. "Call me Mac."

"Mac, right. Of course. Well, Mac, I will see you in three days." He winks at me, making my skin crawl, and then he walks off, leaving through the entrance he came in.

My heart in my mouth, I walk over to the doors that Anna left through. I open them and see her stood, her back turned slightly with her arms crossed tightly against her chest. The beefy man in black is leaning towards her as he talks to her, his hand clasped around her wrist. An anger-propelled green-eyed monster crawls inside my gut. I stride towards her, I slide my arm around her smoothly, turning her towards me and pulling her to me in one swift movement. She relaxes into me; I meet the steely glare of the man in black over her shoulder as she kisses my neck and breathes shakily into my ear, "Thank God…" and I hold her tighter in reaction. Her skin is icy cold.

"Hey, beautiful. Sorry about that," I mutter lightly while the man in black stares me down.

"You should never leave beautiful things unattended; you never know who might swoop in and *take* them," he grunts, his voice harsh. I hear the threat in his words, and Anna's grip on the back of my shirt tightens.

"Ah, well, I would agree except, she is no – *thing* to possess. If I were to treat her as such, then she would leave of her own free will. Because I don't, she *always* comes back to me. I'm sorry, I didn't catch your name," I berate, my smile taunting.

"I didn't offer it."

"Am I supposed to guess? Larry? Boris? Simon? *Dick*?" I goad, and behind the mask, I see his eyes flare coldly at me, and then I hear Lambert chuckling in my ear. My smirk is impossible to suppress.

"Damon. I'm sure I'll see you again very soon, *Mckenna*." Damon sneers, the emphasis sharp in his voice as he speaks my name, and then he walks away.

"He's gone. Are you alright?" I ask Anna as I pull back, but she grips on to me.

"Not yet, please," she whispers.

I hold her tightly even though all I want to do is let her go, but I can feel the fear coming off of her as she trembles against me.

"It's okay, I've got you. What did he say to you?"

"Nothing helpful. He was just really leery, almost threatening. He wanted me to dance with him even though I told him I was here with you. He said he knew that and that you wouldn't mind. He wasn't taking no for an answer, and that is when you came back."

"He was probably trying to get a rise out of me. He's gone now, it's alright," I assure her, rubbing her back. "Agent Holt, did you catch all that?" I mumble.

"Yes, we are running the name Damon too, trying to find connections. Extraordinary work, Agent Scott. Your car is en route, ETA ten minutes."

"Thank you, Agent Holt. Houston, we have a problem," I mutter as I pull away from Anna. I take off my blazer and put it over her shoulders and turn away from her. We stand shoulder to shoulder, gazing over the darkness of Regent Street. The pain in my chest is suffocating; the fantasy is over.

"What happened with Barrett?"

"I have another meet with him in three days, at the brewery."

"Mac… I…"

"The car is on its way. Now Barrett has gone there is no point in staying and putting you at risk. We should go." I cut her off.

Anna walks with me through the ballroom and down the stairs. When we get outside, I pull my mask off, and it is a relief. We walk across the road and wait in the same place we were dropped off. We don't speak, and I don't have it in me to look at her. My head is so messed up, and I feel like I am about to break. The car moves off just as the fireworks light up the sky; I watch them, and they blur colourfully in my teary eyes. The drive back feels like it is never ending. When we finally do get back, walking towards the fire, I just want to be alone. Alfred approaches me when he sees me coming.

"Well done, kid."

"Thank you. Look, I know everyone probably wants a chat, but could you buy me half hour? I need to go shut a door."

"Of course, I was expecting that. Thanks for keeping her safe," he grumbles, and he grabs me for a bear hug. I let him but only briefly because I can feel the tears threatening to overtake me.

I stride towards the barn, feeling the eyes of Anna, Dixy, and Lambert on me at the fire. I walk in, loosening my tie and untucking my shirt, and sit on the end of the couch with my head in my hands. The tears come, hot and fast, and I don't try to stop them. The pain burns in my chest, and I haven't got the strength to fight it; I just want some relief. I let myself get too close, too involved in the fantasy of the moment, of being with her. I only have myself to blame. I don't want to be here anymore; I don't want to be around her. I hear the door open, and anger bubbles in my gut.

"Go away!"

"That's not very nice," Dixy teases lightly.

"I told Alfred I wanted half an hour."

"Yes, you did, and I ignored him."

Dixy sits on the sofa next to me, and I cover my tear stroked face in my hands. She nudges her shoulder with mine, and I groan.

"Please go away, Dixy. I don't want to snap at you."

"Oh, you can try, but I'm not scared of your bite," Dixy teases lightly, and it just agitates the anger inside, flinging me to my feet.

"I can't deal with your playful fucking tone right now, just GO!" I yell through a strangled voice, turning away from her. I storm to the other side of the barn and lean against it, my arms above my bowed head. I breathe long, ragged breaths to try to calm myself down.

"I'm sorry. I'm not so good at the emotional stuff, but after that, I can't imagine what...I don't want you to be alone in this, Mac."

I sigh. Now I feel bad. I guess that isn't a bad thing if it stops me bawling like a pathetic loser. I turn around and face her.

"I'm sorry. I'm fine. Nothing happened that I wasn't expecting. Honestly, I don't know why it got to me so much."

Dixy walks over to the desk and picks up one of the glasses that Alfred bought when I had a drink with him before I left for the ball. She pours a healthy measure of whisky.

"We both know why it got to you. How about you knock that back, you come out and talk through tonight, and then I will take you home?"

I knock the drink back and hold the glass out to her, and she laughs, refilling it.

"Ready?" she asks, and I nod, walking forward and as I do, she grabs my wrist and pulls me in, giving me a hug. At first, I tense, not wanting to get upset again. Then I let go, slumping, and I hug her back because I know it isn't easy for her to make that move. I don't want to reject her for trying. However, this may just be the most awkward hug there has ever been.

"That was sneaky," I mumble into her neck.

"It's easier for me that way. You're not the only one with intimacy issues. Why do you think I flirt with you relentlessly? It's the easiest way for me to show I care."

"There was me thinking it was because you find me irresistible."

"Well yes. Obviously." She scoffs. "But you are my friend, and you are hurting; I want to be there for that. That and there's a man outside that adores you, and he's super worried you are going to disappear on him again. He told me because he's hoping I can help stop that from happening."

"Ugh, that bloody traitor."

"He's not; he loves you. We all do, you idiot, and you love us too. You would be crazy not to. Now let's get this over with so I can take you home. I want to see your place; I've heard it's epic!" she squeaks and laughs.

"Yeah, okay, I do a bit. Don't let it go to your head, you fucking nutbag."

"Too late. Oh no – Mac. Please catch me while I swoon!" Dixy coos, and she falls backwards, fake fainting, and I only just catch her.

We make our way to the fire pit, and Alfred, Lambert, and Anna are there. Anna is still wearing my blazer, and I am careful not to look at her. I walk past Lambert, and he holds his hand out, giving me a high five.

"Well done, Mac! You handled that like a boss!"

"Thanks brother."

I take a seat in my camping chair and sip my whisky and sigh out the heat it burns in my throat.

"I had a lot of people staring at me. I guess they are Culling members, and they know I am Barrett's daughter. There were two people constantly flanking him; it was like they were guarding him. The big bloke, he definitely doesn't trust me. And the way he made a beeline for Anna? I'm sure he was trying to push me. He could be a problem."

"Yeah, I noticed that, and I agree, but the woman in red looked at you like you were food. You may be able to exploit that." Dixy winks, and I cringe.

"Oh, gross. You're not serious?"

"I am. The art of seduction is a real thing, Mac. You could use your powers of seduction to get information, possibly turn her, get her on your side as a potential ally."

"Now I really want a shower." I shudder, and everyone laughs except Anna whose gone back to staring back into the fire with a blank expression.

"Who was that woman in blue?" Alfred asks, and I shrug.

"I wish I knew. She seemed so familiar but… not. I'm probably just imagining it."

"I guess you will find out. There isn't much time till the meet," Alfred grumbles, his expression grim.

"Three days. This time, I have no idea what to expect, except that he clearly wants to be dramatic about it. Why else pick the brewery as the place to meet?"

"If he is going to tell you more about The Culling and it sounds like he is, maybe he is just trying to provoke an emotional reaction from you. Push you to see things from his messed-up point of view, manipulate you. It's the only thing that makes sense to me, kid."

"I agree. He wants to turn you, convert you to his ideology. He wants you angry at the world, maybe even at yourself, so he can take advantage of your vulnerability. You are going to have to convince him he's succeeding but not too quickly. Make him work for it, or it won't be believable," Lambert explains calmly, his voice monotone as always.

"Question is, is he going to take me then for reconditioning or will he wait? I think it is too soon, but I guess there is no way of knowing, so I should prepare for the fact that he could."

No one seems to have an answer for that and soon, everyone falls silent, all deep in their own thoughts. I look over at Dixy, and she smiles.

"Come on, Casanova. Let's get you home."

***

At the apartment, Dixy runs around the apartment like a crazy person. Over-excited and a little resentful. I laugh at her; she is like a hyperactive child.

"I think Lexi must be crushing on you. My first apartment was nowhere near this nice!" She pouts.

"You should have seen me the first time I came here. I was still in prison-issue clothing. Lexi not long bailed me out of a segregation stretch and recruited me, sending my head in the biggest mind fuck ever. God, I must have looked insane. I walked in, and I was just happy to sleep somewhere where the toilet wasn't three feet from my head. I spent far too long opening and shutting the fridge door because it felt like forever since I'd done it."

"So, what you are saying is screw the fact that it was a mansion – there was a real-life fridge in it."

"Basically, yeah. Lexi even put a bottle of Jack in there."

"No way!"

I reach into the cabinet and pull the bottle out. The note from Lexi welcoming me home, still attached. I put it down on the kitchen counter, and she looks at it, gawped.

"She is definitely trying to get in your pants." She smirks.

"Aw! Don't say that; I have enough trouble with the women in my life."

"Can't really argue with that."

CHAPTER 7

Hurricane Anna

"Mac…don't be such a baby. Just jump!" Dixy teases.

"I'm not being a baby; I just don't see the point to this. I don't like doing stuff I don't see the point in."

When I arrived at the farm this morning, I did so in my truck, and it felt awesome to be able to drive again. Now that I am here, they literally want me to jump through hoops. Hula hoops to be more specific. My hip is better, but the idea of running and jumping through hoops and risking it, doesn't sit well with me. I've tried, but I just keep landing in a heap, and the more that happens, the more I don't want to do it.

"The point is, learning to be accurate when on the run and if you make a mistake, learning to land in a way that won't hurt you." Dixy groans impatiently.

"Don't think that would have helped me when the psycho bitch sand bagged me. And I have tried. I can't land right, and it hurts my God damn butt!"

"Oh. Just do it; it isn't even that high. Don't think, just do it, and land in a forward roll. The forward momentum will dull your impact down, and it will hurt less."

I glare at her and huff. I am agitated and moody, and this isn't helping. I stare at the hoop, then at the floor, and I groan, bouncing on the balls of my feet.

"Urgh fuck it."

I blast into a run, my stomach clenching with the horrible feeling of dread you get when you know you are about to fall. When I am roughly two meters away, I pound the ball of my dominant foot into the ground and push off into a jump. I move headfirst through the air, tucking my arms tight at my sides, and I see the hoop getting closer and closer. I sail through it and then I realise I haven't pushed myself forward enough, tucking my head to spin. It's too late to correct myself; the floor is coming fast. I belly flop to the floor with a winding thud. Dixy and Lambert are howling with laughter, and I pound the floor with my fist in frustration.

"Okay, I think that's enough hoop jumping for one day. We're going to pick up some burgers for lunch. You want us to being you back some food?" Dixy asks.

"Obviously."

Dixy and Lambert set off in the hunt for some food, and I collapse in a heap on the grass. It is cold and wet, but it feels nice since I am sweating from all the failed attempts at hoop jumping.

"Kid, you out there?" I hear Alfred buzz in my ear.

"Yeah, laying in the grass."

"Meet me at the pit. I have coffee."

"You wonderful man."

"Houston, we have a problem."

I push myself up off the floor and saunter over to the pit. Today is going to be a physical day; I am glad for that. I actually miss it, but I am still very gun shy about my hip. I have to get over it. There is no pain, no stiffness or sign of it coming back, and with things moving with Barrett, I don't have time to pussy foot around. And yet, I still can't help but feel tentative about it.

"How many times did you face plant the floor?" Alfred teases, sitting down with a grunt.

"Every God damn time."

"Don't envy you there; I couldn't do it. Not even in me younger days."

"You can still move, though, very well for an old boy."

"Oi you, less of the old," he booms. "Anyway, I've got to pop into town for some bits. Just wondered if you needed anything while I was there?"

"Nah, I'm good. I need to go myself in a few days. It's Mum's birthday soon; I need to get her something. God only knows what."

Suddenly, I have the entire farm to myself. I don't think that has ever happened before. It is a weird feeling. It's so quiet; it is actually quite eery.

I stand, staring at the parkour run. After my fall – or rather, push – I'm pretty scared of it. Dixy and Lambert haven't pushed me to go back on; I think they have guessed that my confidence on it has blown. I am tempted to give it a go now that no one is around, but the longer I look at it, the more my stomach tightens. I don't feel ready yet, and I am sure it won't help with whatever is going to happen with Barrett in two days' time.

So far, I can't help but think that the master manipulator has been too easy to manipulate. Then again, both times I have seen him have been in very public places where he has had to be discreet. I wonder how he will change when we are alone together, inside the condemned brewery that I half blew up after a killing spree. Maybe he just wants me to *think* I am manipulating him, a double manipulation. Who knows? Regardless of what he is thinking, of what his intentions are for me, I still have to go. The thought fills me with dread. I can't pretend I am looking forward to going back there and facing all those memories either.

I hear a car engine rumble, and my eyes flick to the sound. Anna is home. I look away quickly and sit on the floor, my back against one of the platforms. I don't want to see her. Last night's encounter with her at the ball is still fresh in my mind, and the pain still burning in my heart. I don't understand her anymore. For a brief moment every now and again, I see the Anna I knew, the girl I fell for. Then, out of nowhere, she will do something to hurt me, push me away, or be so cold I don't recognise her. At this point, my head is so messed up that I don't know what to believe anymore.

I want to believe that she is still in there somewhere, that she isn't lost to me forever, but that hope keeps getting me hurt. The only thing I really know for sure is that she isn't herself; I am as worried about her as I am resentful. It is hard to be here, to watch over her when I feel like she just wants me gone half the time. God, I miss the person she used to be, and yes, I miss her. Being with her, her touch, her kiss, her light but mostly I miss *her*, the her I used to know. I wonder if I will ever see her again.

"Mac!" Anna screams.

Pain shoots across my temple, sending my vision blurred. My back slides sideways down the platform, and I feel the warm trickle of blood dribble down my face as I get a mouth full of grass. It feels like far too long before I find the connection between my brain and my hands. I push myself up on all fours shakily, my vision starting to come back, and then an impact pounds hard into my rib cage, then my face, and I taste blood.

"Houston, we have… a problem," I grunt.

"Stop! Stop! Ahhh!" Anna cries out, and the sound of her pain rouses me.

"I told you, stay back, or I'll kill you." Danni spits.

"Kid, is everything all right? What's that shouting?" Alfred booms in my ear.

The sound of Anna's pain ignites fury inside me. Suddenly all the pain is gone, and I get sharply to my feet. I poise myself to launch myself at her, but Danni points a gun at Anna, and I freeze.

"I am telling you now, Danni, you touch her again, and I will fucking destroy you!" I snarl.

"Oh, shit! I'm coming, kid. Hold her off. I'm coming! Dixy, Dixy do you read?" Alfred yells.

"Loud and clear, farmer Giles, what's up?" Dixy calls in my ear.

Danni laughs, a shrill and high-pitched laugh, her eyes cold and menacing.

"Oh, the irony! You have been here before, haven't you, Mac? Gun pointed at your girl… Oh, wait, she is not *your* girl, is she? I saw to that," Danni jeers, her eyes cold on mine. I look back at her cold stare, the hairs raising on the back of my neck.

"Your problem is obviously with me. Let. Her. Go!" I bark.

"Fuck! Callum, make a U-turn – now! Hold on, Mac," Dixy orders.

"Maybe, but I've been planning this a long time. I want to enjoy the moment a little first, and let's face it, the best way of hurting you – is by hurting her." She taunts, her eyes alight with hate.

I look at Anna, the terror on her face, her cheek glowing red from where Danni hit her. The sight makes my blood boil, and I feel myself tremble.

What the hell is this?!

"There's no point looking at her. Even she doesn't know who I really am!" Danni spits, her eyes wide and bulging. "It was fun, playing with her, forcing her to stay away from you to fuck with you. You seeing us together…oh, I did really enjoy that! How easily you fell for it, resented her for it! I had almost as much fun fucking with her life as I did yours. That was an unexpected bonus," Danni muses with delight.

My stomach drops, shock swooping in my chest. I look at Anna, her pleading eyes full of tears. Her body is shaking from head to toe.

"She told me she lived along Eastfields Street, above the shop you blew up, and that her father was inside and that you killed him. She said that she had proof that it was you, and if I didn't do what she wanted, she would hand the evidence to the police and get you sent back to prison. She showed me a video of you shooting at Jakub's men. I checked, Mac - there was no one living in that building," Anna explains, her voice shaking on every word.

The clarity, the understanding of why she has been so scared, so angry and tired, of why she treated me so coldly, hits me so hard, I feel winded. I've been so blind. I have to find a way to get her out of this. The gun pointed at her makes that impossible. All I have is a knife strapped to my shin that I can't reach without her seeing me. Alfred is our only hope. Surely, he will get here before Dixy. I must stall Danni.

"Who the hell are you? Why would you do this?" I growl.

"Five minutes out, kid. Keep her talking. I'll flank her from behind," Alfred updates.

"All in good time. First, you are going to get on your knees, and I'm going to make you bleed! Anna here is going to watch me, and if you don't sit and take it, she's dead. *Now move*," Danni orders, ramming the gun against Anna's throat, and the fear that courses through me is like nothing I have ever experienced.

"Urgh…Callum, put your foot down! She is dead, she's so fucking dead," Dixy snarls.

I keep my eyes on Danni, my brain moving at lightning speed as I try to find a way to get Anna out of this. All I can think of is stalling her, keeping her attention on me till help comes. I have to do this, while I fear what she can do to me, what I have to allow her to do to me. It is nothing in comparison to the desperate terror possessing me at the thought that I could lose Anna forever. She has been protecting me all along; if I lose her now...

I step forward two paces towards Danni, then drop to my knees, my arms relaxed at my sides.

"Do your worst, you psychotic bitch!" I spit with venom, and her smirk falls, her lips curling around her teeth.

Danni pulls something small and black from inside her jacket. She holds it up for me to see, and there is a click as the blade is revealed on a switch blade, taunting me. My blood runs cold, nauseating fear churning my stomach. I grit my teeth; I don't want to give her the satisfaction of seeing my fear, but there is no denying that I feel it. Danni steps towards me and keeps the gun pointed in Anna's direction, her eyes fixed on me. She hooks the point of the knife in the neck of my t-shirt, and she pulls, ripping it open and revealing my chest. I stiffen, my composure shaking as my chest is exposed, revealing every ugly scar.

"Oh, look at the state of you." She cringes with disgust, and I feel the familiar shame creeping up on me, making my insides shake. Danni turns her gaze on Anna. "And to think you ever wanted to touch this mess. She's making my skin crawl just looking at her."

I know it shouldn't hurt, it shouldn't humiliate me, and yet – it does, so powerfully. For a split second, I couldn't care less how much Danni cuts me. Really… What difference will it make to an already scarred skin such as mine? The heavy weight of resignation tugs my shoulders down as low as my eyes as the grass blurs in my tears.

"Every kind…of beautiful." Anna emphasises every word clear and sure.

Warmth spreads through my chest, and I choke a laugh, scrubbing the tears away roughly with my sleeve. I drag my eyes away from the floor and find Anna's burning powerfully. A look I don't quite understand, and yet it fills me with strength. I can't seem to tear my eyes away from hers, even when I feel the edge of a cold blade pressing against my skin. Danni drags the blade hard and slow. A sharp, hot pain forces my eyes closed and a growl to escape my lips. My body shakes in the effort not to scream, my teeth clamping down.

"Stop it! Please! Stop!" Anna cries.

"Ugh, I'm going to kill her!" Alfred booms in my ear.

"Anna, it's…okay. It's okay," I soothe breathlessly, looking at her with pleading eyes. Willing her to shut up. I need her to stay quiet; I need the attention on me.

"It's okay? I must not be doing a good enough job," Danni utters with sickening playfulness.

She moves fast. I see the glint of her knife, and then I feel the pain as she rams it deep into my arm. White hot agony burns through my bicep, and this time, I cry out. My vision whites out, heat igniting over every inch of my skin as the pain threatens to make me pass out. I am just able to catch my breath when the pain intensifies. A scream bursts from my mouth as Danni twists the knife.

"Argghhhhh!"

"No!" Anna screams.

"Hold on, kid, I'm almost there!" Alfred yells.

"Damn it! It's on you, old man – you're going to beat us there," Dixy growls.

Anna runs towards me, her hands on my face, sobs bursting from her chest. I shake my head to snap out of the spin cycle it's stuck in, and my eyes find hers.

"Anna…you have to move."

She pulls me in, her arms wrapping around my waist, her tear steaked face buried in my neck. I feel a jolt of energy as she presses her lips against my neck, whimpering. Her hand moves down my back, and I feel her slide something into the back waistband of my trousers. Anna pulls back, catching my eye, and I see the briefest smile touch her lips.

"Anna, fucking move away from her, or you're dead!" Danni yells.

Anna moves away fast, and I bow my head, letting it bob to feint that I am weakening, and then I let my hand slide behind my back. I feel the handle, the familiar wooden handle that is beaten and dented, and my heart leaps as I realise it is the knife Alfred gave me. Anna had it all along. My chest floods relief, and a new light burns inside of me, a hopeful one.

Danni steps towards me, and I drop my hand. She looks at me with such vengeful hate, a vicious smile on her face. I stare back at her. The hairs on the back of my neck stand on end, a cold shiver tingles down my spine, and I flinch when, for just a second, her eyes disappear and are replaced with his eyes, his sadistic, predatory eyes as he takes my body for his own. I choke on a gasp and pinch my thumb and finger together.

"Who are you?"

Danni takes a step back, smiling perversely. Her eyes on me, her gun still pointed at Anna.

"My name is Danka Nowak."

"Is that supposed to mean something to me?!"

"How about Tomasz Nowak. Does he mean something to you!?" Danni snarls at me with venom, her eyes deranged with anger.

I recoil, the fear and hatred boil up inside me like heated acid. My stomach tightens, my mind a blur of sickening memories…a crescent shaped scar on a whiskery jaw.

Tomasz…

I look into her eyes and then I see it...the ghost of the sadistic rapist, resembled in her eyes. How could I not of seen it? All this time.

"On site, moving to your position," Alfred growls.

Oh, God…please hurry. She is going to kill us both.

"You see it now, don't you? You destroyed my life. You took my father from me, the only person I ever had! The only person I ever cared about! So, tell me, why shouldn't I kill the person you care for most?"

Danni turns her glare on Anna, and she whimpers, her eyes wide and full of terror, and the fear grips my throat like an iron fist. I see movement, Alfred running – he is too far away; he isn't going to make it. I have to stop her. I grip the handle of my knife…

"Your father was scum, and I made him cry like a pathetic little bitch – I loved every second of watching him die!"

Danni turns on me, the gun pointed at my chest, but I am already moving at savage speed. I pound my left arm into the ground, balancing myself, and the pain sears in my bicep as my arm swings forward. My wrist flicks and my hand releases grip all in one fluid movement. I watch as the knife sails through the air, spinning in ruthless revolutions. My chest explodes with vengeful satisfaction as I see the blade plunge deep into her chest. Her eyes widen in shock, and I see her arm begin drop as the weight of the gun becomes too much for her.

Relief floods me for a fraction of a second, and then I see the fury reignite in her eyes as she grits her teeth, the gun raising back up towards my face. I feel an impact that sends me flying to the floor. Anna tackles me just as I hear the loud crack of the gun going off. She cries out, and it feels like my heart stops.

"Anna! ANNA!" I cry, tears burning in my eyes as I see the blood flow from her shoulder.

Her eyes widen in fear as she looks over my shoulder, and I turn to Danni looming over us. I spread my body to shield Anna just in time to see Alfred's mask of fury pounding towards her from behind. Dani stares me down with a tooth baring grin, the gun directed at me shaking in her hand.

"Tell your father I said hello!" I spit.

Alfred leaps, soaring through the air. His arm hooks around her neck, and he pulls her down with his momentum. He pounds down towards the ground, landing on his knees and snapping her neck in one expert, terrifying, savage movement. He drops her to the ground and is back on his feet in a second, dashing towards us. I turn back to Anna.

"Is she gone?"

"Yes, she is gone. It's over," I say, wiping the tears from her face. "Stay with me, okay? Keep your eyes open, don't…" I sob, and then Anna's eyes flutter closed.

"Anna!"

Alfred skids to a stop by my side. He lifts her up, checking the back of her shoulder.

"Oh, God… No, no, no!" I cry.

"Mac, MAC! Listen to me. It's a through and through. She's going to be okay! Snap out of it, kid! I need you to calm down and help me. Let her go so I can fix it!" Alfred bellows in my face, and he shakes me out of my panic. I hear car tires screech to a stop and see Dixy and Lambert running over at full speed.

"Tell me what to do, Pa."

"Hold pressure on the wound while I carry her."

I whip off my shredded shirt, shivering at the cold against my skin, and I press it hard against the front and back of her shoulder. Alfred slides his hands beneath her and lifts her off the ground; we are on the move in seconds. My heart is aching in a way it never has, my breath ragged in terrified sobs. Dixy and Lambert are hot on my heels as Alfred and I move in pace with each other towards the house.

"I'll grab the first aid kit," Dixy grunts.

We burst through the door, and Alfred sends everything on the kitchen table flying with a crash so loud it jolts Anna awake. She cries out as Alfred lays her on the table, and I grip her hand while I cradle her face softly.

"It's okay; you're going to be okay," I cry, my words coming out strangled.

"Mac, I need to see to your arm. You're losing a lot of blood," Dixy orders, pulling me by the wrist.

"I am not leaving her!" I snap, pulling my arm out of her grasp.

Alfred moves at lightning speed; everything is moving around me in a frenzy, and all I can do is keep my eyes on her.

"I'm sorry, Mac."

"You should be; that bullet wasn't meant for you," I choke, my lips pressing against her forehead.

"Sweetheart, I need to close the wound. It's going to hurt, baby, but once it is done, you are going to be okay." Alfred sniffs, and Anna's eyes widen fearfully, her grip on my hand tightening.

"Don't leave me, p-please."

"I won't. Not now, not ever again."

I look over at Alfred and can see he is struggling, the needle and thread shaking in his hand, tears running down his reddened cheeks.

"Alfred. Alfred…" I call, but he is lost, his eyes tortured.

"PA!" His head snaps round to look at me, "Come fix my arm and let Dixy do that," I order.

His eyes find Dixy, and she moves round to him, cupping her hand on his whiskery cheek.

"I can do it; you have done the hard part. I've got her. Take care of Mac, big fella," Dixy soothes.

He nods and wipes his tears away roughly on his sleeve, then moves out of Dixy's way. I feel him at my arm, and I feel separate from the pain. I keep my eyes on Anna. I rest my cheek on the table, my forehead against hers, my hand stroking her cheek. Her breath is fast on my face as she trembles.

"It's going to be okay; it will be over soon," I whisper.

Then, she screams. The sound is the most painful sound I have ever heard; it tears through me as if it's ripping my chest apart. I hold her through it, feeling more helpless than I ever have in my life, and then – mercifully – she goes silent. Her body flops limply, and she passes out. I break down, hunched over the table, holding her hand to my face. I sob as if no one is listening, loud and unapologetic. Lambert steps in front of me warily and shirtless and at first, I am confused. Then he pulls his t-shirt over my head, covering me up. I had completely forgotten I was topless.

"Th-Thanks."

Huge, strong hands pick me up, and the familiar scent of hay and motor oil engulfs me. Alfred curls me up on his lap, cradling me like a child, his bear-like frame jerking as he sobs.

"Thank you," he struggles. "Thank you so much, kid."

"Don't thank me. I'm the reason she got shot," I cry, the hatred of myself boiling over.

"No…you're the reason that she is alive. You bought me enough time to get there."

"She's all set," Dixy announces softly, and I look up at her, so thankful that there are no words, and she smiles warmly at me.

Lambert offers to carry Anna upstairs to bed, and I am relieved; Alfred looks weak and shaken. I get to my feet to follow Lambert, but Dixy pushes me back down on the chair.

"You can go sit with her after I stitch the gash on your head," She insists forcefully, and I don't have the energy to fight her. Dixy begins cleaning my head wound, and my head swims. I grip the table, closing my eyes. The sting of the needle soon snaps me alert again.

"She… was…" I croak, and Dixy bends to her knees, her eyes tight with concern.

"*His*…daughter. The man. It was her…eyes, the same eyes, triggering me. I didn't realise…" I manage, and I see the understanding flicker across her face.

"Jesus…" he breathes, and she takes my hand, gripping it tightly. "Then she totally deserves the unmarked grave that Lambert is about to bury her in."

I climb the stairs with shaky legs, my body exhausted and my heart heavy. Her bedroom door sweeps open silently as I move into her room. She is asleep, her face relaxed and beautiful but her lips are pale, her skin covered in a sheen of sweat. I sit by her side, hold her hand, and I watch her. My head feels so heavy, blood loss and lack of food making me feel sleepy, but I fight it, too scared to take my eyes off her.

She was protecting me this whole time, and I lost faith in her. I believed her to be cold and cruel; I forgot who she was. After the loyalty she has always shown me, I hate myself for not believing in her more. The hate I feel for myself raises the lump painfully in my throat. I hunch over the bed resting my forehead against it lightly. I grit my teeth, trying to gain some control over myself, and then I feel her hand move to the back of my head. I look up, and she is staring back at me, groggy, pained, but so beautifully alive.

"Hey…"

"I'm so, so, sorry, Anna." I choke, suppressing a sob. She frowns at me, pushing herself up in bed with a wince. Anna takes my hand, and she squeezes it gently.

"You have nothing to be sorry for. I'm sorry for screwing with your head so much. You don't know how hard it was for me, doing that to you. Watching you slip further and further away from me every time I hurt you. I was trying so hard to find a way out. The longer it went on, the more I was convinced you would never forgive me."

She looks wary, like she is waiting for me to bite her head off at any second, and part of me wants to. But most of me is just relieved to see her eyes open. Even now, it is hard for me to maintain that eye contact; the way I feel about her has never felt so raw. I just want to scoop her up, taste her lips on mine. I want to hold her with burning irrational need, a need to know she is safe in my arms.

"I wish you had told me; I knew something was wrong. I would've protected you, Anna."

"I couldn't. You really think I was going to risk you going back to prison? That place almost killed you. You were protecting me; you think I didn't notice that you were watching over me? That if Pa wasn't here, you always were? I was treating you like crap, yet you were here more, not less."

I hunch forward, my head resting on the edge of the mattress. My head is swimming in floaty, nauseating movements. It reminds me of being back on the boat. I feel her hand on the back of my neck lightly, and it amazes me how good that one tiny action feels.

"I would sooner have gone to prison than have her do this to you."

"Why do you think I couldn't tell you?" She giggles playfully.

I push myself back up slowly, trying not to activate the spinning in my head that is making my stomach churn.

"It's not funny, Anna. What were you thinking? If that bullet were a couple of inches lower, we wouldn't be having this conversation," I assert, the edge in my tone impossible to miss.

"It's what you would have done, what you did do. You let her cut you up to save me. She could have killed you, but you did it anyway."

"That's different," I deadpan.

"How is it different?! Oh, I see. You can protect me, or Alisha, or the whole damn world from The Culling, but heaven forbid I try to protect you! What is the difference?!" she snaps.

Tears fill my eyes, and her face softens instantly. She leans forward, her eyes warm and confused on mine. Anna watches me, waiting patiently for me to answer her, and she looks at me in a way that I have missed so much. She places a hand on my face, steadying me, and my eyes close in reaction to the pleasurable purr that her touch brings, blinking my tears away. My heart pounding hard inside my chest, fear threatening to break my resolve.

"The difference is…I love you, Anna. I have *always* loved you and…if it's a choice between you and me, I'll always choose you because, without you, I - "

Her eyes burn with emerald green fire, and her hand trembles on my face. She pulls my face a little closer.

"Then…Mac Scott, there is absolutely no difference at all."

Her lips sink into mine with desperation, and my body reacts instantly with fervour, heating my skin, tremoring my hands, a frenzy of vibrant sparks tingling in every nerve. Anna takes complete possession of my lips with a kiss burning so hot, it could melt steel. Every movement, every taste, pulling me deeper into an ecstasy so intense, I can barely breathe. She is on her feet and then, straddling me, her hands on my face gripping me closer.

I knew I missed her lips, her taste, and my tongue remembers the feel of hers sliding against it perfectly. But never have I experienced a kiss so erotic and yet deep with unparalleled love. Tears well in my eyes, my hands dive into her hair, and I am encompassed by her sweet candy-like scent, intensifying the tingles that are ravaging me. She is saturating my body with desire with every stroke of her tongue. Amidst each blissful passing second, our entwining moans grow more ragged and needy. Anna pulls back, dipping her forehead against mine.

"Oh, God…I love you; I have loved you for so long," Anna sobs.

My body throbs with the pound of my soaring heart as I hear the words. I choke on a sob, smiling, and I wipe the tears away from her pale cheeks, softly showering them with kisses.

"I won't let you go, *ever* again," I promise.

At my words, she breaks down, sobbing into my shoulder. My arms slide beneath her, and I stand, wincing at the pain in my arm. I turn around and sit on the bed, her arms and legs still wrapped around me. Shuffling back, I lay down, and she settles on my chest. I hold her, and she begins to calm, her body melting on top of mine while I feel like I am melting contently into the mattress.

"Say it again…" she whispers sleepily, and I chuckle.

"Savannah Mae Slone, I love you, and when you open your eyes, I'll still be here – loving you. So, close your eyes, beautiful. You are safe; you can sleep now," I utter softly, and she nuzzles into my neck, kissing it and sending shivers down my spine.

"I love you, Mac Scott," she mumbles, and I know right there and then, I will never tire of hearing that.

***

"Alfred… Alfred…" Dixy hisses in a whisper, and I hear his footfall come closer to the bedroom door. "How fucking cute is that?" Dixy hisses with a giggle, and I hear him chuckle. I squint my eyes open, and I see them both in the bedroom doorway, grinning.

"Go away - you creepers," I whisper, smiling, and they both chuckle at me before closing the door, and I fall straight back to sleep.

The next time I wake up, it is Anna that wakes me. My arm is throbbing, and I feel dizzy from the hollowness of my stomach.

"Sorry, I was trying not to wake you, but I had to move." She winces, holding her hand over her shoulder.

"It's okay; I'm glad you did. We need to get some food and painkillers in you. Stay here. I will go get you some." As I get to my feet, Anna grabs my hand.

"No, don't go. Please."

I turn back around and kneel down in front of her. She looks look a rabbit in headlights.

"Talk to me, beautiful. No more secrets."

I watch the fear on her face. She struggles, scared to speak the words. I hold her hands, rubbing the tops of them with my thumbs.

"I know everything that you've been facing. I watched, and I couldn't go near you. The night I was told that you might be tortured again, I felt like I was losing my sanity. Do you know how much it's tormented me? To see you get hurt and scared over and over and not be able to even touch you? It's been excruciating. You're only at the beginning of this. What if you decide it is too dangerous to be with me again? Barrett knows who I am; you could easily let me go again, and I can't take it, Mac. I can't…"

I can see she is about to break, and I can see why. I have given her no reason to believe that I will stick around. In fact, I have given her every reason to believe that I won't. I brush her hair away from her face and cup her cheeks, her eyes closing at my touch, and I wait for her to open them again, my thumbs stroking her cheeks.

"You may know all of that, but what you don't know is the torment I felt. Through everything that has happened, every fall and every break, every win and every loss. All I wanted was you. Every single time and that torture sounds very similar to yours. I never really let you go because you are what my heart beats for. I will do everything I can to protect you but the right way this time. I promise, I won't let you go again unless it's what you ask of me. I know I don't deserve it, but I need you to believe me…please. I won't make the same mistake again, Anna; I can't lose you ever again."

I am scared that after all this, I have caused too much damage for her to ever trust me again. My heart pounds as I look into her eyes, waiting for her to say something, anything to stop the ridiculous fear pounding through my heart. Then she smiles, and I chuckle a sigh of relief.

"God…you really know how to make a girl melt, you know that?"

I lean in, my lips meeting hers feverishly. I nibble at her bottom lip, and the sound of her whimpering in my mouth forces my thighs to clench. She is just as responsive to my touch as she always was and just as honest expressing it. And God, have I missed that. She lifts her arms to drape them over my shoulders, and then I hear her wince. I pull back in an instant.

"You need food and painkillers."

"I know, and I'm not the only one," she insinuates, quirking an eyebrow. "You are a woman of many talents, but cooking isn't one of them. Help me up. I'm coming down with you." She grins cheekily, and I laugh, feeling brighter and lighter than I ever thought I could again.

I get to my feet and help Anna to hers; my head swims a little at the top of the stairs, but I manage to get us both down safely. We turn the corner and find everyone sat round the kitchen table, wolfing down sandwiches and custard creams. Dixy looks up and sees us both walking through the doorway and cheers.

"God, you two can sleep! Anyone would think being shot and stabbed would earn you a holiday in lazy town," she says playfully.

"Don't mess with me before coffee has happened, Dixy," I groan.

"Oh, you're not so scary. You want to be careful, Mac. Anna is getting close to stealing your coveted badassary title." She winks at Anna, who blushes and grins back at Dixy with ease. That is nice for me to see; the tension always being so thick between them. I see a truce forming, and it is a relief.

"Believe me, I'm well aware how badass she is. I finally found out where my missing knife was when someone smoothly handed it to me without the psycho seeing."

"Oho! That's my girl! Now *that* is bad ass!" Alfred booms, and the blush heating Anna's cheeks is adorable.

"I couldn't agree more, but I saw the knife sunk into her chest. Someone's practice is paying off. That was a blade heavy knife as well. You did me proud, Mac," Lambert commends.

We all sit around the table, laughing and joking as if a psycho hadn't infiltrated the farm intent on killing us. I feel Anna's hand on my thigh under the table the whole time, and I feel pure joy tingle in my chest. I can't believe after everything that has happened, she is finally mine. After the food, Alfred breaks out his moonshine, and I look at it with scowling apprehension, cringing at the memory.

"Oh, come on, Agent Scott – grow a pair! It can't be that bad," Dixy teases.

"First of all, the last thing I would ever want is to grow a pair." I cringe and shudder, and everyone howls with laughter at my continued contempt towards anything penis related.

"Second of all, put your money where your mouth is, Agent Dixon," I goad. I pour her a small measure of moonshine and slide the glass towards her with an eyebrow raised. Dixy snorts, picks up the glass, and knocks it back in one cheek bulging gulp. She chokes, spluttering with a beetroot face, and I laugh in victory.

"Oh, good Lord, that tastes like Satan's arsehole!" she chokes.

Anna leans on my shoulder, and I put my arm around her, kissing her forehead, and she melts into me, sighing cutely. Questioning eyes are on me immediately. I look at Dixy, and her face is lit up like Christmas.

"Hold on a minute, what is this? Do I see a Facebook relationship status change in the cards?" she asks grinning, and Alfred looks up, his eyes bright with happiness and pride.

"I don't even have Facebook."

"I know, you fucking weirdo. Stop avoiding the question!" she squeals, and I laugh, looking down at Anna, and her eyes are alight with glittery warmth, her expression darling and tantalising. I lean in, kissing her quickly and sweetly. The kitchen erupts with cheers, and Anna giggles in my mouth.

"About time! Jesus! Okay, I propose we toast with a glass of Satan's arsehole!" Dixy cheers.

***

Soon, the party dissipates, and I walk hand in hand with Anna to the barn. I lead her inside, walk her to the sofa and wrap a blanket around her shoulders. She watches me, her eyes curiously scanning my face, and I smile awkwardly, feeling a little self-conscious. Mostly I feel immensely blessed. I never thought she would look at me like that again. Never has anyone made me feel so precious and wanted just by a single look.

"Just what are you staring at?" I ask, and she smiles at the memory.

"Nothing…everything. It's been a long time since I really got to just…look at you. It was unbearable to even try, plus I was worried you would see through the façade. I'm making up for it now," she says softly, her voice dreamy.

She reaches up, her fingers tracing the lines of my face. I watch her; the intensity in her eyes and her velvet soft touch awakens the warmth inside me. Expelling the lonely pain with such force, it is staggering. It hurts, but it also feels good, like all the aches are being forced out of my system.

"I know exactly what you mean."

Anna's fingers stop tracing my face, and she drops her hands, and they find mine. She looks at me, her eyes thoughtful, and I can feel the nervousness coming off her.

"You almost told me, didn't you? The night of my birthday."

"How did you work that out?" I frown up at her. Her eyes are full of pain, she takes a deep breath, and I listen, her words activating the memories. They play over vividly in the theatre of my mind.

"The way you looked at me was identical to the look in your eyes when you finally did tell me. I wanted so much for you to let me explain; I only accepted the date with Danni because you told me you had seen Alisha. I assumed that you had let me go, and I was broken up by it. Danni had been persistent. I met her at work, and I felt so sad, I just gave in. You gave me the bracelet, and I realised you hadn't completely let me go. I needed you so badly that I forgot she was coming. That kiss was enough to make me forget my own name…" Anna pauses, her cheeks flushing to match mine. Reminding me of that moment is making me need to kiss her all over again.

"She arrived before I could warn you, and I realised I had broken you. I sat by the fire. I saw Pa holding you, and I thought if I could just break it off with her before it starts…if I could just explain myself to you, maybe I wouldn't lose you. I tried, and that's when she started to threaten me. I watched you drive off in Lexi's car and…I thought you were lost to me forever. Little did I know it would only get worse from there."

My heart aches for her pain. The fear and entrapment she must have felt. To know she was surviving all that and no one had any idea the strain she must have been under. The pressure and loneliness of it all.

"I'm so sorry I brought this down on you. I left you alone in it, and I don't know how you got through all of that. I don't think I'll ever forgive myself for that, but I'm here now, and I'm not going anywhere."

I pull her in for a cuddle, but she gently pushes me away.

"Don't do that; this was not your fault! She was the daughter of a man who tortured you and was a complete psycho. You could never have known who she was or what she was doing. Don't take that blame on; it is *not* yours. Do you understand me?!" Anna rants fiercely, and I smile with tingles erupting inside my chest.

"I love it when you're bossy."

"And I love it when you look at me like that; it is irresistible. I tell you what else is irresistible…you in that damn tux – *Jesus*."

"Ugh, don't. You...in that dress…the most devastatingly beautiful and devilishly tempting sight I've ever seen. The only reason I was able to control myself was because you had me utterly convinced that you didn't want me anywhere near you."

"I noticed that. Honestly, Mac, I know I screwed with your head, but how could you still believe that after how badly I wanted you on that dance floor? God, I was desperate to kiss you. How couldn't you feel that?"

I scrub my hand across my forehead, cringing, deciding that the fluff I am picking off the knee of my ripped jeans requires my immediate attention.

"It was too easy to believe that I was what broke you and even easier to believe that you…" I look away, clearing my throat as if it will release the embarrassed clench clutching at it. "That you could never love me. Alfred told me I was wrong many, many times. Dixy did, my mum, even Lambert. They all were trying to persuade me in their own ways and I just…couldn't…"

Anna moves towards me, her hands on the sides of my neck. "Baby, look at me, please."

I can feel the pain building in my throat, and I don't want it. I know where this is going, and I don't know if I am ready to go there yet. I look up, my jaw set, trying to keep myself in control.

"What is it that makes you believe you're so bad? You've always felt that way; you used to tell me that you were afraid your darkness would destroy the light in me. It was never true. You always made me burn brighter, but to believe that I couldn't love you to that extent, that's heart breaking, and it has to stop. Where does that come from? Do you know?"

"I didn't know at the time."

"But you do now?" she asks, and I nod.

She waits patiently, watching me with eyes warm with affection. She is always so patient, much more patient than me. I don't know how she does it; I couldn't feel more frustrated or impatient with myself right now. Then I see a pain flicker across her honest face, a painful understanding, and I flinch back.

"You already know," I breathe.

"For a long time, yes," she confesses with tears misting in her eyes, and I look away, shock and shame flooding through me icily at ferocious speed.

"The hospital?" I whisper, keeping my eyes down.

"No…when you were in the brewery. Something you said before you killed…him."

I shake my head, eyes wide as my mind stretches to try to remember. I feel the panic starting to peak in my chest, and Anna grips my hands.

"I saw a scar o-on his jaw from when I bit him. It triggered the memories and…I don't remember saying anything. I came out of it, I killed him, I don't remember…"

"I think you got confused about what was memory and what was present. You mentioned what he did and that he didn't listen when you said no."

Her voice gets quieter with every word, but it doesn't lessen the impact of them. The images invade my mind with a jolt, and the memory swirls.

"Should I violate you with this knife the way you violated me?" I growl.

"No please..." he begs.

"But you didn't listen when I said no...did you?! DID YOU!?"

"No... No. I'm sorry," he whimpers.

"Oh, God...Mac..." Anna whispers.

"You are so very lucky I am not quite as big of a monster as you," I scathe.

I snarl as I stab him three times in a quick and but controlled frenzy right in the heart.

I jump back stumbling on to the floor, unable to shake the images from my mind. That means if Anna heard, Alfred heard, Alisha... She did know why I wouldn't let her touch me. She never said – she must have been waiting for me...

"Oh God..." I choke, my head in my hands, the shame crashing over me like a tidal wave. I just want the ground to swallow me up. Please...make me disappear. They know, they have all known, this whole time.

"Mac..."

"No, no, no, no..." I mumble as if it will make it all disappear.

Anna slides on to floor and shuffles over to me. She kneels between my legs, and pulls my hands away from my face, and she places them on the sides of her neck.

"You don't hide from me anymore; I've spent too long not being able to see that gorgeous face. Now you take those haunting eyes that make my world stop and look at me!" she yells.

It takes every last bit of strength I have to look at her. My body starts to shake, and the tears well. I want to run, and she can feel it. She grabs my face and holds me there, her forehead dipped against mine.

"What he did to you doesn't dirty who you are. You are not bad; you are so far from bad it amazes me. How you kept hold of that fire inside of you, that love and spirit, I'll never know, but you have, and I fell in love with it all, with every part of you. I've tried, very hard at times - not to love you, and I've never succeeded. You make it impossible. I love you, so much and nothing you could tell me that he did will *ever* change that."

She has hold of me before a single tear falls. She kisses me with such love, I feel it bursting from her. Extinguishing the flames of shame and filling me with all the intensity her heart can hold. Her lips move against mine with furious desperation, her tongue tantalising me with its exploration. She leans into me and knots her hand in my hair, pulling me close, and I can't stop the needy groan that builds in my throat. Never have I felt anything so raw and powerful; she lays herself bare. I feel the love in her heart. It's screaming out my name, and I hear it.

"I love you, Mac. All of you and I need to believe in that, in us. Do you believe it now?"

"With my whole heart," I promise, and she chuckles a sigh of relief.

Anna's eyes alight with desire and invigoration. I want her, so badly, but the fear is still there. The fear of being touched and his eyes flicker across my mind so sharply, I flinch as my insides revolt as if he really is stood in front of me.

"What's wrong? I've seen you do that before."

"I've been having flashbacks and memories for a while. They are all…of him. They kept coming really randomly; there seemed to be no trigger. It was happening out of the blue, and I couldn't find a way out. Then earlier I realised it was Danni. They have the same eyes. I'm remembering everything he…and I'm scared to…I'm not ready to…" I struggle as the embarrassment wins out.

I chance a look at her, and her expression is pained. Her eyes are tight with anger, and it makes me look away, but she stops me.

"I'm sorry," I blurt.

"Please don't be sorry. I just hate that this has been happening to you, and I didn't know. You've been going through this, and I wasn't there. Mostly, I *hate* that anyone could ever hurt you that way," she explains, and I breathe a little easier, a slight smile playing my lips.

"I know how that feels," I quip, pointing out the irony, and she smirks as kisses me lightly, sweet and loving.

"I am yours...we have all the time in the world."

CHAPTER 8

What My Heart Beats For

It takes a lot of willpower to tear myself away from her as she sleeps soundly in my bed at the barn. Her face beautiful and relaxed, and I just want to stare at her. It still doesn't feel real that she's finally mine. It was worth every moment of pain it took to get to this place. I scrawl a note, the words 'I love you' jumping out from the paper, and I leave it on the bedside table before I begrudgingly walk away into the chilly morning. It is an early start, but with everything that happened yesterday, I feel a little behind. My meet with Barrett is tomorrow evening, and I feel underprepared and daunted. The sun is not yet in the sky, but the fire is already blazing, and in its bright glow, I see the dark figure of Alfred, dipping custard creams into a steaming cup of coffee.

"Morning, Pa."

"Morning, kid. How's our girl?" he asks, and I grin.

"She is fast asleep; she seems to be doing okay. Although after everything that psycho bitch put her through, I have no idea how."

"She's okay because she has you. That's all she ever needed."

"Is this an 'I told you so' speech I feel coming on?"

"No, it's a 'It is so good to see both my girls so happy' speech. I mean, I could tell you I told you so, but I'm a bigger man than that," Alfred jokes, puffing out his chest in a mock macho way.

"You are so fucking cute," I tease, and he scowls.

"Am not!" he snaps playfully. "Do you know what you are up to today?"

"No, I just wanted the early start to ram in as much as I can and hopefully get some time with Anna this evening. What are your plans?"

“Now who’s cute? Well, I never got the things done in town yesterday before the psycho bitch came, so I will go back in a bit later to get them done.”

“I was hoping you would say that. Would you be able to pick some things up for me? A little surprise for Anna.”

The grin on his face is adorable; I remember once being scared of what his reaction would be to us being together. I assumed he would think I was bad for her, just as I did. To see him light up, to have his acceptance, makes me stupidly happy.

“Of course!” he booms.

The sun is just beginning to rise when the silver van pulls up into the drive. Dixy is far too chirpy, and she practically skips over to the fire pit with a coy grin on her face. I internally groan, bracing myself for whatever impulsive and uncomfortable thing she is about to say.

“Soooo, it would seem that wedding bells are just not in our future, Max. It’s your loss; I was too good for you anyway.”

“You got over that heartbreak quickly. Max? Since when?”

“Since like 30 seconds ago… Durr. What’s wrong with Max? It’s much better than Mac, rolls off the tongue easier. Oo, I could always call you Maximus!”

“Ugh, Max is fine, you freakin’ lunatic,” I groan, but I can’t help but laugh.

No one has called me Max since I was a kid. I’ve never been much of a fan of Mckenna, and the hate I feel for my second name, Margo, is strong. I sip my coffee and listen to Lambert and Dixy run through the game plan for the day. As I lift my arm to sip the steaming coffee, it feels tight and hot. I guess that is to be expected, and it could have been so much worse, so for that, I’m grateful.

“So, we are going to be teaching the art of manipulation, more about deception, and later, I want to work on some more exposure with you. I don’t think we need to worry about the reconditioning yet; there’s no way he could possibly trust you enough to bring you into his inner circle yet, but we don’t know when that is going to happen. So, I think it’s best to continue while we have the time,” Dixy explains.

“Can’t say I am enthusiastic about the prospect, but I agree that it needs to be done.”

Seeing as Anna is asleep in the barn and it is cold out, we all pile around the kitchen table and get to work. Alfred busies himself cooking everyone breakfast, and I brace myself for the information overload that is about to come.

"A lot of fooling Barrett will come from pulling off convincing lies. You already know this; you are improving, but you still haven't passed the lie detector, which we'll be doing again later. The other thing you need to get to grips with is manipulation. Being able to manipulate Barrett but also being able to see when he's manipulating you. If you can do that, you can seem to give him what he wants, and he will trust you for it. It might seem easy, but he is a master manipulator. To be able to turn previously decent government officials and police officers and God knows who else to his ideology proves that," Lambert explains.

I rub my temples; we have only just started, and I already feel like my brain is being bent. My head pounds right along with the throb in my arm, and I feel weary. I knock back another coffee and hope that it will help. This meeting with Barrett feels vital; I need to have my head on straight for it.

"You've already shown you can manipulate him. Probably by instinct, but you have. At the ball, you played up to his guilt for abandoning you and made him want to tell you more about The Culling by playing the fact it would help you move on and bring you both closer. Guilt is definitely a way to manipulate, but there are many other ways. You could play up to emotions, but I don't think he is capable of empathy; the other way is using logic. Logical people are receptive to rationality, facts, and evidence. With logical people, emotional bribery rarely works; you have to persuade them calmly. Explain how what you want benefits them," Dixy chimes in.

"I'm not sure he is being manipulated by me; I think maybe he wants me to think he is. Like a double manipulation. It all seems too easy. From what I've read about him, he'd respond to logic and guilt."

"I think you're underestimating how much he wants you to join his cause. Not out of love, it's a matter of arrogance and ownership - passing on his legacy. From what we've already seen, I think he plans on love bombing you. He wants to make you feel special; he will go over the top with gifts, love, and affection in order to gain control and significantly influence you. It's a common tactic used by narcissists, cult leaders, and mental abusers and Barrett is practically the definition of all three. He will inspire fear, then offer relief, hurt you, then love bomb you. So, watch out for it and make him think he is succeeding," Dixy explains.

"Ugh, that's gross and probably true. He can be overly affectionate, and it just comes off leery and completely fake." I shudder, and Dixy nudges my shoulder in a playful punch.

"See, none of that. You can't let him see that you are grossed out; control your cringe! There is, of course, the manipulation you will use on others. It will differ from person to person. Take the woman in red. If you're charismatic, make her feel special, and show interest in her interests, she will warm to you. That could fool her into opening up more, and when people are that comfortable, they often give too much away. If that doesn't work, I'm sure you can seduce her into trusting you. She so wants a piece of humble Max pie."

"That is *not* happening, but I see your point. She will be a lot easier to get on my side than that big beefy guy in black. He was suspicious of me and hostile, but I'll cross that bridge when I come to it."

Dixy offers me a break, and I take it gladly; my head is pounding from the barrage of information, and I feel exhausted already. I lie back in the camping chair and close my eyes; the icy air is soothing on my face while to fire keeps the rest of me warm. How am I ever going to remember all of this? I am just beginning to doze when I feel her lips against mine; I jump a little and then groan a happy moan in her mouth as she kisses me.

"Mm, I could get used to this," I smoulder.

"I've wanted to do that for a long time, although you weren't asleep, but it was close enough." She grins, straddling herself on my lap.

"I think I nearly was; I don't know why I feel so beat. I've had like 12 coffees. If that's the way I'm going to wake up, I think I'll have to start having more naps."

"You could, except you don't need a nap to sneak a kiss from me. In fact, you don't need to sneak at all. You can kiss me any time you like for as long as you like."

"Careful… I might not stop…" I growl pleasurably, and then I kiss her hungrily.

Her hands cup my face, willing me closer, and then slide down my neck and onto my shoulders beneath my jumper. Anna's fingers stroke along my collar bones with feather light touches. Her tongue dances with mine perfectly, and I can't get enough of her. Every inch of me craves her so badly, my hands tremble. I skim my fingertips up her back, stroking the dip in her spine and making her shudder her words into my mouth.

"G-god I've missed you…and those hands and these…" Anna trails her tongue across my bottom lip making me whimper, "…lips."

"*Fuck…*" I moan, my lips taking possession of hers. I hold her closer to me, kissing her with pure, unapologetic need. Every lap of her tongue is sending shockwaves through my system, making the ache between my legs desperate to be touched.

"Kid, back to work in five." Alfred sounds in my ear, and I break away from her kiss.

"Got you Pa, thanks. Houston, we have a problem," I growl.

"Did he just…"

"Activate my earpiece while I am getting turned on by his granddaughter's kisses – yes! Ugh!"

"Aw baby…" she coos, but she is crying tears of laughter.

"It's not funny!" I gripe, my voice unusually high pitched.

"It's a little bit funny. What did he want anyway?"

"It was the five-minute warning before I have to get back to work."

"I wish you didn't have to." She pouts and she cuddles up on me, her lips trailing up my neck, sending shivers down my spine.

"You're making me want to leave even less. I haven't even left, and I miss you already."

"Mm… I love hearing you talk like that. Come find me when you next get a break?"

"You can count on it."

***

We spend the next two hours running the lie detector. The first round was a complete failure, the second read as both truthful and inconclusive, which I will take as a win. It's definitely a massive improvement. Of all the things that I expected when I agreed to try to infiltrate The Culling, learning to lie and manipulate people didn't even enter my radar. Although it makes perfect sense, thinking that way is unnatural to me. It isn't something I want to be good at, even though it is vital to my survival.

Now I find myself staring at the trunk in the middle of the field. The very trunk that defeated me within minutes the last time I got inside of it. I remember the panic vividly, and it is not something I want to repeat. Last time I was panicking before I got inside the trunk; this time, I'm trying to calm the anxiety before I get inside.

"Can you tell me what you think when you look at the box? Maybe if we can understand what the fear is, we can help you conquer it," Dixy asks, and I sigh, closing my eyes and letting the memories play over.

"I never knew how long I was going to be in there. It was smaller and hard to breathe. I never knew when they were going to pick the box up and throw it or how many times they would. There was no way to brace myself," I list mechanically.

"Huh… I think I know where this is coming from. Tell me the same thing with waterboarding," Dixy requests. Her face is thoughtful and focused. She's looking at the floor, frowning, which makes it easier for me to divulge.

"Not being able to breath, being held down, not knowing when it would stop." Dixy nods to herself, then she looks up at me, her eyes questioning.

"Electrocution?"

"Being restrained, not being able to breathe, not knowing when they would stop."

"Electrocution is painful, as is waterboarding, and I imagine being stuck inside a tiny box and being thrown repeatedly is also painful. Yet not once is pain one of the things you mention," Dixy points out.

"Pain wasn't the worst thing. Not knowing when the pain would end or being able to see where the hits were coming from and being restrained so I couldn't defend myself. That was all much worse than the actual pain."

"Exactly!" Dixy squeals.

"Exactly what?"

"It's about lack of control! Restraints, blindfolds, not being able to breathe. Not knowing when you are about to be hit, not knowing when it will end. It's all about people having control over you. You also said before about forced self-harm and suicide, that is someone controlling you, making you do something you don't want to do. Not to mention the hallucinations. Being out of control is why people love drugs. They love that feeling, but to you, it was losing control of your mind and not being able to stop it," Dixy rambles excitedly. I am failing to see the reason for the excitement.

"That makes sense, but how does that help?"

"Knowledge is power. If you can understand your fear, you can take the power out of it at least some. Name it in your head. 'I don't like this because…' Make friends with it, understand it. Then we just have to find a way to help you cope with lack of control. We don't even need to use the box; we could use many things. Teach you that you may not have control over the situation, but you can get control of yourself."

"You really think that's possible? Because even though it makes sense, I don't feel like any amount of exposure is going to stop me fearing being drowned again. Does this mean I don't have to get in the box?" I ask hopefully.

"I think that it is possible to at least desensitise you some, but eventually…yes. I need to think about the drowning. I think that fear is as much about drowning as it is lack of control. The only way I can think of exposing you to that – is drowning you again, and that doesn't sit well with me. Nice try, but you are getting in the box, and this time, I'm not going to tell you when you'll be getting out. Only that it will be less than an hour. I'll send Anna when it is time, and then you'll be done for the day."

I groan at her dramatically, and she laughs at me, holding open the lid of the trunk. My stomach is alive with nerves as I step inside, tucking my knees up against my chest.

"Now remember, this is about control. You don't need control of the box; you need control of yourself. This is your box; you are the person with thoughts and feelings. The box is just a box. You can control yourself, Max; you just need to believe you can. If you need out, buzz me. Are you ready?"

"As I'll ever be."

Dixy shuts the lid, and I am left in the cramped darkness. I can feel the anxiety building, and I know I have to do all I can to make sure it stays manageable. I don't want to fail; the embarrassment of failing is enough to keep me in this box. I am still the person that doesn't like to show weakness. Getting out of this box early shows weakness, but that isn't enough to make me succeed. Is it really possible that I can gain control of my fear? Of myself?

I start touching the roof of the lid, my fingertips following the lines in the wood and smooth metal oval bolts, trying to picture what it looks like in my mind. When I get done with that, I play games with myself to try keep my mind moving enough that it is harder for the panicky thoughts to take over.

"This is my box. I don't belong to the box. I can stay in here as long as I want. This is my box."

I mumble to myself, even sing to myself and for what feels like a long time. I keep good control of myself, but eventually, it feels like it is getting harder and harder to keep that control. My thoughts are getting louder and darker with each passing second. This is just fear; my mind is activating that fear so surely, my mind can deactivate it too. I envisage an on-off switch in my mind; I just need to find a way to flick the switch.

"This is my box. I don't belong to the box. I can stay in here as long as I want. This is my box."

It feels like I have been here a while. I am doing much better than last time, but I am tiring. The longer I am in here, the less distracting myself works. How do I get control of my fear? How do I persuade myself that someone else having control of me isn't terrifying? Dixy is probably right about the cause, but that doesn't tell me how to tame the effect. My chest is starting to feel too tight; the unnatural heat is beginning to spread across my skin, and it feels like the walls of the box are closing in. My mouth is beginning to dry out, and my throat is raspy. I have to find a way to take control before it takes control of…

The lid to the box opens, and daylight pours in, burning my eyes in a white out. I sit up and lean over the edge of the box, the cold air hitting my face as I try to catch my breath. I feel familiar, soft hands on the back of my head as

Anna steps forwards and holds my head to her tummy. Her calming touch is magical.

"How long?"

"45 minutes," Anna utters in a tight voice.

God damn it, it felt like double that. Still, better than 15 minutes. I take a deep breath and climb on wobbly legs out of the box. I look up at her and see the stress tugging at her honest face.

"Are you okay?"

"I'm fine, just not a fan of this…purposely scaring you thing," she admits, and I chuckle.

"That makes two of us." I step up to her, my hands sliding onto her waist, "Grab your stuff; I'm kidnapping you."

The stress disappears from her face as it lights up with an excitement.

"I like the sound of that."

***

We pull up outside my apartment and get out of the truck. I reach down, pick up my rucksack from the footwell, and I lead her inside by the hand. Once we are inside, I can feel her eyes watching me curiously as I throw firelighters in the fire and light them. The logs catch, and the fire begins to roar. I take some of the cushions from the sofa and lay them in front of the fire with some blankets. I grab my rucksack and take out the things that I got Alfred to pick up for me. A selection of little sandwiches cut into perfect triangles, chocolate-covered strawberries, a big packet of her favourite sweets, a bottle of champagne, and two glasses.

"You always said you wanted a movie by the fire."

Anna giggles and sits down on the cushions, her eyes twinkling in the firelight. The smile on her face is beautiful, her skin lit up by the flames, and I am transfixed.

"Who would have guessed, Mac Scott is a romantic? You are so sweet. This is… perfect."

I pop the cork on the champagne, fill the glasses, and I hand her one. She takes a sip, and she gazes at me, her eyes expectant and curious, and suddenly, I'm nervous. It feels too good to be true that I am sat across from her, that the loving look in her eyes is reserved for me, and I am scared that one wrong move will burst this perfect bubble.

"I have something for you."

I dig deep inside the rucksack for the last thing inside and pull out a small black velvet box. I shuffle closer to her, take her hand, and put the box in it. Nervous butterflies fly around my stomach as I watch her. I lift the lid and reveal the shiny, freshly cut key inside. She looks up at me with a confused frown, and I chuckle nervously.

"Before the ball, Pa told me that there is more than one way to die. He was scared I was disappearing again. He asked me, "*What's is the point of a pulse, of your heart beating, if it is broken and empty... What's it beating for?*" I grumble in a gruff imitation of his voice, and she laughs brightly. "He said anger and duty will only get me so far, I have to fight to come home to the people I love. I told you yesterday, you are what my heart beats for. I want you to come here *whenever* you want. Because…whatever happens, wherever I am, I'm always going to want to come home to you."

Her eyes burn mistily, and she leans into me, her lips capturing mine wantonly. Her kiss deep, slow, and deliberate. A kiss full of love but also laced with intense desire. I feel her tears on my cheek, and I pull back.

"Why are you crying?"

"Because I finally believe you. I'm not scared of you letting me go anymore, and you have no idea how good that feels. Do you remember at the warehouse, in bed, you asked me why I was crying?"

"Of course. You wouldn't tell me."

"That's because I knew, after the way you touched me, after everything you made me feel, I was so in love with you. You had altered everything I thought I knew about myself in one passionate night, and I knew there was no coming back from that. I was yours regardless of whether you loved me back, and I felt terrified because I could feel you trying not to leave me. I knew I was going to lose you; I could always feel that conflict in you, but I don't feel it anymore, and it's the most amazing feeling. I feel… safe."

"You did your own fair share of altering that night too." I pause to watch her blush. "I was yours, even then. I just wasn't in a place where I could show it. I'm sorry I hurt you so much to get to the place where I could," I sigh, feeling a pang of guilt.

"Stop. We both had a hand in that, and it doesn't matter anymore; you are here with me now, and you were worth the wait."

We never put a movie on. Instead, we talk and talk and talk. We missed a lot of what happened with each other during Danni's control of her. We nibble on the snacks, sip champagne, and laugh as we tell each other everything we missed. I feel relieved. I was worried that giving her a key to the apartment was too bold of a move too soon, but it went down better than I could have hoped. Instead of freaking her out, she seems more relaxed and playful than I've seen in a long time, and I am loving every second with her.

"...Oh God, I could have killed Lexi. The look on your face told me the last thing you wanted to do was go to that ball. I only pulled myself back because Dixy gave me the 'shut the fuck up' eyes, but I was livid."

"I saw that. You were disobeying a direct order, Agent Scott, and it was really quite sexy." She grins daringly. "But you were wrong; I wanted to go. I wanted the chance to be with you in a place I knew I wasn't being watched."

"You were being watched. When I was getting ready, I was looking in the mirror, and then I saw words pop up in my vision, little floating words in red. It was Lexi was wishing me luck on the mission. Everyone could see everything through my contact lenses; it was the weirdest thing."

"Okay, that's just creepy! I knew they could see me, but it wasn't them I was constantly being watched by; it was Danni. I had the chance to be with you where she couldn't see, so I took it."

"That girl has a lot to answer for. I kind of wish I could revive her so..."

I see his eyes flashing across my vision, and my muscle tenses rigidly. My index finger and thumb squeeze together hard. It is like a habit now; I am getting better at it, but it doesn't always work. I feel her hands on my face, but I only see him.

"Come back to me..." she whispers, her lips against my forehead.

I close my eyes, trying to see my good memory clearer. The taste of the lemon lollypop is sweet and sour in my mouth. The sound of the campfire songs being sung merrily, the feel of the rifle kicking into my shoulder. I open my eyes and see Anna's eyes instead of his. They are sad but so rich with green and easy to get lost in. She lifts my hand; my thumb and index finger still locked in a hard press.

"What is this?"

I explain everything that Dixy has been teaching me to try to help me control the flash backs. She listens intently. I watch as the emotions play on her face, I've always been a little bit fascinated by the ease with which she shows how she feels.

"I'm glad she has been trying to help you. I have to admit – I hated her a little. She's very protective of you, and she flirts with you constantly. It drove me crazy," she admits, cringing.

"Dixy has her own…story. One that's not my place to tell, but she has been through some things. Things that make it hard for her to warm to people. She flirts because that is the easiest way for her to show she gives a crap. There was never anything in it; she was pushing me to be honest with you, as much as everyone else, if not more."

Anna smiles at me, a little embarrassed but clearly relieved.

"Thank you for not freaking out at my jealous girlfriend moment. I'm glad she is your friend, that you weren't completely alone in this."

"Your jealously is nothing to freak out about. It is understandable and actually quite adorable."

I take Anna for a tour around the house. She loves the balcony. I stand inside the doorway and let her go out there. It is not my favourite place to be; it may not be that high, but it is high enough for me not to like that the floor is made from glass. It's not a place I feel safe standing, and she smirks knowingly as I hover in the doorway anxiously. When she comes back inside, I watch her walk through the bedroom. Her eyes curiously roam around the place, her fingertips running over the surface of things. It's still as neat as the day I got here - just the way I like it. It's quite easy to keep it that way when I spend so much time at the farm.

The bedroom is a very bright room full of natural light because the back wall is made entirely from glass. Everything is decorated in white, black, and purple. Fluffy rugs and thick carpets make the room feel luxurious, and the modern furniture is mirrored and sharp. The cosy sofa in the centre of the room is black and leather. I don't think I've ever sat on it; it is pointed towards the wall-mounted TV, but I just watch TV in bed. Below it is an electronic imitation fireplace which I've never used; for me, fake fire is no fire. The bed is an unnecessarily large, sleek, white-gloss four poster. White slinky vails hang from the posts; the bed looks cloud-like and bouncy. The sheets are purple satin and there is a black fur blanket tucked neatly and snuggly along the bottom. It's the most comfortable bed I have ever slept in, but now I'm looking at it anxiously.

Anna wanders into the bathroom, and I hear long drawn out "Woooah." She reappears with wide eyes. "Your shower is amazing! It's huge!"

"I know. Imagine walking in there and seeing that after showering in flip flops, in the most disgusting shower cubicles, under the watchful eyes of a prison guard for two months. I dread to think how long I was in there that first time. I looked like a wrinkly beetroot by the time I came out." I scoff, and she laughs easily, walking back over to me. Her eyes fall on my bed, and she looks up at me with a raised eyebrow.

"That is…some bed."

"Yeah… It's bit over the top, but then, the whole place is over the top."

As we both stand there in front of the bed, the atmosphere heats up rapidly. I want nothing more than take her to bed. I want her so badly it is painful, and I can feel her wanting me even though she's trying not to show it. She is trying to be patient with me, but I still feel it, and it's just exciting me even more. I'm so fed up with myself, of not being able to just get over it already. Anna closes the gap between us, her hands on my hips and gives me a look of knowing.

"Remember, we have all the time in the world. I want you, *God* do I want you, but not until you're ready. Don't feel pressure; there is none. I'm just happy to be here with you." Anna cradles my face in her hands, her eyes strikingly green and full of adoration. "This…you, it's *all* I want. I don't need anything else. As long as you never stop kissing me, it's enough, Mac."

Her understanding and patience only magnifies the desire I have for her. My lips brush against hers, slow and gentle at first, but the want I have for her, the want I feel radiating from her, powers through me. And I can't fight my need for her. It burns from inside me and flames across my skin. It urges me to kiss her firmer, deeper. Anna keeps her hands on my hips like she is trying to restrain herself, but her grip on them tightens, and she pulls me closer by them. I trace her bottom lip with my tongue, marvelling at the smooth plumpness of it. The taste of the sweets she has eaten still lingers there.

Anna lets out the tiniest moan, and it is so enticing. The sound of her pleasure sends shockwaves of tingly excitement through my nerves and throbbing between my thighs. No one has ever kissed me so honestly. I feel every ounce of her want, her pleasure, and it is wrecking me. Her kiss becomes more urgent, her thumbs just lightly gazing my hip bones from under my shirt. The smallest touch, and my legs are weak. I pull back breathlessly.

"You are driving me crazy…" I breathe into her ear through heavy panting, and she shudders.

"You only have yourself to blame…God…"

***

We find ourselves back downstairs, cuddled in front of the fire, watching a movie. I feel relief, like the pressure has been taken off. While I want to enjoy every inch of her body, and it frustrates the hell out of me that I am not ready – I know that Anna doesn't feel that frustration. She lays on my chest, her fingertips running up and down my ribs over the top of my t-shirt, and I feel content. The only thing that could make this evening better is if I wasn't so scared of taking that next step, but somehow I know, with Anna – I will be.

"I have to go to my mum's in a few days; it's her birthday. Would you…like to come with me?" I ask her, slightly awkwardly, and she lifts her head, surprise raising her eyebrows.

"Meeting the parents, big step." She smiles sheepishly. "Of course, I'd like to."

"You have already met my evil villain father; this will be a piece of cake."

"How are you feeling about tomorrow? You haven't really talked about it."

"I know. Talking about the doom and gloom of that stuff is hardly fun date materiel. I didn't want to ruin things with it."

Anna props herself up on her elbow, her free hand laying on my chest while her fingertips mindlessly trace my collar bones. Her touch, the simple thoughtless ones, are my favourite. Like she can't help but always be connected in some way.

"I don't want you to hide the things you're going through from me; I want to know everything. I'm not just here for the fun stuff, Mac. I want to be the person you can turn to, just like I was before."

God... She is way more incredible than I deserve.

"Okay then, I'll admit – I'm a little afraid. Not of him, really, just of messing up. There's a lot riding on me getting it right with him every time. I don't really feel like I have any idea what I'm doing no matter how much information Dixy and Lambert cram into my brain."

"They believe in you; we all do. There is a reason for that. You might feel scared, but when the scary thing happens, you always face it fiercely no matter the danger. I wasn't happy about it when you agreed to doing this, to being an Agent, but I can see why they want you."

"I'm not an Agent; they just call me that, and it makes me cringe because it feels like I'm being a fraud. I'm just doing what I have to do, to end it."

"You might mess up; everyone does, but you will find a way through. Try not to think of what everyone expects of you; that's a scary amount of pressure. Just think of what *I* expect of you." She smirks sexily.

"Oh, right, and what would that be?"

"For you to keep your promise and make sure that cute little butt is always coming home to me. That, and pizza. I'm starved."

"Okay, let's order in before you bite my cute little butt." I wink.

"Don't think I haven't thought about it..."

The time with her passes unbearably fast. I don't think either of us wants it to end, but Anna is barely able to keep her eyes open, much as she tries to fight it. We make our way upstairs, and Anna walks over to my chest of drawers and picks out one of my t-shirts. My insides clench as she climbs into bed wearing nothing but that and the tiniest pair of lacy panties.

Damn... She is hot.

Then I realise, I have no idea what I am supposed to wear to bed, and I feel ridiculous. Last night in the barn, we fell asleep in our clothes out of sheer exhaustion. This shouldn't be this hard; I shouldn't be this anxious. It isn't like she hasn't seen it all before or touched it all before in fact. Mm, she was very good at touching it all before.

Not helpful...

"Are you okay?"

"Um yeah, be right there."

I retreat into the bathroom, taking off my jeans and putting on a clean baggy t-shirt. I feel ridiculous. I don't want to be this way, not with her. I splash some cold water on my face, trying to cool the anxiety beginning to burn on my skin. I need to get a grip; this is Anna, and I know that she is the last person that would judge me for this fear. As I walk back out to the bedroom, I still feel anxious, but if I spend any longer in the bathroom, she may think I fell down the toilet or something. I climb into bed quickly and find Anna laying propped up on her elbow, facing me. I smile at her stiffly, but she doesn't smile back. She just reaches for my hand and holds it, keeping her eyes on me. I can't help but look away.

"I don't want you to be scared of me."

"I'm not...I...I'm not."

"If you get any closer to the edge of the bed, you are going to fall off," she utters lightly, her smooth yet gravelly voice dry with tiredness.

"I'm not scared of you, I just...I feel vile and dirty, and I'm scared of your touch bringing on a flash back. They are not always so easy to stop, and it seems like I have an unlimited supply of forgotten memories with him, and I don't ..."

She waits, being patient with me as always. I try to keep myself calm, but the anxiety is getting the better of me. The fear that talking about him might bring on more flashbacks is strong, and yet I want her to understand that it isn't her. I need her to.

"I don't want to remember anymore. The more I do, the more disgusting I feel and the angrier I get that all this time later, it's affecting me so much. It's over, done. It was a long time ago, so why can't I just stop?"

"You lost your memories. Every time you get one back, to you – it *has* just happened. You never got the chance to go through this. You just need time. It will get easier; it will stop, and I'm not here to push you."

"Two years is a long time. A lot of mem…" I gasp.

Excited eyes flash perversely across my mind. I let go of Anna's hand as my finger and thumb pinch together and my eyes squeeze shut. I feel her move closer, her hand on my face, and then the memory swirls…

"How long before she recovers?" Tomasz asks eagerly.

"You want to hope it's quick! I have videos I need to record. You will have to get your dick wet somewhere else," Jakub spits.

"I know. I'm sorry, sir."

"No!" I cry as I half jump, half stumble off the bed and onto the floor. I pull my knees up to my chest and wrap my arms around them tightly.

"Mac…"

"I can still have some fun with you, mala suka," Tomasz leers.

The pain in my hip is excruciating, no way to even move. Yet my wrists are still chained as I lay here on the floor. Tomasz kneels down by my head, unzips his fly…

"Gnnnaahh stop!"

"Mac…look at me!" Anna yells.

Anna pulls at my wrists, unwrapping my arms from the hold I have on my legs. She spreads her legs, slides closer to me, and wraps them around my hips. Then she starts to pull my t-shirt off, and I panic.

"What are you doing?! STOP! My skin is fucking crawling, Anna!"

"I know…I know! Mac, stop! Look at me!" she yells, and I jump as she catches me off guard.

"Just trust me… if it doesn't work, I will stop."

She doesn't wait for me to argue. Taking advantage of my momentary freeze, she whips my top off, then hers and then she pulls me into her. My skin bare against hers, she holds me close as I continue to fight her, shame and disgust crawling over my skin like a rash.

"No, no… I can't."

"Just stop…your skin is not crawling. You can feel my skin against yours; just focus on that, on what that feels like. That is all there is right now, you and me. Can you feel that? Just stop fighting, baby, please."

The sound of her voice breaking shocks me into submission. My breath sounds so loud and ragged in the silence, but I freeze, my body tense as though bracing itself for impact.

"That's good…it's just you and me. This is all we are going to do. You can stop this whenever you want, and I won't be upset, but don't stop it because you assume that I think you're dirty. I don't. You feel… amazing. I'd hold you all day long if I could," Anna coos softly.

Her arms relax around me, she's not holding me so tight, and then she runs her fingertips up and down my scarred back, making me shiver. It feels so good and bad all at once. I'm so tense it hurts. She holds the back of my neck lightly with her other hand, her lips at my ear.

"I love you…"

My body starts to relax one muscle at a time. My neck loosens, and I let my forehead lean forward, my face buried in the crook of her neck. My arms loosen at the sides of me, and my shoulders slump. She exhales in relief and pulls me tight to her. Her skin is so soft against mine, and it feels incredible. The panic starts to loosen its grip, and the itch crawling over my skin retreats; all I can feel is her.

"I'm so sorry; I didn't know what else to do. Please tell me I haven't made it worse?" Anna chokes.

I lift my arms and slide them around her. Skimming my hand up her back and holding the back of her neck as I kiss the crook of it, and her breath shakes.

"O-oh, thank God…"

I feel shell shocked; fear that he could invade my mind again at any moment is rippling through me. I just keep holding her because the feel of her skin against mine is both tantalising and calming all at once. She is the only thing holding me here. My anchor in the now.

"I'm scared to let go…" I confess.

"Then don't…"

Anna pulls back. She keeps her eyes on mine as she gets to her feet and doesn't let go of my hands. She leads me to the bed, and I follow as she gets in and pulls me with her, laying me on her bare chest. I lay my hand over her heart and feel it pound against my palm. She holds me to her, and I melt against her as I feel the fear trickle away. As the fear disappears, the hurt hits me like a freight train, and I am unable to stop the tears that flow.

Anna rolls onto her side, holding me tight to her through the sobs that drag through me raggedly. I don't know how long we stay like that, only that it feels like far too long before I am able to stop. Every time I nearly gain control of myself, images of his violations invade my mind, and I lose control, again and again. Anna just continues to hold me through it, kissing my face, wiping my tears, and keeping her arms and legs caged around me protectively till eventually, I stop.

"I'm sorry… I didn't want you to have to…"

"No, don't you dare. Mac, I can't imagine how long you've needed to do that, and I just…it feels good that when you finally let yourself break, it was me you wanted through it. I know that sounds awful, but I spent so long watching you in pain and not being allowed near you or feeling like you didn't want me to be. I can't really help but love the feeling of you needing…me."

Anna looks at me apprehensively, her face pinkened with embarrassment, and I smile at her because that might just be the sweetest thing I've ever heard.

"I've always wanted you, no matter how hard I've tried in the past not to. Of all things, I thought that was obvious."

"Not to me. You were a master at pushing me away. Especially after Danni, not that I could blame you. At the hospital when we saw those X-rays, I knew what those breaks were. You couldn't have kicked me out of the room faster, and I understood. I'd hurt you so much because of her. Of course, you wanted me gone, but I didn't ever choose to hurt you. To me, the woman I loved was broken and alone and not wanting me, and I understood it, but it was still heart breaking."

I see the tears mist in her eyes, and the guilt I feel is shocking. I never really thought about how hard it was for her; I was too wrapped up in trying not to want her.

"I pushed so hard because no matter how much I got hurt over Danni, it was infuriating that I still wanted you. You once asked me what the hardest part of prison was. I told you it was segregation and that is true. But only because the whole time I was alone, I needed you, and I couldn't have you. It hurt a lot. That's what made me so distant when I came back, why I kept pushing you away, but you don't have to worry about that. My days of pushing you away are long gone…clearly." I quirk an eyebrow, and she laughs through her tears.

I pull her into me. Her cheek rests against my bare chest, and she breathes a long, shaky sigh of relief. She feels so good in my arms. No number of tears and fears will make me immune to the tingles that having her almost naked in my arms will bring. As she falls asleep, I feel a peace that I haven't for a long time or at least the beginning of one. The grip that Tomasz holds on me has loosened, and I can breathe. I fall into a dreamless sleep with a little more hope in my heart and a lot less pain.

***

The pain wakes me, sharp and burning down my bicep as Anna lays asleep on it. I carefully slide it out, and the relief isn't as much as I'd hoped for. It feels tight and hot, and it's throbbing with a strange pulse. My skin is covered in a sheen of sweat. I pop a handful of painkillers and make my way to the bathroom. I unwrap the bandage carefully and check the stab wound. It is a little swollen and red but nothing that isn't to be expected, so I step into a cool shower and let the night's sweat wash away.

When I'm done, I dry off my arm, pull out the first aid box from the bathroom cabinet, and wrap a clean bandage around it. I wrap a towel around my waist and creep back into the bedroom to try to blindly find some clothes in the darkness. As I pull open my draw, I hear her giggle.

"Now *that* is a sight to wake up to," she croaks groggily, and I turn round with a smirk as I feel her come up to me.

"Sorry. I was trying not to wake you."

"No, see, you have this all wrong. You should always wake me when you are walking around in nothing but a towel."

"I'll bear that in mind," I breathe, and then I kiss her, but she pulls back quickly, giggling.

"Mm okay…stop…I only have so much self-control. I think I might go for a cold shower if that's okay?"

"You don't need to ask for anything here…that's why I gave you a key."

Anna giggles and dashes off to the shower, and I get dressed and make my way downstairs. I am pretty sure if she leaves the bathroom wearing a towel that my self-control may not be as strong. I get to the bottom of the stairs and pause as my head swims a little, an unnatural slosh that has me gripping the handrail.

Coffee… I need coffee.

In the kitchen, I fire up the coffee machine and set to work making us both some breakfast. I feel sluggish and the smell of the food is making my stomach churn. I dish up a plate of eggy bread for Anna just as she comes down the stairs.

"Mm, I know that smell. Aren't you eating?"

"Not really hungry. Coffee will do me fine. How's the shoulder?"

"Actually, not bad at all unless I move it. Was amazing to finally have a shower, though. I felt disgusting."

I know that feeling all too well. The wait to be able to shower after a gunshot or stab wound feels like forever. This time, though, it didn't bring me much relief. I feel weary, and my head is pounding to the same beat as the throbbing in my arm. I rub my forehead to try to soothe the pound but closing my eyes makes my head swim.

"Are you okay?"

"Yeah, just feel a bit rough. It's nothing, probably just tired."

We get our things together after Anna is finished eating and make our way to the front door. The dread of the day adding to the uncomfortable churn in my stomach. That is probably what it is; the nerves of seeing Barrett tonight are finally getting to me. I reach for the door handle, and Anna steps in front of me. She slides her hands around my waist and pulls me in. Her hair is still wet and is cool against my skin as I rest my cheek on top of her head.

"I know you probably feel disappointed that things got rough for you at the end of the night, but I'm not. I had the best night with you. I wouldn't change a second of it," she affirms softly, and I smile because that is really good to hear.

I pull back, my hands sliding up the side of her neck, and I kiss her urgently, catching her off guard. I kiss her firmly and I lean into her, pushing her against the door. My hands wander under her shirt, my fingertips tracing her ribs and my thigh pressing between hers. And fuck if I don't love her reaction. Her hands slide under the back of my shirt and down the back of my trouser waistband, and she pulls me into her hard as a soft moan escapes her mouth. I nibble my way down her neck, and the sound of her pleasure is intoxicating me. I let my hands slide up till I am holding her face, her breath rapid on my face and her cheeks flushed.

"I'm not disappointed. I needed you, you were there for me, and now…I can feel myself coming back," I breathe intensely as my eyes smoulder into hers.

"Oh God, baby…so can I."

CHAPTER 9

We, The Culling

The atmosphere in the truck is electric as I drive Anna back to the farm. Her hand resting on my thigh, my eyes on the road, my mind in the gutter. It isn't even like I know for sure I am ready to move to that next scary step. All I know is I want to be ready so badly, and I feel less scared of her touch now. I feel less weighed down by the pain of Tomasz, but I'm still just as scared of the flashbacks and how they feel.

God, do I want her.

I pull to a stop, the tires crunching against the gravel, and I get out the truck. I see the silver van parked up, and then it really dawns on me. Today is the day that Barrett and I meet. I shut the door behind me, and then Anna is there; she rams me up against the truck. She presses her body against me, her breasts aching against mine and her kiss firm and fast. As she nibbles my bottom lip, my legs weaken. The frustration I feel is immense; my whole body is on fire and throbbing with want. She pulls back, leaving me breathless and squirming with need.

"Just wanted to make sure you wouldn't forget about me." She smirks with sexy eyes full of emerald fire.

"I might need more reminders; you know what my memory is like."

"I'm sure I can arrange that. I love it when you smile like that. The dimples in your cheeks make you look so adorable but then those eyes… Mm." She blushes, her gravelly voice sexy and playful.

"I hate my dimples."

"I know you do." She giggles and leans in, kissing my cheeks, and then her lips move down my neck, and then - she freezes before pulling back.

Anna lays her hands on my cheeks, and then they slide down my chest as she looks up to me.

"Are you feeling okay?"

"Yeah. Like I said earlier, I feel a bit rough, but I'm probably just tired. Why?"

"Because you are like a furnace, and it is freezing. Do you feel ill at all?"

"I'm fine, don't worry. I don't have time to be ill, not with Barrett tonight. Probably just tired." I shrug flippantly.

"Can you try to find some time today to rest? Please?"

"If it will stop you worrying, I'll try. Depending on what Dixy and Lambert have in store for me."

"Max, move your arse. You're late!" Dixy yells, and I chuckle.

"Speak of the devil."

"Did she just call you Max?" Anna asked.

"Yes, she did. I'm just thankful she seems to be sticking with that and not Maximus."

We set off hand in hand towards the fire pit. Her concern is really sweet. To be honest, I do feel a bit worn in, sluggish and kind of heady, but I don't think I've slept that much since the show down with Danni. Right now, I don't have the time to think about anything but Barrett.

We reach the fire pit and find Alfred, Dixy, and Lambert all sat around in camping chairs. I take my usual seat, and Anna sits opposite me, looking at me with come to bed eyes, heightening my already burning ache for her.

"You're late!" Dixy grumbles, snapping me out of my lusting trance.

"Barely. What's the plan for today?"

"Well, you are going to do some stick fighting with Lambert, both of you using your non-dominant hand only. I need to run through some exposure with you, and we need to talk about and plan tonight. I think we've rammed enough information into your brain for now; I don't want to make it so full of things that you overthink and don't act naturally with him. Your strength is how you react when you are thrown in the deep end, and I don't want to take that strength away by over rehearsing you," Dixy explains.

I am relieved; I don't think my brain can take much more. I feel too tired to take anything in. Stick fighting with just my left arm although my right arm is painful isn't much of a relief. My left side is weak, and my only consolation is that so is Lambert's. I take a side glance at Lambert to meet his goading gaze, and the familiar excitement fills my stomach.

"Come on then, brother. Let's do this."

Lambert runs off to the van to get the sticks, and I whip off my jumper and jacket and throw them on the chair. It's cold, but I like the soothing feeling against my skin. I walk away from the fire pit and start to psych myself up, activating the adrenalin inside. It feels good, and right now, I need all the energy I can get. Lambert returns with the sticks, and we start to circle each other. Lambert holds his right arm behind his back.

"We are fighting with one hand because your arm is still injured, but it's useful to strengthen your less dominant arm. Try to use your whole body to your advantage; you may only have one hand, but you have legs, feet, and even your own bodyweight that you can use against me. Improvise; don't rely on fighting with the stick alone because you could be disarmed at any moment, and your body will be the only weapon you have. Use it," he instructs.

My lanky butt is like a stick in comparison to his gargantuan hulk of a figure. Using my bodyweight would be utterly pointless; the only thing I can use is my speed. I am faster than him, but he is stronger. I have to play smart, try to think, and make moves in a way that he isn't expecting. I look up at him and give him a nod, the movements we make circling each other slow, and each step becomes lighter and more calculated. His eyes and body language are my complete focus, and everything else begins to melt away as that feeling of calm that I love washes over me.

I make the first move, something I don't think he was expecting, which is what I hoped. I lunge forwards, striking the first blow, and he springs into action just quick enough to block, but I'm moving fast. Dominating may be my only chance of winning the first point. The sound of colliding sticks clanking away is a loud and echoey. I attack as fast and as strong as I can. I push myself towards him, using my body to invade his space so that he is only able to block. I force my left arm out hard; he blocks, and I hold my baton against his, and I run forwards, throwing my weight behind the baton. Lambert steps back once, then I step forward and hook my foot behind his heel as I grunt out one last push. Lambert falls backwards and slides on the grass on his butt, then recovers in a backwards roll smoothly, getting back to his feet.

"First point goes to Max! Whoop!" Dixy announces.

I turn my back to try to catch my breath. I feel wiped out already, sweat already pouring off my forehead.

"Nicely done, but the next point is mine," Lambert taunts, and I chuckle, turning to face him.

"Come get it then."

Lambert lunges for me, fast and powerful, his left baton striking with such power I am barely keeping grip on the baton. I spin away and swing the baton round using my momentum, and he blocks the hit like I hit him with a feather. The force vibrates up my arm, and he spins his wrist, and the baton flies out of my hand to the floor.

"Damn it!"

"Level pegging!" Dixy announces, and my insides burn with annoyance at myself. I feel sluggish, like my body isn't able to keep up with the moves my mind is ordering quick enough. I wipe the sweat out of my eyes and turn to face Lambert.

This time, we both lunge at the same time. I run and then jump, my baton arm swinging down. Lambert cringes into a block, and the fire in my belly fuels me as I attack. We flurry into a frenzy of fast and accurate hits. I bob and weave with ease, fluidly sliding out of reach of his swings in an attempt to tire him, but I am tiring much faster than he seems to be. My arms and legs ache, and my head swims lightly, I can't help but wish I had managed to eat this morning.

I need to make a move; I am losing stamina and speed fast. I weave away, sliding to Lambert's left and spinning the baton at him from behind his back. He spins, dropping to the floor, and sweeps my unsuspecting legs from beneath me. Lambert's shin hits my calves like a battering ram. I hit the floor with force, landing on my injured arm, and cry out. The pain shoots down my bicep all the way down to my wrist, and I drag my knees up to take my weight off it. My forehead sweats into the grass as my head spins in violent, nauseating circles as I grip my arm trying to ebb the pain.

"Mac, are you alright?" Lambert asks, putting his hand warily on my shoulder.

"Yeah, just need…a minute. Dizzy."

"Alright. Stay still; I'll grab you some water."

The sweat pours off me as my empty stomach churns. Now I'm so very glad it is empty. I feel like if I move, I might puke. That horrible feeling you get when you go into shock is powering through me as I hear light footsteps running towards me. Then, her icy fingers touch the back of my neck, and it feels amazing.

"Aw God, baby, are you okay?" she coos.

"Yeah, just dizzy. Can't move…yet."

I feel her cold hand slide under the back of my t-shirt, and the cold air blows up the gap her hand creates between my shirt and my skin, and the momentary relief is awesome. I want to take my clothes off.

"You are roasting and clammy."

"I'm fine. I just had a fight; it's nothing."

Lambert returns with a bottle of water, and he hands it to me. "You are taking a break; you are white as a sheet. I will check back on you in an hour. If you need anything give me a shout, alright?"

"Uh-huh."

Letting go of my arm I try to reach the back of my t-shirt and pull; Anna sees what I am trying to do, and she slides my t-shirt up my back, and the icy air hits me.

"Urgh, thank you."

Soon, I am shivering, the dizziness subsides, and I slowly push myself upright. Anna is staring me down with an unimpressed glare. She slides her hand around the side of my neck and down the back of my t-shirt, clearly checking my temperature.

"You are going to rest in bed *right now*. If I have to tie you down, I will," she orders firmly, and I giggle. "Okay, that was probably not the best choice of words, but the point is the same."

"I disagree; that was a great choice of words. I'm ready when you are," I tease playfully.

"Stop, I'm being serious. This isn't the fight you're burning up, and you look about ready to puke or pass out. Now you are going to bed before either of those things happen. Come on."

I relent, slowly and wobbly getting to my feet. She is right, I'm not feeling great, but it's nothing that some pain killers won't fix. Anna hooks my good arm over her shoulders and leads me to the barn. My hands grab for the painkillers in the bedside table, and I swallow them down before rolling onto the pallet bed. She lays down with me, brushing away the sweaty hair that's stuck to my forehead.

"Close your eyes."

"I really don't have time for this. I'm fine. Nothing pain killers won't – "

"Don't argue with me. Seriously, Mac, you're not well. If you rest now, you might feel better, so just close your God damn eyes."

"Bossy…"

"You love it…" she whispers enticingly.

"Yes, I do."

Anna strokes my face, and I feel myself beginning to doze, but every time I do, my thoughts are invaded with the face of Barrett, and the nerves rouse me awake. I open my eyes, and each time, she is still there lying beside me, stroking my face.

"What is keeping you awake?"

"Can't really get tonight out of my head. The pain killers are working, though; I feel better. You don't have to worry," I croak dryly.

"You are mine to worry about; I take that job very seriously, you know."

"Mm, yes I am."

She leans in to kiss me, slow and deep. The kiss is short, leaving me wanting more, but she pulls back, her eyes full of worry.

"I wish you didn't have to go. I know you have to, but it feels like I've only just got you, and the danger you're going to be in isn't lost on me."

"He isn't going to hurt me; he wants me to join him. Hurting me is counterproductive. I'm coming home to you."

Anna shuffles forwards and curls into my chest, her hand sliding up the back of my t-shirt. Her fingertips are featherlight against my skin.

"Just make sure you do."

When I get to my feet again, my stomach begins to growl with hunger, and I'm feeling much better. I make my way back outside and towards the house, and the smell of bacon rouses my hunger even more. Inside, I take a seat at the table with Lambert and Dixy, and Alfred has a plate of bacon sandwiches in front of me in minutes. I feel Dixy's stare on me, and I meet her narrowed eyes.

"What?"

"Someone told me that you are running a fever," she replies, her tone accusatory.

Damn it, Anna.

"I'm fine. She is just worried, but there's no need for fuss. I've had some pain killers and laid down for an hour. I was just tired, and I hadn't eaten."

"Even so, you should have told us that *before* you entered the fight. You weren't up to full form, and you paid for it."

"Ugh, point taken; now can we move on?" I say, exasperated.

We all eat in silence, and I feel more human for it. The rest and pain killers seem to have done the trick, and I'm relieved. I don't need anything making my meet with Barrett tonight any more complicated or daunting than it already is. I am nervous, the unknown always makes me nervous, and the wait for the unknown is, as always, nerve-racking and no doubt much worse than what I am actually going to face.

I get the feeling the only reason for meeting me there is for him to watch my reactions as he pushes me. Is he looking for me to show him something he can trust or relate to? He will have his people watching, no doubt, hidden in the shadows. I can't imagine after I saw him flanked by the big guy dressed in black that he would ever do something like this without cover. They will be watching me and watching for any sign that I didn't come alone or that I've tipped off the police. I'll be in this alone.

"You will need to wear your contact lenses and keep your earpiece activated. We will monitor everything, but there is no way we can cover you without drawing attention. You can't take any weapons, except the ghost knife. He's going to try to intimidate you and provoke you, and you are going to have to let him, but not too much. He knows you are not weak; he chose a meeting place where you killed a small army of men that were there to kill you, so he won't expect you to just bow down. Make him work for it, show emotion but keep control. You will know what he wants from you; you just need to show balance, make it believable. This is just another test he is throwing at you, and we can be sure there will be more," Lambert explains in his almost hypnotic monotone voice, and I nod, my head a buzz of 'what if's.'

"What if he provokes me too much, and I lose it at him? It's not exactly a place full of happy memories, which is what he is counting on," I ask Lambert, but Dixy is the one that answers.

"We will be monitoring your heart rate and stress levels through your watch; you may have to lose it because that might be what he wants, but we will talk you down if you are losing it at the wrong time. Trust yourself, Max; he wants to break you so he can put you back together in his own vision. You just have to make it seem like he is succeeding. He won't do it all at once, or he risks you pulling back. You will be able to see his manipulation. You *are* ready."

I lean forward at the kitchen table with a sigh, rubbing my eyes, and I feel a giant encouraging hand on my shoulder. Alfred, lending me his strength as always.

"Alright, so what's the plan?"

We talk through everything, all the behaviours and body language to watch out for, both his and my own. Dixy and Alfred will be in my ear mostly while Lambert examines every detail of the video link through my contact lenses in real time. Lexi is on route to Bosnia to question the Agents that last spoke to the man that died after Barrett's reconditioning. She won't be monitoring the meet. I'll drive my truck to the meet, activate my earpiece, and from then on, I am on my own.

I have to make him trust me; that is my objective. Gain more trust, and it's a step closer to The Culling. In my head, though, all I can think is the more he trusts me, the closer I get to this…reconditioning, and that terrifies me. I still don't feel ready for that, and I have to wonder if I ever will.

I take a walk around the grounds, giving myself a chance to process. The physical movement helps, and so does the privacy and freedom to be able to let myself show a little fear without the eyes of everyone on me. The last thing I need is for them to doubt me now.

When I reach the back fence, I'm not surprised to find Dixy there waiting for me. I walk over to her, lean against the fence, and stand shoulder to shoulder with her.

"What's on your mind, monkey butt?"

"I'm okay, just processing." I huff, knowing lying to her is pointless.

"Pants on fire, Agent Scott. We both know the plan is pretty simple, and you're very well prepared and aware of what's coming. Lying to your instructor is pointless; lying to your friend is just down right an-noy-ing," she emphasises.

I groan loudly, and she chuckles but falls silent quickly, waiting for me to talk. She doesn't watch me. Somehow, I think she knows I find that more difficult when I am trying to talk about what's eating at me.

"I want to do it right tonight, but if I do, I am one step closer to the reconditioning."

"That is something to be afraid of. No one can fault you for that, Max."

"I'm not…" I start, my voice coming out with an edge.

Dixy moves her hand from the fence, wraps it around my wrist, and I take a deep breath, calming myself.

"Yes, you are, and that's okay. When tonight is over, the reconditioning will be our focus. I have a plan, and we will do all we can to prepare you. But I know that when it comes down to it, no amount of preparation is going to get you through it. The only thing that will is your strength and your fight, and you have that in spades."

"I think you overestimate me. I know he can't do worse than I've already had, but I'm not used to…*that*, anymore. Prison almost broke me because I didn't have the strength of mind that I needed to get through it, and now, I have a lot more to lose," I admit.

"You are not talking about the pain, are you? You are worried about the same thing that Alfred is. That you will lose yourself."

I just nod. I didn't even realise quite how worried about it I was till now. The more time I spend with Anna - the more scared I am that I'll lose myself and that she will lose me too. I promised I'd never leave her again, but what if that isn't within my control? Anna has always been able to bring me back from the darkness inside, but how many times can I fall down that rabbit hole before it is just two hard to claw myself back up?

"It is…gorgeous to see the side of you that girl brings out. You light up, and I see the playful side of you that was always there but hidden somehow. She gives you strength," Dixy assesses, giving my wrist a squeeze, and I turn my head to look at her. Her eyes look haunted and sad.

"You all do that, in your own ways. Especially you, you creepy little weirdo. Your friendship means a lot to me."

She smiles at me warmly, her eyes welling, and then she looks away laughing.

"Soppy git," she jibes.

"Oh, shut up. You love it. I see your misty eyes over there."

"You are imagining things, Max. You're too late; I'm totally over you."

I chuckle, her avoidance of intimacy coming out in its usual quick-witted snipes. She is a good friend, good people. Like the many other good people that surround me. I know I'm lucky to have them; I just hope I don't let them all down.

Dixy steps out in front of me, her eyes determined and her hand still holding my wrist, and she speaks fiercely.

"I don't underestimate you; you're much stronger than you realise. We won't let you lose yourself and neither will Anna. That girl has more strength than I ever would have given her credit for, and she adores you... Don't you tell her I said that!" she warns, and I snort. "Use her as your anchor; use all of us. When you feel like you're losing your way, we will ground you. Trust that...trust us. You've got this, one battle at a time, and while you have it, we will have you."

She holds my gaze as my eyes become tight. I nod with a clenched jaw and look away.

"Thank you…"

"Don't mention it. I have left some clothes for you to wear in the barn. Just a selection of plain clothes, but they are your style. You only have combat clothes here, and you can't wear those to see Barrett. Make sure you hide that arm and wear your boots. You can keep the clothes; the jumpers are Kevlar lined. I will leave you be. You have a couple of hours to prepare. If you need anything I will be here."

"I thought you wanted to run through some more exposure?"

"I think you have enough on your mind for now. It can wait till tomorrow."

Dixy walks down the hill back towards the farm, and I watch her leave. The sky is getting darker, and I have just under two hours before I have to leave for Eastfields Street. My heart palpitates unevenly inside my chest, and I take slow, deep breaths as I try to calm it. I can't let this fear dominate me. This is not the reconditioning; this is just a chat with dear old Dad. The overly tactile, raving lunatic with eyes that resemble mine. My skin crawls. I need to get a handle on that too; shuddering at his touch is not a convincing move.

I make my way down to the barn, my feet drag with every step. I'm starting to feel sluggish again, and my skin stings as my clothes rub against it. It feels like my clothes are made out of sandpaper, and by the time I make it to the barn, I'm sweating, and my arm is throbbing in rhythm to the beat of the pounding in my head. I knock back more pain killers and lay on the sofa, my legs curled up into my chest.

Something is definitely not right; I don't feel good. My muscles ache, and I feel hot and cold all at once. My arm feels tight, and hot pain shoots down to my wrist whenever I move it. I close my eyes and will the pain killers to kick in again. The anxiety is tightening my chest and making me wheeze. I need to get a grip; I don't have time for whatever this is.

The barn door opens, and I hear Anna approach. She puts her hand on my face, and I open my eyes. "Hey beautiful," I croak.

"Mac, you are burning up again. What's going on? You can't meet Barrett like this."

"I just took some more pain killers, and I'll be fine in a bit. It's not like I can call in sick. Don't worry; it's nothing. I just need a minute."

Anna moves away and walks over to the sink, turns on the tap, and soaks a flannel. When she returns and starts dabbing it on my head and neck, I moan at the relief.

"Ugh, that's good."

"Just close your eyes for a bit. Don't worry, I'll make sure you are up in plenty of time. *Don't* argue. I'm not happy about you going, but it isn't like I can stop you. The least you can do is rest for me," Anna demands, but her voice is soft, loving.

"I can do that."

The cold against my skin feels so good. I just want more, lots more. My eyes close, and I feel the pain in my arm start to melt away. Anna disappears off, and I hear the tap running. When she comes back, I feel her wrap it around the back of my neck, and I shiver. She strokes my face, and this time, I fall straight to sleep.

***

"Dixy, she is running a fever. She isn't well; she shouldn't go!" Anna hisses.

"Is she showing any other symptoms?" Dixy enquires.

"She hasn't told me anything; she just says she's tired. There is no way that's just tiredness. She was on fire and white as a sheet."

"I hear you, Anna, and believe me, if I could stop it, I would, but there's no way to contact Barrett. No one can go in her place, and there are too many lives riding on this. You said the fever has broken. We just need to get her through the meet, and then we can deal with whatever is going on with her," Dixy assures, and Anna growls.

I pull myself upright on the sofa. My clothes are sweaty, and I feel gross, but I feel a lot better than I did. I rub my eyes and get to my feet slowly, my head still swimming a little.

"I'm fine; I am good to go. How much time do I have?" I croak, and they both turn and look at me.

"You have to leave in 15 minutes if you want to be there before Barrett, presuming he doesn't get there early," Dixy informs me.

"Alright, then I need to get changed."

Dixy leaves the barn, and I feel Anna's eyes on me as I walk over to the sink and splash cold water on my face. I find the clothes Dixy left on the arm of the sofa. I lift my jumper up and over my head with my good arm, and then Anna is there, carefully pulling it down my arm. She helps me change into clean clothes, then I sit back down and watch her worried face as she laces up my boots. She looks up at me, shuffling forward between my legs, and she rests her arms on my thighs. The way she is looking at me, the fight I see in her eyes as she tries to keep her composure, makes me never want to leave her again.

"It will be alright; I'll get back as quick as I can."

"I'll be waiting," she whispers, and then she gets to her feet and walks slowly out of the barn. I don't watch her leave; I can already feel the worry she is struggling with, and my resolve is shaky enough. I get to my feet, pick up the little black box that houses all my contact lenses, and I put a pair in. My eyes must be a little dry; they feel scratchy at first, but they soon settle. My feet move with more confidence than I feel as I walk my way out of the barn. Alfred approaches me with a bear hug which I gladly take.

"It's your arm, isn't it?" he grunts discreetly.

"Think so."

"Get the job done and get home. We will sort it," he assures, and I nod, letting him go.

I walk away, and I don't look back. Too quickly, I am pulling out of the drive and watching the farm disappear in my rear-view mirror. The anxiety hits my pounding heart hard. I've left just in time; I should just barely have enough time to get there before 8pm. I'm not trying to beat Barrett there; something tells me he will be there ahead of time. My fists grip the steering wheel too hard as I feel the doom begin to wash over me. The tendrils of darkness are creeping up, but I can't succumb to them. Tempting but I am going to need my emotions if I'm going to be convincing, so I just keep breathing and driving as I try to hold back the nagging thoughts that are feeding my self-doubt.

"I can do this. I have to do this. I *will* do this."

I drive deeper into the centre of London, and darkness has fallen, sucking the colour from everything in sight. My breath shakes out of my mouth in shivery clouds as the iciness of the wintery night sets in. I welcome it; the cold has always been calming for me. Plus, if it keeps the fever at bay, it is worth every shuddering moment.

"I am a mouse, and I *will* shout about this house," I chant.

A mantra that my mum used to say to me whenever I was scared of something as a kid. Knowing I'll be seeing Barrett forces her face to the front of my mind. How much of the monster inside him will he reveal now that we'll be alone? I have no idea what to expect. All I know is I hope it's over quickly. My head swims as I drive, not making me feel altogether safe behind the wheel. I feel weary and weak, and all I can do is hope the pain killers I took last long enough to get me through this.

"Mac, do you read?" Alfred sounds in my ear.

"Yeah, loud and clear. I'm two minutes out."

"We know, you doughnut. We can see what you see," Dixy jibes.

I look up to the rear-view mirror, and I lift my middle finger giving her the bird, and quickly put my eyes back on the road.

"Oh, you are in trouble, Agent Scott!" Dixy threatens, and I chuckle.

"Audio and visual…confirmed." Lambert manages through his laughter.

My heart begins to pound as I slow down the truck and pull into Eastfields Street. I come to a stop just outside the brewery, and the memories start to flow. The police caution tape has all been removed, but from what I can see down the street, it still looks like a warzone. I peer out at the brewery, and the memories flood me – of Alisha, Jakub but mostly Tomasz. I flinch as his eyes invade my mind, and I look away as my finger and thumb pinch together.

"We are with you, Max," Dixy sounds, her voice firm and calm.

I pull out the small torch I had stashed in the glove box, get out of the car, and face the brewery. The entrance is completely caved in where I blew the doors with C4; my only option is to go round the back. I stand completely still and listen as an eerie feeling creeps over me. Out the corner of my eye, I see a tiny movement.

"I'm being watched," I mumble, trying not to move my lips.

"We saw. Not surprised he didn't come alone," Alfred confirms.

My feet start moving me forwards. They crunch on brick dust and rubble with every step I take, and it's so loud in the silence. I move down the side of the brewery and stop as the memory hits. My hand plunging the knife deep into the man's throat while my other hand gags his screams. The vision is so vivid, I can almost feel the warmth of his blood spraying over my hand from his throat. I stand at the back door, hesitating. It was right there I sat, feeling I was dead for sure. I remember the pain, the fear that I would never see Anna again.

"If there is a way through this alive, I will find it, Anna - I promise you."

I shake away the memories and push through the door, clicking on the torch as I go. I see the metal steps on either side of me that lead to the balcony that skirts all around the space; the huge copper tanks look creepier in the dark. Instinctually, I go the same way I did on that fateful day, moving to the right and following the wall along. My legs feel weak and shaky. My feet pound against the metal grate of the balcony floor too loudly, and the sound echoes.

I hold the guard rail and pause as my head spins but only for a moment. I need to keep moving. The worry in my chest tingles as I realise that the pain killers are already beginning to wear off. At the end of the balcony, I reach the top of the stairs, and I freeze. My stomach swoops horribly as I see the dark bloodstain at the bottom of the stairs. In my mind, I see him crumpled at the bottom of the stairs, a wedding band on a dead man's finger. I drop to the step, sitting down hard, my eyes transfixed.

"Max, is everything okay?" Dixy asks.

"Just give her a minute. There are a lot of things to haunt her in that place. Kid, remember the code. If you can't talk but need to answer a question, just cough once for yes or twice for no. Are you rubbing some dirt in it?" Alfred grumbles.

"Ahem."

"Good job, kid."

My hand grips the handrail as I pull myself back up to my feet, and I make my way down the stairs, stepping over the bloodstain because, in my mind's eye, he is still lying there. I turn the corner and see the door with the small window that I saw Alisha through. The glass is gone, and the door is barely holding onto its hinges. The wooden kegs still line the walls, and I take a deep breath as the memories invade me.

"That's the room. Barrett should be in there," I hear Alfred confirm.

Now more than ever, I long to be home and in the arms of one gorgeous red head. I don't want the memories that come with this room; now that I'm here, I feel a fool. I should have come here to face this before I came to meet him. I can feel the burn of the fever beginning to return as sweat beads at the back of my neck. My head spins, and I hold the wall and lean my forehead against the cool hard surface.

"Ugh..."

"What's happening? I can't see anything; her eyes must be closed," Lambert reports.

"Kid, is that fever coming back?" Alfred asks.

"Ahem."

"Damn it…"

I open my eyes and push forward. The door creaks as I force it open and enter the control room. Walking forwards into the room, I am hit with a barrage of memories. They are like echoes, faint sounds. Manifestations and spirits of a past life I still see as clearly as if it were happening right now. I force my index finger and thumb together hard to block them. It works, mostly. I can still see the frozen shock on Jakub's face, the terror on Alisha's, and the pain on Tomasz' as I pull the blade slowly out of his ribcage, but the effect is lessened by the flicker of the good memory I force into my mind's eye.

"There must be a lot of memories for you here," Barrett muses softly as he comes out from the shadows. I look in the direction of the sound of his voice.

"Yes. It makes me wonder why you chose this place to meet? They aren't good memories; you must know that."

"I do. They may not be good memories, but maybe you are looking at this from the wrong… perspective. I chose this place because it is ground zero. The moment of complete collision, the moment you rose like a phoenix from the flames. You see, no one can doubt your strength after surviving that boat, but this place shows more than your strength…" Barrett speculates in a pompous tone. He steps forwards and stops close enough that I can see him clearly. He is watching me intently, his eyes unreadable. I look down, trying to convey pain and discomfort at being here. It isn't difficult to do so.

"It shows your animal instinct; it shows that you're a formidable force…just like *me.* The difference is, I embrace my dark side, but I don't think you do. I can see it in your eyes, McKenna. You reject the monster within you that created this carnage. Why? Don't you see that if you were to, instead, *embrace* that darkness, you would be at peace? More than that, you would be savagely unstoppable. Who would dare threaten you again?"

God, he likes the sound of his own voice.

"The threat is over. I killed them all,"

"The threat is never over!" Barrett barks, and I look up at him. His eyes bear down on me coldly, and I want to cringe away as I see the monster in his eyes beginning to make its appearance.

"Yes, you destroyed your enemy, but do you feel better for it?!" he presses, taking another step towards me.

"No…"

"Why? They no longer threaten you. You snubbed out each and every one of them. So why don't you feel better?" Barrett goads.

"I don't…know."

"Yes, you do. Come on, McKenna!? Don't be so weak. The person that did this isn't weak! You executed them! The people that stole you away and took your life, that tortured you! You tore them to pieces so why don't you feel better?!"

My mind is reeling, I don't know what the answer is, and the more he badgers me, the angrier I get and the harder it is to think clearly.

"WHY!?"

"Killing them doesn't delete what they did to me! That will be with me always! There is no peace from that!" I spit venom.

Barrett's features soften to a calm mask as my chest heaves with anger. He wants me angry; that is what this is. Anger I can do.

"You are angry. That's good. Anger I can work with; anger I understand. I built my foundation using the anger I had burning inside of me, and that same anger is burning inside you right now. So, tell me, who are you angry at?"

"At them. How could I not be?" I shrug, looking away from him. I know what he wants and that is not the answer, but I need to make him work for it.

"No, it's bigger than that. They're dead. You may hold the memories and bear the scars, and that may be where your anger began, but it is not the source of the anger burning inside of you now. Tell me, who are you angry at?" Barrett probes as steps forward and pushes me hard against the chest.

"What the fuck is wrong with you?!"

"Tell me, who are you angry at?" he goads, his eyes cold and wide, and he pushes me again. The anger flares, and I step towards him and push him back forcefully.

"Back off!"

"Oh, there she is. There is the monster in your eyes. I knew she was in there somewhere; that's who I want to see. Let her out – I would like to meet her." Barrett smiles at me savagely, his handsome face twisted by sick delirium.

"You don't know what you're talking about."

"Yes, I do. Now answer me! Who are you angry at?!"

Barrett steps forward, pushing me hard in the chest again, the impact not especially hard but enough to jolt through my aching muscles as I try to stay on my feet. I glare at him, jaw clenched, and I hold my ground. He swings his arm back and slaps me around the side of my head, hard and fast.

"Tell me!"

Fury seethes inside my chest, and I lunge for him, grabbing him by the collar, and I ram him hard against the wall. His eyes burn into me but not with rage – with smug satisfaction.

"Everyone! The whole fucking world! How easily was I lost? How quickly was the search called off? Why did no one find me?! How did no one find the sick fucks that destroyed me? Why did I have to end this myself?! I was forced to end this myself and then they locked me away to rot for it. As if I had a choice!"

I drop his collar and walk away wide eyed, dropping to my knees dramatically. My head spins, and my heart pounds unevenly. The fever is really helping me sell it. Sweat is pouring down my back. I lift my hand to wipe my brow and almost cry out as pain shoots down my arm.

"Damn she is good. Well done, Max," Dixy encourages.

I'm not good. The anger burns in my belly, and my own resentful words rattle me as I realise that not all of that was an act. Barrett walks around to face me; he holds his hand out, and I hesitate before I take it and allow him to pull me to my feet. He pulls me by the hand and drags me in for a hug. I tense and then force myself to relax. My insides crawl at his touch, at the smell of his overly sweet aftershave. I feel his hand patting my back, and I want to snap it off.

"You're angry at the world because they let you down. Every system that was in place to protect you failed. You were lost, and no one came for you. They gave up on you; they left you to snivel in your own piss like you were nothing because to them, you are *nothing*. The world doesn't care about you because it is run by the rich and selfish. To them, you don't affect their bottom line. Why should they care?" Barrett muses in a soft patronising tone.

"He's gaslighting you, Max - trying to destabilise you so he can twist your beliefs. He will try to make you question your own judgement. Make him think he's succeeding," Dixy voices furiously.

Barrett finally pulls back, but he keeps hold of me. His hands on my biceps, and the pain in my arm starts flourishing. He looks at me intensely, and I hold his glare with unsure eyes.

"They never came for you… but I did. You're my daughter. I left you, yes, but I never stopped watching over you; I didn't abandon you. We're both angry at the world because every system within it is broken and corrupt. The only difference between us is that I found a place to direct my anger, and you haven't. This world is full of degenerate scum, of leeches and parasites and evildoers that are capable of destroying lives with their cancers, and they lose no sleep over it. They are corrupting this world, and even worse, they breed more parasites to suck the life out of it."

Barrett's grip on my arm gets tighter, and I can't take the pain. I look down, and make a frustrated noise, pulling myself out of his grasp and stepping away from him.

"I didn't come here to be spoken to in riddles and elusive hints! You talk of the triangle of truth. Why not just speak it now? Tell me what you want from me! You tried to save me; I will always be grateful for that, but that will only afford you so much. I want the truth. What do you want from me?!"

My impatience is not put on; I am feeling more ill by the second. The pain in my arm is so unbearable and every muscle aches. The fever is in full swing, and I'm terrified I won't be able to get through this. Barrett looks at me, his eyes analysing my face. The pain in my arm is good for one thing. It's very easy to convey emotional pain when you are in physical pain.

"Do you want a place to direct that anger? You know what I am, you know what I fight for, and you know that the path I am fated to walk *has* and *will*, cost lives. A cost that's for the greater good. We, The Culling, have a mission, yes, but we are also a brotherhood, a family. Inside our circle, you would never feel alone. The question is, do you want a seat at the table? What I want is you by my side, taking your rightful place at my mantel. As my daughter and as the enforcer of my will."

Barrett walks towards me, closing the gap between us once again; he looks at me with obvious fake affection and puts his hand on my clenched jaw.

"As I stare into those eyes that are so similar to my own, there is no doubt in my mind that you are capable. The monster I need lives there inside you, but will you embrace it? Will you help me cull those who are destroying our world? Does it burn inside you hot enough – the need for vengeance on those evildoers? The very people who abandoned you? I ask you in the place where your last crusade ended - will you join mine?"

My heart is pounding inside my chest as I realise that this is the moment, the moment I must sell so perfectly. My mouth turns dry as I lift my injured arm slowly, flexing the muscle in my bicep and causing the pain to flare and my eyes to water. I lay my hand over his holding my face.

"Yes, Father, I will," I choke, and Barrett's eyes flash in victory. The smirk that pulls on his lips is repulsing me, but I hold my intense and teary stare.

"You will be tested. It takes commitment, absolute strength of will, and total belief and fidelity in our cause. Many before you have failed," Barrett alludes, and I let go of his hand.

"Then you will be all the prouder when I succeed," I growl.

Barrett's smile is vile; he really is insane. My legs are beginning to shake; I need this to end now. My head is swimming, and it is becoming impossible to maintain eye contact.

Oh, God – don't pass out.

"I have faith in you. I must return to Bosnia; I'll be gone for just over a week. On my return, you will be tested. You will not be warned. It will happen exactly when I plan it to. Be prepared; these tests may seem harsh, maybe even a little cruel, but each step is vital in the journey into your rebirth. You *must* be strong, and you *must* prevail. Only then can you truly be free of the chains that bind you. Only then will you see the *truth*."

My stomach swoops, terror runs through me like a jolt of electricity, and there is no hiding it. I look away, and the simple movement sends my head spinning. I can't hold on much longer.

"It's okay to be scared, McKenna, but that fear won't last forever. You will join our family where you will never have to be scared again," Barrett says softly, and I look back at him.

"I won't fail you. You've given me purpose and your faith; I take that seriously," I mutter evenly, and he nods at me, giving me a childlike grin that looks so sweet that it doesn't look like it belongs on his face.

"Then I shall take my leave. I'll see you soon…Mac. You can be sure of that."

Barrett walks away, and I freeze in place, waiting for him to disappear out the door. I wait, my breath held, my body rigid. I stumble forwards against the wall and brace myself against it as my entire body begins to shake.

"Ugh, fuck."

"Max…we are so proud of you; you could not have done better," Dixy says warmly.

"I…uh…"

"Max? Are you okay?"

I stumble out the control room to check that he's definitely gone. Every footstep I take sends jolting pains up my muscles, the sweat pouring off me rapidly and stinging my eyes. I drag myself up the metal steps and across the balcony. The floor beneath me warps as my vision bends with sickness.

"Kid, do you read? Answer us please."

"Her heart rate is through the roof. Max, do you read?!" Dixy says urgently.

I burst out the back door of the brewery, and the cold air hits my face. I breathe it in and stumble towards the truck. My chest tight with wheezes; my arm is on fire. I open the door and stumble into the truck.

"I read. I had to make…sure I was…clear."

I struggle with inserting the key into the ignition, and my vision blurs nauseatingly as the truck moves forward. Panic pounds through me; something is wrong. I feel more ill than I ever have in my life.

"Pa, n-not going to make it to the farm. Something is wrong – I don't feel good," I blurt fearfully.

"Get yourself to the apartment. We're coming, kid. It's alright. Open all the windows in the truck and just get there in one piece," Alfred orders, and I could kick myself for not thinking of that. The air blasts in and clears my head a little. My driving is dangerous, and all I can do is pray I don't hit anyone. The road in front of me is blurring; the lights from lamp posts and oncoming cars streak in long bright glows that burn my eyes.

"Keep talking, Max. We need to know you are safe," Dixy prompts.

"N-nearly there."

It is hard to talk. The dizzy nausea is making my mouth feel tired and dry. I am scared; I can't deny that. My arm is burning, the pain is incredible, and it is throbbing so hard, I feel like I should be able to see the throb like a beating heart. I screech to a stop on my driveway and stagger out of the truck. I make it about four steps before the world decides it is going to swoop to one side like a gigantic swing. I fall, landing flat on my face.

"Ugh, G-god."

"Mac, where are you?!" Alfred calls urgently.

"Home. It h-hurts. I need…is Anna there?" I whimper pathetically.

"Of course, she's here, darling. We won't be long," Alfred coos in his gruff voice.

I need to get off the ground. If I stay here, Alfred could run me over. I drag myself along the floor. It hurts. My skin feels like it is covered in sun burn, and I am dragging it along concrete. I push through, spit flying out of my mouth from the exertion, and I just about make it across my doorstep when my body gives up. The shakes rock through my body violently, jarring every aching muscle.

"P-p-please h-u-rry."

Fear grips me; I've never felt anything like this. Tears burn my eyes, and all I can do is shake. My teeth are chattering and my breaths are coming out ragged, and it is a lonely, pathetic feeling. Headlight's glow, whiting out my vision. I have never been so relieved to hear car doors slam.

"Mac!" Anna screeches.

"A-n-n-nna." I tremble as I feel her hands on my face.

"Oh, God…she's on fire. It's okay; we've got you," Anna coos as I grab the front of her shirt.

"Savannah, get the door open," Alfred commands. "Lambert, can you help?"

"It's alright, I've got her. Mac, I am going to lift you now, okay?" Lambert requests politely, but he doesn't wait for permission.

He slides his hands under me and lifts me with ease. Pain shoots up my arm, and I cry out; my body is rattling so hard it comes out in a strangled, vibrating wail. Lambert crosses the room fast and lays me down gently on the sofa. My vision spins in the movement, and I gag, but nothing comes up. Anna is at my side in seconds.

"You are going to be okay, baby."

"H-h-hurts."

"I know, I know…we're going to make it stop," she coos softly and looks behind her. "Pa?! Where is he?!" Anna shouts.

"He won't be long; he's gone to get some wet towels to bring her temperature down. Let me take a look at her."

Dixy kneels down next to Anna; she presses her fingers to my throat and holds them there, and holds her hand over my forehead.

"Hey rock star, it's all right. You will feel better soon." She smiles at me, but her eyes are clearly concerned as she turns to Anna.

"Her pulse is erratic, and her body isn't able to control the temperature spike, so she is convulsing. You need to keep her calm, and you need to get her jumper and jeans off. If we can bring the fever down, the shakes will stop. I need a first aid kit. Any ideas?"

"Bathroom, upstairs," Anna directs.

She looks at me with pained eyes, wiping the sweat and tears from mine. "I need to lift you up; we need to get your clothes off, okay?"

I nod, bracing myself as Anna pulls my jeans off, the shakes somehow becoming more violent. Then she slides her good arm under my shoulders, and she pulls me upright. She carefully peels the jumper off me, and I wince as she coaxes it off of my arm. I fall into her, my fists grabbing at the hem of her shirt, fear rocking me riotously. She pulls back, holding my face, and her eyes are determined on mine.

"S-s-cared."

"Hey…it's okay. I'm here, and there is *nothing* in the world that could make me leave you right now. I need you to trust that, okay?"

"O-o-kay," I manage, and she pulls me to her gently, holding me.

"That's good. I've got you. Jesus, you are soaked through. Pa! Hurry up!" Anna yells, and I wince at the loudness as it pounds in my head.

Anna lays me carefully back down, standing leant over me, and then she kisses my forehead lightly as she holds my face still. Her eyes glitter with tears as she strokes my face. Dixy returns at the same time as Alfred, and Anna moves out of the way. She kneels at the end of the sofa, and her arms curl over my shoulders. I wrap my hand around her arm and hold it tight as I wince at the cold, wet towels being laid over my legs and chest.

"Hey, kid, I know it hurts, okay, but I need to get that bandage off your arm. I can already see the swelling has tightened it. Dixy, if I hold her arm still, can you try cut it off? You got more of a delicate touch than me."

I feel giant hands holding me still, then I feel the cold metal of the scissors touch beneath the bandage.

"Arghh, God!"

"I know, I'm sorry, Max! I've almost got it." Dixy cringes.

I feel the bandage fall away but no relief. If anything, the pain is worse.

"Damn it. Dixy, can you get IV antibiotics?" Alfred growls. The worry in his tone is making me panic.

"Yes, I can! Callum!?" Dixy shouts.

"Wh-a-a-t's go-ing on, Pa?"

"You have a nasty infection, but Lambert is going to get you some IV antibiotics, and it will kick the crap outta' it. It will be fine, but I am going to have to wash out the wound, and it's going to suck. First, we are going to pound you with some of my kick arse pain killers. You remember them?" he says softly, and I nod.

After Alfred puts the pain killers in my mouth, Anna pours water in which I choke on, but thankfully, I manage to swallow the pills.

"Okay, kid, Anna is going to hold you nice and tight, and I'm going to clean your arm. I'll be as quick as I can, but feel free to call me every name under the sun. I won't take offence."

Anna leans forward so her cheek is against mine. Her arms cross over my heaving chest tightly. There is no warning. The pain is excruciating and not the kind of pain that knocks you out, the kind that makes you wish it did. My arm is burning as if someone poured acid over it, and I scream.

"It's okay. It will stop soon," Anna cries.

I pull at my arm and jerk, and then I feel more hands, small cold hands holding my arm still.

"Argh fuck!!!"

"Done! We're done, kid. Just got to wrap it loosely to keep it clean, but the hard part is done."

I sob into Anna's neck, all dignity well and truly lost.

"Pa, stop. Can you lift her up? I am getting on the sofa with her. She isn't shaking anymore; her fever has broken."

Alfred lifts me upright, and when I am lowered back down, I lay between Anna's legs, my head on her chest, her hand stroking my cheek.

"Close your eyes, baby. I'll be here when you wake up," she whispers.

Calm washes over me. Her touch is magical, and so are these painkillers.

Darkness.

Chapter 10

Expendable Asset Agent Scott

"Three bags? Surely that's overkill? I don't even know what's in them; I don't want to overdose her," Alfred hisses.

"Just trust me, big fella. The dose is correct, this stuff is amazing, and it is tried and tested. Lexi only gave it up because to her, Mac is now a priceless asset," Dixy whispers.

"She isn't an asset; she's family!"

"Easy, Alfred… You know I don't see her that way. She is my friend - I just had to play up to that to get Lexi to give up the medication. It isn't cheap stuff."

"I know, I'm sorry. I shouldn't have…it's been a long night."

"Don't mention it. I know you are worried, but she is going to be okay," Dixy soothes.

I open my eyes to disorientation; I'm no longer in the living room. The satin sheets are soft against my skin as I lay in my cloudlike bed. My body aches, but the pain is bearable; my head is fuzzy from the drug haze. I feel her hand laying on my chest and turn my head to see her lying beside me, her eyes flooding with relief as I look at her.

"You scared the hell out of me, Mac Scott," Anna gasps, exhaustion thick in her voice.

"I scared myself a little too, to be honest. Thank you for staying with me," I mutter, my voice a dry shriek.

She leans forward and gives me gentle kisses, sweet but still enticing.

"I wouldn't want to be anywhere else. As much as I hate seeing you hurt, it's nice that I get to be here for it. Even nicer that you seem to want me to be."

Her expression is serious, but her eyes are full of love. The way she is looking at me is enough to make my insides melt. Like I am precious, like I'm hers.

"You still doubt that? I've always wanted you to be here, Anna. Good or bad, I just want you."

"Ugh…stop being so God damn delicious. You're not well and making me want you right now is making me feel perverse!" she growls, her tone a lowering an octave, and I chuckle. Only Anna could make me tingle right now.

"Mm…I've never wanted to get better quicker."

"Well, that's good, because until you are better, you are not leaving this apartment, and neither am I."

"I don't expect you…" I begin, but she places her hand over my mouth, quieting me, and I chuckle, but she doesn't laugh. Her eyes are full of pain so raw, it silences me.

"I meant what I said; you scared the hell out of me. I felt completely helpless. You always seem so… unshakable. I've seen you in pain many times, but I've never seen you that scared. I'm not leaving you until I know you're okay again. Please don't ask me to."

"You were not helpless. I'm just embarrassed because you are right; I was scared. I'm not used to needing anyone, not like that, but I needed you - it just isn't always easy for me to admit that."

"Why?"

"You're not the only one that gets afraid of being left. I have my own reasons for fearing that. Admitting I need you feels like tempting fate."

She looks at me thoughtfully. At first, she is completely puzzled, then I see the recognition, and her eyes clamp closed.

"Because I left you…just before you went to prison. Ugh, you know, I've never regretted anything more in my God damn life," Anna groans, flinching at her own memories in unison with me.

"You shouldn't. I was going to prison; it was the right thing for you."

"I was being a coward; it wasn't right for me at all."

"Anna, we talked about this. It's in the past. I don't blame you; I never did. I just wanted you to be happy. I understood why you did what you did."

I can tell I am not getting through to her, but Alfred and Dixy approach the bed and end our conversation. It feels a little strange having them in my bedroom. Alfred looks so stressed it is making me sad just looking at him. Dixy doesn't look much better.

"Hey, how are you feeling, kid?"

"Like I was hit by a truck twice," I reply, and he chuckles.

"Well, Dixy is going to hook you up with some IV antibiotics. They should knock the infection out, but you are going to be out of commission for a few days."

My heart sinks. A few days? I'm not surprised, but now that I'm coherent and not racked with fever, Barrett comes straight to my mind. I only have about a week to prepare. Recovering could cut that time in half.

"I don't have much time; Barrett will be back in just over a week."

"Don't worry about that; this stuff is amazing. As long as we are careful and you do as you're told, then you will recover quickly. I have to administer these three IV bags one after another, so I'm going to make friends with your couch. When you are a bit stronger, we will talk about Barrett. Till then, you need to put it out of your mind and relax. You did incredible, Max, but now you need to get better," Dixy orders, giving me her best, 'don't mess with me' face.

Dixy hangs the IV bag off the top post of the four-poster bed. With a quick scratch, the needle is in my hand and taped secure. The liquid invading my veins is cold, and within minutes, I am shivering. I send Alfred home to bed; it is almost morning, and no one but me has slept, although I still feel exhausted. Dixy disappears downstairs to catch up on some sleep with orders to be woken when the IV bag runs out, and I am left alone with Anna, who looks about fit to burst with tears.

"Anna, you have to let this go. It doesn't matter anymore."

"Of course, it matters! You are scared I will leave you because I already did. First, when you went to prison, then again with Danni, and because of that, you worry about needing me just in case I disappear on you again. I could feel it coming off of you; you were scared I was going to leave you!" Anna rants furiously, pacing around the room.

"Can you come here, please?"

Anna walks over to the bed and sits facing me, but her head is bowed, and she is tightly wound like a spring. I'm struggling to understand why this is such a big deal.

"Most people fear getting left. It isn't your fault; things happened. Besides, I had abandonment issues long before I met you. First with the absent terrorist dad and then with the boat. I mean, really, what chance did I have?" I joke, but she doesn't laugh; she doesn't even look up. "Why is this bothering you so much?"

Anna shuffles closer and takes my hand gently not to knock the IV line that is plumbed into my vein. I'm choosing to ignore its presence because looking at it makes me queasy. Instead, I watch Anna struggle with herself.

"I know what that fear feels like. I don't want you feeling that. So, please don't freak out when I tell you this."

There is no way not to freak out when someone says, 'don't freak out.' Just the words are enough to make my heart rate pick up speed.

"You don't need to be scared of me leaving you. You are…*it* for me. I know that sounds sudden and completely mental. Please don't freak out, but I just know, you're all I want and that isn't going to change. You are my endgame… There's no way I could leave you now, not unless you wanted me to," Anna speaks clearly and calmly, and then she goes back to looking at my hands.

My heart bursts with both shock and a powering gush of love. I feel tears prick my eyes as I watch her keep her eyes down, clearly terrified to look at me. My body throbs with tingles because suddenly, I know that everything inside me has changed. I'm not afraid anymore. I sit up in the bed and wince as my muscles protest at the movement, and then I hold my hands out to her. She takes them, and I pull her towards me till she is straddled on my lap. She sees the tears in my eyes and fear washes over her face.

"What…" she begins.

"Now who is the blind one?" I ask, and she frowns. I dip my forehead against hers, and the tremble in my chest shakes my voice. "I don't know what is going to happen next. Everything always feels so full on and unpredictable. The only thing I know for sure is… whatever it is – I want it to be with you. I hope you know what you are saying because…you are my happy ending, Savannah. It's you and me, and I'll always want it to be."

I kiss her before she has the chance to speak with purpose. Her breath comes out in adorable, ragged huffs as she kisses me, cries, and moans all at once. It is the kind of kiss that should definitely be done in private, messy, loud, and passionate. The kind of kiss that makes you feel like you can't bear the intensity of it but also you can't bear to stop. Through every stroke of my lips, I feel the ache inside me being soothed, and yet somehow, I still feel an inferno of desperation blazing inside me for more of her.

"Ugh, God…please…Mac. Don't ever stop…needing me…" Anna gasps between kisses. "I need you…and I can't…s-stop."

"I couldn't if I wanted too…believe me, I've tried. But I don't have any reason to try anymore."

Anna buries her face in my neck. Her arms wrap around me gently, and we stay that way, enjoying the moment and catching our breath for quite some time. It is long enough that the sight of her collarbone, exposed by how loosely her jumper hangs off one shoulder, becomes too hard to resist. I dip my head and map her shoulder with my lips, delighting in the sound of her quickening breath. She has the most gorgeously prominent collar bones that I've spent too long desiring. I can't stop myself from adoring it with my tongue. Anna's hand dives into my hair, a whimper escaping her mouth. I kiss and suckle my way up her neck, pausing to nibble on her ear lobe, and her thighs clench. The sound of the needy groan building in her throat is pulsing throbs between my legs.

"God, Mac…I need you to touch me *so bad.* So…you should… probably…"

My lips trail along her jaw line, and I pause just short of her lips, my nose brushing hers, our breath hot and laboured. Her words and the desperate dragging in her gravelled tone are enough to make me squirm. More than that is the need for closeness with her that only getting lost in her body will bring me.

"I'm not going to apologise…" I grin into her lips, kissing her lovingly. "Not when I'm aching for you so badly."

Anna's groans against my lips, and I shiver as her hands slide down my neck. Then her kiss becomes gentle and hesitant. She pulls back, peering at me with thoughtful eyes and huge, aroused pupils. Anna her skims her hand down the back of my t-shirt, then across my forehead.

"You're clammy; I think your fever is spiking again."

"I don't feel hot. Ugh, no, I can't...n-not again."

"Hey…it's okay; your pain killers are just wearing off. The drip bag is almost empty. I'll go get Dixy, and we will stop it before it starts," she reassures.

Anna disappears downstairs, and I'm left to try to get a grip on myself. To be this scared of a fever is ridiculous, but the lack of control I had over my body. The fear I wouldn't last out before my meet with Barrett ended. The fear I wouldn't make it home in one piece. The pain that tore through my body as it shook so violently and unnaturally is still only a couple of hours fresh. My arm begins to throb again in beat with the pounding of my head, and I know it's coming back. Anna returns with a groggy Dixy, and she touches my forehead the same way Anna did, and then she swaps out the IV for a fresh bag.

"Your temperature is definitely going back up, but we have caught it in time. Take these and drink the whole glass of water. How are you feeling?" Dixy asks, and I swallow the pain killers immediately; I can't knock them back quick enough. I sip the water, and it makes me shiver.

"Not…brilliant. Arm and head are pounding, dizzy again, but I don't feel hot like I did before. I'm actually cold."

Anna pushes me backwards against the pillows and pulls the duvet back up over me before disappearing off to the bathroom. Dixy perches on the end of the bed awkwardly; I can tell she is uncomfortable and exhausted.

"The IV is probably helping keep the fever at bay, but the pain killers should stop the spike altogether. If it doesn't, then get Anna to wake me up again, but I'm pretty sure those pain killers could knock out a fever ten times over." Dixy yawns.

"I'm sorry you have to be here, but…I'm glad you are too. I hope you know I appreciate it."

"Yeah, well, I have to keep you around. Who else am I going to rag on? You can't just bug out on me; it will spoil all my fun."

"That might just be the worst deflecting I've ever seen, and I thought you was meant to be a good liar."

"Oh, come off it, Max! Nothing beats your 'It is just low blood sugar' deflection after you passed out!" she teases, her voice imitating mine in a not so favourable light. I laugh, but then my head starts to swim heavily.

"Woah…"

"Hello painkillers," Dixy giggles.

"How are we doing?" Anna asks, returning with a cold, wet flannel.

"Great, awesome sauce, super-duper-reindeer-pooper," I ramble.

"Pain killers are in full swing," Dixy says, winking at Anna, and they both laugh animatedly.

Dixy goes back downstairs to get more sleep, and Anna dabs the flannel over my face. I watch her, examining every perfect line and curve. She is so gentle in everything she does.

"You need to sleep, beautiful," I croak.

"I'll sleep when you do, which by the look of it isn't long away."

Anna climbs into bed with me. She holds the side of my neck, running her thumb up and down my jawline as my eyes start to droop. She keeps her body away, trying not to overheat me.

"I love the magic that makes you," I mumble as sleep overcomes me.

***

The next 48 hours are very repetitive and frustrating. Being in bed all that time, knowing that time is slipping away, that Barrett's return is just getting closer and closer, has been enough to make me go crazy, but I didn't. Anna never left my side; she kept my spirits up, kept me laughing, and kept me feeling safe at the toughest times. She took care of me in a way no one ever has, and that is the most frustrating part of all.

Ever since she spoke those words on that first horrific night, the words that melted away my fears and made me feel totally safe to need her, I've needed her so badly that the word frustration doesn't begin to cover it. Of course, I've been too ill to act on it, so when she walks around in my t-shirt and little boxers, completely unaware of how sexy she actually is, the desire burning in me just becomes all the more intense. Oh, how I want her.

Now though, after three days spent mostly in bed sweating out fevers, I'm finally allowed to go for a shower, and my God, do I need one. My arm feels slightly stiff, but the pain is gone, as is the swelling and gross puss that was apparently leaking from it. Very glad I never saw that. The fevers have stopped, and although I feel weak and wobbly, I am able to move around without aches in my muscles, and after a three day fast – my appetite is finally back.

Stepping into the shower makes my skin sing in jubilation. I don't have it anywhere near as hot as I usually would; the fear of bringing on a fever is still very much present. We are finally leaving the apartment today and going back to the farm. I've loved having Anna all to myself, but it really isn't the same when you are gross with illness. I'm keen for some normality and for her to see me looking and smelling much less vile. Lexi will be coming for a debrief. Although it is something that doesn't surprise me, I can't say I'm looking forward to it.

Alfred has promised us lunch when we arrive, and I really have my heart set on bacon. I step out the shower feeling much more human and relish in the spraying of my aftershave… Bad fever smell be gone! I look in the mirror and decide that a little make up is a must. I look much more like myself but still a little zombie-like around the eyes. Tonight, I'm taking Anna with me to see my mum on her birthday. No amount of makeup will stop her telling me I am too thin, but it can't hurt my case.

Soon, I'm dressed and ready, and when I get downstairs, I find Anna making us both a steaming hot latte. The smell of the bitter coffee makes my insides smile; I've missed coffee. She sees me coming, and her face lights up.

"You look gorgeous." She beams brightly, and I chuckle.

"That's way too generous, but you are cute for saying so."

I take a seat at the breakfast bar and take my first sip of something in three days that isn't water, and it is amazing. We leave the apartment, and the fresh air that hits me as I walk outside is invigorating. We set off towards the farm,

Anna's hand on my thigh as I drive, and my mind wanders, thinking about what today will bring.

The subject matter of Barrett has been strictly prohibited for the duration of my recovery as if not talking about it would stop me worrying. How could I not? He was pretty clear; whatever is coming my way will not be fun. Harsh and cruel were the words he used, and it makes my gut clench just thinking about it. Is this the dreaded reconditioning or just another step closer to it? I have to try to prepare for the worst, but how can I prepare for that?

I saw the monster in his eyes, his eyes that look like my own, and it made me want to claw at my own eyes just for bearing a resemblance. He's a mad man, and he totally believes in his own madness; it's clear that there isn't anything he won't do to further his cause. There is no line he won't cross. His words, or parts of them, are whizzing around my mind. They make me itch almost as much as his touch does.

I pull up on the drive at the farm, it's really good to see the place, especially the soft plume of smoke dancing up into the sky.

"I can feel it coming over you," Anna says softly, and I smile a little at all the memories of her saying that. Memories that no longer hurt.

"I know. I guess…you can only hide from reality for so long."

"You haven't been hiding. You think I don't know that he hasn't really left your thoughts? I don't see how he could after what he said to you," Anna remarks, and I whip my head around to look at her, dumbstruck.

"You were watching?"

"Of course, I was," she utters softly.

I thought, from how worried she was when I left, that watching it all happen was the last thing she would have done.

"You didn't say anything."

Anna turns to look at me, her eyes serious but warm. She is wearing one of my old band t-shirts and a pair of my jeans, and she looks so cute in them.

"Because when you are ready to tell me whatever it is that's getting to you, you will. Till then, I'll wait. You are, however, going to promise me that you will tell me *immediately* if you start to feel unwell again. You're not all the way back yet, and I don't want you slipping back because you pushed yourself too hard."

"Mm bossy."

I lean in and give her a cheeky kiss, short and sweet and as always, it leaves me wanting more. Then we set off for a walk down towards the fire pit. The welcoming smell of burning wood makes me feel at home; it is good to be back. It's as if the place itself gives me strength. As we draw nearer, we see Dixy and Lambert sitting around the fire pit, and they greet me with grins as I take a seat.

"Agent Scott, you are looking almost human again," Dixy jibes.

"Um thanks, I think."

"I'm glad you are back. With you gone, she was even more annoying than usual," Lambert gripes.

"Again…thanks, I think."

"Hey! I am not annoying," Dixy pouts.

"GRUBS UP!" Alfred shouts out of the kitchen door.

We make our way inside, and the smell of bacon makes me salivate. Alfred has pulled out all the stops, and my eyes widen at the sight of feast laid out on the kitchen table. Bacon, eggs, freshly baked bread, sausages, beans, tomatoes, hash browns, everything you could wish for from a hearty English breakfast.

"Pa, there is enough food to feed an army here," Anna points out.

"It's Mac's favourite. Thought I'd put a bit of extra effort in, you know. Help her back on her feet." He fidgets awkwardly.

"I know that, but how much do you think she can eat?" She giggles.

She is right; as much as I would love to take full advantage of the amazing spread, I'm disappointed with the amount of food I'm able to put away. My stomach must have shrunk, and I am so stuffed I feel verging on 'food coma' territory. Lambert, however, does not have this problem. He is already halfway through his second helping and showing no signs of stopping any time soon. Eventually, the table is cleared, and I can feel the tension in the room starting to build. It is great to be around everyone, but it's clear that the Barrett topic is on everyone's minds as we wait for Lexi to arrive.

"What time is she coming?" I ask Dixy.

"Any time now. We should probably go outside to meet her. You holding up okay?"

"I'm fine. I'll be even better when people stop asking me that."

Everyone makes their way outside and takes a seat around the fire pit just as we see Lexi's car pull up. My stomach tightens. I'm never sure what to make of Agent Holt. While she has done a lot for me, I can never quite get myself to trust her fully. Lexi approaches silently as always. She is wearing a long, heavy looking black coat. Her clothes are sensible, smart, and plain. Nothing flashy but they do also ooze of expense. She walks confidently to the empty chair opposite me, and everyone falls silent.

"Agent Scott, it's good to see you looking so well. From what I heard, you have had a rough week. I trust the recovery is going well?"

"Thank you. Yes, I'm feeling much better." I smile politely.

"Good, that's what I like to hear. Now, I've reviewed the footage of your latest meet with Barrett, and I have to tell you, I am very impressed with the progress you have made. He seems to be beginning to trust you, and things are moving quicker than I could have hoped for."

"I'm not sure he trusts me as much as he trusts his own ability to manipulate me. I think trust will only begin to develop after I pass whatever tests he has in store for me."

"I think you're probably right about that. Now, we do have eyes on him in Bosnia. The moment that he makes a move to return to the UK, we will know, and you will be notified. Unfortunately, that's the only real lead time that we can offer you," Lexi explains bleakly.

"It's better than no lead time."

Lexi nods, her face a smooth mask that is impossible to read. She leans forward and digs through her bag, pulling out a brown file.

"I have the coroner's report of the man that failed Barrett's reconditioning. It doesn't tell us too much but enough that it might be helpful to look at when it comes to preparing yourself for what is to come."

"I think you would be better off giving it to Dixy. Whatever is in that file, I'm sure can be applied to my training, but I don't need to see it."

"Fair enough. I have Lambert along with some of our behavioural analysts reviewing the footage. If there are any clues in what Barrett said, any tells in his behaviour that could give anything away of what his intentions are, we will find them. I did wonder, is there anything that stood out for you?"

“Most of it was raving madness but one thing stood out. He said he wants me to be the ‘enforcer of his will.’ That seemed a strange thing to say, almost like it was some kind of job title. Surely, *he* is the enforcer of his will? This is his screwed-up agenda, wanting me to join him - I understand. Wanting me to lead my generation under his regime - I understand, but being the enforcer of his will? That…almost sounds…”

“Like he wants you to kill for him? I thought the same, and when you consider the place, he chose to meet you and how much he mentioned your battle there and ‘the monster inside’ I can only surmise that’s exactly what he wants from you. The Culling works very similarly to any other organisation in the sense that there are job roles. Maybe the job role he expects from you is to intimidate people or even execute those who are disloyal or might be getting in the way of his cause.”

My stomach churns, and my heart thuds with a deep pound that hammers inside my ears. My eyes flick to Anna just for a second, and I see her mirroring my disgust.

“She’s not an assassin,” Alfred chimes in.

“No, we all know that, but that doesn’t mean that isn’t what he expects of her,” Lexi replies coolly.

“And what is it that MI5 expects of me?” I ask firmly, my eyes fixed upon Lexi’s. She holds my gaze with zero emotion, and the atmosphere has turned as icy as the chilly winters air.

“We are not there yet, Agent. For the moment, this is all just speculation. I suggest we table this conversation unless it becomes more than that. For now, your focus needs to be on the potential reconditioning that is looming and how you are going to pass it successfully. Where are we with the training regarding that?” Lexi asks turning to Dixy.

“There has been improvement, but there is only so much that can be done to desensitise Max without actually repeating those…acts, and I’m in no hurry to do that. I’m working on a plan; it shouldn’t take too much longer. If all goes well, then I’m confident that Agent Scott will pass the reconditioning,” Dixy explains vaguely.

Lexi nods thoughtfully, shifting around uncomfortably in her chair as she takes her focus from Dixy and back onto me. I can see that she's wrestling with something. For once, she doesn't look cold; she more resembles the woman I first met and ate KFC with in the police questioning room. I haven't seen that side of her for a while.

"Could I possibly have a moment alone with Mac?" she asks eventually.

Yep, something is definitely up.

Everyone leaves the fire circle and heads inside. I can feel from the tension in the air that they're not happy about it. I keep my eyes down while they leave, and when they are out of ear shot, I look back up at her, bracing myself.

"I don't want to see you subjected to any kind of unnecessary trauma, believe me. My concern is, though, if we don't subject you to it, will it be harder for you when The Culling eventually does? Or will it be easier? Only you can answer that, Mac. What do you need, to get through this? It's important that you're honest with me because this isn't just about passing the reconditioning. If they break you and you begin to divulge sensitive information, there is a protocol in place to protect MI5. A protocol I don't want to have to execute."

"What protocol?"

"It is called, the gag protocol. If you are seen to be divulging too much information, we remotely activate the cyanide needle inside your boot, silencing you."

I laugh darkly. "Now why doesn't that surprise me?!" I scoff with edge.

"Mac, that is the last thing I want. I meant what I said to you that first day. I want to see the day you get to live in peace, but that won't happen if you keep looking at me like I'm the enemy."

Her tone is soft, she even looks like she means it, but I am livid. There is an odd sting of betrayal in my chest, and I feel inches away from blowing. Even the people on my side are willing to kill me.

"I'm not looking at you like you are the enemy, Lexi. I am looking at you like someone I don't know how to trust!"

"Then tell me why you can't because that needs to change," she says diplomatically. Her calm is just winding me up further.

"Okay, tell me, why is it when people are around you are cold and detached? When people are around, I am expendable asset,, Agent Scott! When people are not, you want me to believe that you care and I'm Mac again. I don't have a problem with whatever side I land on; I accept that I am expendable. I could probably even accept that it bothers you, but your back-and-forth inconsistency is hard to trust because I don't know what's real."

"That's… fair. I'm both sides; it's my job to make hard decisions. To do that, I have to remain detached. I have to think of the survival of the many over the few, but I'm human. It's not always that easy. With you – I don't find that easy. Just as I didn't with Dixon. The stories of how you both became Agents are very similar, and I guess by now, you already know that?"

"She told me."

"Right. I took you from a place that you didn't deserve to be because I wanted to help you. Yes, there is a purpose to your release from prison, but that doesn't change *why* I did it. I made you an Agent because I wanted to help you and because you show extraordinary potential, but I always wonder. Am I doing you more harm than good? Just as I did with Dixon. Only with you it's worse; Dixon wasn't facing torture for the second time under my orders. Can you imagine how hard an order that is to give? You have suffered enough; I worry I'm making it worse and when that worry takes hold, I turn into an icy bitch."

I can't stop the laugh that bursts from me. I don't mean to, I just didn't expect to hear that, and she laughs too, breaking the tension a little.

"You are not making it worse, Lexi – you saved my life and Dixy's. It helps to understand, but it's much easier to go to war with a person leading you rather than a robot. My choices are my own burden to bear – not yours."

Lexi smiles at me, relieved, and I give her a rigid smile back. I'm still trying to wrap my head around the gag protocol. Though I'm not surprised, it still isn't easy to hear. Now more than ever, my ability to withstand torture is life and death.

"That's kind of you to say, and I will try not to get quite so icy. That hang up is mine, and I don't want it affecting your progress or your trust in me."

I nod and Lexi gets to her feet. She walks towards me and hands me the brown file, and I take it.

"As for your original question, from my experience – there is nothing that can prepare you for torture. The experiences I have had have left their mark. For me, the hardest part is not letting those marks overcome me, and that's what I am working on with Dixy. Other than that, I'm not sure what else I can do to prepare," I explain with a dead tone, and she reaches out and puts her hand on my arm.

"Thank you for being honest with me. If you need anything, please tell me. At this point, I'd welcome it if it gave me the chance to show you that *I am* here for you. I know it probably doesn't mean much, but I am proud of you, Mac. You've come a long way from the girl in chains."

Lexi walks away without another word, and I am left standing, shell shocked and brain bent. I still don't know what to make of her but right now, working her out isn't the priority because she is right about one thing: the focus is the reconditioning. It isn't just about infiltrating The Culling anymore. If I fail – if I break, Lexi will silence me, and I'll lose everything and…everyone. I drop into the chair and stare into the fire with wide eyes. I knew it wouldn't be long before everyone came back to the fire pit.

"What happened, kid?" Alfred asks, and I look up.

"Uhhhh…" I breathe before looking at Dixy. I pass her the folder and look back at the fire.

"Nothing really. She just wanted to warn me about a protocol I needed to be aware of, and she asked me if I needed anything to help with my training for the reconditioning. We had a bit of a barny, but it's fine now." I shrug my shoulder.

"What protocol?" Dixy asks.

"Can't remember what it's called, not a big deal anyway. Like I said, we had a barny, but it's fine now. She is right, though; we need to focus on the reconditioning. I say we get back to work tomorrow; we don't have much time, so we need to hit it hard."

"Yes, I have to agree. I have some ideas. We can start in the morning; I just need to wait to confirm some details on something."

I look at Dixy, and I can see she isn't buying what I am selling, but she is at least playing along, thankfully. I'm lying to everyone; I already feel crap for it, but I am not sure how to tell Anna or even if I should. I know her well enough to know this will freak her out, and if she finds out, it shouldn't be in front of everyone else. I'd be lying if I said it didn't freak me out too. At the push of a button, I can be executed in seconds – the lack of control over that is terrifying.

Everyone starts chatting amongst themselves, and Anna gets up and walks over to me. She kneels between my legs and scrutinises me. She has that look like she is examining every inch of my face.

"I have to get ready to meet your mum. Is there a specific dress code?" She smiles cutely, and I laugh, relieved that it wasn't the deep question I was expecting.

"Wear whatever you want. You will look stunning regardless."

She smiles through a blush and kisses me sweetly, then she moves to my neck, her lips trailing open mouthed kisses up to my ear.

"Mm…you smell good," she breathes.

She pulls back giving me daring eyes before she gets up and walks away towards the house. Excited tingles mixed with pangs of guilt swirl in my stomach. I get to my feet and walk into the barn because this is definitely a moment where I feel the need to shut a door. I walk over to the table and pick up the throwing knives and decide it is a great time to start practicing with my left nondominant arm, which is piss poor.

It helps, even when I miss, because that just makes me angrier, and that makes me throw harder. I don't last out very long, clearly still weak from the infection; I'm soon out of breath and fatigued. I lay back on the sofa and inspect the ceiling, my mind busy. That is until the gold star irritant pops her head over the back of the sofa, making me jump half a mile.

"Argh! Did you really need to creep!?"

"I wasn't creeping; you are just totally unaware. You need to work on that. It's kind of spy 1-0-1." She winks.

"What do you want, Dix?"

"I want to know what you are lying to everyone about. Dix? Since when?"

"Since, 30 seconds ago. Dur."

"Huh, I like it. Max, what did Lexi actually say? You know, lying to your instructor never goes down well."

I huff. The woman is annoyingly relentless.

"I'm not lying; I'm delaying telling the truth till I can get my head around it."

"Fine, I can wait. Just let me know when you head is firmly around it," she says, and then she sits on my legs that are stretched out on the sofa.

"Ugh, why are you so annoying!" I groan, pulling my legs free and getting to my feet.

"I am adorable." She grins angelically.

"Dix…can you just give me till morning? Please?"

Her face turns serious, and she nods. "If that's what you need."

After getting changed into a clean white shirt and blue skinny tie, I pick up the gift for mum that, thankfully, Alfred was able to collect for me, and I leave the barn. I find Anna in the kitchen, her back turned as she pulls a chocolate cake out of the fridge. The royal blue dress she is wearing is understated and loose fitting, but the materiel is thin and is very teasing to look at. When she moves, it clings and reveals her curves just enough to be sexy. The colour against her pale skin and rusty red hair is gorgeous. She turns to find me propping up the doorway, mentally ripping her dress off and taking her.

"Mm…that look in your eyes is enough to drive me crazy, Mac Scott."

I can think of better ways.

***

The drive to mum's is fast, and I can tell all the way there that Anna is nervous. She has a chocolate cake on her lap, and she is inspecting it with a little too much interest. When we pull up outside, she takes a deep, shaky breath, and I giggle.

"She is going to love you. Don't be nervous."

We walk up the garden path, and Mum spots us approaching from the kitchen window, and she grins from ear to ear. I swear that woman is always washing up. I wrap an encouraging arm around Anna. The door opens, and mum squeals with happiness.

"Yay! I'm so glad you came, sweetheart."

"Of course, I came, Mum. It's your birthday!"

"Well, come in, come in! You both look gorgeous! Although you're clearly still not eating enough, Mckenna."

I groan, and Anna giggles sheepishly as we follow Mum down the hallway and into the dining room. I put her present down on the table and pull her in for a big squeeze. I've missed her, and I didn't realise quite how much till I saw her.

"Happy Birthday, Mum." I pull back and look at Anna. "You remember Anna."

Mum lets me go and goes straight in to hug Anna. "Of course, I do! It is lovely to see you again, darling, I have heard a lot about you."

"Oh, have you?" Anna asks raising an eyebrow at me, and I blush.

"Yes, I've been looking forward to meeting you properly. I wondered if the day would ever come. She has never bought a girl home before, you see." Mum winks at Anna.

"OKAY…time for presents."

I see Anna immediately relax as we watch Mum unwrap her presents. Her face lights up as she opens the small leathery box revealing an elegant diamond necklace. The box of Ferrero Rocher also went down well, her favourites – an easy win. She admires the necklace with twinkly eyes.

"Oh, Mac, it's beautiful, but this is far too much."

"Actually, it is just enough, Mum. I missed two birthdays and Christmas's while I was away. I am just making up for lost time."

"Aw, thank you. sweetheart. Well, what are you waiting for? Help me put it on!" she squeaks.

I grin at her excitement; it makes my insides swell. It really feels good to see her so happy and for once to be the cause of that happiness. I get to my feet and start fiddling with the clasp. Anna is busy admiring Mum's large country-style kitchen when Mum addresses her, but she doesn't miss a beat.

"So, Anna, where did you first meet my Mckenna?"

"Actually, it was at a photo shoot at The Shard, and she was absolutely terrified. It was adorable," Anna coos.

"*Terrified* might be a little strong…" I gripe, and she raises an eyebrow. "Okay, yes… I was terrified, but I still stayed for coffee."

We all tuck into some chocolate cake with monkey tea, and it's the perfection combination. The conversation is smooth, Anna has relaxed quickly, and it is a happy relief for me. Mum is right; I have never bought a girl back home to meet her. My nerves were never due to worrying Anna and Mum getting along. I am pretty sure Anna could get along with anyone; she just radiates a warmth that's impossible to dislike. But this is the first time I really wanted this to happen with someone, and it only hammers home more how much Anna means to me.

"Mac love, have another slice of cake will you, you look so skinny. Don't you ever eat?" Mum prattles.

"I eat loads, Mum; we bought the cake for you. I don't need another slice."

"She actually does eat, but she trains like a gladiator and doesn't eat extra to compensate for the calorie burn," Anna interjects.

"Hey, whose side are you on?"

"Oo I like her! She isn't afraid to tell you what's what. Good for you, sweetheart. She can be very stubborn, *our* McKenna," Mum quips with a quick pat on Anna's hand, and my insides warm as Anna's whole face lights up with my favourite, infectious laugh.

"That's it, gang up on me!"

I pick up the plates and start to wash them up before Mum gets the chance. I listen to them talk and laugh, and I am loving every second. That is until…

"Oh, you have to see my favourite photos of baby Mac! They're in the living room – come on, love," Mum squeaks as she drags Anna away.

Oh, sweet Jesus.

Once I'm done, I follow them to the living room and pause in the doorway to watch them. They are both standing by the fireplace looking at a picture of me. I know the picture; I am about 3 months old, and I am laughing. All gums and dimples with a head of curly brown hair. Thankfully, I lost the curls as I grew up.

"Oh, she's so cute! I love them dimples; I'm glad she didn't lose them," Anna coos.

"Me too! She was such a happy kid, loving and full of life. When I lost her, it was excruciating. To have her come home felt like the biggest miracle. But she was so broken, I never thought I would see that lively side of her again. She was a ghost; she wouldn't even hug me. And then, she met you, and I'm so thankful because somehow, you bought her back. Thank you so much, Anna." Mum chokes, and she pulls Anna in for a hug.

Anna spots me over her shoulder and looks at me lovingly while she rubs Mum's back. I smile at her, tears pricking my eyes, and I sneak away and let them have their moment. It's hard to hear Mum talk like that. She has always been so honest with her feelings – not a trait I inherited. I have caused her a lot of pain; all I want is to bring her happiness, and whatever it takes, I am determined to be the source of that. When they return to the table, I notice that Mum has her tell-tale worried look.

"Are you alright, Mum?"

"Yes, I was just wondering. How…everything is going with…Barrett? Has he…have you…?" she stutters awkwardly, and I stiffen a little, but I try to keep my face calm.

"Yes, I've met him twice. It's going okay; he is just as creepy as I expected him to be, but you don't need to worry, Mum. I'm being careful, and I have plenty of people keeping me safe," I assure her.

My eyes flick to Anna briefly, and she offers me a sad smile, knowing how much I hate to lie. I look back at Mum, and she is looking at my hand holding hers, her eyes a little misty. She lets out a big sigh and looks up at me with a forced smile, and it hurts to see the pain she is trying very hard to hide.

"It will be alright, Mum. He doesn't know what he is dealing with. I am quite the scary monster, you know," I joke lightly.

"Don't lie to your mother. You are not scary or a monster. Just you make sure you stay safe or you are grounded with no monkey tea, and don't think I won't do it!" she rants, playfully stern.

Leaving her never gets any easier but missing her is worse. I hate that I give her so much reason to worry. I dream of the day that I am not the cause of that for her, a day where I can just pop round for tea and a catch up and leave without the panging guilt in my chest. She hugs us both goodbye with parting orders to come back soon.

"So, your mum is super cute. Almost as cute as you," Anna coos, and I chuckle.

"I told you she would love you."

***

I lean against the wall of cold, smooth glass of the bedroom wall, loosening my tie, and she walks up to me. Her expression is quizzical, her arms draped over my shoulders, her slight smile affectionate.

"Are you going to tell me what Lexi said?" Anna asks.

"Yes, but not right now."

"Why?"

"Because right now, I have more important things to say."

I take her waist in my hands, and my lips descend on hers. I kiss her with hunger, my tongue exploring hers as I drag my hands up her satin-soft thighs beneath her dress. Her reaction tells me she knows exactly what I want to say. A deep groan escapes her mouth, and the sound sends tingling pleasure pulsing between my thighs. I turn her around, pressing her against the glass as my hand slides down her thigh and hooks under the back of her knee. I lift her leg, my thigh sliding between hers, grinding against her, and I am relishing at the needy whimpers falling from her mouth. Anna's hands unknot from my hair and grip on my hips, and she pulls, driving my thigh harder against her excited heat.

I press my body against hers. Anna licks into my mouth, her tongue sliding against mine in deep slow strokes that set my skin on fire. I have never felt so thoroughly…kissed. A kiss that alone is enough to enliven every cold and broken part of me with salacious, loving, rapture. Anna steps into me, and my hands slide up her waist and onto her back where I unzip her dress. I guide it off her shoulders, and my lips are trailing down her chest before it hits the floor. My hands tremble over her heated skin, but it is not enough, not nearly enough. I need all of her.

"You are so fucking beautiful it hurts in the best way," I mutter breathlessly into her mouth.

"I need you to take me. Show me that I'm yours and always will be."

I catch the tear rolling down her cheek, her words both fearful and full of desire. Enough to intensify the ache just when I thought I couldn't need her more. I hold her face delicately as I pull her eyeline up to mine.

"*You. Are. Mine*...as much as I am yours," I whisper, the power and sureness of my own words shocking even me. I watch her eyes darken from crystal emerald to opaque, ruinous green with arousal, and she sinks her lips into mine.

Her fingers fumble, urgently unbuttoning my shirt. As our clothes fall away, I slow down my kisses, and I lead her to the bed. She trembles beneath me, my kiss deepening to a slow, loving rhythm while my hand explores her body. She shudders at my touch, her hips bucking, hungering for more, and I couldn't be more desperate to satisfy her. I kiss and bite down her neck and onto her perfect full breasts. I take the soft swell of them in my hands as I tease her aching nipples with my tongue, and she moans breathlessly. Anna's hands knot in my hair, urging me not to stop, and I massage her breasts harder, dragging my teeth over her nipples.

She is still just as responsive to my touch, so free and expressive with everything she feels. I am lapping up every utterance, every moan and squirm, every honest look. I am drunk on her reactions, overwhelmed by how much it sets my skin ablaze and just how much I want to devour her beautiful body.

I work my way back up to her lips and slide my arm under the back of her neck, my other hand hooking the back of her knee and pinning it up by my hip. I manoeuvre myself, spreading my legs and lowering myself into the perfect scissor position and I hover. I pull back and look into her eyes. Powerful need and anticipation burn there, and they clamp tightly closed as I lower myself against her. I feel the wet flow of her hard clit throbbing against mine as we finally connect. There is no closer feeling than that, her hands holding my face, her eyes locked onto mine as she moans deliciously. I grind against her slowly, teasing her, feeling her warm slick wetness sliding against mine.

"Oh, fuck, Mac..."

Anna never really swears. To hear the words strain pleasurably out of her mouth is almost enough to make me come. I whimper in the effort not to, my self-control weakening. I'm teasing myself as much as I am her. The look in her eyes, desperate, wanting, adoring. The panting whine of pure arousal escaping her, heightening my need to make her feel good. My need to dive into the innermost essence of her. My rhythm picks up speed as I thrust, her wetness sliding against mine, the sensation so unbearably heavenly I could scream. Her hips begin to thrust in perfect rhythm with mine as she moans fiercely and freely, her hands on my hips driving me into her.

Heat builds, rumbling from my deepest core, resonating intense pleasure through every nerve and cell till every inch of me is pulsating. Complete white out, a blind, blissful rush echoes through my system and is only intensified by Anna's every joyous scream. Our moans intwine, my name falling from her lips as we begin to climax together, gushing all over each other, and I fight to keep the movement going as long as I can physically bear.

I lay on top of her, our bodies trembling as I kiss her through rapid breaths, my hand soft against her warm rosy cheek. The love I feel is bursting from me so powerfully, I don't know what to do with it. I pull back and see her beautiful green eyes alight with exhilaration and glistening with tears.

"Are you alright, baby?" I ask. She gasps with a smile, and her tears escape.

"Just…so happy. I've never felt so connected, so...ugh, Mac…"

Her kiss is desperate, loud, and shameless. She rolls on top of me, and my excitement is renewed as she confidently explores every inch of my skin with her lips. She moves her body with such teasing sensuality, her hands moving softly but with complete certainty, trailing hot tingles in their wake. Her unexpected dominance in the moment enchants me with wild rhapsody as she reveals a side to herself I've never seen before. Anna claims me with a confidence I didn't know she had, and it is driving me wild. It's all I can do not to beg her to fuck me, to let her take her time when every touch she graces me with is making me writhe and plead for her to sink inside of me.

Anna straddles me, she scoops the back of my neck, and she pulls me upright and into her urgent kiss. Again, I am struck by how a kiss can be so erotic and still so loving; it is all encompassing the power her kiss has over me. Anna sucks and bites wet, feverish kisses down my neck as her hand slides down between my legs. Her breath catches in her throat at the feel of my excitement pooled between my thighs. Her lips are on mine, and I groan in her mouth as her fingertips trail up and down, teasing every swollen, dripping fold of me. Then her fingertip circles my clit sending me closer to the edge, and I am so desperate to topple over.

"A-anna…"

She slides a finger inside, then another, and it feels so good, my eyes open to see hers locked onto mine, and then…

I freeze, as her eyes are replaced with his. I cry out a pained moan as I bury my face in her neck. Anna pulls back, her hands on my face as she forces me into her eyeline.

"Hey…hey…it's okay, just look at me."

"Anna…he..." I whimper as I squeeze my finger and thumb together. The fear grips me so fast, it is jarring. Anna reaches for my other hand and lays it over her heart; I feel its fast beat against my palm.

"It's just you and me. You are *beautiful*, you are *safe*, and you are *mine.* That is all there is ever going to be. I love you so much, Mac – please, come back to me."

I kiss her, open eyed, softly, through shaken breaths. Unsure if I really have control, testing myself. Anna stays completely still like she can feel the fear still rippling through me, her eyes on mine, her lips never leaving mine as she whispers.

"I would wait a whole lifetime for you if it meant I would get to have you in the next. We can stop. It's okay. Everything is so much more than okay; it's beautiful."

My eyes close of their own volition as her words wash over me, the tears escaping. Her patience seems never ending, and it only makes me ache for her more.

"I don't want to wait anymore…I need you." I whisper shakily.

I let my hand slide down her chest to feel the warm wetness of her excitement. Calm returning, I kiss her like there may be no tomorrow. Her hand slides back into position, and we move in rhythm with each other, slow, deep, and building. Heated goosebumps flee across my skin, our eyes locked as we climax together. Her body shakes with mine, ecstasy powering through me in an electrical surge, and I fall into her. Anna climbs off my lap and lays down, pulling me down with her. Her lips are soft against my forehead, and then she pulls back, keeping her eyes locked on mine.

"I'm sorry," I choke.

"You better not be," she breathes, tears building in her eyes, and I frown. I go to speak, and she gently covers my mouth with her finger. "The only thing that is wrong here is your need to be sorry for something that couldn't have been more perfect."

Anna pulls me snugly into her chest, and I melt into her, knowing she is right; there is no way that could have been more perfect. I feel the calm wash over me as I lay securely entangled in her arms and legs, feeling more safety and love than I ever thought my heart could hold. My breathing slows, and the raspy sob in my throat quietens. My eyes are getting heavier and heavier as I kiss her softly.

"You were so worth the wait," I mumble sleepily, and she smiles into my lips, her chuckle low and gravelly.

"Mm, so were you. Close your eyes, beautiful. Meet me in dreamland."

***

Eyes.
Hollow, unforgiving, cold eyes.
Manic, delirious, emotionally barren eyes.
Devoid and loveless,
Scrutinising, analysing, an evil X-ray,
Windows into the soul,
Yet no soul resides there.
Crystal-like blue, large and round,
I see the monster that resides there
Staring down with a knowing smile
Familiar and haunted.
Reflections, perceptions, misconceptions.
Are they my eyes? Or are they his?

I jump awake searching for a threat that isn't there, sweat glowing off my skin. The nightmare still etched behind my eyes. Carefully, I creep out of bed and tiptoe my way to the bathroom. I run the cold tap and splash icy water over my face, and it doesn't feel enough, I want to bathe in the cool of it.

Looking up, I see my reflection in the mirror. I watch as a lone droplet of water trickles down my nose and onto my lips. My eyes pick out the various scars I've collected, one to my temple, the slit across my eyebrow, and one at the bottom of my chin, which I still have no memory of getting.

My sight fixes on my eyes, crystal-like, blue, big, and round and framed in dark circles beneath pale skin. My vision flashes, and I see his familiar eyes, similar to mine, not as soft and much more crazed, and I flinch. Then the savage eyes of Tomasz invades, and my blood runs cold. I look away from the mirror sharply as if his ghost lives there, as if it will melt the horror away, but it doesn't, and the panic takes hold.

Within seconds, I am sat inside my large walk-in shower, the cold water freezing against my skin, numbing my mind and calming the crawl on my skin, my forehead bouncing on my knees with every shiver and shake. Every time I decide it is time to get out, I find another reason why another sixty seconds can't hurt. Am I losing my mind? Or is it just being invaded by the eyes of monsters? The list of them just gets longer, and I wonder – is my name at the top?

T

CHAPTER 11

Reminiscent Purgatory

"Mac… What are you…? Jesus! What are you doing? It's freezing!" Anna snaps.

The water stops flowing, and I feel a towel being wrapped around my shoulders. My insides clench. I really hoped she wouldn't wake up.

"Mac…"

My neck is stiff as I lift my head up to look at her, and her expression turns from mad to concerned instantly.

"Come on. You are getting out now."

My body has seized, my joints stiff, and getting to my feet isn't easy or graceful. Anna wraps another towel around my waist and pulls me by the hand back into the bedroom, where I sit on the sofa. I stare dazed back at Anna as she kneels down in front of me.

"I'm okay. Just a bad dream; I like the cold."

"I just found you at 4am sat in a shower of ice water after you have been fighting fevers for 3 days, and you are telling me that you're fine," Anna says, her voice calmer now, but I can tell she is still mad, and I don't have a fight in me.

"Please…don't."

"Then tell me what is going on, don't tell me it's just bad dreams. You've always had bad dreams, and I've never found you in the shower freezing yourself."

"I can't tell you what is going on because I don't know." I groan, leaning my head in my hands. I feel her move away, and guilt pangs in my chest, but then I feel a blanket being wrapped around me. Anna slips between my rattling knees and gets inside the blanket with me, her arms warm around me.

"You told me it's you and me, and it always will be. If you shut me out, how is that ever going to happen? It isn't just you anymore, Mac, it's us."

I nod into her neck. "Just need a minute."

"That's okay," she whispers, rubbing my back, her anger completely melted away.

I breathe her in and try to clear my mind of the haunting eyes that are etched there. I focus on the motion of her hand moving slowly up and down my back, the feel of it. The sound of the swish her hand makes against the blanket with every movement. I count the strokes till calm returns, and then I lean back a little. I can feel her eyes on me, but I don't look up.

"I wasn't being a jerk; I don't know what's going on with me. I've been seeing Tomasz eyes and dreaming of them for months. Now it's not just his eyes, it's Barrett's. At least, I think they're Barrett's."

"What do you mean - you think? Who else could they be?"

I grit my jaw, my throat a little tight as the anxiety claws at the edges of me. Talking about this is only provoking it. I feel like I am precariously poking a wounded bear. Anna holds my face, her eyes warm and determined.

"Just look at me till it stops. I could look at those gorgeous eyes all night long."

"That's just it… I t-think they are mine. The way he looked at me at the brewery, there's no humanity there. He pushed me, and I saw the monster there, the same monster I saw in my own eyes when I killed Jakub's men. I don't know if it's his eyes or mine. I got up from the bad dream, looked in the mirror and saw my eyes, then Barrett's, then Tomasz, and I just…freaked out, and the cold always helps me calm down."

The look in Anna's eyes doesn't waver, warm, beautiful, and full of love. Her thumbs stroke my cheeks, and she keeps me held in the now. I don't know how she does it; it is as if she knows how to keep me grounded.

"Your eyes are similar but barely. I should know; I'm frequently lost in them. They are bright blue, especially in the sun. Even though they have a gorgeous, haunted look to them, they are also warm, soft, and full of love, and there is no monster there. Barrett's eyes are almost grey; they are cold and piercing. The resemblance is there in the shape, but it's not obvious, and I think you must know that. So, what is really scaring you?"

"You heard what I said to him. Not all of that anger was put on, Anna. He says I'm just like him, that he wants me to embrace the monster inside. A monster I know is there, the monster that killed over 40 people. He pushed my anger, and I could see what he was doing, but what if he pushes me so far I can't come back? What if he wants me to kill for him? How much more can my soul take? And what if underneath it all…I really am just like him?"

Anna looks at me with thoughtful eyes and then walks over to her bedside table, taking out her mobile phone. I watch her, totally confused as she walks to the middle of the room, her fingers punching against the touch screen. Then she looks up at me with a sheepish smile, blushing a little. She lays the phone on the end of the bed and pulls me to my feet. When Anna turns back to the phone, she hits the screen one more time, and then it comes to life.

The intro sings loudly from her phone, and the memories make me smile instantly, and then then I turn to her with a curious frown. The lyrics begin to sing loudly, filling the room with the words of Sweet Home Alabama. Anna begins to dance on the spot, and I chuckle.

"I will tell you who you are, Mac Scott. You are a terrible dancer, but you get away with it because you are just so damn goofy! You are a nerd who quotes movies with childlike excitement at every possible opportunity, and if it wasn't so cute, it would be annoying. You are a terrible cook but a master at making coffee, and you've never failed to make me one. Even when we were hardly speaking. You're a loyal friend, the most loving partner, and a brave and sexy soldier. You always step up regardless of the danger, first protecting the people you love and now the whole world. You are thoughtful, playful, and romantic, and after all you have seen and survived, it amazes me and just proves that your soul is far from broken. You feel guilt for killing people that were trying to kill you because you have your humanity, your compassion, and empathy. You are…"

I chuckle as I stride towards her and silence her with my kisses, and she giggles and kisses me sweetly but pulls back quickly with serious eyes.

"You are *nothing* like him. There is no monster inside of you, and it doesn't matter what he does to you, he can't change that. Everyone has anger inside, and you have more rights to feel that than most. It doesn't make you bad. The good inside of you will always win out because that's all there is. He can't break you and reveal an evil inside that isn't there."

I tense at her words, and I sigh. She frowns at my reaction.

"We really need to hope you're right," I state grimly.

"What do you mean?"

I lead Anna back to the sofa, and the music stops playing. The sudden silence hammers in my ears. I put the blanket over us both and meet her questioning gaze as I try to summon the courage to explain myself.

"Lexi told me that infiltrating The Culling isn't the only reason I need to pass the reconditioning. There is a gag protocol in place to protect MI5. It's used when an agent divulges too much information. If Barrett breaks me, if I say something I shouldn't, then they activate the cyanide needle inside my boot remotely, so…I can't…talk anymore. I didn't say anything before because I didn't want to tell you in front of everyone else."

"You mean… t-they will kill you?"

I watch her face turn from disbelief to anger to pain and then fear. I was expecting it; her emotion always plays out honestly on her face. Expecting it doesn't make it any easier to see. The devastation in her eyes is raw and enough to bring pain to my chest.

"Yes…but that isn't going to happen, Anna."

"I…" Anna struggles, the tears in her eyes building, and I hold her hand, waiting for her to find her words. Her eyes are strained like she has a thousand thoughts inside her head, pain written all over her face. She gasps, eyeing me imploringly, and her words come out furiously, not with anger but with urgency.

"When you got those boots, you said that you knew what it is like to be captured and have no way out. You said it like – it was something you would seriously do if you had to. That you would end your life if there was no way out. Is that still true? N-now that we…"

"No! There isn't anything I wouldn't do to get back to you. I wouldn't give up on that; it was different then."

"And you mean that? You are completely sure about that?" she presses firmly.

"Yes, I am sure."

I feel like I am missing something. Things have changed since I thought I could pull that trigger. Now that I have her, there isn't anything I wouldn't endure if it means I could find my way back to her. That thought is terrifying; there really is no potential easy way out if I'm not willing to pull that trigger.

"I can't leave that to chance. You are finally with me, finally mine as much as I am yours. The idea that they could push a button and…I can't bear it, Mac. I can't lose you. And now, I have to do the most selfish thing I have ever… Oh, God - I really hope you can forgive me. I just…I can't…" Anna babbles through tears, and my chest tightens in fear. I can barely breathe.

"What are you saying?"

"I'm so sorry…" she chokes, and she gets to her feet. I stiffen, bracing myself as she walks away and then… I am confused; she doesn't walk out the door. She walks over to the window, and I get to my feet just as she picks up my right boot.

Anna turns the boot upside down and then slides the heel right and left, right and left, over and over again. I see a small trail of white liquid squirt out of the foot hole from inside the boot as she activates the cyanide needle. She turns the heel over and over till the liquid stops, and then she breaks down, dropping the boot, and I finally understand. My stomach drops just as she drops on the floor, sobbing.

"I'm sorry…I am so sorry. Please…I know you wanted that out just in case, but that out will *destroy* me. You have to come back…you have to! No m-matter what! If you don't tell them…it's empty, they can't…oh, God! I'm so sorry!"

I pull her to me, tight against my chest as she sobs violently. I am reeling from the shock of what she has just done.

"It's okay, I get it. I don't need it anymore, okay? I am coming home to you. Whatever it takes. I won't tell them, and I'll come home. There's nothing I won't do, I promise. It's you and me just like I said; it always will be." I reassure her, holding her tight.

Please, don't let me be lying to her.

I cradle her on my lap, and she curls up against my chest. She looks so tiny. I want to be mad because I did feel safer with it there. I felt safer knowing there was a way out if I needed it. But the thought of not coming home to her, of ever making the choice to end my life and leaving her forever. I know I'd never be able to do that because she is right. It isn't just me anymore; it's us. I have to survive what is coming, whatever it takes.

"I'm sorry..." she struggles.

"No, look at me. I don't need it anymore; it's no longer a choice I could have made. So, don't be mad at yourself, because I'm not mad. I'm even a little impressed. Some spy I am, I didn't think of doing that."

She chuckles a little, her face nuzzled in my neck.

"Taking that choice away from you, I know how selfish I am being, and I know I have to live with that, but if it means you come home, I'll find a way."

"Don't torture yourself, please, for me? I'm yours to be selfish over, and I couldn't be happier about that. It's done now, so you may as well kiss me and just get over it," I utter playfully, and she giggles, turning her head to kiss me.

We begrudgingly move off the floor and start to get ready to go back to the farm. When I said I wanted an early start, I didn't quite mean this early, but if either of us were to fall asleep now, we would probably sleep the whole day away. I start ramming clothes into a rucksack and then pick up my usual items from my bedside table. Keys, wallet...I see the message window light up as I pick up my mobile phone.

Dixy Mobile:

Pack for a few days, we are all going to the seaside! YAY! 6.00am at the farm, don't be late! We need a covert exit in case Barrett has eyes on you.

"What the hell?"

"What's up?" Anna asks, looking cute in one of my combat jumpers. I hold up the phone to Anna so she can read the message, and she raises an eyebrow.

"We are going to need a lot more coffee."

***

The coffee didn't work. An hour into the drive, Anna falls asleep in the passenger seat of my truck while I continue to down unhealthy amounts of coffee. My eyes are dry and scratchy as I try to keep a good pace behind Alfred's Land Rover. This is not good beach weather; winter is fast approaching, and I really don't want to imagine what training is in store for me and why we have to drive to Southend-on-Sea to do it. The only thing that comes to mind fills my stomach with dread. The one thing the beach has plenty of is water. Water I want to stay very far away from.

I can swim, although it has been a long time since I have. The water didn't scare me, but since I came back from the boat, I've made a point of avoiding it. I wasn't really sure why till memories came back of the waterboarding. Now that I can clearly remember what it feels like to be drowned over and over, the idea of getting into a body of water that isn't a bath, sends my anxiety bells ringing. Dixy knows this; of all the things I had to live through on that God forsaken boat, that was definitely one of the worst. I might fear lack of control, but I fear the actual drowning just as much.

"Mac, you read me, kid?" Alfred sounds inside my ear.

I am getting used to having him inside my head for the most part. It doesn't even make me jump as much anymore, and it can be convenient, if not a bit intrusive.

"Yeah, Pa, I read."

"We are pulling in at the next services to take a break and get some food."

"Copy that, I'm Hank Marvin."

"You what now?"

"I am Hank Marvin…starving! My old buddy, old pal," I ramble, putting in the strangest failed pompous accent I can muster.

"I think someone has had too much coffee." Alfred chuckles.

"True that."

"What's true?" Anna mumbles through a yawn.

I turn to see Anna rubbing her eyes and stretching in her seat; she still looks like she could sleep for ten more hours. Anna turns to me with groggy eyes, putting her hand back on my thigh, and I smile. She always has to be touching me in some way; it is adorable, and I have no complaints.

"Hey, beautiful. It is true that I have drank too much coffee. Pa was just letting me know we are making a food stop."

"That's good; I'm hungry. How far have we got left do you think?"

"Umm, the satnav says 45 minutes to the hotel. One day, I'm going to take you to a hotel for entirely normal reasons. Ones that do not involve being invited to a ball by my psycho dad to mingle with his evil clan, or me being practice tortured on by government spies. It will happen…I'm determined."

"You can take me anywhere you want. In fact, when this is all over, I think you should kidnap me, take me away from everyone and everything. I want at least two weeks where it's just you and me. Preferably somewhere that you have no need for clothes." Anna smirks sexily, and I chuckle as my face flushes warmly.

"You are on, Princess, but I don't think two weeks will be nearly long enough."

Alfred finally pulls off into the services, a petrol station with a coffee shop and a convenience store all bundled together. I feel myself creak as I get out the truck and straighten up. The air is bitterly cold and jarring, and I eagerly head towards the warmth of Starbucks. The aroma of pastry and coffee beans is thick in the air as we look for a table big enough for five. Lambert automatically picks a table at the back and sits with his back against the wall, next to Dixy and Alfred, and Anna and I take the tub chairs opposite them. We all order cheese toasties and hot drinks, and even though they are not as good as Mum's, the salty oozy cheese certainly hits the spot, and I feel much less ratty for eating. I'm known for my hangry mood swings for a reason.

"We should be at the hotel soon, but you won't be staying long, Max. We have an appointment." Dixy fidgets uncomfortably, paying close attention to her empty plate.

"What kind of appointment?"

"Umm, I think it is best we wait till…"

"Dixy, don't spring it on the kid. Tell her or I will," Alfred grumbles, and Dixy inhales deeply, her eyes narrowing in Alfred's direction.

"I'll tell her when we get there, Alfred. I know what I'm doing," Dixy asserts firmly.

The atmosphere between them is immediately icy, and I am shocked. I've never seen either of them act that way towards each other or anyone else for that matter. My stomach twists in knots as the nerves hit.

"O…kay, what's going on?"

"If you wait till then, you take away her right to shut a door and her right to have someone go in with her. It isn't right, Dixy," Alfred argues calmly but with an edge to his tone. I look at Anna, and she shakes her head, her expression as perplexed as I feel.

"Alright, stop talking like I'm not here and tell me what is going on. Seriously, you are both freaking me out. Just spit it out… Dixy?" I snap, and she looks at me, her jaw clenched in anger, and then she sighs. Her eyes soften, and she nods.

"Lambert, let's go get some cakes," Alfred suggests, and they both get up from the table and walk away with all the subtlety of a battering ram.

The look in Dixy's eyes is making me nervous, mainly because I can't understand what that look is. She leans forward, tucking the loose tousle of escaped hair behind her ear before her honey-brown eyes find mine.

"Okay, so I wasn't going to tell you till later because I know if this was me – I wouldn't want the anticipation. I think I know you well enough to know you won't want this eating at you, even for a short while. I know that Alfred knows you, but my…story, helps me understand…the mindset. I wasn't disrespecting Alfred's view. Do you understand, Max?" Dixy explains calmly, looking at both me and Anna.

Oh, God...what is happening?

"Yeah, Dix, I get you. Just hit me with it. It's okay." I gulp.

It really doesn't feel okay. The anxiety is building in my chest, threatening to make me panic. I freeze statue still, my breath held. I watch her struggle, willing her to rip the plaster off fast but also not wanting the plaster off at all.

"I have found the Seabird, Max. It is here; we have it. You are going back on the boat."

My stomach just fell out of my butt and all the moisture in my mouth evaporates.

"Ughh…" I moan as I look away from Dixy, and I hold my dizzy head in my hands, and my ears start to ring.

"Jesus..." Anna exclaims as she gets to her feet. She stands behind my chair, and her hands lightly hold the back of my neck.

The memories instantly flash across my mind, fast and blurring, and my hands ball into fists as I press them hard against my eyes. I feel disorientated, and terror is threatening to take me. I feel like I am falling, a horrible swooping sensation in my stomach that doesn't seem to want to stop. Anna pulls my hands away from my face and holds them tightly, her arms crossing over my chest, and it helps a little like she is grounding me to the spot.

"Max...are..."

"How?" I croak, my voice gravelly.

"We have been looking for it for a while now, ever since we found out about the reconditioning. Ever since Alfred said he was worried about you losing yourself again, I've been working on a plan to make sure that doesn't happen. There are a lot of boats with that name; it took a while to trace it," Dixy explains calmly, and my head snaps up at her.

"How do you know it is the right boat? Have you seen it?" This time I definitely see sadness in Dixy's eyes, and my hope dwindles away in seconds.

"Because...it still has...I've seen video footage of inside, and it still has...things inside that you have described."

Unnatural heat burns against my skin like someone poured hot water down my back. The panic grips my throat, and I let go of Anna's hands, scrambling to my feet.

"Back in a minute."

My vision is darkening at the edges as I stumble my way clumsily through the coffee shop. It's like tunnel vision, only the tunnel is getting smaller and darker with each passing second. The cold air freezes the beads of sweat building on my forehead as I burst outside. I rip my jumper off as stride towards my truck. My vision blurring, I stumble against the truck door, gripping the wing of the truck, bracing myself. I feel Anna's hands on my face as my legs begin to give way. Her mouth is moving but there is no sound. My vision blackens as I slide down the door, but when my butt hits the floor, I jolt awake again.

"Mac...?" Anna mouths, and I strain my eyes to focus on her.

"Ouch...my butt." I groan, and her lips press into a tight line.

"It's okay, you can laugh," I wince giving her a crooked smile, and she chuckles, but the smile doesn't reach her eyes. She pulls me against her snuggly.

"Baby, you don't have to do this. In fact, I really, really don't want you to. This is going to hurt you; it's going to mess with your head. I don't want you to go through this."

"I know, but I have to. I told you, I'll do whatever it takes to get back to you. If this helps me pass the reconditioning, I have to do it, Anna."

"Maybe you do, but you don't have to do it alone."

The tension when I get back to the table is palpable. No one is really looking at each other. Alfred is pushing cake crumbs into a pile on his plate, Lambert is still eating, and Dixy looks at me with such sad eyes, it's painful. I walk round to the other side of the table between Alfred and Dixy. I put one hand on Alfred's shoulder and the other on Dixy's.

"You two overprotective, stubborn, pains in the butt better make up! Seriously, I can't have this; I love you both, and you love each other! This is juvenile. Now you are going build a bridge, and you are going get the fuck *over* it. Am. I. *Clear*?" I assert firmly, probably a bit too firmly.

"Crystal, kid. She's right; I'm sorry Dixy."

"Me too, big fella."

I walk away with a nod and take my seat next to Anna with a huff, and she leans in, her lips at my ear. "Apparently, I love it when you are bossy too."

***

We pull up outside the Edge Bay Hotel. I welcome having something to distract me, and at this point, I have to say, Dixy was right. I would have been better off being told closer to when we were about to leave for the boat. The knowledge, the impending doom, has been playing with my head for the hours' drive. Eating at me. I've already imagined and reimagined all the possible embarrassing and horrific outcomes that could come of this outing down memory lane.

The hotel is tall and white, the top floors boasting large balconies, and all the windows pop out like huge bay windows. The place looks modern and chic. The wooden deck walkway into the hotel is lit up brightly, and attached is a large glassy building glowing with purple backlights. The outdoor seating area is neat and sharp with black furniture and blue lighting. The overall look is quirky enough to have a boutique-style, but the expense put into it makes it look classy rather than gaudy.

We enter a warmly lit entrance, and the reception is clean, wooden and samey. Nothing really sticks out except that it looks neat and minimal. The walls brown and cream and lit up with wall-mounted uplighters. Dixy talks to the lady at reception while the rest of us hold back, taking the place in. Dead ahead are numerous seating areas with comfy looking purple armchairs, sofas, and tub chairs. Behind them are some doors that I can see lead to a bar to the far left. Dixy hands me, Lambert, and Alfred key cards after explaining that all our rooms are on the bottom floor.

"Max, meet me back here in 15?" Dixy asks, and I give her the nod.

Anna and I make our way through the hotel. We pass the seating area and move to the right through a breakfast area that adjoins the restaurant. It is bustling with people, and the smells of fried food and coffee fill my nose. The hallway curves, and we pass a series of doors and notice that Lambert and Alfred disappear into rooms along the way. The smell of chlorine burns my nose as we pass a swimming pool. The glass windows along the wall are slightly steamy, and the pool area is empty aside from an old man sitting in a hot tub with his greying wife. Finally, Dixy enters a room on the left, and our room is a couple of doors down from hers. I slot the key card into the reader and with a click, the door unlocks, and we enter our hotel room.

It isn't too flashy, plainly decorated in white and rose gold. The light fittings and feature furniture add some luxury to the room. There are two soft, dusty pink velvet armchairs by the window. The furniture is all white gloss with flashes of pink ornaments that add colour and interest. Opposite the armchairs is a glass dining table and chairs and a matching desk built into an alcove. The carpet is soft pink with white geometric patterning that matches the backlit wall that surrounds a king-size white bed. The hotel seems to use a lot of lighting features to add unique style and warmth.

The ensuite bathroom is a nice touch; the taps and sink are gleaming gold, the walls black with glittering gold marble with an oversized walk-in shower cubical. Complimentary soaps and shampoos sit on top of a cabinet with two white and fluffy, neatly folded bathrobes and some flimsy white slippers wrapped in cellophane packaging.

I drop our bags on the floor by the built in, mirrored wardrobe and take a seat on one of the armchairs. It is soft to the touch, and it feels new like I don't want to sit on it through fear of dirtying it. Anna sits in the chair opposite me; I can feel her eyes on me as I look out the window at the sea. You can just see the top of it, a line of blue. If we were on a higher floor, I'm sure we could see more. It isn't far – a few minutes' walk at most. I am glad we aren't; staying low to the ground suits me fine. Anna gets off her chair and kneels down in front of me. She takes my hands, and I look down at her.

"If it would be easier to go without me, you can tell me. I won't be upset. I just want to give you whatever you need. But if you do need me, please don't be afraid to tell me. I want to be there for you in any way you need me to be."

I grip her hands a little tighter, fear beginning to get the better of me. The conflict of making this choice is weighing on me, and she obviously knows it.

"I need you, I just…don't know what I'm going to find or how I will react when I see it. You always look at me like I am strong. That place shows how weak and pathetic I actually was. I don't want it to change how you look at me," I confess.

"Whatever your reaction is, it will be the right one. You are wrong. Seeing that place won't be nice for me, but it will only confirm what I already know." Anna gets to her feet, and she tugs my hand, pulling me to mine. She leans in close and keeps her eyes on mine. "That the love of my life really is a miracle.

***

The Land Rover rumbles along the roads, the reverberation buzzing in my chest as I stare wide-eyed out the window from the back seat. I feel weary and disconnected; the only thing really keeping me anchored to the present is the feel of Anna's fingers interlocked with mine. Dixy drives as smoothly as the Land Rover will allow. No one speaks, and it feels like we are driving a long time before we park up on the sandy dirt road parking area of the Leigh Marina.

The large farmhouse looking buildings are wood slatted, painted in green and dark blue, and they're the only things about the place that looks clean and new. The boats bobbing in the water's soft current, anchored and lined up in a uniform manner, are old and decrepit. The place looks haunted and eerie.

This must be the place where boats go to die.

The hairs stand up on the back of my neck as we walk along a small beaten pier. Slats are missing, and the wood feels soft underfoot and creaks precariously as my weight shifts from step to step. Rotting cargo nets and lobster pots, broken masts and collapsed hulls of splinted wood and rusted metal, algae stained, paint peeled wooden structures of once glorious boats float sadly in the water while the odd boat hand strips them bare and attempts to salvage anything of worth.

I follow Dixy as we weave through section upon section of piers through the graveyard of corpse boats. The deeper in we go, the tighter my chest becomes. I float along, feeling like my body is moving, my feet walking, my legs striding without my permission or know how. We cross the water to a larger group of boats, the gaps opening up between moors making way for larger vessels. And there, the space opens up widely with only two boats docked.

The breath catches in my chest as I see, set furthest away in the background, is a large, dark blue and white fishing vessel. My feet come to an abrupt stop as my eyes are just about able to read the plaque on the ships bow. 'The Seabird' glares in white chipped paint proudly. It is so much bigger than I thought it would be. If it wasn't for the name of the boat, I'd never have known the difference. I feel no connection to what my eyes are seeing.

My feet start to move again. Now instead of floating, they drag heavily as if I am wading through thick treacle. From further away, the ship looked quite grand. Now I draw nearer, I see it for what it actually is: beaten, weather worn, and shabby. The paint, although glossy in some places, is mostly peeled and dented, the wood scratched and gouged. I stop metres away from a wooden ramp that bridges the gap between land and boat. Rope hangs taught either side at hip height for balance when crossing the ramp.

"Inside has been left exactly how we found it. You can leave whenever you want to, and we will be with you every step of the way," Dixy says softly.

"Are you coming inside?"

"Yes. It will help me to help you if I know what triggers you. By the time we go home, you will be free of this place in every way. Trust me on that, Max, and trust yourself. You are in control. This is your boat; it doesn't own you anymore," Dixy encourages me as I look at her fearfully, and I nod rigidly.

"Anna, this is going to trigger memories and flashbacks. It's important that we let that happen. Be there for her but don't try and snap her back. It will be hard to watch but it's part of the process, and it will help her in the end. Can you do that?"

I look around to Anna, her eyes strained, and I give her an encouraging nod, and she takes a deep breath.

"You better know what you are doing, Dixy," Anna jabs icily.

"I can assure you, I do," Dixy states calmly and unphased. "Max, can you tell me anything about what you see?"

"No, I don't recognise it, but I don't remember getting on or off. I only remember being in the cargo hold. I escaped to the top deck once, but it was dark, and I was stopped before…I only saw the water, no land, and then…nothing."

The memories of the moment that I thought I had finally managed to escape. The brink of freedom and then my hopes dashed when I soon realised there was nowhere to run. I stood on the deck, and there was nothing to see but water. I feel the weight, the tension of trying to stay in the now while my mind pushes, attempting to transform me to a place in time that I'd do anything not to return to.

"That's okay. From what I've been told, there is a cabin with five cot beds, and the navigation room has one, plus a kitchen and bathroom area. There were definitely six people living on the boat beside you. Maybe we just get you on the boat, and you could look around those first. There is no hurry to go below deck; this takes as long as it takes," Dixy suggests.

I stand still for too long; my feet feel welded to the floor. I don't want the memories that I know will come with entering that cargo hold. I don't want the fear or the pain. I keep urging myself to move, and nothing happens, and I grow more embarrassed by the second. Dixy stands on one side of me, Anna the other, her hand still holding mine. They don't say anything, they don't even move, they just stand shoulder to shoulder with me, eyes fixed on the Seabird.

I squeeze Anna's hand slightly, then I let it slide slowly out of mine as I take my first steps forward. My hands grip the ropes as I stand at the bottom of the ramp, fear pumping through my veins like a potent shot of adrenalin as I hesitate there. It's irrational, I know it is, but I can't help it – I'm terrified of being trapped back on the boat again.

"Who…has…are there keys?"

Dixy steps forward. She takes me by the wrist, turns my hand over so it's palm up, and then places a set of keys in my hand and closes my fingers over them. "This is *your* boat."

Dixy steps back, and I feel a tiny sense of safety as I slide the keys into my pocket. I take hold of the ropes again and try not to look at the water below as I walk across the ramp. The moment my boot hits the deck of the boat, I feel my heart rate accelerate. I quickly step away from the door that I know leads down to the cargo hold. Instead, I move around to the starboard side of the boat.

I know without looking that they are just behind me, keeping a foot or so away, being there but giving me space. I come to a door, and I put my hand on it; it is made from steel, and it's icy cold. There's a deep gorging dent and a twist in the metal near the handle and frame of the door.

"That is the cabin. The keys were inside, so we had to use the jaws of life to prise it open. You should be able to push it open," Dixy explains.

I push it open, and it groans as metal drags along the wooden deck of the floor. The first thing that hits me is the smell; it is musty and damp like there is no clean air. I walk inside and find a very dirty room. It's almost hexagonal with five bed cots lining the walls; each one has a small cupboard at the head of each bed. Empty food wrappers, waste paper, dirty rags, sheets, and beer cans line the floor. The cots still have blankets on them as if they were all expecting to come back.

There is light coming in through small rectangle windows at the top of each panel. The walls are soiled with finger marked and stains. I turn in a slow circle, my eyes scanning each bed, and then I see at the end of one is a pair of old boots, boots that I recognise. I take a step forward and pull them closer with the toe of my boot. I stare at them, transfixed, and I flinch as the memory flashes.

"What is it, Max?"

"This bed belongs to the mala suka man."

"Mala suka man?" Dixy asks.

"Anna…can you…"

I am trying really hard to hold myself together. I feel like it is taking all my fight and focus to stay on the boat and keep myself in the now.

"They used to call her mala suka; it means little bitch. The man that did most of the torture and called her it the most. He is the man that tracked her down at the docks and who she killed at the school," Anna explains.

"Brown bread dread," I mumble as I turn slowly around the room.

The next bed looks the most disturbed and dirty. The little cupboard is slightly open, and I can see little white pieces of card falling loosely from the gap. I open the door, and there is a photo taped to the inside of it. A face smiling up at me with cold eyes that I recognise. I drop to one knee, pull it off, and take a closer look at the now dead and buried Danika 'Danni' Nowak. She would almost look sweet in the photo if it weren't for those eyes that still raise the hairs on my neck. I turn to Anna, her eyes questioning.

"What is it?"

"Tomasz bed," I mumble, handing her the photo, and then I turn back to the cupboard.

"Ugh gross," Anna groans.

I slide the little white cards towards me. They are glossy like photos only thicker and squarer. I pick them up and get to my feet, turning them over in my hands. My stomach bottoms out, pain shooting across my chest as I see the evidence of horror in the polaroid photos. My hands begin to shake as I flick through the crystal-clear images of myself that scream at me. There are so many, and although not all are very clear, all are compromising. All are violating and all make my stomach revolt.

"Gnnaar," I choke, and I drop the photos as my vision begins to blur. I lean forward against the wall with my palms out bracing myself. I feel Anna's hands on my back.

"Don't look! Don't..." I trail off.

The memory swirls...

The protruding bones of my shoulder blades dig against the wooden floor of the boat. I lay shaking, from cold, from hunger, from the pain and shame that still lingers between my legs. I stare up at them, too tired to even glare as they watch my naked and dirty body, chained to the floor.

"Why take photos of the skank? It's not like she is going anywhere?"

"Cos' if the skank doesn't do what I ask, I put them on the internet and send them to her mother." Tomasz leers.

"Not like she can stop you taking a piece, clearly."

"No but it stops her biting off a piece." Tomasz leers.

"You mean...?"

"Yeah. Look, I'll show you."

Tomasz steps towards me, eyes savage and excited as he unzips his flies.

"NO!" I yell, and I pinch my finger and thumb together tightly; I feel Anna's arms tight around my waist and across my chest as she whispers in my ear.

"It's okay, it's okay, it's okay."

"Where are...the...photos?"

"I'm standing on them. It's okay. We hardly saw anything, I promise," Anna whispers and then she kisses the back of my neck. "I'm so sorry."

The sound of the painful break in her voice breaks my resolve. The sobs rack through my body silently, my arm shoots out, and I punch out at the cabin wall as rage burns through me. Anna slides around my body and underneath my rigid arms braced against the wall. She steps into me and holds me tight.

"Let go of the wall; I've got you."

I wonder how long I was stuck like that because it actually stings when I let my arms drop. I fall into her and try to get control of myself. I just want to scream and scream, and it's taking all my will to remain silent.

"I'm going to give you guys a minute," Dixy announces.

Anna pulls back, holding my face in her hands, and I can't look at her. The shame is itching all over my skin and burning in my heart. I don't want to be here; I don't want to be seen.

"Look at me," she says softly.

"I can't…I feel so fucking vile. Please don't."

"Mac…"

I pull away, keeping my head down, and I cross my arms tight across my chest. I feel so dirty; the shame is harrowing. She reaches out to put her hand on my arm, and I flinch away.

"Why won't you let me touch you?"

"Feel…dirty. You shouldn't have…" I struggle, trailing off.

"I shouldn't have to touch you?"

Anna moves so fast I don't see it coming. She pushes herself up against me hard. Her hands on the side of my neck, her face an inch from mine, shocking me into submission.

"There is nothing in the world that can make me stop wanting you! Not with my body or my heart. One day, you will know that, but I'll continue to show you long after you do," Anna emphasises fiercely.

Her lips are on mine gently, I can feel her nerves, her fear of doing the wrong thing. She is barely touching me; I don't think she's even breathing. I kiss her back but just barely. The torment of wanting her and despising myself conflicting loudly in my head, but the longer she stands there, the louder the wanting becomes. My body lets go of its tension; I pull her close, my lips firm against hers, and she finally breathes. Long ragged breaths of relief burst from her as she kisses me feverishly. The itch on my skin starts to soothe, and I break away from her kiss.

"I'm sorry, I couldn't…"

"No, no, no…it's okay, I understand. I'm just glad you are back."

The thought of going into the cargo hold is terrifying. I wasn't prepared to find anything up here. I felt almost complacent that as I'd never seen any of the upper deck, there wouldn't be anything to trigger me. What I did find couldn't have been much worse, but as horrific as it was, now I remember those photos being taken. I'm glad that I can now destroy their existence.

"I need you to give me a minute. I can't leave them there, and I don't want you to see."

"I'll meet you outside." Anna smiles softly.

As soon as she leaves the cabin, I start picking up the photos and doing my best not to look at the images as I go. I search all the little cupboards, through the rubbish on the floor, and under all of the cot beds. Once I am satisfied that there are no more, I jam the wad in my pocket and vow to burn them the first chance I get. It is only when I step outside, I realise how stuffy it was in there, and it is a relief to breathe in the cold fresh air.

I find Anna and Dixy on the bow of the boat sat on some upturned crates. When I reach them, Dixy hands me a bottle of whisky and I smirk, taking it gratefully. I open the bottle and the potent alcohol fumes tickle my nose. I take some sizeable gulps, and I feel the burn of them all the way down into my belly. Some whisky should not be drunk neat; it's like drinking lighter fluid. No taste, just bitter burn, but right now, I'll take it.

"You came prepared." I cringe as I knock back another mouthful.

"Nah, I bought it off a fisherman named Earl. Nice chap but stunk of fish. I knew if I asked enough of them, I was bound to find some old boy with a stash somewhere."

I snort a laugh. "To Earl," I toast.

No matter how shell shocked I feel, I can't help but see an opportunity that my nerdy little heart can't resist. I put the bottle onto the deck and walk around Dixy and Anna to bow of the boat. I stand at the point of the bow, stepping up onto the ledge, and my arms stretch out at the sides of me - palms up.

"I'M THE KING OF THE WORLD! HA-HA-HA WHOOOP!"

I turn round to the booming laughter of Dixy and Anna, and I grin, quite impressed with myself. It feels so good to laugh and even better to shout.

“I’m so disappointed with myself for not seeing that coming.” Anna cackles.

“Either that whisky is getting to you, or you my friend are the biggest nerd I’ve ever seen,” Dixy jeers in mock repugnance.

“It’s not the whisky,” Anna confirms.

From up here, there is a winning view of the entire docks. My head swims a little at the height, or maybe it is the whisky. I hold the rail and take it all in; the graveyard of skeleton boats looks much prettier from this distance. If I hadn’t already walked through them, I could easily be fooled that they were a fleet of gleaming pleasure boats. The water stretches out as far as the eye can see. In the distance, I can just see the yellow swirl of metal that makes the big roller coaster I saw when I drove past the pleasure beach.

“You don’t have to go any further here today. We are here for a few days; we can always come back tomorrow. I have training planned for you in the cargo hold, so we will definitely be coming back anyway. There’s no pressure,” Dixy encourages.

“Actually, there is. The more we get done, the better. I have five, maybe six days till Barrett comes back. I don’t have the time to waste. As tempting as is to take the out, I don’t want to delay the inevitable. So, tell me what I have to do.”

I crouch against the wall of the boat, opposite Dixy and Anna. Anna is back to looking stressed; I can tell she doesn’t want to go below deck just by the worry that is pulling at her face. Dixy leans forward on her knees and rests on them with crossed arms, her eyes scrutinising my face as if she is trying to make sure I mean what I say. Eventually, she smiles a little and nods.

“Okay, so I want you to do exactly what you did in the cabin. Move around the room, touch things, but talk about what you see. Be vocal about what you see and remember because I need to know those triggers for step two of this.”

“What is step two? How many steps are there?”

“I will tell you tomorrow, and there are three but don’t worry. You are going to love step three,” she insinuates vaguely with an encouraging smile, but I don’t return it. Nor do I believe it.

"I know it's hard, but you need to let the flashbacks happen. Talk them out, tell us what you see, make friends with them, just like the box. They are just flashbacks and memories, horrific ones, yes, but you already know you can stop them. Now I want you to take the power out of them, so they are less scary. Hopefully then, with whatever Barrett has planned, you will be able to focus more on enduring the reconditioning and less on trying not to let the flashbacks take hold."

I can see the method through the madness, it does make sense, but it doesn't make me any more eager to go down there. There is so many what if's running through my mind, loud and overactive fears, both rational and irrational. The idea of going down there feels very much like standing on the edge of a cliff and being told, 'don't worry, there is a crash mat at the bottom.'

"What if all my memories come back all at once?"

"I think that's extremely unlikely. Your memory wasn't just lost because of trauma; there were drugs involved in making that happen. It has caused intermittent gaps that you simply can't remember, and I think that's why it doesn't all come back smoothly. Your memory isn't working in a continuous reel; there are breaks that interrupt the flow. It will probably always come back in pieces till it eventually stops."

"Okay, but if there any flashes of Tomasz, I'm not talking them out, and I'll be stopping them as quick as I can. I don't think anything that happened with him is likely to come up with Barrett. I'm not willing to relive it unnecessarily."

"That's okay, Max. I agree. Are you ready?"

I get to my feet, breathing in a long, deep gust of air.

"Nope, but let's just chuck it in the fuck-it-bucket."

CHAPTER 12

Purging the Demons

My instincts scream at me to turn around run as I stand with my hand hovering on the door handle. Anna and Dixy stand on the stairs behind me, waiting patiently for me to work up the nerve to open to door. Behind this door is my own personal hell. Right now, I feel numb, and after everything that triggered in the cabin, it feels wrong to force the relief of that numbness away. I want to stay there on holiday from the pain.

Trust, that is what I need. Trust that Dixy knows what she's doing, that this will all be worth it. Trust in my own ability to withstand this. The demons behind the door are dead; I already killed them. Only their ghosts remain and all I have to do is open the door exorcise them. As long as I fear them, as long as I allow them refuge inside me, they'll continue to possess me with their ghastly grip.

"I am a mouse, and I will shout about this house," I mutter.

Without really thinking, my wrist twists, the handle turns, and I push the door open with a creak. The cargo hold is dark; only shadows and shapes are visible as I hesitate in the doorway. Little rays of light uselessly attempt to peek through the six small round windows, unable to penetrate filth obscuring the glass. I take one step forward with my eyes on my feet and lift my right hand. It finds the light switch with ease, flicking it on as if I had done it a thousand times before. In reality, I've only *wanted* to a thousand times before; I hated being left in the dark.

The smell is pungent, like the home of a crazy cat lady who houses 50 cats with no real way of keeping up with the cat piss. I lift my head, and the scene that meets my eyes is hideously familiar and every bit as disturbing as I expected it to be. The arched walls of curved wood are varnished in deep burnt red and are reinforced with cold steel girders. Ropes hang in coils loosely from the walls. The ceiling structure is joisted with the same varnished wood and steel rafters. The steel rafter dead ahead towards the bow of the boat still bears the chains that bound me. It hangs there silent and still, the slack of it balled on the floor, the shackles still attached.

My heart remembers the loneliness like a phantom limb pain, the affliction severed but the pain is still there. It's so real that you question if the diseased limb was ever actually removed. I lean my forehead against the doorframe and close my eyes. My breath is embarrassingly loud as I try to keep control of myself. The emotion is thick in my chest, my hands rubbing my wrists like I can feel the cold steel entrapping them.

"Max…use your voice," Dixy reminds softly, and I groan in frustration.

"The chains, I can feel…"

"Don't just rub them; look at them. Connect your vision with the feel of it," Dixy instructs.

I do as I am told, and it helps almost instantly, but I can't seem to get a hold of myself. I grip hold of the door frame and breathe through clenched teeth as the memories bombard me. Pain seers inside my chest, and I want to scream to relieve it. I hear movement from behind me.

"Anna, don't. You need to…" Dixy begins.

"You are not going to stop me going to her, Dixy. She isn't triggered; she is upset," Anna snaps.

I jump at her touch even though she is being incredibly gentle. Her hand slides just under the back of my t-shirt, and I open my eyes.

"Tell me," she utters softly.

The lump rises in my throat no matter how hard I try to swallow it down; the tears threatening to spill over, and I don't want them to. I don't want to lose grip on the tiny grasp I have hold of myself with.

"It's…the same. Everything…"

Her eyes are intent upon mine. It would be easy for her to show sadness, but instead, I see fiery determination, and I am grateful for it.

"This room didn't defeat you then, and it won't defeat you now. This room should be afraid of the unstoppable force that is Mac Scott." She smiles lovingly and leans in closer, whispering so only I can hear. "If you need to leave, no one will blame you for it, but if I know you, you won't because you never back down from a fight. Whatever you choose to do, you are not alone this time, and whatever happens, when you leave, you will leave holding hands with the proudest girlfriend."

I take one hand off the door frame and hold it out till I feel her warm hand holding mine, my breath beginning to slow.

"…magic." I breath, and then she giggles sweetly. "Thank you…"

I lean back off the door frame and squeeze her hand before I take a deep breath and let her hand slide out of mine, and then I look up to Dixy.

"Keep the door open," I mutter, and she smiles at me proudly before giving me a nod.

Taking my first tentative steps into the room. I move to the right-hand side, and I hear their footsteps clonk down the wooden stairs as they enter the room behind me. Then the quietest, tiny gasp from Anna escapes. I keep my back to them and approach a beaten and old chest of drawers that is bolted to the floor, and I lay my hands on the top of it. The top drawer has a hole, an old-style keyhole, and I run my finger over it and flinch as I see the mala suka man clear in my mind, his hand twisting a long, old-fashioned key in the lock before putting the key inside his jeans pocket.

I pull out the keys from my pocket, searching for the key, but I knew that was pointless. The key wasn't a part of a bunch. Whatever is in the drawer, it is something the mala suka man wanted kept hidden. I move to the next drawer down, and my stomach swoops with a nauseating churn. Inside the drawer are the mala suka man's choice tools of torment. My hand shakily reaches in, and I grip the handle of a hunter's style knife; the blade is long and smooth, the handle heavy and slightly rubbery.

"Max?" Dixy calls, and I turn round with a clenched jaw and meet her gaze, then Anna's, and they both look at me, and then their eyes glance to the knife. I answer the question in their eyes by lifting the knife and tracing the point across the scar that jaggers across my throat, and I turn away.

"This is the mala suka man's toy drawer; they are self-explanatory," I say dismissively as I shut the drawer.

Upon opening the bottom and final drawer, I find a mess of rusty tools and junk. Gaffer tape, matches, broken pencils, coils of wire, screwdrivers, batteries, a hammer, some spanners, spark plugs, bolts, and screws. I pick up a flat headed screwdriver and the hammer and shut the drawer. The head of the screwdriver just fits inside the keyhole. I hold it steady while I take aim, and I bring the hammer down on it. After three hits, I feel the lock collapse and shatter.

There is no resistance as I tug on the smooth, round handles of the drawer. Sadness tugs on my heart as I see my own possessions that I thought were lost forever. Things I was wearing when I returned home after leaving Alisha at the hotel. My favourite black skinny tie, a gift from my mum when I landed the job at PIC. It is rolled neatly into a reel. I pick it up and feel the heavy fabric, soft and made with quality.

It doesn't feel real or possible. My fingers unravel it, and my eyes well as I see the message sewn into the back in white embroidery. 'Love you lots, Mum x' I choke on a sob, the lump rising in my throat, but I swallow it down. Anna moves to my side, her hand light on the bottom of my back. I hand her the tie, and she takes it, her thumb running over the embroidery.

"Aw, Mac..."

Inside the drawer, I also find my black polished dress shoes, my mobile phone, and my wallet. I open it and see my old bank card and store cards, money still inside, and a piece of folded up hotel paper with Alisha's phone number scrawled neatly by her hand. My heart aches. It is like a time capsule. The part of myself that I lost is still here, and too much time has passed, too many scars have formed to ever get that part of myself back. The only thing I can do is open the drawer, release my possessions, and let that ghost of myself finally rest in peace. They are not his trophies anymore.

The last thing inside of the drawer is a small wooden box, the surface of it clean and smooth light-coloured wood. I flick the tiny catch with the tip of my finger and lift the lid.

"Oh, Jesus...Dixy?" I growl, and she comes straight over, standing at my other shoulder.

The box is lined in red velvet materiel and split into two sections. On the left is a neat stack of plastic cards. Upon closer inspection, they are all photo ID cards, mostly driving licences, and all are bearing the faces and names of different women, both British and Polish. I hand them to Dixy, and her face gawps in disgust. "Oh, my God. There are so many."

In the right section are various pieces of jewellery, mostly rings, all different shapes and sizes and showing different degrees of tarnish. It is there I spot the cufflinks I was wearing that night. How many lives has this man destroyed? My stomach churns, and I have to look away. I definitely feel less guilt for the murderous frenzy of stab wounds I rained down on him at the school.

Next to the chest of drawers is a pile of damp sandbags, I step around them to follow the wall of the boat. When I walk past, I see leant up against it a white moulded plastic box. It is smaller than I even remembered, dented and yellowing with small holes in the top. The top is catch down with an unlocked padlock loosely threaded through it, securing it shut. I stand frozen, unable to look away, the memories flashing across my mind.

"Ughh," I groan, my palms ramming into my eyes.

"Max…don't fight it. Voice it!" Dixy commands.

The memory swirls…

"Arrrgghhhh stop!! STOP! Let me out!" I scream in unison with my past self.

"Mac…" Anna calls.

"Anna, no! You have to let her pass through this!" Dixy snaps, and Anna growls. I drop to my hands and knees, my fists pounding on the deck.

"LET ME OUT!" I wail.

I pound my fists against the box as I am dangled over the edge of the boat, suspended by a chain that is fixed to the padlock. Through the holes in the lid, I see the water get nearer as I am lowered towards its icy depths. Waves of saltwater thrash against the box, leaking in through the holes.

"Max, use your words!" Dixy shouts.

"Box, chain…locked, the sea, drown…" I choke.

The box submerges, and the water starts pouring in. Panic takes hold, and I thrash and pound until I have nothing left. The water starts to creep up my neck, and I sob.

"Please don't let me die like this, any way but this," I gurgle in terror-stricken sobs.

I can taste the saltwater as it leaches into my mouth. I start to choke, and then I feel a sharp lunge. The box is yanked out of the water, and the water starts to pour back out. I gasp for air, coughing and spluttering.

"Oskar! What the hell are you doing?! Jakub yells, the words repeat in my strangled sobs.

"Just having some fun, Jakub. Leave it out," Oskar snipes.

"If the catch on that box breaks and you lose her to the sea, you are as dead as she is! Pull her up now!" Jakub barks.

"Ugh, fuck," I sob.

I feel the hard wood of the deck against my knees as my limbs shake. My breath ragged, I swear I can still taste the salt water.

"Mac…" Anna says softly, her voice pained.

"No! On your feet, Agent Scott," Dixy orders.

I whimper, wiping the snot from my nose on my sleeve.

"I said, ON YOUR FEET, AGENT SCOTT!" Dixy yells.

Anger burns inside me like acid as I drag myself up. I glare at Dixy with venom. She holds my gaze with strength and then she lifts her arm and points at the box. My eyes stare fixed at it, fury building inside, and I launch myself towards it. I kick it over and over and over, snarls of rage escaping my mouth. It is painful, it doesn't dent the box, but my foot keeps kicking and stomping with every ounce of strength I possess until I run out of steam. The tears return, and I drop onto the sandbags.

"Now, you can go." Dixy says in a pained voice, and I hear Anna dash towards me. Her arms are around me in seconds.

"I'm alright, I'm alright,"

"Yeah well, it's not all about you," she jokes through a sob, and I chuckle, pulling her as close as I can possibly can, my face buried in her neck. I breath in her candy scented perfume, and I feel the calm sweeping over me. I feel a pang of guilt when I see the redness of her eyes. I cup her face in my hand.

"I have to finish this," I groan in a gravelly tone, my throat burning from all the screaming. "But you don't have to stay," I offer, and her eyes intensify on mine, determined.

"I am *not* leaving you."

Pulling myself to my feet, I see Dixy standing over on the other side of the boat near the bow with her hands on her hips, her back turned, and her shoulders shaking. I look at Anna, confused.

"I was mad at her till I realised that wasn't easy for her to do," she whispers, and I nod.

I walk over to her, approaching her carefully till I stand shoulder to shoulder with her, and I drape a hesitant arm over her shoulder. She flinches, but she doesn't pull away.

"I'm sorr…"

"Dix, you have nothing to be sorry for. I'm starting to see what you are trying to do. Don't lose trust in yourself now. I'm grateful you exist, Kate Dixon. Now rub some dirt in it, and let's finish this."

"Hah. Thanks, dweeb."

I let her go and turn back towards the centre of the cargo hold when something flashes across my mind, and I stop in my tracks. I turn back around, step around Dixy, and then the image flashes. This is where I was sat when I noticed they had left the video recorder on, right before I left the video message. The image is clear in my mind; it feels almost natural when I habitually lower myself to the floor and sit back in the spot. My back leans back against the curve of the boat. It feels like sitting in an old chair. I close my eyes. I felt safest here, hidden in the corner, and it was always the least painful place to sit.

My hands run across the smooth wood, and then I feel something that isn't smooth, something out of place, and I open my eyes and investigate. I see the words gouged deep into the wood, smudged with dried up blood drops and smears. The strangest noise escapes my mouth, a cross between a whimper and groan, and my hand covers my mouth. The lump rises back up in my throat with force, and the tears fall from my wide eyes. I pull my knees up to my chest, just as I always did, and my body rocks back and forth slightly, my mind starting to slide in that horrible familiar swirl.

Anna kneels in front of me, holding my knees and stopping the rock, and I jump. I point rigidly to the etchings.

HERE LIES MAC SCOTT

GONE AND FORGOTTEN

The memory swirls, but I don't move. The scene doesn't change but Anna and Dixy disappear.

My body rocks as I hold my bony, naked legs tight against my chest. The terror I feel is so raw and so piercing, I feel like I'm losing my mind. My body racked with painful tremors. The chains cold against my bruised and bloody wrists clink with every shake that convulses through me.

"This is good, Mac. It w-will be over soon; it will all stop," I ramble in sync with my past self.

"I can't take…anymore. I can't…I wonder if there is a heaven. If there is a God…why d-did he leave me here? I thought if I held on long enough…but no one is…I don't exist. I'm already dead."

My wrists itch so bad. I scratch wildly under the shackles and growl when I can't reach the itch. Rage burns up inside me, and I slam my wrists hard on the deck either side of me, over and over again. The chain attached whips hard against my knees, and I cry out.

"Argh! Why don't they just get it over with!" I snarl.

I feel my heart break with pain as the sobs start to roll through me. I lean to my left and lift up the loose plank, pulling out a small bloody screw. My fingers raw and bloody, I focus on finishing my epitaph. I look down and start gouging the F.

"Forgotten… I wish I could go back. All this time…for what? I may as well have given up a long time ago. I hope there is a heaven and…I hope they have ice cream. Maybe if…I pray…maybe…I don't know if I remember…

"Now, I lay me down to sleep…I…

"Ugh come on! Just one fucking prayer, Mac! Oh…swearing, great! That's really going to please God!" I chuckle darkly.

"Now, I lay me down to sleep, I…pray the Lord…my soul to take…no…keep…my soul to keep. Guard me Jesus…through the night…ugh…something, something…morning light."

I look down, satisfied with my work, I hold the screw tight in my palm as I curl my arms back around my knees and rock. Maybe I can ram it into one of their necks before they finish me off.

"I pray the Lord my soul to keep, I pray the Lord my soul to keep, I pray…"

I see a flashing blink in the corner of my eye, and I turn and look at the video camera mounted on the tripod. Even as I squint my blurry eyes, I can't see from here. I lean forward, crawl slowly on my hands and knees. Fuck, it hurts, everything hurts, and the chain is so God damn heavy. The drag of it is hard, sapping the last bit of energy I have. When I am close enough, I stop, inspecting the blinking light.

"It's still switched on. Why..."

Is this a trick? My brain drags too slow as I try to figure it out, but I'm dead anyway, so really...what does it matter? I look into the camera lens; it is hard work keeping my head upright. I just feel so weak but maybe, one day, someone will find this.

"I don't know if anyone will ever see this. I've been here too long. I don't know what day it is. What year it is...I have been in the dark so long, I can't remember people's faces anymore. I would...give anything to see...

"Mac... Mac..."

"What are you doing, Anna?!" Dixy spits.

"She already has this memory! She doesn't need to go through it twice. Mac..."

"Good catch."

"Mac...come back..."

I gasp, choking on air, disorientated as my eyes come into focus. I am sat in the middle of the bunker; Anna's sat on the floor in front of me with her hands on my face. Dixy kneels down beside Anna, both of them wearing matching masks of horror. I cringe, looking down in embarrassment.

Sharp pain stings in my palm, and I look at my hand, releasing the grip of my fist. There, glistening with my blood, lays the screw from under the floorboard. The sight of it hammers down the reality, the lonely fear of waiting for death weighing heavily on my heart. My hand tremors, and I drop the screw from my hand in revulsion.

"Oh fuck..." I whimper.

Anna pulls me to her, and I break. The past, the present, the memories, the reality all hit me like a hurricane. I cry so hard I have to force myself to stop as a feeling of nausea hits.

"It's okay...it's okay, it's over. I've got you," Anna cries. "Dixy..."

I feel Anna lean then Dixy fall against my back, and they both sandwich me as all three of us cry. Anna is kissing my neck, Dixy is awkwardly rigid, patting my shoulder, and suddenly, my laughing bursts through the sobs.

"Dixy hates hugs!"

"Hey! Shut it you, I am trying!" Dixy gripes.

Before I know it, we are all laughing. Hysterical laughs through painful tears, and Dixy pulls away. Her playfully annoyed face just makes Anna and I howl harder. When the laughing stops, I wipe my eyes and take a deep shaky breath. My chest hurts, and I'm exhausted.

"I think that's enough for one day, Max. Let's get the hell out of this horror house and get us all some food and many a strong drink!" Dixy announces.

***

I walk in autopilot, being led by Anna's hand back to our hotel room. She leads me to the bed and sits me on the end of it, kneeling in front of me.

"I don't even know what to say to you right now. I don't know how… Tell me what you need baby. Please, anything that will help?"

"I need…a shower. I feel..."

"Okay, we can do that."

Anna unlaces my boots, pulling them off, and then she leads me to the bathroom. She turns on the shower and then turns back to me, taking my clothes off. I walk into the huge, steamy shower cubical. I step under the hot water, my hands leaning against the cool marble. I close my eyes and let the water pound down on me. Once I do, the pain starts to engulf me. It is inescapable, inevitable, and I don't have the strength left to stop it.

Then I feel her hand on my back as she moves in front of me. She steps under the water with me and pulls me to her. I fall apart, the water hiding my tears, but the sobs break through me violently, and she just holds me tight against her. Then I feel the sobs shake through her, and guilt pangs in my stomach.

"I'm so sorry, I don't mean to…just seemed s-so real. I was scared just watching you, like it was really happening. I don't know how you survived this, and after that, I don't know how I'll ever let go of you again."

"That's okay. I'm in no hurry for you to let me go."

***

I feel dazed and weary as she pulls me in into the crisp, clean bed. Anna lays on her side facing me, her hair hanging in damp, loose, red wine curls. She holds my hand over her heart; it is comforting to me, and she clearly knows that.

"How do you know to do that?" I squeak, my voice still raw from the screaming.

"In the field, after you let me touch you for the first time. You were crying, and you laid your hand over my heart. It seemed to calm you, and then you kissed my fingertips... God, it was the sweetest thing. I can still see your face when you realised you could touch me. You looked so free and elated. It was so beautiful." She smiles warmly, and I smile a little as the memory hits.

"I remember. It was the moment I knew there was no fighting how I felt about you."

Anna smiles at me but looks at me with wary eyes, like she is worried I will shatter into a million pieces. Her fingertips absentmindedly trace up and down my forearm, and I shiver at the goosebumps her touch brings.

"I'm okay. You don't need to worry."

"If you were okay right now, I really would be worried. I'm just struggling to know what to do or what to say, and I'm not used to that feeling."

"Say what's on your mind; I always want to hear that. You look scared of me, and that is really hard to take," I admit.

"Oh God no! Of course, I am not. I'm sorry. I'm just scared of saying something that will make it worse. I promise, I'm not scared of you. In fact, I wish I felt like you wanted me closer. You feel really far away."

I feel a pang of guilt as I hear the sadness in her voice. I shuffle a little closer and lay my hand on the side of her neck, my thumb tracing her sharp jawline.

"I'm sorry. I am just embarrassed. I'd never have chosen for you to see those parts of me; I didn't even want to see them myself. I feel absolutely mortified, weak, and pretty pathetic, but I'll get over it. It isn't you," I assure her.

"You are so wrong, Mac. You always talk about the magic of me, but today, I saw your magic. I've seen it before, but it wasn't till today that I really registered it."

I frown at her. Now I'm really lost. The only magic of today is that somehow, I still have my marbles intact…I think.

"You left the cabin after horrific flashbacks, and moments later, you were stood on the bow of the boat yelling that you were the king of the world. Then I heard you in your memory trying to pray. You sounded so terrified, clearly sure you were about to die, and then I heard you swear as you couldn't remember the words, joking that God was going to be pissed. You laughed, and so did we, just for a moment. Just like when you sung Sweet Home Alabama when you were under Billy's control or when you told Jackson that your name was Groot. You face the most horrific things, and somewhere inside of you, you hold this endearing, beautiful, strength that keeps you holding on. No matter how bad things are."

I smile in spite of myself. She is damn good at speeches, and she knows just how to bring the light when I need help out of the dark.

"So, what you are saying is…I'm the biggest nerd you've ever known, and you freaking love it!" I grin brightly, and she laughs musically.

"Well, that and…you have magic inside of you, Mac Scott, and it's the furthest thing from weakness I've ever seen."

I pull myself towards her, kissing her lovingly. My body tingles as I pull her close as if it has suddenly realised that we are both naked. No matter how messed up I am feeling, she is gorgeous, and I'm only human. My hands start to wander, relishing in how responsive she is to my touch. My hand follows the dipping arch of her waist, and I feel goosebumps irrupt on her heated skin beneath my touch. Anna's hand rests at the bottom of my back, her fingertips stroking the space between my tail bone and bum. It's a touch I have never experienced before, and the sensation is singing, the echo of her touch making me squirm. I roll on top of her, my thigh hanging and creating heavy pressure against her excitement.

"Mac-attack, you read me, kid?" Alfred sounds in my ear.

I pull away suddenly, laying on my back panting breathlessly with my hands covering my face.

"Mac…"

"Yeah, I read you Pa," I reply through the worst cringe I have ever suffered in my life, and Anna starts cackling with laughter. I roll over to her, playfully covering her mouth.

"I just wanted to check on you, see how you were holding up. We're all going down to the restaurant for food and drinks. You fancy meeting us there in 10?"

"Yeah, sure, Pa. We'll see you in there."

"Great. Love you, kid."

"Love you too, Pa. Houston, we have a problem."

I let go of Anna's mouth, and she howls with laughter. I just want the ground to swallow me whole, but I am laughing too.

"Ugh…I'm so grossed out. Ugh, God damn it!" I winge.

"Ha-ha! I don't blame you. I don't want to go; I was really enjoying where your hands were going. Did he tell you he loved you?"

"Yeah, that's the only reason I am getting out of this bed right now. He's worried."

I dig around in my rucksack for some clean clothes. I make a mess of it but manage to pull out some jeans and a not too creased black shirt.

"That's so freaking cute. I never really told you, but I love the way you are with him. When Danni was around, I'd watch you both get closer and closer, and it would make me melt. He adores you," Anna coos, and I blush.

"Well, I love him, too."

"I know. You are so damn cute - I could just eat you!" she squeaks.

We both get ready at super speed, and we are just about to leave when Anna stops me, tugging on my wrist till I turn to face her. She pulls up the collar to my shirt and slides the tie around my neck that I found in the drawers on the boat. She begins tying it for me, and I watch her intently.

"Back where it belongs," she mutters.

"I don't know what I would do without you, girl."

"I don't plan on letting you find out."

We make our way to the restaurant, and it is only when we leave the hotel room that I realise how hungry I am. I notice the light is fading outside; it must be a lot later than I realised. How long were we on that God forsaken boat? We find the restaurant entrance, and I hold the door open for Anna she grins at me cutely. There is a fire in her eyes tonight, a fire that makes my legs weak, and my insides throb.

I feel underdressed and a little uncomfortable, and by the look on Anna's face, she feels the same. This restaurant is fancy. It's dimly lit with moody purple uplighters that beam warmly across glittered silver wallpaper on some walls and silver and dark purple geometric patterns on others. It is almost dark but bright enough to see; it has a sexy nightclub vibe. The soft grey chairs are neatly arranged around heavy white marble tables. Between them are privacy screens made from dark wood structures that look like trellises only the gaps form intricate geometric patterns.

I crane my neck around in search of everyone. By now, I should have learnt better because they are, of course, sitting hidden at the very back of the restaurant. I feel relieved as we draw nearer and see not one of them has dressed up. We will make a misfitted ragtag bunch, and the hotel staff will probably be glad we are hidden in the back. Alfred gets to his feet with a big, crooked grin. He kisses Anna on the cheek and gives her a hug. Then he turns to me and gives me a big bear hug.

"Glad you made it, kid. Was worried. Dixy told me it was a shit storm," Alfred grumbles.

"I'm alright. Had to rub a lot of dirt in it, but I'm good." I pull back and blush at the sight of his proud grin.

"Well, I think you'd better let your Pa buy you a well-deserved drink. Take a seat; I can bring them over." He winks, and he scurries off. Anna leans in, her lips at my ear.

"Seriously, I will eat you," she whispers deep and gravelly, and I smirk at her, the thought spurring on a heavy assault of butterflies in my tummy.

Not if I eat you first...

Anna and I take the empty seats next to Alfred, and we sit opposite Lambert and Dixy. Lambert tears his eyes away from the food menu and grins upon my arrival, giving me my obligatory high five. Dixy rolls her eyes, scoffing.

"What?"

"You two are so blokey! You have like this, macho, gun envy, let's fight each other – bromance going on," Dixy jeers sarcastically.

"Aw, I think someone feels left out because she never gets high fived by anyone," Lambert snipes playfully.

"I will high five your face, *Callum*," Dixy threats.

"I would like to see you try, *Kate*," Lambert retorts.

I can't help but laugh; they are like spatting siblings. As always, I feel Anna's hand resting on the inside of my thigh. I love that about her, her need to always have contact even if it's in the smallest way. The truth is, after the day I have had, I long for more closeness with her. I still feel shell shocked. As much as I want to be here, it's also not easy to be. I rest my arm across the low back of her chair, my hand light against her ribs, and I take a deep breath. Alfred returns from the bar, and not a moment too soon; he is carrying a tray full of drinks, and I raise an eyebrow at him.

"Thought I'd get a good few in, save us going back and forth. Everyone has a double whisky plus two shots of tequila."

"Nice one, Sarg!" Lambert booms

"I see a hangover in my future," Dixy winces.

"Pa, are you trying to get everyone hammered?" Anna asks.

"Hammered is such a strong word, Savannah. I was thinking more like…trolleyed." Alfred beams, and I snort.

"Are you already a little lightly trolleyed, Pa?" I ask.

"No…I mean, I had a few shots of this purple stuff while I waited at the bar. It was complimentary, you know. Would've been rude not to."

Alfred passes all the drinks out to everyone, and I feel the warmth of the whisky begin to relax my muscles. Everyone chats excitedly about what food they are going to order, especially after Dixy announces that dinner is on MI5. Alfred and Lambert don't waste any time ordering their pricey filet mignons. I ordered a modest pizza meal and salted caramel chocolate lava cake, which I'm way more excited about than I should be.

Alfred gets to his feet, his handed extended with a shot glass brimming with tequila, and everyone picks up their first shot. I am filled with dread; I absolutely loath tequila.

"I'd like to propose a toast. It's good to be here with family, which I consider you all to be, and I hope you'll all join me in toasting Mac, who today kicked ten bells out of the suck, and I for one am proud as hell. So, to Mac-attack!"

"To Mac-attack!" everyone cheers.

"Oh, Jesus…"

My nose crinkles as I knock back the shot of tequila, and I shudder as it goes down. I look at Anna, and she giggles, her eyes sparkling magically.

"You hated every second of that, didn't you?"

"Hated, loathed, detested… Pick a word, beautiful, any word." I grimace.

The food arrives, and I look at my pizza with wary eyes. There are things on there I don't really recognise, and it is covered in raw green foliage. I start pulling it all off to try to find the pizza underneath.

"You alright there, Max?" Dixy asks, suppressing a laugh.

"I'm trying to find my pizza; I wasn't aware I ordered a forest, and there is weird stuff on it like… What is this?!" I gripe dramatically, and Dixy howls.

I hold up a little green, round, slimy disk that looks a bit like a sliced grape.

"That is an olive, baby," Anna chimes in, her smirk adoring.

"Oh…I don't think I like olives."

"Have you ever tried it? You should; they're nice." Dixy encourages, her face serious.

"No, but look at it. It is green and slimy; it just screams gross."

"Oh, just try it. You never know, you might love it," Dixy presses.

I put the olive in my mouth and instantly regret it. The texture is mushy, and my mouth fills with bitter saltiness. Dixy is beside herself laughing at the faces I am pulling; I swallow it down and chase it with my drink.

"Ugh! It's making my ears giggle! How can you like that?!"

"I don't; I think they are the devil's work. I just wanted to see you try it." Dixy smirks, winking at Anna.

I decide this would be a great time for another drink, especially as I downed mine trying to wash down the vile aftertaste of the olive. I disappear off in search for the bar, which is conveniently just around the corner some. I'm waiting to be served when Alfred pops up behind me.

"Thought I'd stretch my legs before desert arrives," he mutters.

"You are as useless of a liar as me. You don't need to worry; I'm okay."

"Busted… You can't blame me for checking. Dixy didn't give any details, but she was shell shocked when she came back. Had me worried 'cos if it upset her that much, I can only imagine."

"It was the day from hell, and it wasn't easy on Anna and Dixy either. Honestly, I don't know how I would have got through it without them, especially Anna. Although, if I could make it so she never had to see any of that, I would."

Alfred rubs the whiskers on his cheek with his hand, his eyebrows crumpling.

"Nothing would have stopped her going with you, kid. All the bad stuff aside, it's great seeing you both together. You both look besotted and 'on top of the world' happy, and it makes me happy to see."

"Thanks, Pa. I am happy in spite of everything. She's just… incredible."

"Of course, she is. She's a Slone! Or at least, for now she is." He nudges my shoulder with a wink.

"Woah, slow your roll, old timer! Bit early for wedding bells, don't you think?"

"Well, I married her grandmother after two months. Best thing I ever did in my life, but I guess those were different times. Life is short, and when you know, you know, but you're right; there's no hurry. Just make sure it happens in my lifetime. I want to be there to walk her down the aisle."

"No pressure then, Pa."

That was not the conversation I was expecting. I never thought he would be so eager to marry Anna off. Although I see why he wants to walk her down the aisle when she has already lost her parents. I feel a tad daunted by it, but not for the reason I expected. I am daunted that the thought doesn't daunt me at all. If anyone knows that life is short, it's me. I've been with enough of the wrong people to know when I feel like I have found the right one. Yeah…I think I will drink my whisky and torture myself with that knowledge another day.

Thankfully, dessert does not disappoint like dinner did. My eyes light up as a perfect chocolate sponge dome twinkling with glitter is placed in front of me. I slide my spoon into it and giggle to myself like a child when the thick, hot, salty caramel oozes out. I polish it off with ease, and it might just be the best dessert I've ever had.

"Oh, I forgot to tell you guys. Something really weird happened earlier on the boat." Dixy frowns, and my insides clench.

"What happened?" Alfred asks, and everyone quietens down to listen. My heart begins to pound uncomfortably.

"Well, we were taking a break, and then suddenly, Max was standing on the bow, arms stretched out, yelling, 'I'm the king of the world!'" Dixy bellows, and I cringe at her volume, but the relief washes though me as the table irrupts in booming laughter.

"No way! I'm gutted I missed that!" Alfred booms.

I'm blushing again; it seems to have happened a lot tonight. I've had a blast with them all. As much as I didn't want to come at the beginning, I've laughed so much having dinner out with people I love. But I am exhausted, and right now, all I want is to be with Anna. I slide my hand onto her thigh, feeling the softness of her skin just under the skirt of her summer dress. I feel her hand grip my thigh slightly; I can't suppress the smirk. Anna leans into me, laying her head on my shoulder, and then she turns her head, discreetly kissing my neck. I feel my face flush, and my hand slides a little further up her skirt. My grip tightens as she bites my ear lobe, her breath shaky in my ear.

"I need you," she breathes, and the tingles double their assault in my chest.

"Guys, I'm going to have to bail. I'm beat, and I am guessing I have another early start tomorrow?" I ask Dixy, and she gives me a knowing smile.

"I think I can allow a little lay in, Max. I'll be knocking on your door at 8am. Bring spare clothes. Anna, you probably won't want to come; it's going to be a particularly rough day so you might want to…look after her tonight," she insinuates with all the subtly of a rusty teaspoon.

We slip out of the restaurant and walk hand in hand back to the hotel room. With every step, I am aching for her more and more. I have never felt such relentless need to touch someone, to make them feel good. In most relationships I've had, I've been considered a giver, and I've been fine with it. With Anna though, I crave her touch as much as I crave to touch her. The connection I have with her is electric, a magnetic pull dragging me in. It's always felt that way, but when we collide, it's nothing short of earth shattering.

I watch as Anna slips the card into the slot and smile with satisfaction when I see the slight tremble in her hand. The door opens, and the moment we are inside, my lips are on hers. I push her feverishly against the door. I kiss her with urgency, nibbling on her bottom lip. My hands run over her body firmly with nothing short of animalistic need.

I spin her round, lifting her dress off above her head and flicking off her bra. My lips travel down her spine, and I fall to my knees as I slide her panties down. On my knees, I turn her back around, and my lips explore the crease of her groin. Her legs squirm as I spread them gently apart. Anna whines gravelly deep inside her throat as I taste her, my tongue teasing her with every flick and stroke.

"God…you taste amazing…"

"O-Oh, you f-feel so fucking good." Anna moans, her hands pulling me in deeper.

I look up to see her watching me through heavy-lidded eyes. Her legs shake as I suck her clit; it hardens inside my mouth as I roll my tongue against it. The sight of her falling apart as she shamelessly watches me make it happen is so beautiful, I never want to stop. I kiss my way back up her body, pausing to lap my tongue around her aching nipple. Anna's breath hitches any time I get close, and I smile as I continue to tease her, my hand engulfing the swell of her other breast. Anna's hand curves around the back of my neck, gripping needily, and it's enough to stop me teasing. My finger and thumb pinch in perfect time as I suck her other nipple into my mouth. I relish in the moans that follow, straining from her mouth as her hips buck against me. I pull back, my lips possessing hers again, and she utters breathlessly into my mouth.

"I need you naked… I need to feel you..." She groans, her fingers unzipping my flies.

I rip open my shirt, half the buttons falling on the floor, and she makes quick work of the rest. I lead her backwards, my lips never leaving hers, past the bed and into the bathroom. My palm slams on the shower power button as I pass, and she giggles into my mouth musically.

The shower beats down on us both as I kiss her; the sensation of her body sliding against mine is heavenly. My hands slip over every beautiful inch of her adoringly, her touch stimulating every nerve ending within me with electrifying excitement. Anna nibbles at my neck as my fingers tease her warm delicate folds. She impatiently bites down harder, sending spikes of arousal hotly through me. I lean her against the marble of the shower wall and lift her till her legs curl around my hips, her arms hooking over my shoulders. Anna's eyes lock onto mine, she bites down on her bottom lip, and muffles her moan as my hand slides between us till I feel the warmth of her entrance on my fingertips.

God, if it doesn't break me how much I want to make her come undone. I want to wait so I can savour every moment, but I can't. I slip a finger inside her, and her moans get louder with every thrust, setting my world on fire. Anna pulls back, her lips stained with the bruising of my kiss. Her hands clutch in my hair, and her eyes are dark and pleading with mine with sincere, aching, need.

"H-harder…" she whimpers.

"Fuck…"

Just when I thought I couldn't love her more…

The guttural growl that escapes my mouth at her words surprises even me, and I sink another finger inside her. I thrust harder, my fingers curling and stroking on every thrust. Anna's delicious cries echo off every wall of the bathroom as I bring her closer and closer to the edge. Her body shakes against mine with ripples of pleasure, and I slow my thrust but deepen it, dragging the palm of my hand against her swollen clit with every stroke.

"F-fuck, baby…don't stop…"

There is no possible way I could stop. The look in her eyes is so fucking beautiful, desperate, loving, pure uninhibited pleasure, and it's almost too much and yet somehow – not nearly enough. Her thighs clench around my hips as she powers over the edge, weakening my knees with overwhelming arousal as she cries out. I watch her cum as I drag out every last second of orgasm she can bear.

I carry her over to the bed, sitting on the edge with her straddled on my lap, my fingers still inside her as she gasps hot, breathy kisses. Anna traces her fingertips down my arm till her hand grasps my wrist. Her breath catches as she pulls my slickly coated fingers out of her. She lifts my wrist, her eyes locked on mine as she sucks her own wetness off my fingers.

Just like that, I am ruined, totally and beautifully ruined by her.

She ravishes me with confidence, her hands firm and feverish, her lips loving. I fall into bliss as my body tremors beneath hers. I am certain there is no more heavenly place to be than at her mercy. Anna follows the blade-like scar that runs over my hip and down to my groin with her tongue until it sinks exactly where I'm aching for it. My body is no longer acting under my will, my fingers interlocked with hers tightly as she teases every sensitive fold of me.

Heat begins to build inside me, my back arches, and all I can do is moan her name in unbridled pleasure. Anna presses on my clit with her thumb as her tongue enters me, and my thighs shake as I gush in her mouth. Tears prick my eyes as I kiss her through rapid breath, my hands knotted in her damp, rusty red hair. She sees my tears, and her eyes widen, and I laugh a dragged gasp.

"Nothing…happened. It was just you…"

"That's so good, baby, so good," Anna chokes, her eyes twinkling brightly with happiness that matches my own.

"You're telling me!" I blurt with a grin, and she roars with laughter, and it is infectious.

Today has been the day from hell, going back on that boat was one of the hardest things I've ever had to do, but somewhere inside I know it has brought me a little closure. The memories are horrific, and I can feel the grief of them, but to see the boat empty of monsters inside, to walk in and out freely in a way that I was never able to before…to touch the things that were out of my reach while I was chained in place…to kick the hell out the box that filled me with such fear and pain, it was all liberating.

I feel a little hopeful ember smouldering inside. Hope that passing the reconditioning may not be such an unattainable feat. I have a long way to go, I know that, but if today has taught me anything, it's that I'm able to withstand more than I thought. I am letting go and moving forward, and I'm surrounded by the strength and faith of the people I love. The demons that haunt me are a little less powerful, and I feel stronger for it. This, of course, could all change when I find out whatever it is that Dixy has planned for me tomorrow. But I have a certain faith that she knows exactly what she's doing, and I know that whatever tomorrow brings, it will be worth it.

Alfred's words are buzzing around my head. It seems utterly ridiculous given all I am facing that marriage has even entered my mind. But it's hard to ignore the implications of that conversation or the fact that the idea didn't seem as insane as I thought it would. The truth is he's right; life is short, and that is a knowledge that never leaves me. Not since the moment I escaped the boat. Now, with the dangerous prospect of attempting to infiltrate The Culling and destroy them, it definitely rings true in my mind. Life. Is. Short.

As she lay in bed beside me, her eyes full of love as she traces her fingertips over my scarred, battle-worn skin. It is impossible to imagine my life without her. She has hold of my heart in the palm of her tiny hand, and I feel complete trust that she will look after it. I adore her, and I don't doubt that I would love to marry her one day. That fact is terrifying, but the truth is, there is a very real possibility I won't survive all of this. How could I ever make that leap of faith knowing I can't promise her forever?

Of course, there is also the flip side to that. Part of me wants to declare myself, tie myself to her so that if the worst should happen, she and the whole world knows that she was it for me. She was everything. I can all too easily imagine the immense pleasure and pride of putting a ring on her finger. I can imagine her holding Alfred's arm as he leads her down the aisle towards me. I can imagine his face full of pride as he sits in the front row next to my mother, crying happy tears.

"What I'd give to know what it is you are thinking to make you look at me that way," Anna utters softly, and my already flush cheeks heat rapidly.

"Oh…I definitely can't tell you that."

"That is frustrating as hell, you know that, right?"

"Yeah, I can imagine."

I shuffle closer to her, my hand light on her face. Her eyes are paralysing, and I feel the strength and weakness they inspire melting me inside. I don't fear dying, I've learned that there are far worse fates, but as I trace her face with my fingertips and her eyes burn into me with love and curiosity, I fear the chance that I could die and her never really know how much I want forever with her.

"You are everything I hoped for and even more, that I was too blind to even begin to wish for. I just wanted you to know that," I say with certainty.

"You have no idea what hearing that from you does to me. Now I really want to know what is going on in your mind. Can't you at least give me a clue?"

I pull her in and give her deep, passionate kisses, relieving myself of the loving throb that is burning in my chest.

"Maybe someday."

***

I almost launch the alarm clock across the room as its loud siren obnoxiously wakes me long before I am ready to wake up. My eyes scratch dryly as I force them open and groan. I don't want to move, and Anna isn't helping. She latches onto me, her body warm and naked, and she grumbles at me cutely when I try to get up.

"You're infuriatingly tempting, Savannah Slone, but if I don't get up, I'll still be naked when Dixy arrives."

"The door has a lock; I could hold you hostage and order room service. There would be no need for clothes or to leave this bed."

"Ugh…God, stop!" I groan, and she giggles.

Anna lets me go, and I sit up rubbing my eyes, grumbling. I'm stupidly tired, and my head feels thick with alcohol haze. I sleepily get to my feet and drag my clothes on with resentment after I ram a spare set in a bag on Dixy's orders. The hint from Dixy that I need spare clothe is already twisting nervous knots in my gut. Somehow, I'm ready just in time.

"I will be here when you get back, but if you need me, you better call," she utters softly, concern playing in her eyes.

I walk out of the hotel room just as Dixy comes strolling around the corner. My nerves are playing on me already, but the sight of her doubles them.

"Let's go get some coffee and breakfast. we can talk through what we are doing today. It isn't going to be an easy day, but we're just going to take it one step at a time," she reassures as if she can read my mind.

We make our way back to the restaurant where we had dinner last night; the place looks much different in the daytime. All the tables have been moved to one side of the room and in their place, a 'help yourself' breakfast buffet has been organised. Catering trays loaded with steaming food provide everything you could dream of for an English breakfast. Further along, there are a selection of pastries, muffins, and breakfast cereals along with icy cold fresh orange juice and tea and coffee being served. I really wish my stomach felt up to the task of taking full advantage of this, but as it stands, the nerves churning in my belly are destroying my appetite. I settle for two croissants and a huge mug of coffee.

"How are you holding up after yesterday?" Dixy asks as she makes easy work of a bowl of cornflakes and a chocolate muffin. I pick apart my croissants and sip my coffee.

"Okay, I guess. Not going to pretend that it didn't shake me, but I can see why I have to do it. There were moments it felt…liberating, but all in all, it pretty much sucked." I chuckle uncomfortably.

"Yeah, I wasn't quite prepared for how hard I'd find it, and I was only in that cargo hold for a couple of hours. I can't understand how you survived two years in there. It wasn't easy, forcing you to relive that, but I promise, there's a reason for everything I am doing, and it *is* going to help you," Dixy presses, her eyes sad and guilty.

"It isn't very heroic; I survived because they needed me alive, but I know you and Anna didn't have it easy in there. I must have been a scary sight. Don't feel bad; I trust you. I'm just a bit nervous about what today will hold."

"You hate showing weakness, but you also won't take credit for your own strength. You are a conundrum, Agent Scott. You weren't scary; if it wasn't so painful to watch it would've been fascinating."

"Fascinating?"

"Well, yes. Don't look at me like that, I'm not a weirdo!" She scowls playfully.

"You really are but explain anyway."

"Okay, umm... Well, when people fall deep into flashbacks, they are completely unaware. That's what makes them so scary because they feel like it is happening in real-time. With you, you have moments where you can communicate during the flashback. You can even speak through the memory, reciting what's being said by the people in your vision, and yet, you're completely unaware of what you were physically doing."

"I'm never aware I'm doing anything. I can only talk through it if I feel tied down somehow. Like sometimes, I hold Anna's hand; I always see her as like an anchor holding me in the now. I can talk through what I see in the past, and she keeps my foot in the door in the now. It wasn't like that yesterday, though; I had no anchor. It felt like it was real, and I don't remember trying to talk anything out or moving. I couldn't understand how I had moved."

"I know, you said every word like it was real, and your body shook and rocked like it was real, and that was the hard part to watch. You didn't know we were there, and we could feel the fear coming off of you. What was fascinating to watch was when you lent over to move a plank of wood without looking at what you were doing. To pick up a screw you left there three years ago and up until that point, you had no memory of the screw or scratching those words into the wood. You actually scratched over the letters already etched there perfectly. You moved like your hands were still chained. Anna had to move out of your way so you could crawl across the room, and I could see you dragging the weight of the chains."

I shudder, my mouth going dry. That might just be one of the most head screwy things I have ever tried to wrap my head around. I shift in my chair, feeling embarrassed. I had no idea I was doing any of those things in the present, I just remember doing them in the past. It's like Dix and Anna had a front row set to the movie I was unknowingly in.

"That sounds more creepy than fascinating, like I was possessed. I remember all the things you said, but I remember doing them years ago - not yesterday. And yesterday, I couldn't remember doing them at all," I explain but even saying the words is making me feel like I am cuckoo.

"I've freaked you out, haven't I? Don't be freaked out; it *is* like you are being possessed but by the memories you have lost. It makes complete sense; it is just unusual because there's a distinct difference in your control between a flashback and a memory. The flashback, you seem at times, fully aware it is happening, and you want to make it stop - when most people are unaware during flash backs. The memories, you are completely unaware and not fighting to stop because you think it is actually happening. It doesn't enter your mind to try and snap out of what you think is present reality. The reason this is good is that means if you're already aware of the flashback and trying to stop them, it shows you can control them a little. We just need to push that awareness harder and that is what we are doing today."

I hate how much sense she is making right now because that can only draw me to one horrible conclusion.

"We are going back to the boat, aren't we?" I groan in a deadened voice.

Dixy reaches out for my hand and holds it tightly. My heart pounds unevenly, forcing me to take a deep breath. I squeeze her hand back and look back at her as her eyes bore into me with determination.

"Yes, Max, we are. Only this time, you are going to *fight*, and you are going *win*."

CHAPTER 13

Sink or Swim

"How is this going to be any different from yesterday?"

I stand at the top of the stairs that lead down to the cargo hold. I don't quite feel the fear to go in that I did yesterday, but that doesn't mean I want to go back in or that I'm not still scared.

"Yesterday, I wanted you to let everything trigger you, so I could learn and also so you could. I wanted you to be able to experience these flashbacks from when you were powerless. Show the power that you now have and then give you brand new memories that will empower you. Show you that you are not the same person that was trapped on this boat. What is the first thing you think when I say – the box?"

The memory flashes, the rage all too easy to recall.

"Me kicking the crap out of it."

"Exactly. Now, I'm not going to pretend it will magically erase your bad memories of the box; I'm just planting seeds in your mind. Give you memories with empowering emotions attached that will conflict with your bad memories and emotions of trauma."

"That still doesn't tell me how this is going to be any different from yesterday," I point out.

"The difference is, today, instead of letting the flash backs dominate you, I'm going to show you while you are triggered different ways that you can gain control. It means I'll be provoking you. It means you have to trust me because it is going to be hard, but you will come off the boat today with more knowledge of how to control yourself."

"Oh, that sounds fucking delightful."

"I know you're scared, but I will be with you every step of the way. I promise, I know *exactly* what I am doing. I just need you to trust me and remember…whatever happens in there, I am your friend. I don't want to hurt you, so everything I do is for good reason."

"Sounds fun. You should have led with that. What are we waiting for?" I joke darkly. "If this is what we are doing, why do I need spare clothes?"

"For what we're doing later with Lambert. I wouldn't worry about that now."

"Ugh. There better be a whisky fountain at the end of this."

I walk down the stairs and open the door, and Dixy follows me. She slides around me and stands in front of me, blocking the doorway.

"Yesterday, you stopped here because you could feel the shackles on your wrists. You rubbed them, trying to show yourself they weren't real. Do you remember what I said?" Dixy asks.

"You told me to look at them, connect the feeling with my sight or something?"

"Yes, exactly. There is a technique called grounding. It's a coping strategy used to help combat the flashbacks and disassociation that come with PTSD. It's a way of connecting yourself with the present, the here and now. Yesterday, you used this coping mechanism instinctually, but today, I want to show you how to use *all* of the strategy to your advantage. You were using your sense of touch to ground yourself, but if you use all of your senses, it will give you more options to work with and will create a stronger connection to the present. Are you following me?"

"I think so. That's why you told me to look at my wrists. Instead of just feeling that the shackles were gone, seeing that they are gone gives me more…evidence that it isn't real."

"Good! So, the flashbacks aren't always as intense as they were yesterday and sometimes you are able to stop them before they get that far. I've seen you do it, using the pinching technique or even just distracting you mind with a physical task. Today and from now on, I want you to apply it using all of your senses.

"Use your sight to take a mental inventory of the things around you, analyse patterns in wallpaper, count items of furniture, do a crossword puzzle.

Use all your senses. Suck a sweet lollypop, bite into a sour lemon, feel the texture of carpet, take a cold shower, let an ice cube melt in your hand. Listen to a loved one's voice or a favourite song, talk out loud about what you see or feel if it helps, but the aim is to connect to what is in the now. If you can do this, you can stop a flashback before it takes hold of you or stop it once it has. It takes commitment; you're altering the way you think. It's a mindset, but over time, it will become second nature."

My brain is connecting to that easily because I already do half of the stuff she just mentioned, just in an unfocused way. If I can just focus it, maybe it really will change everything.

"Okay, I can do that. I already use this, I just never really tried to find other ways to use it. The cold always helps, I have freezing showers, but I never thought of an ice cube. When it is that extreme, an ice cube wouldn't be enough, but if I did it before that extreme hits, it could work."

"Yes, and it will be very personal to you. What will ground you is dependent on what you connect with, and it could be completely different to what grounds me. One of the things I use is pain. Even a slap of an elastic band on my wrist can be the quick reality check I need. It's all down to what you respond to."

Dixy takes me gently by the wrist and leads me to the middle of the room. I keep my eyes on her because it is easier than seeing everything around me that could trigger me, both in flashbacks and in pain. Looking up feels like a risk, a danger, and I can already feel the fear building as I know she wants me to look. She wants me to be triggered. Dixy keeps hold of my wrist, not in a comforting way. More of a way to keep me anchored and focused on her.

"Yesterday you moved around this room, jumping from trigger to trigger. You confronted a lot of fears, and I'm sure if we stayed in here for days and days, you would find more and more. But there was one thing that you avoided. You didn't go near it once; you made a point of going around the edge of the room even though there's an elephant smack bang in the middle of it which means, it's the thing you fear the most."

My eyes close as the panic swoops in my chest, my heartrate accelerates as dread gnaws in my stomach. I know exactly what she is talking about, and now I know why we are here; I want to run more than ever. I feel her hand apply a little pressure to my wrist. I take a deep breath and open my eyes again, keeping them on Dixy.

"I don't even want to look at it, let alone go near it, and that's exactly what you want me to do, isn't it?"

"Yes. we aren't leaving till we make those chains as insignificant to you as the feel of my hand on your wrist is. Remember, there was once a time you wouldn't allow that touch. This is no different. You may always fear the chains a little, and that's okay, but letting that fear dominate you is not. People are scared of heights, but they still get on a plane. You can be scared of the chains but not to the point that the fear controls you."

The fear is starting to really set in. The ammonia smell is repugnant and is burning my nose. My legs feel full of lead, and I feel an invisible danger that is urging me to run. I stare wide eyes at Dixy's hand holding my wrist, trying to keep myself calm. Trying not to allow the cold grip of the invisible chains to replace her hand.

"What do I have to do?" I croak without looking up.

"First, you are just going to look at them and keep control while you are doing it. If you lose control, then get it back; look at them till you feel the fear is less intense. Then, we repeat the process, taking harder and harder steps. You've got this, Max. I know that to you, the idea of this is intolerable, but you have already proven time and time again that you don't run from a fight. You run towards it. So, don't run from this one. Dominate those chains; I just know you have a kinky side," she teases.

"I'm going to choose not to answer that one." I chuckle dryly.

"Good, you are respecting your woman – that's what I like to see. You're not the player I expected you to be, Max-a-million."

"I have been; I was terrible, I can't deny that, but I grew up, and well, kidnapping has a way of ruining your game."

"Hah! I knew it! Aw, does this mean Max is settling down? Is that the distant chime wedding bells I hear?" Dixy squeals.

"Seriously, don't go there."

"Feel calmer?" she asks, and I nod, and she lets go of my wrist. "You've got this. We are just going to take a couple of steps closer and then, you are going to look. If the flashback starts to happen, use your senses and try to stop it. You move when you are ready."

I keep my eyes focused on hers for just a minute while I run over the possible ways I could use my senses. Smell and taste are out; the place stinks of piss, and I don't have anything to taste. That leaves sight, touch, and sound. I can hear the water, a soft lap of the current hitting the boat. It's quiet, but it is there. I could sing, but I feel too self-conscious, and my throat feels tight. It has to be mostly about vision and touch.

I square my shoulders, my fists clenched tightly, and I walk around Dixy, keeping my eyes on the floor till I'm about a metre away. The chains are fixed to the centre supportive cross beam. The silvery grey chains are slack and coiled onto the floor in warped circles; the cuffs are thick and lay open like claws. Inside the claws are dark brown smudges of dried blood.

My blood.

It happens so quickly, too quickly with no real warning. I feel the cold metal grip my wrists, the pain of the bruises and abrasions. Then the weight of the chain attached, pulling at my wrists, and I gasp. I grab at my wrists; I stare at them intensely, willing the chains to disappear. The vision starts to flash, and then my thumb brushes the silver bangle on my wrist. I run my thumb along the engraving of the coordinates to the farm, picturing the tiny swirly script word 'goof' in my mind. My chest fills with warmth, and the cold grip around my wrists begins to loosen.

I look back up at the chains, keeping my thumb rubbing up and down the engraving. I try to guess the tiny little numbers that are etched there while my eyes stay fixed on the chains. My shoulders begin to relax, and I sigh a breath of relief. It's working; I can't believe it.

"Well done, Max. Stay focused, stay in control. You can only let go when looking at them doesn't scare you as much. They are just chains, chains you broke free of. You survived this, not because they needed you alive, but because you fought to stay alive long enough to come home," Dixy growls passionately.

"They are just chains." I croak.

"That's right, just chains, Max."

It feels a long time that I stand there. Long enough to decide that Dixy has a lot of patience. Much more than me and after what could have been hours, or maybe even minutes. I stop rubbing the bangle engraving, and my arms fall to my sides, palms out and hands relaxed. I take a step forward and then another so that I am standing beneath the beam, between the chains that hang either side of me. They are just inches from my fingertips, my head bowed and my chest heaving in and out. I feel Dixy's hand on my shoulder as she stands behind me.

"They don't hold you anymore, do they?"

"No…" I choke.

"Then hold them! Prove you have control! Hold those chains the way they once held you! Take control of them! Take control of yourself!" Dixy barks.

My hands shake as they reach out, I feel the cold metal touch my palms, and I close my grip tightly around the chain. Panic starts to take hold almost immediately; my arms begin to shake, and the chains clink loudly at my movement. The sound is so familiar, and it sends ice through my veins, making my blood run cold.

"Urghhh."

My sense of touch is useless because I have to keep hold of the chains. All I have is sound and vision, and my vision is flashing with tormented horror. Bloody wrists, the chain wrapped around Tomasz neck, the mala suka man pulling the chains hard and fast, and my arms extending high above my head.

"Gnnaarhhh."

My shoulders burning with pain, my arms numb from the blood drain. My wrists itchy and stinging from stinking, fetid, wounds.

"Take control, Max!"

Oh God, I can't do this. I can't focus on anything. There's no sense I can draw from, no sound except my own scream inside my head. No taste but salty blood, no sight but the horror in my mind. No smell but the pissy ammonia of this retched boat. I feel nothing but the chains in my hands and the pain of the memories. Pain…

I need pain!

I look at the chain on my left hand and twist my wrist so that it wraps tight around my hand. I do the same on my right and then – I push. The metal digs into my hands and pinches at my skin, and I whimper at the stinging pinch as blood starts to draw. The visions slow but they don't stop.

My eyes water at the pain, but it's not enough, the panic starting to rise again. I grit my teeth and lean my weight on the chains, and pressure tightens the coil around my hands, crushing them, and I cry out. The vision disappears, the screaming in my head quiets, and I drop to my knees, taking the weight off my hands.

Dixy dashes in front of me and starts uncoiling the chains from my hands. I look down and see purple and blue bruising forming and red blood blisters filling. I shove my hands under my armpits to numb the ache. I feel dizzy with exhaustion, barely able to hold my head up. Dixy kneels in front of me, and I can only hope she isn't going to start barking orders at me again just yet.

"So…using pain is great and all but usually as prevention. Then the pains and are smaller and less damaging."

"It didn't really feel like I had many options. I can't taste anything; I can't feel anything holding the chains. The place stinks of piss; I can't see or hear anything except the flashbacks. It was the only thing I could think of." I wince, my hands throbbing.

"I know, I'm not knocking you; that was commitment, I'll give you that. Hopefully with practice, you will find lots of grounders. This technique has only just been sprung on you, and you are dealing with powerful triggers. You are doing well. Let me have a look at those hands."

I shuffle off my knees and onto my butt, sitting cross legged, and I hold my hands out. They hurt, for sure, but the flashback stopped. For now, it is hard to care about anything except making them stop; they are worse than any physical pain. Dixy inspects the damage gently, and I attempt to catch my breath.

"They are going to be colourful in a few hours, and they will hurt tomorrow. Make sure you ice them tonight. How are you feeling?"

"Tired, but I'm fine."

"Well, let's take a break, but you are not moving. The longer you sit making friends with those chains, the better."

I just want this day to be over. I despise this place. I lay down. The deck is gross, but I am past caring. The filth is mine; it's three-year-old filth, but it is still mine. My blood, sweat, and tears, my piss and excrement. Again, it almost feels like returning to an old chair. I spent most of my two years bound to this spot. Whether the chains kept me standing or I was afforded the privilege to lay down, it was still mostly here I was stuck. I know every line and mark on the ceiling as well I know any face.

"What's on your mind, monkey butt?" Dixy asks.

"Uh…it feels almost like home lying here. Everything is the same. It amazes me how much of it hasn't changed. I was triggered because the shackles still have my blood on them. It's like someone hit the pause button on the place."

"Everything is the same, except you."

"I don't feel that different, not when I'm here. Even before I came back here, it felt like a part of me was still trapped here waiting for me to come back, and I just want that part of myself to give up already. Just die and let me move on."

Dixy shuffles closer from behind me and puts her hand on my shoulder, and I jump a little, but she doesn't move. It isn't easy when I can't see the contact coming, and I feel jumpy as hell. Jumpier than I have in a long time.

"That's because even though you left, you never let it go. That's what you are doing now. By the time we go home, you will feel free of this place. We have one more thing to do here today, and then tomorrow will be the last time you ever come back. Are you ready?"

"Let's get it over with."

Dixy shuffles around till she is sat in front of me and holds her hand out to help me upright. I take it with a wince; gripping her hand shoots pain into my knuckles. She pulls me up and straight into her for a hug, which is both awkward and unexpected. Her breathing sounds unnaturally heavy; I hug her back.

"I'm sorry, Max," she whispers.

Dixy moves fast, so fast I don't see it coming. I am too slow to react, trying to understand, and it is too late. Dixy grabs my wrists, encasing them within the claws of the cold steel shackles, locking into place with a clink.

"No…NO! What are you doing!? Dixy, please don't do this to me! No, no, no! Take them off, please! DIXY!" I cry fearfully.

Dixy is on her feet, her back turned, her fists balled.

"DIXY!" I yell, and she turns around, her expression blank, and storms towards me.

"You want out, Agent Scott? Then get control of yourself and get yourself out!" she barks.

Dixy grabs my hand and places a thin piece of metal in my hand, straight and strong, the end of it bent into a right angle. I look at the lockpick in my hand in horror as my arms shake in panic, and I almost drop it.

"No! You can't do this to me! I can't – please, please, please! Let me out, LET ME OUT!" I scream.

Dixy turns her back to me again, and the panic intensifies. I thrash against the chains, angry snarls of terror spitting from my mouth.

"Oh God…please, make it stop…make it stop…make it…"

The memory swirls.

I am sat back on the floor in the same spot, alone, with my knees pulled up against my chest, my body naked and shivering violently.

"I have to make it stop. I can't do this anymore. He is going to come back and do it again; he always comes back. I need to end it, I can't..."

My skin crawls, and I scratch at my bare legs, straightening them out so I can claw at the itch on my thighs. I can feel him crawling all over me, inside me. I whimper, sobs rattling in my chest.

"There is only one way out."

I push myself up to my feet and lift my knee up, pulling it up to my chest and balancing on one foot. I wrap the chain attached to my right wrist around my lifted foot securely, and then I stand on it, giving myself the height needed. Without hesitation, I wrap the left-hand chain around my neck and then...kick the chain off both my feet. I drop, and the chain tightens around my neck painfully tight, cutting the airflow.

"MAX!!!"

"No! Max! *Fuck*!!"

"Come back!!! Max!"

My eyes snap open, and I can't breathe. Dixy has her arms wrapped around my waist and is lifting my weight off the chain. I pull at the chain desperately, and I gasp as t comes uncoiled, and my air way opens. I drop to the floor as the extra weight overwhelms Dixy. I choke and gasp trying to get oxygen back into my lungs. I scramble to my knees, trying to get myself upright.

"Take…them…off."

Dixy crawls over to me. She grabs the collar of my shirt, her eyes full of tears but anger is dominating them.

"Max! Get control! Use your senses; ground yourself! This is your boat; these are just chains. Now rub some fucking dirt in it and get yourself out! Now!!" she bellows, putting the pin back in my hand and turning her back.

"Fuuuuck!"

The tears flow hot and fast as I sob like a child. My head begins to swim, the flashes of horror flickering in my vision. I need to stop this; I need to stop this now. I grip the pin tight in my shaky hand. Two locks, two shaky hands; I need control. I drop to the floor and focus on my hands.

"Why do we fall? So, we can learn t-to pick ourselves back up. Batman." I stutter, and the image flashes.

"Gnaah!"

I tip the lock pick from my right palm to my left.

"If the world is too big…m-make it small. Man of steel." I tip the lock pick from my left palm to my right.

"No money…ugh…no *amount* of money ever bought a second of time. Iron Man."

I tip the lock pick, and the tremor in my hands stop. Out of the corner of my eye, I see Dixy take a step towards me. I put the pick in the keyhole of the left shackle and focus on the lock, feeling my way through the mechanism. These are old locks; they should be simple to unlock, but my focus is so split. The struggle to stay in the now is harder than it ever has been. My bruised and swelling hands are struggling to keep hold of the pick.

"For every minute, t-the future is becoming the past. Thor. Ugh come on, come on!" I growl.

"With great power…"

The mechanism clicks, the shackle claws fall open, and I whimper a tearful moan as the cuff falls to the floor with a clunk. I slide the pick into the right lock; my left hand feels awkward as I try to manoeuvre it around the lock.

"…comes great responsibility. Spiderman."

I can feel the panic creeping back in, and it is terrifying. My head is starting to swim, and I'm losing control.

"Ugh, no."

My mind flickers with a flash. Tomasz looming over me, his body overpowering mine, and he presses me into the deck.

"Gaaah!! Either you die a hero, or y-you live long enough to see yourself as a villain. Arrow. God, come on!" I snarl. "Just because someone stumbles and l-loses their path doesn't…doesn't…"

Clunk!

"Arrrgghh!!" I wail as the shackle falls off my wrist.

"You did it, oh, God! You did it! I'm so sorry! I am so, so sorry," Dixy cries.

Dixy launches at me from across the room, pulling me to her. At first, I fight her because I am livid and hurt, but then I feel her body shake with sobs as the girl that is scared of hugs holds on to me for dear life. As she breaks, it shakes my resolve.

"Max, I am so…oh…" Dixy lets me go and runs to the back of the boat and vomits. I drag myself to my feet and stumble over to her just as she stops puking. She wipes her mouth, straightens up and turns around, her eyes on the floor. I pull her in and she breaks again.

"Dix…it's alright. I was mad but only for a minute. I know what it cost you to do that. Let it go, I already have," I reassure.

"I don't know how to do that yet, I thought…I…the chain was around your –"

"Don't! I am not ready to think about…I can't. It isn't your fault; I didn't know that was going to happen. I didn't remember…so how could you know?"

"You think that matters?! I thought I wasn't going to be able to…" Dixy chokes, her eyes are bulging, seeing things I can't see.

"Dixy…Dixy! Stop. I am fine because you made sure I was fine! This wasn't your fault, and if you want me to continue to fucking trust you, then you better trust me! I'm telling you, it isn't your fault! You are trying to help me no matter how hard it is for you; you are here. Now let it go!" I yell.

Dixy bites her bottom lip to stop the wobble, nods, and throws a curious glance my way.

"What was the end of that quote you were saying as you unlocked the second shackle?"

"What? Oh, yeah. 'Just because someone stumbles and loses their path doesn't mean they're lost forever.' It's from the X-men."

Dixy simpers warmly, and I chuckle because the irony isn't lost on me either.

***

Once we get back to the van, I can feel the tension coming off her. Dixy starts the motor and the revs roar as she pulls away. Her hands are white knuckled on the steering wheel, and she's rigid. I want her to be okay. The truth is, I was hurt by what she did and angry, but I know that she is trying to help me. Just as she has been trying since she came into my life.

"What are we doing now?"

"Depends whether you feel up to being cold and wet now or this evening. Either way – first, we need a drink," she sighs.

"I couldn't agree more."

We drive back towards the direction of the hotel but thankfully, Dixy stops before we get there. I don't think I could carry on if we went inside and saw Anna. We pull into a car park right near the pleasure beach, and I follow her toward The Cobblers Tap, a dingy looking pub that juts out at the corner of the street. It looks old and very British. The sort of place you would expect to find your drunk uncle, hugging a pint of Guinness.

As we walk, it's easy to imagine what this place would be like in the summer. The laughs and squeals coming from the amusements of the pleasure beach. The roller-coaster thundering along the tracks. The smell of freshly fried doughnuts and candy floss, and the beach brimming full of sunbathers and sandcastle makers. As it stands though, it is bitterly cold and gloomy; the place is pretty lifeless.

The Cobblers Tap is a pleasant surprise. The outside appearance is deceiving. Inside, I find a traditional, old man style pub with ugly carpet and sticky varnished tables. It smells like real ale and old spice aftershave, and 80s rock plays softly in the background. Although a little dingy in appearance, the place has a warmth. The bar staff are polite and welcoming as Dixy orders us both a drink. We find our seats at the back of the pub in a small den type area. The seats are plush, stained, green striped benches.

"What is it going to take to get you to let this go?" I ask Dixy as she stares into her glass.

"I don't know. I guess seeing that it worked would help. I'm sure tomorrow, we'll find out if it did."

"Dixy, it doesn't matter if it worked or not. You ask a lot of my trust, and I give it to you without question; that's not an easy thing for me to do. I think I deserve the same trust in return. If I tell you this isn't your fault, that you are my friend and that won't change no matter how annoying you can be – then I think I've earnt the right for you to believe me with that same unquestioned trust."

Dixy looks up from her glass and smiles a little, and I feel relieved. The last thing I need right now is for her to lose faith. My faith is shaky enough as it is.

"You're right; I know that. Thanks for forcing me to hear it. I think I'll almost be as glad as you when this is over, and we never have to see that boat again. I'm sorry I had to do that to you. I think it's obvious I felt vile doing it. But if I'm right about what I think will happen because of it, it will be worth every second of today."

"Well, as much as I just want to go crawl into a dark hole. I don't want to delay whatever is next till this evening. So, what is next?"

"Next, we drink a little more, order some hot seaside chips, and call Lambert. We are going to do a little bit of water exposure, and he's going to help with that. Plus – I plan to have enough whisky that I can no longer legally drive. Care to join me my friend?"

"Finally, something I'm good at."

Dixy calls Lambert, and we order the saltiest, fluffiest mountain of chips I've ever had the pleasure of eating. I didn't think I was going to be able to eat, but once the alcohol starts to relax my tight muscles and settle the anxiety, I realise just how hungry I am. However, it's actually a little sore to eat. I bring my hand up to my throat and apply a little pressure with my fingertips and feel a dull ache.

"Yeah…I expect your Mrs is going to be pissed at me. It isn't pretty." Dixy winces, her eyes on my throat.

"No, she won't be… Okay, yes, she probably will be, but she has seen me gain more memories than anyone. She knows what it like. I'll talk to her; she'll be fine."

"You two seem to be going well. You look so much more at peace with her around and so does she. It's nice to see. I know she isn't my biggest fan, but I like her a lot more now. Without Danni's control, I can see who she really is. You both bring each other out, and yesterday, she earnt my approval. She held it together much better than me."

"You held it together fine, and I don't think she has a problem with you anymore. She told me she's glad that you're my friend. I am at peace with her, as much as I can be with everything so uncertain. It's hard to think of a future with someone when you don't know if you'll be around for it," I admit grimly with a dark chuckle.

"You will be. You two have a connection that is nothing like I have ever seen or had. It is actually quite annoying how well you fit together. Like, I hate you both a little bit." She sneers playfully. "You will fight with all you have to keep that connection alive and that will keep you alive. Before you know it, you will be having a little farm family…OH! I need to buy you plaid baby grows! Yes! It will be adorable!" Dixy squeals.

I down my drink and groan at her, scowling. "Don't you start. You're as bad as Alfred. He was eagerly talking about marriage last night which was the last thing I expected to hear. You keep your mouth shut to Anna; it would scare the life out of her."

"Oh, come on. I don't think you get how this friend thing works. I don't tell people the stuff you tell me. It is like pirate code or something. Why are you so certain it will scare her? The girl is clearly head over heels for you. Maybe it is just you who is scared."

"I was more scared that it didn't scare me, to be honest. I have no doubts about her, but you can't take that leap with someone if you can't promise them forever. Plus, I really do think it would scare her. It's a bit soon, don't you think?" I say raising an eyebrow.

"Not really. It clearly isn't too soon for you. So why would it be for her?"

"That is different. I live every day fighting one God damn battle after another. I'm fully aware how short life is because mine is always under threat. With everything that has already happened and everything that is about to. My life span never feels very promising and that makes me less fearful of that step. Anna doesn't have that threat."

Dixy snorts, sneering with a mouth full of chips.

"You are delusional, Agent Scott. Her physical life may not be under the threat that yours is, but she's clearly devoted to you. And that means that the threat to your life will be just as damning to her and just as scary. Her life and future are just as dependent on you surviving as yours is, and she will feel as threatened by the prospect of losing that as you do. When it comes to protecting her, it isn't just about making sure she doesn't get physically hurt. You have to protect her heart too. Would her knowing that you want to make that commitment to her forever be so terrible? Or would it tell her that no matter what happens, you have chosen her?"

My stomach swoops, and I am massively regretting this conversation.

"Shut up; you are freaking me out."

"That's because I'm making too much sense, and you don't like it," she teases, smirking in victory.

What she says does make sense, I know that, but I don't want to hear it. I don't think Anna is anywhere near ready for that and neither am I. My lack of fear doesn't make me ready; the only thing that will ever do that is knowing that I can keep the promises that a ring on her finger proposes. I don't know that I'll ever be able to do that and that hurts to think about. I don't know that I'll survive, and that means I don't know that I can ever have the future with her I want. All I can do is live in the now and appreciate every moment I have with her. Lambert arrives and doesn't hesitate to steal chips off of Dixy's plate. He takes a seat next to Dixy, and his arrival makes my stomach twist.

"How are we doing?" Lambert asks.

"Slightly tipsy so, pretty good," Dixy replies.

"Was asking Mac but thanks for the update, Kate. I'm guessing this is why you told me to walk?"

Dixy hands him the keys to the van and grins. "You are a smart cookie." She grins, slapping his cheek patronisingly.

"I'm good. I just want to get this over with, whatever this is," I reply.

"Then let's do this."

We leave the pub, and I follow behind Lambert as we walk across the street and along the promenade to the beach. It's pretty much deserted, and that isn't at all surprising. The wind is blowing bitterly cold, whipping my hair up into my eyes. Along the beachfront are six towering white columns that lean slightly forwards. They are 100ft tall lighting masts that beam light across the beach at night, creating moving shapes and words in different colours that glow on the sandy beach. My boots sink into the damp sand as we draw nearer to the tide. I love the sound of the waves crashing onto the shore; it is much different from what I heard on the boat. The water foams white and frothy as it hits the toes of my boats.

"The reason we are here, Mac, is quite aptly known as surf torture. It's a technique many branches of the military have used for physical training over decades. It is effective and gruelling and has a habit of sorting the men from the boys. Which is why when it comes to navy seal and SAS selection, it's used so regularly. This one challenge in PT has a significantly high dropout rate."

Delightful.

"The pressure points are the extreme cold. Combine the water temperature with the wind chill and the cold soon becomes painful, cramping your muscles and bringing on fatigue. Which makes the next pressure point even harder. Drowning. You must lay on the flat of your back, facing the shore with your body straight, and allow the surf to wash over your head. It's difficult to breathe and exhausting to keep your head held up just enough to be able to get air. The anticipation of each wave is worse than the one before. That would be the second pressure point.

"This challenge is dependent on you staying calm in the water. If you panic and gasp, you will choke, and that's how people drown. A bit like when you walk over an ice lake and fall through the ice. The shock of the cold causes a panic reaction, and you gasp, sucking in the water. It's a natural reaction that you have to try to suppress. This will teach you to control your breathing through fear which is pivotal to surviving waterboarding.

"Ordinarily, this technique is done with many soldiers linking arms in the water. It stops the surf washing them back onto shore and obviously stops them from using their arms to support themselves, creating more fear. It also helps boost morale amongst comrades. We don't have anyone, so you are going to have to cope with my holding you still and trust that I am not actually trying to drown you. Time your breaths, keep your arms crossed over your chest, and stay calm. I'm guessing you can swim?"

"Um...yes. I haven't for a long time," I respond a little too slowly. My throat is dry. I am bricking it.

"Good. You don't need to swim, but for safety, it's good to know," Lambert explains.

I look at the water with dread. I don't even want to think about how cold it is. I'm already cold just stood here. The only saving grace is I'm sure that if I had elected to do this this evening, it would've been even colder. A small comfort in the face of the loud thrashing waves being catapulted onto the shore with the force of the wind. Dixy comes and stands shoulder to shoulder with me.

"This is going to trigger your fear of drowning; you have to try to stay grounded and in control. You are not going to drown; you are going to focus and find a place of calm. Find a rhythm in the waves. Focus on the cold, the sound of the water. If you need to stop, just say so, and Lambert will pull you out, but the longer you can withstand this, the more you solidify the message in your brain that you're in control. Just like the box, it doesn't own you. The waterboarding will always scare you; it would scare anyone. The key is controlling that fear inside yourself so that it doesn't become panic," Dixy explains, her hand on my wrist again, grounding me.

"Ugh, I hate you a little bit right now."

"I can live with that." She chuckles.

My numb fingers fumble with the laces of my boots as I try to mentally prepare for the hell that is about to come. I step out of them, stash my wallet and phone inside them, and walk back to the edge of the tides icy flow, my feet not quite daring to touch it.

"Right, Mac, you're going to face me, and I'm going to walk you backwards till the water is about half way up your shins. Then I will lower you into the water. All I'm going to do is hold you still by the legs so the tide doesn't wash you back in while you float on your back. Are you okay with that?" Lambert asks.

I turn round to face him and nod, trying to seem more confident than I feel. Lambert holds my forearms and steps towards me. I step back and cringe as the icy water freezes against my feet.

"Oh, holy guacamole that's cold!"

"Couldn't agree more," Lambert grunts through tight lips.

He watches my feet as we walk, and I try to control my breathing that is already beginning to become erratic in the frigid cold and anticipation. He stops and stands still, tightening his grip on my forearms, and I grip onto his. Lambert lowers me into the water, and as it touches my skin, my nerve endings scream. I force my mouth closed, trying not to gasp at the shocking feeling that swoops in my chest.

Lambert moves quickly to my feet; he kneels down with a growl at the cold water and then I feel hands on my shins. The first wave crashes over me before I have a chance to hold my head up at all. Salty ice water burns my eyes and nose. I manage to control my gasp, but the panic hits me with an iron fist. My arms thrash, and my vision begins to flash.

"Mac, cross those arms, soldier. Take control!" Lambert booms.

I cross my arms and take a deep breath, holding it, and when the next wave hits, I exhale through the wash. The cold is painful already, the panic rising in my chest. I take another deep breath and hold it.

"That's it, Mac. Calm yourself. It's just water – fucking cold water!" Lambert yells.

The wave hits and I growl an exhale, I would laugh if I wasn't so scared. I force my stinging eyes open as I take another deep breath and hold it, trying to find something to focus on, but my vision is beginning to swirl. The tell-tell sign I'm losing control and a flashback is coming. The wave hits, and this time, I yell my exhale, shivering breath.

"Big wheels…keep on turning, carry…me home…to see my kin!"

Inhale! Splash!

"Singing…songs about the southland, I miss Alabamy once…again…I think it's a sin, yes!"

Inhale! Splash!

My legs are cramping; my chest hurts from the unnatural breathing and fear. The vision is just tugging at the corners of my mind, threatening me with its presence. I have to keep it at bay; a flashback like this means choking on sea water and complete failure. The pure terror of the vision and the cold is forcing violent shivers through me; laying still takes every ounce of fight I have.

"Keep going, Max!" Dixy yells.

"Sweet home Alabama, where the skies are so blue!" I yell, and Lambert is singing along with me.

Inhale! Splash!

"Sweet home Alabama, Lord I'm coming home to you!"

At this point, I am struggling to think as if the cold is numbing my brain. I lose track of the words and just repeat the chorus in time with the waves over and over. Soon, my energy is sapped, and I can barely speak let along yell song lyrics. I need it to be over; everything hurts. The only good thing is that the mind-numbing cold is, along with my ability to think clearly, helping to keep the vision at bay.

"Pull her out, Lambert!" Dixy shouts, and relief floods through me.

Lambert grabs at my arms. He pulls me upright to my feet and scoops my arm over his shoulder, dragging me to shore. When the wind hits my soaking clothes, I really learn what cold is. Lambert lowers me to the floor, and Dixy wraps a thick and scratchy blanket around me.

"You killed it, Max! You had control almost immediately!!" Dixy beams, and I chuckle a shivery chuckle.

The truth is, as scary as it was, it was nothing on what has happened over the past two days. It was a lot easier to get control than I expected. Probably a fluke, but I will take it. I am so relieved, but the cold is painful.

"Can you make it to the van?" Lambert asks.

"Th-i-i-ink so."

"Tell you what, I'll run ahead and bring the van closer. I can park on the promenade and meet you both there." Lambert is off running in a shot, and Dixy helps me to my feet.

"You need to change your clothes in the van; they'll sap any heat you gain. When we get you back to the hotel room, *don't* get straight into a hot shower. It's dangerous to heat back up too fast. Just sit with a blanket till the shivering stops and then get in. You hear me? Nod so I know you are hearing me?" Dixy orders with a raised eyebrow, and I nod.

"Good. You killed it today. I'm so proud of you, Max."

I look up at her and give her a crooked smile. "Tha-a-a-nks."

We reach the van, and Lambert is waiting with the rear doors open. He helps me inside and my rucksack with spare clothes is waiting for me. They shut the doors behind me, and I begin striping the wet clothes off my skin. My skin is red raw and itchy, and the bruising to my hands is suddenly glowing dark purple and blue. It isn't an easy task, and I only just manage it when the van comes to an abrupt stop.

I try to ignore the people looking at my oddly as I shiver my way through the hotel, wrapped in a blanket. I probably look as gross as I feel. I knock the hotel room door, remembering that Anna has the key, and couldn't be happier to see her when she opens the door. Her face lights up only momentarily as the sight of me wipes the smile off her face. She pulls me inside and sits me on the end of the bed, kneeling in front of me and getting inside the blanket with me.

"Oh God-d you are so war-m-m-m."

"And you are like an ice cube. What the hell have you been doing?" She mumbles into my shoulder. Before I can answer her, there is a knock at the door, and Anna gets up to answer it.

"Make her drink this and don't let her in a hot shower till the shivering stops. I'll come check back in a bit," Dixy informs her and then scurries away quickly.

Anna returns with a cup of hot coffee in a takeaway cup and hands it to me, her face an irritated mask of concern. I sip the coffee, and it quickly starts to ease the shivering; it feels amazing. Anna's eyes fall on my hands, and she looks back up to me.

"I've mis-s-s-ed you." I shiver, and she smiles in spite over herself. She takes the coffee out of my hands and leans in.

"I have missed you a bit too much; it's a little embarrassing," She admits, and I smile into her kiss. Even her lips are warm. Her hands slide on to the side of my neck, and I wince.

"What's wrong…what is that?!"

Her fingertips lightly touch my neck, and my jaw clenches as the lump in my throat starts to rise. She looks at me, and I look away before my tears betray me.

"I should get in the shower. I am…gross."

"Don't do that; don't run from me. We don't do that anymore. Tell me please," she utters affectionately.

I lean into her, burying my face in her neck, and I tell her about the memory. I know if I look at her, I will break, and I don't want to. I am fed up with breaking. All I want is to shower and to climb into bed and sleep.

"Oh God, baby, I…"

"I'm alright. I can't…I don't want to…I just want to stop," I interrupt.

"That's okay, you told me, and I know. That's enough. Now, let's get you in the shower and in bed. You and I are putting a movie on, ordering room service, and we are not leaving this room for the rest of the night."

"That sounds so perfect."

The hot water is heaven, warming me to the bone, and scrubbing the salt and sand off my skin is a relief on the itch. I have sand in places no one should ever have sand. Anna comes into the bathroom and hands me a pair of the softest, heavy flannel, red and black plaid PJ bottoms.

"I bought you them from the hotel gift shop because I thought you would look cute in them but turns out they are a practical gift today." She smiles cutely.

"You are adorable. I love them; thank you."

Climbing into bed and cuddling up on Anna's chest is the most amazing feeling. The warmth of her envelopes me as she pulls me tightly to her. Her fingers brushing through my hair, I feel the hell of the day begin to melt away, but as the fear begins to calm, it leaves nothing to distract from the grief. The pain in my chest over that memory, over feeling that brief moment of relief when I thought death would free me, feels so present and fresh. People wonder how I survived those two years; they call me brave and strong like surviving was an achievement. I've always rejected that notion, and now I know for sure.

"I know you don't want to talk about it and that's okay, but I can feel it coming over you. If I can do anything at all, please tell me," Anna utters carefully, and I sigh.

"I'm not as strong as everyone seems to think I am; I'm so fed up with people telling me how brave I am. I always knew that I didn't survive out of bravery. I survived because they needed me to. Remembering when I tried to hang myself only brings that home more."

Anna is quiet for so long that I start to feel awkward and embarrassed. I am about to apologise for being so blunt when she slides me off her chest a little and props herself on her elbow and looks down at me. She skims her hand up my t-shirt and lays it on my chest. There is nothing remotely sexual in it. It is comforting, warming, and it makes me feel cared for and protected in a way I've only ever felt with Anna.

"The bravery and strength I see in you, that everyone sees in you, doesn't come from the fact you survived. It comes from the fact that surviving all of that didn't destroy everything that makes you. You kept your humanity; they weren't able to stamp out the warmth, kindness and compassion in you. The nerdiness of you survived, your personality, your love for people, it all survived, and that's what people see the strength in. It would have been so much easier to succumb to that place. Now that I've seen it, I know just how much easier it would've been to cope if you had become cold, emotionless, and harsh, but you didn't, and that *is* brave."

I am losing the fight against the tears. Her words hurt to hear because they are beautiful, but they couldn't feel less true.

"I don't feel brave, Anna. I just want to go h-home; I just want it to stop. I can't take much more of this, and I still have to get through tomorrow," I choke, my voice breaking.

"I know. Come here…"

Anna pulls me back onto her chest, holds me tight, and rocks me as the tears fall hotly down my face.

"You're going to be okay; I'll make sure of it. I promise you."

It doesn't take long before I fall asleep. The hurt in my chest didn't ease but exhaustion hit. I don't even remember feeling like I was going to fall asleep. It isn't long, I know it isn't, because a knock on the door wakes me, and my eyes ache to stay closed so I don't move. Anna pulls the duvet up, covering my bare back. I'm just coherent enough to realise how sweet that is. Even when I am supposedly asleep, she covers my scars, knowing I wouldn't want to be seen.

"Come in.," Anna hisses. "Sshh…"

"Sorry," Dixy whispers. "I just wanted to check how she was doing?"

"Not great. Are you going to tell me how the hell she managed to get a chain around her neck without you seeing?!" Anna hisses.

My insides clench. Now I want to go back to sleep more than ever. I thought I had been clear with Anna; this isn't Dixy's fault. Not clear enough apparently.

"I…cuffed her in the shackles. It was a necessary part of the process, but it wasn't easy to do. I knew if I gave her the lock pick and if she could control the flashbacks, she would get free, something she was never able to do before. But…when I cuffed her, she broke down. It wasn't easy to watch or hear so I turned my back, hoping she would see there was only one way out of the cuffs. By the time I realised she had slipped into a memory, it was too late; it happened in seconds. You can be mad at me. I don't blame you, Anna, but you will never be as mad at me as I am."

Anna stays quiet for a moment, and the tension in the room is thick. There is no way I am getting back to sleep now.

"Mac already told me she doesn't blame you, and I guess…I can see how easy that could happen, but seriously she could have – "

"I know!" Dixy hisses.

"What are your plans for her tomorrow?" Anna whispers more calmly.

"I can't tell you that, but it is going to help, and I need you to trust me on that."

"Trust you? You're breaking her; she can't take much more! You don't have to tell me because tomorrow, I *am* coming with her."

"Anna, that isn't a good idea. I know you're upset, but she is my friend. I'm not doing this to hurt her. I am trying to help her, and this will work."

"I know she is your friend, and I know today was an accident. That is the only reason I'm not losing my shit at you! I will *not* risk her, not for a single second. I am coming, and I really wouldn't argue with me on this one, Dixy," Anna whispers but somehow still manages to be firm, and the finality in her words is clear.

I don't know whether to feel awkward and embarrassed over Anna being protective or touched and slightly aroused.

All of the above.

"Fine, but don't get in the way of this, Anna. The past two days have all been for this – the past few weeks in fact. This *will* help her and to stop it would hurt her much more than you realise. Everyone is meeting for breakfast at 8am. We leave after that; she needs to bring two spare sets of clothes."

I hear Dixy leave the room and then I feel Anna stroke my face. "You were not supposed to hear any of that."

"It was hard not to; I didn't mean to eavesdrop, but I really didn't have it in me to make my presence known and join the argument either."

"Are you mad at me?" she asks warily.

I sit up, rubbing the sleep out my eyes. From the look of the light outside and how much my stomach is growling, it must be around 7pm. I mustn't have been asleep very long, but I am glad. I don't want to sleep the evening away and waste the time with Anna.

“No, not at all. It is actually quite…sexy to hear you go off like that,” I smirk, and she giggles. “but try not to be too hard on her. Today really messed her up.”

“I know, I was trying to bear that in mind, but I had to get my point across so she could see there is no way I’m not coming tomorrow.”

“I don’t want you to feel like you have to come. I had a freak out, but I’ll be okay. I know how much it hurt you being there last time. I don’t…” I begin, but I am quickly silenced by Anna’s finger placed on my lips.

“You might not want to finish that sentence; I know you can do this without me. This is not me doubting you, but after today, I’m not leaving you alone in this again. I could have so easily lost you, Mac.” Anna’s voice is more gravelled than ever. Her eyes fall on my bruised throat, and she lightly traces her fingers down my neck. “I am not leaving that to chance. I’ll stay out the way, but I’m not risking you. I am going to make sure you get through this in one piece, and then you and I are going *home*.”

CHAPTER 14

Release Me from These Chains

"Morning, kid. How are you holding up?" Alfred asks in a groggy grumble.

"I'm alright. Missing the fire pit."

Alfred and I are in line at the breakfast buffet. I'm nervous and food is the last thing on my mind, but it was the perfect excuse to get away from the world's most awkward breakfast table. Anna and Dixy are being rather icy with each other, talking in clipped, formal speech. Lambert is stuffing his face, completely oblivious. While I understand the tension between them, I also don't have the head space to deal with it. Dixy's secrecy on the subject of today is making me more nervous than ever.

"Yeah, I'm with you there. It would be nice to get away one day, but this is as far from a family holiday as it can get. The only thing that rings true is the family spat. What is going on with Savannah and Dixy?"

I load my plate with everything a heavenly fried breakfast of champions could hold, hoping it will rouse some appetite, and order a huge mug of coffee. I had the best evening with Anna, ordering dinner in bed and watching movies. I spent the evening laughing, and I didn't want it to end. After all this time, you would expect that we would run out of things to talk about, but we never seem to. For this reason, not much sleep was had, and the coffee is very much welcome.

"Ah, yeah. They had a little bust up over something that happened with me yesterday. Anna thinks Dixy dropped the ball and told her that she is coming with me today. Dixy isn't happy about it. I'm sure they will work it out. I hope so anyway," I explain exasperatedly with a huff.

"Well, I don't know what happened, but if Anna feels she needs to be with you to watch your back, it mustn't have been good. She wouldn't interfere for nothin' so I am inclined to agree with her."

"I don't disagree with Anna being there, I just don't like her seeing bad stuff. It's bad on there, Pa." Alfred's brow furrows, and he scratches his whiskers with the palm of his hand.

"I get you, but it wasn't easy for her waiting around yesterday either. She knows the whole time you're gone you are suffering, and she can't see that you're okay. Remember in Wales, when you were with Billy and Jackson? Even though it was hard to watch, she couldn't look away from the screen. The only way she could cope was if she could see you. This is no different, kid."

"Huh…didn't think of it like that. Thanks, Pa. Feel a little less crap about it now."

I make my way back to the breakfast table, take my seat next to Anna, and find that the atmosphere is no different to when I left. I listen as Alfred and Lambert discuss different alcohol they have discovered while on missions around the world. I push my food around my plate with no real interest in eating it.

"You need to eat, Max. First thing we are doing is going back to the surf. The cold will burn through your energy in minutes," Dixy informs me, and I groan.

"The *first* thing? What about the rest of the day?"

"You don't need to know that," Dixy replies.

"Surely it would be easier if she did," Anna interjects.

"Easier isn't what we are here for, Anna."

My patience is being tested; my nerves are not taking to this hostility well. I drop my knife and fork with a clang onto the plate and rub my temples with a growl.

"Okay, ladies. I'm not going through the whole day like this because it is likely to suck enough without this. We are all on the same side. Can we try to remember that? I know you both have…disagreed, and that's fine, but I need you to try to get along, please."

Anna leans into me, kisses the side of my neck quickly, and whispers, "I'm sorry," into my ear. Then she pulls away to look at Dixy.

"She's right; it's done now. So, let's just let it go," Anna says sincerely, and Dixy smiles.

"Consider it done."

I am definitely relieved, and things do feel less icy almost immediately. I force some food down me, focusing on my favourite things on the plate, and before I know it, it's time to go.

"Alfred, meet us at the rendezvous with the supplies we talked about say about 5pm?" Dixy announces, and I frown at her, then at Anna, and she shrugs.

"Sure, no problem. If the time changes, let me know," Alfred replies, and then he looks at me oddly, a look I can't quite work out.

"Good luck, kid," he grumbles, and then he pulls me in for a bear hug.

"Uh…thanks, Pa."

Well, that is enough to make me nervous. Clearly, he knows something that I don't. Anna and I follow behind Dixy and Lambert as we leave the hotel. The tension is definitely less, but now I have my own tension to worry about. We pile into the van, but because there isn't enough room for us all, Anna and I are sat in the back of the van on the floor. The first thing I notice is that there is a spade that wasn't there yesterday along with a large cardboard box with a long sheet of thick plywood on top.

"The last time I was in here, we thought you broke your hip, and you fell asleep with your head in my lap. It was the first time I'd really touched you in a long time. Although you were asleep, so you won't remember that," Anna mutters thoughtfully, holding my hand.

The memory is easy to recall. The fear, the pain in my hip, the flashbacks, and the good and bad feelings of her being close to me again.

"That isn't a day I'm likely to forget. I was convinced I'd broken my hip until I remembered what it actually felt like to break my hip. It was the day I remembered the butcher. I wasn't very nice to you that day. The flashbacks were in full swing, and I wanted you but couldn't have you. It turned me into an uber arsehole." I chuckle uncomfortably.

"You weren't an arsehole; you had the right to push me away. Who the hell is the butcher?"

"The creepy man who operated on my hip on the boat. Jakub told Tomasz to call the butcher after he broke my hip."

Anna looks at me; I can tell she isn't sure what to say. So, in the end, she leans in and gives me slow, teasing kisses, but then she giggles, pulling away.

"I feel like a terrible person. The scar he gave you, the way it smoothly runs from the dip in your groin in an arch over your hip and…ugh! It has always been one of scars I find the sexiest. As you may have noticed last night..." She pauses, her eyes darkening sexily, and my stomach flutters. "But now you put it into context…" I blush and raise my eyebrow, and she giggles cutely, hiding her face in her hands.

"Mm is that so?" I tease, pulling her hands away from her face which is flushed ruby red with embarrassment. "Don't feel too bad. You like the things about me I find hideous. That isn't a bad feeling for me."

She looks at me with darling eyes, and I love that look. It is a look that never fails to make me tingle. Her lips are on mine with kisses so tempting, I could easily forget we are rumbling along in the van.

"I think it's obvious there isn't a single inch of you that I find hideous."

God damn it… Why are we in a van right now?

I am just about to lean in to kiss her again when the van stops. She groans, and I chuckle. At least I'm not alone in that frustration. The doors swing open, and I am filled with dread as I walk back down the promenade towards the beach. I'm really not looking forward to getting soaked and freezing cold again, but the fact that Lambert is carrying the spade is bothering me more right now. Again, the beach is deserted save a few joggers and dog walkers. Most normal people wouldn't want to be on the beach in this cold. Dixy comes to an abrupt stop just in front of me.

"This should do," she alerts Lambert, and he nods. He then stomps the spade into the sand and starts to dig.

"Okay, so you won't be doing surf torture just yet. First, I want to work some more on your triggers with being trapped. We have learnt that all the triggers are based on fear of someone having control over you and being trapped is an easy way to trigger that. It's also the least evasive thing on the list, and Barrett is almost guaranteed to confine or restrain you in some way," Dixy explains.

Suddenly, it is pretty obvious to me why Lambert is digging in the sand, and I'm nervous, but so far, I feel in control of myself.

"With confinement, we have a lot of options. The box was one, and you said one of the things that was hard was that it was so tight, you couldn't breathe easily or move. We are already working on you being restrained, and I think this will be a good way to push this trigger. You won't be able to move once you are buried.

"You have to find new ways to adapt your grounding techniques. Once buried, you won't be able to use your sense of touch or taste. This limits your options to sound, sight, and smell, and that could be the case wherever you're triggered. Being able to adapt to your surroundings and circumstances quickly can mean the difference between stopping a flashback before it starts or having to try to claw your way out of one in full swing. Once we have done this stage, we'll move you to the water. Then, I think we are all going to need a coffee break to warm up. Sound okay?" Dixy asks, and I do a double take. Dixy never asks, she tells. Something tells me that was for Anna, not me.

"Yeah, I'm good with that."

I watch as Lambert digs what looks like a shallow grave in the sand. Nerves are now starting to twist in my gut. Anna comes over, wrapping her arms around my bicep, her teeth chattering on my shoulder. I take off my jumper and hand it to her, the wind chill making me shudder.

"No, it's freez – " she protests.

"It isn't going to do anything to keep me warm. Plus, I have spares in the rucksack." She puts it on, and I smile. "Looks better on you anyway."

Lambert finishes digging, and I start unlacing my boots. In my head, I try to run through all the things that I can use to ground myself as the familiar sensation of anxiety begins to creep into my chest, tightening it. The rectangular hole is just over my length and width and roughly a foot and a half deep.

When I was a kid, I remember giving my mum a fright at the beach. I dug a deep hole; it took me hours. I must have been 5 years old, and by the time I had dug the hole deep enough for me to jump in, the tide had crept in. I jumped in my hole. I remember patting the walls of it, trying to make it neat and smooth. I shouted for my mum, impressed with my efforts. The hole filled with water as the tide washed over it and completely submerged me with murky sea water. Luckily, she heard my shouts and was already running over to me when the hole filled up.

I still remember the taste of the sea water and the panic of choking on it. I remember not quite understanding at first why mum was so mad at me. Most clearly though, I remember what happened afterwards. She took me to the public tap that is for washing the sand off your feet, and she stuck me under its icy flow. She washed the sand out of my hair and wrapped me in a fluffy beach towel.

Then she took me to a café, and we drank monkey tea and ate chocolate muffins. I asked her why she likes tea so much and she said, "Because, my darling, tea makes the world go round." Still to this day, I don't really know what that is supposed to mean or why it makes me so happy thinking about it. But right now, as I lay myself down in the cold sandy hole, that's what I'm thinking about. As Lambert shovels piles of sand over my feet, I picture my mums round face. Her dimples pronounced as she smiles warmly at me over a mug of monkey tea. What does tea really taste of anyway? I mean, I like it, but I can't think of a way to describe it. Not like I can with bitter, dark, smoky coffee.

Laying on the flat of my back, looking up at the sky, I let my mind ramble and surf through memories of mum while I try to make pictures with the clouds. Somewhere behind me, Anna is sat with Dixy, watching as Lambert continues to cover me with sand. The drops of cold sand are now just above my knees and he pats the sand down with the flat of the spade. I listen to the waves crashing onto the shore and try to count the seconds between each crash. I know I don't have much to work with. I can't really smell anything but the salty seaside smell. The only thing I really have to ground myself with is sounds, sight, and keeping my mind busy.

It isn't till Lambert starts putting the sand over my stomach that I really start to feel the panic setting in. I want to lift my arms out of the sand to feel more in control, but I know that's an instinct that Lambert would quickly call me up on. As the abrasive sand hits my cold, bare arms, it stings my skin like a cold sun burn.

"Can someone help keep the sand out of Mac's face while I cover her shoulders and chest?" Lambert calls.

I wish he hadn't said that; his words are like pulling the trigger of a gun. Once I hear them, the panic I am trying to keep hold of slips from my grasp as easily as sand through fingers. I feel my body tremble oddly as it is immobilised by the heavy sand. Anna kneels by my head and puts her hands in front of my face. She manages to block most of the sand and then a puff of air is forced from my lungs as the weight of the sand falls on my chest.

"Ugh, fuck nuggets."

It doesn't take long. Once my face is blocked by Anna's hands, Lambert picks up speed. The last shovel full of sand falls, and I am completely paralysed. I can't so much as wiggle a finger.

"Okay, Anna. I am done; you need to walk away from her now. Mac, focus – if you need me to pull you out, just shout. I am within earshot," Lambert advises.

Anna runs her finger down my cheek quickly and then walks away. That small touch tells me it isn't easy for her to step away, but I feel better not being watched. My jaw is set; the fact that I can't move at all is shocking. I knew I wouldn't be able to but knowing it and feeling it is completely different. My chest is attempting to heave for breath but there is no room for it to expand. It feels like I'm slowly suffocating, only able to draw a little air in.

No. This is in my head; I am panicking. There is room to breathe as long as I don't panic. I need to focus on something, anything. I can only just see the sea. The position my head is stuck in is the position it was in when I was looking at the sky. I can't find anything I can see that can help me. I only really have one thing: my mind.

My eyes close, and I try desperately to open the curtains to the cinema of my mind. It has been a long time since I've been to this theatre, my place of sanity on the boat. I need movies I know well; I need to picture every scene as perfectly as I can. In vibrant colour and rich sound. It's impossible for me to play a whole movie from memory, so I pick scenes from my favourites, and I speak the lines out loud.

I picture that scene in The Matrix, where Neo is at the train station and he decides not to run but to fight Agent Smith.

"What is he doing?"

"He's beginning to believe."

The image morphs and flickers into the scene of the cargo hold, and my eyes shoot open.

"Ugh…" I groan.

This isn't working. I was on the boat when I did that. Doing it now just makes me feel like I am back there, trying to save my sanity. My mind is blank. The corners of my mind are darkening as the flashback tries to take hold. I am losing grip of my control. It feels like time is moving too slowly, and although the presence of the flashback is there threatening me, the strength behind it seems to be less.

By the time Lambert starts digging me back up, I feel a little disorientated and confused but relieved. I never fully lost control, but I have no idea why. It doesn't feel like such a victory when it feels like I've fluked it. I felt like I was on the edge the whole time, but everything I did to ground myself failed, and I don't know how I didn't succumb to it. Lambert pulls me to my feet, and I breathe some long sucking breaths, dust the sand off my arms, and stretch my back.

"How are you holding up?" Dixy asks.

"Um…okay."

"Are you sure because you look out of it?"

"Yeah, I just don't know how I kept control. It felt like I was just…on the edge of the flashback the whole time. I failed to ground myself but there was no flashback," I explain.

"Because you are taking the fear out of them, the trigger was probably weaker, but because of that, it made it easier for you to see the difference in the intensity. That is good sign, Max."

"Probably a fluke," I say, shaking my head.

"Well, get your butt in the water, and let's find out, shall we?"

I am already cold; the sand seems to have chilled me to the bone. I figure it will be less of a shock to the system as Lambert lowers me to the water, but I am so wrong. I forget to close my mouth or even try to supress my gasp, but luckily, the first wave doesn't hit till seconds after. I cross my arms over my chest as I feel Lamberts hands on my shins, holding me in place.

Like yesterday, the panic rises quickly, but I'm ready for it this time. As soon as I find rhythm with the waves, I sing though the wash and inhale in the break. My body shakes violently from the cold, and I feel my brain going numb again. I lose the ability to shout the lyrics; the effort to hold my head up out of the water is exhausting. Somewhere I know, I'm tiring quicker than I was yesterday. I'm losing track with the rhythm of the waves, and my mouth fills with salty water, and my head begins to swim and blur.

The memory swirls.

"Wash off your filth!"

A steel bucket is kicked towards me. Murky sea water sloshes over the sides, and attached to the handle is a rough bristle scrubbing brush. The same brush I just used to scrub the deck of the cargo hold. My body is exhausted from playing Cinder-Goddamn-rella, and my arms shake as I dip the brush into the water. I begin to scrub it against my arm slowly, my head bobbing with the effort to stay upright.

"I said wash!" the mala suka man yells.

I don't feel the pain at first, only the winding impact as his boot hits me square in the chest. The force knocks me back, banging my head on the deck and sending my head in a spin. His foot holds me down, suffocating pressure in my already winded lungs, and I see the bucket upturn above me.

Salty water burns my nose and throat as I choke, unable to sit up as he holds me in place under his boot.

I am choking...I'm going to die...God, it hurts. My vision begins to blacken, my body jerking as I drown. The mala suka man yanks me upwards...

Choking... Spluttering... Gagging...

My eyes shoot open.

Choking... Spluttering... Gagging... Pain.

A stinging pain burns up my back as I feel a hand slap the centre of my back w, and I gasp as the water clears from my throat and lungs. My fingers clench into the sand as I spit salt water. I feel a blanket being draped over me and then Anna pushing me upright. The air swells into my lungs. I see the fright on Anna's face and cringe.

"Ugh. Well, tha-a-a-at sucke-d." I shiver, and she smiles a little.

"You okay to move, Max? You need them wet clothes off," Dixy urges.

"Le-t-tss go."

I get to my feet, holding the blanket tight to me. The van is closer this time. I walk as fast as I can away from the sea, and I'm glad to see the back of it. This time, Anna helps me get changed which means I'm out of the wet clothes and into a dry set before the van has barely moved. She pulls my hands to her mouth, blowing hot air onto them, and it feels amazing.

"It was a memory, wasn't it?" Anna asks.

"How d-did you kn-now?"

"Because you went into the water calm like you didn't know you were in it. You didn't even struggle at choking," she utters, mouse-like.

"I'm o-okay," I assure her with a shiver, and she smiles, not completely convinced.

I am led to the back of the closest coffee shop, which just happens to be a Starbucks. Lambert disappears off to order coffees without even asking what anyone wants and returns with a caramel latte for me and then takes everyone else's orders. I smile; he is quite the gentleman when he wants to be. I'm not used to that kind of treatment from men. They always seem to want challenge me and treat me like one of the lads.

Lambert brings everyone melty cheese toasties, and I eat and greedily gulp the coffee down. Soon the shivers slow down, and I start to feel more human. I'm disappointed that it didn't go better, but the feeling is overshadowed by the relief of knowing I won't have to do that again. We are leaving in the morning, and I can't wait.

"How you doing?" Dixy asks.

"Fine now I am warm."

"You held out well. The memories will always be harder to block out. It is seeming like your mind is determined to remember once it starts, but you blocked the flashbacks both times, and we only have one more stop before you are done."

"Let me guess: you saved the best till last?" I groan, and Dixy smiles warmly.

"It is the last time you will ever have to go back. Let's make every second count." She winks, and I chuckle as she uses the words that she had inscribed on the inside of the watch. "We have some time; it's only 1pm. I think everyone has earned an hour in the warmth. Plus, I want some cake!" Dixy squeals.

When Dixy mentions the time, I remember what she said to Alfred about a rendezvous at 5pm and bringing supplies. Does that mean we will be done before 5pm in order to meet him somewhere? Or is the rendezvous at the boat, and he is bringing more stuff to torture me with? No, that doesn't make any sense. Whatever it means, I don't really want to wait an hour. Whatever is going to happen, I just want it over with. Anna curls her arms around my arm and leans her head on my shoulder.

"You okay, beautiful?"

"Yeah, just thinking." She yawns cutely.

"Do I get to know what about?"

"Yeah…but not yet."

"That is frustrating as hell. You are up to something, I know that look."

"Well, you could wait…or you could tell me what you were thinking the other night that you wouldn't tell me. Then I'll spill my secrets in return," Anna teases, looking up to me with challenging eyes.

"I can wait."

"Oh, damn you, Mac Scott! I will get it out of you somehow. Trust me, I am determined."

"That isn't happening, Savannah Slone."

"We'll see."

The time drags. As much as I enjoy casual chat in a coffee shop, I'm glad when we are finally on the move again. The fear is present, gnawing in my gut as we rumble along in the van on route to Leigh Docks. But the draw to this being the last time I have to enter the vile purgatory is spurring me on.

As the van pulls to a stop, I get out, and I don't hesitate as I begin the walk along the docks, weaving in and out of the graveyard of boats.

Dixy and Lambert lead the way while me and Anna follow, her hand firmly holding mine. I can feel the dread coming off her, and I can't say I blame her. Whenever I get on this boat, I seem to go full-on exorcist, and I can imagine how jarring that is to see. It's not my most attractive quality. Lambert is carrying the cardboard box and sheet of plywood from the van. I know better than to bother asking what they're for, regardless of my curiosity. Dixy is carrying a takeaway tray loaded with coffees, which makes me wonder how long I am going to be stuck on this boat for the final time.

My feet pound across the ramp as I cross the water on to the boat. Lambert walks around to the bow of the boat as I lead the way down the stairs and back into the depths of the cargo hold. My body tightens as soon as I enter but the initial fear walking in is less potent; it's more of an anxious nag. I stop in middle of the room, and I turn my back on the chains to look at Dixy. She walks over to the chest of drawers and puts the tray of coffees on top of it, and then turns back to me.

"Can you tell me about the last memory you have before you came home?" Dixy asks.

"Not very well. The memories only come back in shards, not a complete picture, and the timeline is mixed up. It gets a little clearer the more I remember. I can sometimes tell that one memory came before others, usually by the timing of injuries, but it still isn't a continuous line. The last thing I remember is walking into A&E."

"Tell me about that memory, about walking into A&E," Dixy requests. Her expression is warm and careful, much different to the last time I was here. She stands with her back leant against the slope of the wall, mimicking Anna who stands further down the wall, closer to the chains. Anna's eyes are focused on me, warm with affection and encouragement, telling me she is there but giving me space.

"I was told to get out of the van, and when I did, the van drove away. It took a long time to walk into A&E. By the time I got to reception, I was just able to tell them my name before I passed out."

"Somewhere in this room, there is a trigger, and that trigger holds the key to open the door to the memory of *how* you got off this boat that day. I want you to find it; I want you to remember getting off the boat."

"How am I going to do that? It isn't like I can choose what I remember."

"Your mind has never been more open to remembering than it is right now. These past three days, you've gained a lot of memories. The memory you just described was clinical and says nothing about how you felt, physically or emotionally. Talk about it in more detail, connect to it, and use this room to trigger you. Then you will find the memory. Walk around the room, stay calm and grounded, block out the flashbacks, and keep your mind open for the memories. You have already proven that you are gaining control. The memories are a lot harder to stop than the flashbacks because they are real and although forgotten, they are a part of you."

I rub my eyes and groan, turning my back on her. She makes that sound a lot easier than it actually is. I don't have confidence in my control. I don't fear remembering, part of me wants to remember, but I do fear the pain that comes with it.

"What do you want me to do?" I huff.

"Tell us the memory again with as much detail as you can. Follow your instincts, move around the room, and try to connect to that day. The answers are here you just have to find them, Max."

It is blind faith that makes me turn back around and look at her. I don't know why this is so important. I left the boat. What difference does it make if I remember leaving? Like everything I've done since being here, it doesn't really make sense to me, but I have come this far trusting Dixy. I can't fall short in the eleventh hour or everything I've done will have led to nothing. Whatever the point of all of this was, my only chance of understanding it is if I see it through. It may lead to nothing or it may, as Dixy has said hundreds of times, help me.

"I didn't get out of the van right away. They told me to but…I thought it was a trick. They had played that game before, pretended to set me free only to punish me when I tried to run. When I hesitated, they kicked me out, and the van sped away."

"That's better, Max. Keep going."

"I was weak, and it hurt when I tried to get up off the floor. My ribs were broken again, my shoulder dislocated but…not from the fall out the van, from…something before. Everything felt…heavy, like I was dragging my legs through treacle. I didn't have shoes or socks, but it didn't really bother me after so long without them. Cars were moving around me, real life cars with real life people inside them." I look at Anna and chuckle a little. "They were like spaceships, zipping past me faster than I could really register. They didn't seem real, and it didn't feel like I had control. I just kept walking.

"When I got to the entrance, the doors slid open, and the brightness of the hospital lights was blinding, a complete white out, but I could hear people muttering. As my eyes adjusted, I saw them all staring at me sat in the waiting room. I realised then it wasn't a trick, I was…I…" The lump in my throat cuts off my voice, and I turn away, my eyes blurring with tears.

"Don't stop, Max. You are connecting. I know it hurts, but you need to keep going," Dixy encourages.

I wipe my eyes roughly and try to collect myself. I don't want to feel this; it is all too easy to recall how I felt in that moment. I feel it now just as purely as if I am back in that waiting room. I see their faces staring at me with crystal clear clarity. I start to move as I speak, wide eyed and not really seeing the cargo hold anymore but feeling the creak of the deck below my feet.

"People are…w-were staring at me, strangers with shocked and disgusted faces, but I didn't really care. They were real people the first people I had seen in two years, and I just wanted to reach out and touch them. I knew that…now I'd been seen, it wasn't a trick. They had let me go. I can't really explain…what that…felt like."

I walk over to the doorway, my eyes falling on the wooden steps that lead up the top deck. There are only four steps; the varnish has worn off the centre of each step showing the number of times that these steps have been walked up and down. The sound of the hollow knocking I would hear whenever someone came down them to torment me is still so clear in my mind. I was only ever once able to scale the steps; the time I tried to escape but the memory of being kicked back down them is much stronger.

"The walk to reception was…the hardest part. My head was swimming. I was so past hungry and tired, I didn't really feel…present. I was scared I wouldn't be able to speak my name. My mouth tasted like blood and it is…was…so dry from…"

My mind flashes, just for a second. I bring my fingers up to my mouth, my head begins to swim, and I can almost feel it there. Tightly bound and sucking the moisture from my mouth. I turn away from the stairs and walk back towards the centre of the room.

"I was…gagged." I gasp.

I walk over to the chains and pick up the shackles from the floor, holding the steel hoop that fixes the chains to the shackles. I hold one in each hand as my arms hang loosely at my sides. I walk forwards; the chains clink as they run through the steel hoop that that secures it to the steel ceiling cross beam.

Clink-Clink, Clink-Clink, Clink-Clink.

I walk till I feel the tug against the chains as I meet the boundary of how far the chains length will allow me to go. Then, I crouch down to the floor, sit cross legged, and hold the chains tightly. My vision begins to blur and then focus, blur and then focus as it starts to swoop in that familiar swirl.

"I need…" I struggle as my head bobs, "… you to gag me."

I hear a rip of fabric, and Dixy dashes up to me; I feel the materiel wedge between my teeth and then it drags roughly against the corners of my mouth as it tightens. My mouth starts to dry up, and my head begins to swim, the corners of vision blackening. I lay on my side, my knees pointed towards my chest, and the cold chain drapes over my hip heavily. My right arm bends awkwardly beneath my head, the chain coldly digging into the crook of my neck.

"Ughh…"

My eyes droop closed, and the memory swirls.

I hear the clonk-clonk-clonk as footsteps pound down the stairs, and my eyes shoot open fearfully. I cringe against the chains, pushing myself upright. Groggy and shivering as my eyes come into focus. I see them charging towards me, and I jerk backwards with a terror-stricken whimper, but I am out of length of chain.

The mala suka man, Tomasz, and Jakub stand over me, and I shrink. they must be here to kill me. I hope they actually do it this time.

"Gag her," Jakub orders, but the words come out of my mouth mumbled from the gag.

Tomasz lunges for me, and I fight him off, squirming out of his grasp, kicking and punching uselessly. There is no weight or force left for me to hit with. I watch as my arms, bony and atrophied, squat at him like a fly. Tomasz grips my throat and slams my face to the floor, and my head spins, blood trickling warmly down my cheek. He pulls me upright, his nails digging into my throat.

"Stay still, or I will squeeze the pathetic life out of you!"

Tomasz holds me in place, and the mala suka man ties a rag around my mouth. Terror rocks my tired bones and then...Tomasz lets go of my throat and the shackles are unlocked, freeing my wrists for the first time in what feels like forever. I gasp. The lightness feels alien, and my adrenaline begins to pump. I can't help it; I have to try, I lunge forwards and launch myself, slamming at the gap between Jakub and Tomasz.

I am forced to a stop as Tomasz grips my hair. He holds me by it as his fist pounds against my jaw, and I collapse to the ground. Blood fills my mouth, and I rip the gag out of my mouth, spitting blood. I crawl towards the stairs and bone crunching pain explodes in my ribcage.

"Arggghh!"

The pain paralyses me. I try to get up, once, twice, but the pain buckles my legs in seconds. It is hard to breathe; the pain is all consuming. I see shiny shoes step towards me as Jakub crouches in front of me.

"Now, McKenna, it is in your best interest that you behave yourself," Jakub leers, and his leer comes clearly out of my mouth in the present.

"What is...the point? I am dead anyway," I gasp.

"Oh, but you're not dead. Not yet. I am not here to kill you; I'm here to free you."

This is a trick; they are fucking with my head again. Why must they play with their food before they eat it? Just fucking end it.

"You're a fucking liar!"

"Yes, I am, but not about this. I should correct myself. I am here to ***release*** *you, not free you. We will be watching you; you will never truly be free. Your father will find you, and then I will find him. Then I will extinguish the entire bloodline of your family, starting with you. Your father will learn the agony of watching his daughter die slowly, just as he forced that fate upon me. Until then, McKenna Scott, I bid you goodbye," Jakub said lightly, his tone playful and light.*

The vision distorts. I lay curled on my side a few feet from the stairs. As the past becomes the present, I push myself upright.

"They tied me up, gagged me, and threw me into the back of a van. When we reached the hospital, they untied me and…that's it," I choke, my eyes dazed and unfocused.

"Anna…" Dixy says softly.

I feel her come up behind me. She sits on the floor and slides her legs apart so I am sat between them, her arms wrapping tightly around my waist. I jump at the contact and then cross my arms over hers, my body relaxing into hers. Dixy sits down in front of me, her eyes determined on mine.

"You never let this place go because somewhere inside your head, that memory of Jakub telling you that you will never be free has been stuck there. You feel like they let you go but kept you on a piece of string because that's exactly what they did do. That restraint didn't release when you killed them. Your fear was always that you would end up back here, you just didn't know why, and this memory is why. The string is tied to this place and when we leave, I promise you, you will cut that string, and you will finally be free," Dixy assures me, but the words just hurt; they're not so easy to believe. I choke on a sob but manage to control myself.

"H-how can you know that?"

"Just trust me one more time, Max. It's almost over; I'm asking you now as your friend not your instructor. Trust me and trust yourself, please. Can you do that for me?"

"Yeah,"

"Good. Now just take a few minutes, cuddle your girl. I will grab you a coffee," Dixy says, getting to her feet.

Anna slides round me, and I melt into her. It is so magical, the effect her touch has. Dixy hands me a warmish cardboard takeaway cup of coffee, and I down half of it in one gulp, soothing the dryness of my throat.

"I don't know how you do this; I just want to take you away," Anna whispers.

"I would totally be okay with that. Let's make a run for it."

The coffee is super sweet; it's kind of gross. I am hoping the sugar and caffeine will rouse some life back into me. My eyes droop as I try to fix them on bright green eyes.

"Are you sure you can run? You look exhausted, baby." She smiles warmly. I am exhausted; I just want to sleep.

"I feel it. This coffee isn't doing anything to…"

An unnatural tiredness pours over me with dizzying power, and I slide away from Anna, dropping my coffee as my head hits the deck.

"Mac…what's wrong?!" Anna shrieks franticly.

"I don't feel good. Oh, God, w-what's happening?" I blurt fearfully.

Dixy pulls me back upright and holds my face. It does nothing to stop my head swooping. I feel like someone turned up the gravity, and now, I am sinking through the floor.

"Don't panic; you are fine. I put sleepy stuff in your drink. Sorry, Max. You will wake up again in a bit. Trust yourself, Max!" Dixy says firmly.

"What?! No! Wh…" I begin, but my mouth is no longer connected to my brain.

"Dixy, what the hell!?" Anna rages, and she pulls me from behind into her arms and out of Dixy's grasp. The tug sends my head in a tailspin, a blur of colour, and then my eyes close as gravity takes me.

Darkness…

***

My eyes shoot open, but all I see is darkness. I jerk around in a fright to find - I can't move. Panic surges through me at an electrifying rate. I can't see; I'm hooded with something. I try to shake it off, but it is snug around my neck somehow. I can't lift my arms to pull at it or bend forward. I am fixed to the spot.

"Oh, God…what has she done?!" I choke.

I try to move my legs, but they are fixed too. Then I hear the clink of the chains, and I flinch. Horror sweeps inside my gut. The only things I can move are my hands, wrists, and feet. Understanding suddenly hits me. I am bound and chained to a chair. I feel disoriented and dizzy, like I am swaying…no. I am not swaying, the boat is!

"Oh, God…no, no, no…" I whimper.

My fists clench in terror, and then I feel something in the palm of my hand. I touch for it, my fingertips investigating, and I feel something is taped to my hand.

"Argh, fuck!" I scream.

Taped to the palm of my hand is a lockpick. I grip it with shaky hands as fear and pain explode in my chest, and I sob.

"Why would she do this to me?! Why?! Oh God, I can't do this…I can't."

Panic grips me, and my mind flashes…

"No…calm the fuck down!" I yell.

My chest heaves but is gripped tightly with whatever has me bound to the chair. I need to slow my breathing and work this out. Dixy did this for a reason. She told me to trust her, then I had better do it. No one else is getting me out; I have to get myself out. This is just a game, a puzzle. I can do this. This is the end game that she wouldn't tell me about; she wants me to escape. I'm not trapped again, not really. This is a just a game, a screwed-up game, but a game nonetheless. I can do this. My arms are bound down to just below my elbows, giving my lower arms a little movement. I feel for the bangle around my wrist, tracing the feel of the numbers engraved inside, and I take deep, shaky breaths. I feel my mind begin to clear as I ground myself.

"I am a mouse…I will shout about this *fucked up* house!"

"This is *my* boat!"

"They are just chains!"

"You are all dead, now *get the fuck out of my head!*"

I growl, spitting the words furiously. The anger and resentment I feel for this boat and every haunting psychopath that resided in it is burning in my chest and bursting out of me.

Yes…that's better.

I chant to myself while I grip the lock pick with my thumb and palm, using my fingertips to find the keyhole on the lock of the shackle around my left wrist. I find it and hold my fingertip to the hole to help guide the pick to it. My hands are steady as I chant my vengeful words over and over again. The lock clicks, and the left claw of the shackle opens and falls away. A smile plays on my lips. I am in control. The fear is still there, but the venom I feel, the determination to escape in a way I never could before…

Oh! That's what Dixy is doing. She is giving me the escape I never had before!

That woman is as clever as she is brave. I am both grateful and pissed as hell at her. I make quick work of the second shackle, and I feel the weight of the chain fall away with a loud clank to the floor. It is a small victory; I am still hooded, completely blind, and just as tightly bound to the chair. I try again to lean forward, pushing with everything I have, my hand stretching painfully to try to reach the hood, but it is no use.

I need to cut the rope. I have the ghost knife attached to my shin, just above my boot near my knee. I stretch my hand down to see if I can feel and reach the hilt of it through my trousers. My heart flies when I can just feel it. I start dragging and clawing at my trouser leg. It is slow but it is moving up my leg. The hard part is getting enough pull to untuck it from my boot. I am soaked with sweat, my throat dry, but I keep chanting, the anger keeping me calm. I feel the skin of my bare knee, and my fingers desperately grope for the hilt of the ghost knife.

"Come on, come on, come… YES! Thank you, Lambert, you wonderful man!" I cheer.

The easiest place to reach is my inner elbow, but I can only just reach it. I try to hook the tip of the blade under the rope. I manage it, but I wince as I feel the knife slice into my inner bicep, right near my elbow. The blade catches on my skin over and over as I drive the knife back and forth.

"Gahh…" I growl at the pain.

The pain is good. It, along with the anger is keeping me grounded. I keep pushing; I keep slicing. Sweat pours off me as I grunt through the pain of the repetitive slices to my inner arm, and then, I feel movement in the rope, the knife no longer slicing at my skin because it has room to manoeuvre. The realisation spurs me on with excitement. I drive the knife harder and the I hear a snap. The ropes around my chest and arms loosen, and I wriggle.

My chest explodes with excitement as my arms break free, I grab for the hood, and now I see why I couldn't shake it off; it is tied with a drawstring around my neck. I use the knife to cut the string and inhale a long breath as I rip the hood off my head. My eyes are blinded in a white out that takes a few seconds to adjust my vision to. I can't believe it – I did it! I want to laugh and cry all at once. As my eyes adjust, they zero in on a large cardboard box sat on the deck just in front of me. Scrawled on the front of it in big chunky marker penned letters are the words:

"Cut the string!"

I look down and begin unwrapping the ropes around my chest. The excitement feels incredible; my heart is flying. Once the rope is off my chest, I'm able to lean forward and begin cutting at the ropes around my ankles. My hands are shaky now, adrenaline pumping through my veins. Excitement, fear, anticipation – all dance inside me making me feel giddy. Blood is pouring down my arm, and I don't care. For once, it is blood that I am proud of spilling.

The ropes come loose, and the feeling that runs through me when I finally cut myself free is overwhelmingly liberating, an absolute high. I get to my feet and go straight over to the cardboard box, opening the flaps, and then, my eyes light up. Inside is a jerry can full of petrol and a grenade. Attached to the Jerry can is a note scrawled in the same handwriting:

"Blow the bitch!"

I laugh, tears stinging my eyes, the lump rising my throat as my heart swells, but I swallow it down. This is not the time to lose control; this is the time to end it. I slide my ghost knife back in its sheath, pick up the grenade and pocket it, and pick up the jerry can. By the weight of it, I'd guess it's brimming full. As I stand, I feel the movement of the boat and then I understand. They must have moved it a safe distance away from the docks so I can blow it, but then…how the hell do I get off? I put down the jerry can and make my way to the door to go up on the top deck to find it locked.

"Seriously!?" I growl with an exasperated laugh.

I walk over to the chest of drawers. I saw loads of tools in there before; hopefully, there is something in there I can use. I scramble through it. The only thing semi helpful is a hammer, but I am not sure it will work. I look at the door. It's old. The wood isn't strong, it's light and weathered. Maybe if I just run at it, I can barge it open. I drop the hammer and walk to the far end of the boat; I have a fair length run up, but that doesn't mean I am strong enough to barge it open.

"Oh, this is going to suck."

I launch into a run powering towards the door. At the last second, I turn my body, so that I hit the door shoulder first. The impact is shocking, but not from hitting the door. The door shattered with ease, sending me through it and landing hard on the stairs and sliding back down them.

"Ugh. Well, that worked."

I scramble to my feet and climb the stairs. When I get to the top and see that is starting to get dark, that in between stage where the sky glows a rich dark blue. I get to the stern of the boat and my chest drops as I see open water. Fear and doubt jolt through me. I walk down the starboard side of the boat towards the bow and stop in my tracks. The plywood that Lambert was carrying has been leant up against the rail of the bow, making a ramp. There is red spray paint glowing off the wood, an arrow pointing upwards, and messily scrawled words advise me of the way out.

"Jump - You are the king of the world!"

CHAPTER 15

King of the World

I stare, fixed and immovable, at the ramp, the hairs rising on the back of my neck. I can't be certain, but I suspect the colour just drained from my face along with my brief confidence. My eyes flit to the water below, and my legs weaken - it is a long way down. I peek around the wood ramp and see the land where the boat was originally docked. It has to be about 150 meters to shore, maybe more. That is not an easy swim for me.

"I'm not a strong swimmer."

On the floor, I spot a flare gun lying next to an upturned can of spray paint. Fear and self-doubt are creeping up on me fast. How the hell am I going to do this?! The thought of leaping into the unknown deep water – Jesus…how deep must that water be? How far will I fall before I hit it? I lean over the side to try to get a better sense of the length of fall and then…

…I see them.

My heart fills with warmth and hope. Gathered around a fire pit, all their eyes are on the boat. They are all there - waiting for me. They believe in me, and that belief brings a renewed strength. Their faith in me never seems to waiver. Maybe it is about time I start having a little faith too. I move out of sight and try to calm the fear that is thick in my chest. They are all waiting for me; I have to do this. This is it, the last push. This is what it all comes down to, facing my fears. Breaking free of the chains, cutting the string, and finally escaping with my freedom. All I have to do is take one last leap of faith.

"Fucking huge leap."

I take a deep breath, and my eyes back fall on the flare gun, and I frown. Is that to shoot for help if I bottle it, and I can't jump? Or to let them know when I am about to jump? I pick it up and open the slot to see the flare inside. It's white; probably a parachute flare. I have learnt a lot about distress signals and military operations from both Alfred and Lambert. If I am right, then this flare will burn white, deploying small parachutes that keep the flare up in the sky illuminating everything below for around 30 seconds. Red flares are for distress signals. I grin. This is to let them know when I am about to jump and to ensure they can see me when I do. I wedge it into the back of my trousers and climb the stairs back down into the cargo hold.

Pleasure, ridiculous pleasure, and fiery vengeance tingles over me as I pour petrol all around the cargo hold, making sure to soak the most hateful areas of pain the most. The box, the epitaph I etched into the floor, the chest of drawers – I even open and fill the mala suka man's toy drawer, dousing the weapons of torment that he used on me. My final fuck you.

Once I feel satisfied with my work, I pour a trail up the stairs and all around the opening to the entrance. I follow the trail around the starboard side of the boat towards the bow, stopping near the cabin. Then I walk down the port side of the boat and use the jerry can to block the gap of the on ramp to the boat. The last thing I need is the grenade rolling through the gap and off the end of boat. The smell of the petrol is pungent, and I feel a little unsafe floating on a boat soaked in petrol. I need to get off as soon as I can. I walk back to the front of the boat and stand in front of the cabin in line with the ramp.

This is going to be tight; I'm going to have to roll the grenade and run full pelt for the ramp and jump without hesitation or…I'm going down with the ship. I pull the grenade from my pocket and examine it; the cool ridged metal feels familiar and comforting somehow. It looks like one of Alfred's grenades, identical to the ones I used in the battle on Eastfields Street. Which means I have 8 seconds before it detonates after I pull the pin.

"Jesus…"

Can I really do this? I am scared of heights, not the best swimmer, and I could end up chargrilled or lost at the bottom of the sea. But that's probably why Dixy has done this. She has crammed a bunch of my ultimate fears into a floating box for me to conquer, for me to destroy. The time for self-doubt has passed. The gun is loaded - I have to pull the trigger.

My hand closes around the flare gun, and I pull it from the back of my trousers. I let my arm fall loosely at my side. Flare gun in my right hand, grenade in my left. I think there is only one way to do this, one way to make sure the grenade blows near the other end of the boat and as far away from me as possible. Once I hit the water, I am going to have to swim for my life. The explosion from this boat will be huge when it finally blows; I will need as much distance as I can get. I have to run as hard and as fast as I can, hopefully giving me a good distance jump.

I need to do this; I need this to be it. This boat has haunted me too long; the ghost of myself is still trapped inside, and I am tied to it. It is time to finally let it go. Jakub released me, but now it's time to set myself free. Never again will I fear this boat. I will burn it to the ground, and every haunted soul inside can burn in hell fire.

I feel a calm sweep over me, a calm I haven't felt in a while. That feeling I love where everything slows down, a hyper focus. A peace that happens when I find acceptance. I adjust my stance so that I am standing slightly off centre, a step closer to my right and to the trail of petrol that leads down the starboard side of the boat. I plant my dominant foot behind me and crouch slightly. My hand points the flare gun skyward but dipped slightly towards the shoreline.

"My name is Mac Scott, I am an Agent of MI5, but I have been many things, thanks to you. Photographer, captive, slave, hunter, executioner, soldier, prisoner, spy…*survivor*. I will burn this boat to ashes; its bones will turn to dust – Just. Like. Yours."

I pull the trigger, the gun explodes with a crack, and I hear a whistle very similar to the build-up sound a firework has it climbs up into the sky. The sky lights up brightly, the flare's bright beam reflecting along the waters ripple, lighting the way home. The gun drops from my hand, and I pass the grenade from my left hand to my right, gripping it. My left index finger tugs on the hoop attached to the firing pin, and I pull it.

I swing my right hand up and fling it back on my first pounding step forward, my legs exploding from their coiled position. When my hand slides past my hip, I release the grenade down the starboard side of the boat. I hear it roll along the deck for a fraction of a second before my feet pounding is the only sound I hear.

Seven…

Everything slows down, my jaw set. I pump my fists backwards hard, driving my feet into the deck of the boat, propelling myself forward.

Six…

Adrenaline is fizzing through my veins. Fear, excitement, determination, and fortitude burn through me like rocket fuel as my toes touch the tip of the ramp. I inhale a deep breath and hold it.

Five…

My feet pound up the ramp in three aggressive, unhesitating strides, my sights set forward, my heart in my mouth. On the fourth step, I push off the top of the ramp, the true scale and height hitting me hard in the face. Cheers erupt from the shoreline, and I see the knot of them jumping up and down, fists pumping in the air.

Four…

I exhale with a "WOOOOOOOOOOOOOO!!!!!" as I fly through the air. My arms and legs still pumping in a run as I sail through the air at an incredible speed. The cold wind stinging my eyes, my heart swelling with happiness, my nerves thrumming with electric liberation. My flight path begins to dip as the momentum is lost, the icy waters creeping closer.

Three…

I pull my arms and legs in tight to my body, tensing rigid and as straight as an arrow. As I watch the black icy depths of the water get closer, I drag a long, deep breath in and hold it, pushing my lips together hard and bracing myself. My feet pound hard into the water, sending a jarring jolt into my spine. I plunge deep into darkness, my nerves screaming at the sudden cold. The water slows my decent, and I kick back up toward the surface, swimming diagonally to try to gain distance from the boat, as well as reach the surface for air.

Two…

My boots and trousers are slowing me down. My lungs are fit to burst, burning as I break the surface of the water with a huge gasp. Cheers boom from the shore again warming my insides like Ready Brek despite the icy water. I made good distance; I must be 40 metres closer, but there is no time to waste. I throw myself forward, swimming as hard and as fast as I can.

BOOM!

The grenade explodes, and by now, the boat is ablaze. How long before the whole thing blows? Fear prickles in my stomach, and I know I have to push. I immerse myself in the element that feels to me like soft satin. My arms gliding through its icy depths, my neck arching to the side to draw the breath that gives my limbs the power to kick and stroke.

My trousers and boots weigh heavily, forcing me to drive my limbs harder to keep speed and momentum. I push, kick, and stroke my way through the water, moving faster than I thought I could, and yet, it doesn't feel fast enough. Doubt starts to scream in my head; I can't keep this pace all the way to shore. This will be the longest swim I've ever done. Can I even make it that far?

You don't have a choice.

I don't look up at the shore, I just keep powering forward. The cold is making my arms and legs feel seized and cumbersome. They are not moving as smoothly as they were. My lungs are bursting from the effort, and I long to stop, but I know if I do, there will be no starting again.

My speed is slowing, exhaustion taking over as the muscles in my limbs begin to cramp and then…I hear a deafening boom, the loudest boom I could ever imagine hearing, and my whole body cringes. Suddenly, I feel so small and vulnerable in the water. The explosion causes a ripple in the water, the flames burning bright, and I can see the eery yellow glow reflected in the surface of the water.

As the boat starts to explode and fear burns though me, I am scared to look back. A chain reaction of smaller booms echo in the air, and I can smell the smoke. I feel too close; ashes and glowing embers begin to float down like giant fireflies. Fear spurs me on as the adrenalin surges once more, and I find a new gear. I hear the cheers from the shoreline grow louder and louder.

I push, pummelling the water with my legs, dragging the water with my hands, propelling myself forwards, the salty water stinging my eyes. Darkness is beginning to fall and so are my energy levels. My stamina is draining away as fatigue aches in my cramping muscles, the pain getting hard to bear. I don't have the nerve to look up, fearful that I will still be so far from shore that it will destroy my spirit and fight.

"Gwaaaan, kid!"

My heart soars! Cheers loud and booming erupt from the shore, so close I can pick out the voices. Alfred's deep gruff cheers are very prominent. My legs kick the soft, silty ground as the water shallows, and I collapse onto my hands and knees. I'm gasping for breath, too exhausted to even lift my head. Hands grab at me, and I don't even care whose hands they are because they are pulling me under the armpits and dragging me to land.

Land!

Lambert wraps a blanket around my shoulders as I hear the cheers thundering closer.

"Well done, Mac!" he cheers. "You fucking legend!"

I laugh hard, elation and relief so powerful in my chest, I could cry. Lambert pulls me to my feet; I turn to meet the cheers charging towards me just in time to stop myself being knocked back to floor as Anna ploughs into me. Her lips are hot on mine for nowhere near long enough, and then she showers my face in kisses. She laughs in relief, her eyes glowing with teary intensity.

"I promise, I had nothing to do with what is about to happen." Anna winks.

"What do…"

The floor disappears beneath me with a fast swoop. Alfred and Lambert lift me into the air and onto their shoulders before I can even protest. They begin strolling around the fire, with me held up in celebration.

"KING-OF-THE-WORLD… KING-OF-THE-WORLD… KING-OF-THE-WORLD!" they chant in unison, their voices loud an echoing.

"Oh God!" I gasp, embarrassment flushing my face.

"KING-OF-THE-WORLD… KING-OF-THE-WORLD… KING-OF-THE-WORLD!"

I look down at Anna and Dixy, their faces bright with happiness and laughter, and then I am laughing too. I can't help it. For a fleeting moment, I feel like the king of the world. I laugh and whoop, pure joy and jubilation singing inside me. Somehow – the implausible, the improbable and the absolutely absurd has happened…I did it. Alfred and Lambert let me down, and then I am scooped up into a huge bear hug.

"Atta girl! Atta girl! That was bloody brilliant kid! Come on, it's drinking time!" Alfred beams.

"I already bought her one," a careful voice calls from behind me.

I turn around and see her proud and teary grin, and it slips a little as I meet her gaze. My expression blank, I see the concern cross her face. But I can't keep up the act; my grin betrays me just before launching myself towards her and grabbing her for a hug. A half whoop, half laugh, loudly escapes my lips, and she roars with laughter and relief.

"Well done, Max. I knew you could do it! Does this mean you forgive me?" Dixy laughs, hugging me back substantially less awkwardly. I pull away, she hands me a generously filled glass of whisky, and I take it gladly.

"I won't lie, I was *pissed* when I woke up, but I soon understood, and there is nothing to forgive. You are the most incredible friend, Kate. Thank you for being brave and insane enough to do that and for believing I'd find a way through it."

"Naw, shut up. You are going to make me cry, soppy git. You're my friend till the end Max. Now – turn around," she orders. I turn, obeying her guiding hand on my shoulder, and my eyes fall on the flaming boat across the water.

"You are *free*, Max-a-million. You did that," Dixy utters passionately, her voice breaking before she squeezes my shoulder and walks away.

I see the billowing smoke and blazing inferno of the boat, flames of orange and white glowing and throwing light across the water. The tears fall, and I don't care to stop them. I watch the flames roar. The relief, sadness, and happiness all conflict in my heart like a tug of war, but it isn't a bad feeling. It is over; there is no possible way I can be dragged back onto that boat again. As I watch it burn, I say goodbye to the part of me I lost, the part of me that was trapped there, and it hurts, but for once, I know – the hurt will stop. I feel her hand in mine, warm and soft as she stands by my side. She drops my rucksack in front of me and brings her lips by my ear.

"I am so very proud of you, my beautiful, brave soldier, and God… do I love you."

I pull her in, looking away from the blaze, and wrap her up inside the blanket with me. My body begins to shake. The adrenalin has all but burnt through, and now I am feeling the cold.

"I love you; I always have," I mutter with my lips on hers between kisses, and she groans.

"Ugh, as much as I want you to keep kissing me because that was in fact, the sexiest thing I've ever seen - you need to get changed. There is a party waiting for you, and you, Mac Scott, *definitely* deserve to celebrate."

Peeling my wet clothes off in the dark behind a bush is not the easiest thing to do, but I really don't want to walk all the way to the van. It is a such a warming feeling to have dry clothes on, almost like they have been heated on a radiator. It isn't till I get dressed that I notice or even remember the cuts on my inner bicep from cutting the ropes. After the infection I just got over, I can't really ignore it. As I walk towards the fire pit, I smile. Everyone is sat on camping chairs, drinks in hands, a stack of pizza boxes lay on the floor near Alfred. My mouth waters.

"Bout time, kid. I am wasting away here!" he booms.

"Oh man, food! Dig in, Pa. I'll have some in a minute. Is there a first aid kit handy?"

"Right here. I had a feeling your clumsy arse wouldn't get through that completely unscathed. take a seat," Dixy orders, and I obey, taking the spare camping chair next to Anna.

My body sinks into it and relaxes. I'm not going to want to move for a good long while. I sip my drink and make easy work of annihilating the pizza handed to me while Dixy cleans and bandages my arm.

"What the bloody hell did you do? Gnaw into your arm with a kitchen knife?" Dixy berates playfully.

"Well, it wasn't very easy to cut the ropes away. If it wasn't for the ghost knife, I'd probably still be there tied up," I comment with a wink at Lambert, and he chuckles.

"Handy, aren't they? You would have found a way. You made good time as well. How did you unlock the door?"

"I, um… ran through it," I say sheepishly, and he laughs.

"Legend."

I feel myself sink into the chair, the fire we all surround making me feel at home. It is warm and comforting like being back at the farm. My body aches from the stress of the day, but it is a good ache, an accomplished one like that feeling you get at the gym after a good work out. The whisky, belly full of pizza, warmth of the crackling fire and the company I keep are all playing their part in making me feel content, cosy, and very much at peace.

"Gotta hand it to you, kid, that was some jump. Not sure I could have done that," Alfred commends.

"Ah, well, when I saw that ramp, I didn't think I was going to be able to either. I won't lie – there was definite butt clenching the whole…way…down," I joke, my hand making a nose-dive movement to emphasise my words, and everyone laughs.

"Oh, you loved it! We heard you whoop from across the water!" Dixy teases.

"I think 'loved' might be a bit ambitious, Dix."

"Hey! I thought I was forgiven!?"

"You are, but I know one thing's for sure…I'll never, ever…be accepting a coffee from you again!"

"Yeah…I kind of, maybe, already – tore her a new one for that," Anna interjects. "Sorry again, Dixy." I look at her, her lips pressed into a hard line as she stifles a laugh, and I snort.

"No worries. I drugged your girl, tied and chained her up, and forced you on a getaway boat to leave her there. I was anticipating you might be a little pissed." Dixy grins.

That scene is all too easy to imagine. Anna was as clueless as me about what was going to happen on that boat. It isn't hard to envisage her going off; she doesn't pull her punches when she is mad. Poor Dixy. As the evening grows later, I feel my eyes begin to droop. It has been one hell of a day, and there isn't an inch of me that isn't exhausted, but I feel lighter and less burdened for it. I listen to them all laugh and joke as I start to doze. Then I feel soft, warm lips that taste like champagne warm mine deliciously.

"Mm…I knew if I waited long enough I would get to do that eventually. Come on. We are going back to the hotel," Anna coos.

***

By the time we have waited around in the cold for the taxi to pick us up, I am wide awake again. Now I find myself sitting on our bed in the hotel room, showered and warm, trying to process the day. I find myself distracted as Anna darts around the room. Her hair still wet, looking cute in the PJ bottoms that she bought me and one of my t-shirts. The sweet smell of her candy perfume in the air. I am happy to be distracted by her.

"Right, you are going to have to fill me in on what I missed after Dixy drug-napped me," I ponder, and she cringes before coming and sitting on the foot of the bed opposite me.

"Okay, but the record, I did apologise…eventually. Um…well, as soon as you passed out, she called Lambert, telling him to prep for pick up or something. I didn't quite register it straight away. You were passed out on my lap, and I was livid. Dixy dragged you along the deck and started to tie you to the chair, chaining you up, and then pushed me out of the room and locked it behind us. At that point, I kind of lost it. I may have called her a psycho bitch."

Anna cringes with an uncomfortable chuckle, her face flushing red, and I restrain myself from laughing, but I also wince. I am feeling pretty bad for Dixy.

"She moved the boat out to sea, and then I started to understand what she was doing, but it didn't calm me down, it just made me worse. In my opinion, it was a risky move that could have easily gone horribly wrong. After what has happened during the memories you have regained, I thought it was reckless and a risk that I didn't want to take. She dropped anchor, and Lambert picked us up in a dingy and bought us back to shore. My God, I lost my shit!" Anna explains, covering her mouth with her hand.

"I can see why that wasn't the easiest scenario to deal with. You hadn't built the trust with her in this that I had, and even I woke up furious at first. What made you apologise in the end?"

"She showed me a video link. There was a camera in the cargo hold and one up on the top deck of the boat. We could see you, so we take the dingy back if you weren't able to keep control. I still wasn't happy about it, but it did show that she was not *completely* abandoning you."

Huh…I didn't see anything. I guess I'm not surprised that Dixy was taking precautions; it wasn't the safest position for me to be in. I am glad that I had no idea that I was being watched. It would have added to the pressure that was already hard enough.

"I'm suddenly relieved that I was hooded; at least it hid how much I freaked out trying to get out of the restraints. I'm glad you both seem okay now."

"It looked like you got control pretty quickly. Maybe it just didn't feel that way to you because you were the one tied up. The whole thing was…actually, really damn sexy." Anna sighs, her sultry tone sending a frisson of want descending down my spine.

"O-okay, you are going to have to explain that one."

"I don't know how well I can." She giggles sheepishly, biting her lip. "It's this… shift. You go from scared to determined, and the look on your face when it happens…ugh. So hot. You were stood at the cabin, and you held the flare gun in the air, and you got that…*look*. You were smouldering, like a moody aggressiveness. Not angry just commanding and…ugh, don't laugh at me you jerk!" Anna shrieks.

Anna launches at me from the other end of the bed, jumping on my lap, her fingers tickling my ribs roughly, and I howl. I'm too ticklish; my limbs flail, but she tickles me relentlessly till I throw myself forward, and Anna flies backwards onto the bed. I land on top of her, pinning her arms down and grinning in victory.

"You really shouldn't have done that." I grin, and she laughs brightly, her whole face lighting up, and I am so enchanted by her. The vibrance of her smile and how it makes my insides soar have me fixated; I can't take my eyes off of her. She smiles at me, but her eyes grow thoughtful as they analyse my face, her expression serious but gentle somehow. I let go of one of her hands and hold her face instead. The sudden fear in her eye's pangs in my chest.

"I am so lost in you, it terrifies me," she whispers.

I slide my hand under her neck, lowering my lips to hers. I kiss her softly as I pull her upright, and then I break away as I hold her face in both of my hands, meeting her fearful eyes.

"Savannah…I'm just as lost in you. I am not going to let you go. Of all things, don't ever be afraid of that. I love you so much, and every second I am with you, I love you even more because there is so much of you to love, so much I adore. You are safe. Whatever happens, I am yours, and that is all I want to be. You have no idea how lucky I feel because I haven't had the chance to begin to show you, but I promise you – I will. And long after you finally see it, I will still be here showing you, for as long as you will have me."

I watch the tears escape her gorgeous eyes, and I catch them with my thumbs, her breath catching in her throat.

"Now who is magic?" she breathes softly with a loving smile. "You should be really careful what you say though, Mac."

"Why?"

She leans in, her eyes locked onto mine, and they are teasing. Her smiling lips just barely touch mine as she lays her hands on my chest.

"Because, for as long as I will have you…" she utters softly, her lips delicate against mine, giving me the gentlest, slowest, and most enticing kisses. "Is always…" she whispers. I smile, my chest full of butterflies, and I kiss her just as gently, my lips not leaving hers as I speak.

"Now I think that it is you who should be careful," I whisper, exhaling a shaky, excited breath into her mouth, and her eyes twinkle with a satisfied smile.

"Oh yeah… why is that?" she breathes, her hands softly sliding up onto the sides my neck as she continues to tease me with her light kisses, making me crazy with lust.

"Because…I might just hold you to that." I groan, my tongue tracing her bottom lip, and she moans softly. I shudder at the tingles the sound inspires.

"I am ready when you are, McKenna," she breathes, her lips teasing mine, the groan in her voice is so tantalising. "What exactly are you waiting for?" she whispers and smirks into my kiss. Her whispered tone as sexy as it is loving, and I am completely enthralled. This is a whole different kind of magic, and I am bewitched.

***

I have no idea what was on her mind as she said those words; the conversation felt laced with double meanings. I only know what I wanted to be on her mind. I could be misreading her; in fact, I probably am, and yet it was all I could think about as she fell asleep curled up on my chest, and it didn't leave my mind for the entire drive home. Now, back in London, that thought has me staring through the glass of a jewellery shop window. My eyes wandering over the twinkling diamond rings. I am exhausted from the long drive home, and yet here I stand, trying to decide whether I should go inside.

I was so sure that she wasn't ready, and I was okay with that. I was happy to wait because there is so much danger that I might not come home that it felt wrong to give her a promise that I might not be able to keep. Only, somewhere over the past few days, or maybe it has been weeks, with every moment I spend with her, I've become sure of what I want. The surer I am, though, the more I fear she might never know that it is her I wanted forever.

My stomach flutters with butterflies as I enter the brightly lit shop, closing the door behind me with a soft click. It is too warm, that is the first thing I notice. Maybe from the number of lights brightening the place, or maybe the staff enjoy the feeling of being slowly roasted. Either way, I feel beads of sweat glow off the back of my neck instantly. My boots clonk against the buffed, smooth stone floor, and I suddenly feel too scruffy to have entered this place. I feel uncomfortable, that familiar feeling of not belonging and the dread of judgement that accompanies it. Just like the feelings the bespoke suit shop I visited with Dixy inspired.

I roam around the store, my eyes searching the tall backlit glass cabinets of fine jewellery. It all glitters superbly. Necklaces with sparkling pendants, bracelets, and broaches. I walk up two steps onto smooth cream carpet, and the area changes. Although still brightly lit, the cabinets are now low and angled to make the space circular. In the centre is a small round, dark-wood table, and two ornate chairs. On the table is a cardboard sign that reads 'Experts in Engagement.'

Shit just got real.

Behind the centre of the cabinet circle is a woman dressed in a smart grey suit with a starchy white shirt and a floaty red scarf tied loosely around her neck. She smiles at me in welcome, and I return it, my feet turning in her direction. The nerves in my stomach are shivering as I realise I have not one single clue what I'm looking for. The woman has a kind, aging but attractive face, long wavy greying hair that doesn't appear to move, and perfectly manicured nails. She eyes me curiously as I approach her.

"Good afternoon. My name is Joy. Can I help you at all?" she says in a musical tone.

"I hope you can." I grin sheepishly, and she smiles at me with understanding.

"Let me guess. You are looking for an engagement ring with no idea where to start?" she utters with a knowing smirk.

"Spot on, Joy."

"Well, that is perfectly fine my dear. It is my job to show you where to start. There are so many to choose from; looking at them can be terribly daunting. The best thing we can do first is narrow the choices."

The lady leads me to the table and chairs and gestures me to sit down, I oblige with a smile and she sits opposite me. Her face is lined, and she is wearing far too much make-up, probably to attempt to hide her age, but she is still very attractive.

"Now, first let me congratulate you. If you are here, then that means you have found the love of your life and are ready to pop the big question."

That's it, Joy. Put the fear of God into me.

My face flushes hotly, and I smile as I fidget nervously in the chair.

"Thank you, Joy."

"You're welcome. Now, before we look at anything, can you tell me anything about what you are looking for or even things you know for sure you don't want?"

"Uh, well… not much. I'd say something in gold because it looks incredible against her skin. Something elegant and not too gawdy. I want it to make the clear statement, but she doesn't wear much jewellery so something delicate. Ugh, umm…" I wince apologetically; I have no idea what I am talking about.

"Don't panic. That is actually more helpful than you think. It sounds like you are looking for a solitaire ring; they are simple and classic but very eye catching and clear cut. There are different cuts of diamond shape, so let's go look at some examples. I am sure the right thing will grab you."

In the space of almost two hours, I learn more about diamond rings than is necessary for any person to ever know. I'm sure Joy is glad to see the back of me, but I wanted every detail to be perfect. I float out of the door with a satisfied smile and a rumble of excitement in my chest. When I find myself sat back in my truck, I am unsure what to do about the little bit of extra weight that hangs from the inner pocket of my jacket. I have no solid plans to propose. All I know is that I want to.

"Houston, we have a problem. Pa, do you read?"

"Yeah, kid, I read. What's up?" Alfred grumbles.

"Uh, could you meet me at Umber? Just you. There is something I want to talk to you about."

"Sure, kid. I will be there in 15."

***

The last time I was here was the first time I met Barrett. I am sat at the very same table with my back against the wall. The memory of him sat in front of me, his blue suit immaculate and his grin smarmy, is all very easy to recall. Today is day seven; he said he would return in just over a week, and I'm acutely aware that doesn't leave me much time. The doom in the pit of my stomach seems to gnaw deeper with every passing moment.

This weekend has been punishing, gruelling, and arduous. Every memory has left its pain, and I am exhausted to the core, and yet, I feel lighter somehow. While I don't think I will ever be truly ready for what is to come, I do feel more equipped to face it. Dixy was right; I feel free of the string that tied me to that place of hell, and for that, every terrifying moment was worth it.

He approaches me with a sceptical look through narrowed eyes and a crooked smile, and I tense nervously as I return it. I slide his coffee towards him. Now that he's here, I feel like I've lost the ability to talk.

"So, are you going to tell me why I am here? As much as I like a good coffee and chat with you, kid, we could have done this at home. You obviously bought me here for a reason."

"I did, I just…"

"Speak your mind. Isn't that what you always say?" he encourages.

I look up at him and chuckle. The nerves are prominent. The moment I tell him is the moment that it all becomes real. I take a deep breath and steel myself.

"Now we are back, it's only a matter of time before Barrett takes me, and we don't know how long I'll be gone, or if I will be coming back. I need…"

"You are coming home, kid," Alfred interrupts firmly. "These past few weeks, you've been through hell and back preparing, facing demons, kicking the hell out of the suck. I might have knocked Dixy, quite few times in fact, but I can admit when I'm wrong. She knew exactly what she was doing, and she had the strength do it. I know I couldn't have. The point is, you've got this, and now more than ever, you have a very strong, red headed motivation to get the hell home."

"Yeah, well, that is kind of what I wanted to talk to you about. At the hotel, you said some things that got me to thinking. A lot," I insinuate.

"I did?"

Seriously? He is going to make me spell it out for him.

"When we were standing at the bar, you mentioned walking Anna down the aisle."

"Oh, yeah. I probably shouldn't have said that. I was a little merry and loose tongued. Sorry if I scared you. Wasn't me place."

"Well, yeah, it was a little unexpected, but you didn't scare me. More shocked me than anything. You've always treated me like family. To me, you are my Pa. You accepted Anna and I, even though I always felt she deserved someone better and more whole. You made me feel worthy of her and that has always meant a lot to me."

Alfred peers at me with narrowed eyes and his lips are pressed hard together, like he is supressing a grin.

"Is this you asking for me blessing? I think it's obvious you already have it."

"No…yes…well, kind of. Listen, I know you don't want to hear it, but just humour me, alright?" I ask, and he puts his serious face on and gives me a nod. "There is a chance I might not come back; you can deny it, but I'm asking you to be *real* about it. I'm not saying I am about to propose because I can't help but think that making that promise to her when I can't actually promise her forever isn't right. But…I don't want to die and her not know that I wanted to make that promise. That I would've done it if I'd had the chance."

Alfred leans forward in his chair and hesitantly reaches for my hand, his hand freezing above mine, and he frowns. I take his giant of a hand, wrapping my hand over the top of it, and he smiles briefly. Then his wise eyes turn intense and powerful as he gives me his best 'no bullshit' look.

"Mac, no one can promise forever. There's no safety in love; it is a leap of faith. Marriage is a way of saying you want to hold that person's hand and take that leap *with* them, whatever happens. Yeah, it's a contract, a promise, but there's nothing saying either person will live forever cos' they won't. You could come home from the reconditioning, propose, and then get hit by a campervan full of clowns the next day. There's no guarantees; it's about living in the now and saying whatever happens, this the person you want to face every day with."

His words come out slowly and assured, almost as if he planned them. He is damn good at speeches, just like Anna. Clearly, the apple doesn't fall far from the tree. I huff at him, and he grins cheekily.

"You soppy bugger, you are quite the romantic, Pa. But the point is…I may never get the chance. If the worst should happen, I was wondering if you would give her something, so she knows that she was it for me."

I reach into my inside jacket pocket, pull out a box, and place it on the table in front of him. The box is polished wood, smooth, and amber in colour. His eyes fall on it, and he sighs before looking back up at me with sad eyes.

"Give it to her yourself!" he growls.

"And if I don't come home, then what? The only reason I am doing this is because you once convinced me to give her a bracelet, so she knew what I felt for her was real. If you are telling me that if I don't make it, she would be better off never knowing – I'm okay with that. I'll put it away and hope I get to give it to her one day, but don't refuse me out of hope I'm coming home; we both know that isn't certain."

Alfred rubs his palm over his whiskery chin and sighs, his eyes analysing me for so long that the silence is starting to make me uncomfortable. Then his eyes leave my face and fall onto the box. He reaches out and picks it up.

"Can I?"

"Of course, Pa."

He opens the box with gentle hands and his eyes light up, twinkling and glassy. He smiles at me warmly, and I know right away that the ring has his approval. It feels good to share this moment with him, to know that whatever happens, I at least got to have this.

"It's perfect for her." He grunts, clearing his throat and then he shuts the lid and places it back on the table gently as if it were made of glass. "Tell me, kid. What is the hold up? You have the ring, so why are you stalling?"

"I'm not sure she's ready. Even if she is, to propose and then be taken to a reconditioning, I…can't do that to her. So, I am going to hide it inside the garment bag of my tux in the wardrobe at my apartment. If I don't come home, will you give it to her?"

Alfred growls an exasperated huff, his eyes sad and his expression irritated. I hold his gaze, but it is difficult to do. He has the disappointed parent look, and he knows just how to use it.

"I want to be clear: I understand why you're doing this, and I believe that for her to never know you intended this would be a crime. But for the record, I think you're kidding yourself. You say you think she isn't ready, and yet you clearly thought about every detail of that ring. You don't do that if you are not sure and ready to ask, and you wouldn't want to ask if you didn't have some inkling that she's ready."

I go to speak, and he holds his hand up, stopping me in my tracks.

"I'm not done," he utters and I bite my tongue, supressing a nervous laugh because the look on his face tells me I should definitely shut up.

"You are going to leave her, who knows how long for, and she'll have nothing to hold on to but hope! Now is clearly the perfect time to give her that ring. Whatever's holding you back, I just hope you don't regret not asking her sooner. I will, if the worst should happen, give her the ring, but make no mistake, kid - I think your stalling is a severe miscalculation and so far, I can't see a solid reason for it. Maybe you should think about what that reason is."

My jaw is clenched, and I am tense. The dressing down was to be expected, but I didn't think it would be that hard hitting. He has me doubting my own damn decisions, and it's screwing with my head. I lean forward, elbows down and my head in my hands, my eyes fixed on the small wooden box. I feel his warm hand on my arm, and I look at him, his eyes much warmer and less aggravated.

"As for my blessing, you clearly already have it. I've never seen her so happy and at peace, and considering the pressures you are both facing, that fact is not to be underestimated. You both bring the best out of each other, and I'd be proud to call you my daughter in law. You're already family, but I look forward to the day that you finally make it official. I might not agree with your stalling, but I'm proud as punch of the person you have become, Mac."

My eyes prick in perfect mirror image to his, and I chuckle in relief, sliding the ring back inside my jacket pocket.

"Thanks, Pa. That means everything to me."

***

Back at my apartment, I hide the ring just where I told Alfred I said I would, and then I zip the garment bag up and shut the wardrobe door. I walk over to my bed, flinging myself backwards onto it in a huff as Alfred's words ring noisily in my ears. He's right, of course; my stalling isn't about her not being ready. I don't know if she is, but isn't that part of what makes a proposal scary? The fear that they may say no? But I don't want to propose and then disappear on her, propose and not even get to enjoy the time with her if she says yes before I am taken.

Screw that.

He's also right that it would give her something to hold on to, whatever happens. Am I robbing her of that? Probably…but I have to try to have faith that, when the right moment arises, I will know it, and right now doesn't feel like that moment. I can take comfort in knowing that whatever happens, she will know; it was her that I wanted forever with, but the idea that I might now get to…

Stop it.

"Max-a-million, you reading me, grass hopper?" Dixy screeches in my ear, making me jump.

"Yes, Agent Annoying, loud and freakin' clear."

"Oo someone's grumpy. You skip a meal or something?"

"Funny… What's up?"

"Nothing, I just thought I'd give you the heads up that I'm on my way over," Dixy informs.

"Okay, how long…" The door knocks a with an over enthusiastic tap, and I groan. I head to the door and open it, certain my face conveys the irritation I feel.

"Don't look at me like that. I gave you some warning!"

"Yeah, about 15 seconds. Very considerate of you, Dix."

Dixy walks in and heads straight for the fridge, helping herself to a can of Dr Pepper before making herself at home on the sofa. I take a seat opposite her. She is watching me oddly, and it's making me self-conscious.

"Are you going to tell me why you are here or keep looking at me all weird?"

"A couple of reasons. First, I wanted to see how you were feeling after this weekend. Second, if you think I have forgotten about the explanation that you owe me regarding what Lexi spoke to you about, you are very much mistaken. Lastly but very much by no means least - I should warn you that all your bank transactions are watched but mostly ignored. It is a safety measure to keep track of you, just in case. However, when a rather large transaction to a very high-end jewellers is flagged. it's certainly going to pique my interest," Dixy hints, her eyebrows raised so high they could almost reach her hairline.

"Oh, for the love of…urgh! Seriously!? Is nothing secret round here?!"

"Not really. You are a secret spy. If you want your transactions remain a secret, you may want to get creative in future. Don't get pissy; it isn't like I'm going to tell anyone."

I lean my head back on the sofa and hold my hands over my face with a dramatic sounding groan, which only makes Dixy giggle more.

"I'm not worried you will tell anyone; I just don't want the lecture that I'm positive I'll get. I've already had it from Alfred."

"Huh, why would I do that?" Dixy asks, her tone a little more serious, and I lean forward to see the confusion written all over her face.

"Because I don't intend to propose before the reconditioning. In fact, I don't know when I will or if I'll even live long enough to get to. I just know that I want to. So, I got the ring and told Alfred to give it to Anna *if* I don't come back so she knows that I wanted to. He thinks me stalling is a mistake, that if I did it before I left, it would give her something to hold on to while I am gone."

"I'm sure it would give her that but that isn't a reason to propose to someone. You have to do it when you feel it is right. If you propose now *because* you are leaving, then she may think that's why you are doing it. Instead of all the right reasons that you have for wanting to."

My jaw drops a little, and she laughs.

"What?"

"I just wasn't expecting that, I guess. Where the bloody hell were you when I needed you an hour ago?"

"Mac, follow your own instincts. It doesn't matter what Alfred or I say. You know what is right for you and Anna. If you don't feel the time is right, then it isn't."

The tightness in my chest eases, and I take a deep breath. This is the right choice, I know it is, even if I am not altogether sure why.

"Thank you, Dixy."

"Don't mention it. Your secret is safe with me, but I don't want you talking about not coming home anymore. I understand the need to put your affairs in order, but that's where it ends. You are coming home, Max. I need you to believe that because we all do; you didn't go through all of this for nothing. You've shown incredible strength in the face of nothing short of hell, and in doing so, you have proved that you have control over your own mind. Whatever happens, when Barrett takes you, there's nothing he can do to break your spirit. The force is clearly strong in you, Max-a-million." She winks with a proud smile.

"Ohhhh, you are more of a nerd than you let on!"

"Oh, hell no! I just know how to speak your language at this point."

I narrow my eyes at her, and she giggles.

"Okay, fine, I like some nerdy films but not so much that I'm no longer cool. You, on the other hand…" she jibes.

I laugh, but it is short lived. My chest is tightening. I'm going to have to lie to her, and I hate myself for it already. There is no way she can know that the cyanide capsule in my boot is now empty. As much as I hate to lie to her, the alternative is to betray Anna, and that is something I'll never do.

"What is it, Max?" she asks softy.

I look up at her and sigh. Her face is calm, but I have learnt over time to read the concern in her eyes. She's not so good at hiding that from me anymore.

"Lexi warned me that I need to pass the reconditioning because if Barrett breaks me and I let slip something about MI5, she will have to execute the gag protocol," I blurt flippantly, shrugging my shoulders.

"What?!" Dixy snaps.

"What's the problem?"

Her eyes widen and darken as she leans forwards, her hands covering her mouth and nose, and her eyes become distant. I've never seen the look on her face. Whatever it is, it isn't okay.

"Dixy, what's wrong?"

"I...uh...just..." she struggles, and then she looks up at me, her eyes pained, and a fearful swoop hits my stomach. I stand up from the sofa and cross the room, sit on the coffee table just in front of her, and I take her hand.

"Talk to me, please. You're freaking me out. I'm not used to seeing you wig out."

"Uh...sorry, I am just...shocked. That protocol is designed to only ever be set up in the worst possible circumstance. It's rarely mentioned, and it's barely ever been done. In most cases, the agents have asked their operator to activate the protocol because whatever position they are trapped in meant they couldn't activate the heel shot their selves and consider themselves to be a threat to national security. I know of only one time it was actually used for its intended purpose. There probably are more cases, but like I said, it is rarely talked about, and in most cases, agents prefer to pull their own trigger," Dixy explains, and then she uses her hand like a gun, mimicking shooting herself in the head.

"That's what bothers me. I'm as prepared as I can be for the fact that I might not make it; the cyanide in the heel was actually a comfort to me. A way out that I would have loved on the boat. But the idea of someone else having control over the trigger...that wigs me out," I admit.

She is so statue still, it's unnerving. My gut is twisting in uncomfortable knots because she is always so unphased, and right now, she looks rattled.

"Dix, why is this messing with you so much?"

"The one case that I know of where the gag protocol was executed, it was Lexi. She executed an agent that said too much, and that agent was her best friend. Although a lot of people presumed, he was much more to her than that. There were discrepancies in the voice records – there were concerns she may have pulled the trigger too soon in some attempt to save her friend a painful death, but nothing ever came of it. At one-point, people thought she'd be dismissed. Instead, she was promoted."

"And what do you think?"

"It's above my pay grade to think anything, and I never heard the voice records to judge, but I've been an agent for five years, Max. I have been on a lot of missions in deep cover. I have *never* been warned of the gag protocol," she says grimly.

"It's probably because she knows for certain I'm going to be tortured. She has reason to be concerned that I won't be able to take it." I watch her, her eyes flitting around, her mind clearly going a million miles an hour. "But you don't think it's that."

"I don't know what I think. I'm probably being paranoid, I trust Lexi, but...whatever happens, we can't let the gag protocol be executed, Max."

She has got me worried. now I'm paranoid. I've always struggled to trust Lexi, and Dixy's reaction isn't helping me with that.

"Who is my operator?"

"Me, but Lexi can order me to execute the protocol."

I wish I could tell her the truth; her eyes are pained, and I can tell she is struggling with the idea she may have to pull the trigger, but I can't take that risk. The guilt burning in my chest is ridiculous.

"Then, there's no point in worrying about it. It's out of our control. I just have to keep my mouth shut, and it will all be okay. If I can't, then that is an order you'll have to obey. I understand that, Dix."

She looks up at me, her eyes analysing my face as if she has X-ray vision, and I do my best to keep my face slack.

"You are *lying* to me, Maxwell Margo Scott!" she spits, and I laugh.

"Okay seriously? Do you have an arsenal of Max related nick names on hand or what? And what the hell are you talking about? I told you what Lexi said; I'm not lying."

Fuck... Fuck... Fuck.

"Not about that. You seem awfully nonchalant about me having a trigger that could end your life. What are you not telling me?" she presses.

"Nothing. I guess I've just had time to get my head round it. A lot has happened since then. Of course, it bothers me, but I've accepted it." I shrug.

"Bullshit! You fear people having control over you, you wouldn't just accept it, so why is it you seem completely unphased by this? Don't lie to me. You are much better at it than you were, but I know you too well to be fooled that easily."

I get up from the coffee table and walk away, the fury at myself pumping coldly through my veins. How the hell did I manage to screw this up so badly? I sit down on the opposite sofa with my head in my hands. I can't tell her;

how do I get out of this without telling her? I hear her move off the sofa, and I flinch a little as she kneels down in front of me, her hands pulling my hands away from my face, and I look her square in the eye.

"Please, Dixy, if ever I need you to trust me, it's now. Please, don't ask me," I beg, my voice strangled by the lump in my throat.

She searches my eyes for the longest time, and my heart flies with a fast pound inside my chest. I can barely breathe. Then, she pulls me into her by the wrist and gives me a hug which is, surprisingly, her least awkward yet.

"Alright, my friend, I won't – but I swear, if whatever you are hiding puts me in danger of losing my friend, there will be hell to pay. I'm trusting you, Max. Don't break that trust by doing something stupid. I am not a forgiving person," Dixy warns.

I exhale in relief, my body trembling as I try to catch my breath.

"Thank...you," I manage.

"You can thank me by staying alive long enough for me to buy a hat. I do love weddings," she says lightly as she rubs my back, and then she freezes. Dixy pulls back suddenly, and I look up at her focused eyes.

"Yes, I read you, Agent Holt," Dixy utters.

CHAPTER 16

Trojan Horse

My stomach lurches as though tugged with a fishhook from inside my belly button as I watch her face. Dixy keeps her eyes on me; they're unreadable, and I'm both desperate to know what is being said inside of her ear and desperate not to.

"I understand. See you in an hour." She pauses. "But why is the rum gone?" Dixy sighs, and I stiffen, waiting for her to fill in the blanks.

"We need to get the farm; Lexi wants to debrief us on some developments."

"Marvellous," I groan, and Dixy looks up at me thoughtfully, her eyes slightly tight with stress.

"Max, don't mention the gag protocol. She told you in private, so I'm not sure I am supposed to know about it. I will do whatever I can to make sure that protocol is never activated, but I don't want to draw attention to the fact that I know."

"I'm not in any hurry to bring it up. Don't worry. It's the last thing on my mind right now." I huff, slumping back into the sofa. The pit of doom in my stomach smoulders.

"I know. We don't know for sure that is why she is coming," Dixy offers, and I raise my eyebrow. "Okay, I admit, the chances are pretty strong. You are ready, Max."

"I'm fine. In a way, it will be a relief. I'm never very good at waiting for the suck. I'll meet you there in a few…wench," I jibe with a wink.

"Um, what?"

"Your earpiece activation phrase is a Pirates of the Caribbean film quote." I scoff. "And you call me a nerd."

"What can I say? Pirates are hot." Dixy shrugs.

The moment the front door closes behind her, the nerves accelerate, and I am stood in an icy cold shower before the panic takes hold. The cold water eases the unnatural fever racing across my skin, but my body is trembling. I need to pull myself together; this is ridiculous. I knew this was coming. I have been preparing for this. Now is not the time for losing my shit. Now is the time to grit my teeth and embrace the suck. The sooner I get this over with, the sooner I can come home to Anna.

Anna... Yeah, that's it. The reason for the panic. The idea that...

Nope!

Anna is going to be scared; I have to get it together for her. I can't tell her that everything is going to be okay if I don't believe that myself. It *is* going to be okay; I have worked too damn hard for it not to be okay. I have too much to come home for. Alfred's words ring in my head, and I take a deep, steadying breath.

"You can't just fight to save the world from The Culling. Anger and duty will only get you so far. You have to fight to come home to the people you love. If you close yourself from that love, it is going to be much easier to lose yourself."

"What my heart beats for," I mumble.

***

The drive back to the farm is mercilessly fast, but when I pull up on the gravel drive, I am at least relieved to see that I have beaten Lexi here. As I walk down towards the house, I still feel the relentless doom gnawing in my stomach, but I feel much calmer. The fire pit is blazing, but no one is sat around it. When I walk into the kitchen, I find Alfred sat at the table leant over a cup of steaming coffee. He looks up at me as I arrive, giving me an unconvincing smile.

"Whatcha, kid."

"Hey, Pa. Where is everyone?"

"Dixy and Lambert are picking up surveillance kit and supplies; they shouldn't be long. Savannah left as soon as she heard that Lexi was coming.

She said there was something she needed to do. She didn't elaborate." Alfred sighs, and an unease sweeps across my chest.

Why would she leave?

I get to my feet and busy myself making coffee that I don't really want to drink. I hate the wait, the sitting and the watching as the suck creeps closer. At this point, I feel the wait has been so long and the build-up so large that I'd almost welcome the kidnap just to stop the tiring, stomach-churning wait. Where will I be taken? When? Barrett will already have plans set firmly in place, that much I'm certain of. I stand at the window, allowing my eyes to stretch aimlessly over the fields of the farm. The greens grow richer in colour in the distance. The fields there are far less touched and trodden. I rarely see Alfred venture to them except to cut the grass on his ride-on mower.

I step outside, and the cold is bitter on my cheeks. There is a cold dampness clinging to the air, a promise of rain to come. The indigo blue sky is morphing into sapphire and darkening with charred, ashen clouds.

A storm is coming.

Just as I take my seat at the fire, I hear the familiar crunch of tires grinding on gravel, and I suck in a long, smoke-tainted breath. I hear the car door open and shut with a soft clunk, and I exhale. My widened eyes daze into the dancing flames, and I feel rather than see the chairs around me become occupied. I hear Alfred grunt on creaky knees into his chair on my left and Lambert land next to him with an energised thump. I feel a squeeze of my shoulder as Dixy passes before dropping soundlessly into the chair on my right. Lexi moves around the circle of chairs, her feet moving as silent as always till finally, I look up from the flames and into her eyes as she sits opposite me.

"Agent Scott, I know that you bear my same impatience for pussy footing around, so I will skip the pleasantries. Barrett is booked onto a flight back to the UK that boards in," Lexi looks at her watch, "just under thirty minutes. Which means he will touch down in London in three hours from now at 9pm," Lexi announces, her voice taught.

I hold her x-ray like stare, aware she's watching for my reaction, and I nod, ignoring the swooping sensation in my gut.

"You can relax, Agent Holt. This isn't surprising news; we all knew it was coming, and we are all more than prepared for it," I assure, and I see a warmth arrive in her eyes.

"I know, Mac, but that doesn't make breaking the news or hearing it any easier." Lexi pauses, looking at me with sad eyes that I immediately look away from. "However, I did also hear that you surpassed predicted expectations in conquering 'Project Seabird.' I must confess, I had my doubts when Agent Dixon proposed this…left of field idea, but I am happy to admit when I am wrong. Now I wish I could have been there the moment you jumped ship. I'm sure that was some spectacle to witness," Lexi concludes with out of character excitement and the circle of chair occupants laugh.

"If it helps, it lasted all of a few seconds before I hit the water. You didn't miss much." I chuckle with ease, which earns another laugh. It's nice to see a more human side of her.

"Nevertheless, I commend you, Agent Scott. As I said before, you have come a long way from the girl in chains."

I do my best to hold her ardent gaze even though I feel a warm blush heat my cheeks. Still, even now, I can't quite bring myself to trust her completely, but I can tell that she is trying to earn it by being less cold in front of others than usual. My phone vibrates in my pocket, a short, barely audible buzz that means I have received a text message, and the urge to reach for it is strong. There is only one person that could be.

"Anyway, I do have something for you," Lexi interjects, pulling out a small black box from her overpriced handbag. The box is about the size of a necklace gift box. Lexi flips the lid open for me to see inside.

"These autonomous lenses are a substantial upgrade to the ones you already have. They do everything your current lenses do but unlike those which must be changed every 24 hours, these can be worn for a month continuously, maybe a little more. After that, your bloodstream will absorb them, and they will disintegrate without a trace. I would advise you put them in tonight, then no matter when Barrett comes for you, they will be ready."

"That sounds a lot less complicated. I don't think he will come for me tonight; he has a flare for the dramatic, and to take me tonight will leave him little time to set up, but I'll put them in anyway, just in case."

“You seem ready, calm even. Is there anything else you need? Anything that may help before I take my leave, Mac?” Lexi asks.

“Only one thing. That first night here on the farm, I asked you to take care of something for me. If you have, then I’m ready, Lexi,” I allude, and she gives me a knowing look and gets to her feet, stepping towards me. I follow suit.

“It is handled, I promise, but have faith. I believe it is a precaution I won’t have to act on. You should believe that too,” Lexi mutters softly, holding out her hand, and I take it firmly. “Luck be with you, Agent Scott.

“Thank you, Agent Holt.”

I wait as long as it takes for Lexi to step around me and take a mere three steps away before I slide my hand inside my jeans pocket and pull out my phone.

7.00pm
Anna Mobile:
Meet me at the apartment, 8pm.
Don’t keep me waiting, McKenna Scott.

I smile involuntarily at the brightly lit screen and the ball of tension in my chest eases as I slump back in my chair.

7.10pm
I wouldn’t dream of it, Savannah Slone.

A solemn silence falls around the fire circle for what feels like too long. This is it; it is finally happening. I look around at their faces, at Lamberts furrowed thoughtful brow. At Alfred as he stares into his coffee cup, scratching his whiskery chin. And then round to Dixy, who is watching me watch the others and smiles softly when I catch her. I wait for someone to speak, for the parting advice I was so sure I would get. And yet, no one speaks. Then I wonder if they are waiting for me to speak which I attempt to do a few times. My mouth opens and shuts with a soft pop that I imagine gives me a look of impersonating a goldfish.

And then it dawns on me. These three teachers of my life have taught me everything they can because the time is spent. There really isn't anything left to say except goodbye, and it seems that no one wants to say those words, myself especially. I get to my feet slowly but steadily, and I feel their eyes follow me as I do. The first spatters of raindrops fall lightly on my face. They all stand just as wordlessly, and as they do, I take my first tentative steps towards Lambert. He holds his hand out for a stomach level high five, and I oblige him with a light slap on contact. I grip his hand and pull him in.

"See you soon, brother," I mumble to his ear as I pat his back, and then he pulls back, my fist still clutched in his, his dark eyes forceful.

"You will, soldier. The hardest battle you are going to have to fight is self-doubt and when it creeps in, when you can't find that belief in yourself - you call to me in any way you can, and you borrow mine because mine is unwavering. You get me – sister?"

For once, Lambert's voice is far from monotone; it is impassioned and reedy. The impact of this rare change and his words fills me with his hearty strength.

"I get you, brother," I manage with a nod, and he releases my hand before turning and trudging away towards the barn.

My shoulders hitch up and down with a resolve building sigh, with my head bowing slightly, I close the gap in three fast strides. All expected awkwardness is non-existent. Dixy holds on tight, and I rest my chin on top of her head. Suddenly, she seems smaller than she ever has, childlike and uncharacteristically silent. With a quick squeeze and a sigh of her own, Dixy pulls back, but her hand finds my wrist, and she grips it gently. Her move to keep me grounded.

"I'm taking up residence in your barn for the foreseeable. So, if there's anything you don't want me to find - porn stash, secret love letters to me – make it known now or forever hold your embarrassment, Max-a-million." Dixy winks, and I chuckle before frowning in confusion.

"Why are…"

"Because one of us will be here watching over you, 24 hours a day, until you come *home*. You are not going to lose yourself; you've got this, and we have got you. If at any time you need to be reminded of that, of who Max is,

I'll be here; I *promise* you," Dixy assures softly, all mocking wiped from her expression, and then her grip on my wrist tightens before she lets go. Dixy tiptoes up, placing her lips on my forehead, and then turns sharply away, following in Lambert's footsteps.

The rain is getting heavier now, more in splats than in spits, the volume increasing from a fizz to a patter. The air smells earthy as if the raindrops that coat the grounds are heightening the scents of nature. I can feel him behind me, but I don't turn around when I speak.

"So, we don't have to be all soppy and hug it out…right?"

"Nah, us? We're made from tougher stuff than that," Alfred grunts in true farmer twang, and I chuckle lifelessly.

A shiver runs up my spine as the rain begins to penetrate my jumper. I know I should leave, but my feet are not cooperating. I lift my wrist, and my watch reads 7.35pm; I still have plenty of time to get to Anna. I can't wait to see her, to touch her and breathe her in, but also, I'm dreading it. While I refuse to say goodbye, I know at some point, it will feel like goodbye. I feel a giant hand land softly on my shoulder just as my eyes begin to pinprick.

"You get the job done, and you get the hell home, kid. Whatever it takes," Alfred orders softly, and I nod stiffly.

"Y-you will watch out for her, Pa?" I choke, and Alfred steps around me, pulling me in for a bear hug.

"I'll watch out for *both* of my girls."

***

My clothes are heavy, saturated from the rain as I pause on my doorstep for just a moment, steeling myself, trepidation heavy in my chest. I check my watch, and I'm home just on time. When I open the door, I am hit with warmth and the delicious scent of her candy-like perfume, and I can't help but smile. God, I am going to miss coming home to that smell, to knowing I will find her here.

There is music playing softly in the background, and the lighting is dimmed low. My eyes are drawn to the living room, which is glowing in warm light, and when I notice something out of place, curiosity carries me forwards. Dropping my rucksack, I walk past the kitchen, and then I notice the fire roaring brightly and candles flickering moodily all over the room. In the centre of the living room on top of the red fur rug, the end table has been moved, and there on top of it is a note:

Put on the suit. You have five minutes.

At first, I feel a little excitement as I crane my neck in search of my suit bag. Then, recollection hits me, and my mouth dries up.

The ring.

I turn on my heels with urgent speed, and then I find it, hanging from one of the steps of the spiral staircase. I dash to it, unzipping it, and my hands frantically search for the small amber-brown box still nestled inside the bottom. The relief when I find it there is astronomical. I whip off my wet clothes and start dressing in the suit, leaving the suit bag still hung up, and zip it closed. The moment I am dressed, it feels like seconds later I hear movement upstairs. Breathless and flush cheeked, I move to the bottom of the staircase just as I hear heeled shoes clink-clonk down the staircase.

I see the flash of green grow closer, and my eyes trail after her. The illusion of leaves cascading down her chest once again stirs tingles though me. Even the second time around, she takes my breath away. If anything, I am more moved by her. The knowledge that this impossibly beautiful woman is mine captivates me all the more. The warmth in her gold glittered eyes when she sees me waiting for her. And her mischievous smile as her eyes trail up and down me melts the trepidation from my chest. I hold my hand out to her, guiding her down the last few steps until she stops just in front of me, smiling at me with such ardour that I feel invincible.

"Thank you for indulging me in this." Anna smiles through shimmery pink lips.

"Well, I don't really know what *this* is, but I already think it's the best idea ever." I pause, blowing out a breath. "You look magical, Anna."

Anna steps a little closer, her head bowed slightly as she watches me from beneath her eye lashes and her hand finds mine.

"Follow me…"

With a tug of my hand, she steers me to the living room. I follow her until we stand toe to toe in front of the fireplace. Her arms drape over my shoulders, and without conscious thought as if we had been doing it for years - my hands find her waist and then our bodies begin to move and sway to the soft background music. The movement is slow, and my eyes never leave hers. The fire is glinting off them, making them hypnotically translucent, although still powerfully green. All my words fall away as I stare at her, wondering if it's possible that I can memorise every perfect line of her face. Maybe then, I won't miss it so much. Maybe then, it will be there every time I close my eyes.

"No one has ever looked at me the way you do," Anna mutters softly.

"How is it that I look at you?" I ask, wondering if my eyes really do betray my thoughts as I've been told.

"Searching…like you really *see* me, and yet, you are always looking deeper, searching further still, and it is magnetising. I can't look away, and I could never want to. It makes me feel both vulnerable and safe all at the same time."

Everything, my eyes betray everything.

"Why vulnerable?"

She sighs, and I feel the warmth on my face as her eyes wrinkle with uncertainty.

"Because you might see something that I don't want you to see. Something bad that could make you stop looking at me."

I unwrap one of my arms from around her waist and cradle her cheek in my hand. Her skin is warm against the coolness of my hand, not yet warmed from the downpour I was caught in. I let it slide down the side of her neck, and she shivers as I hold it there, my thumb resting on the soft point of her chin.

"No one is entirely good; we all have darkness. I believe it was you who told me that. It was you who made me feel worthwhile in spite of my darkness." I smirk, and she returns it. "You are right though, I do see you, but…I'm just as incapable of looking away because your gaze and your touch make me feel precious in a way that no one ever has."

I watch as Anna's eyes glisten. She bows her head and rests it against my shoulder. Her hand reaches up and holds my neck, and I can feel her breath tickling my throat.

"That's because you are precious," she whispers and then her lips brush my neck in a warm kiss, just once. An action that has come to hold unspoken meaning between us. It still sends goosebumps racing across my skin.

We sway together in the warmth of the nearby fireplace, words unexchanged for quite some time, and I am okay with that. I will steal each moment I can with her and treasure it. It is that thought that encourages the rush of memories from the ball. The symmetry of it, of the moment I let go and allowed myself those stolen moments on the dance floor with her. The thought has me curious and pushes me to finally speak again.

"This all feels a little familiar, kind of," I probe, and Anna pulls back and drapes her arms over my shoulders once again.

"It was meant to." She smiles, her fingers nestling in the back of my hair. "I wanted to realign this event for us. I wouldn't change anything about how we got to this place. It's our story, and every plot twist and every page turn was worth it to be here with you now. But I still wanted a metaphorical do-over of this night. Not to delete our night at the ball, just to add to it. I wanted you to take me on this make-believe dance floor. Only instead of believing that there was no way I could ever love you, as you did in that moment, I wanted you to believe the undeniable truth and take that truth with you wherever you go," Anna mutters softly but deliberately, and then she leans in, her eyes locked onto mine and her lips just inches from mine.

"There is no way that I *couldn't* love you, Mac Scott," she whispers forcefully. She closes the gap, her top lip just brushing mine, and then freezes there. "That, and I wanted to see you in that suit and be able to touch you in all the ways that were forbidden to me that night."

She swallows my gasp with her lips.

***

The rain is ricocheting thunderously off the wall of glass in the bedroom, the heavens have opened, and it sounds incredible. My eyes are closed, but I can feel her gaze on me as I lay naked with my head in her lap, her fingers raking softly through my hair. I'm scared if I open my eyes, we are going to have to talk about it. It's inevitable, but I don't want to. I want to stay in this post-orgasm bliss, the sweat trickling down my abdomen making me shiver while I dive deeper into the magic of Anna. I open my eyes, and sure enough, she is staring down on me. She doesn't smile, but she doesn't look sad either. Her hand moves from my hair and rests cupped along my jaw, and I can tell she is in no more of a hurry to burst this bubble than me.

"Do you know what this reminds me of?" Anna asks.

"Uh…no." I grimace, worrying I have forgotten something important, and she laughs.

"Don't worry; it probably isn't similar for you. It's a good memory for me, but I doubt it is for you."

"Tell me?"

"Okay, well, it was quite a long time ago now. You were asleep on me in a very similar position to this. You had just watched a video on the memory stick you took from Alisha's office."

"I remember. It unlocked some memories, and it wasn't pretty." I cringe. "*I* wasn't pretty."

"Hey, this is my story - don't commentate it with inaccurate information!" Anna scowls playfully. "Anyway, at that point, you still wouldn't allow anyone to touch you. But you were asleep and so peaceful, and it was really hard to resist. At first, you fell asleep hugging me sat upright. Do you remember?"

"Actually, no. I don't remember falling asleep. What I remember is waking up with my arms wrapped round you, and they were completely dead. I was confused how I ended up that way."

It is hard to forget the embarrassment of waking up in that moment, Anna having had a front row seats to my psycho show and a rather grim view up my nose while I slept.

"You fell asleep with your head on my shoulder, so I eased you down till your head was in my lap. Then, I watched you for a while, and I couldn't stop wanting to touch your face. I didn't even know why I needed to so badly, but I couldn't bring myself to. It felt like I'd have been violating your trust if I did. But then you started muttering and flinching in your sleep like you were having a bad dream. I didn't think; I put my hand on your face just like it is now, and I stroked your cheek, and you just…stopped. You smiled into my hand, and then wrapped your arms around my waist, and your body completely relaxed. The feeling that surged through me was…insane. Your touch, even while asleep…excited me, but also, I knew in that moment that I would do just about anything to keep you safe."

I see the sadness in her eyes. It fills them slowly, and suddenly, this story takes on a whole new meaning. With a subtle pop, I feel the bubble burst. I prop myself up on my elbow till I am able to sit up.

"Anna…"

"When is he coming back?" Anna interrupts, and I sigh heavily.

"Beautiful, he's already here."

I feel it before I see it, her entire body seizing up, tightly winding like a coiling spring. Her fists clench, and she stands up, turning her back to me.

"Anna, you always keep me safe in the best possible way. As I've always said, you light up my darkness, and I…"

Anna spins round, eyeballing me incredulously before laughing darkly. It stings like a bitch slap.

"No, you are not going to do that!" I snap, almost shocking myself as much as Anna, and she shrinks a little, but her tone is still harsh.

"Do what?!"

"Shrug this off as if it's nothing without even hearing me out. You've always…listened when I needed..." I lose my words, and Anna loses the anger on her face.

"I'm sorry; you're right. It's just…being the light for you won't protect you from the cuts, the bruises, or any pain they can physically inflict on you. It *feels* like nothing in the face of that," Anna chokes, her voice small, and I melt. I pull her to the edge of the bed and kneel between her legs.

"It's not nothing. It is…*everything*. Anna…cuts heal, pain dulls, bruises fade, but the loss of who I am, that's lasting. That is so much worse. I know; I've been there already. I was there the day I barrelled into the farm with a bullet in my shoulder and very nearly there again in prison. You keep me safe and anchored to the now, to who I am. The ability to take those physical pains, to see through the darkness and not succumb to it, to hold on to who I am, comes from your light. Whether I am here or taken, in prison, or chained to a boat, I hold on to who I am because no matter how lost I feel, you are my home, and that is *everything*."

Anna folds into my chest, her legs and arms wrapping around me. It is bittersweet. While I love the cute little knots that she ties me up in, I know this one comes from fear and an ache of not wanting to let go.

"I'm sorry. I wanted to be stronger than this for you. I will be, I promise," Anna mumbles into my neck sleepily.

"Don't be sorry. I don't want you to put on some act. I want you to be you. We do need to go through some things before you fall asleep on me." Anna squeezes me a little tighter with both her arms and her legs and snuggles her face a little deeper into the nook of my neck.

"Just five more minutes, please," Anna murmurs.

Fucking adorable.

***

Five minutes turned to ten. Ten minutes turn to twenty, and at that point, being on my knees perched between Anna's thighs meant that I no longer felt like I had legs. By the time we moved, Anna was wide awake again, and it was getting on for midnight. We took a shower and made our way downstairs. On Anna's instruction, I sit in front of the fire while she makes the floor a picnic. I watch as she lays out some of my favourite foods, way more than I can eat. And then she finally sits down, bringing with her a white cardboard box and a tiny black envelope.

"This is…a lot of food." I puff, my eyes lighting up greedily.

"Well, I know that in the past you mentioned that food is something that you always miss…when, uh…you've been gone."

I look away from her nervous eyes for just a moment, and my chest swells. She has thought of everything. There's even a large tub of cookie dough ice cream. As always, I am bowled over by how much she just…thinks, and how lucky I am to be the one she thinks of. We eat far too much, and I can feel a food coma coming on. Inside the white cardboard box is a cake that she had made to taste like the white swiss meringue cake we ate at the ball. Then, we fall silent, which is only made louder when the rain just suddenly stops.

I watch her, and then I see the determination wash over her. She squares her shoulders and sucks in a deep breath. The sadness in her expression is engulfed with strength and warmth, and she looks at me in that way that always makes me feel strong.

"I had this made for you," Anna utters, passing me the small black envelope.

I take it, apprehension tingling in my stomach. The envelope is small, black, and slightly shimmery. I open it, sliding out a rectangular metal disk the same size, shape, and thickness as a credit card. My breath catches as I see a picture of Anna emblazoned on the surface in black ink. Her smile is sweet in the photo and the glint in her eyes is bright even without colour. I bite my bottom lip to stop the pathetic tremble.

"I thought… it's small enough to take with you, to hide inside your boot," Anna explains. She leans into me, turns the steel card over in my hands, and I see a message. The lettering is raised like brail.

As long as the stars are above.

All the strength in my resolve begins to crumble. The ache in my chest flares, and the lump in my throat feels melon-sized as I fail to swallow it down. I cannot afford to break; if I admit the fear I feel, the ache will almost certainly suffocate me. I look down at my hand holding the card and out of Anna's gaze, and it blurs as I try to get a grip on myself. I bought her something too, but with how much this hurts, I don't know if I can give it to her. It feels so insignificant in comparison to what I really want to give her. The fact that it is sat metres away in my suit bag almost feels mocking.

"I, uh… it's perfect, really perfect. Thank you so much."

"Mac?" I feel her hand cup around my cheek, and I stiffen.

"Please, I…I just need a minute," I manage, and I tense, bracing myself for her to fight me, for her to be hurt. Instead, I feel her fingers interlock with mine.

"That's okay.," she whispers. "I'm just going to sit here for however long that minute is and hold your hand. When it's over, you are going to tell me everything you need no matter what it is. And then, you are going to take me to bed and kiss me till we fall asleep."

I nod and squeeze her hand. For a while, it is all I can manage.

***

She flinches when I finally move. It makes me wonder how long we have been sat, silent, unmoving, her hand clutching mine. I lift my head, and my neck feels stiff. The tears never dropped. She holds my gaze; the strength and warmth in her eyes is still smouldering, and I have never been so grateful for her. The way she gets me, the way she sees me.

"I need you to understand – I can't say goodbye to you. I need you to know that there is a gun in my bottom bedside drawer. This is your home too, but if you do stay here, I need to know you're safe. I need you to hold me till we fall asleep knowing…I will be gone by the time you wake up. I need you to know I love you, Savannah Slone, and there is *nothing* I won't do to come home to you."

I see the fight it takes for her to keep the hurt from spilling over. Part of me wants to let her break, but I know, and it is clear she knows, it would be impossible for me to leave her if she did. She pulls me to my feet and leads me up to the bedroom where she wraps herself around me, and we lay nose to nose.

"I love you, Mac Scott. Just you make sure that cute little butt is always coming home to me," she whispers. The memory jogs of the last time she said that and I smile into her kiss.

Anna fights sleep. We don't speak; we just kiss. And yet, it feels like we are still talking, like I can taste the words that she is not saying. The kisses get lighter the closer to sleep she gets. She almost succumbs, then jumps before her kisses become hungry and deep again. Soon though, she loses the fight, and I watch her, knowing if I move to quickly, I will wake her. I know there is no chance of sleep for me tonight, so I perform the delicate operation of creeping out of bed, picking up my tux from the floor, and tiptoeing downstairs without waking her.

As much as I hate to leave her, it's good to move around and to have things to do. I set about quietly cleaning up the apartment so that Anna won't have to face it in the morning. Then I re-hang my suit up inside the suit bag and zip it up, completely ignoring the existence of the ring box sitting snug in the bottom. I retrieve my still-damp rucksack from the hallway and upturn the contents to the coffee table. I scan the items: my mobile phone, wallet, ghost knife, the small black box that encases my upgraded autonomous contact lenses, spare clothes, and finally, my gift to Anna.

I haven't had a chance to really look at it, so I pick it up and run my hand over the smooth leather surface that binds the large photo album. It's made from crazy horse leather, warm looking and strong. On the bottom right corner of the cover, the words *'what my heart beats for'* are burnt in deep elegant script.

I begin flicking through the photos, and immediately a smile blooms on my lips. A photo of me asleep in my camp chair, of Alfred shouting at me while I press another push up, a picture of us in the barn, watching Harry Potter on the big screen, one just before we left for the ball, at the beach, a picture of Anna and my mum on her birthday to name a few. It took some sneaking of pictures on Anna's laptop, combined with my own collection, but I think I have managed to get pictures that show a lot of the chapters of our story. On the last page, which is roughly halfway through the book, I have left her a message.

'To be continued...'

***

You have never had a wardrobe crisis until you ask yourself, what might one wear to be kidnapped? The answer? Whatever is in the bottom of my rucksack. I managed to pull together some black jeans, the black and blue plaid shirt that Alfred bought me all that time ago, and some clean underwear. My boots are on; I took a knife to the inner lining on my boot and stashed Anna's gift safely inside. I strapped and unstrapped the ghost knife to my leg countless times before deciding not to take it. I'm sure it will only be taken from me when the time comes, but man do I feel naked without it. My contact lenses are in, scratching at my dry and sleep deprived eyes. My watch from Dixy is strapped to my wrist, telling me it is 4.30am.

My boots are heavy, but I fight to move them silently as I climb the spiral staircase. It's a risk, I know, but I *have* to do this. I inch along the bedroom floor and slide the suit bag back into the wardrobe, and it's a relief knowing it is back where I told Alfred it would be, should he need it. Then I turn and hunch over Anna and lay the lightest of kisses onto her forehead. She looks tired, even while asleep, but no less beautiful. The ache in my chest is deep-seated. My hands tremble as I stick a Post-It note to her bedside table and turn away.

'I love you, goof!'

The whisky trickles down my throat with a bittersweet burn. This is definitely a neat whisky moment. A fearful current is rippling through my body; the ice clinks in the glass as I lift my unsteady hand to drain the last of the ginger-brown liquid. My eyes are trained on the front door, unblinking. Not that I think anyone will break in to take me, but fear is making me paranoid of every unfamiliar noise that clicks and scratches in the night. I will be taken; it is just a matter of time and place.

I clamp my eyes shut.

Ten seconds, Mac, that's all you get. You can let the fear in for ten second and then you must banish it, kick it away.

Ten…

I don't know if I can do this again, I know I have to but…

Nine, eight…

Will purgatory be easier to survive if I walk into it of my own free will? If I knowingly lock the shackles and relinquish my freedom?

Seven…

Six…

Anna…gorgeous, stubborn, brave holder of my heart. We have survived so much. Surely, we can survive this too?

Five, four…

Three...

Captive, enforcer of his will, daughter of a demon, Agent of MI5. Where will Mac Scott be at the end of all of this?

Two...

Here. I will be here; I am coming home! I am Mac Scott, enforcer of my will, escapist of chains, daughter of Caroline Scott. This is my life.

One...

I am ready.

Acceptance is extinguishing the fever across my skin. My heart slows to a deep, heavy thud. The tremor in my hands fade, and I step, sure-footed, grabbing my keys off the kitchen side as I go. My eyes still trained on the front door, the door to vulnerability. I lift my chin and swing the door open without hesitation. A blast of cool air hits me as I cross the threshold and then turn and lock the door. My nerves are firing on all cylinders. I get inside my truck and turn the key in the ignition and then red writing blazes across my vision, clear and bold.

`I am with you, Max.`

I puff out a choked laugh in visible misty clouds through the icy night air. My eyes flick up to the rear-view mirror, and the wideness of my eyes startles me. I close them, breathing deep and ordering my body to relax, muscle by muscle. Starting from my head, moving all the way to my toes. I look back at the rear-view mirror, give Dixy the nod, and then train my eyes out of the windscreen.

"Come and get me, you fucking monster."

***

I drive around for long enough that my stomach starts to growl. Slowly but surely, the sun is beginning to rise over London, and my eyes burn from sleepiness. I'm loathe to eat right now but the fact is, Barrett could take me in two minutes, two hours, two days, two God damn weeks. There's no sense in starving myself when I don't know how long I will be dangling myself like bait before he makes a move on me. It's probably wishful thinking on my part that he will take me so soon.

I want this over with; I don't think my nerves can take much more. There is the fleeting thought that maybe after a long day of baiting, I will be forced to go home and fall into the arms and warmth of my ravishing red-head. But no. I don't think either of us can endure another not-goodbye. What am I supposed to do if he doesn't take me today? I'd have to go back to the apartment and ask Alfred to make sure Anna goes back to the farm. It's the only option. Sleeping in my truck wouldn't come off as normal, and this needs to look normal. The thought makes me chuckle darkly.

A normal kidnap.

Hunger gets the better of me, and I pull into a McDonald's drive-through and score myself a hot-ish breakfast. I eat in my truck, slurping on a coffee as dark as Barrett's soul, but it doesn't stop the 'full tummy tiredness' that is crawling over me. My eyes are dry, the lids are heavy, and I tell myself that I will just rest them, just a few minutes. I lock myself in the truck. Kind of counterproductive to kidnap, but I don't want to be taken half asleep. I at least want a few seconds of coherency first.

But then there is a loud rapping of knuckles on glass, and I am jumping out of my skin. I flail, neck craning, eyes searching.

"Miss, excuse me. Miss!" a voice calls, and I squint at the woman in the McDonalds cap. Her eyes are bulgy, and the lashes are thick with clumped mascara. My heart rate begins to slow. I drop the window a few inches and squint back at the bulgy eyes.

"Sorry, miss, but you are parked up in one of our waiting bays. I am going to have to ask you to move."

Her voice is high pitched, and I'm groggy, so I grunt an apology and start the engine. However long I slept, it doesn't feel nearly long enough, but I do feel safer to drive. My chest is hurting; the constant tenseness and waiting are draining on me, prickling over my skin. What if I am driving around hoping to be found, and Barrett has no clue where I am? Maybe the best thing to do is go to some places I regularly frequent, like Umber. I need to be visible, and let's face it, caffeine couldn't hurt my case.

Umber is on the other side of the Thames, quite a drive, but short of going back to the brewery where I last met Barrett, I can't think where else he would link to me. If he has been watching me as much as I suspect, he knows I don't go that many places regularly. The traffic is beginning to build in the morning rush, and I note I must have been asleep for at least an hour to be hitting rush hour traffic.

I check my mirrors, hit my indicator to sweep over to the left-hand lane to turn off at the next junction, and hear an obnoxious car horn. My chest lurches. My eyes jolt back up to the rear-view, fearing that I may have cut someone off even though I was sure I had a clear gap. Sure enough, the only person behind me is a black, shiny BMW owner, and he is a far enough distance away.

Nice car.

Not that I would ever have a BMW. Fast, yes; practical, no. I have gone through a lot of cars, and while I love the speed and the look, the boot space sucks. The hairs rise on the back of my neck. I glance up again, about to take the turn.

Is he watching me?

The thought is fleeting and a testament to my own paranoia as I turn off the exit and the BMW sails by, undeterred by my turn off. I'm not sure what is more prominent, the relief or the disappointment. Either way, it feels like it is going to be a really long day.

***

I sip my second cup of coffee and breathe in the sweet scent of the glistening cinnamon whirl that had been tempting me from the counter for at least an hour before I folded. The coffee shop is quieter than I have ever seen it; I've missed the morning rush and strolled into a lull. I've seated myself at the back, not for the strategy of an easy escape through the fire exit to my right but so I can see the comings and goings. There are two baristas, one cleaning tables, the other behind the counter replenishing disposable cups into stacks. There is an old man seated by the window with his delicately frail-looking wife; she is dabbing his lips with a napkin and shaking her head with a soft smile. I look down at my cinnamon whirl, then flinch.

"Mac-attack, you read me?" Alfred buzzes into my ear, and I pick up my cup, my lips mumbling in response.

"Loud and clear, Pa."

"How you holding up? That pastry looks bang on," Alfred grumbles with enthusiasm, and I smirk.

"I needed a sugar hit. I'm fine just - the waiting sucks. I don't know what he is waiting for, but it could be days before he takes me for all I know." I sigh.

"The waiting sucks here too, but we both know you don't think it's going to be days."

"What makes you…"

The door to the coffee shop swings open, and my eyes dart, but I can't make out the guy's face. It's hidden beneath the peak of a baseball cap. I take a bite of my cinnamon whirl and let my eyes dart back and forth. The pastry was a mistake; anxiety dries all the moisture from my mouth and swallowing is suddenly impossible. The man turns towards the counter and lifts his head to make his order, and I exhale dusty pastry.

"False alarm?" Alfred comments, and I get to my feet.

"Yeah. I need to get out of here. Sitting here is just making me jumpy of every God damn person," I mutter in a growl, annoyed at myself. After throwing a tip on the table, I am already on the move, nodding to the barista on my way out.

"Take a breath, kid. You're doing great. Trying to be captured, forcing yourself to be exposed, well…it goes against every instinct in a soldier. You're doing alright," Alfred soothes.

The contrast in temperature when I leave the heat of the coffee shop to the icy chill of the street is calming. I pause to gulp in the air before turning and colliding with someone in a blue denim blur.

"Oh, God, I'm sorry!" I blurt.

"That's okay, no big…M-McKenna?"

My insides seize; I know that voice. I look up into the scrutinizing eyes of Nicole, and for a moment, I am relieved, but it is a very short moment. The memory of our last encounter in the park plays over in my mind with crystal clear clarity.

"Nic. Uh hey," I utter awkwardly because what do you say to your ex-best friend of over a decade who you cut off without explanation? I brace myself, waiting for the onslaught of shitiness I know I deserve, and then, the corner of her mouth tugs into a smile.

"What? You go to prison, you don't call, you don't write?" Nic jibes, and I chuckle.

"Ah, you heard about that, huh?"

"Mac, you were all over the papers and the news. I'd have to be dead not to hear about that!" Nic beams, her laugh bright and easy, and the sight blasts me with memories.

We were friends for a long time, close friends. We met at a gig at my old local pub. It was that nightmare situation where you turn up to a night out and someone is wearing the same as you. Only for us, it came to be the start of a long friendship. She approached me after eying our identical Pink Floyd t-shirts, and from moment one, it was easy with her. The pang of guilt resurfaces.

"Good point." I sigh, my smile wavering. "I…uh, Nic…"

"Before you say it, there is something I would like to say first if that's okay? I can walk with you if you want?" Nic offers.

"You need to cut her loose ASAP, kid."

"Ahem," I cough, signalling Alfred with a yes. "Sure. I was just on my way back to my truck."

We start walking, a slow meandering walk. The truck isn't far, two streets away, and the perfect opportunity to bail out. Plus, I can hear what she has to say while avoiding the eye contact that makes me feel like the world's worst human.

"You don't need to be sorry, Mac," Nic begins, and my head shoots in her direction, but she is watching her feet.

"I really do, Nic. I treated you like…"

"No, listen. I don't know what happened to you, but it's obvious when you came back whatever it was wasn't over for you. When I saw you in the park, I was so pissed at you. But over time, especially when I saw you in the paper and stuff, I started to realise that I was being selfish. Yes, you could have handled it better; you were a bit of a jerk." Nic smiles, rolling her eyes, and I chuckle. "But I wasn't listening. You needed time. I could see that you were trying to tell me that. I just didn't want to hear you. If I had, maybe you wouldn't have blown up, and maybe we would have been friends again when you were ready."

The ball of guilt plummets deeper into my gut, the weight becoming heavier. We turn onto the next street that leads on to the car park, and I pick up the pace just a little, hopefully unnoticed by Nicole. I would love to have this conversation with Nic. Only now with her laughing and ribbing me do I realise I've missed her. But now isn't the time for this. I'm a target, and I could be in Barrett's sights this very second, and I can't have her become collateral damage.

"You were not being selfish; I get why you had questions. I'm sorry that I wasn't in a place to give you answers. I do need to be sorry because I treated you like crap, Nic, and I do regret it. But I also know the place I was in; I wasn't able to be your friend. I wasn't even able to be me. That's not an excuse, it's just the truth, and I'm sorry."

We stop outside my truck, and I look up at her. She hasn't changed much. She is still wearing band tee's – today's edition being Black Sabbath, which is framed in a denim jacket. Her hair is longer and darker than it was, and she looks skinnier, but her face is the same. Her brown eyes are small and squinty and made to look darker by the thick black eyeliner that outlines them. She is looking quite tan, not a real tan, the kind that comes in a spray bottle. She uses it well; she hasn't reached that Oompa Loompa stage of fake tan. She gives me a soft smile, and I feel the relief, the guilt a little lighter.

"Thanks, Mac. I didn't need or expect an apology, but I appreciate it, and maybe one day soon, we can have a fresh start."

"I'd like that. It was good to see you, Nic."

"Yeah, you too."

We both turn away; we were never the types of friends to hug. I unlock the truck, and I can't help but smile. Being able to apologise after all this time felt really good, and although I feel better with her walking safely away, it was also a welcome distraction.

"Oh, and Mac…"

There is no time to turn round. The sound is immense, not of the glass shattering as my head is rammed through it, but of the ripping of my flesh, of my scalp being torn open. The pain is hot and sickening. Hunched through the driver's window, jagged glass boring into my palms, the blood is dripping into a pool on the car seat. Panic surges through me; I didn't get away quick enough. Nic must have seen them.

They are going to take her too.

"Mac!" Alfred booms inside my ear. "Mac! Come on, kid, you've got to move, move so I know you are okay. Dixy, come in."

I try to respond, but my mouth doesn't seem connected to my brain.

"Mac – MOVE!" Alfred roars.

The pain sears in my palms as I push myself slowly up and outwards from inside the windowless truck window.

"N-n Nic!" I groan.

"Oh, thank God. She's moving."

"I'm here. What happened? Why wasn't she moving? Max?" Dixy blurts urgently.

Just as I am upright, I feel hands digging into my ribs, and as I am turned around, the world spins, and the blurred features of Nic swim across my vision.

"Nic…run…you need…you are not safe!" I pant, blinking to try to stabilise my vision. Nic frowns at me, and then I feel her fist close around my throat.

"Safe from who? *Barrett*?"

Darkness.

CHAPTER 17

Veritas

"She is okay; her vital readings from the watch are strong. She's just knocked out, but we need to figure out who that girl is," Dixy urges.

"She said her name was Nic; seemed like they knew each other well but had a falling out or something. There was *no* indication that she was a threat," Alfred growls.

"She's going to be okay, big fella. Do you think Anna will know who she is?"

Anna...

"She's on her way, so we'll soon find out."

"Okay, Lambert – go back through the footage and screengrab this Nic girls face. Run it through facial recognition just in case Anna doesn't know who… Max? Her eyes are opening – look! Max, can you hear me?"

My body is vibrating, a dense pulse resonating inside my bones. A high-pitched ping is singing in my ears. I can see the ping; it is dancing with the distorted shapes and colours in my eyes.

"Max, it's Dixy – I need you to keep your eyes open."

Aren't they open?

"She's disorientated; she needs a fixed point. Mac – it's Pa. Keep them eyes open; it's time to work now. That Nic girl banged your head pretty good. Everything probably feels screwy, but I need you to snap out of it. Rub some dirt in it, look around you, and get your bearings."

Nicole...

A scorpion tail sting of betrayal, harsh and needle-pointed emitting pinpricks of light through the veil of darkness. Shafts of clarity, streaks of hurt, glares of anger. Each beam burnishing the dust and clearing my mind.

My senses sharpen, and my body awakens, my mind reconnecting the dots between body and brain, and then, there is *pain.*

"Ugh… That *bitch*," I groan, and then a collective of relieved shouts sound in my ear.

My eyes blink and strain, like the focusing of a camera lens, and my vision begins to sharpen. I am laying on my side; my hands are resting in front of my nose, obscuring my vision. I push them away and feel the unnatural movement, the restrictive tug of them bound together at the wrists. Dipping my chin down, I look towards my feet to see that the silvery duct tape is also corkscrewed tightly around my ankles. My eyeline raises above my feet to see metal panelling and the arch of a wheel well. Using my elbows, I push and shuffle myself upright. My head spins, and my stomach revolts at the motion, and I freeze while my head searches for equilibrium.

"Looks like the inside a van. Can you see the driver?" Dixy asks.

Tentatively, I bum shuffle back till my back hits the wall of the van and turn my head to the right to see the partition wall blocking any sight.

"Well, that's good. If you can't see her, she can't see you and probably can't hear you either. Max, who is she?"

"She was my friend before the boat. I cut her off when I came back because I couldn't…but I don't understand…we were…she was…for over ten years," I ramble, dazed.

"Barrett must have planted her to watch you. I'm sorry, Max." Dixy pauses, her voice apologetic. "What is her last name?"

Hurt floods my chest, hurt and embarrassment. All that time, all those moments, watching movies, going to gigs, drunken heart to hearts. Late night phone calls and coffee shop catch ups – a lie? A fiction to gain my trust? My mind is reeling, scrambling through the hours we spent together, trying to find a clue, a hint of deception. It all felt so real; how could anyone keep up a lie for that long? How did I not see?

"Chambers. Nicole Chambers."

The pain throbbing in my head and burning in my scalp is clearing the fog. I've been taken by The Culling, by *Nicole!* It is unfathomable; therefore, to analyse it is a waste of time because her deception, her betrayal, is something I'll never understand. I feel a warm trickle down the side of my neck. I lift my hands to investigate for them to slide in dark scarlet blood. Head wounds bleed a lot, I've learnt. But that doesn't stop the nauseating swoop in my abdomen at the sight of it coating my fingers.

"Max, you need to keep your eyes open; you have a concussion," Dixy asserts firmly, and I groan.

"I'm aware of that. What are you, the nap police?"

"Snarky!"

"That's because I have a concuss…" I smirk, and it freezes and dies on my face. My senses fire up, ears pricked, heart hammering.

"What is it, Max?"

"The van has stopped."

"Alright, time put your game face on. You've got this."

I don't look up when the doors open to the back of the van. I keep my body loose, my eyes fixed forward, and my face slack. I am humiliated and hurt but determined she will not profit on that. The van dips with her weight as she clambers in, her feet pounding towards me.

"Hello, old friend," Nic leers, and my blood runs cold, hardening me.

Yes… Burn, burn, burn.

Nicole tares the duct tape from off my ankles and then drags me to my feet, her nails digging into my under-arms. She steps into me, her eyes colder than I ever knew they could be, and I hold them.

"What? Nothing to say? You going to re-adopt your pussy whipped prison silence?" Nic goads, and I smirk.

"Oh, Nic, I'm sorry. You seem to be operating under a misconception. I have plenty to say but only to people who actually matter, and you, sad girl – *don't*," I belittle, and her cheeks redden, swirling guilt in my already churning gut.

Don't feel bad. Ten years of lies!

Burn, burn, burn.

"Move…" Nic growls, pushing me towards the van doors.

Outside of the van, the air is brisk, and I gulp it in, welcoming the shiver running through me. My eyes dart, analysing every detail I can for my contact lenses to pick up. I make a point of looking at the numberplate to the van before I am nudged forward. There are no street signs. I am surrounded by buildings sprawling on all sides, and I feel hemmed in by the mass of them. Nicole pushes me forwards in the direction of the largest building. On top is a clock tower. The windows are long and slatted with frames of peeling white paint. The building looks old and forbidding; it has an eerie, haunted, boarding school feel to it. The closer, I get the smaller I feel and the less I want to venture inside.

"Hold on a minute. I know that building. Ha!" Alfred booms, and the tightness in my chest eases a little. "It's the abandoned military hospital in Aldershot. That's where they used to take soldiers during the First and Second World Wars. It's about an hour's drive from here, been shut down since the late 90s. As far as I know, the building was left to nature after that."

Ugh – I hate hospitals.

"That fits with the timeline; it was an hour and ten minutes from Max being taken to her arriving there. Hold on, isn't that where they filmed *28 Days Later*?" Dixy muses, and I suppress a grin.

"Ahem." I answer yes covertly, which earns a laugh singing inside my ear.

"Course she knows that, gigantic nerd."

I want to say that she is just as much a nerd for pointing it out; I want to say, 'Okay, that's enough, shall we go home now?' But of course, I can't say anything of the sort while I drag my feet and the creepy building inches closer. It would be comforting that they know where I am, except Lexi made it clear there will be no rescue mission. It is too high of a risk to expose MI5 agents. I can easily picture that the buildings were probably handsome once; it has survived war, and I am sure it is the treasure of this town, but it also looks condemned, and I have to fight the quiver running through me as I enter.

The inside of the main building makes the outside look like a holiday camp. Nature has, in fact, attempted to claim this building, along with graffiti artists of varying degrees of talent. Mould and damp are creeping up more walls than not; there is debris, dust, and glass crunching under my boots. It is cold, the temperature difference to outside must be minimal, and the air smells frowsty and stale. We come to what looks like it may have been a main reception area; there is a large dark-wood U-shaped counter and some upturned file boxes, and we pass them. Above the reception desk, painted on to the white brick wall, are the words 'I am the resurrection and the life.'

The deeper we delve, the tighter my chest becomes. There is no sound but the crackle of my boots against grit and rubble, and yet it is so loud. We enter a corridor with high arched ceilings; there is moss and algae on the windowsills. The emptiness of it, the stillness and the shadowy vastness, prompts the hairs to stand up on the back of my neck.

Yeah...this is where ghosts come to hang out.

We pass some faded green doors to operating rooms. The rust on the bolts and handles has liquified and oozed, streaking down like blood. If I had thought to attempt to memorise the route I am being taken on, with so many twists and turns, I would have quickly forgotten it. We finally pass a green stencil-painted sign that reads 'women's service wards,' then take one last corridor. This corridor is longer, and there is less debris on the floor as if someone came along and swept it up. I can see in the distance that there are dark-wood double doors at the end. Closed, but there is a warm glow seeping through the gap at the bottom edge.

Every fibre of my body tightens as we draw closer, the long corridor not long enough. Then, a flash of red blinks in the top right of my vision.

`Luck be with you, Agent Scott.`

Metres away, Lexi's message fading from my sight. I make the conscious effort to square my shoulders, lift my chin, and straighten up my posture. I suck in a long breath silently through my nose as Nicole crosses in front of me, pushing open the doors with an echoey thump of her palms. The room is huge, spacious and church-like, and we keep walking towards the centre of it. It is hard to make out what it once was during its glory days. The ceiling is high, all the walls are white painted brick, and the floor is dark wood and gleaming, not a speck of dust or rubble in sight. Most noticeable is the stark difference in temperature. In each corner of the room, there are elegant looking fire pits made from black marble, coal embers smouldering away. Along the back wall, there is steel shelving with plastic trunks lining the shelves neatly.

Nic holds her arm out in front of me, and I stop in my tracks. Barrett stands front and centre, smartly dressed in a dark blue suit. He is flanked by three others, all of them wearing long, royal blue hooded robes. When I approach, they take their hoods down in perfect timed unison. Two of the faces, I recognise from the ball and from the background checks I have since studied on them. Farah Fadel, long face, olive skin, perfect white teeth, and a scar across her lip. Her hair is long, slinky, and jet black. Her expression curious. There wasn't much to read about Farah. She was orphaned at 11, had limited education growing up in Bosnia, and is the widow of her husband Azem, a drug kingpin.

My eyeline flicks to Damon Anders. Beast-like to the point it makes you wonder if steroids are sprinkled daily on his morning bowl of cornflakes. He has deep black eyes, the bushiness of his eyebrows darkening them further. According to his military jacket, he has an explosive temper and a tendency to disregard orders. He was given a dishonourable discharge from the special forces under suspicion of using undue deadly force, cruel and unusual punishment, and a pending charge of statutory rape. He is eying me with malice, and it is a little harder this time around to not fear that look. A look I have seen in the eyes of many cruel men.

The last face is new to me, and the eyes that belong to it are framed in chunky framed glasses and are struggling to make eye contact with me. This man is skittish, biting his nails, painfully skinny. His arms are long, pale, and veiny. He has boyband-long messy hair that falls in front of his eyes, and I suspect he uses it to hide behind.

I look back to Barrett to find him looking at me with an irritated, questioning look that has my stomach clenching. He steps forwards, his hand reaching for my chin and gently turning my face. His eyes dart to Nicole, and then he drops his hand.

"Was *that* really necessary?" Barrett asks, his voice sharp.

"Yes, Noah, I-I couldn't leave room for mistakes. I wasn't about to fail you." Nicole wobbles.

Noah?

"Go get yourself robed and join your siblings," Barrett orders, and Nicole nods and disappears out the doors behind him. He turns back to me, reaching out for my hands, and rips off the duct tape before meeting my gaze again with a sigh.

"I am sorry that you were handled this way, McKenna. I don't condone *unnecessary* violence."

What do I call him? Barrett, Noah, Father, demon-daddio?

"No apologies necessary, but I appreciate that," I utter smoothly, and he nods before turning sharply away and returning to his centre spot.

Nicole returns, robed in royal blue and standing next to Damon, evening out the sides. The sight of them, still and staring at me intensely, incites both terror and revulsion inside me. I refuse to tremble but inside, my heart is beating so fast it is tripping over itself, skipping beats, making me feel breathless.

It's then it hits me. As my eyes fall on the royal blue robes Nicole now adorns, an image flashes faintly in my mind. As I see the familiar smirk she is so coldly displaying, the image sharpens, and the memory swirls.

My gaze falls on a woman; she is dressed in a royal blue dress and mask. Her back is turned to me but her head turns towards me, eyes fixed. The hairs rise on the back of my neck as she stares at me. Anna's hands slide onto my hips, her lips at my ear.

"Who is that?" she whispers, her voice shaken.

"I don't..."

The woman in blue smirks, and it feels so familiar and yet so cold, a shudder runs through me.

I blink hard, clearing the memory from my mind.

My stomach plummets as if realising that it was Nicole who barged into me at the ball has somehow made it more real. As if ramming my head through a car window and kidnapping me wasn't enough. Our friendship really did mean nothing. The hurt is draining away, making way for disgust.

"By now, I am sure you have noticed that not all know me by the name Barrett. Some know me as Noah. I am also sure you are familiar with the tale of Noah's Ark. In the story, God tasks Noah with saving the very best examples of the world's animals from the Genesis flood. A flood of His own creation designed to destroy the entire population of mankind because they had become evil. God saw a purity within Noah; He sought to spare him, his family, and two of each of His greatest creations of animals. He sought a world of peace and a world without the wickedness that humanity had become. You might say, He sought to *cull* them," Barrett muses softly.

"Remember, Max, passive face. You are not disgusted," Dixy utters softly.

Oh, but I am.

"Culling…the rejection and removal of inferior individuals from breeding. The act of selective breeding in accordance with pedigree. Animals are spayed and neutered when they are deemed not to measure up to the standard of their breed. And yet we as humans, with finer intelligence, are free to breed with lesser, weaker, humans. Now, centuries have passed since the story of Noah's Ark, and the world is brimming with inferior humans, and the world is suffering for it. Without intervention, without realignment, we are all doomed."

Barrett takes a step closer, his jaw clenching and his expression hardening.

"Uneducated, homeless, criminals, drug addicts, disabled, unhealthy, lower classed, below average intelligence, poor, lazy, unemployed, *weak*! The leaches of society! Teen mothers, council estate dwellers, benefit scroungers, thieves! They drain society and then they fuck, reproducing new generations of inferior humans to siphon the life from this world!" Barrett raves, his rant spewing out of him as rage fuels his momentum. His eyes display the madness within.

I watch as the vein throbbing in his forehead deflates and the heat reddening his cheeks subsides, and then he takes a step back.

"Ask yourself, Mckenna - what if the weak were culled, leaving only the strong?" he asks, all calm returned, although his voice is now hoarse. "Intelligent, wealthy, educated, higher classed, artistically genius, athletically gifted, healthy, *strong*. If humanity were to impose selective breeding from a pool of the elite, the superior pedigree of humans - then we would be paving the way for a superior-race. We would be paving the way to the creation of a thriving utopian world built by the ultimate human race.

"Now, I do not claim to be chosen by God. I am merely enlightened and fated to change the catastrophic trajectory of our world. Not with a genesis but with a culling. By being here today, you are pledging your commitment to not only our family but our cause. To grant you admittance, you must prove your absolute elegance and fidelity. To do this you must triumph the tests of Veritas. To fail…is to die."

It takes everything, every ounce of will, to hold his stare. To block out the fear seizing in my chest and the revulsion bubbling in my gut. Everything, and somehow, I do, and I feel all the colder for it.

"I am aware of what is being asked of me. Aware and ready to show my devotion to this mission and to you."

I see the glint in his eye. The glint of satisfaction I was hoping for, and yet my heart plummets at the sight of it.

"Then let us begin," Barrett announces, and then Damon and Farah both step out of line simultaneously. They walk…unnaturally in a slow march, their steps in line with one another and their heads bowed.

"Veritas, the triangle of truth. Like a triangle, Veritas has three points. Three peaks you must climb and conquer in order to gain the understanding and strength required to reach Veritas, to reach enlightenment, to reach – the *truth*," Barrett emphasises egotistically.

I watch as Damon and Farah come back into sight, still walking as if in some ceremonious parade, only Damon now carries a cast iron chair. His bulging muscles are a clear indication of the weight of the chair. Farah carries an old beaten wooden box. They come to a halt in front of me, standing facing each other, statue still. Barrett steps forward and stands centred, just behind them.

"The first peak you must scale is *restraint*. Self-restraint takes strength; it takes willpower, and it takes courage. Restrain yourself of the need to depend on others, and you become formidable."

My heart rate skyrockets; the blood rushes till I can hear it pumping in my ears. Damon places the chair down and walks back to his spot in the centre of the room. My eyes dart back to Barrett while I fight to keep the fear out of them. Barrett turns to Farah and opens the box, taking out three very old-looking pairs of shackles and a brown leather collar.

"Dix, her heart rate is flying," Alfred advises.

"I know. Easy, Max, take a deep breath. They're just chains, remember. They can't hold you," Dixy soothes, and I follow her instruction.

Just chains, just chains…

Red words float up to the right-hand corner of my eyeline once again as Lexi leaves her message:

`You've come a long way from the girl in chains.`

Barrett looks at me, a look I can read all too well; he is still testing me. He has only really begun to test me. Fighting every instinct that screams in my mind and bubbles in my blood, I hold my wrists out to him, and his eyes flash with gratification. I watch as Barrett encloses the cold steel around my wrists, the weight of them horribly familiar, and then he inclines his head towards the chair. The chair is a highly ornate, antique occasional chair decorated in feathers of thick swirls cast in iron. I sit, feeling the iciness of the iron through my shirt, and I shiver, causing the iron to dig into my spine. Barrett takes a knee and begins fixing my ankles to the chair using the last two pairs of shackles.

"Without pain, there is no glory. Being able to function through pain, restrain your mind to focus in spite of it, is a skill. Like any skill, it is honed with practice. Without restraint, you cannot hope to protect the secrets of The Culling," Barrett muses lightly as if discussing an afternoon tea, and he gets smoothly back to his feet. He leans in and places the collar around my neck, then fixes it to the back of the chair with such a light touch, it makes my skin crawl.

It is not so tight that I can't breathe or move my head, but it is a clear and humiliating deterrent from being able to get off the chair, and the terror grips me. My jaw is clenched in the effort to stop my teeth chattering. My brain feels waterlogged; I cannot think through the tidal waves of fear crashing inside my head.

"People bond in pain. Soldiers on the battlefield talk not of fighting for their country or to win the war but of fighting for the brothers dug into the trenches beside them. You are a soldier; this is a war. We must be united as one." Barrett's eyes bear down on me, his expression void of emotion. "I have high hopes for you, daughter. Do not disappoint me."

Barrett holds out his hand, and Damon steps forward. He makes point of slowly opening his robe so that I have a clear view of the hunter's knife sheathed to his belt. He hands it to Barrett who steps forward and uses the knife to cut the sleeves off of my shirt and the legs off my jeans halfway up my thighs. How stupid that, in this moment, instead of fear, I feel hurt? A guttural hurt because he has ruined a shirt bought for me by Pa, my black and blue plaid shirt.

The memory hits me with vivid full colour clarity. The memory of hobbling down to the fire pit using a crutch, finally feeling clean after my first post-bullet wound shower. I'm wearing the plaid shirt. The curious grin that warmed Anna's face as her eyes swept over me stirred everything inside of me.

"What?"

"Suits you," she replies, blushing slightly. I am not sure if she is joking or not.

"I fit in with you farmer folk now," I reply, sticking my tongue out.

My eyes close of their own volition, and the image sharpens. The scent of the smoking fire pit, Alfred chugging a Budweiser in his camping chair, Anna's curious grin – a grin I fell in love with, a grin I want to come home to again. My chest swells with warmth, the tautness of my muscles sag, and I open my eyes.

My farmer folk...

Barrett looms over me, the monster in his eyes clawing at the edges of his grey-blue piercing irises.

"People bond in pain," Barrett mutters, and then I watch as he presses the cold steel of the blade into my forearm and drags in one measured, fluid motion. I gasp at its hot sting, my fists clenching.

Barrett straightens up and holds out the knife. Nicole steps forward to take it, and Barrett turns away and strides out of the room. She meets my glare with cold amusement before holding the blade against my shoulder.

"People bond in pain," Nicole repeats, and then she pulls the blade hard and fast against my skin. Hate is fuelling me; the action feels like being whipped. Painful but fast, and I barely flinch. Which, by the look in her eyes, is a massive disappointment.

Nice try, psycho puppet.

Burn, burn, burn.

When Farah steps forward, for a split second, I see a hint of hesitancy. She is unable to maintain eye contact, and her hand trembles when taking the knife from Nicole. She bends down and holds the knife to my shin.

"People bond in pain," Farah repeats, and then she drags the knife in a quick slash before turning away.

The skittish skinny guy approaches me. For some reason, it really irks me that he is going to cut me, and I don't even know his name. From his nervous disposition, I expect him to be timid and tentative, and I almost want to apologise for his having to do this. He steps forwards and holds the knife against my uncut inner forearm.

"People bond in pain," he repeats, voice unshaken and overly soft. He presses down hard on the blade and then drags it slowly.

This time, I almost cry out. A whimper escapes my lips, my chest heaving; there is no doubt in my mind that his cut is the deepest. I shake my head to try shake off the swimming and sloshing, threatening to make me pass out. Then my eyes find him, eying me with venom, his face a picture of excitement.

Damon takes the knife, and I am left with him, alone. He steps towards me, and the hate I feel is only magnified by the memory of his hand, clamped around Anna's delicate wrist.

Burn, burn, burn.

Damon runs the point of the knife up the inside leg of what's left of the leg of my jeans. I watch as the tip of the blade draws closer to my groin. Every muscle in my body clenches, fear and humiliation burning like acid in my stomach.

"Sick bastard," Alfred growls. "He better watch himself; she will break his nose in seconds."

Damon pushes his fist against my thigh as he draws out the point of the knife, the tip jabbing the fly of my jeans. My head snaps up, and I snarl, fury igniting inside and burning away all the fear in its path. With a rip, I feel my thigh exposed, then the cold knife edge pressed firmly against my inner thigh, and then he meets my hateful gaze.

"People bond in pain."

The pain is electric as he drags the knife deep and slow, and I growl through clenched teeth, spit bubbling through the gaps. My head sags, chin bouncing off my chest as my vision darkens. Damon clamps his hand hard around my cheeks.

"You will not pass this evolution; you will fail, and you will *die*," Damon seethes, and then he thrusts my head back sharply and storms away.

"Oh yeah? *Watch me*," I choke.

Darkness.

***

I like the cold, so much so, I dream of it sometimes. Where most dream of summer holidays, the sun, sea, and flip-flops slapping on blistering hot sand, I dream of the deep reds and browns of fallen autumn leaves. The flames of a warm fire, the stillness of a morning fog. I love the frost that crunches underfoot on an icy morning. And the need to wear thick, unflattering, woollen jumpers and bobble hats. Most of all, I love the calm it brings me, like balm on a rash. I like the cold but maybe not today.

When I come to, I am sure it was the cold that roused me, my shivers jolting me awake. I find myself in a different, much smaller, and colder room. It is dimly lit and featureless. There is no glass to the windows. They are covered in metal gridded sheeting; the holes would be large enough to see through if it weren't dark. The floor is dusty concrete and covered in grit and glass. The walls are peeling with paint so evenly that it looks like some eerie artistic feature. A dank and dirty dungeon. When my body catches up with my mind, I discover I am chained to the wall with my arms strung up, sat on the same ornate cast iron chair. My cuts are bandaged up, and my restraints have been removed from my legs and neck.

"Hey, Max-a-million, how are you holding up? You were out for about an hour. I heard Barrett order Farah to tend to your wounds. There was a lot of moving around but not much else. Looks like you woke up in Creeps-Ville," Dixy mutters.

My knees creak as I get to my feet, turning to face the wall and leaning my forehead against it. I mumble my shivery response as quietly as possible; I don't think I can be overheard, but I am pretty sure I am being watched.

"F-fine, I guess. Y-yeah, no zombies s-so far though. Bonus." I shiver, my mind wandering to the *28 Days Later* movie.

"Oh well, if no one is looking to eat your brain, then this should be a walk in the park for you."

I chuckle very quietly. The dizziness in my head is finally gone. What isn't is the sting to my pride. I still can't wrap my head around the idea of Nicole being a member of The Culling. It hurts, the knowledge that none of our decade long friendship was real. It is also a testament to how much Barrett enjoys control and how far his followers will go to please him. I can't help but wonder if there will be any other surprise members creeping out of my past.

Three stages to conquer Veritas to become a member of The Culling. How long will each stage go on? I knew there would be pain; pain I can deal with but never knowing when it will end is the real torture. There are no safe words this time. This isn't a simulation. Although people are watching, they can't rescue me. I knew once I was here it was do or die; Barrett would never let anyone walk away. The risk of exposure to him and The Culling would be too great. What I didn't know was that there would be a gargantuan man-beast hell bent on me failing. I have no doubt he will do whatever he can to ensure I fail, the question is – why?

"Zombies would be refreshing; they are just h-hungry. They don't have the brains to hatch evil villain plans to m-march selected humans two by two and wipe out the rest of humanity with the s-second coming."

"He really is a mad man and completely unoriginal. Twisting religion to serve his ideology – cult leader 1-0-1."

The door swings open with a long clang as it hits the wall behind me. I turn, my eyes failing to register anything before my nerves begin to scream. It is familiar but no less shocking, water so cold it saturates iciness into my very bones. It is familiar, and yet the water's flow seems relentless and never-ending. Through the powerful water's spray, I see a hose, a huge fireman-type hose. The water pressure is so high, my skin is burning, and I ram my face into my armpit to shield it. I fight the urge to gasp, my chest heaving at the shock of it, and then, it stops. His fist is clamped around my throat quicker than I can blink.

"Welcome to *my* evolution. It's my job to test and push your boundaries of restraint. If you feel you cannot continue with this evolution, you will utter the submit phase, *I am a dirty dyke.* The evolution will end shortly, followed by your life*,"* Damon spits, and I chuckle.

"That's original.," I choke, and the squeeze on my throat gets tighter.

"Those words will be coming out of your mouth, McKenna; it's only a matter of time," Damon leers, and then he releases my throat and rips open my shirt, his expression jeering.

My breath shakes from the cold and from the shame as his eyes scrutinise inside my open shirt with disgust. Goosebumps flee across my skin, and I set my jaw, burning him with all the hate my stare can muster.

"You will resist the need…to scream."

He moves so fast, I feel the pain before I can brace myself. The sound of the hollow slap echoes off the walls as his open palm lashes against my abdomen. My skin cold and wet from the hosing only intensifies the pain. The whimper escapes my lips, heat radiating from my torso as his hand swings for another smack. The pain is searing, my head bobbing and jerking with every strike, the impact so forceful, my back hits the wall with every blow.

Thwack… Thwack… Thwack.

My vision clouds with tears, but I will be damned if I let them drop. I lift my head to see him skulk out of the room, then I clamp my eyes shut just as I see the hose in his hands. The water hits my skin so hard, it feels like sand blasting through the hose. At first, it is hot, and then the flow stops, and the cold seeps into my bones. Damon drops the hose, reaching for something out of sight, and then drags it across the floor. A white wire trails behind him, and he sits it just in front of my feet. My eyes fall on a heater, and I watch as he flicks it on and off, and then he looks up at me.

"Resist…" Damon utters smugly, then he drags the cast iron chair out of my reach before walking away and slamming the door behind him. I don't watch him; my eyes are on the heater, the power switch a toe nudge away, but it may as well be a mile because if I flick that switch – I am dead.

I like the cold, but maybe not today.

The pain in my abdomen is forcing me to slightly hunch forward, and I am desperate to hold my hands against the ache. I turn back to facing the wall, my forehead scraping the rough surface, the chains chinking as my arms shake above my head. The cold air blowing across my skin from the glassless windows is already rocking my body with shivers.

"Dix…"

"Yeah…I'm here," Dixy responds, her voice gravelled and pained.

"I need you not to be…for a while. I need radio silence. I can't…"

The words get stuck in my throat, cut off by the lump rising. I thought the familiar voices inside my ear would be comforting. But really all it does is make me long for home, for safety and for Anna. I can't focus. The warmth of their voices is holding back the cold darkness, and although I fear letting it inside, I know I won't survive if I don't.

"I know; you don't need to say it. Listen, I'll make sure everyone keeps radio silence unless we feel it is necessary, but only if you keep your earpiece activated. We need to hear if you need us and know everything that's happening there." Dixy pauses, and I hear her sigh shakily. "Max, can I do anything for you?" she asks, her voice breaking.

"Yeah...don't let her see too much. Don't let her live at those screens."

"Oh, we are *trying*, trust me, but your woman is a force to be reckoned with."

"I know…" I smile, and the ache in my chest smoulders.

***

The shivering is relentless, and my muscles ache from the constant shudder. I have been here for a while now, I think. If the hunger pains are anything to go by. I can't quite see my watch to figure it out; the chains I am strung up by are keeping it out of my sight. I could ask whoever is listening, whoever is seeing through my eyes, but I know no matter how long I *feel* it has been, it has no doubt only been half of that time in reality. I am not sure I can take hearing that.

Old habits die hard. I became quite accustomed to the art of dozing while standing strung up by chains on the boat. It isn't real sleep, more of a dozing daydream, teetering within the in between. That place you visit just as you wake up, the place between asleep and awake. It passes the time, but sometimes I topple off the teeter into the asleep. Till my unconscious legs give in and my bodyweight sags, tugging on the chains and crushing the joints in my wrists.

"Argh…fuck sakes." I rasp, whimpering pathetically as I jolt against the chains, eyes wide and bleary.

The cold is tiring. And in this position, strung up next to the draft of the windows, in wet rags for clothes, there is no way to shield myself. It is a constant aching numbness that I am now struggling to endure.

"Superman doesn't f-feel the cold. He lives in his fortress o-of solitude in the middle of t-the Artic, surrounded by… *Ice-ice baby*," I rasp, chuckling lifelessly. "G-great…well done, now that s-s-song is stuck in my God-d damn head. C-c-couldn't h-have referenced a rock song, could you? No."

My gaze falls on the heater and I glare at it resentfully. I have no temptation to turn it on, regardless of how cold I am. To do that would be a death sentence, but the sight of it licks anger against insides. How long am I going to have to stare at the thing? How long before they see I am not going to turn it on and move on? I am past the stage of fearing what is next. The mundanity of this unchangeable hell is beginning to weigh too much; my thoughts are getting louder.

The girl in chains…

"Ugh s-stop…"

My head begins to swim, a heavy familiar drag of my mind as the corners of my vision darkens, and I begin losing grip of the now.

"Stop…m-make it stop," I whimper pathetically.

"Mac-attack, you read me?" Alfred booms.

The memory swirls.

"I have to make it stop. I can't do this anymore. He is going to come back and do it again; he always comes back. I need to end it. I can't…" I croak weakly in present time.

My skin crawls, and I scratch at my bare legs, straightening my legs out so I can get to my thighs. I can feel him crawling all over me, inside me. I whimper, sobs burning in my chest.

"There is only one way out."

"Mac! Come on kid, Answer me. Why isn't she answering me?"

"She is triggered in a memory, the worst possible memory she could be… Anna! Get Anna!" Dixy orders.

"Gnnnaaaah!" I growl, forcing my thumb and index finger into a hard press.

The vision is flashing and pixelating. The boat, the chains, the pain, the fear, the cold chains coiling tightly in my fists…

"Nooo!"

"Max! Focus! This is your boat; you are in control!" Dixy yells.

I press my thumb and finger as hard as I can and pull down on the chains, digging the shackles into my wrists. The biting pain interrupts the images. The vision warps, the rifle kicking against my shoulder, the campfire songs. I clamp my eyes closed to try and keep hold of the vision only for it to warp again.

I wrap the chain attached to my right wrist around my foot securely and then I stand on it, giving myself the height needed.

"Mac! Mac. it's Anna. Please come back to me. I'm here, and I need you to hear me. Come back, please," Anna pleads, her voice breaking.

I shake my head as the vision pixelates, the sounds merging in chaos.

"Gnaaah – Stop! Make it stop!"

"Mac Scott, I know you can hear me. Baby, please – I need you. I need you right now! Please come back to me…"

Anna's face flashes across my mind, her eyes determined and burning with emerald-green fire. The chains drop from my grip and my head swims, disorientated and swooping as my back thumps against the wall. Chest heaving, throat sharp with parched dryness, my eyes unblinking.

"Anna?" I whimper.

"Mac! Oh, God! Oh, thank God! Yes, baby, it's me! I'm here, it's okay." Anna cries, and I turn my back and face the wall. The tears catch in my throat, and all I can say is her name.

"Hey, you. I know it's only been five days, but I miss you so damn much. I keep looking at the photo album you made me, at our story. It's so beautiful, laid out so perfectly, but it is *not* finished. We still have so much left to w-write." Anna chokes on a sob, and then her voice fires, emboldened. "I know you are hurting, but I need you to *fight* now. Fight to come home to us because every time you do, you are *unstoppable!* They have no idea who they are dealing with, and I want you to *show* them!"

My chest swells with her warmth in the silence that follows as I try to find my words, my mind fills with a memory that I have replayed so many times. A memory that changed everything inside of me forever. A memory that still makes me wonder if that moment meant the same thing to her as it did me…

"For as long as you will have me," I whisper, and I hear her gasp, the most gorgeous happily tearful, chuckling gasp. I can see it on her face so clearly in my mind.

"I am right here, Mckenna. What exactly are you waiting for?" Anna whispers.

The rush is astounding. I have no idea if those words mean to Anna what they mean to me. But she remembers them, and it is enough to burst through any pain, any exhaustion, and any doubt. The warm blanket of calm, the focus of acceptance, encompasses me. I scrub my eyes over the sleeve of my arm and breathe.

"I *am* coming home, Savannah. I promise," I vow, my voice strong despite the exhausted rasp.

"Mm, there she is," Anna groans, her tone doing delicious things to me. Only Anna could send jolts of tingles between my thighs at a moment like this. "I'll be waiting…"

I turn away from the wall, my mind clear, my resolve hardened. And suddenly, I know exactly what I need to do. My eyes fall back down to the heater, and I smirk and then feel a rush of satisfaction as I kick out at the heater. I watch as it flies across the room and crashes against the opposite wall.

"Come and get me," I growl.

***

It only takes moments; the door swings open, and I grin with mirth at the bitterness in his expression. Damon crosses the room, and without a word, he pulls a hood over my head. My legs buckle and I sink to my knees as the shackles grip on my wrist's releases; the relief on my arms is exponential. Damon scruffs the back of my shirt, dragging me to my feet and shoving me forward. I stumble along, shoulders and elbows bashing into walls and door frames, led roughly by the fist gripping the back of my neck.

The disorientation is at a maximum with no sight and going without food and sleep for five days. My head is swimming. I am almost grateful for the rough grasp of Damon's hand around my neck, guiding me. Five days. I was right; the reality is sobering. It definitely felt like more, but the world isn't crashing down inside me. It is time to fight. It is time to remember everything I have learnt. I am at his mercy physically, but I have been at others mercy many times before. The way to win a physical game with your hands tied is with your mind and mine is awake.

Damon tugs me to a stop, turns me to face him, and then lifts me, his hands gripped under my armpits. My back hits something solid with a creak, and my feet find a ledge. He keeps hold of me, pressing me even though I am not putting up a fight.

"Hands," he grunts, and before I can question it, cold hands grip my wrists, and then I feel a tightening.

Both of my hands are fixed in place, palms out, my arms spread just a little further out than feels natural. The image of my statue made by Alfred flashes across my mind. Her arms spread out in the same stance; the words 'blessed mess' ironically flash across my mind.

"Ankles."

My feet are spread shoulder width apart, and while Damon's hold on me stays unperturbed, cold hands fix them in place too. The hood is ripped off, and my eyes adjust quickly to the dim scene. I look down to find myself fixed to a wooden surface by leather straps, and if it weren't so obvious that this is going to lead nowhere good, I would be quite comfortable. In comparison to the chains that held arms above my head, it is heavenly, but soon I lift my chin to find the speculative stares of Damon and Nicole.

Two psychos for the price of one.

Burn, burn, burn.

"You know what you have to do to end this. Say the submit phrase, and I will end it quickly." Damon utters coldly.

"What, and spoil all this bonding we are doing?" I mock.

"Oh, McKenna, I have no interest in bonding with you. I tell you what, though; I can't say the same about your red headed friend." Damon sucks in a breath through his teeth and leans into me, his knee pressed against my groin. "Maybe once I'm through with you, I can pick up where I left off. I am sure it won't take much…pressure before I am so deep inside her, she forgets your name."

Damon presses his knee harder at his words, and the fury inside me burns hotter than it ever has, but I am in control now. I lean forward slowly, my eyes soft and sincere, my voice steady and firm.

"Let's not pretend the only way you could ever get a woman like that is by force and…I will kill you, long before you *ever* get the chance because - *I am Mac Scott, and I will come for you!"*

The crack is sickening, loud, and I think it is the most beautiful sound I could possibly hear in this moment. That is, until he cries out. A strangled, blood choked, garbled cry at the perfectly directed hit of my forehead hammering into his nose.

"Ha-ha-ha! That's my girl! I knew it, I fucking knew it! Gwaan kid!" Alfred booms inside my ear.

"Oh, so sexy its unfair," Anna groans.

"Motion seconded," Dixy chimes.

"Legend!" Lambert cheers.

Damon straightens up, blood flowing in a gush, his face a mask of fury, and while I know I am going to pay, this feeling cannot be crushed. Nothing can beat the thrum of liberation pulsing through my veins. The frenzied torrent of vivification, of restored certainty and faith. Take my body, do what you will, but you will never take my mind.

And so, he does.

The blows rain down, fists forcing the air from my lungs. Sharp, short jabs to my ribs, and I am glad he started there. I'm too winded to give him the screams he so desires. My head sags, chin bouncing off my chest. I am only just aware of the scream inside my ear because the blows are dizzying, and I am falling into the teeter. The place between the asleep and awake, and I like it there.

"Submit, and the pain will stop!" Damon barks.

It has stopped, hasn't it?

"Fuck…you."

The high-pitched clack of the back handed slap to my cheek has my ears ringing in an instant. My neck jerks from left to right with every stroke, and I am not on the teeter anymore. The sting is burning, white hot and eye watering. It hurts, there is no denying it, and while I try to choke out the scream with every lash, the cry escaping my lips grows louder and louder until my vision begins to blur.

"Submit, and the pain will stop."

I taste iron and spit blood, my chest heaving for breath. I try to make it look like I am considering it, like the pain is too much while I use the stall to catch my breath. Damon lifts my face using a fist full of my hair, his eyes squinting in questioning. My answering smirk infuriates him, and he growls in frustration. He lashes out, fists pummelling my face.

Thump… Thump.

"Damon, stop! Damon, she has resisted!" Nicole yells.

Thump.

"Damon! Noah will –"

Everything stops.

CHAPTER 18

The Foreplay of a Monster

"Send for Farah. Get her to clean and dress her wounds and then continue with the final stages of resistance. She has exceeded my expectations, but the real test will come in the next two evolutions."

"I don't trust her, Noah," Damon declared.

"I never asked you to. I and I alone will determine the validity of her pledge. To question my insight would be ill-advised to say the least, and it speaks to your lack of trust in me. Be sure you remember that should you choose to question me again," Noah scolds smoothly.

"Understood."

"Good. Now you are dismissed, Damon. I am sure you need to prepare."

My ears could not be more strained as I attempt to hear over the blood pounding through my head. Boots scuff, and the door opens and then closes with a click.

"Nicole, you are to stay for the final stage. It is important that every recruit is given the same treatment. If you suspect that personal feelings are clouding Damon's judgement and that he is breaching the confines of the reconditioning in order to prevent Mckenna's ascension, you are to report to me immediately. I need you to be objective. Can you do that?"

"Of course, Noah."

"Even though she was once your friend?" Noah presses.

"She was my friend because you asked it of me," Nicole counters, her voice even, emotionless.

"Don't pretend you never cared about her, Nicole. I never asked you not to care; I asked if you can be *objective*."

"I haven't let you down as of yet, have I...*Father*?" Nicole snipes, an edge to her tone.

My heart seems to have rolled over inside my chest, a cold hand squeezing the blood out from within, and I cannot breathe.

No...

The sound that follows is unmistakable, the harsh whip of a palm slapping against a cheek followed by a cry escaping Nicole's lips.

"I said, can you be objective?!" Noah hisses.

"Yes, Noah, I can."

At the sound of the door opening and closing again, I choke on the metallic blood pool that is puddled in my mouth, my eyes flying open. My body throbs like a beating heart, the exhaustion heavy and the confusion volume set to maximum.

"Dix..."

"We heard everything; we know. Close your eyes, Max. Rest while you can." Dixy soothes.

***

I like the cold; there is always something you can do to warm up and be cosy. Put on a jumper, sit by the fire. Have a steaming mug of caramel latte, cuddle the woman you love. Being too hot is much harder to regulate. I am happy in 't-shirt weather,' which is usually around 24 degrees. Anything hotter, and I become very British - bitching and moaning about the sweltering, sticky heat that should be reserved for countries that have air conditioning systems in their homes. I don't like the heat, especially not today.

"McKenna..."

"McKenna, wake up."

"Oh, for fuck sakes, she's barely been asleep an hour. Give her a break already," Lambert huffs.

"Ugh...stop. Don't," I mumble.

"McKenna, you must wake..."

"Don't touch me!" I snap.

My eyes shoot open, and I jerk at the contact of an unfamiliar hand cupping my face, the motion sending shooting pains up my ribs. Farah's eyes widen in shock, and she whips her hand away, holding it up in surrender. My heart races, panic kickstarting the speed like a horse out of its gate.

"I-I'm sorry. I need to clean and dress your wounds. My aim of waking you was an attempt *not* to startle you," Farah utters nervously.

"Easy soldier, take a deep breath. You have to let her help you. You are not eating, barely sleeping, and you have taken a beating. In the condition you are in, coupled with the condition that hospital is in, you're a prime candidate for infection," Lambert informs, his monotone voice soothing.

The word infection is the only thing that has me leaning back against the wooden base of the contraption I am bound to. I give Farah a nod, and she smiles, a smile I fail to return. Farah wheels over a cart that is neatly stacked with first aid supplies and two bottles of water. She opens one and douses a pristinely white towel with it before tentatively bringing the towel up to my face. Wary eyes watch me as she cleans blood off my face and neck. I grit my teeth, but I have to admit, the cool water against my battered face feels good. Her eyes dance over my face, and I look away, eyes glazed.

"The good news is, it doesn't look like anything needs stitches, and your nose isn't broken. Can't say the same for Damon's, though," Farah says softly, and I don't miss the amusement in her tone.

My eyes dart, and sure enough, there is a smirk playing on her lips, but I am quick to look away again before she notices.

Interesting...

"You have a couple of cuts that need dressing. I'm going to take an educated guess that your tummy and ribs are probably hurting too," Farah probes, and I flick my eyes to her.

"They don't require attention; it's nothing," I mumble as she attempts to close the split on my lip with a steri-strip. She drops her hands, openly staring at me enough to make me uncomfortable. Eventually, she nods and picks up the other bottle of water.

"You are going to need to drink some of this." She twists off the cap. "Can I?"

My throat is burning with thirst. I can't remember the last time I drank water that hadn't come out of the hose. After I nod, she holds the bottle to my lips and pours it into my mouth. I swallow a few sizeable gulps, and the relief to my throat almost makes me moan. Farah pulls back to let me breathe.

"How much am I allowed to drink?" I ask, and she smiles softly, lowering her voice.

"I would say as much as you can. You're going to need it."

She eyes me with a strange, thoughtful look, and I don't have the energy to figure out what it means, although it sounded ominous. I drink the entire bottle, more out of thirst than following her advice.

"I think you're about done. Is there anything else I can do for you, McKenna?" Farah asks like this situation is completely normal.

A taxi ride home.

"Uh…no. Thank you, Farah."

I watch her leave and sigh a strained exhale of relief as soon as the door shuts.

"Dixy is right, that woman *does* look at you like you are food," Lambert reports, and I snort, which is a mistake with how delicate my nose is right now.

"That's it, dude, just make it creepier," I mumble, and he chuckles.

"You should try to get some sleep, Mac. You have barely caught any in five days."

"I don't think I can; I know who I'll be waking up to next time. I can't… It's harder being surprised than it is to see it coming."

I'm eager for things to move forward. The faster they do, the faster I can go home, but that doesn't mean I am eager for Damon and Nicole to darken the doorway.

Nicole…

"It could be an hour or ten hours before that meat head comes back. You need to take sleep whenever you can get it. I understand why it is hard, though, so - I bought a secret weapon. Or shall I say, *Anna* gave me a secret weapon. I brokered a deal with her; she goes to bed and in exchange, I use the secret weapon if you wake up and won't go back to sleep."

"Uh…what?" I ask, perplexed and a little curious.

There is a moment of silence, followed a rustle of paper, and then, it is all I can do to supress the sob that is fighting to burst out of my throat. Lambert, in his soft monotone utterance, begins reading aloud the first chapter of Harry Potter and the Philosophers Stone. Tears well in my eyes and break free as I let them fall closed.

***

Sleep never came for me, much to Lambert's dismay, but my body hurts. Sleeping standing tied to a wooden board isn't easy regardless of how tired I am. The fear of being woken by Damon got the better of me. Mostly though, I just couldn't switch off from the conversation between Nicole and Noah revolving endlessly around my mind. Did she mean father literally? Or as a creepy mark of cult leader respect? I know I heard him tell her to join her 'siblings' when I first arrived. What if she did mean it literally?

When Damon comes striding through the door, my fears are momentarily disrupted by the sight of his blackened eyes and crooked nose. It takes a lot of effort, but I manage to supress my smirk. His expression is emotionless as he unbuckles the straps to my wrists and ankles. He grabs me from under my armpits, lifts me down to the floor roughly, and then he nudges me in the back.

"Walk over to that wall and stop four feet in front of it. Keep your back to me," Damon grunts.

I follow his instruction. Although it takes me longer than it should because my joints quite literally refuse to move as if they are glued stuck in a straight standing position.

"Now lean forward, hands bracing the wall, fingers touching."

It is then I realise exactly what this is, and my heart drops, because I know I'm far too weakened to withstand this. When I look back at my time in Wales, when I was forced into stress positions by Billy and Jackson, it isn't difficult to recall how hard that had been to endure. This time around, the consequence of failing is death.

You don't have a choice.

I can hear Damon dragging things across the floor, then some flicks of switches, and then he appears in front of me with a bottle of water.

"Resist."

I feel it before he has even left the room. I crane my neck over my shoulder to see five heaters, much larger than the one I kicked across the room. Each of them is glowing molten lava red. A rush of panic sweeps through me, feverish across my skin, my throat instantly parched.

No... Calm your shit and think smart.

This is just another test, and if it is a test, there are answers. There is a way to end it. There has to be more to this than just standing in a stress position in heat. Noah wanted Nicole to watch Damon in case he...what? Over-reacts? He isn't in the room, so does that mean the over-reaction would be to let me bake to death? Will Nicole intervene before that happens? No...I can't and won't depend on some psycho puppet to save me from becoming human jerky. As my mind reels to try to find answers, my arms begin to ache and fatigue very quickly. I can feel the beads of sweat bubbling on my skin, dripping down the back of my neck.

I don't like the heat, especially not today.

I can't help but wonder what would happen if I threw the water bottle over my shoulder quickly and then re-assumed the position. I guess it's wishful thinking that the thing that seemed to get me out of the cold room would also get me out of this furnace. I was in that room for five days. There is no way I or anyone else could survive five days of this, so it has to be shorter. The sweat is starting to sting my eyes, and I scrub them with my shoulder. It is when I move my head I realise that my vision is dragging, and nausea churns.

"Oh no, not today Satan ... You will not puke the only water you have in your system, not smart and not fun." I grimace, taking a deep breath.

That's it, Mac. Keep it light, keep your brain moving.

"Let's play a game, Mac-attack... Easy one to start. Angelina Jolie was in *Mr and Mrs Smith* with Brad Pitt, and Brad Pitt was in *Meet Joe Black* with Antony Hopkins, and uhh..."

"What is she doing?" Lambert asked, chuckling.

"She's fighting," Dixy replies proudly.

"He was in *The Mask of Zorro* with Catherine Zeta-Jones, and Catherine Zeta-Jones was in... Oh, God - you can't fold this... *The Terminal*! Aha! With only the easiest actor to partner up ever – Tom Hanks, ladies and gentleman! Oh, there are so many - bonus points for a movie quote there, Mac-attack..."

I pause just for a moment because I hear the quietest of laughs so bright and captivating that my breath catches in my throat. I love to make her laugh, and I love that even now, when I feel so far away, burning in the depths of hell - I am the cause of that sound.

"Well...I'm going to go with *Castaway* just for the chance to shout 'Wiiiiilllson!'" I yell, at the top of my lungs, and it feels so good. "Tom Hanks was in *Castaway* with Helen Hunt, and Helen Hunt was in *As Good as It Gets* with Jack Nicholson, and Jack Nicholson was in *The Departed* with Leonardo DiCaprio, who shouted 'I'M THE KING OF THE WORLD!' in *The Titanic* with Kate Winslet!"

The chorus of laughs booming inside my ear is enough to rocket fuel my dwindling strength, and I'm laughing too. The release I feel from shouting is liberating and to make them all laugh makes me feel *present* like I haven't lost myself yet. And really, that is all I can hope for.

***

It doesn't feel like nearly long enough before my body begins to abandon the fight. My arms, locked at the elbows, burn from shoulder to fingertip. My legs are shaking, trying to bear my own body weight, and the sweat is pouring off me. I know somewhere in my mind that dehydration has set in because my head is pounding, my tongue feels furry and swollen, and the dizziness and nausea are now constant. Worse than all of this, I have no idea how to get out of this. Try as I have to think about it from every angle, I cannot predict what the winning move is. At this point, my mind is so sluggish, my thoughts are as slurred as my words. A whimper escapes my lips as the hopelessness I feel begins to overwhelm me.

It happens quickly then, as if the sound of my whimper is a signal to my body – *that's enough*. My knees buckle beneath me, my hands slide down the wall, and I fall on my side. The dry heaves of an empty stomach rack through my system. The world is coiling around me, colours and shapes intwining. I grip the floor, grit embedding under my nails so I might not be flung from this revolving floor.

"Don't try and move, kid. You are severely dehydrated; your heart is beating faster to compensate for the loss in blood volume. You need to stay still and calm," Alfred warns.

"Pa…I have…I…"

"No, you listen to your Pa! Stay down!"

He doesn't understand; I can't lay down. I have to get back up. There is no choice. I drag my knees and push on my hands till I manage to wobble on all fours. Then I shuffle forwards, my forehead and hands braced against the wall. Panting breath, sweat stinging my eyes, Alfred's grumbling protests buzzing in my ear, I inch my knee up and plant a foot on the floor. My head spins, a sneaking sweep like my brain is going to sleep without my permission.

And then I feel hands pulling me backwards, wrists hooked under my arms and dragging me across the floor. Exerted grunts are loud in my ear, my eyes straining to focus on the fisted hands jerking in front of my face. A small tattoo the size of a ten pence piece, a music note darkly glaring between her thumb and index finger.

Nicole…

"Turn the heaters off and get Farah, now," Nicole snaps.

"Oh, thank fuck." Alfred groans.

"You don't order me around; this is my evolution, and I say she isn't done," Damon grunts.

"Do you think Noah will agree with the fact she has been in for double the time of other recruits? Should we ask him?"

"You fucking nark."

"I didn't think so. Now go get Farah!" Nicole orders, and then the dragging stops. I am leant back against the wooden bench, the footrest digging into my back.

"Drink. Not too fast; I would rather not see it come back up," Nicole jeers, lifting the bottle of water to my lips and tipping it. It takes a lot of effort not to guzzle it greedily, the icy water extinguishing the fire in my throat.

It is hard to see anything clearly, my vision dragging and swirling. But I can make out her facial expression, and it is completely void of anything I recognise. Still, I feel a rush of gratitude – gratitude I don't want to feel let alone convey. Nicole pours the remainder of the bottle over my face; it feels good but does nothing to stop the ache and spin in my head. I let my eyes close, and I can tell she has left my side. I can hear her dragging the heaters out of the room and feel the draft from the open doorway that she was blocking.

"McKenna," Farah utters, her tone even, and I open my eyes. "I need to get you on the rack and give you a saline drip. Is that okay?"

"W-what is the rack?" I stutter, and she smiles, slightly blushing. Like she finds me amusing when I am not at all trying to be.

"What you are leant against, what you've been stood on. We call it the rack."

Sounds like a medieval torture device. How fitting.

I blink my eyes hard, planting my hands on the floor and turning myself to reach for the rack. Slowly, I pull myself upright, and then the world begins to move, buckling my knees. Hands grab under my armpits to stop my fall, and I have nothing left to protest with, my energy bottoming out. It feels very similar to when Dix drugged me except my eyes are wide open with no sleepiness tugging them closed.

"Nicole…a hand?" Farah grunts.

More hands grab at me, and the panic begins prickling in my chest. But its seconds before I am held against the rack, strapped back in place, and then the hands release me. My head has never been heavier, my neck muscles incapable of holding it up.

"Okay, McKenna, you're going to feel a slight scratch; it's just me placing the IV," Farah informs, the scratch in quick masterful succession, and I note she must be well practiced because I hardly felt a thing.

"Can't we lay her down?" Farah hisses.

"Not until she moves to the next phase; no special treatment. You know that," Nicole deadpans.

"What about unfair treatment? No recruit has been in resistance this long. Medically, the final stage of resistance in her condition is – "

"Farah!" Nicole barks, and the room falls silent, the atmosphere icy. "You have treated her, now we should go. Just be on standby for the final stage. That's all you can do," Nicole concludes, her voice calmer.

The door shuts with a click, and my heart plummets.

"Pa…"

"I'm here, you stubborn pain in the arse," Alfred grumbles lightly.

"I w-want to come home," I confess, dry sobs wracking through my chest.

"I know, darling, and you will. I promise."

For once, I wish I could cry, anything to stop the vulnerability I feel, the hopelessness aching in my chest. I am losing my way. To feel this broken and be nowhere near the finish line - it all feels inevitable and impossible.

"You can't promise me that."

"Yes, I can, because I know you, kid. You are exhausted and hurting and scared, but that's usually when you kick the most arse. Do you remember that day in Wales, just before you shipped out?"

I close my eyes, watching it over in the theatre of my mind. I remember the fear, my fingers trembling as I buttoned up my camo shirt. I remember sitting with Alfred, leaning into him and borrowing his strength as time ran down. I remember the affection that washed over Anna's face when she saw us there, huddled together.

"Yeah, I remember."

"Course you do but do you remember what I said?"

My brain is too tired to conjure up that much detail, but it doesn't matter because Alfred soon reminds me.

"I told you that you had no belief in yourself and to borrow mine until you could prove it to yourself. Now, you have even more people that believe in you," Alfred asserts softly.

"That was a simulation, Pa. It wasn't real. I could have said the word at any time, and it would have ended. Here, saying it means getting dead."

"True but…both of the men in that room wanted to hurt you. That wasn't a simulation. You knew that long before I did. You could have said the safe phrase at any time, but you didn't because, for you, failing is never an option. If I know you, saying the safe phrase hasn't even entered your mind, has it?"

I have to laugh, and it feels good to, especially as Alfred laughs right along with me. Silence passes for a while. I can see him in my mind's eye, sipping a whisky, scrubbing his palm over his whiskery cheek. His brow furrowed as he watches the screens.

"Pa, is she…"

"She is holding it together as best she can. But you know Savannah, she doesn't talk to me about that stuff. I know she's missing you a lot; anyone can see that. Mostly she's just… quiet. Like she is somewhere else. I'm guessing that somewhere else is with you."

My eyes close of their own volition, a smile playing on my lips in spite of the heaviness his words bring to my chest because my *somewhere else* is with her too.

"Thank you, Pa."

***

Time has ceased to have any real meaning; I don't know how long it has been since I last spoke to anyone, how long it is since I slept, and I'm definitely clueless as to how long I have been here. My mind is splintering, I know that much. My thoughts are barking and unorganised, like a drunk man trying to tell a story in a pub. Tiredness is playing with my mind. I don't know how long I will be here; I know that time is passing. However slow, it is still passing. How much of it will pass? Will I be home before Alfred's birthday? Or Christmas? I have never really put much thought into Christmas. It isn't something I get excited for, but I know Anna does, and that is something I don't want to miss.

Time is passing. I think the drip bag is helping; things feel less screwy. I watch the drip bag slowly drain down. I can't help but wonder how so much liquid can be syphoned into my body, and yet, I have no need to pee. The thought makes me chuckle and then giggle, and then I can't stop laughing.

My ribs aching, my eyes watering, pure ridiculous hysteria. The feeling in my chest is like being tickled relentlessly by invisible fingers causing uncontrollable, nonsensical, deep belly laughs. Then I hear laughs inside my ear, and it only fuels the delirium.

"What is she laughing at?" Lambert manages, his laugh deep and throaty.

"Not a Scooby Doo…Max? Where's the punch line?" Dixy giggles.

The door flies open, and Damon, Farah and Nicole enter, and while I know I should stop, the laughter still bursts from my throat, unstoppable. My eyes fix on Damon's.

"Hello darling!" I blurt, and Nicole snorts a laugh while Damon's jaw tightens.

Farah approaches me. I watch as she slides the needle out of my hand, presses a wad of cotton wool firmly in its place, and tapes it down. I look up her to thank her and find that her eyes are ringed in dark red, and her lip is split and glowing with red blood. Her eyes looking anywhere but at me.

The laughing stops.

"I hear someone was a little dehydrated. How about now? Still *thirsty*?" Damon asks, a smirk playing on his lips.

The hairs rise on the back of my neck. The look in his eyes is so familiar; I have seen glints of it in his eyes before, but never to this extent. This is his final showdown, his final chance to break me. Even if I hadn't overheard enough of Nicole and Farah's conversation to tell me this, his eyes tell me all I need to know. Sadistic eyes, predators' eyes, with a look of anticipation at the pleasure of playing with his food before he eats it. The foreplay of a monster who enjoys inflicting pain and inciting fear.

Don't let him have it.

"Not especially but if you are offering, I would love a Jack and Coke," I retort, keeping my face slack, but the fear inside is frenzied no matter how much I try to hide it. I am all too aware of how much he wants to break me, how much he doesn't want me to ascend. He doesn't want me to be a member of The Culling. He won't be happy till I am dead.

The question is – why?

"I have learnt a lot about you," Damon presses, ignoring my jibe.

"I'm touched."

"I wouldn't be. None of it was anywhere near as impressive as you seem to think you are."

"And yet you took the time anyway."

Damon takes some measured steps forward till he is stood a foot or so in front of me. Nicole doesn't move, her eyes are staring off, distant, bored.

"I did. You see, I have a *thirst* for knowledge, and with someone with a body as mutilated as yours, I saw it fit to do my homework. Make sure I knew exactly how to get beneath that ugly skin of yours," Damon muses, his index finger running down my stomach through the gap in my open shirt.

The panic is instant. My fists clench and I jerk against the restraints. Damon's smile grows, and it is all I need to know I was right; he is getting off on this.

"No, that would be too easy. I could inflict pain you can't even imagine. Hurt you in ways even your nightmares couldn't dream up. I could take you, enter you, split you open, just like the men on that boat did. I'd have to put a bag over your head, of course. Think of someone less repulsive, but with enough imagination, I'm sure I could get it done."

My body tenses, and I flinch as Damon's eyes warp, and all I can see is Tomasz, my head beginning to swim. I need to ground myself, but I have nothing; I can do nothing. I look down at my hand, my thumb and index finger in a hard press, knowing Dixy can see. Sending her a mayday.

"I hear you, Max. Uhh…I never told you, I've wanted to for a while, but you know us – feelings aren't our strong suit. I…used to have a little brother. He was my best friend, and while I was gone, stuck in that place I told you about, h-he died. He was brave and funny, and he challenged me, pushed me to accept myself. Love myself. I miss him every day…" Dixy's voice is soft, pained, and I feel a pang deep in my chest. How useless of a friend I am to have never even asked about her family, "What you should know, w-what you should hear, is that his name was Max."

And just like that, Tomasz eyes disappear.

It has never been so hard to keep my mouth shut. I'd give so much to say thank you to her for being the friend I didn't know I needed. Instead, I thank her in the only way I can when I smile as I look up at Damon. My voice unshaken, my head clear.

"I am sure you could. I'm sure the only way you can get it up is with the thrill of taking it from women who would otherwise laugh at you and your limp dick."

The answering giggle inside my ear tells me she *knows*.

His answering glare tells me I'm going to pay.

"I imagine that a dirty dyke like you wouldn't understand what it is to be *wet* for a man. I'm going to fix that because I've figured it out," Damon mutters lightly, and then his hand hurls towards my throat, his fingers squeezing. "Someone like you will take pain after pain, because deep down, you are a scared little girl who is terrified of dying. See, I believe that scares you more than anything. So, what better way to test your resistance then…" Damon leans in, his grip tightening, his breath hot on my face. "Killing you over and over again. *Drowning* the breath inside your lungs and then pulling you back, right before you die."

I choke but do not drown, I drown but do not die.

I know the terror that has gripped me is evident in my eyes from the satisfied glint that flashes in his. Damon turns away, dashing out the room, and my widened eyes trail after him. My ears ring, my heart flies, and I want to cry out, scream like a child.

"Fuck," I curse, barely audible.

Damon reappears. In one hand, a smaller, thinner hose. In the other, a towel. The panic kicks up yet another gear, every inch of me trembling.

"Lambert, get Anna; we are going to need her," Dixy orders.

What? No!

"Ahem, ahem!" I signal no.

"Max, you need an anchor! No one anchors you like Anna; you can be mad at me later. I need you to focus, ground yourself. You *can* do this. All of us are here. *Use* us."

There is no time to argue. Damon stands inches from me, watching. Marvelling at my fear, fear I have no power to hide. Damon leans in, reaching for something out of my sight. I hear a clank, and the rack lunges backwards till all I can see it the ceiling. The trembles intensify, my body vibrating against the wood, my chest heaving rapidly in and out as if it knows there are limited breaths left to take.

"Anna, keep her in the now. Whatever it takes!" Dixy commands.

"What is happening? Oh, God…"

Damon looms above me, the smile on his face vile as he lowers the towel over my mouth.

"Anna!" Dixy yells.

"M-mac, do you remember the first time we danced? It was at the warehouse. You hugged me for the first time; you were so scared. I remember how hard it was not to hold you closer, to let you take your time because I had wanted your touch for so long. It felt better than I had ever imagined it could. And then when you let go…you looked so alive, so happy. You ran over to the laptop and hit play…"

Damon grips my chin in a vice-like grip, his eyes alight and gleaming, his stare cold-blooded, and his smile hungry. I try to focus on Anna's voice, on her words, her gorgeous gravel tone.

"Hose," Damon grunts.

"I couldn't stop laughing, so goofy and so God damn cute. You pulled me to you, and you danced with me to our song." Anna chokes on a sob, and then her words fire, impassioned and sure. "Now, I need you to remember the last time we danced. It was magical. Like we could have been dancing on our tenth anniversary. And yet, I knew even if we were, you would still look at me in a way no one ever has. Go to that place, Mac. Dance with me. Dance with me and never stop."

I can see it so clearly. The gold glitter to her eyes, emerald-green, hypnotically translucent in the fire light. I can smell her candy-like perfume, feel the warmth of the fire on my legs as I hold her, sway with her.

"You can see it, can't you? I know you can; I can see it too. Stay with me there, then come home and kiss me till we fall asleep," Anna rasps, her voice low and needy, wanting. The sound brings an assault of butterflies in my chest, forcing me to inhale a deep steadying breath.

Then, the water fills my mouth.

My breath held, my eyes dazed, I hold the memory, gripping it as tightly as my fists are clenched. The taste of her lips, the sound of her laugh, the feel of her fingertips light on my face. I stay completely still, holding the memory, holding my breath, holding Anna. The water is icy cold in its relentless flow, and I am grateful for it because I like the cold, especially today. It is starting to hurt, my held breath slowly escaping my lips. The sheer pleasure radiating from Damon's face is sickening. My ribs are being pulled apart, chest fit to explode, and then I can't stop it. The gasp is small, but it is enough. Water catches in my throat, and I choke, my head bucking up and side to side.

The bench lunges upright, water spluttering from my mouth. I retch and cough, gasping for the air my lungs so desperately crave.

"Say the submission phrase, and this will end," Damon urges.

"Stay with me, baby. Dance with me and never stop," Anna chants softly.

And then I hear it, clear as day. The unmistakable tang of the guitar riff, its melody loud and rich inside my ear. Sweet Home Alabama plays, and the memory invades, filling every corner of my mind. I meet Damon's stare, cold as ice.

"This is how you get off, isn't it? You limp-dicked psychopath. Well, you might as well stick it in your wank bank because you'll never break me, Damon. You just aren't *man* enough."

I take pleasure in the very short seconds when I see the anger shake him, the tic in his jaw flickering. A few seconds, and then he slams the rack backwards again. The motion is so fast, it swoops in my stomach like I am on a park swing. The song continues to blare in my ear, the hose is turned back on, and I manage to suck in a breath just in time.

The water powers down, and Damon's grip on my cheeks is so tight, it forces my mouth open. My mouth is full of water in seconds. Panic is making it nearly impossible not to gasp. I struggle against his hand, jerking my head from side to side, but his hold is unyielding. Damon rams his elbow into my gut, the blow enough to force my sharp inhale, a gush of water trapping it inside my windpipe.

"What the fuck, Damon?!" Nicole snaps.

The rack lunges upright, but this time I can't clear my airway, choking, gagging, wheezing. Damon watches in amusement, and then Nicole reacts, the movement fast and shocking. I feel a sharp, short, slap thwack against my chest, and then drag in a long, rasping breath. The inside of my throat and chest are burning and aching, a deep whimper leaving my throat with every breath. Damon's face is a mask of fury. He lunges for Nicole, hand around her throat, and he slams her against the wall.

"Interfere again, and I'll put you on the rack when I'm through with her," Damon spits, and then he turns back to me, walking back to the spot he left me in. "Still thirsty? Or are you going to use the submission phrase?" Damon jeers, his face smug.

"I… am…" I struggle, my head bowed and bobbing.

"Yes? Say it, McKenna. *I am a dirty dyke*. Say it, and this will end."

"Oh, fuck. I… am…*sorry*, but could you get out of my face? Your breath is fucking dyer." I look up, grinning with mirth before spitting in his face.

Damon throws himself against me, his body impacting hard enough to wind me. He grips my face and runs his tongue up my cheek before ramming it into my mouth. My insides revolt, and the panic surges. Anna growls inside my ear, and then fury surges through me. I bite down till he screams in my mouth, jerking his face away while his lip is clenched between my teeth. His blood salts my mouth, his fist pounds into my gut, and I release. Gasping for breath, I spit blood, repulsed by its presence in my mouth. Damon is spitting too, his mouth pouring with blood in a satisfyingly fast flow. The anger flowing though me is intoxicating, fizzing through my blood, pulsing in my heart. Fuelled by the hate the mere sight of Damon now brings.

Burn, burn, burn.

I need this to be over; I am running on empty. My body weakened and my mind fracturing, memories jarring in my mind. I don't want to wait for whatever is coming. I am done waiting. It always comes down to this. Billy, Jackson, Jakub, the mala suka man, Tomasz. When it came right down to it, their undoing was their loss of control. A loss of control I forced by provoking them. While I know I should be scared, and a part of me definitely is, all I can feel is hate. Pure, clean, cutting hate overriding everything. A hatred so strong, it is making my hands shake.

"You know, Damon…" I gasp, spitting once again. "For someone who regards me as nothing, you sure are threatened by me. All of this to break me, to stop my ascension!" I pause, my laugh dark and incredulous. "All you have really done is show me how fucking weak *you* are! Really when you think about it, doesn't that make *you* a scared little boy?"

"Max, what the hell are you doing?!" Dixy snaps.

"She's ending it," Alfred grunts grimly.

"So come on, *big man*, get it over with! Because I will die before you come close to breaking me!" I yell, lunging against my restraints, a feral snarl bursting from my mouth.

It is like he is moving in slow motion. My body is tensed, bracing for the impact, but it feels like it is taking so long to hit. A cold numbness spreads through me like I am floating through this weird zone of shock. I barely feel the impact when he ploughs into me, blood spilling from his mouth, his pupils blown, a vein throbbing down the centre of his forehead.

"Then you will die, Mckenna," Damon utters softly, so softly it almost sounds affectionate, and my skin crawls.

"Wouldn't be the first time, and I am willing to bet it won't be my last."

Damon slowly leans the rack backwards, his eyes on mine every second. After all the malice I have seen from them, the benign calm in them now is somehow worse. The rack clicks back, and he looms over me again, his expression relaxed as his eyes roam my features thoughtfully. My chest begins to hitch, the speed building in my breaths, and then he looks at me, eyes still soft and unthreatening, as soft as his voice.

"I am guessing you are not accustomed to deep throating?"

I don't make the connection quick enough. I guess it wouldn't have mattered if I had. A cold fist of understanding squeezes the breath out of me as Damon prises my unsuspecting jaws open and rams the hose into my mouth hard. The force of it hitting my throat makes me gag. Then the water flows fast and icy down my throat, paralysing it in seconds, and I thrash wildly. The only sound is Anna screaming inside my ear, and the pain of it is so much worse than anything I have endured. So much so, I fall still.

"Get her out! Hold on, Max! Hold on!" Dixy yells. "Don't you fucking give up!"

I choke but do not drown, I drown…

"Fuck! Damon! You are going to kill her!" Nicole shrieks. "Damon if you don't stop, Farah will get Noah. Farah…Farah!?"

My limbs jerk even though they feel as though they are made of sponge. The corners of my vision darkens, and I let my eyes fall closed because his face isn't the last I want to see. I am inside the teeter between asleep and awake, and I like it here. I don't know why I ever worried I wouldn't be able to see it. Why I felt the need to try and memorise every perfect line and curve. Her face is so easily summoned while I balance on the teeter. Gold glittered, emerald eyes, thick rusty red hair, warm ivory skin, a bright disarming smile… Everything my heart beats for.

And just like that, the teeter shatters.

Anna…

What my heart beats for…

I have to keep my heart beating.

"She's not breathing. Get her on the floor now!" Farah orders.

I'm not?

Pain, crushing pain compressing my chest in a thumping, rhythmic beat. Pressure aching inside of my throat. If I am not breathing, why does it hurt? If I am not breathing, why am I scared? If I am not breathing, why can I hear? I need to open my eyes; I need to open them and breathe right now.

Oh God, where are my eyes?

"Come on, Max, breathe! Don't you do this; you are not going to do this! We are waiting, just fucking breathe!" Dixy shrieks, her voice broken.

I am trying. Don't you know I am trying?

Thump, thump, thump, thump.

"Breathe!" Farah yells.

"Dixy, you have to do it!" Lambert barks.

"Don't you think I know that?! The moment I push that button, I risk them seeing the watch shock her. It will blow her cover, and then she is fucking dead anyway! I have to time it; they are giving her chest compressions. Look at the heartrate monitor," Dixy yells.

Thump, thump, thump, thump.

"Mac! Come back to me. You promised! And I am here, just like I said I would be. Please baby, come back to me!" Anna cries.

I don't know how; why won't anyone tell me how? The fear and need build in my chest so much I want to scream. Like I can hear my life slipping away, hear their voices growing further away, and I'm useless to stop it.

Thump, thump, thump, thump.
Jerking, jolting, bitter pain,
Writhing, splintering, silent screams,
Burning, glaring, cold and hot,
Blowing, hissing, whispering storm,
Throbbing, pulsing, frenzied rush,
Yanking, stretching, in and out,
Brazen, glowing, blinding light.

CHAPTER 19

In Her Eyes

"Pa! Let me go!" I shriek, struggling out of his grip.

"Alright, alright… Savannah, take a breath, I'm –"

Raking my hands through my hair, I turn on him, anger seething so hot in my chest, I don't know what to do with it. I am trembling with it.

"Don't you… How *dare* you kick me out of that room?! Mac could be dying right now, and –"

"Exactly! That is something you can't unsee! I'm trying to protect you. Do you really think Mac would want you to see that?" Alfred grovels, rubbing his hand nervously over his whiskery cheek.

"This isn't about what Mac would want. She has a hose…" I bite back the sob. "She won't know if I am there, but I will! I could lose her forever, and you are taking away what could be my last moments with her. My last chance to be there for her. I promised her I would never leave her when she needed me again! What if it was Nan?!"

Low blow, instant regret.

I see the pain in his eyes as it crumbles his resolve, and I don't wait for an answer. I dash past him, pounding into the barn door. Dixy is on her feet, yelling at the screen, her fist pounding into the table.

"Come on, Max, breathe! Don't you do this; you are not going to do this! We are waiting, just fucking breathe!" Dixy shrieks, her voice broken.

I stumble into the desk, knees buckling. The screen is blank; her beautiful eyes are closed. The sharp pain ripping in my chest is breath-taking. I cannot move, I cannot…anything.

Please, baby…

"Dixy, you have to do it!" Lambert barks.

"Don't you think I know that?! The moment I push that button, I risk them seeing the watch shock her. It will blow her cover, and then she is fucking dead anyway! I have to time it; they are giving her chest compressions. Look at the heartrate monitor!" Dixy yells.

My head whips to the next screen, and I watch as her heart pounds unevenly. The readings spike high with every compression then plummet, immediately flatlining. I turn to find Dixy looking at me, her eyes wide, brimmed with red and questioning, pleading. My eyeline roams to see her finger hovering over the button. The button that has stared me in the face for two weeks now. The button I had convinced myself we would never have to use. My eyes dart back to Dixy as I lay my hand over hers, and she nods, the movement barely visible.

My heart pounds so hard I am convinced it could pound for us both. I watch the screen with my eyes and Farah pounding Mac's chest in my mind. My hand trembles on top of Dixy's while hers remains steady. I want to scream at the screen. I want to tear away Farah's hands as much as I want her to pound even harder into Mac's chest. I feel Pa's hand, strong and warm on my shoulder. The blip on the screen blurs in my tears, I feel Dixy tense beside me, and I know I only have seconds.

"Mac! Come back to me. You promised! And I am here, just like I said I would be. Please baby, come back to me!" I beg, the words burst from me, and then Dixy's hand jolts beneath mine.

The barn has never been so silent, so still. Not even a breath can be heard. It's as though time is standing still; a second may as well be an hour. Inside my head I plead… *Please, please, please*. Pa's hand grips harder on my shoulder, and then I realise the strained chant is whispering desperately on my lips for everyone to hear. It is hard to care, to feel embarrassed because I am desperate. Because the idea that this is where it ends, *how* it ends, that I will never again see those haunting eyes or touch that perfect face...

"Sinus rhythm!" Dixy shrieks, her hand suddenly gripping my wrist.

And then time kickstarts, everything happening all at once. I hear coughing, a ragged deep breath, and then, I hear her tiny, haggard voice, and it storms a gush of warmth into my chest.

"Anna…" Mac chokes, and my heart flies, ragged breaths dragging of my own.

"Mac! I'm here; I'm right here. Oh God, you are breathing; please keep breathing." I blurt, tears flowing freely.

The room erupts around me, cheers so thunderous it startles me. The blank screen flickers as Mac tries to open her eyes. Farah and Nicole come into view.

"She's back," Farah breathes, the relief evident on her face.

"Guys, quiet!" I snap.

The barn falls quiet, and my eyes are fixed, unblinking at the screen. Mac's eyes roam over the room, her eyes blinking slow and heavy. I breathe a sigh of relief to see that Damon isn't in the room. Her head jerks forwards, and I wince as she cries out. The sound of her pain, as always, makes my tummy burn and swoop, and I wrap my arms tight around myself.

"You might not want to move, McKenna. I'm almost certain I cracked one of your ribs resuscitating you," Farah warns. "You should rest now; you have a few hours before your next evolution."

A mix of gratitude, anger, and jealousy swirls inside my chest. It is irrational, I know it is, but I hate that I'm not there and Farah is. I also hate the way she looks at Mac because I know that *look*. How can I be both grateful and livid that she broke her ribs? Nicole and Farah get to their feet and leave the room, leaving Mac laid on the floor.

"Ugh, Max, you jerk! You are not allowed to die. That is like - spy rule number one! Did I teach you nothing?!" Dixy jibes, her voice seemingly unaffected. Her eyes, however, tell a different story. Red rimmed from tears and shadowed from little sleep.

"Max?"

Mac brings her wrist up to her field of view, turns the dial, and clicks the face. The sound of the watch clicking is silent, but the next time she clicks the face, it booms through the computer speakers that usually sounds her voice. Lambert dashes forward, grabbing a pen, and scribbling lines and dots onto paper.

"Is that morse code?" I ask, and Lambert smirks.

"It is rather poor morse code. Unless Mac is actually saying, 'I am a liver, I can't heart you.' Her earpiece must have been fried in the defibrillation; we can hear her, but she can't hear us," Lambert concludes, and my heart sinks.

"We will have to use her contact lenses." Dixy sighs and finally sits down; she pulls the keyboard closer and begins to type.

`Max, your earpiece is fried. We can hear you, but you can't hear us.`

"Just as well, I've got a banging headache," Mac jibes, her voice croaky, and I can't help but smirk, because it's just so *Mac* to make a joke right now.

`Glad to see kicking the bucket hasn't dulled your sense of humour.`

"Who said I was joking? Don't rain on my undead parade. I'm a real-life zombie in the set of *28 Days Later*. You wish you were this cool."

Her laugh is tired and easily drowned out by the boom of laughs around me. The relief is astounding, and I can practically feel the weight lifting off of my chest. But now more than ever, I just want her home. I can hear the pain in her voice, and all I want is to soothe it. The need I feel is staggering, and as if she can feel it radiating from me…

"Is Anna there?"

`Of course. We are going to give you guys a minute. Standby.`

"Okay, lets clear out. Anna, try and make her go to sleep. Farah said she had a few hours," Dixy requests, and then one by one, they all leave the barn. I take Dixy's seat, my fingers trembling as they hover over the keyboard.

`It is so good to see your eyes open. I've never been so scared. I thought you weren't coming back.`

"I know. I…could hear you," Mac rasps softly, and I blink, squinting at the screen, my heart hammering hard and slow because that isn't possible.

`What do you mean? You weren't breathing. How?`

"I know, but I heard you asking me to come back to you. I tried to answer you but…I couldn't. Like I was screaming a-and nothing was coming out."

My eyes close of their own accord, a smile playing on my lips even as the lump rises. It shouldn't be possible that Mac heard me, and yet somehow, she did. I take a deep breath and wipe my fingertips across my eyes, a strange giddiness wanting to giggle out of my chest.

`I really must be what your heart beats for.`

Her answering chuckle is delicious, smooth in spite of the obvious rasp of exhaustion. So close to the chuckle that never fails to make me throb. What I would give to feel her lips against mine; I didn't think it was possible to feel such an ache for a person.

`Mac...`

"Yes, princess?"

My cheeks flush; she hasn't called me that in a long time. I both love it and hate it in equal measure, and she knows it. The grin on my stiff cheeks feels alien and welcome.

`Oh, come here and say that ;)`

This time her chuckle is even smoother, a groaning chuckle that I recognise. I can easily picture the knowing, irresistible look in her eyes that accompanies it. It inspires a fluster inside that I am totally weak for. A fluster that has me crossing my legs.

`As if I didn't miss you enough.`

Her chuckle stops, and the screen goes dark, her eyes closing, and I hear her breath huff heavily.

"I miss you and…I hate this. I don't…" Mac struggles. The pain is thick in her voice, and my eyes close in reaction to it just for a moment before I type again.

`Tell me...`

I hear her choke on a sob, and it wrecks me like a punch to the chest. But Mac being Mac, she soon swallows it down. I wait, stewing in the helplessness that I have felt for two weeks now. Utterly powerless.

"I don't know how long I can…I'm so *tired*, and I…" Mac pauses, sucking in a breath, gathering strength. "Whatever is coming next, my body…I am…hurting already."

The weakness she hates to admit is right there, hanging honestly in the air between us. I always feel a mix of pain and privilege at hearing it. Because I know how much it takes her to admit it, to be that vulnerable. And I love that she shares it with me as much as I hate that there is nothing that I can do to make her pain go away.

`I know. You have been so brave baby, but I need you to be brave a while longer. I need you to keep breathing. Keep fighting so you can come home where I can take care of you. Now, I need you to rest; it will help. Can you do that for me?`

The movement in the screen catches my eye, and then I wince as I hear the painful grunt of her trying to roll onto her side. Her eyes still open, I see her hand laying relaxed in front of her face on the dusty ground. Knuckles grazed, purple with cold and trembling. Never have I needed more to reach out and hold it, steady it, warm it between my fingers.

"Anna…" Mac rasps sleepily.

`Yeah, I'm here.`

"Stay till I'm asleep?"

`There is nowhere else I would rather be.`

The tears flow easily then, hot and fast, the sobs deep in my throat. Because she is alive and still my Mac, but there is no telling if or how long she will stay that way.

***

Her breath is heavy and rhythmic, a sound I know well. The sound of her sleeping dreamlessly, and I am grateful for it. The steady beat, loud in the silence of the barn, is making me sleepy. I scrub my fingers into my eyes, trying to press the sleepiness out of them, and then my eyes roam around the barn. It looks completely different now, but the memories are still clear and easy to summon. It feels like so long since we slept here together, even though, in reality, it hasn't been.

My eyes sweep to the pallet bed that Dixy and Lambert now take it in turns sleeping in. I remember waking up there after Mac carried me to it, back in the days where Danni made it impossible for me to sleep. I woke up with the scent of her aftershave all around me, woody and vanilla. Just for a moment, I thought I would wake up to find her there. So much so I didn't want to open my eyes to find I was wrong. Then my eyes flew open because I heard her scream after Danni knocked her off the platform.

The memory is enough to make me want to look away, and when I do, I catch sight of the stacks of hay piled up and moved to the side of the barn. Goosebumps race across my skin; I can see it so clearly. The tightness in her jaw, the fear in her downcast eyes as she took her top off and revealed herself to me. I remember how much she trembled as my fingertips traced every scar. Battle worn, brave, and beautiful. The self-control it took me to resist kissing her all over. The shame she was carrying was so out of balance with how much I wanted her, it was almost funny.

"You are somewhere happy," Dixy says hesitantly, and I blink.

"Uh, yeah. Just remembering something."

Dixy walks over to the desk and sits opposite me, turning her body to face me a little. There is still this awkwardness between us, and at this point, I am not even sure why. The days of me being jealous are long gone, yet the air between us is always slightly thick.

"It looked like a happy something; I'm sorry I interrupted it. I just…I wanted to check on you," Dixy utters awkwardly, and my head snaps up, attention grabbed.

"On me? Why?" I ask, and Dixy sighs, her eyes glancing up very quickly and then back down to her lap as she tugs at an elastic band that hangs loosely around her wrist.

"Well, because Max would want me to and because this is hard for me. If it is hard for me, I can only imagine…" Dixy pauses, her brow furrowing. "I know we don't exactly get on, but that isn't because I want that or because I don't care."

Dixy is statue still, her head still bowed down, and I am glad because it gives me a few seconds to adjust this really unexpected moment. To try to think of what on earth I am supposed to say.

"I don't have a problem with you, Dixy. I mean – you haven't always made it easy." I grimace, an awkward laugh bubbling in my throat, and she grins a little as she looks up.

"I know. I'm sorry for that. It isn't easy for me to show I care or express it. Even this is hard, I …"

I feel a pang. For once, I see that it really isn't easy for her. I turn my chair towards her and watch as she starts flicking the band on her wrist again.

"Mac told me a little about that. She said you have a story that makes it hard for you to show you care. Since she did, it hasn't been a problem for me."

"That's all she said?" Dixy asks, looking up again.

"She would never tell someone else's story. I trust her; that's all she needed to say," I assure her, offering a soft smile. She returns it, and this time, she doesn't look away.

"My story is quite similar to Max's, only nowhere near as bad."

But bad enough.

My stomach clenches as I feel a pang of sadness for her and understanding. I hold her gaze with difficulty because her eyes look haunted. But I hold it anyway because suddenly, I feel like a complete arse.

"I'm sorry, Dixy. I had no idea."

"Don't be. I can't say I'm glad it happened, but I wouldn't be here if it hadn't. I guess, because of my story, it's hard not to be protective of Max. If I've stepped on toes, I never meant to. For what it is worth, it isn't just Max I care about. All three of you have got under my God damn skin, and I kind of hate you for it. Stupid-plaid-shirt-wearers." Dixy smirks, playfully scowling, and out of nowhere, the laugh bursts from me quickly and easily.

As we laugh, I feel the tension between us dissolve, and it is a relief. I never expected Dixy to be so honest, but it's good to understand her more. She is offering an olive branch, and I am genuinely happy to take it. As the laughter quietens, I find my eyes flicking to the screen for the millionth time, checking Mac is still asleep, and my eyes don't leave it as I speak.

"It was harder at the time - seeing you be there for Mac because I could see her struggling, but Danni was stopping me going anywhere near her. How I felt wasn't just about you. It was about me feeling like I was watching her slip away, and I was powerless to stop it. She told me how you helped her; I've always been grateful that you were there for her when I wasn't."

I rub my eyes, elbow on the desk, and then lean my chin against my fist. My chest is heavy, as though there is an elephant sat on it. It is like a constant nervousness waiting for whoever is going to enter the room and wake her next.

"You were there for her; you were protecting her. I know you probably feel powerless right now, but you're not. You just...*get her*, and she really needs that right now, Anna. I know we are all supposed to be keeping you out of this room. I know Mac doesn't want you to have to watch this but selfishly, I'm glad you are here because no one can break through to her like you can."

***

Four hours, six cups of coffee, and two false alarms later, I hear Farah's voice through the computer speakers and instantly, my heckles are up, any tiredness dissolved. Twice, I mistakenly took Mac talking in her sleep to be her waking up. Mac's eyes begin to open, and Farah comes into view; she is knelt at Mac's side with a neatly folded pile of towels on top of her lap.

"Sorry to wake you, but I've come to take you for a shower before you begin the next evolution," Farah explains.

Heat radiates across my chest and onto my cheeks. I'm very much glad that Mac can't hear the growl fleeing my throat right now. Mac doesn't say anything. Instead, she pulls her arm beneath her and pushes herself upright, a pained grunt escaping her mouth as she goes. By the time she is on her feet, she is breathless, but she follows Farah out of the room and into a hallway. Mac walks slowly, a metre or so behind Farah, and her eyes dart, taking in every detail of her surroundings. With how grim that hospital looks, it is hard to imagine a working shower in the place. Let alone one that wouldn't make you feel dirtier for being in it. They pass through two corridors, then Farah stops outside a door and turns to face Mac, waiting for her to catch up.

"There are some clean clothes in there. They will be too big, they're Noah's, but they are clean. You have twenty minutes; do you need a hand?"

Oh, you doe-eyed, mega-slut.

"I can manage," Mac mutters, taking the towels out of Farah's extended hands.

The bathroom is bright, floors and walls gleaming in what is obviously brand new, bright gloss-white tiles. Mac's eyes roam, taking in the place; it isn't massive, but it is modern. There is a double shower cubical with a glass door, a toilet, and two bathroom sinks below a mirror that stretches the length of the wall. Mac stumbles forwards, her eyes on the sink. She frantically turns the tap lever and then holds her mouth under it, gasping and gulping the water down.

And then I choke, my hands flying up over my mouth as she slowly straightens up in front of the mirror and looks at her own reflection. Her face is bruised, her cheeks hallow, her lips chapped, and her eyes dark and pained. What is left of her clothes seem to be hanging off her, covered in dirt and dust. Mac looks at her own eyes; it is almost like she is looking right at me, and then she smiles a soft smile.

"I've looked worse," Mac mutters with a wink, and I chuckle. God, I can't help but find her strength sexy. Then, I see her thoughtful frown in the reflection, and then she brings up her finger to her ear, then her eyes, and then tugs on her shirt.

`It's okay; it's just you and me.`

I watch as her eyes dart to read the message and then back at her own eyes in the reflection again. She lifts her hand, pointing her index finger to her eye, then at her heart, then at the mirror. I giggle a teary giggle, my chest warming so powerfully, it makes me sigh shakily.

`I love you more.`

She looks away as she smiles and then takes a deep breath. I never thought there could be a scenario where watching her get naked would cause me anything but overwhelming arousal, but I was wrong. As she eases what is left of her plaid shirt off of her shoulders, the true scale of what she has endured is revealed. Both sides of her ribs are black and blue, her wrists are raw from restraints. There are cuts and bruises up both arms, and there is obvious weight loss. All I can feel is pain and anger. Why do people keep hurting her? She turns away from the mirror quickly, I hear the shower turn on and the water beat down. My heart drags as that powerless feeling engulfs me again.

***

The blue hooded cloaks give me the creeps, and I can't stop the shiver from running down my spine as I see them again. Just like when Mac first arrived, she finds herself back in that large room stood before Noah and his four hooded disciples. After her shower, Farah took Mac to an equally bright, clean, and shiny kitchen. She gave Mac a cheese sandwich and a cup of coffee. As relieved as I am to know she has eaten, it all seems a bit odd, and I can't help but be distrustful. The last time Mac was given water, they roasted her in a hot room.

Noah steps forward, this time donning a light blue suit, and the hooded figures around him take down their hoods. Immediately, Mac's eyes dart to Damon, who isn't hiding his contempt, and then she glances back to Noah just as he speaks.

"Mckenna, congratulations on your ascension. It pleases me that you have made it this far. Although I confess, I never really doubted that you would. You possess enduring strength, regardless of the *physical* pain that is bestowed upon you," Noah muses, his tone as leery as ever.

"I am grateful for the opportunity to prove myself," Mac imparts, her voice stronger than it was but still not the honey-smooth tone that I miss.

"There will be plenty more opportunity for that. The next evolution is called *cleanse.* And it is so named because just like the world must be cleansed of weakness, you must be cleansed of your weaknesses in order to ascend to the final evolution. Cleanse yourself of all selfishness; dissolve the *you* and become an *us*. You will be cleansed of the preconceived notions of what you have been programmed to believe is right and wrong. Because only then will I know that you possess the fortitude to make the hard sacrifices to protect your siblings and carry the responsibilities you will shoulder in saving our world."

My hand grips the arm of the office chair, my mouth running dry, fear jittering inside my chest.

"T-that sounds like brainwashing. Can they…" I gasp, turning my head to look at Dixy.

"No. They will try to manipulate her, twist her beliefs, but she has had a shed ton of training on this. I'm not worried about that," Dixy explains, trying to soothe, but the look in her eyes tells me she *is* worried.

"Then what are…" I begin, and then it dawns on me. "Her flashbacks. Oh, God, and we can't even talk to her." I groan.

"I know. We can still type her messages, but ultimately - it's down to Max."

I look back up at the screen and watch as they take her away. No words being exchanged, she is being led by a thin, jumpy-looking guy who needs a haircut. I know how tired she must be; we have all seen how little she has slept or eaten. Damon put her through so much her heart stopped. Yet somehow, suddenly I have no doubt that the magic about her, that spirit…the king of the world inside of her – will win.

"I have seen her battle with her mind so many times, and only once did she break. Even then, she didn't break till the battle was over. It's as if she can't give up; it just isn't a part of her. If she breaks, it won't be until she's home, until she feels safe to. There isn't anything they can do to stop her," I assert, and Dixy nods, the stress in her expression loosening a little.

Mac is taken back to the hot room. She enters, her eyes falling on the rack, and the weedy man gestures with his hand towards it. Mac climbs on the rack and watches as his thin veiny hands buckle the restraints to her wrists and ankles. He is young, maybe mid-twenties, and his eyes shift around nervously.

"My name is Ethan, and this is my evolution," Ethan shares, his voice high and nasal.

"Hello, Ethan, and how do you plan to torture me today?" Mac asks lightly, amusement in her tone.

Ethan's face flushes red, and he runs his hand through his flopping fringe. His stance shifting from one leg to the other.

"I don't appreciate being mocked, McKenna. I'm not here to torture you; I am here to educate you."

"I can see this is going to be fun. But no math, okay? I suck at math, and I'm hungry, which means I'm cranky. You don't happen to have a pizza in your pocket, do you? Because I am sure you will have my brain growing in no time - *if* there is pizza. None of them pizzas with a forest on top, and hold the olives because they taste like Saddam Hussein's left flip flop."

Dixy and Lambert are in fits of hysterics on either side of me while I grin smugly because there she is, proving me right. Using her magic, fighting.

***

It's been six days since we've really heard from Mac. The cleanse evolution is its own brand of torture known as sensory disorientation. It turns out that 'education' is blasting high pitched hissing noises into her ears through headphones or repetitive screams and chants. It was like that for two days solid with a hood over her head. In darkness and unable to read the messages we typed into her contact lenses.

Ethan then stepped it up, playing disturbing videos through a virtual reality headset. It wasn't long before I couldn't watch. While everyone wants to turn off the sounds of the screams and chanting and switch off the grotesque images burning into her eyes, we have to stay connected in case she reaches out.

Every morning, noon, and night, Ethan recites mantras about weakness, about letting go of McKenna Scott. About how doing the right thing doesn't always feel good but that it's her own weakness standing in her way. That she is responsible for blocking her own path to her ultimate potential. Every couple of days, he allows her a few hours rest, still strapped to the rack with the hood over her head. At first, she talked to herself, played games with herself. But the sheer exhaustion was so clear in her voice, and she got quieter and quieter till finally, she fell silent. She is fighting, but there is only so much a person can be subjected to before they begin to withdraw from reality. With nothing but Ethan's voice, darkness, and disturbing videos and sounds to guide her, how long can she hold on?

The fire crackles, but it is not enough to keep me warm; the weather has become bitter, that type of cold that hurts your bones and burns your skin. I sit on Mac's chair wearing her cargo jumper. I watch the glow of the fire reflecting on the gold bangle on my wrist as I slide it round and round.

"Thought you had left already?" Alfred grunts, sitting down in the chair opposite.

"Soon. Dixy is programming the feed into my phone so if Mac talks, I'll be able to message her lenses."

"I'm surprised you haven't tried to do that yourself, computer wizard that you are," he teases, and I smirk. "Oh, so you did try?"

"Dixy has very extensive firewalls; it is MI5 software. I was never going to crack that, Pa."

"I am not going to pretend I know what that means. Are you sure you want to go back there on your own?"

I sigh, my suspicion he wouldn't be happy about it - confirmed. It has been twenty days since I woke up in the apartment without her. Twenty days wanting to go back but not wanting to leave the screens, to leave her.

"I have things I need to do there. The food will all be off. I bought food to replace it, some first aid supplies, and some Christmas decorations for when she comes home. I don't want her to come home to a mess," I list and then look away from the sadness in his eyes.

It's not a lie. I plan to do all of those things, but it isn't what is compelling me to go back. It is Mac's apartment; she never actually asked me to move in. But since she gave me a key and we spent so much time there, it feels like ours. Over time, more of my things have made their way there. My clothes, my favourite books. Even my smoothie maker has found a home on the kitchen side despite the fact Mac hates smoothies. I want to be there, just for one night, in our bed, surrounded by our things. Our memories.

"I miss her too," Alfred huffs. "It doesn't sit well; she is an hour away and I…I said we were in this together…me and her till the end, that I'd have her back. I don't feel much like I've got her back. I said I'd look after you, she asked me to, but I don't feel like I'm doing a good job of that either. You don't…you're so quiet. You don't talk about it, you just…"

I feel a pang of guilt, and it forces me to meet his gaze, his eyes full of concern.

"I'm sorry, Pa. I know you miss her too. You have got her back; she knows that. You are her hero, you know that, right?" I assure, and he smiles, looking into his coffee cup. "I don't mean to be quiet. I just – I want her back, I want her safe, with me. I want it over, I want my life, with her, *our* life."

Alfred looks up, his smile bright, his eyes glistening.

"You sound pretty sure about that." He grins quizzically, and it seems so weird like I am missing the punchline to a joke.

"I am. Why are you looking at me like that?"

Dixy strides out of the barn, interrupting my confusion. She hands me my mobile phone with the promise to call me if anything changes. With the feed uplink streaming to my phone, I can hear Mac at the push of the button and type messages to her contact lenses. It feels like I am holding a lifeline, like I can take her with me, and it means I can finally go home.

***

Christmas is my favourite time of the year. I love that you can drive around and see the lights that people have decorated their houses with, twinkling in the night. From minimalist dangling snowflakes hanging off edges of rooftops, to the full-on Santa's grotto explosions of festivity, I love it all. I love that a lot of people seem to be in merrier spirits as time draws near. People are more polite, brighter, looking forward to family fun, over-indulging in food and days off from work.

The living room has been transformed, and I have taken my time with every detail. The Christmas tree is stood twinkling, bathed in red and gold by the side of the fireplace that now houses two stockings. Beneath the tree are the Christmas presents I have bought for Mac. Even those, I took my time wrapping, getting lost in imagining her face when she opens them. I had fun stringing fairy lights around the spiral staircase because Mac loves fairy lights. It took so many of them that the room is now glimmering in a multicoloured glow that seems to reflect off of every gloss white surface in the living room and kitchen.

The kitchen has been restocked and not a moment too soon because the food in the fridge was undergoing its own green, furry transformation. The first aid supplies have been replenished, so whatever happens, I am prepared for whatever she needs when she comes home. I have given the place a dust and clean, not that it really needed it much because Mac is always military neat and tidy. But I was running out of jobs to do, so I began trying to *find* jobs to do because it felt good to do something for her, anything.

Finally, in the early hours of the morning, after a hot shower, I snuggle down in our bed, and even though I changed the sheets to some festive, thick, soft, red tartan bed sheets, her pillow still faintly carries the scent of her aftershave. I allow myself a moment, a few moments, to indulge in the smell and the memories it inspires.

I remember the first time I really smelt it. She arrived at the farm carrying cakes and coffee. She had been training with Billy and took a baton to the eye. She looked gorgeous, smiling radiantly and wearing new clothes that had me staring at her longer than I should have. I leaned in close to clean and bandage the cut on her eye. So close, her breath tickled my lips, and it was intoxicating. Then I smelt it, that vanilla sweet, woody scent. Somehow managing to be both masculine and feminine and utterly delicious. Just as I dropped my hands, our eyes caught, and I was paralysed by her. I couldn't take my eyes off her face. I was so taken by it; I always had been. Even that first day at The Shard, but with her so close, closer than she'd ever let me be, I couldn't stop my eyes from admiring every perfect inch.

Then I noticed that her eyes were dancing round my face too, and…I liked it. That alone was enough to send goosebumps burning over my skin. But then her eyes paused on my lips, and suddenly, all I could think about was tasting hers. She moved just a fraction, or maybe I just hoped she did, but it was enough to power tingles so strong I felt it all over. Her face has always had a gravity to me, a pull that I couldn't resist but *those lips*. I have never needed to kiss someone so badly.

I had a date with Billy that night, and I spent it trying not to daydream about her because I was sure she wasn't daydreaming about me. I failed; I only wanted her more and more from that moment. And still now, I am taken by her face, intoxicated by her smell, crazy for her lips, and daydreaming about her. Because even though she is mine, I still can't have her.

***

It hasn't been long enough. The heaviness in my limbs and the scratchiness of my eyes squinting at the screen of my phone tells me I have not been asleep nearly long enough.

"Hello," I mumble, my eyes still refusing to open.

"Hey, it's Dixy. Sorry to wake you, but you asked me –"

"What's happened?!" I interrupt, suddenly alert and anxious, which is apparently written all over my voice.

I am on my feet and already scrambling to pull on my clothes awkwardly while still holding the phone, my eyes wearily glancing at the window wall. It is barely daylight.

"It's okay, it's good news but you might want to come back soon," Dixy blurts, and I freeze, one leg in my jeans, one leg out. "She did it, Anna, she fucking did it! She is moving onto the final evolution!"

For a moment, I forget how to make words, my brain disconnecting from my mouth. All I can do is breathe through the sudden palpitations fluttering in my chest.

"Oh God! She…" I choke on a laugh. "Is she okay?"

"She…hasn't spoken much yet; she is disorientated, which isn't a surprise, but I could do with your help bringing her back. She is okay; she just isn't…herself."

"I'm already on my way."

***

I practically run to the barn after breaking every speed limit to get here. Dixy and Lambert are both sat at the desk, and Lambert jumps up to his feet on my arrival. My eyes must say a lot because immediately he holds his hand up gesturing me to slow down.

"She is okay, her stats are okay, but she isn't really talking much. The evolution ended, and Farah gave her a plate of food and a drink, but she hasn't touched it. We are now three weeks in, very little sleep, and now the disorientation they have subjected her to, its …" Lambert pauses, rubbing his fingertips against his temple. "She has withdrawn. What we need is for you to talk to her about things that connect her to what she knows but in short sentences and slowly. After the darkness, virtual reality videos and sounds, her head is probably hurting, and her processing is slow."

I nod, trying to take in all the information as Lambert steps aside, and I see on the screen she is laying on the ground again. It vexes me. Would it be so hard to give her a pillow, a blanket, anything? I can also see the sandwich in front of her and a mug of coffee. I take a seat near Dixy, and she turns my way.

"Has she said anything?" I ask, pulling the keyboard my way.

"Um, when they first took the headset off her, she kept saying, 'my eyes or his,' but she has stopped now. Other than that, she is just answering yes or no or not at all."

I look back at the screen, and suddenly, I don't know what to do. She is always so responsive to my touch; without it, I feel cut off. She can't even hear me. To her, I am just some disembodied text in her eyesight. How can I connect to her that way?

"Do you know why she would say that? I mean, she sounded scared at the time, but now she doesn't sound...*anything*," Dixy presses.

"Yeah, I know exactly what she is saying. That's not the problem. I don't know how to reach her this way. If I was there, if she could see..."

And then it hits.

"Are you okay? You look kind of gawped." Dixy frowns.

"I know what to do." I smile, looking back at the screen.

`Hello, beautiful.`

"Anna?" Mac answers, her voice tiny and unsure.

`Yes, Mac-attack, it's me.`

"Hey..."

`Hey, yourself. What's for breakfast?`

"A sandwich and coffee, but my stomach doesn't want it," Mac replies. She doesn't sound like herself; she sounds wary and childlike.

`What does your stomach want?`

"Monkey tea."

`Okay, so your tummy hurts?`

"Yeah...inside."

"Okay, Mac-thesaurus, how did you get that from Monkey tea?" Dixy snorts.

"Her mum and her drink monkey tea. She would give it to Mac when she didn't feel well. It's *PG Tips*; the adverts have monkeys in them."

`A bit will help. Maybe in a little while.`

I wait for her eyeline to flick up and to the right and back again so that I know she has read the message. Lambert was right; it is taking her longer than usual to read the message like she is having to really try to absorb every word.

`Mac, are you wearing your boots?`

I watch the screen as Mac's eyeline pans down. She is wearing a baggy light blue t-shirt and even baggier dark blue jeans about five inches too long. The toes of her boots are just poking out from the bottom of the trousers.

"The fact that she had to look to see if she is wearing them worries me a little," Dixy mumbles but I ignore it.

`Good, that's good. Now, there is something hidden inside your boot. Do you remember?`

There is a pause, and even though I can't see her face, I can easily imagine the creasing between her eyebrows as she thinks. It always looks quite childlike, endearing. Like I've just told a five-year-old that the world isn't flat.

"Anna's face is in my boot?" Mac askes, the tiniest thread of excitement in her voice, and I chuckle, the palm of my hand rubbing the ache in my throat.

So cute.

`Yeah, that's right. I want you to get it for me.`

Mac shuffles, bending to tug up the trouser leg of her jeans to reach the top of her boot. The action looks like a lot of effort. She grunts and winces and then brings the credit card sized metal disk into view. Her hand is trembling, her breath hitching. A barely audible whimper escapes her mouth.

"Anna, you're a genius," Dixy whispers as if she is intruding on a private moment; she kind of is. "I think you have this under control. I'm going to give you a minute." Dixy smiles, and I am relieved because I was about to ask for that minute. I don't want to openly discuss Mac's fears on screen for everyone to see.

Mac holds the card in one hand, while the other trails fingertips tracing the image of my face. It is gut-wrenching because I can almost feel her doing it. Almost. I look away for a moment, bowing my head and gulping in breaths to collect myself. When I look back up, the image of myself is still there, and Mac is rubbing her thumb up and down the embossed words on the back of the card.

It's just you and me now…

I need you to hear me. I need you to trust me.

Mac Scott… You are NOTHING like him…

There is no monster in those loving eyes…

Look at the photo, at me, and ask yourself…

If you think I'm this light in your life, this source of good…

How could I ever love a monster?

I space out my messages giving her time to read them. It feels too long that she falls silent. Long enough that I am already desperately searching my mind for what else I can say to connect with her. Until the sound of her voice snaps me back.

"Anna…"

Yeah, I'm here.

"I'll be home for Christmas."

***

"Welcome, McKenna, to my evolution," Noah announces. "The final evolution to reach Veritas may be an obvious one, but I consider it the most important and the most *telling*. To scale this final peak, to conquer the triangle of truth, you must prove yourself in telling the *truth*. With the truth comes trust. Without trust, we cannot protect each other, and we have no hope of reaching our goal."

Mac is back in the large room with blue robed psychopaths for company after only two hours sleep. I managed to get her to eat half of the sandwich. The picture worked; she came back to me, almost sounding like herself. She is so close to the end of this, but she is exhausted, and it is obvious that this last evolution is the worst to be tired for. She is sat on the cast iron chair, but this time, she isn't bound to it. Noah is in a royal blue suit, matching the colour of his robed devotees perfectly.

It is the last evolution, but I'm more fearful now than with any other. The truth is what Noah wants, and if he somehow gets it, either he will kill Mac, or the party crasher will. Or at least, she'll try to. I can't quite relax with Agent Holt sat beside me, her eyes trained on the feed streaming into her personal laptop. I never really thought about her watching and listening to every word. I have been so wrapped up in Mac, in trying to endure watching her endure that, I had completely forgotten about the gag order. It was a swift reminder when she informed Dixy she was coming. Dixy, who looked just as apprehensive of her coming as me.

She has the power to order Mac's execution. At the push of the button, a cyanide shot would burst from a needle, piercing the heel of her foot and killing her in minutes. Except I emptied the canister of cyanide. If she gave the order, Dixy would have to follow it; Mac told me that much. What if Dixy disobeyed? Does Lexi have the remote access of the trigger via her laptop? Not that it matters, there is no cyanide left, but I can't help but wonder what it would take to push Lexi to give that order.

"People have and will come after us. The police, the government, even the military. They will always come after revolutionists because they are weak! They fail time and time again because we, The Culling, have trained for decades for this. We have bonded in pain, we have grown in strength, and we have protected each other. We prevail because we trust each other, and we have shared the truth with each other," Noah muses, stepping closer to Mac, his gaze fixed on her, and she is holding it unblinking, but her heartrate is beginning to accelerate. As is mine.

"I expect the absolute truth from you. I expect you to be faithful to me, your siblings, and to our cause. But trust is earned, is it not? It is a respect that is earned...mutually. To do this, I will offer you a truth of my own discovery. A truth that is of benefit to you, a gift of sorts that you will receive if you pass Veritas. I will give you fair warning: I don't look kindly upon those who have declined to accept my generosity."

A gift with a warning label attached. Nice.

"Be candid, prove your intentions pure, and it will be your deliverance. Be deceitful and prove your intent counterfeit, and you, shall, *fall…*" Barrett warns, his grey eyes piercing as he emphasises his point. "We will not leave the fate of the world to happenstance! We are the guardians; we will cull the unworthy! Are you worthy, McKenna Scott?!"

"*Try me!*" Mac booms thunderously, enough to make Noah flinch, followed by the grossest self-righteous grin I've ever seen.

Noah gestures his hand up and out to the side in a lazy wave, and Farah begins marching forwards, holding another small box in her hands. This time it is metal, smooth matte silver, and about the size of a handgun case. My chest tightens; it doesn't take long to learn that anything concealed inside a box in that place is never good. Farah stops just in front of Mac, her arms extended and offering. Noah opens the case; he pulls out a gun very much like the ones MI5 uses to inject earpieces into the inner ear. He holds up the gun resting in his open palm, his finger loose on the trigger.

"I am under the impression that you are familiar with this particular brand of truth serum." Noah muses.

No…

"Damn it!" Dixy snarls. "Lambert, increase the text size by double. We need to make sure our messages are clear for her and centre them. If her eyes quirk up and to the side, Noah will view it as a lying tell."

"On it; I need 30 seconds," Lambert reports.

"Dixon, you are running point on this. Why are you giving your keyboard to Anna?" Lexi asks, her tone noticeably icy.

"I am plugging in an extra for me. Mac responds to Anna. Trust me, Agent Holt, we want her in reserve just in case," Dixy throws back firmly, and I feel my cheeks redden.

"I have no objections as long as Anna can remain *objective*," Agent Holt comments, her eyes on her laptop.

We can't all be ice queens.

"Calling for a visual test, Dix?" Lambert requests, and Dixy types at a speed close to rivalling me.

`We are with you, Max. Read our messages, use our words.`

"Ahem," Mac signals.

"Visual test confirmed," Dixy announces. Her hands are poised, frozen over the keyboard, and her body is arrow straight and statue still. Her eyes focused on the screen.

Mac looks down as Noah grasps her wrist and holds the nuzzle of the gun to it. The blipping rhythm of Mac's heartbeats tempo speeds rapidly. The barn falls silent, making the sound of Noah pulling the trigger even louder and menacing.

Kutissshh.

"With her heart rate going that fast, it won't take long for the serum to take effect," Alfred informs.

"You have experience with this serum?" Agent Holt asks in a hushed voice.

"Not as much as Mac. It slows your ability to think. If you can't think, then it is harder to lie," Alfred explains.

"McKenna, why are you here?" Noah asks.

"I want…to be a member of The Culling," Mac murmurs, her voice sounding as though every word weighs a ton.

"Why do you want to be a member of The Culling?"

"To be…to save the world, to have a family," Mac stutters but recovers.

"You said 'to be' and stopped yourself. What were you going to say?"

Mac hesitates just a second too long. It is barely a second and Dixy taps her keys.

`Safe.`

"To be safe…I want…safe," Mac struggles.

I don't think my body could be more tense staring at the screen, willing Mac to pull through. One false move and everything I know and love will be obliterated.

"Is there any other reason you are here, a reason not to do with joining The Culling?" Noah asks softly.

"Yes."

Oh, God...

"What reason is that?"

"To know my father," Mac mumbles, fast, sure sounding, and the whole barn exhales.

"Oh, well done, Max," Dixy praises, and I'm smiling slyly at the look of adoration washing over Noah's face.

That's my girl.

"Will you serve me faithfully?"

Mac's head bobs down, her eyes shutting, and then opening again. Noah lunges forward; he grabs her by the face, and her heart races again. Noah's expression is demanding, almost desperate.

"Will you serve me faithfully?! Will you die for me?!"

Mac holds his gaze with heavy eyelids; Noah's eyes are wide and maddened. Dixy leans forward to type and then –

"Yes, Noah…I will."

Noah stares into Mac's eyes, still holding her face. He is so close it's unnerving, like he is staring back at me. Mac's blink is slow and dragged, but she keeps her eyes fixed on him as he searches hers. Whatever he is looking for, his eyes seem to glint when he finds it.

"Congratulations, McKenna, that is the end of my evolution," Noah utters softly.

The barn erupts in cheers. I roar a cheer of my own that I didn't know I was capable of. Even Agent Holt is punching the air, her grin wide and her laugh bright.

"Now it is time for your gift. Damon?" Noah requests.

Damon leaves the room, striding out the back doors towards the cold and hot room, and our attention is snapped back.

"When you were taken by Jakub, many people held the responsibility of finding you, but the man leading the charge was one Chief Superintendent Andrew Hicks." Noah spits the name, disgusted.

Damon bursts back through the doors, and he is not alone. He is dragging a man, bound at the wrists and ankles, gagged, and his face his bruised and bloodied. He is quite a large man; his police uniform is soiled, and the buttons of his shirt stretch over his gut tightly. Damon drags him across the room, dropping him at Mac's feet. Her eyeline pans down to see his fearful eyes peering back up at her again.

"Fuck… Anna, I'm going to need you here." Dixy gripes.

"What? Why?"

"Because I think Noah is about to give an order that…"

"Andrew Hicks has served over 25 years in the London Metropolitan Police Force. His background was long and distinguished. That is until five years ago when his wife left him. After that he became *this*." Noah pauses, his eyes on the police officer, cold and livid. "Lazy, fat, incompetent, alcoholic! This man was the sole driving force behind finding you, Mckenna, and at first, the search was thorough. But that search was called off by *this* man after only two weeks, having never investigated the docks as a possible means to stow you away."

I am too slow to catch on to what is happening. It isn't till Noah reaches inside his blazer to retrieve a gun that is holstered there that the penny finally drops. A heat spreads over my body, pulsing from my chest.

"You want me to persuade her to execute this man?!" I snap, and Dixy whips her head around, her eyes tight.

"If you don't…she'll die," Dixy mouths, sadness thick in her throat.

"She…this will *break* her Dixy."

"Savannah…" Alfred grumbles, and I catch his eyes. "You can bring her back from this."

Noah holds the gun out to Mac and she takes it with a steady hand, her eyes roaming over the dark glimmer of black metal. Mac tosses her hand up and down, a slight movement as though to evaluate the weight of the gun in her hands, and her heart rate begins to slow. Her thumb taps the gun grip three times. The movement looks nervous.

"Wait a minute…" Alfred gasps. "Rewind the feed 10 seconds."

"Alfred, what…" Dixy begins.

"Just do it!" Alfred snaps, getting to his feet and leaning over my shoulder to access the secondary screen. The video plays back, once again showing Mac's hand seeming to weigh up the gun and then her thumb tapping the gun grip three times.

"The gun is empty! It's a signal. I taught her how to judge the weight of an empty gun from a loaded gun. She is telling us the gun isn't loaded!" Alfred fires.

"You can't know that," Agent Holt interjects. "We can't rely on that."

"*Yes, I can*. I trained her; I know how she thinks," Alfred deadpans, the pride in his voice so blatant it warms my chest. "Lamb, do a background check on Andrew Hicks," Alfred commands.

Mac takes her gaze away from the gun and back up to Noah.

"This man is a prime example of weakness. It was his job to search for you, his duty, and he didn't just fail, he gave up. Do you understand, McKenna? Do you see? Because as not only a member of The Culling but an entrusted member within my inner circle, sometimes I need you to see, to act, without my instruction. I will have to trust your devotion, your ability to act, as the enforcer of my will."

"Andrew Hicks, deceased, died in action 18 months ago. He's a plant!" Lambert calls.

My heart soars, and I can't contain the rush of adrenalin zinging through my veins. My breath is laboured, my jaw clenched in the effort to subdue the overwhelmed tingle threatening to burst out of my chest.

She's got him.

Dixy lunges for the keyboard, her fingers moving furiously.

```
Signal received, gun empty, that is not Hicks.
I repeat - NOT Hicks.
```

Mac gets to her feet and takes a step back from the cowering man on the floor. She looks back up at Noah and then her hands move masterfully at speed, her eyes never leaving Noah's. She slides back the barrel, her hand swooping down out of sight, and then …

Click.

Noah's answering smile is vile. Mac looks down, her gaze following her extended hand past the gun, and then falling to the man's face which is grinning. He sits up and slides his hands out of the restraints.

"Well done, McKenna. You have made me proud," Noah oozes, his voice a soft, sickening purr. "And now, there is only one more thing left to do."

The doors to the room fly open as robed hooded figures march into the room, a chant repeating from their lips.

"Cull the weak, harvest the strong. Cull the weak, harvest the strong."

"Well, I'll be damned," Agent Holt breathes.

Mac's eyeline roams as the room begins to fill with blue robed figures, circling, lining up, layering each wall in uniformed rows as Mac slowly revolves on the spot. The sea of royal blue thickens, revealing the sheer mass of figures. The chanting getting louder with each passing second till suddenly, everything stops. The room falls silent, each figure inhumanly still. Their presence seemingly alien, transcendental and lethal.

"There has to be over two hundred of them," Dixy gasps.

Noah holds his hand out, and Mac passes the gun back to him. He places it back inside his holster and takes a deep breath, a smile playing on his lips before his own voice begins to chant. The moment the words burst impassioned from his mouth, the hooded figures all take down their hoods in perfect, practiced sync. They begin to follow Noah's chant; the sound is thunderous.

"Our path is righteous; our path is pure! Our path is righteous; our path is pure!"

Mac's eyes dart to Nicole as she steps out of line and walks with parade-like steps towards the corner of the room. On her return as she passes Damon, he breaks away from the line, following her step. As they draw nearer, the scene becomes too easy to predict. My heart sinks with a burning, hateful sadness, and my grip on the table tightens. Dixy places her hand on top of mine, and I grip it gratefully. My breath is hitching in sharp sucks as Nicole stands before Mac, carrying a metal poker, the end glowing lava-orange in the shape of a triangle.

No words are spoken as Damon approaches Mac. He grasps her wrists, places her hands on his chest, and holds them there. Her hands are relaxed, fingers extended against the bright blue of his robes. His eyes bear down on her savagely as she stares into them. Then she looks down at her hands gripping his robes and she screams a blood-boiling wail of agony. My eyes blur on the screen as I exhale through clenched teeth, Dixy's grip strong on my hand.

The pained growl coming from Mac's throat as she tries to steady herself is guttural and angry. Her eyeline meets Damon's once again as he lets go of her wrists and reaches inside his robe.

"Welcome to The Culling!" he spits.

He moves fast, so impossibly fast that Mac is only just able to follow the movement with her eyes as he lunges for her arm. He grips her arm with one hand while the other hammers down, ramming a needle deep into her bicep. The screen goes black.

***

"Don't tell me everything is okay; you don't know that! She hasn't opened her eyes in two hours. It's supposed to be over!" I seethe, and Alfred recoils, his eyes wide and uncertain.

"Savannah, her vitals are strong. All I'm saying is she's alive, and I'm sure we will know more soon. Why don't you take a walk, get some air?"

It has been the longest two hours of my life; I haven't been able peel my eyes away from the blank screen since Damon drugged Mac. There was the sound of movement and muttering but nothing concrete to go on. Pa is right, her heart is beating strong, but it isn't enough. I need her eyes to open. I need to hear her voice. I need…her.

"I'm sorry for snapping, Pa, but please stop. I'm not leaving her. Not till I see her eyes open. I can't so please, stop asking me to," I plead, and he sits down, taking the chair next to me.

"Then we will both wait for her, together."

My eyes burn as time winds down. I stare, transfixed, at the blank screen. The only sounds inside the barn are the heavy breaths of Pa and the twang of Dixy flicking the elastic band on her wrist. In the background, the soft blip of Mac's heartrate, slow, even, and strong. My whole body seems to thrum in a slow vibrate, my stomach clenching in knots as inside my head, I plead.

Please, Please, Please.

The screen flickers, a second of the blank interrupted with bright white speckled with warm haloed orbs of multicoloured light and then blank again.

"What the fuck was that?!" Dixy gasps, but her voice is drowned by the pounding of blood in my ears. I push out from the desk, the office chair wheeling back. A strange swooping wave hits my chest, an out of body shock as everything slows down.

"Anna, what is –"

The wave crashes, a swell of emotion, reality hitting inside the waters whitewash. I gasp as if coming up for air because I know them multicoloured orbs of light as well as I would know any beacon guiding me home.

"We have to go - *now*!"

CHAPTER 20

Let There Be Light

Basking in this seething swelter,
Drowning, falling, helter-skelter,
Skin of fire, bones of grief,
Crawling out of the darkness beneath,
Slide the vale, move the sun,
Light up the dark as she comes undone,
Lightest touch, guiding hand,
Lead her out of the arid wasteland.

I know I need to open my eyes; I know, and yet they are so incredibly heavy. If I open my eyes, I might know where I am, and they will see *where I am, but they are so very heavy. I am heavy. The ground is cool and smooth beneath my face, but the heat is radiating over my back. Like the sun is beaming down far too hot on my naked skin. Am I naked? I don't feel naked, but I do feel pain. Pain in my bones and simmering under my skin; it didn't hurt till I realised it did. Oh, why did I have to realise it did?*

That is enough to open my eyes for just a moment. It's so bright and colourful, a rainbow on white shine. And then it's gone, it all turns dark... Colour bleeding into black. Am I here, or am I back? I can't be back because I feel her soft, loving hands holding my face delicately. That heavenly hold that makes everything inside feel calm and precious and warm. And that hurts the most because I can't be back, and I miss that hold, those hands, that touch.

"Open your eyes, please," Anna whimpers.

I don't want to; you will be gone when I do. Just a little longer.

"I'm here, please baby, just open your eyes."

"Savannah, we need to check her over…"

"No, just give me a minute, Pa."

Yes, please. Just a minute longer.

"Mac…it's Anna. I need…I can't wait anymore…"

Warm, full lips brush against mine softly, and I taste her on my still lips. The taste is awakening, scuttling shivers down my spine, and I don't care this is a dream. I will take her any way I can get her. My lips respond, and the sound of her shocked inhale flurries a current of pleasure through my chest. This has to be the best dream ever. My eyes open as her lips break away from mine, and I miss them. Her eyes bright and glistening green.

"Anna…please t-tell me you are real? Don't go again, please?" I croak, grabbing the hem of her shirt.

I am lying propped against her chest, my head cradled in her arm. Anna rests her nose against mine, her thumb rubbing my cheek, her breath ragged and tickling my lips.

"I'm real; you are home. You came back to me," Anna whispers and pulls back a little. She takes my hand, sliding it inside her shirt and right over her heart. "Oh God, thank you for coming back to me. I won't leave you – I promise, Mac. You're safe; it's over."

I can't take my eyes off her. Mostly because she is so damn beautiful, she is glowing brightly like a daydream. But also, because I'm scared this is just my mind giving me what I want again only to take it away. But I see the fear in her teary eyes; I feel the pound of her heart against my hand. I smell the candy-like scent I've missed so much, and then everything shifts. I slide my hand up her chest onto the side of her neck and nuzzle my face into her chest.

"Anna…" I groan, the sob almost overwhelming my throat, and she pulls me closer gently as if I am made out of glass, her breath heavy with relieved huffs as her hand rubs up and down my face and neck. It is instantaneous. My body loosens, sinking against her. Aware it has found safe harbour. It feels so good to be in her arms.

"It *is* you. I'm sorry…I-I got confused."

"I know; it's okay," Anna whispers, her lips finding my forehead, and then she eases back so she can see me. I watch as her mouth opens, and I'm not sure what she was going to say. Whatever it was, it got silenced by my lips. I kiss her deeply, revelling in the softness of her lips and the sound of her whimper. Every stroke of her lips is an awakening. She tastes every bit as perfect as I remember. I pull back a little, just enough to speak, my lips still brushing hers.

"I love y-you…" I wince, pain seething up my spine.

"I love you. I'm not going anywhere, I promise - but we need to get you checked over." Anna sniffs.

"We?"

"Yes, we…" Anna whispers, and then she looks away from me, towards the front door. I follow her eyeline, and then I see them all standing there.

Dixy's eyes are glittering, her smile soft, her head resting on Lambert's shoulder as he smirks boyishly. Pa, already approaching, easing to his knees and grinning with tired eyes.

"Pa…they ripped my shirt,"

Alfred frowns, his eyes dashing to Anna, and she gently pulls my face back to hers.

"What do you mean, baby? What shirt?"

"T-the plaid one Pa bought me when I got shot; they ripped it. It's gone," I choke, my throat tightening from the lump continuing to rise, but its Anna's tears that fall.

"It's okay, we can get you another one. Maybe a few; you do look gorgeous in them," Anna soothes, sweetly kissing my fingertips.

"Yeah, almost as gorgeous as me." Pa winks, and I manage a raspy chuckle. "We need to get you off of this floor, okay, darling?"

"I don't…I don't think I can, Pa."

The surrealistic haze is beginning to lift. Pain is sweeping back in fast, enough to make my head swim. Pa smiles reassuringly, but now the idea of even trying to move scares me.

"That's okay; we can help you." Alfred cranes his neck behind him. "Dix, Lamb," he calls.

They stride over. Dixy drops to the floor next to Pa, and Lambert kneels just behind her. Dixy's eyes are dark, shadows circling them in ways I have never seen before, but her smile is bright. She is unscrewing a bottle of water, and suddenly, I realise how thirsty I am.

"Hey, Max. Lambert is going to carry you upstairs, but I want you to drink some of this first and take some pain killers."

"Max…" I gasp, managing a smile as I remember the story about her little brother. Dixy's eyes well a little, her smile full of knowing.

I take the bottle with a shaky hand, and I can't drink it fast enough, Dixy gives Anna the pain killers, and she places them in my mouth. The water has soothed the blades in my throat, but I am sure I could drink at least four more bottles and still be thirsty. I feel like my bones are on fire, and the last thing I want to do is move, but Lambert is already approaching.

"Hey, sister, you ready for lift off?" Lambert says smoothly in his monotone calm. Even now, he still asks permission before touching me, which I can't help but find sweet.

"I d-don't… It's going to hurt. Make it quick."

"Copy that."

Lambert slides his hands under my armpits, and my body tenses, bracing itself, but it doesn't matter. It does nothing to lessen the pain as Lambert smoothly lifts me to a standing position, and I feel him wince as I cry out, but he doesn't miss a beat. He bends forwards, lacing my arms over his shoulders, and crosses his forearms under my butt. He lifts me like I'm weightless and carries me like a child. My head slops on his shoulder as he starts to cross the floor over to the spiral staircase. He smells like Lynx Africa; the smell jogs memories of my nightclubbing days. I dread to think what I smell like.

"There are lights…" I mumble, and Lambert chuckles as we reach halfway up the stairs.

"Yes. Anna has been busy," he clarifies, and my chest swells a little, the smile on my face unstoppable.

Lambert stops next to the side of the bed and leans to perch me on the end of it, and Anna is already at my feet unlacing my boots. My head is sloshy; I feel like heat is radiating from my bones, feverish down my back. Anna places her hands on my hips, her eyes fixed on mine, and I stare back while Dixy hangs an IV bag off of the top brace of the four-poster bed.

"Tell me…" Anna mouths.

"My back…it's burning. They..."

Anna's jaw clenches and she leans forwards, pulling me gently against her chest, her hand on the back of my neck. "Where?" she whispers.

"At the bottom. I t-think my t-shirt is stuck to it." I sob, the lump in my throat finally triumphing. My skin crawls feverishly at the admittance. I knew it was a possibility they would brand me again. I knew it, and yet I didn't know it would make me feel so vile inside.

"Okay, it's okay. I can fix that," Anna soothes, her fingertips trailing up and down the back of my neck as she whispers in my ear. "How do you feel about a cold shower with me?" she asks, and I nod into her neck.

"Right, the IV is ready. The electrolytes and fluids you've lost need replacing, Max. You'll feel a lot better after," Dixy informs.

"We can't do that yet, Dix. I need to get her in the shower," Anna explains.

"Uh…why?"

"The brand; her t-shirt is stuck to it. I need cold water to get it off her."

"…bastards. Okay, I'll get Lambert."

"I can walk. Please," I mumble.

Anna and Dixy help me to my feet and then cradle my arms over their shoulders. We make it to the bathroom, and Dixy stays holding me up while Anna goes to fetch clean clothes. The pain killers are hitting, the fire in my bones is dying out, and tiredness is weighing heavily.

"How are you doing, rock star?"

"I don't know. I feel a bit…screwy," I admit.

"That's okay, Max. You are exhausted, and you still have whatever drug that psycho gave you a hot shot with swimming around your system. Things will unscrew when you've had some sleep."

Taking off my clothes is not as difficult as I expected. Barrett's clothes are miles too big; the jeans practically fall off. What isn't easy is seeing the shock on Anna's face when the ice water finally does its job and she turns up the water temperature and takes my t-shirt off. I know she tries valiantly not to react but there is no mistaking the tightness of her jaw, the almost silent, sharp intake of breath, and the tightening of her eyes. Instantly, the embarrassment is almost too much to handle, and my arms cross tightly across my chest.

"I t-think you should go. I know I look… I can do this on my own," I struggle, looking down at my ugliness, pain burning behind my eyes.

The weight loss is significant; my ribs and stomach are black and blue. I am covered in filth, there is bruising running up my arms and legs, and cuts everywhere, the vilest being the deep slice to my inner thigh, courtesy of Damon. I don't even want to know what my face looks like. All I know is the last person I want to see me looking this hideous is Anna. I stiffen as she takes a step closer, her hand light on my forearm, her eyes wary.

"You don't want me here?"

"I can see how you are looking at me, and I don't blame you, okay? I'm not blind. I look..." I grimace, chuckling darkly, "I'm not upset with you…but I can't take it. C-can you go, please?"

Anna steps into me lightly pressing her body against mine. Her hands slide up my chest, smooth against the hot water beating down on us.

"Mac, look at me please."

It really doesn't help; in fact, it only deepens the shame because she looks practically edible. Her skin flawlessly creamy, her rusty red hair darkened to a deep scarlet in the water, her eyes luminously green in the brightness of the bathroom. She is so damn beautiful, I didn't need to look to know that, but she gently but firmly pulls me to her eyeline as my arms stay tautly crossed over my chest.

"I'm sorry, my face doesn't lie - especially to you, but you are reading it wrong. It hurts, Mac. That is what you can see. Not repulsion, hurt. I can see the evidence of what they have done to the woman I love, and it *hurts*." Anna brushes her lips lightly against mine; it feels tender and loving. There doesn't seem to be a time that her lips won't excite me. "You are so beautiful and sexy, and Jesus…I've never felt such unrelenting desire for someone. I just…I hate them, I hate them *so bad.* I just want you, us…I don't want you getting hurt anymore. I just want to be us; I want our life together."

I uncross my arms, and I can't supress the smile her words inspire.

…our life together.

She smiles back at me, her nose crinkling between her eyes. "What's that smile for?"

"It's just nice to hear you talk about us that way regardless of the situation. I'm sorry I misunderstood. I don't…I'm not feeling good. Everything has been too loud for too long; I just need it to stop. The only thing that makes any sense, the only thing I know for sure whether it's loud or quiet, is that I want that too."

"Don't be sorry. Now we are on the same page, you're going to let me take care of you. Let's get you showered, and then I will do everything I can to make it quiet again."

Anna is so gentle; she delicately lathers every inch of my skin, the iridescent bubbles popping as she rinses away the weeks of dirt and ugliness. I can't help but watch her; the affection in her eyes is fierce and undiluted. If it wasn't for how much my legs don't want me to be standing, I'd happily stand here and watch her for hours. After we are both washed and dried, Anna helps me back into the bedroom where Dixy is waiting. It isn't till I am sat on the bed that the tiredness hammers my system again, making everything feel heavy.

"Do you think I can persuade you to eat?" Anna asks, kneeled between my legs, and I grimace.

"I really don't have much of an appetite."

"I know, but it will help. You don't have to eat a lot. What if I make you toasted cheese sandwiches? I can't promise they will be as good as your mums, but I'll do my best." Anna grins sweetly.

"Okay, I'll try. Thank you."

Dixy plumbs in the IV with expert hands. With a quick scratch, the needle is taped securely to my hand. She asks to take a look at the branding on my back, and I wince as she lifts my t-shirt.

"H-how bad is it?"

"Anna did a good job cleaning it, and if I cover it in gel treatment and a bandage, it will be fine," Dixy assures.

"That isn't what I meant."

Dixy kneels down in front of me, her hand firm around my wrist, eying me with understanding.

"I know. It doesn't look bad. If it wasn't for the meaning behind it and the way they did this to you, it would look quite cool. You did so well, Max. I know that doesn't help right now, but I'm so proud of you, and I am not the only one. I don't know how you got through that."

"With a little help from my friends," I smile, "and Anna. There were moments I know I wouldn't have got through without her."

"She was incredible, I have to agree. I wouldn't let that one go if I were you."

"I don't intend to."

I manage to eat half of my toasted cheese sandwich; the food feels alien in my mouth even though it looked mouth wateringly yummy. My stomach just doesn't seem to want food. Lambert and Pa go back to the farm to catch up on some sleep; Dixy goes downstairs to sleep on the sofa so that she can be on hand to change my drip bag. Anna finally helps me lay back onto the bed, my broken ribs screaming in protest. And then she props herself up on one elbow while her fingertips trace my face.

"I didn't miss Christmas?" I utter, and she smiles, twinkling with excitement.

"No, you kept your promise. You kept all your promises. I know you're not a massive fan, but I can't wait to spend Christmas with you."

"I'm not usually…but while I was gone, I kept picturing you in a Christmas jumper, drinking Baileys, all excited and warm – I really didn't want to miss that. I didn't want to miss you opening your presents either."

Anna arches her eyebrow, her surprised smirk delicious. "Mac Scott…when did you have time to buy presents? Is that where you went when we came back from South End on Sea?"

I can feel my cheeks flush, which really isn't helpful. I did get Christmas presents then, fearing I wouldn't get time any other time, but my mind wanders directly back into the jewellery store, and her eyes are definitely curious.

"Ahem…yeah, I wanted to make sure I had everything I needed before I…b-before they…" My words are cut off by the memories invading my mind. Powerful enough to force my eyes closed and make me tremble. Anna shuffles closer to me, wrapping her arms and legs around me.

"It's okay; it's just you and me now. You don't have to hold this back," Anna whispers.

"I know…but I don't…I can't, not yet. It's too much."

"And that's okay too. I'll be here when you are ready. Till then, tell me what you do need, anything you need."

I open my eyes and meet the eyes I have missed so much. Eyes so mesmerising and full of love, they have the power to make me confess every last fear and pain. But now is not the time. Now, there is only one thing I need.

"Kiss me till I fall asleep," I choke, and she dips her forehead against mine.

"Baby, I will kiss you even when you are asleep."

***

"She is looking better; her temperature is down; heartrate and blood pressure are going back to normal levels. She has some colour in her cheeks," Dixy whispers.

"That's probably me; I can't seem to keep my hands off of her face," Anna whispers, and her hand pauses on my cheek, holding my face softly to her chest. I couldn't feel more content.

"What's that?"

"Broad spectrum antibiotics. I'm probably being overly cautious, but the wound on her thigh is deep, and it hasn't healed nearly enough considering it happened on the first day. After her last infection, I'm not taking any chances."

Anna sighs, and I feel my head go up and down with her gentle deep breath, her heartbeat pounding rhythmically against my ear. Her thumb lightly strokes my cheek, and I feel peace as the weight of tiredness starts pulling me back down.

"Thank you, Dixy."

"Don't mention it. She's going to be okay."

"I know, I just… God, Dixy, I don't want her to hurt anymore. People have been hurting her since before I even knew her and every moment since. I would give anything to make it all stop, for her to be happy and safe."

My heart aches, and it is hard to keep my eyes closed when I hear the pain in her voice. I feel the bed sink a little as Dixy's voice draws closer.

"Anna, she *is* happy – with you. And when this is all over…because it will be all over one day, she will be safe. She is going to get through this. I don't know her like you do, but I know her enough. I know some of what it takes to survive what she has, and I know there is nothing that can bring her down. Because you're right, giving up just isn't a part of who she is. In the meantime, just look at her, bundle of cute." Dixy chuckles, and Anna chuckles with her. "She looks like she feels pretty damn safe right now if you ask me."

It is almost impossible to supress the grin trying to betray my 'sleeping' face as I listen to them both giggling together. Obviously, while I was in the pits of hell, something has evolved between them. An unmistakable ease of friendship, and I couldn't be happier to hear it.

***

I have been asleep a long time, I'm sure of it. When I open my eyes, the light is dim and the room quiet. The cannular has been removed from my hand, and I find it resting on Anna's hip as she lay sleeping, her arms wrapped snuggly around my arm. I take my eyes away from the adorable sight to find Alfred on my other side, sat on a chair, smiling softly.

"Hey, kid," he grumbles as he leans forwards and hands me a glass of water which is drained before I even realise how thirsty I was.

"Hey, Pa. How long have I been out?"

"Almost a day, but you needed it. You look less zombie-like. How do you feel?"

I think about that. My body still aches, but it is a dull ache, the type you get the day after you have been to the gym. My head feels clear, although a little light.

"I feel alright, I think. Better than I expected to and…hungry." I groan and my stomach growls in agreeance. Alfred chuckles a long sigh, his eyes falling to Anna, and mine follow. My chest warming at the sight of her.

"I'm so glad you're home, kid. I hope you don't mind that I was sat here. I came to check in, but it's just nice to be sat with you both. The only person that needed sleep half as much as you was her."

I feel my smile fall as the guilt pangs deep in my stomach.

"I know. I've put her through a lot."

"No, you haven't, *they* have. Don't go taking that on. It's not on you; it's on them. Fucking monsters," Alfred growls, and I flinch at the sting in his words.

"I'm one of them monsters now, Pa."

Alfred takes my hand; it feels tiny inside of his giant clasp, and I can't help but think back to a time when I couldn't have allowed that touch. It feels so long ago now. Even though I still can't easily allow it to most people, with Alfred, it is now easy and natural. Inside the touch of his rough calloused hand is a strength that I have many times borrowed. A father's touch so alien to me and yet so familiar by his hand.

"Mac, you are not now, nor will you ever be one of them. You are not theirs; you are ours. Our family, our Mac, and I'm proud of you."

I look up at him, his stare insistent, and I gulp the lump down that drags in my throat, my hand gripping his.

"Pa, can you do something for me?"

"Course, kid. Name it."

I look over to Anna, and I bite my lip, still fast asleep, but I am not going to take any chances. I let go of Alfred's hand and quietly ease my bedside drawer open, retrieving a pad and pen from inside. Leaning it against my leg, I scribble down a few lines, tear the sheet off, and hand it to him. I watch as his eyes brows raise higher with every flit of his eyes.

"Ahem - Copy that, Mac-attack," Alfred whispers before his hand gently cups my face. "Now, how about a bacon sandwich?

***

As I dance on the teeter between asleep and awake, I feel her lips press warmly on the back of my neck as her fingertips map my tummy. The hot tingle her touch brings is enough to quicken my pulse and open my sleepy eyes with sudden alertness. I can tell that the kisses Anna is trailing down my shoulder are those purely with the intent of being loving. And yet, my whole body is set ablaze by them with want.

I am blissfully saturated by her skin, the velvet smoothness of it pressed up against my back as she spoons me. Like many things with Anna, this is new for me. I'm so used to being the big spoon. I never really even thought about what it would feel like to fall asleep this way - to be held and not always be the one holding. Maybe because I've never allowed myself to be as vulnerable as I have with Anna. It's an equality I never thought I needed, and I am happy to be proven wrong.

I reach behind me and skim my hand over the gorgeous curve of her arse. I trace down her thigh and stop at her knee, curving my hand around the back of it. As I roll over to face her, it only takes a small firm tug of her knee before her leg hooks over my hip. Her legs spread; I pull her closer until there isn't so much as a breath between us. Her eyes are alive with the excitement I was anticipating, and I can't help but be infected by it.

"Merry Christmas, beautiful."

"Mm … Already the best Christmas ever," Anna murmurs into my lips.

It has been two days since I woke up from my 24-hour sleep. Since then, there has been no talk of The Culling or Barrett. In fact, the only mission-based conversation was about my earpiece, which has now been replaced. I never thought I'd feel relieved to hear the voices back in my ear. But the truth is, I've come to like the connection being there if I need it. Dixy has regularly checked on my recovery. With my appetite returning and the steady flow of IV bags pumping life back into my veins, my body has begun to respond. Lambert drops in to play cards, Alfred to make the fattiest foods you could ever wish for, and Anna hasn't left my side for a moment. She hasn't pushed me to talk; as always, her patience is unwavering.

It's my first-time wearing clothes that are not PJs and feeling semi-human in what feels like too long. I look myself up and down; my favourite dark red shirt is hanging off me more than it used to. The weight gain is still not where it needs to be, but as I knot the tie around my neck and feel the cool the mist of my aftershave tingle on my skin, I feel much more myself than I could have hoped for.

I find Anna loading hot croissants and freshly brewed coffee onto the coffee table in the living room. I watch her arranging them neatly next to a stack of Christmas presents. Completely unaware of my presence, she hums and murmurs along to the cheesy Christmas music playing in the background. I can't help but stare. Her is hair hanging in loose curls that fall over her face as she bounces slightly to the music. The deep red of it is in stark contrast to her pale skin but matching perfectly with her short burgundy corduroy dress. My chuckle has her cheeks pinkening and her eyes narrowing playfully in my direction. Then her eyes trail over me, and she closes the gap between us.

"Screw breakfast; can I just eat you?" She smirks into my lips. "You look gorgeous."

"What a coincidence, I was just about to say the same thing."

Anna guides me towards the sofa, helping me lower myself down while I try not to wince at the sharp screaming of my broken ribs. As we eat breakfast together, the fire is smouldering, the embers just enough to radiate heat. The Christmas tree glitters in red and gold, and the fairy lights are glowing in multicoloured twinkles reflecting all over the living room.

"You decorated, even though I might not be home in time?"

"I knew you would be home; I don't know how, I just did. Plus, even if you weren't, I wasn't going to miss Christmas with you. We would have just postponed it till you were home," Anna explains, her voice sure.

"Thank you, it looks beautiful. I like the mental image of you doing all of this while I was away, but next year, we'll do it together."

I am loving every second of watching Anna open her presents. As always, everything she feels is openly displayed on her face, so when she opens her presents, I feel every bit of excitement with her. Her gifts for me are just as thoughtful as always, and we laugh hard as we simultaneously open the tackiest Christmas jumpers that either of us could have ever found. Anna straddles my legs, her knees hugging my hips, her morish lips adoring mine.

"Thank you for all of my presents, they are just…perfect," Anna sighs, her lips melting into mine.

"Being here with you…is perfect. You're perfect."

"Mm keep talking like that and flashing those dimples, and I'll melt into a puddle." Anna bites her lip, and I dip my head, trailing my lips down her neck.

"Is that right?" I whisper, nibbling on her earlobe.

"Mmhmm – yep, puddle."

I slide my hand up her thigh, dragging over her heated ivory skin as her muscles flex beneath my touch. I feel the heat of her through her lacey pants as I run my finger up her channel. Anna's thighs clench, her hips lift, and I smile my whisper hotly into her ear.

"It would seem you're already a puddle…"

I slip her damp panties to the side but resist the urge to touch her where I know she really needs me to. My eyes are locked on hers as I lightly run my fingers over every swollen, sensitive inch of her. Barely touching, and yet it's enough to coat my fingertips in her wetness.

"F-fuck … Please, baby…"

"Please what?" I ask, circling my fingertips teasingly around her aching entrance.

I am drunk on her reactions once again. On the openhearted honesty that burns through her eyes, at how deeply she is biting her bottom lip as she gasps, at how uninhibited her hips freely roll against me with need.

"P-please, I need …" Her eyes express such vulnerability it melts my heart, and yet her body moves with audacious certainty as she lowers herself against my fingers. "I need you so deep inside me that all I know is that…you are Mac Scott, and you have come for me."

Christ...she has me wrapped around her finger. At her words, I feel myself swell and gush inside my pants, and my heart flies. I slide two fingers inside her with ease, and they are engulfed with her heat. Her dripping excitement trickles down my wrist, and I watch her with worship as she rides my fingers. I match my slow, deep thrust with every stroke of my tongue and brush of my lips as she moans lusciously and freely. My chest is fit to burst with an overwhelming rush of love so powerful it hurts.

"I will always come for you, Savannah," I promise, mumbling into her lips before I pull back to see her heavily hooded eyes telling me, she is close to the edge. "…now, *come* for me."

***

"Mum, I'm so glad you could make it," I manage through her tight squeeze of her hug. She smells like lavender, and the diamond pendant necklace that I bought her for her birthday glitters proudly on her chest.

"It's our first Christmas together since you came home. Of course I made it, love."

She turns to Anna, giving her an equally big squeeze, and all of Anna's nerves seemed to have completely evaporated as she hugs her back with ease.

The farmhouse is warm, full of cheer and fragrant with the festive smell of mulled wine heating on the stove and chicken roasting in the oven. While I can't stand the taste of mulled wine, the smell is cosy and merry. Dixy and Lambert are sat at the dining table, looking hungry eyed in Christmas hats and laughing at the lame jokes they have pulled out of their Christmas crackers. Alfred steps away from the stove, prompted by the melody of Mum's voice sounding in the dining room.

"Oh, that smells delightful. What a lovely home you have, Alfred; thank you so much for having me." Mum hands Alfred a large bottle of Woodford Reserve bourbon.

"Oho! Thank you, Mrs Scott, and you are most welcome. Can I tempt you to a glass?"

"I would love some of that mulled wine you have bubbling away, but please - call me Caroline."

While Alfred focuses on his – no doubt, winning Christmas banquet, Anna serves everyone up healthy glasses of mulled wine.

"Thank you, Anna. You are looking just radiant; I love those boots!" Mum gasps.

"Aw, thank you - so do I. I'm extremely lucky; your daughter has excellent taste," Anna coos, side glancing me sweetly.

Hell yeah, I do.

I can feel my mother's eyes on me as I struggle to manage a child sized portion of Christmas dinner. She doesn't voice it, but I can feel the worry coming off of her, and I'm defenceless because who can blame her? I look much more human than I could have hoped for after just a few days, but there is no escaping the bruises to my face that make up fails to completely hide or the obvious weight loss. Thankfully, she doesn't comment. Probably because it would prompt a conversation that doesn't fit with the festivities booming around the table. I know it is a conversation that will have to happen eventually, but I am determined to delay it for as long as possible because there is no way for me to ease that worry.

"Excellent spread, Sarg!" Lambert commends with a nod towards Alfred.

"Yes, because annihilating your third helping isn't a subtle enough indication that you are enjoying the food. Honestly, Lamb, you eat like a pig. Its mildly morbidly fascinating to watch, but mostly - just gross." Dixy scrunches up her nose.

As night begins to fall, the party moves outside to snuggle with blankets around the fire, and the real drinks begin to flow while presents are exchanged. All eyes are on me as I struggle to find words after opening my gift from Alfred. I turn the compass over in my hands, the cold brass surface of it smooth under my fingers and shining. It looks antique and weighs more than you might consider to look at it.

"These compasses were issued in 1918 to officers of the First World War, and that one was my grandpa's." My head shoots up, my throat tight, and Alfred eyes crease with a soft crooked smile. "It has bought me home to my family from every war, and something tells me it will do the same for you."

"I..."

Anna grips my hand when she sees me struggle, knowing I hate being the centre of attention this way.

"Pa, I think you knocked that one out of the park," Anna jokes lightly.

"Oh, McKenna, what a beautiful gift," mum gasps. "Can I see?"

I place the compass back inside its worn leather pouch and get to my feet. As I pass it to her, I take a deep breath and stride over to Alfred and right into a bear hug.

"Thank you so much, Pa."

"Anytime, kid. Remember, we're partners. We will end this shit storm together."

There is a long road of uncertainty ahead. While it feels like I achieved the impossible in becoming a member of The Culling – I know that there is still so far to go to end this war. The army of The Culling is so much bigger than I feared it could be, a true force of heinous corruption. They are coming, and if they're not stopped, there is no limit to the devastation they will cause. Today of all days, I don't want to be weighed down by the albatross of the coming battles. I want to eat, drink, and be merry with my family, but no matter how hard I try, I feel the drag of that weight pulling on my shoulders and seizing in my chest. I could lose any one of them, *every* one of them. The cost of my failure would be everything I know and love. Anna leans into me and plants a kiss against my throat, snapping me back to the present.

"I can feel it coming over you. Do you want to go inside, take a minute? I can stay here or…"

"Take a walk with me?"

No one seems to look our way as we get to our feet and walk away. It's so still; the air is bitter cold, but there is no wind, and the moon is ensuring it's a bright, midnight blue night. My feet direct us exactly where they always do when I need to shut a door. I lean against the back fence, and Anna takes my hands in hers. They are so warm and steadying. I keep my eyes on her fingers interlocked with mine.

"I know I haven't talked about it. I just…I don't know what to say or where to begin, and I feel like if I do talk about it, I will lose control of myself. I don't want to do that any day but especially not today. I don't want to ruin…"

Anna drops my hands, and they find my face as she steps a little closer.

"I don't care what day it is; I am here for every day. I got to wake up with you on Christmas morning, laugh with you wearing that ridiculous Christmas jumper and still managing to look gorgeous. I got to have you make me feel wild in a way," Anna leans in, her lips soft against mine as she bites down on my bottom lip, "that only you, ever has." Then she releases it and pulls back a little. "You begin with whatever is on your mind the most. You tell me that one thing when you are ready to and then another and another. Because I am not going anywhere, Mac. It takes as long as it takes."

I dip my head into the crook of her neck and pull her close, and she slides her hands beneath my jacket. I feel the icy heaviness that seized in my chest begin to melt away, and I breathe her in before I pull back again.

"Whatever is on my mind the most?" I ask, immediately annoyed at the shake in my voice betraying the fear I'm trying so hard to hide. But the warmth in Anna's eyes, the heavenly hold she has on my cheek, steadies me once again.

"Tell me, Mac." Anna whispers.

I step into her, my hands gently on her hips, turning her gaze away from me and towards the farm. My chin resting on her shoulder, my arms around her waist, I hold her there, and she waits for me to find my words. The farm looks magical, so clear and glittering with the beginning of frost, the fire pit glowing and illuminating the small circle of family gathered. I turn my head and plant my lips just under Anna's ear.

"For as long as you will have me," I whisper, and Anna chuckles gorgeously in her gravelled tone.

"I am right here, Mckenna. What exactly are you waiting for?"

"I am done waiting," I announce, my voice clear and emboldened - no longer a shaken whisper. "Houston, we have a problem. Pa…you are a go."

Everyone at the fire pit stands and turns to face the big red barn as it illuminates bright and colourful in the darkness. There, clear as day – Anna's eyes are fixed on the words 'Marry me' spelt in masses of threads of fairy lights across the roof. Fear runs through me as I hear her breath shake. I unwrap my arms from her waist and step to her side, bending to one knee. Her eyes are brimming and wide as I take out the ring and present it to her, placing the warm amber wood box in her hand.

"Mac…"

"I am sure a day will come that I tell you about everything that happened. But when you ask me what is on my mind the most, what was on my mind the entire time I was gone – the answer is this." I open the lid to the box, and as her eyes fall to the ring, her tears fall with them. Fear is tightening my throat once again as I fail to read her honest face, and my hands tremble holding hers.

"Savannah Mae Slone, it's you and me, and I will always want it to be. Will you be my wife?"

Anna looks up from the ring, and my legs weaken. It feels like time has ceased to exist as I wait for moments, far too many moments. And I am sure I have ruined everything. Because a yes surely wouldn't take so long to say. Anna cups my cheek in one hand and bends down, her eyes completely unreadable.

"You goof – of course I'll marry you. Any time…anywhere. I will marry the hell out of you, Mac Scott."

Anna's hand slides from my face on to the collar of my shirt and she pulls, and somehow, I find my way back to my feet. With shaken hands, the ring is out of the box, and my chest is bursting with pride as I slide it onto her finger, and I can hardly breathe. Her smile is brighter than I can recall ever seeing it, her glimmering green eyes sparkling as perfectly as the ring on her finger. I slide my hands on to her waist firmly, and Anna's breath catches as I dip her backwards like a scene from a 1950s movie.

"Houston, we have a problem," I mumble, and then my lips melt into hers.

Cheers erupt from the fire circle, and fireworks screech and detonate in the sky above us. The smell of gunpowder fills my nose, but nothing can deter my lips from claiming hers. Goosebumps race across my skin, and yet my body burns and throbs. Anna's hands grip my face closer, and she sobs and moans into my lips. I lift her back upright, my lips pulling back from their heavy assault enough to take a breath.

"Oh, God…I love you, s-so much," Anna gasps, and I choke a laugh, my body shaking and tingling all over, but Anna isn't laughing. Her hands slide on to the side of my neck, her gaze is questioning. "You looked so scared."

"I…was scared. I love you; I love everything we are. How could I not have been scared?"

Anna takes her left hand away from my neck, and her eyes fall on the ring before they find mine again. The look in her eyes is without a doubt the most captivating look I've ever seen.

"Maybe when I take your name…you will finally see just how yours I always have been and forever will be."

The cheers grow louder with every step closer, and we brace ourselves. Dixy and Lambert pop corks on champagne bottles while the arms of my mum and Alfred envelope us.

"Oh, congratulations, sweetheart! I'm so proud of you," mum coos as she pulls back revealing a big grin on her beautifully plump, tear-streaked face.

"Thank you, Mum. I'm so glad you were here for this."

"Well, it all makes sense now, why Alfred was so insistent I came here for Christmas. That was such a beautiful surprise. Aww, my baby is growing up! And oh… Where's my future daughter-in-law?"

Just as Alfred lets Anna go, she is almost bowled over by my mum. I watch as they hug and both giggle teary excited squeals as they gush over the ring until Pa steps in my sights, snapping me out of my daze.

"You know, I don't like being wrong, but I'll always admit when I am," Alfred grumbles, his expression serious, and I gulp.

"Uhh…what do you…?

"I never understood. I was convinced you were wrong for waiting but…" Alfred pauses and stands by my side, his giant hand on my shoulder, and we both watch Anna, absolutely beaming with my mum. "…you were right. This was the perfect moment. Because she knows that you have asked her for forever for all the right reasons. You stood up to me, held your ground for what you felt was right for her, protecting her heart the way I know you'd protect her from any harm. And that is one of the many reasons I feel completely sure you will take care of her." I turn to look at Alfred, his eyes a little misty as he looks back at me, grinning crookedly.

"Aw come here you big softy!" I jibe, pulling him in for a hug. "Thanks, Pa, for everything."

I catch Anna's eye from over Pa's shoulder, and they burn with a look that inspires completely inappropriate bodily reactions while holding Pa.

"Hey! Stop monopolising the future bride, big guy!" Dixy whines playfully, and she hands me a bubbling champagne flute. "Congratulations, Max-a-million. I'm so happy for you both. And just so you know, I'm a spectacular wedding organiser." Dixy grins, and I frown, sighing.

"I don't know, Dix; I really don't think you will have time. Maid of honour duties can get a little hectic – so I've heard."

It takes longer for the penny to drop than I anticipated, her face gawped for long enough that I have to supress my laugh.

"A-are you serious? I…" Dixy stutters, putting up a valiant effort to hide her misty eyes. "Oh, my God… I'm going to throw you best hen party ever! There will be cocktails and canapés and –"

"No strippers, Dixy. That's a deal breaker."

"Pssst strippers…who do you think I am? I'm way classier –"

"Dix…"

"Okay…okay…no strippers." Dixy pouts, and then she laughs as she looks down at her feet. "It means a lot, Max. Thank you."

I pull her in for the hug I know she is quite able to give. "Well, you mean a lot. I mean, you are completely loopy and a master annoyance…but you mean a lot to me."

"Right back at you. Now let's get drunk – shall we?"

When everyone stops pulling me from left to right, showering me in so many hugs you would think no one knew I had an issue with touch, I find myself searching for the only touch I really want right now. I find her pouring herself another glass of champagne, her back turned as I slide my arms around her.

"There's my fiancé," I mumble into her neck, and she turns in my arms.

"Mmm … Call me that again, and I'm going to rip your clothes off – I don't care who's watching." Anna growls playfully, pulling me in, but our attention is diverted.

The unmistakable ping of a spoon being tapped on glass has us both turning to Lambert whose eyes are on Anna and me.

"Ahem…I would like to say a few words. Dixy and I, we uhh - came here to do a job. We came here to mentor and train a scrawny little runt named Mckenna Scott," Lambert begins, and the chuckles that surround us seem to put him at ease.

"But the job didn't remain just a job for very long. Soon I learned that, that scrawny little runt wasn't fearless - No, far from it, but who is? What was she was in spades was *brave* and unbelievably stubborn. And somehow, with every battle she won, Dixy and I came to care more and more. First for Mac, my sister from another mister – and then, for you all. You became our family, and to misfits like us, that counts for a lot." Lambert pauses, bowing his head a little, and my chest swells.

"It has been a privilege to watch you grow, Mac, and to see you and Anna *finally* start the journey we all saw long ago that you were destined to. I wish you both a lifetime of happiness…. To Mac and Anna." Lambert toasts.

"Mac and Anna!"

***

The night has been magical; there is no other word for it. It doesn't feel real or possible that Anna has agreed to be my wife. But I am aching for some alone time with her, to make it feel real, and by the look in her eyes, she feels that too. Lambert offers to take Mum home and I am grateful. I don't much like the idea of her in a taxi at night when she is slightly merry on champagne and mulled wine.

"Congratulations again, both of you. I honestly couldn't be happier for you, and you must come for dinner soon," Mum insists with her best stern eyebrow raising.

"Of course, we will. We'll even bring more cake." Anna beams as Mum taps her cheek dotingly before turning her gaze on me, her smile slipping.

"I can't pretend I don't see how poorly you look love or that it doesn't scare me. I won't ask; just please be careful, Mckenna, and keep coming home."

"I will, Mum. It's going to be okay," I soothe as she squeezes me a little too tight.

"Agent Scott, do you read?" I flinch, stepping back abruptly.

"Mac…are you okay, sweetheart?" Mum gasps, and then all eyes fall on me.

"I read, Agent Holt."

"Agent, there isn't much time. We have had eyes on Barrett since you returned, and he is heading in the direction of the farm. If he is heading to you, then he will be there in less than two minutes."

Fear tightens my chest, and my hand reaches out reactively as my head spins. Anna grabs my wrist, stepping in front of me.

"Mac…"

"Agent Scott, respond?!" Lexi barks inside my ear.

"U-understood, Agent Holt. I will handle it. Houston, we have a problem."

I imagine the fear in Anna's eyes matches my own, and the sight of it snaps me out of my freeze.

"He's coming. I need you to get inside," I say softly and directly to Anna, and then I look up. "All of you, inside - now. Dix, Lamb, Pa – activate your earpieces, keep the line open. He is 60 seconds out. Get Anna and Mum inside – they don't leave your sights for a single second till we are clear."

"Copy that. You heard her – let's move," Dixy responds.

"He's here? Y-you mean Barrett?" Mum gasps, but Pa is already leading her inside.

"Mac…" Anna chokes, and I pull her in, my lips descending on hers in a quick but loving kiss.

"I'll be right back, okay? We have celebrating to do…" I smile reassuringly - a pointless effort. "But I need you to go inside; I need to know you're safe." I move to turn away, and Anna grabs my collar roughly, pulling me back.

"You come right back; I mean it!" Anna orders. She kisses me hard and turns away. I don't have it in me to watch her leave.

I busy myself cleaning up the mess of the party around the fire pit. I can't just go to meet him; how would I explain knowing he was coming? Instead, I pick up cups and fold down chairs. I focus on keeping my breathing even, even though my heart is racing so hard I feel breathless. Why would he just turn up and why now? Whatever his reason, I can't just go with him. I am not in any way prepared for that, and I'm scared. I told Anna that I would be right back, but how would I tell him no if he asked me to go with him? Would he even give me a choice? Maybe he wasn't even coming here; the two-minute ETA Lexi gave has been and gone.

"Max, you copy?"

"Yeah, loud and clear."

"We have Anna and Caroline secure; you don't need to worry about them. We've got them, you've got this – okay?"

"Dix…I wasn't ready. I'm not…"

"I know but you can do this. I have eyes on headlights; you have about 40 seconds."

My chest tightens as I turn to see lights crawling down the drive towards the farm. I focus on loosening every muscle one by one as I take my first steps forward. Whatever this is about, I am already a member of The Culling. I passed his tests, I proved myself. Now all I have to do is keep up with the lie I've sold and keep selling it. It makes sense he might want to talk, seeing as we barely spoke during the reconditioning. How would I feel if I really wanted this? Would I be excited to see him after passing his tests? Proud? Eager for his recognition, his approval? And what would he want? What is he hoping to see from me?

The tyres of a very sleek black Mercedes roadster crunch on gravel just as I make it back to the back fence. I watch, easily portraying the confusion of his appearance as he smoothly steps out. He approaches, and I notice he is more dressed down than I've ever seen him, wearing a blue button-down polo and sandy chinos. He is carrying a fight case the size of a briefcase only chunkier.

"Good evening, Mckenna. I hope you don't mind me dropping by."

"Not at all. It's good to see you, although it does seem out of the blue. Is everything okay?"

His eyes are piercing even in the dark as they scrutinise me then lift over my shoulder. There is something about the tightness in his jaw that is making me anxious. My instinct is to look behind me and follow his gaze, but I feel planted to the spot.

"Yes, everything is perfectly fine. I just came to check on you and give you this; it is Christmas after all." Barrett hands me the case, and I take it. "Think of it as a welcome pack. You will find everything you need in there for your first assignment, plus my gift to you."

Worst Christmas present ever.

"Thank you. Now I feel bad – I didn't get you anything." I chuckle awkwardly. "I already have an assignment?"

"Don't feel bad; it was my pleasure. Yes, the details are in the case. It may seem quick, but your performance and handling of Veritas pleased me. I have no doubt that you are ready. I trust you are still happy to have joined us?"

"Of course. I appreciate your faith in me. It's just a shame that not everyone is as happy at my ascension as you are."

Barrett considers that for a moment, his eyes seeming to X-ray me before flitting over my shoulder again.

"Ah…you mean Damon? He will come around. He is just having a little trouble accepting the new order of things…which brings me to the other reason I am here. And just in the nick of time, I see." Barrett looks over my shoulder and nods towards the farm, and this time I do turn to follow his gaze. My stomach fills with ice as I turn to see my proposal still brightly shining off the barn roof. I don't know why, but every instinct in my body is screaming.

"What do you mean, just in the nick of…"

"Mckenna, I am sure you are no doubt aware that a part of my mission is to pave the way to the ultimate human race," Barrett interjects harshly.

"I am aware of that."

"Then, I am sure you also remember *how* I said I intended to achieve that."

My brain is scrambling. What has me proposing to Anna got to do with paving the way… I turn away from Barrett and brace myself on the fence just in time for my head to swim.

The memory swirls.

"Ask yourself, Mckenna - what if the weak were culled leaving only the strong?" he asks, all calm returned although his voice is now hoarse. "Intelligent, wealthy, educated, higher classed, artistically genius, athletically gifted, healthy, strong. If humanity were to impose selective breeding from a pool of the elite, the superior pedigree of humans - then we would be paving the way for a superior-race. We would be paving the way to the creation of a thriving utopian world built by the ultimate human race."

I am snapped back to the present by Barrett's hand squeezing my shoulder, and it's all I can do not to scream as I feel my heart break.

"I have no issues with your sexuality, Mckenna. But you are a leader in my inner circle now, and you must lead by example. The example that we must be matched to breed with the most superior pedigree of mate." Barrett turns me to face him, and I don't bother trying to hide the hate written all over my face.

"I am marrying Anna!"
"No, Mckenna – you are not, because you are already betrothed to Damon."

The End

The story concludes in:
Retrospect – The Reckoning of Mac Scott

Coming Soon!

ABOUT THE AUTHOR

A.J. Forton is a newly emerging author who seeks to shock and thrill readers with brutal and honest action, shamelessly scorching intimacy, and unforgettable goosebump-inspiring moments. As a member of the LGBTQ+ community, she aims to bring strong queer characters boldly into the limelight with realism and authenticity. Parallel to this mission, she hopes to break the stereotype that many people on the Autistic spectrum have no imagination.

A.J. is studying for her BA in English Literature and Creative Writing. However, her most notable qualification as a writer is the lifelong obsession with creating other worlds. She enjoys cake, a dash of whiskey, and consuming unhealthy volumes of cheese, as should all right-thinking people. She's a terrible cook and an enthusiast in all things good and geeky.

My website: https://www.ajforton-author.com
My Author Facebook page: https://www.facebook.com/inthewordsofaj/
My Author Instagram page: https://www.instagram.com/aj_forton_author/
My Author Twitter page: AJ Forton (@AjForton) / Twitter

Made in the USA
Columbia, SC
16 July 2022

62999189R10272